THE APOCALYPSE WATCH

Robert Ludlum

An Orion paperback

First published in Great Britain in 1995
by HarperCollins*Publishers*
First published in paperback in 1996
by HarperCollins
This paperback edition published in 2004
by Orion Books Ltd,
Orion House, 5 Upper St Martin's Lane,
London WC2H 9EA

An Hachette UK company

9 10 8

Reissued 2010

A CIP catalogue record for this book
is available from the British Library.

ISBN 978-1-4091-1990-6

Printed and bound in Great Britain
by Clays Ltd, St Ives plc

The Orion Publishing Group's policy is to use papers
that are natural, renewable and recyclable products and
made from wood grown in sustainable forests. The logging
and manufacturing processes are expected to conform to
the environmental regulations of the country of origin.

www.orionbooks.co.uk

NOTE FROM THE AUTHOR

I've rarely written a dedication longer than two or three lines. This current one is different, the reason self-evident.

To my lovely and compassionate bride, Mary, of forty-plus years; and our children, Michael, Jonathan, and Glynis, who displayed strength, determination, and unfailing good humour (a mainstay of our family) throughout everything. They could not have been finer, nor could I ever express my love and gratitude sufficiently.

'Your father's off the operating table and on the recovery floor.'
'Who's going to pick him up?'

To the brilliant cardiologist Jeffrey Bender, MD, and the superb cardiothoracic surgeon Dr John Elefteriades, as well as the surgical crew and all those in the CTICU of Yale-New Haven Hospital, whose skills and concern passeth all understanding. (Although it could be argued that I was a glorious patient – unfortunately, not very convincingly.)

To our nephew, Dr Kenneth M. Kearns, also an extraordinary surgeon, who puts up with his less than saintly uncle with a tolerance known only to martyrs. And, Ken, thanks for the 'Listerine'. And to brother Donald Kearns, PhD-Nuclear Medicine. (How did I ever marry into such an accomplished family?) Thanks, Don, for your daily calls and visits. And to their medical associates Drs William Preskenis and David 'the Duke' Grisé of the pulmonary team. I hear you terrific guys, and I'm doing my damnedest to behave.

To our cousins I.C. 'Izzy' Ryducha and his wife, Janet, who were always there when we needed them.

To Drs Charles Augenbraun and Robert Greene of the Emergency Clinic at Norwalk Hospital, Connecticut, and all those wonderful people who made a pretty sick stranger feel as though he might see another sunrise. No mean feat.

Lastly, despite all efforts to keep the event under wraps, to those scores of people, friends, and those I've never met but whom I certainly consider friends, thanks for all the cards and notes expressing your good wishes. They were gratefully received and avidly read.

Now, let's lighten up; there's always something funny even in the worst of times. During a perfectly normal sponge bath a day or so after surgery, a kindly nurse turned me over and with great dignity, as well as a glint in her eye, said: 'Not to worry, Mr L., I'll still respect you in the morning.'

Amen. And to all once again, my deep thanks. I'm ready to run in a marathon.

To any sane person there has always been an unfathomable mystery about the systematic evil the Nazi regime perpetrated. Like a moral black hole, it seems to defy the laws of nature while being part of that nature.

DAVID ANSEN *Newsweek*, December 20, 1993

PROLOGUE

The Alpine pass, high in the Austrian Hausruck, was swept by the winter snow and assaulted by the cold north winds, while far below, a valley sprouted crocuses and the jonquils of early spring. This particular pass was neither a border checkpoint nor a transfer post from one part of the mountain range to another. In fact, it was not on any map issued for public scrutiny.

There was a thick, sturdy bridge, barely wide enough for a single vehicle, that spanned a seventy-foot gorge, several hundred feet above a rushing offshoot of the Salzach River. Once crossed, and passing through a tree-notched maze, there was a hidden road cut out of the mountain forest, a steep, twisting road that descended well over seven thousand feet to the isolated valley where the crocuses and the jonquils grew. The much warmer flatland was dotted with green fields and greener trees ... and a complex of small buildings, the roofs camouflaged by slashing diagonals of painted earth colours, undetectable from the skies, merely a part of the mountainous terrain. It was the headquarters of Die Brüderschaft der Wacht, The Brotherhood of the Watch, the progenitors of Germany's Fourth Reich.

The two figures walking across the bridge were dressed in heavy parkas, fur hats, and thick alpine boots; each turned his face away from the blasts of wind and snow that buffeted him. Unsteadily, they reached the other side and the traveller in front spoke.

'That's not a bridge I'd care to cross too often,' said the

1

American, slapping the snow off his clothing and removing his gloves to massage his face.

'But you will have to on your return, Herr Lassiter,' countered the late-middle-aged German, smiling broadly under the protection of a tree, as he, too, brushed off the snow. 'Not to be annoyed, *mein Herr*. Before you know it, you will be where the air is warm and there are actually flowers. At this altitude it is still winter, below it is springtime . . . Come, our transportation has arrived. Follow me!'

There was the sound of a gunning engine in the distance; the two men, Lassiter behind, walked rapidly, circuitously, through the trees to a small clearing, where there stood a Jeep-like vehicle, only much larger and heavier, with balloon tyres of very thick rubber, deeply treaded.

'That's some car,' said the American.

'You should be proud, it is *amerikanisch*! Built to our specifications in your state of Michigan.'

'What happened to Mercedes?'

'Too close, too dangerous,' replied the German. 'If you care to build a hidden fortress among your own, you don't employ the resources of your own. What you will see shortly is the combined efforts of numerous nations – their more avaricious businessmen, I grant you, merchants who will conceal clients and deliveries for excessive profits. Of course, once the deliveries are made, the profits become a loaded gun; the deliveries must continue, perhaps with more esoteric merchandise. It is the way of the world.'

'I bank on it,' said Lassiter, smiling while he removed his fur hat to relieve the hairline sweat. He was a shade under six feet, a man of middle years, his age attested to by streaks of grey at his temples and crow's-feet at the edges of his deep-set eyes; the face itself was narrow, sharp-featured. He started towards the vehicle, several steps behind his companion. However, what neither his companion nor the driver of the outsize vehicle saw was that he kept reaching into his pocket, subtly withdrawing his hand and dropping metal pellets into the snow-swept grass. He had been doing so for the past hour, since they had stepped out of a truck on an alpine road between two mountain villages. Each pellet had been subjected to radiation easily picked up by handheld scanners. At the point where the truck had stopped, he had removed an electronic transponder from his belt, and feigning a fall, had shoved it between two rocks. The trail was now clear; the homing device of those following would reach the top of its dial at that spot, accompanied by sharp, piercing beeps.

For the man called Lassiter was in a high-risk profession. He was a multilingual deep-cover agent for American intelligence, and his name was Harry Latham. In the sacrosanct chambers of the Agency, his code name was Sting.

The journey down into the valley mesmerized Latham. He had climbed a few mountains with his father and his younger brother, but they were minor, undramatic New England peaks, nothing like this. Here, as their steep descent progressed, there was change, obvious change – different colours, different smells, warmer breezes. Sitting alone in the backseat of the large open truck, he emptied his pocket of every hot pellet, preparing himself for the thorough search he anticipated; he was clean. He was also exhilarated, his excitement under control from years of experience, but his mind was on fire. It was there! He had found it! Yet, as they reached ground level, even Harry Latham was astonished at what he had really found.

The roughly three square miles of valley flatland was in reality a military base, superbly camouflaged. The roofs of the various one-storey structures were painted to blend in with the surroundings, and whole sections of the fields were beneath a latticework of ropes fifteen feet high, the open spaces between the ropes and poles filled with stretched, translucent green screening – corridors leading from one area to another. Grey motorcycles with sidecars sped through these concealed 'alleyways', the drivers and their passengers in uniform, while groups of men and women could be seen in training exercises, both physical and apparently academic – lecturers stood before black-boards in front of serried ranks of students. Those performing gymnastics and hand-to-hand combat were in minimal clothing – briefs and halters; those being lectured were in forest-green fatigues. What struck Harry Latham was the sense of constant movement. There was an intensity about the valley that was frightening, but then, so was the Brüderschaft, and this was its womb.

'It is spectacular, *nicht wahr*, Herr Lassiter?' shouted the middle-aged German beside the driver as they reached the bottom road and entered a corridor of roofed rope and green screening.

'*Unglaublich*,' agreed the American. '*Phantastisch!*'

'I forget, you speak our language fluently.'

'My heart is here. It always has been.'

'*Natürlich, denn wir sind im Recht.*'

'*Mehr als das, wir sind die Wahrheit.* Hitler spoke the truths of all truth.'

'Yes, yes, of course,' said the German, smiling with neutral eyes at Alexander Lassiter, born Harry Latham of Stockbridge, Massachusetts. 'We'll go directly to the *Oberbefehlshaber*. The *Kommandant* is eager to meet you.'

Thirty-two months of gruelling serpentine work were about to bear fruit, thought Latham. Nearly three years of building a life, *living* a life that was not his, were about to come to an end. The incessant, maddening, exhausting travels throughout Europe and the Middle East, synchronized down to hours, even minutes, so he would be at a specific place at a given time, where others could swear on their lives that they had seen him. And the scum of the world he had dealt with – arms merchants without conscience, whose extraordinary profits were measured by supertankers of blood; drug lords, killing and crippling generations of

4

children everywhere; compromised politicians, even states-men, who bent and subverted laws for the benefit of the manipulators – it was all finished. There would be no more frenzied funnelling of gargantuan sums of money through laundered Swiss accounts, secret numbers, and spectograph signatures, all part of the deadly games of international terrorism. Harry Latham's personal nightmare, as vital as it was, was over.

'We are here, Herr Lassiter,' said Latham's German companion as the mountain vehicle pulled up to a barrack door under the roped green screening high above. 'It is much warmer now, much more pleasant, *nicht wahr*?'

'It certainly is,' answered the deep-cover intelligence officer, stepping down from the rear seat. 'I'm actually sweating under these clothes.'

'We'll take the outerwear off inside and have yours dried for your return.'

'I'd appreciate it. I must be back in Munich by tonight.'

'Yes, we understand. Come, the *Kommandant*.' As the two men approached the heavy black wooden door with the scarlet swastika emblazoned in the centre, there was a whooshing sound in the air. Above, through the translucent green screening, the large white wings of a glider swooped in descending circles into the valley. 'Another wonder, Herr Lassiter? It is released from its mother aircraft at an altitude of roughly thirteen hundred feet. *Natürlich*, the pilot must be extremely well trained, for the winds are dangerous, so unpredictable. It is used only in emergencies.'

'I can see how it comes down. How does it get up?'

'The same winds, *mein Herr*, with the assistance of disposable booster rockets. In the thirties, we Germans developed the most advanced glider aircraft.'

'Why not use a conventional small plane?'

'Too easily monitored. A glider can be pulled up from a field, a clear pasture. A plane must be fuelled, be serviced, have maintenance, and frequently, even a flight plan.'

'*Phantastisch*,' repeated the American. 'And – of course –

the glider has few or no metal parts. Plastic and sized cloth are difficult for radar grids to pick up.'

'Difficult,' agreed the new-age Nazi. 'Not completely impossible, but extremely difficult.'

'Amazing,' said Herr Lassiter as his companion opened the door of the valley's headquarters. 'You are all to be congratulated. Your isolation is matched by your security. Superb!' Feigning a casualness he did not feel, Latham looked around the large room. There was a profusion of sophisticated computerized equipment, banks of consoles against each wall, starchy-uniformed operators in front of each, seemingly an equal mix of men and women . . . Men and women – something was odd, at least not normal. What was it? And then he knew; to an individual, the operators were young, generally in their twenties, mostly blond or light-haired, with clear, suntanned skin. As a group they were inordinately attractive, like models corralled by an advertising agency to sit in front of a client's computer products, conveying the message that potential customers, too, would look like this if they bought the merchandise.

'Each is an expert, Mr Lassiter,' said an unfamiliar, monotonic voice behind Latham. The American turned abruptly. The newcomer was a man about his own age, dressed in camouflage fatigues and wearing a Wehrmacht officer's cap; he had silently emerged from an open doorway on the left. 'General Ulrich von Schnabe, your enthusiastic host, *mein Herr*,' he continued, offering his hand. 'We meet a legend in his own time. Such a privilege!'

'You're far too generous, General. I'm merely an international businessman, but one with definite ideological persuasions, if you like.'

'No doubt reached by years of international observation?'

'You could say that, and not be in error. They claim that Africa was the first continent, yet, while others have developed over several thousand years, *Afrika* remains the Dark Continent, the black continent. The northern shores are now havens for equally inferior people.'

6

'Well said, Mr Lassiter. Yet you've made millions, some say billions, servicing the dark and darker skins.'

'Why not? What better satisfaction can a man like me have than by helping them slaughter each other?'

'*Wunderbar!* Beautifully and perceptively stated ... You were studying our group here, I watched you. You can see for yourself that these, every one, are of Aryan blood. Pure Aryan blood. As are those everywhere in our valley. Each has been carefully selected, their bloodlines traced, their commitment absolute.'

'The dream of the Lebensborn,' said the American quietly, reverentially. 'The breeding farms – estates actually, if I'm not mistaken, where the finest SS officers were bred to strong Teutonic women—'

'Eichmann had studies done. It was determined that the northern Germanic female had not only the finest bone structure in Europe and extraordinary strength, but a marked subservience to the male,' interrupted the general.

'The true superior race,' concluded Lassiter admiringly. 'Would that the dream had come true.'

'In large measure it has,' said Von Schnabe quietly. 'We believe that a great many here, if not a majority, are the children of *those* children. We stole lists from the Red Cross in Geneva, and spent years tracking down each family where the Lebensborn infants had been sent. These, and others we shall recruit throughout Europe, are the Sonnenkinder, the Children of the Sun. The inheritors of the Reich!'

'It's incredible.'

'We're reaching out everywhere, and everywhere those selected respond to us, for the circumstances are the same. Just as in the twenties, when the stranglehold of the Versailles and Locarno treaties led to the economic collapse of the Weimar Republic and the influx of undesirables throughout Germany, so has the collapse of the Berlin Wall led to chaos. We are a nation in conflagration, the lowborn non-Aryans crossing our borders in unlimited numbers, taking our jobs, polluting our morals, making whores of our women because where they come from it's perfectly acceptable. It's totally *un*acceptable and it must stop! You agree, of course.'

'Why else would I be here, General? I have funnelled millions into your needs through the banks in Algiers by way of Marseilles. My code has been *Frère – Bruder* – I trust it is familiar to you.'

'Which is why I embrace you with all my heart, as does the entire Brüderschaft.'

'So now let's conclude my final gift, General, final, for you will never need me again ... Forty-six cruise missiles appropriated from Saddam Hussein's arsenal, buried by his officer corps, who felt he would not survive. Their warheads are capable of carrying massive explosives as well as chemical payloads – gases that can immobilize whole areas of cities. These are included, of course, along with the launchers. I paid twenty-five million, American, for them. Pay me what you can, and if it is less, I will accept my loss with honour.'

'You are, indeed, a man of great honour, *mein Herr*.'

Suddenly the front door opened and a man in pure white coveralls walked into the room. He glanced around, saw Von Schnabe, and marched directly towards him, handing the general a sealed manila envelope. 'This is it,' the man said in German.

'*Danke*,' replied Von Schnabe, opening the envelope and extracting a small plastic pouch. 'You are a fine *Schauspieler* – a good impersonator – Herr Lassiter, but I believe you lost something. Our pilot just brought it to me.' The general shook the contents of the plastic bag into his hand. It was the transponder Harry Latham had shoved between the rocks of a mountain road thousands of feet above the valley. The hunt was finished. Harry swiftly raised his hand to his right ear. 'Stop him!' shouted Von Schnabe as the pilot grabbed Latham's arm, yanking it back into a hammerlock. 'There'll be no cyanide for you, Harry Latham of Stockbridge, Massachusetts, USA. We have other plans for you, brilliant plans.'

CHAPTER ONE

The early sun was blinding, causing the old man crawling through the wild brush to blink repeatedly as he wiped his eyes with the back of his trembling right hand. He had reached the edge of the small promontory on top of the hill, the 'high ground', as they called it years ago – years burned into his memory. The grassy point overlooked an elegant country estate in the Loire Valley. A flagstone terrace was no more than three hundred metres below, with a brick path bordered by flowers leading to it. Gripped in the old man's left hand, the shoulder strap taut, was a powerful rifle, its sight calibrated for the precise distance. The weapon was ready to fire. Soon his target – a man older than himself – would appear in the telescopic crosshairs. The monster would be taking his morning stroll to the terrace, dressed in his flowing morning robe, his reward his morning coffee laced with the finest brandy, a reward he would never reach on this particular morning. Instead, he would die, collapsing among the flowers, an appropriate irony: the death of consummate evil among surrounding beauty.

Jean-Pierre Jodelle, seventy-eight years of age and once a fierce provisional leader of the Résistance, had waited fifty years to fulfil a promise, a commitment, he had made to himself and to his God. He had failed with the lawyers and in the sacrosanct court chambers; no, not failed, instead, been insulted by them, scorned by all of them, and told to take his contemptible fantasies to a cell in a lunatic asylum, where he belonged! The great General Monluc was a true hero of France, a close associate of *le grand* Charles André de

Gaulle, that most illustrious of all soldier-statesmen, who had kept in constant touch with Monluc throughout the war over the underground radio frequencies despite the prospect of torture and a firing squad should Monluc be exposed.

It was all *merde*! Monluc was a turncoat, a coward, and a *traitor*! He gave lip service to the arrogant De Gaulle, fed him insignificant intelligence, and lined his own pockets with Nazi gold and art objects worth millions. And then in the aftermath, *le grand* Charles, in euphoric adulation, had pronounced Monluc *un bel ami de guerre*, a man to be honoured. It was no less than a command for all France.

Merde! How little De Gaulle knew! Monluc had ordered the execution of Jodelle's wife and his first son, a child of five. A second son, an infant of six months, was spared, perhaps by the warped rationality of the Wehrmacht officer who said, 'He's not a Jew, maybe someone will find him.'

Someone did. A fellow Résistance fighter, an actor from the Comédie Française. He found the screaming baby amid the rubble of the shattered house on the outskirts of Barbizon, where he had come for a secret meeting the following morning. The actor had brought the child home to his wife, a celebrated actress whom the Germans adored – their affection not returned, for her performances were dictated, not offered voluntarily. And when the war ended, Jodelle was a skeleton of his former self, physically unrecognizable and mentally beyond repair, and he knew it. Three years in a concentration camp, piling the bodies of gassed Jews, Gypsies, and 'undesirables', had reduced him to near idiocy, with neck tics, erratic blinking, spasms of throated cries, and all that went with severe psychiatric damage. He never revealed himself to his surviving son or the 'parents' who had reared him. Instead, wandering through the bowels of Paris and changing his name frequently, Jodelle observed from a distance as the child grew into manhood and became one of the most popular actors in France.

That distance, that unendurable pain, had been caused by Monluc the monster, who was now entering the circle of

Jodelle's telescopic sight. Only seconds now, and his commitment to God would be fulfilled.

Suddenly there was a terrible crack in the air and Jodelle's back was on fire, causing him to drop the rifle. He spun around, stunned to see two men in shirtsleeves, one with a bullwhip, looking down at him.

'It would be a pleasure to kill you, you sick old idiot, but your disappearance would only lead to complications,' said the man with the whip. 'You have a wine-soaked mouth that never stops chattering craziness. It's better that you go back to Paris and rejoin your army of drunken vagrants. Get out of here, or die!'

'How . . . ? How did you know . . . ?'

'You're a mental case, Jodelle, or whatever name you're using this month,' said the guard beside the whip master. 'You think we haven't spotted you these last two days, breaking the foliage as you came to this very accessible place with your rifle? You were far better in the old days, I'm told.'

'Then kill me, you sons of bitches! I'd rather die here, knowing I was so close, than go on living!'

'Oh, no, the general wouldn't approve,' added the whipper. 'You could have told others what you intended to do, and we don't want people looking for you or your corpse on this property. You're insane, Jodelle, everyone knows that. The courts made it clear.'

'They're corrupt!'

'You're paranoid.'

'I know what I *know*!'

'You're also a drunk, well documented by a dozen cafés on the Rive Gauche that've thrown you out. Drink yourself into hell, Jodelle, but get out of here before I send you there now. Get up! Run as fast as those spindly legs will carry you!'

The curtain rang down on the final scene of the play, a French translation of Shakespeare's *Coriolanus*, revived by Jean-Pierre Villier, the fifty-year-old actor who was the reigning king of the Paris stage and the French screen as well as a nominee for an American Academy Award as a result of his first film in the United States. The curtain rose and fell and rose again as the large, broad-shouldered Villier acknowledged his audience by smiling and clapping his hands at their acceptance. It was all about to erupt into madness.

From the rear of the theatre an old man in torn, shabby clothes lurched down the centre aisle, screaming at the top of his coarse voice. Suddenly he pulled a rifle out of his loose trousers, held by suspenders, causing those in the audience who saw him to panic, the panic instantly spreading throughout the succeeding rows of seats as men pushed women below the line of fire, the vocal chaos reverberating off the walls of the theatre. Villier moved quickly, shoving back the few actors and members of the technical crew who had come out onstage.

'An angry critic I can *accept*, monsieur!' he roared, confronting the deranged old man approaching the stage in a familiar voice that could command any crowd. 'But this is *insane*! Put down your weapon and we will talk!'

'There is no talk left in me, my son! My only son! I have failed you and your mother. I'm useless, a *nothing*! I only want you to know that I tried . . . I love you, my only son, and I tried, but I failed!'

With those words the old man spun his rifle around, the barrel in his mouth, his right hand surging for the trigger. He reached it and blew the back of his head apart, blood and sinew spraying over all who were near him.

'Who the hell *was* he?' cried a shaken Jean-Pierre Villier at his dressing-room table, his parents at his side. 'He said such crazy things, then killed himself. *Why?*'

The elder Villiers, now in their late seventies, looked at each other; both nodded.

'We must talk,' said Catherine Villier as she massaged the

aching neck of the man she had raised as her son. 'Perhaps with your wife too.'

'That's not necessary,' interrupted the father. 'He can handle that if he thinks he should.'

'You're right, my husband. It is his decision.'

'What are you both talking about?'

'We have kept many things from you, my son, things that in the early years might have harmed you—'

'Harmed me?'

'Through no fault of yours, Jean-Pierre. We were an occupied country, the enemy among us constantly searching for those who secretly, violently, opposed the victors, in many cases torturing and imprisoning whole families who were suspect.'

'The Résistance, naturally,' interrupted Villier.

'Naturally,' agreed the father.

'You both were a part of it, you've told me that, although you've never expounded on your contributions.'

'They're best forgotten,' said the mother. 'It was a horrible time – so many who were stigmatized and beaten as collaborators were only protecting loved ones, including their children.'

'But this man tonight, this crazy tramp! He so identified with me that he called me his *son*! . . . I accept a degree of excessive devotion – it goes with the profession, however foolish that may be – but to the point of killing himself in front of my eyes? *Madness!*'

'He *was* mad, driven insane by what he had endured,' said Catherine.

'You knew him?'

'Very well,' replied the old actor, Julian Villier. 'His name was Jean-Pierre Jodelle, once a promising young baritone at the Opéra, and we, your mother and I, tried desperately to find him after the war. There was no trace, and since we knew he had been found out by the Germans and sent to a concentration camp, we assumed he was dead, a non-entry, like thousands of others.'

13

'Why did you try to find him? Who was he to you?'

The only mother Jean-Pierre had ever known knelt beside his dressing-room chair, her exquisite features bespeaking the great star she had been; her blue-green eyes below her full, soft white hair were locked with his. She spoke softly. 'Not only to us, my son, but to you. He was your natural father.'

'Oh, my God! . . . Then you, *both* of you—'

'Your natural mother,' added Villier *père*, quietly interrupting, 'was a member of the Comédie—'

'A splendid talent,' broke in Catherine, 'caught in those trying years between being an ingenue and being a woman, all of it made horrid by the occupation. She was a dear girl, like a younger sister to me.'

'Please!' cried Jean-Pierre, leaping to his feet as the mother he knew rose and stood by her husband. 'This is all coming so quickly, it is so astonishing, I . . . I can't *think*!'

'Sometimes it's best not to think for a while, my son,' said the elder Villier. 'Stay numb until the mind tells you it is ready to accept.'

'You used to tell me that years ago,' said the actor, smiling sadly, warmly, at Julian, 'when I had trouble with a scene or a monologue, and the meaning was escaping me. You'd say, "Just keep reading and rereading the words without trying so hard. Something will happen."'

'It was good advice, my husband.'

'I was always a better teacher than I ever was a performer.'

'Agreed,' said Jean-Pierre softly.

'I beg your pardon? You agree?'

'I meant only, my father, that when you were onstage, you . . . you—'

'A part of you was always concentrating on the others,' jumped in Catherine Villier, exchanging a knowing glance with her son – and not her son.

'Ah, you both conspire again, has it not been so for years? The two great stars being gentle with the lesser player . . .

Good! That's over with ... For a few moments we all stopped thinking about tonight. Now, perhaps, we can talk.'

Silence.

'For God's sake, tell me what *happened*!' exclaimed Jean-Pierre finally.

As he asked the question, there was a rapid knocking at the dressing-room door; it was opened by the theatre's old night watchman. 'Sorry to intrude, but I thought you ought to know. There are still reporters at the stage door. They won't believe the police or me. We said you left earlier by the front entrance, but they're not convinced. However, they cannot get inside.'

'Then we'll stay here for a while, if need be all night – at least I will. There's a couch in the other room, and I've already called my wife. She heard everything on the news.'

'Very well, sir ... Madame Villier, and you also, monsieur, despite the terrible circumstances it is glorious to see you both again. You are always remembered with great affection.'

'Thank you, Charles,' said Catherine. 'You look well, my friend.'

'I'd look better still if you were back onstage, madame.' The watchman nodded and closed the door.

'Go on, Father, what *did* happen?'

'We were all part of the Résistance,' began Julian Villier, sitting down on a small love seat across the room, 'artists drawn together against an enemy that would destroy all art. And we had certain capabilities that served our cause. Musicians passed codes by inserting melodic phrases not in an original score; illustrators produced the daily and weekly posters demanded by the Germans, subtly employing colours and images that sent other messages. And we in the theatre continuously corrupted texts, especially those of revivals and well-known plays, often giving direct instructions to the saboteurs—'

'At times it was quite amusing,' interrupted the regal Catherine, joining her husband and taking his hand. 'Say

15

there was a line like "I shall meet her at the Metro in Montparnasse." We'd change it to "I shall meet her at the east railway station – she should be there by eleven o'clock." The play would finish, the curtain fall, and all those Germans in their splendid uniforms would be applauding while a Résistance team left quickly to be in place for the sabotage units at the Gare de l'Est an hour before midnight.'

'Yes, yes,' said Jean-Pierre impatiently. 'I've heard the stories, but that's not what I'm asking. I realize it's as difficult for you as it is for me, but please, tell me what I must know.'

The white-haired couple looked intensely at each other; the wife nodded as their hands gripped, the veins showing. Her husband spoke. 'Jodelle was found out, revealed by a young runner who could not take the torture. The Gestapo surrounded his house, waiting for him to return one night, but he couldn't, for he was in Le Havre, making contact with British and American agents in the early planning stages of the invasion. By dawn, it was said that the leader of the Gestapo unit became furious with frustration. He stormed the house and executed your mother and your older brother, a child of five years. They picked up Jodelle several hours later; we managed to get word to him that you had survived.'

'Oh . . . my God!' The celebrated actor grew pale, his eyes closed as he sank down into his chair. 'Monsters! . . . No, wait, what did you just say? "It was said that the leader of the Gestapo—" It was *said*? Not *confirmed*?'

'You're very quick, Jean-Pierre,' observed Catherine. 'You listen, that's why you're a great actor.'

'To hell with that, Mother! What did you mean, Father?'

'It was not the policy of the Germans to kill the families of Résistance fighters, real or suspected. They had more practical uses for them – torture them for information, or use them as bait for others, and there was always forced labour, women for the Officers Corps, a category in which your natural mother would certainly have fallen.'

'Then why were they killed? . . . No, first me. How did I survive?'

'I went out to an early dawn meeting in the woods of Barbizon. I passed your house, saw windows broken, the front door smashed, and heard an infant crying. You. Everything was obvious and, of course, there would be no meeting. I brought you home, bicycling through the back roads to Paris.'

'It's a little late to thank you, but, again, why were my – my natural mother and my brother *shot*?'

'Now you lost a word, my son,' said the elder Villier.

'What?'

'In your shock, your listening wasn't as acute as it was a moment before, when I described the events of that night.'

'Stop it, Papa! Say what you mean!'

'*I* said "executed", *you* said "shot".'

'I don't understand . . .'

'Before Jodelle was found out by the Germans, one of his covers was as a city messenger for the Ministry of Information – the Nazis could never get our arrondissements straight, much less our short, curving streets. We never learned the details, for as impressive as his voice was, Jodelle was extremely quiet where rumours were concerned – they were everywhere. Falsehoods, half-truths, and truths raced through Paris like gunfire at the slightest provocation. We were a city gripped by fear and suspicion—'

'I understand that, my father,' broke in the ever more impatient Jean-Pierre. 'Please explain what I *don't* understand. The details that you were never given, what did they concern and how did they result in the killings, the *executions*?'

'Jodelle said to a few of us that there was a man so high in the Résistance that he was a legend only whispered about, his identity the most closely guarded secret of the move-ment. Jodelle, however, claimed he had learned who the man was, and if what he had pieced together was accurate, that same man, that "legend", was no great hero but instead a traitor.'

'Who was he?' pressed Jean-Pierre.

'He never told us. However, he did say that the man was a general in our French army, of which there were dozens. He said if he was right and any of us revealed the man's name, we'd be shot by the Germans. If he was wrong and someone spoke of him in a defamatory way, our wing would be called unstable and we would no longer be trusted.'

'What was he going to do then?'

'If he was able to establish his proof, he would take the man out himself. He swore he was in a position to do so. We assumed – correctly, we believe, to this day – that whoever the traitor was, he somehow learned of Jodelle's suspicions and gave the order to execute him and his family.'

'That was it? Nothing *else*?'

'Try to understand what the times were like, my son,' said Catherine Villier. 'A wrong word, even a hostile stare or a gesture, could result in immediate detention, imprisonment, and even, not unheard of, deportation. The occupation forces, especially the ambitious middle-level officers, were fanatically suspicious of everyone and everything. Each new Résistance accomplishment fuelled the fires of their anger. Quite simply, no one was safe. Kafka could not have invented such a hell.'

'And you never saw him again until *tonight*?'

'If we had, we would not have recognized him,' replied Villier *père*. 'I barely did when I identified his body. The years notwithstanding, he was, as the English say, a "rackabones" of the man I remembered, less than half the weight and height of his former self, his face mummified, a stretched, wrinkled version of what it once was.'

'Perhaps it wasn't *he*, is that possible, my father?'

'No, it was Jodelle. His eyes were wide in death, and still so blue, so resoundingly blue, like a cloudless sky in the Mediterranean . . . Like yours, Jean-Pierre.'

'Jean-Pierre . . . ?' said the actor softly. 'You gave me his name?'

'In truth, it was your brother's also,' corrected the actress gently. 'That poor child had no use for it, and we felt you should have it for Jodelle's sake.'

'That was caring of you—'

'We knew we could never replace your true parents,' continued the actress quickly, half pleadingly, 'but we tried our best, my darling. In our wills we make clear everything that happened, but until tonight we hadn't the courage within ourselves to tell you. We love you so.'

'For God's sake, stop, Mother, or I'll burst out crying. Who in this world could ask for better parents than you two? I will never know what I cannot know, but forever you *are* my father and mother, and you know that.'

The telephone rang, startling them all. 'The press doesn't have this number, does it?' asked Julian.

'Not that I'm aware of,' replied Jean-Pierre, turning to the phone on the dressing table. 'Only you, Giselle, and my agent have it; not even my attorney or, God forbid, the owners of the theatre . . . Yes?' he said gutturally.

'Jean-Pierre?' asked his wife, Giselle, over the telephone.

'Of course, my dear.'

'I wasn't sure—'

'I wasn't either, that's why I altered my voice. Mother and Father are here, and I'll be home as soon as the newspapers give up for the night.'

'I think you should find a way to come home now.'

'What?'

'A man has come to see you—'

'At *this* hour? Who is he?'

'An American, and he says he has to talk to you. It's about tonight.'

'Tonight . . . here at the theatre?'

'Yes, my dear.'

'Perhaps you shouldn't have let him in, Giselle.'

19

'I'm afraid I didn't have a choice. Henri Bressard is with him.'

'*Henri?* What does tonight have to do with the Quai d'Orsay?'

'As we speak, our dear friend Henri is all smiles and diplomatic charm and will tell me nothing until you arrive . . . Am I right, Henri?'

'Too true, my dearest Giselle' was the faint reply heard by Villier. 'I know little or nothing myself.'

'Did you hear him, my darling?'

'Clearly enough. What about the American? Is he a boor? Just answer yes or no.'

'Quite the contrary. Although, as you actors might say, his eyes have a hot flame in them.'

'What about Mother and Father? Should they come with me?'

Giselle Villier addressed the two men in the room, repeating the question. '*Later*,' said the man from the Quai d'Orsay, loud enough to be heard over the telephone. 'We'll speak to them *later*, Jean-Pierre,' he added even louder. 'Not tonight.'

The actor and his parents left the theatre by the front entrance, the night watchman having told the press that Villier would appear shortly at the stage door. 'Let us know what's happening,' said Julian as he and his wife embraced their son and walked to the first of the two taxis called from the dressing-room phone. Jean-Pierre climbed into the second, giving the driver his address in the Parc Monceau.

The introductions were both brief and alarming. Henri Bressard, First Secretary of Foreign Affairs for the Republic of France and a close friend of the younger Villiers for a decade, spoke calmly, gesturing at his American companion, a tall man in his mid-thirties with dark brown hair and sharp features, albeit with clear grey eyes that were disturbingly alive, perhaps in contrast to his gentle smile. 'This is Drew

Latham, Jean Pierre. He is a special officer for a branch of US intelligence known only as Consular Operations, a unit our own sources have determined to be under the combined authority of the American State Department and the Central Intelligence Agency ... My *God*, how the two can get together is beyond this diplomat!'

'It's not always easy, Mr Secretary,' said Latham pleasantly, if haltingly, in broken French, 'but we manage.'

'Perhaps we should speak English,' offered Giselle Villier. 'We are all fluent.'

'Thank you very much,' the American responded in English. 'I don't want to be misunderstood.'

'You won't be,' said Villier, 'but please be aware that we – I – must understand why you are here tonight, this terrible night. I have heard things this evening that I have never heard before – are you to add to them, monsieur?'

'Jean-Pierre,' broke in Giselle, 'what are you talking about?'

'Let him answer,' said Villier, his large blue eyes riveted on the American.

'Maybe, maybe not,' replied the intelligence officer. 'I know you've talked to your parents, but I can't know what you talked about.'

'Naturally. But it's possible you might assume a certain direction in our conversation, no?'

'Frankly, yes, although I don't know how much you'd been told before. The events of tonight suggest that you knew nothing about Jean-Pierre Jodelle.'

'Quite true, said the actor.

'The Sureté, who also know nothing, questioned you at length and were convinced you were telling the truth.'

'Why not, Monsieur Latham? I *was* telling the truth.'

'Is there another truth now, Mr Villier?'

'Yes, there is.'

'Will you both stop talking in circles!' cried the actor's wife. 'What is this truth?'

'Be calm, Giselle. We are on the same wavelength, as the Americans say.'

'Shall we stop here?' asked the Consular Operations officer. 'Would you rather we speak privately?'

'No, of course not. My wife is entitled to know everything, and Henri here is one of our closest friends, as well as a man trained to keep his own counsel.'

'May we sit down,' said Giselle firmly. 'This is too confusing to absorb standing up.' When they had taken their seats, hers next to her husband's, she added, 'Please continue, Monsieur Latham, and I beg you to be clearer.'

'I should like to know,' broke in Bressard, every inch the government official, 'who is this Jodelle person, and why should Jean-Pierre know anything at all about him?'

'Forgive me, Henri,' interrupted the actor. 'Not that I mind, but I'd like to know why Monsieur Latham saw fit to use you as a means to reach me.'

'I knew you were friends.' The American answered for himself. 'In fact, several weeks ago, when I mentioned to Henri that I was unable to get tickets to your play, you were kind enough to leave a pair at the box office for me.'

'Ah, yes, I remember . . . Your name seemed somehow familiar, but with everything that's happened, I didn't make the connection. "Two in the name of Latham . . ." I *do* recall.'

'You were wonderful, sir—'

'You're very kind,' interrupted Jean-Pierre, dismissing the compliment and studying the US intelligence officer, then looking at Bressard. 'Therefore,' he continued, 'I may assume that you and Henri are acquainted.'

'More officially than socially,' said Bressard. 'I believe we've dined only once together; actually it was an extension of a conference that was largely unresolved.'

'Between your two governments,' Giselle observed aloud.

'Yes,' agreed Bressard.

'And what do you and Monsieur Latham confer about, Henri?' pressed the wife. 'If I may ask.'

'Of course you may, my dear,' replied Bressard. 'Generally speaking, sensitive situations, events that are taking place or have taken place in the past that might harm or embarrass our respective governments.'

'Tonight falls into that category?'

'Drew must answer that, Giselle, I cannot, and I'm as eager as you are to learn. He roused me out of bed over an hour ago insisting that for both our sakes I bring him to you immediately. When I asked him why, he made it clear that only Jean-Pierre could permit me to have the information – information that pertained to the events of tonight.'

'Which is why you suggested we speak privately, is that correct, Monsieur Latham?' asked Villier.

'It is, sir.'

'Then your arrival here tonight, this *terrible* night, falls under the blanket of official business, *n'est-ce pas?*'

'I'm afraid it does,' said the American.

'Even considering the lateness of the hour and the tragedy we alluded to?'

'Again, yes,' said Latham. 'Every hour is vital to us. Especially to me, if you want to be specific.'

'I do care to be specific, monsieur.'

'All right, I'll speak plainly. My brother's a case officer with the Central Intelligence Agency. He was sent out undercover into the Hausruck mountains in Austria. It was a survey operation involving a spreading neo-Nazi organization, and he hasn't been heard from in six weeks.'

'I can understand your concern, Drew,' interrupted Henri Bressard, 'but what has it to do with this evening – this terrible night, as Jean-Pierre called it?'

The American looked at Villier in silence; the actor spoke. 'The deranged old man who killed himself in the theatre was my father,' he said quietly, 'my natural father. Years ago, in the war, he was a Résistance fighter. The Nazis found him and broke him, drove him mad.'

Giselle gasped; her hand shot to her left, gripping her husband's arm.

'They're back,' said Latham, 'growing in numbers and influence beyond anything anyone wants to believe or talk about.'

'Say there's even a granule of truth in what you say,' pressed Bressard. 'What has it to do with the Quai d'Orsay? You said "for both our sakes". How, my friend?'

'You'll get a full briefing tomorrow at our embassy. I insisted on that two hours ago, and Washington agreed. Until then I can tell you only – and it's all I really know – that the money trail through Switzerland to Austria and the growing Nazi movement is secretly funnelled from people here in France. Who, we don't know, but it's immense, millions upon millions of dollars. To fanatics who are rebuilding the party – Hitler's party in exile – but still in Germany, hidden in Germany.'

'Which, if you're correct, means there's another organization here, is that what you're saying?' asked Bressard.

'Jodelle's *traitor*,' whispered an astonished Jean-Pierre Villier, leaning forward in the chair. 'The French general!'

'Or what he created,' said Latham.

'For God's sake, what are you two *talking* about?' exclaimed the actor's wife. 'A newly discovered father, the Résistance, Nazis, millions of dollars to fanatics in the mountains! It all sounds crazy – *fou!*'

'Why don't you start at the beginning, Drew Latham,' said the actor softly. 'Perhaps I might fill in with things I knew nothing about before tonight.'

CHAPTER TWO

'According to the records in our possession,' began Latham, 'in June of 1946 a repatriated member of the French Résistance, alternately using the names of Jean Froisant and Pierre Jodelle, appeared repeatedly at our embassy in various simple disguises and always at night. He claimed he was being silenced by the Paris courts regarding his knowledge of the treasonous activities of a leader of the Résistance. The traitor supposedly was a French general under privileged house arrest accorded by the German High Command to your general officers who remained in France. The judgement of the OSI investigators was negative, the determination being that Froisant/Jodelle was mentally unbalanced, as were hundreds, if not thousands, who had been psychologically crippled in the concentration camps.'

'The OSI is the Office of Special Investigations,' explained Bressard, seeing the bewildered expressions on the faces of both Villiers. 'It's the American department created to pursue war criminals.'

'I'm sorry, I thought you knew,' said Latham. 'It operated extensively here in France in conjunction with your authorities.'

'Of course,' acknowledged Giselle. 'It was the formal name; I'm told we had others. Collaborationist-hunters, pig-seekers, so many names.'

'Please continue,' said Jean-Pierre, frowning, disturbed. 'Jodelle was dismissed as a madman – just like *that*?'

'It wasn't arbitrary, if that's what you mean. He was interrogated at length, including three separate depositions taken independently of one another to check for inconsistencies. It's standard procedure—'

'Then you have the information,' interrupted the actor. 'Who was this general?'

'We don't know—'

'You don't *know*?' cried Bressard. '*Mon Dieu*, you didn't *lose* the material, did you?'

'No, we didn't lose it, Henri, it was stolen.'

'But you said, "according to the records"!' Giselle broke in.

'I said "according to the records in our *possession*",' corrected Latham. 'You can index a name in a particular time frame, and the index will summarize without specifics the substantiated case histories where procedures were followed and final determinations were made. Materials such as interrogations and depositions are in separate classified files to protect the privacy of the individuals from hostile inquiries . . . *Those* were the files that were removed. Why, we don't know – or perhaps now we do.'

'But you knew about me,' interrupted Jean-Pierre. 'How?'

'As new information comes in, the index summaries are updated by the OSI. About three years ago, a drunken Jodelle accosted the American ambassador outside the Lyceum Theatre, where you were appearing in a play—'

'*Je m'appelle Aquilon!*' Bressard broke in enthusiastically. 'You were *magnifique!*'

'Oh, be quiet, Henri . . . Go on, Drew Latham.'

'Jodelle kept shouting what a great actor you were, and that you were his son, and why wouldn't the Americans listen to him. Naturally, the theatre's attendants pulled him away as the doorman escorted the ambassador to his limousine. He explained that the old drunken tramp was unbalanced, an obsessed fan who hung around the theatres where you were playing.'

'I never saw him. Why is that?'

'Also explained by the doorman. Whenever you appeared at the stage door, he ran away.'

'That doesn't make sense!' said Giselle firmly.

'I'm afraid it does, my dear,' countered Jean-Pierre, looking sadly at his wife. 'At least according to what I learned tonight . . . So, monsieur,' continued the actor, 'because of that odd yet not unusual event, my name was included in the – how do you say it? – your nonclassified intelligence files?'

'Only as part of a behaviour pattern, not taken seriously.'

'But you took it seriously, *n'est-ce pas?*'

'Please understand me, sir,' said Latham, leaning forward in the chair. 'Five weeks and four days ago my brother was to make contact with his Munich runner. It was a specific arrangement, not an estimate, every logistic was narrowed down to a time frame of twelve hours. Three years of a high-risk, deep-cover operation were finished, the end in sight, his secure transportation to the States arranged. When a week passed and there was no word from him, I flew back to Washington and pored over everything we had, everything there was, on Harry's operation – that's my brother, Harry Latham . . . For one reason or another, probably because it was an odd reference, the Lyceum Theatre episode struck me, stayed with me. As you implied, why was it even there? Famous actors and actresses are frequently bothered by fans who are obsessed with them. We read about that sort of thing all the time.'

'I believe I said as much,' interrupted Villier. 'It's an occupational sickness and, for the most part, quite harmless.'

'That's what I thought, sir. Why *was* it there?'

'Did you find an answer?'

'Not really, but enough to convince me to try and find Jodelle. Since I came back to Paris two weeks ago, I've looked everywhere, in all the back alleys of Montparnasse, in all the run-down sections of the city.'

'Why?' asked Giselle. 'What partial answer did you find? Why was my husband's name forwarded to Washington in the first place?'

'I asked myself the same question, Mrs Villier. So while I

was in Washington I looked up the former ambassador –
from the last administration – and asked *him*. You see, the
information could not have been forwarded to the intelligence community unless he authorized it.'

'What did my old friend the ambassador say?' Bressard
broke in, his tone unmistakably critical.

'It was his wife—'

'*Ah*,' said the Quai d'Orsay official, 'then one should
listen. She should have been the *ambassadeur*. So much more
intelligent, so much more knowledgeable. She's a physician,
you know.'

'Yes, I spoke with her. She's also an avid theatregoer. She
always insists on sitting in the first three rows.'

'Hardly the best seats,' said the actor softly. 'One loses the
perspective for the immediate. Forgive me, go on. What did
she say?'

'It was your eyes, Mr Villier. And those of Jodelle when he
stopped them on the pavement and shouted hysterically.
"Both their eyes were so intensely blue," she said, "yet the
colour was extraordinarily light, extremely unusual for blue-
eyed people." So she thought, delusions or not, that there
might be substance to the old man's ravings because the
similarity of such unusual eyes could only be genetically
transmitted. She admitted it was a speculative call, but one
she couldn't overlook. And, as Henri mentioned, she is a
doctor.'

'So your suspicions proved to be accurate,' said Jean-
Pierre, nodding his head reflectively.

'When the news came over the television that an
unidentified old man had shot himself in the theatre after
screaming that you were his son – well, I knew I'd found
Jodelle.'

'But you didn't, Drew Latham. You found the son, not the
father he never knew. So where are you now? There's little I
can add that you don't already know, and that much I myself
just found out tonight from the only parents I've ever
known. They tell me Jodelle was a Résistance fighter, a

baritone at the Paris Opéra, found out by the Germans and sent to a concentration camp from which he supposedly never returned. Obviously he did, and apparently the poor soul recognized his infirmities and never revealed himself.' The actor paused, then added sadly, pensively, 'He gave me a privileged life and rejected any worthwhile life for himself.'

'He must have loved you very much, my darling,' said Giselle. 'But what sorrow, what torment he had to live with.'

'They looked for him. They tried so hard to find him – he could have been given medical treatment. *God*, what a tragic waste!' Jean-Pierre looked over at the American. 'Again, monsieur, what can I say? I can't help you any more than I can help myself.'

'Tell me exactly what happened. I learned very little at the theatre. The police weren't there when it happened, and the witnesses who remained – mainly ushers by the time I arrived – weren't much help. Most claimed they heard the shouts, at first thinking they were part of the "bravos", then saw an old man in dishevelled clothes running down the aisle, yelling that you were his son and carrying a rifle, which he turned on himself and fired. That was about it.'

'No, there was more,' said Villier, shaking his head. 'There was a brief hush in the audience, a momentary pause, that shock of astonishment before the vocal reaction begins. It was then that I clearly heard several of his statements. "I have failed you and your mother – I am useless, a nothing. I only want you to know I tried – I tried but failed." That's all I recall, then there was chaos. I have no idea what he meant.'

'It has to be in the words, Mr Villier,' said Latham rapidly, emphatically, 'and it *had* to be something so vital to him, so catastrophic that he broke the silence of a lifetime and confronted you. A last gesture before killing himself; something had to trigger it.'

'Or the final deterioration of an unbalanced mind pushed over the edge into utter madness,' suggested the actor's wife.

'I don't think so,' the American courteously disagreed. 'He was too focused. He knew exactly what he was doing –

what he was going to do. He somehow got into the theatre with a concealed rifle, no mean feat, and then waited until the performance was over and your husband was accepting the praises of the crowd – he wasn't going to deny him that. A man gripped in the emotional frenzy of an insane act would be prone to interrupting the play, pivoting the entire attention on himself. Jodelle didn't. A part of him was too rational, too rationally generous to permit it.'

'Are you also a psychologist?' asked Bressard.

'No more than you are, Henri. The bottom line for both of us is studying behaviour, predicting it if we can, isn't that so?'

'So you're saying,' interrupted Villier, 'that my father – the natural father I never knew – rationally calculated the moves for his own death because he was motivated by something that happened to him.' The actor leaned back in his chair, frowning. 'Then we must find out what it was, mustn't we?'

'I don't know how, sir. He's dead.'

'If an actor is analysing a character he must bring to life on the stage or in a film, and that character is beyond the clichés of his imagination, he has to study the reality, expand upon it, doesn't he?'

'I'm not sure what you mean.'

'Many years ago I was called upon to play a murderous Bedouin sheikh, a very unsympathetic man who ruthlessly kills his enemies because he believes they are the enemies of Allah. It brought to mind all the clichés one expects: the satanic brows; the sharp chin beard; the thin, evil lips; the messianic eyes – it was all so banal, I thought. So I flew to Jidda, went into the desert – under luxurious conditions, I assure you – and met with several Bedouin chieftains. They were nothing of the sort. They were religious zealots, indeed, but they were calm, very courteous, and truly believed that what the West called the Arab crimes of their grandfathers were entirely justified, for those ancient ene-mies *were* the enemies of their God. They even explained that after each death, their ancestors would pray to Allah for the safe *deliverance* of their enemies. There was a true sadness in what they felt was necessary slaughter. Do you see what I mean?'

'That was *Le Carnage du Voile*,' said the Quai d'Orsay's Bressard. 'You were superb and stole the film from its two stars. Paris's leading critic wrote that your evil was so pure because you clothed it in such quiet benevolence—'

'*Please*, Henri. Enough.'

'I still don't know what you're driving at, Mr Villier.'

'If what you believe about Jodelle . . . if what you believe is true, then a part of him was less mad than his actions would indicate. Isn't that really what you are saying?'

'Yes, it is. I believe it. That's why I've been trying to find him.'

'And such a man, regardless of his infirmities, is capable of communicating with others, with his equally unfortunate peers, not so?'

'Probably. Sure.'

'Then we must start with his reality, the environs in which he lived. We'll do it, I'll do it.'

'Jean-Pierre!' cried Giselle. 'What are you *saying*?'

'Our revival has no matinees. Only an idiot would play Coriolanus eight times a week. My days are free.'

'And?' asked a disturbed Bressard, his eyebrows arched.

'As you have so generously implied, Henri, I am a passably adequate actor and I have access to every costume establishment in Paris. The attire will be no problem, and extremist makeup has always been one of my strengths. Before he passed away, Monsieur Olivier and I agreed that it was a dishonest artifice – the chameleon, he called it – but nevertheless more than half the battle. I will enter the world where Jodelle existed and perhaps I'll get lucky. He had to talk to someone, I'm convinced of that.'

'Those environs,' said Latham, 'that "world" of his is pretty sordid and can be violent, Mr Villier. If some of those characters think you have twenty francs, they'll break your

31

legs for it. I carry a weapon, and without exaggeration, I felt I had to display it on five separate occasions during the past weeks. Also, most of those people are tight-lipped and don't like outsiders who ask questions; in fact, they resent it strongly. I didn't get anywhere.'

'Ah, but you are not an actor, monsieur, and in all frankness, your French could be improved upon. No doubt you prowled those streets in your normal clothes, your overall appearance not much different from what we see now, *n'est-ce pas?*'

'Well . . . yes.'

'Again, forgive me, but a clean-shaven man in rather decent attire and asking a question in hesitant French would hardly inspire confidence among Jodelle's confrères in that world of his.'

'Jean-Pierre, stop it!' exclaimed the actor's wife. 'What you're suggesting is out of the question! My feelings and your safety aside, your run-of-the-play contract forbids you to undertake physical risk. My God, you're not permitted to ski or play polo or even fly your plane!'

'But I won't be skiing or on a horse or flying my plane. I'm merely going across the city into various arrondissements to research atmosphere. It's far less than travelling to Saudi Arabia for a secondary film role.'

'*Merde!*' cried Bressard. 'It's preposterous!'

'I didn't come here to ask such a thing of you, sir,' said Latham. 'I came hoping you might know something that could help me. You don't and I accept that. My government can hire people to do what you're suggesting.'

'Then without false modesty I suggest that you wouldn't be getting the best. You do want the best, don't you, Drew Latham, or have you forgotten your brother so quickly? Your anxiety tells me you haven't. He must be a fine man, a splendid older brother who undoubtedly helped you, guided you. Naturally you feel you owe him whatever you can do.'

'I'm concerned, yes, but that's personal,' interrupted the American sharply. 'I'm a professional.'

'So am I, monsieur. And I owe the man we call Jodelle every bit as much as you owe your brother. Perhaps more. He lost his wife and his first child fighting for all of us, then tragically consigned his own existence to a hell we can't imagine so that I might thrive. Oh, yes, I owe him – professionally *and* personally. Also the woman, the young actress who was my natural mother, and the child whose first name I bear, the older brother who might have guided me. My debt is heavy, Drew Latham, and you will not stop me from paying something back. None of you will ... Be so kind as to come here tomorrow at noon. I'll be prepared and all the arrangements will be made.'

Latham and Henri Bressard walked out of the imposing Villier house on the Parc Monceau to the official's car. 'Need I tell you that I don't like any of this?' said the Frenchman.

'Neither do I,' agreed Drew. 'He may be a hell of an actor, but he's out of his depth.'

'Depth? What depth? I simply don't like his going into the bowels of Paris where, if he's recognized, he could be assaulted for his money or even kidnapped for a ransom. You're saying something else, I believe. What is it?'

'I'm not sure, call it instinct. Something *did* happen to Jodelle, and it's a lot more than a deranged old man killing himself in front of the son he never acknowledged. The act itself was one of final desperation; he knew he had been beaten, irrevocably beaten.'

'Yes, I heard Jean-Pierre's words,' said Bressard, rounding the trunk to the driver's side as Latham opened the door at the kerb. 'The old man shouted that he had failed; he had tried but failed.'

'But *what* had he tried? What did he fail to do? What *was* it?'

'The end of his road, perhaps,' replied Henri, starting the car and heading into the street. 'The knowledge that at long last the enemy was beyond his reach.'

'To know that, to really know it, he had to have found that enemy, and then understood that he was helpless. He knew he was considered a madman; neither Paris nor Washington thought he was credible, and he'd been rejected, hell, thrown out of the courts. So he went out on his own to find his enemy, and once he found it . . . him . . . they, something happened. They stopped him cold.'

'If that was the case, instead of merely stopping him, why didn't they kill him?'

'They couldn't. Because if they did, it would raise too many questions. Kept alive until he died, and at his age and in his condition, that wasn't far off, he was just another delusional drunk. But if he was murdered, his crazy accusations might appear more credible. People like me might begin digging, and his enemy can't afford that. Alive he was a nothing, killed he's something else.'

'I fail to see your point as it pertains to Jean-Pierre, my friend.'

'Jodelle's enemies, the group here in France that I'm convinced is linked to the Nazi movement in Germany, are way down deep, but they've got eyes and ears above the ground. If the old man made contact, the least they'll do is follow up on his suicide. They'll be on the lookout for anyone asking questions about him. If there's any truth in what Jodelle claimed, again they can't afford not to . . . And that leads me back to the missing OSI files in Washington. They were stolen for a reason.'

'I see what you mean,' said Bressard, 'and now I'm definitely against Villier's involvement. I'll do my best to stop him; Giselle will help. She's as strong as he is, and he adores her.'

'Maybe you weren't listening a while ago. He said none of us could stop him. He wasn't acting, Henri, he meant it.'

'I agree, but you've brought in another equation. We'll sleep on it, if any of us can sleep . . . Do you still have your flat on the rue du Bac?'

'Yes, but I want to stop at the embassy first. There's

someone in Washington I have to call on a secure line. Our transport will get me home.'

'As you wish.'

Latham took the elevator down to the embassy basement complex and walked through a white, neon-lit corridor to the communications centre. He inserted his plastic access card into the security receptacle; there was a brief, sharp buzz, the heavy door opened, and he walked inside. The large air-cooled, dust-filtered room, like the corridor, was pristine white, the panoply of electronic equipment lining three walls, the metal glistening, a swivel chair placed every six feet in front of its own console. Due to the hour, however, only one chair was occupied; traffic was lightest between two and six o'clock in the morning, Paris time.

'I see you've got the graveyard, Bobby,' said Drew to the sole occupant across the room. 'You holding up?'

'Actually, I like it,' replied Robert Durbane, a fifty-three-year-old communications specialist and senior officer of the embassy's comm centre. 'My people think I'm such a good guy when I assign the shift to myself; they're wrong, but don't tell them. See what I have to work on?' Durbane held up a folded London *Times*, the page displaying the infamous *Times* crossword puzzle and lethal double acrostic.

'I'd say that's adding masochism to double duty,' said Latham, crossing to the chair to the right of the operator. 'I can't do either one, don't even try.'

'You and the rest of the youngsters. No comment, Mr Intelligence Man.'

'I suspect there's gravel in that remark.'

'Wear sandals on the driveway ... What can I do for you?'

'I want to call Sorenson on scrambler.'

'He didn't reach you about an hour ago?'

'I wasn't home.'

'You'll find his message ... that's funny, though, he spoke as if you and he had been talking.'

'We did, but that was nearly three hours ago.'

'Use the red telephone in the cage.' Durbane turned and gestured towards a built-in glass cubicle fronting the fourth wall, the glass rising to the ceiling. The 'cage', as it was called, was a soundproof, secure area where confidential conversations could be held without being overheard. The embassy personnel were grateful for it; what they did not hear could not be extracted from them. 'You'll know when you're on scrambler,' added the specialist.

'I would hope so,' said Drew, referring to the discordant beeps that preceded a harsh hum over the line, the signal that the scrambler was in operation. He rose from the chair, walked to the thick glass door of the cage, and let himself in. There was a large Formica table in the centre with the red telephone, pads, pencils, and an ashtray on top. In the corner of this unique enclosure was a paper shredder whose contents were burned every eight hours, more often if necessary. Latham sat down in the desk chair, positioned so his back was to the personnel operating the consoles; maximum security included the fear of lip-reading, which was laughed at until a Soviet mole was discovered in the embassy's communications during the height of the Cold War. Drew picked up the phone and waited; eighty-two seconds later the beep-and-hum litany was played, then came the voice of Wesley T. Sorenson, director of Consular Operations.

'Where the devil have you been?' asked Sorenson.

'After you cleared my contacting Henri Bressard with our promise of disclosure, I went to the theatre, then called Bressard. He took me to the Villier house on Parc Monceau. I just got here.'

'Then your projections were *right*?'

'As right as simple arithmetic.'

'Good Lord . . . ! The old man really was Villier's father?'

'Confirmed by Villier himself, who learned it from – as he put it – the only parents he'd ever known.'

'Considering the circumstances, what a hell of a shock!'

'That's what we have to talk about, Wes. The shock produced a mountain of guilt in our famous actor. He's determined to use his skills and go underground to see if he can make contact with Jodelle's friends, try to learn if the old man told anyone where he was going during the past few days, who it was he wanted to find, and what he intended to do.'

'*Your* scenario,' interrupted Sorenson. 'Your scenario, if your projections proved accurate.'

'It had to be – if I was right. But that scenario called for using our own assets, not Villier himself.'

'And you were right. Congratulations.'

'I had help, Wes, namely the former ambassador's wife.'

'But you found her, no one else did.'

'I don't think anyone else has a brother in a tight, no-answer situation.'

'I understand. So what's your problem?'

'Villier's determination. I tried to talk him out of it, but I couldn't, I can't, and I don't think anyone can.'

'Why should you? Perhaps he can learn something. Why interfere?'

'Because whoever triggered Jodelle's suicide must have faced him down. Somehow they convinced him that he'd lost the whole ball of wax, he was finished. There was nothing left for the old man.'

'Psychologically that makes sense. His obsession had nowhere to go but to destroy him. So?'

'Whoever they are will certainly follow up on his suicide. As I told Bressard, they can't afford not to. If someone, no matter who it is, shows up asking questions about Jodelle – well, if his enemies are who I think they are, that someone hasn't got much of a future.'

'Did you tell this to Villier?'

'Not in so many words, but I made it clear that what he wanted to do was extremely dangerous. In essence, he told me to go to hell. He said he owed Jodelle every bit as much, if not more, than I owe Harry. I'm supposed to go to his place tomorrow at noon. He says he'll be ready.'

'Spell it out for him then,' ordered Sorenson. 'If he still insists, let him go.'

'Do we want his potentially shortened future on our slate?'

'Tough decisions are called tough because they're not easy. You want to find Harry, and I want to find a rotten cancer that's growing in Germany.'

'I'd like to find both,' said Latham.

'Of course. I would too. So if your actor wants to perform, don't stop him.'

'I want him covered.'

'You should, a dead actor can't tell us what he's learned. Work it out with the Deuxième, they're very good at that sort of thing. In an hour or so I'll call Claude Moreau. He's head of the Bureau and will be in his office by then. We worked together in Istanbul; he was the best field agent French intelligence ever had, world class, to be exact. He'll give you what you need.'

'Should I tell Villier?'

'I'm one of the old boys, Latham, maybe that's good and maybe that's bad, but I believe that if you're going to mount an operation, you go the whole nine yards. Villier should also be wired; it's an added risk, of course, and you should spell out everything to him. Let him make a clean decision.'

'I'm glad we're in sync. Thank you for that.'

'I came in from the cold, Drew, but I was once where you are now. It's a lousy chess game, specifically when the pawns can get killed. Their blips never leave you, take my word for it. They're fodder for nightmares.'

'Everything everybody says about you is true, isn't it? Including your predilection for having us in the field call you by your first name.'

'Most of what they say I did is totally exaggerated,' said the director of Consular Operations, 'but when I was out there, if I could have called my boss Bill or George or

Stanford or just plain Casey, I think I might have been a hell of a lot more candid. That's what I want from you people. "Mr Director" is an impediment.'

'You're so right.'

'I know. So do what you have to do.'

Latham walked out of the embassy on avenue Gabriel to the waiting armour-plated diplomatic car that would take him to his flat on the rue du Bac. It was a Citroën sedan, the rear seats far too shallow, so he chose to sit in the front next to the marine driver. 'You know the address?' he asked.

'Oh, yes, sir. Surely I do, certainly.'

An exhausted Drew looked briefly at the man; the accent was unmistakably American, but the juxtaposition of words was odd. Or was it simply that the was so tired that his hearing was playing tricks on him. He closed his eyes, for how long he did not know, grateful for the nothingness, the blank void that filled his inner screen. For at least several minutes his anxiety was put on hold. He needed the respite, he welcomed it. Then suddenly he was aware of motion, the jostling of his body in the seat. He opened his eyes; the driver was speeding across a bridge as though he were in a Le Mans race. Latham spoke. 'Hey, guy, I'm not rushing to a late date. Cool it on the accelerator, pal.'

'*Tut mir* – sorry, sir.'

'*What?*' They sped off the bridge and the marine swung the car into a dark, unfamiliar street. Then it was clear; they were nowhere near the rue du Bac. Drew shouted, 'What the hell are you doing?'

'It is a shortened cut, sir.'

'Bullshit! Stop this fucking car!'

'*Nein!*' yelled the man in the marine uniform. 'You go where I take you, buddy!' The driver yanked an automatic from his tunic and pointed it at Latham's chest. 'You give me no orders, I give *you* orders!'

'Christ, you're one of them. You son of a bitch, you're *one* of them!'

'You will meet others, and then you will be gone!'

'It's true, isn't it? You're all over Paris—'

'*Und England, und die Vereinigte Staaten, und Europa! . . . Sieg Heil!*'

'Sieg up your ass,' said Drew quietly, levelling his left hand in the rushing shadows beneath the weapon, his left foot inching across the Citroën's floorboard. 'How about a big surprise, blitzkrieg style?' With those words Latham jammed his left foot against the brake pedal while simultaneously smashing his left hand up into the elbow of his would-be captor's right arm. The gun spun in the neo-Nazi's hand; Drew grabbed it and fired into the driver's right kneecap as they crashed into the corner of a building.

'You *lose!*' said Latham breathlessly, opening the door and grabbing the man by his tunic. Stepping outside, he yanked him across the seat, throwing him to the pavement. They were in one of the industrial sections of Paris, two- and three-storey factories, deserted for the night. Beyond the dim street lamps, the only brightness came from the damaged Citroën's headlights. It was enough.

'You're going to talk to me, *buddy*.' he said to the false marine curled up on the sidewalk, moaning and clutching his wounded leg, 'or the next bullet goes right through those two hands around your knee. Shattered hands never fully recover. It's a hell of a way to live.'

'*Nein! Nein!* Do not shoot!'

'Why not? You were going to kill me, you told me so. I'd "be gone," I distinctly remember. I'm much kinder. I won't kill you, I'll just make your staying alive a mess. After your hands, your feet will be next . . . Who *are* you and how did you get that uniform, that car? Tell me!'

'We have uniforms . . . *amerikanische, französische, englische.*'

'The car, the embassy car. Where's the man whose place you took?'

'He was told not to come—'

'By whom?'

'I do not know! The car was brought to the front. The *Schlüssel* – the key, I mean – was in it. I was ordered to drive you.'

'Who ordered you?'

'My superiors.'

'The people you were taking me to?'

'*Ja.*'

'Who are they? Give me some names. *Now.*'

'I do not know any names! We are reached by codes, by numbers and letters.'

'What's your name?' Drew crouched by the impostor, the barrel of the gun jammed against the nearest hand around the bleeding kneecap.

'Erich Hauer, I swear it!'

'Your code name, Erich. Or forget about your hands and feet.'

'*C-Zwölf* – twelve.'

'You speak much better English when you're not scared shitless, Erich-buddy . . . Where were you taking me?'

'Five, six avenues from here. I would know by the *Scheinwerfer*—'

'The what?'

'Headlights. From a narrow street on the left.'

'Stay right where you are, Little Adolf,' said Latham, rising and sidestepping to the car door, his weapon on the German. Awkwardly, he backed down into the front seat, his left hand thrusting below the dashboard until he found the car phone with a direct line to the embassy. As the transmitting mechanism was in the trunk, the odds were favourable that it would be operational. It was. Glancing quickly, Drew pressed the zero button four times in rapid succession. The signal for emergency.

'American Embassy,' came Durbane's voice over the speaker. 'Your status is Zero Four. On tape, go ahead!'

'Bobby, it's Latham—'

'I know that, I've got you on the grids. Why the big Four 0?'

'We were sandbagged. I was on my way to a fast execution, courtesy of our Nazi nightmare. The marine driver was a phoney; somebody in the transport pool set me up. Check that whole unit out!'

'*Christ*, are you all right?'

'Just a tad shaken; we had an accident and the skinhead didn't fare too well.'

'Well, I've got you on the grids. I'll send a patrol out—'

'You know exactly where we are?'

'Of course.'

'Send two patrols, Bobby, one armed for assault.'

'Are you crazy? This is Paris; it's French!'

'I'll cover us. This is an order from Cons-Op . . . Five or six blocks south, on the left, there's a car parked on a side street, its headlights on. We've got to take that car, take the people in it!'

'Who are they?'

'Among other things, my executioners . . . There's no time, Bobby. Do it!' Latham slammed the telephone back into its receptacle and lurched out of the car to Erich Hauer, who could lead them to a hundred others in Paris and beyond, whether he knew it or not. The chemicals would open the doors of his mind; it was vital. Drew grabbed his legs as the man screamed in pain.

'*Please* . . . .'

'Shut up, pighead. You're mine, you got that? Start talking, it'll be easier on you later.'

'I do not know anything. I am only C-*Zwölf*, what more can I say?'

'That's not good enough! I have a brother who went after you bastards; it was the last leg of a rotten trip. So you're going to give me more, a lot more, before I'm finished with you. Take my word for it, Erich-buddy, you really don't want to deal with me.'

Suddenly, out of the deserted dark street, a black sedan came screeching around the corner. It slowed down rapidly, briefly, as the gunfire erupted, a deadly fusillade, slaughter for everything in its path. Latham tried to pull the Nazi behind the shell of the armour-plated diplomatic car; he could not do it and save himself. As the sedan raced away, he looked over at his prisoner. Erich Hauer, his body riddled, blood covering his face, was dead. The one man who could supply at least a few answers was gone. Where was somebody else, and how long would it take to find him?

CHAPTER THREE

The night was over, the early light creasing the eastern sky as an exhausted Latham took the small brass elevator to his flat on the fifth floor in the rue du Bac. Normally he would have used the stairs, figuring it was physically good for something or other, but not now; he could barely keep his eyes open. The hours between shortly past two and five-thirty had been filled with diplomatic necessities as well as providing Drew with the opportunity of meeting the head of the powerful and secretive Deuxième Bureau, one Claude Moreau. He had called back Sorenson in Washington, asking *him* to reach the French intelligence officer at that hour and persuade him to go immediately to the American Embassy. Moreau was a middle-aged, medium-size balding man who filled out his suit as though he lifted weights for a good part of every day. He had an insouciant Gallic humour that somehow kept things in perspective when they were in danger of getting out of control. The potential loss of control first came about with the unexpected appearance of a furious and frightened Henri Bressard, First Secretary of Foreign Affairs for the Republic of France.

'What the *hell* is going on?' demanded Bressard, walking into the ambassador's office, instantly surprised yet accepting Moreau's presence. '*Allô*, Claude,' he said, reverting to French. 'I'm not entirely stunned to see you here.'

'*En anglais*, Henri . . . Monsieur Latham understands us but the ambassador is still with his Berlitz.'

'Ah, American diplomatic tact!'

'I *did* understand that, Bressard,' said Ambassador Daniel

44

Courtland, behind his desk in a bathrobe and slippers, 'and I'm working on your language. Frankly, I wanted the post in Stockholm – I speak fluent Swedish – but others thought differently. So you're stuck with me as I'm stuck with you.'

'I apologize, Mr Ambassador. It's been a difficult night . . . I tried calling you, Drew, and when all I got was your machine, I assumed you were still here.'

'I should have been home an hour ago. Why *are* you here? Why did you have to see me?'

'Everything's in the Sûreté report. I insisted the police call them in—'

'What happened?' interrupted Moreau. He raised an eyebrow. 'Your former wife is not becoming hostile, surely. Your divorce was ultimately amicable.'

'I'm not sure I'd want it to be she. Lucille may be a devious bitch, but she's not stupid. These people were.'

'What people?'

'After I dropped off Drew here, I drove to my apartment on the Montaigne. As you know, one of the few privileges of my office is my diplomatic parking space in front of the building. To my surprise, it was occupied and, adding to my irritation, there were several other nearby open spaces. Then I saw that there were two men seated in front and the driver was on his car phone, not exactly a normal sight at two o'clock in the morning, especially when the driver was subject to a five-hundred-franc fine for parking where he did without a government plate or the Quai d'Orsay emblem on the front window.'

'As always,' said Moreau, nodding his head appreciatively, 'your diplomat's penchant for introducing an event with perception and suspense is evident, but *please*, Henri, the personal insult to you aside, what happened?'

'The bastards started shooting at me!'

'*What?*' Latham leapt out of his chair.

'You heard me! My vehicle is naturally protected against such assaults, so I backed up quickly, then smashed into them, pinning their car to the kerb.'

45

'*Then* what?' cried Ambassador Courtland, now standing up.

'The two men got out the other side and raced away. My heart pounding, I called the police on my car phone, demanding that they alert the Sûreté.'

'You're something else,' said an astonished Drew softly. 'You rammed them while they were firing at you?'

'The bullets could not penetrate, even the glass.'

'Believe me, some can – like full jackets.'

'Really?' Bressard's face grew pale.

'You were quite right, Henri,' said Moreau, once more nodding his head, 'your former wife would have been much more efficient. Now, shall we all calm down a bit and look at what our brave hero has achieved for us? We have the vehicle, a licence plate, and no doubt several dozen fingerprints which we will immediately deliver to Interpol. I salute you, Henri Bressard.'

'There are bullets that can penetrate *bulletproof* automobiles . . . ?'

The connection to Jodelle's suicide and the subsequent meeting at the Villier house on Parc Monceau was all too obvious. Coupled with the attack on Latham, the situation demanded several decisions: both Bressard and Drew would be protected around the clock by Deuxième personnel – the Frenchman conspicuously, Latham less obviously, at his own instructions. Which was why the unmarked Deuxième car would remain across the street from Drew's building until relief came to replace it or the American emerged in the morning, whichever happened first. Finally, under no conditions could Jean-Pierre Villier, who would also be guarded, be permitted to prowl the seamier sections of Paris in search of anyone.

'I myself will make that absolutely clear to him,' said Claude Moreau, chief of the Deuxième Bureau. 'Villier is a treasure of France! . . . In addition, my wife would either kill me or have numerous affairs in our own bed if I permitted anything to happen to him.'

The disturbing doubts about the embassy's transport pool were resolved quickly. The dispatcher was a substitute no one knew, but he had been accepted for the night shift because of his credentials. He had disappeared minutes after Latham's car drove off down the avenue Gabriel. A French-speaking American in Paris was part of the Nazi movement.

The hours before dawn had been taken up with endless analyses of the situation – the question of who and who not to include being a priority – as well as lengthy conversations on open scrambler between Moreau and Wesley Sorenson in Washington. The two specialists in deep-cover intelligence sounded like dual practitioners of the darkest arts, creating a scenario of deep-cover pursuits. Drew approved of what he heard. He was good, not as coldly intellectual as his brother Harry, but surely superior when it came to quick decisions and physicality. Moreau and Sorenson, however, were the masters in deception and penetration; they had survived the unpublicized slaughter of spies during the bloody depths of the Cold War. He could learn from such men, even as they programmed him.

Latham walked sleepily out of the elevator and down the hall to his flat. As he started to insert his key, his eyes were suddenly riveted on the lock. It wasn't there! Instead, there was a hollow circle. The entire lock had been surgically removed, either by a laser or a high-powered miniature hand saw. He touched the door; it swung open, revealing the shambles within. Drew yanked his automatic out of its shoulder holster and cautiously slipped inside. His apartment was ravaged, upholstery was knifed everywhere, cushions torn apart, their stuffing scattered; drawers were pulled out, their contents dumped on the floor. It was the same in the two bedrooms, the closets, the kitchen, the bathrooms, and especially his study, where even the rugs were sliced. His large desk had been literally hacked to pieces, the assault team looking for hidden caches where secret papers might be concealed. The destruction was

47

overwhelming; nothing was as it had been. And in his exhaustion Latham simply did not want to think about it; he needed rest; he needed sleep. He briefly considered the waste and how illogical it was; confidential materials were kept in his office safe on the second floor of the embassy. Old Jodelle's enemies – now *his* enemies – should have guessed that.

He rummaged in one of his closets, sardonically amused to find an object that intruders would have taken or smashed had they recognized what it was. The twenty-six-inch steel bar had large rubber caps at either end, each cap holding an alarm mechanism. When he travelled and stayed in hotel rooms, he invariably braced it against the door and the floor, activating the alarms by twisting the caps. If whatever door he shoved it against was opened from the outside, a series of ear-shattering whistles went off that would shock the interloper into racing away. Drew carried it to the lockless door of his flat, activated the alarms, and, anchoring it to the floor, braced it against a lower panel. He walked into his destroyed bedroom, threw a sheet over the ripped mattress, removed his shoes, and lay down.

Within minutes he was asleep, and within minutes after that his telephone rang. Disoriented, Latham lurched off the unbalanced surface of the bed, grabbing the phone from the bedside table. 'Yes? . . . Hello?'

'It's Courtland, Drew. I'm sorry to call at this hour, but it's necessary.'

'What happened?'

'The German ambassador—'

'He *knew* about tonight?'

'Nothing at all. Sorenson called him from Washington and apparently raised hell. Shortly thereafter Claude Moreau did the same.'

'They're pros. What's going down?'

'Ambassador Heinrich Kreitz will be here at nine o'clock this morning. Sorenson and Moreau want you here too. Not only to corroborate the reports, but obviously to protest vigorously the personal attack on you.'

'Those two old veteran spooks are mounting a pincer assault, aren't they?'

'I haven't the vaguest idea what you're talking about.'

'In World War Two it was a German strategy. Close in on both sides, squeeze the enemy so he has to run north or south or east or west. If he chooses wrong, he's finished, which he will be because the points are covered.'

'I'm not military, Drew, but I really don't think Kreitz is an enemy.'

'No, he's not. In fact, he's a man with a historical conscience. But even he doesn't know who's in his ranks here in Paris. He'll damn well stir up the waters, and that's what Sorenson and Moreau want him to do.'

'Sometimes I think you people speak a different language.'

'Oh, we do, Mr Ambassador. It's called obfuscation in the interests of deniability. You might say it's our lingua franca.'

'You're babbling.'

'I'm dead tired.'

'How long does it take you to get from your place to the embassy?'

'First I have to go to the garage where I keep my car—'

'You're in a Deuxième vehicle now,' Courtland interrupted.

'Sorry, I forgot . . . Depending on the traffic, about fifteen minutes.'

'It's ten past six. I'll have my secretary wake you at eight-thirty and I'll see you at nine. Get some rest.'

'Maybe I should tell you what happened—' It was too late, the ambassador had hung up the phone. It was just as well, thought Latham. Courtland would want details, prolonging the conversation. Drew crawled up on the bed, managing at the last to replace his telephone. The only good thing to come out of the night was the fact that he'd be spending a week, or however long it took to restore his flat, at a very fine hotel, and Washington would pick up the bill.

*

The white glider swept down in the late afternoon crosscurrents into the valley of the Brotherhood. Upon landing, it was immediately hauled under a covering of green screening. The Plexiglas canopies of both the forward and aft cockpits sprang open; the pilot in pure white coveralls emerged from the former, his very much older passenger from the latter.

'*Komm*,' said the flyer, nodding towards a motorcycle with a sidecar attached. '*Zum Krankenhaus.*'

'Yes, of course,' replied the civilian in German, turning and lifting a black leather medical bag out of the aircraft. 'I presume Dr Kroeger is here,' he added, climbing into the sidecar as the pilot mounted the seat and started the engine.

'I would not know, sir. I'm only to bring you to the medical clinic. I do not know any names.'

'Then forget I mentioned one.'

'I heard nothing, sir.' The motorcycle raced into one of the screened corridors and, making several turns, sped across the valley to the north end of the flatland. There, again covered by the screening, was the usual one-storey structure, but somehow different. Where the other structures were basically solidly built of wood, this was heavier, sturdier – cinder block layered with concrete – with an enormous generator complex on the south side, the continuous hum low, powerful. 'I'm not permitted inside, Doctor,' said the pilot, stopping the motorcycle in front of the grey steel door.

'I'm aware of that, young man, and I've been told how to proceed. Incidentally, I'm to leave in the morning at the earliest light. I trust you know that.'

'Yes, I do, sir. The winds then are the best.'

'They couldn't be any worse.' The doctor got out of the sidecar; the flyer sped off as his passenger walked to the door, looked up at the camera lens above, and pressed the round black button to the right of the frame. 'Dr Hans Traupman by orders of General von Schnabe.'

Thirty seconds later the door was opened by a man in his

forties dressed in white hospital attire. 'Herr Doktor Traupman, how good to see you again,' he said enthusiastically. 'It's been several years since the lectures in Nuremberg. Welcome!'

'*Danke*, but I wish there were a less arduous way of getting here.'

'You would dislike the mountain approach even more, I assure you. One walks for miles, and the snow gets heavier with every few hundred metres. Secrecy has its price ... Come, have some schnapps and relax for a few minutes while we chat. Then you'll see our progress. I tell you, it's remarkable!'

'Drinks later, and we'll chat as we observe,' countered the visiting physician. 'I have a lengthy meeting with Von Schnabe – not a pleasant prospect – and I want to learn as much as I can as quickly as I can. He'll ask for judgements and hold me accountable.'

'Why am I excluded from this meeting?' asked the younger doctor resentfully as both sat down in the clinic's anteroom.

'He thinks you're too enthusiastic, Gerhardt. He admires your enthusiasm but he doesn't trust it.'

'My God, who knows more about the process than I do? I *developed* it! With all respect, Traupman, this is my field of expertise, not yours.'

'I know that and you know that, but our nonmedical general can't understand it. I am a neurosurgeon and have a certain reputation in cranial operations, therefore he turns to that reputation, not to the real expertise. So convince me ... As I gather, according to you it's theoretically possible to alter the thought process without drugs or hypnosis – that theory is somewhere in the ozones of para-psychological science fiction, but then so were heart and liver transplants not too many years ago. How is it actually done?'

'You practically answered that yourself.' Gerhardt Kroeger laughed, his eyes bright. 'Take the "trans" out of "transplant" and insert the letters *i* and *m*.'

51

'Implant?'

'You implant steel plates, don't you?'

'Of course. For protection.'

'So have I . . . You've performed lobotomies, not so?'

'Naturally. To relieve electrical pressures.'

'You've just said another magic word, Hans. "Electrical", as in electrical impulse, the *brain's* electrical impulses. I simply microcalibrate and tap into them with an object so infinitesimal compared to a plate that it would be a mere shadow on an X-ray.'

'What in hell would that be?'

'A computer chip entirely compatible with an individual brain's electrical impulses.'

'A what . . . ?'

'Within years, psychological indoctrination will be a thing of the past. Brainwashing will be history!'

'Come again?'

'Over the past twenty-nine months I've experimented with – operated upon – thirty-two patients, often with five or more in varying stages of development—'

'So I've been given to understand,' interrupted Traupman. 'Patients provided by suppliers, from prisons and elsewhere.'

'Scrutinized, Hans, all male and all with above-average intelligence and education. Those from the prisons were sentenced for such offences as embezzlement, or selling inside corporate information, or falsifying official government reports for personal gain. Crimes of subterfuge requiring some degree of expertise and sophistication, not violence. The violent mind as well as the less intelligent can too easily be programmed. I had to prove that my procedure could succeed above those levels.'

'Did you prove it?'

'"Sufficient unto the day," as the Bible says.'

'Why do I hear a negative, Gerhardt?'

'Because there is one. To date, the implant functions for not less than nine days or more than twelve.'

'What happens then?'

'The brain rejects it. The patient rapidly develops a cranial haemorrhage and dies.'

'You're saying the brain explodes.'

'Yes. Twenty-six of my patients so expired; however, the last seven lasted progressively from nine to twelve days. I'm convinced that with further microsurgical techniques I can eventually overcome the time factor. Ultimately, and it may take years, it will function permanently. Politicians, generals, and statesmen everywhere can disappear for a few days, and thereafter become our disciples.'

'But for the present circumstances, with this American agent Latham, you believe he's ready to be sent out, am I correct?'

'Without question. You'll see for yourself. He's in his fourth day, leaving a minimum of five left and a maximum of eight. As our personnel in Paris, London, and Washington inform us that he is needed for no more than forty to seventy-two hours, the risk is minimal. By then we'll know everything our enemies know about the Brotherhood with the much more important benefit of Latham sending them all off in wrong directions.'

'Let's go back, if you please,' said Traupman, shifting his legs in the white plastic chair. 'Before we get to the procedure itself, what exactly does this implant of yours do?'

'Are you familiar with computer chips, Hans?'

'As little as possible. I leave that to my technicians, as I do the application of anaesthesia. I have enough to be concerned about. But I'm sure you'll tell me what I don't know.'

'The newest microchips are barely three centimetres in length and less than ten millimetres wide, and they can hold the equivalent of six megabytes of software. That's sufficient to contain all the works of Goethe, Kant, and Schopenhauer. By using an E-PROM Burner to insert the information into the chip, we then activate the ROM – Read-Only Memory – and it reacts to the sonic instructions delivered to it in the same way a computer search reacts to the codes a programmer enters into a processor. Granted, there is a slight delay as the brain, the *thought* process, adjusts to the interception, the alternate wave-length, but that in itself can only persuade the interrogator into believing the subject is truly *thinking*, preparing a truthful response.'

'You can *prove* this?'

'Come, I'll show you.' The two men got up and Kroeger pressed a red button to the right of the heavy steel door. Within seconds a uniformed nurse appeared, a surgical mask in her hand. 'Greta, this is the famed Dr Hans Traupman.'

'Yes, I know,' said the nurse. 'A privilege to see you again, Doctor. Please, your mask.'

'Yes, of course I know you!' exclaimed Traupman warmly. 'Greta Frisch, one of the finest surgical nurses ever in my operating room. My dear girl, they said you had retired, and for one so young it seemed not only regrettable, but quite unbelievable.'

'I retired into marriage, *Herr Doktor*. With this one.' Greta nodded at Kroeger, who was grinning.

'I wasn't sure you'd remember her, Hans.'

'Remember? One doesn't forget a Nurse Frisch, who anticipates your every demand. To tell you the truth, Gerhardt, your credibility just went up the scale . . . But why the mask, Greta? We're not operating.'

'My husband will answer you, sir. These things are beyond me, no matter how often he explains them.'

'The ROM, Hans, the Read-Only Memory. With this patient we don't care to have too many images of identifiable faces, and yours could fall into that category.'

'Way past me too, Nurse Frisch. Very well, let us proceed.' The trio walked through the doors, entering a long, wide, pale green corridor with large, square glass windows on either side. Beyond the windows were pleasantly appointed rooms, each having a bed, a desk, a couch, and such items as a television set, a radio, and a door that led to a bathroom with shower. Also, there were other windows on the outside walls that looked over the meadows, profuse with weaving high grass and springtime flowers. 'If these are the patients' hospital rooms,' continued Traupman, 'they're among the most pleasant I've seen.'

'The radios and the television sets are preprogrammed, naturally,' said Gerhardt. 'It's all innocuous fare, except for the radios at night, when we transmit information as it pertains to the individual patients.'

'Tell me what I'm to expect,' said the neurosurgeon from Nuremberg.

'You'll find an outwardly normal Harry Latham who still believes he's fooled us. He answers to his cover name, Alexander Lassiter, and he's extremely grateful to us.'

'Why?' interrupted Traupman. 'Why is he grateful?'

'Because he believes he was in an accident and barely escaped with his life. We used one of our huge mountain vehicles and staged the event most convincingly, over-turning the truck, "pinning" him under it and employing surrounding bursts of fire . . . Here I did permit the use of drugs and hypnosis – immediately, so as to erase his first minutes here in our valley.'

'Are you *sure* they're erased?' They stopped in the corridor, the Nuremberger's gaze fixed on Kroeger.

'Completely. The trauma of the "accident", along with the violent images, as well as the pain we induced, superseded any memories of his arrival. They're blocked out. Naturally, we reemployed hypnosis to make certain. All he remembers are the screams, the excruciating pain, and the fires he was dragged through while being rescued.'

'The stimuli are psychologically consistent,' noted the neurosurgeon, nodding his head. 'What about the time factor? If he's aware of it, how did you explain the passage of time?'

'The least difficult. When he awoke, his upper skull was heavily bandaged, and while under mild sedation he was told – over and over again – that he'd been severely injured, that he had gone through three separate operations while in a prolonged coma during which he remained completely silent. It was explained to him that had his vital signs not remained remarkably strong, I would have given up on him.'

'Well phrased. I'm certain he's grateful . . . Does he know where he is?'

'Oh, yes, we withhold nothing from him.'

'Then how can you send him out? My God, he'll disclose the whereabouts of the valley! They'll send in planes; you'll be bombed out of existence!'

'It will not matter, for as Von Schnabe will undoubtedly tell you, we won't exist.'

'*Please*, Gerhardt, one thing at a time. I will not take another step until you explain yourself.'

'Later, Hans. Greet our patient first, then you'll understand.'

'My dear Greta,' said Traupman, turning to the wife. 'Is this husband of yours the same logical human being I knew before?'

'Yes, Doctor. This part, the part he will explain to you, I *do* understand. It's brilliant, sir, you'll see.'

'But first see our patient; he's the next window, the next door on the right. Remember, his name is Lassiter, *not* Latham.'

'What should I say to him?'

'Whatever you like. I'd suggest congratulating him on his recovery. Come along.'

'I'll wait by the desk,' said Greta Frisch Kroeger.

The two physicians walked into the room where Harry Latham, his head bandaged around his temples, stood by the large outside window. He turned and smiled; he was dressed in shirtsleeves and grey flannel trousers. 'Hi there, Gerhardt. Lovely day, isn't it?'

'Have you been for a walk, Alex?'

'Not yet. You can damage a businessman, but you can't take the business out of the man. I've been playing with figures; there are fortunes to be made in the Chinese mainland. I can't wait to fly over.'

'May I present Dr . . . Schmidt from Berlin?'

'Glad to meet you, Doctor,' Latham walked over, his hand extended. 'Also glad to see another doctor in our amazing complex here, just in case Gerhardt louses me up.'

'I gather he hasn't so far,' said Traupman, shaking hands. 'But then, I hear you're an exceptionally good patient.'

'I don't think I had a choice.'

'Forgive the mask, Herr . . . Lassiter. I have a slight cold and the resident surgeon is a stickler, as you Americans say.'

'I can say it in German, if you like.'

'Actually, I like to practise my English. Congratulations on your recovery.'

'Well, I'll give Dr Kroeger some credit.'

'I'm curious, from a medical point of view. If it's not too difficult for you, what do you recall when you reached the flatland of our valley?'

'Oh.' Latham/Lassiter paused briefly while his eyes were momentarily glazed, unfocused. 'You mean the accident . . . Oh, Christ, it was terrible. A lot of it's a blur, but the first thing I remember is the shouting; it was hysterical. Then I realized that I was stuck under the side of that truck, and a heavy piece of metal was pressed against my forehead – I've never *felt* such pain. And people were all around, trying to lift whatever it was off me – finally freeing me, and dragging me across the grass, where I screamed because I saw the fires, felt the heat, and thought my whole face was going to be burned. That's when I passed out – for a hell of a long time, as it happened.'

'A terrifying experience. But you're on your way to full health, Mr Lassiter, that's all that matters.'

'If in the new Germany you can find a way to get Gerhardt a mansion on the Danube, I'll pay for it.' Latham's eyes were now totally clear, completely focused.

'You've done enough for us, Alex,' said Kroeger, nodding at Traupman. 'Dr Schmidt here merely wanted to say hello to our generous benefactor, and to make sure I performed as he taught me to . . . Take your walk anytime you like – after you've finished figuring out how to extract many more millions from Asia.'

'It's not that difficult, believe me. The Far East doesn't merely like money, it worships it. When you decide I'm ready to leave, Gerhardt, the Brotherhood will be richer for it.'

'You are forever in our Teutonic prayers, Alex.'

'Forget the prayers, just bring about the Fourth Reich.'

'We shall.'

'Good day, Herr Lassiter.'

Traupman and Kroeger left and walked up the corridor to the pristine anteroom. 'You were right,' said the doctor from Nuremberg, sitting down. 'It *is* remarkable!'

'You approve, then?'

'How could I not? Even to the pause in his voice, his clouded eyes. *Perfect*. You have done it!'

'Remember, Hans, it is flawed, I cannot be dishonest about that. Conditions remaining stable in their abnormality, I can guarantee but five to eight days longer, no more than that.'

'But you say London, Paris, and Washington insist it is sufficient, no?'

'Yes.'

'Now, tell me about this nonexistence of the valley. It's a shock. *Why?*'

'We're no longer needed. We're dispersing. Over the past years we've indoctrinated – trained – more than twenty thousand disciples—'

'You like that word, don't you?' Traupman broke in.

'It fits. They're not only true believers, they are also leaders, both minor and potentially major . . . They've been sent everywhere, mostly throughout Germany, but those gifted in foreign languages and with appropriate skills, to other countries, all financed, ready to take their places in carefully selected professions and occupations.'

'We've progressed so far? I had no idea.'

'Then in your haste you didn't notice that we have far

fewer people here now. The evacuation began weeks ago, our two mountain vehicles operating night and day to remove personnel and equipment. It's been like a colony of ants deserting one hill for another – our destination and our destiny – the new Germany.'

'About the American, this Harry Latham. Beyond staying in contact to learn what he learns, which probably could be accomplished with paid informers, what's his function? Or is that it? That and proving your theory for future use.'

'What we learn from him will have value, of course, and will require the use of a miniaturized electronic computer at close range. It can be easily concealed in a small object. But Harry Latham has a far higher calling. If you remember, I mentioned that he will send our enemies scurrying off in different directions. That, however, barely scratches the surface.'

'You're practically salivating, Gerhardt. Tell me.'

'Latham said he was working on figures, numbers as they pertain to his making millions from the Chinese economic expansion, yes?'

'He's probably right.'

'Wrong, Hans. Those figures have nothing to do with finance. They're codes he's devised so he'll forget nothing after he escapes.'

'*Escapes?*'

'Naturally. He has a job to do, and he's a professional. Of course, we'll let him.'

'For God's sake, be clearer!'

'During his weeks here, in our sessions and over lunches and dinners, we've fed him hundreds of names – French, German, English, American.'

'*What* names?' Traupman interrupted impatiently.

'Those men and women in Germany and abroad who silently support us, who contribute heavily to our cause – in essence, people of influence and power who actually work for the Brotherhood.'

'Are you *mad*?'

'Among this silent, unrevealed elite,' continued Kroeger, overriding Traupman's vehement interjection, 'are American congressmen, senators, and captains of industry and the media. Also, members of the British establishment, not unlike the Cliveden set that gave Hitler his supporters in England, including clandestine policy-makers in British intelligence—'

'You've lost your *mind*—'

'Please, Hans, let me finish ... In Paris we have influential sympathizers in the Quai d'Orsay, the Chamber of Deputies, even the secret Deuxième Bureau. And finally in Germany itself, a number of Bonn's most prestigious authorities. They yearn for the old days before the Fatherland was polluted by the screaming weak who want everything but contribute nothing, the inferior bloodlines that corrupt our nation. Latham has all of this information, all the names. As a trained deep-cover intelligence officer, he'll report the vast majority.'

'You are *certifiable*, Kroeger! I will not permit it!'

'Oh, but you must, Dr Traupman. You see, except for a small number of legitimate supporters who are expendable for establishing credibility, everything that Harry Latham carries out of our valley is false. The names he has in his head and concealed in his codes are, indeed, vital to us, but only in the sense that these people be discredited, even destroyed. For, in truth, they deeply oppose us, many stridently vocal in their opposition. Once their names are flashed secretly to the global intelligence networks, the witch-hunts will begin. As the most sincere among them fall through official suspicion and manufactured innuendo, the resulting vacuums will be filled by many of our own ... yes, *disciples*, Hans. Especially in America, the most powerful of our enemies, for it is also the most susceptible. One has only to recall the frenzied Red-baiting of the forties and fifties. It became a nation paralysed by fear, thousands upon thousands tainted with the Soviet brush, whole industries caving in to the paranoia, the country weakened from within. The

Communists knew how to do it; Moscow, as we have learned, secretly funnelled both money and ersatz information to the zealots . . . One man can start this process for us. Harry Latham, code name Sting.'

'*My God!*' Traupman sank back in the chair, his voice barely above a whisper. 'It *is* brilliant. For he's the only person who's penetrated the core, found the valley. They'll have to believe him – *everywhere*.'

'He will escape tonight.'

CHAPTER FOUR

Heinrich Kreitz, German ambassador to the Republic of France, was a short, slender man of seventy years with a gaunt face, silklike white hair, and sad hazel eyes, perpetually creased. For years a professor of European political development at the University of Vienna, he had been plucked from academia and recruited into the diplomatic corps, due mainly to his numerous papers detailing the history of international relations during the nineteenth and twentieth centuries. These lengthy articles were combined into a book entitled, quite naturally, *Discourse Between Nations*, a staple for diplomats in seventeen languages, as well as a foreign services text in universities across the civilized world.

It was 9:25 in the morning and Kreitz, seated in front of the American ambassador's desk, stared in silence at Drew Latham, who stood to the left of Ambassador Courtland. Against the wall, on a couch, sat the Deuxième's Moreau. 'My shame is my country's guilt,' said Kreitz finally, in his voice a sadness that matched his eyes, 'the guilt of having permitted such monsters, such criminals, ever to have ruled our nation. We will increase our efforts, if that's humanly possible, to root them out and destroy whatever nucleus they have. Please understand, gentlemen, my government is *dedicated* to exposing them, to eliminating them, if it means building a thousand new prisons to contain them. We, above all, cannot afford their existence, surely you know that.'

'We know it, Monsieur *l'Ambassadeur*,' said Claude Moreau from the couch, 'but it seems you have a strange way of going about it. Your Polizei are aware of the leaders of these disrupting fanatics in a dozen cities. Why are they not incarcerated?'

'Where violence can be proved against them, they *are*. Our courts are filled with such indictments. But where mere dissent is concerned, we are also a democracy; we have the same freedom of speech that permits you your peaceable strikes, the Americans their rights of assembly, frequently producing marches on Washington, where men and women harangue their followers from platforms and – how is it said? *oh*, yes – the "soapboxes". Many of both your countries' statutes allow such displays of anti-government displeasure. Are we then to silence everyone who disagrees with Bonn, including those who crowd the squares *against* the neo-Nazis?'

'*No*, goddammit!' roared Latham. 'But you *do* silence them! We didn't create concentration camps, or gas chambers, or the genocide of an entire people. *You* bastards did that, not us!'

'Again in our shame we permitted it ... just as you permitted the enslaving of an entire people and stood by while black men were hanged from ten thousand trees in your Southern states, and the French did much the same in Equatorial Africa and their Far East colonies. There is both horror and decency in all of us. In all our histories.'

'That's not only nonsense, Heinrich, it doesn't apply here, and you know it,' said Ambassador Courtland with surprising authority. '*I* know it because I've read your book. You called it "the perspective of historical realities". What was *perceived* to be the truths of the times. You can't justify the Third Reich in such terms.'

'I never did, Daniel,' rejoined Kreitz. 'I strenuously condemned the Reich for creating *false* truths, all too acceptable to a devastated nation. The Teutonic mythology was a narcotic that a weak, disillusioned, famished people plunged irrationally into their veins. Did I not write that?'

'Yes, you did,' acknowledged the American ambassador, nodding. 'Let's say I just wanted to remind you.'

'Your point is well taken. However, as you must protect the interests of Washington, I have my obligations to Bonn . . . So where are we? We all want the same thing.'

'I suggest, Monsieur *l'Ambassadeur*,' said Moreau, getting up from the couch, 'that you allow me to put under surveillance a number of the upper-level attachés at your embassy.'

'Beyond the intrusion of a host government on a diplomatic level, what can that serve? I know them all. They're decent, hardworking men and women, well trained and trustworthy.'

'You cannot really know that, monsieur. The evidence is beyond debate: there is an organization here in Paris dedicated to the new Nazi movement. All the signs indicate that it may well be the central organization outside of Germany, conceivably as important as the one inside your country, for it can operate beyond German laws, German eyes. Further, it has been all but confirmed, lacking only the specifics of transfer, that millions upon millions are being funnelled to the movement by way of France, no doubt through the efforts of this organization whose origins may go back fifty years. So you see, Monsieur *l'Ambassadeur*, we have a situation that goes beyond narrow diplomatic traditions.'

'I'd need the approval of my government to give you that, of course.'

'Of course,' agreed Moreau.

'Information of a financial nature could be relayed over our secure channels by someone on the embassy staff to those here in Paris who are aiding these psychopaths,' said Kreitz pensively. 'I see what you mean, as disturbing as it is . . . Very well, I'll give you an answer later in the day.' Heinrich Kreitz turned to Drew Latham. 'My government will, of course, absorb all costs for the damages you sustained, Herr Latham.'

'Just get us the cooperation we need, or your government will be responsible for damages you could never pay for,' said Drew. 'Again.'

'He's not *here*!' cried Giselle Villier over the telephone. 'Monsieur Moreau of the Deuxième Bureau was here four hours ago and told us about the horrible things that happened to you and Henri Bressard last night, and my husband appeared to accept his instructions not to interfere. *Maintenant, mon Dieu*, you know *actors*! They can convincingly say anything and your ears and your eyes believe them even while they're thinking something entirely different.'

'Do you know where he is?' asked Drew.

'I know where he *isn't*, monsieur! After Moreau left, he seemed resigned, and told me he was going to the theatre for an understudy rehearsal. He said – and he's said it many times before – that his presence at such rehearsals lends enthusiasm to the minor players. I never thought to doubt him, then Henri called from the Quai d'Orsay, insisting that he talk with Jean-Pierre. So I told him to call the theatre—'

'He wasn't there,' interrupted Latham.

'Not only was he not there, the understudy rehearsal isn't today, but tomorrow!'

'You think he went on with his own plans, as he described them last night?'

'I'm sure of it, and I'm frightened to death.'

'Maybe you don't have to be. The Deuxième has him under protection. They'll follow him everywhere.'

'Again, our new friend, Drew Latham, and I hope you *are* a friend—'

'Completely. Believe that.'

'You really *don't* know talented actors. They can walk into a building looking like themselves, then reappear on the street as someone else. A shirt stuffed under their jackets, their trousers baggy, their walk different, and God forbid there's a clothes shop inside.'

'You believe he might have done something like that?'

'It's why I'm so frightened. When we spoke last night, he was very strong in his decision, and Jean-Pierre is a strong man.'

'That's what I told Bressard when he drove me to the embassy.'

'I know. It's why Henry insisted on speaking to him, to lend his voice against any involvement.'

'I'll check with Moreau.'

'You will call me back, of course.'

'Of course.' Drew hung up the phone in his embassy office, checked his index for the Deuxième Bureau, and called its chief. 'It's Latham,' he said.

'I was expecting your call, monsieur. What can I say? We lost the *acteur*; he was too clever for us. He went into Les Halles, a circus of confusion to begin with. All those stalls – meats, flowers, chickens, *légumes* – total chaos. He passed through a butcher market and not one of our people saw him come out either side!'

'They were looking for someone he wasn't. What are you going to do now?'

'I have units checking out the less desirable of our streets. We must find him.'

'You won't.'

'Why not?'

'Because he's the best actor in France. But he's got to show up at the theatre tonight. For Christ's sake, *be* there, and if you have to, put him under house arrest tomorrow . . . If he's still alive.'

'Please, do not suggest . . .'

'I've been down in those streets, Moreau; I don't think you have. You're too elite; your sophisticated strategies have nothing to do with the sewers of Paris, where he probably is.'

'Your insult is unwarranted; we know more about this city than anyone on earth.'

'Good. Then go *look*.' Drew hung up the phone, wondering whom else he could call, what else he might do. His thoughts were interrupted by a knock on his office door. 'Come in,' he said impatiently.

An attractive dark-haired woman in her early thirties and wearing large tortoiseshell glasses walked in, carrying a thick file folder. 'I believe we've found the materials you asked for, monsieur.'

'Excuse me, but who are you?'

'My name is Karin de Vries, sir. I work in Documents and Research.'

'A euphemism for everything from "sensitive" to "maximum classified".'

'Not all of it, Monsieur Latham. We also have road maps, as well as schedules for airports and rail transport.'

'You're French.'

'Flemish, actually,' corrected the woman, her accent soft but unmistakable. 'However, I've spent a number of years in Paris, including studies for my degrees at the Sorbonne.'

'You speak excellent English—'

'Also French and Dutch, including the Flemish and Walloon dialects, of course, and German,' interrupted De Vries quietly, 'with equal reading skills.'

'That's some talent.'

'It's not at all unusual, except perhaps the in-depth reading, the abstractions and the use of idioms.'

'Which is why you're in Documents and Research.'

'It was a requirement, naturally.'

'Naturally . . . What did you find for me?'

'You asked us to research the laws of the Ministère des Finances, explore whatever cracks might exist with respect to foreign investment, and bring the information to you.'

'Let's have it.' The woman came around the desk, placed the file folder in front of Drew, and opened it, revealing a sheaf of computer printouts. 'That's a lot of data. Miss de Vries,' said Latham. 'It'll take me a week to go through it, and I haven't got a week. The world of high finance isn't one of my strong suits.'

'Oh, no, monsieur, most of this contains extracts from the

laws supporting our conclusions, and case histories of those caught violating those laws. Their names and short summaries of their manipulations are on only six pages.'

'Good Lord, it's far more than I asked for. You did all this in five *hours*?'

'The equipment is superb, sir, and the ministry was extremely cooperative, even to the point of intercoding our modems.'

'They didn't object to our invasion?'

'I knew whom to contact. He understood what you were after and why.'

'Do *you*?'

'I'm neither blind nor deaf, monsieur. Enormous funds are being transferred through Switzerland into Germany to unknown illegitimate individuals or accounts using the Swiss procedure of subjecting handwritten numbers to spectographs.'

'And the identity of those numbers?'

'Wired instantly back to Zurich, Bern, or Geneva, where they are inviolate. Neither confirmed nor denied.'

'You know a great deal about these procedures, don't you?'

'Allow me to explain, Monsieur Latham. I worked for the Americans in NATO. I was cleared by the American authorities for the most highly classified materials because I frequently saw things and heard things that escaped the Americans. Why do you ask? Are you suggesting something else?'

'I don't know. Maybe I'm just overwhelmed by your efficiency – you're responsible for this folder, aren't you? I mean you alone, correct? I can ask others in D and R.'

'Yes,' said Karin de Vries, walking slowly around the desk and standing in front of Latham. 'I saw your request – flagged red – in our department chief's file. I opened it and studied it. I knew I was qualified to expedite it, and so I removed it.'

'Did you tell your superior?'

'No.' The woman paused, then added softly, 'I understood immediately that I could analyse and develop the information quicker than anyone else in our section. I've brought you the results – in only five hours.'

'You mean nobody else in D and R knew you were working on this query, including your section chief?'

'He's in Calais for the day, and I saw no reason to go to his deputy.'

'Why not? Didn't you need authorization? This is a matter that required special assignment. The red flag spells that out.'

'I told you, I was cleared by the American authorities in NATO and by your own intelligence specialists here in Paris. I've brought you what you wanted, and my personal motives are irrelevant.'

'I guess they are. I've also got a few motives of my own, which means I'm going to check and cross-check everything in this file.'

'You'll find the entries accurate and confirmed.'

'I hope so. Thank you, Miss de Vries, that'll be all.'

'If I may correct you, sir, it's not Miss but *Mrs* de Vries. I'm a widow. My husband was killed in East Berlin by the Stasi a week before the Wall came down – the Stasi, monsieur. The name was changed but they were as vicious as the most savage units of the Gestapo and the Waffen SS. My husband, Frederik de Vries, was working for the Americans. You may check and cross-check that also.' The woman turned and left the room.

Stunned, Latham watched as the door was closed so sharply, one could say it was slammed shut. He picked up his phone and touched the buttons on his console for the embassy's director of security. Once past an irritating secretary who kept practising her college French, which was less adequate than his own, thought Drew, the security head was on the line.

'What's up, Cons-Op?'

'Who the hell is a Karin de Vries, Stanley?'

'A major blessing contributed by the NATO crowd,' replied Stanley Witkowski, a thirty-year-plus veteran of Army Intelligence, a colonel transferred to the State Department because of his extraordinary success in G-2. 'She's quick, bright, imaginative, and reads and speaks five languages fluently. Heaven-sent, my friend.'

'That's what I want to know. Who sent her?'

'What are you talking about?'

'Her work habits are a little strange. I sent a sealed red flag down to Research, and without authorization or assignment she removed it from the file and processed it herself.'

'A red flag? That *is* strange; she knows better than that. A flag has to be signed off by the section chief and his deputy, the assignee approved and registered.'

'That's what I thought, and where this operation is concerned, I'm paranoid about leaks and false information. Who sent her here?'

'Forget that, Drew. She requested Paris, and from the supreme commander down she was golden.'

'There's gold and there's fool's gold, Stan. She inferred things that went beyond her clearance in this matter, and I want to know how and why.'

'Can you give me a clue?'

'I'll go this far. It concerns the new bad dudes marching around Germany.'

'That doesn't help me much.'

'She said her husband was killed by the Stasi in East Berlin. Can you confirm that?'

'Hell, yes, even personally. I was stationed on our side of the Wall, busting my balls around the clock making contact with our people on the other side. Freddie de Vries was a young, smart-as-a-whip infiltrator. The poor son of a bitch was caught just days before the Stasi became history.'

'Then she would legitimately have a serious, even obsessive interest in events in Germany.'

'Sure she would. You know where most of the Stasi went when the Wall came tumbling down?'

'Where?'

'Right into the welcoming arms of the skinheads, those goddamned Nazis ... Oh, speaking of Freddie de V, he worked with your brother Harry. I know because my G-2 coordinated with both of them. Harry wasn't just upset, he was mad as hell when he heard about Freddie. Almost like he was a kid brother, like you maybe.'

'Thanks, Stanley. I think I just made an insulting mistake. Regardless, there are a couple of gaps that have to be filled.'

'What does that mean?'

'How did Mrs de Vries know about *me*?'

In the shadows of the afternoon sunlight, Jean-Pierre Villier, his face unrecognizable, the nose twice its true size, his eyelids equally bulbous, his clothes tatters and rags, stumbled down the dark alley in Montparnasse. There were drunken bodies intermittently sitting on the cobblestones, their backs against the walls, most slumped, others having collapsed into foetal positions. He sang in an alcoholic sing-song cadence, the words slurred.

'*Écoutez, écoutez – gardez – vous, mes amis!* I have heard from our dear companion Jodelle – is anyone interested, or am I wasting my old breath?'

'Jodelle's crazy!' came a voice on the left.

'He gets us in trouble!' cried a voice from the right. 'Tell him to go to hell.'

'I must find friends of his, he tells me it's important!'

'Go to the northern docks along the Seine, he sleeps better there, steals better there.'

Jean-Pierre wandered up to the Quai des Tuileries, stopping at every darkened back street and alley he came across, plunging into each with essentially the same results.

'Old Jodelle is a pig! He doesn't share his wine!'

'He says he has friends in high places – where *are* they?'

'This great actor he says is his son – such *shit*!'

'I'm a drunk and I do not care any longer, but I don't burden my friends with lies.'

And then, as Villier reached the loading piers above the Pont de l'Alma, he heard the first words of encouragement from a derelict old woman.

'Jodelle is mad, of course, but he is always nice to me. He brings me flowers – stolen flowers, naturally – and calls me a great *actress*. Can you believe that?'

'Yes, madame, I believe he means it.'

'Then you are as mad as he is.'

'Perhaps I am, for you are a lovely woman.'

'*Aiyee!* . . . Your eyes! They are blue clouds in the sky. You are his ghost!'

'He is dead?'

'Who knows? Who are *you*?'

And finally, hours later, as the sun descended behind the tall structures of the Trocadéro, he heard other words, shouted in another alley, far darker than any previous one. 'Who speaks of my friend, Jodelle?'

'*I* do,' yelled Villier, walking farther into the darkness of the narrow enclosure. '*Are* you his friend?' he asked, kneeling beside the collapsed, dishevelled beggar. 'I must find Jodelle,' continued Jean-Pierre, 'and I have money for anyone who can help me! Here look! Fifty francs.'

'It's been a long time since I've seen fifty francs.'

'See them *now*. Where is Jodelle, where did he *go*?'

'Oh, he said it was a secret—'

'But he told *you*.'

'Oh, yes, we were like brothers—'

'I am his son. Tell *me*.'

'The Loire Valley, a terrible man in the Loire Valley, that's all I know,' whispered the derelict. 'No one knows who he is.'

A silhouetted figure suddenly came out of the bright shaft of sunlight into the alley. He was a man of Jean-Pierre's size when the actor stood upright and was not hunched over as

72

he was then. 'Why are you asking about old Jodelle?' said the intruder.

'I have to find him, sir,' replied Villier, his voice wheezing and tremulous. 'He owes me money, you see, and I've been looking for him for three days now.'

'I'm afraid you won't collect the debt. Don't you read the newspapers?'

'Why spend what money I have to read about things that do not concern me? I can laugh over the comics in yesterday's thrown-away paper, yesterday's or last week's.'

'An old tramp identified as someone named Jodelle killed himself in a theatre last night.'

'Oh, that bastard! He owed me seven francs!'

'Who *are* you, old man?' asked the intruder, approaching Jean-Pierre and studying him in the dim light of the alley.

'I am Auguste Renoir and I paint pictures. Then sometimes I am Monsieur Monet, and often the Dutchman Rembrandt. And in springtime I like to be Georges Seurat; in winter I'll be the cripple Toulouse-Lautrec – all those warm bordellos. Museums are wonderful places when it rains and is cold.'

'Ah, you are an old fool!' The man turned and started walking towards the street as Villier hobbled rapidly after him.

'Monsieur!' cried the actor.

'What?' The man stopped.

'Since you were the bearer of this terrible news, I think you should pay me the seven francs.'

'Why? What kind of logic is that?'

'You've stolen my hope.'

'I stole what . . . ?'

'My hope, my expectation. I did not ask you about Jodelle, you accosted *me*. How did you know I was looking for him?'

'You shouted his name a few moments ago.'

'And on that trivial excuse you enter my life and destroy my anticipation? Perhaps I should ask who *you* are, monsieur. You're dressed too richly to be acquainted with my friend Jodelle – that son of a *bitch*! What is Jodelle to you? Why did you come in here?'

'You're a lunatic,' said the man, reaching into his pocket. 'Here, here's a twenty-franc note, and I apologize for coming into your life.'

'Oh, thank you, sir, thank you!' Jean-Pierre waited until the curious stranger reached the sunlit pavement, then raced up the alley, peering around the corner as the man approached a car parked at the kerb twenty metres up the street. Again feigning a half-mad vagabond of Paris, Villier lurched onto the sidewalk, prancing like a deformed court jester, shouting at his benefactor. 'May God love you and may the holy Jesus embrace you, monsieur! May the glories of heavenly paradise be—'

'Get the hell away from me, you drunken old tramp!'

Oh, I certainly will, thought Jean-Pierre, studying the licence plate of the departing Peugeot.

It was late afternoon when Latham took the elevator down to the embassy basement complex for the second time in eighteen hours, not, however, to head for Communications, but instead to the sacrosanct Documents and Research. A marine guard sat at a desk to the right of the steel door; he recognized Drew and smiled.

'How's the weather up there, Mr Latham?'

'Not as cool and clean as yours, Sergeant, but then, you've got the most expensive air-conditioning.'

'We're very delicate down here. You want to enter our hall of secrets and hard-core porn?'

'They showing dirty movies?'

'A hundred francs a seat, but I'll get you in for nothing.'

'I could always count on the marines.'

'Speaking of which, the fellas in the squad want to thank you for the freebies you set up for us at that café in the Grenelle.'

'My pleasure. You never know when you might want to see a dirty movie ... Actually, the people who own that place are old friends and your presence had a calming effect on some unattractive regulars.'

'Yeah, you told us. We dressed to the nines, like we were in an operetta or something.'

'Sergeant,' interrupted Drew, looking at the guard. 'Do you know a Karin de Vries in D and R?'

'Only to speak to – "good morning, good night", that's about it. She's a real good-looking girl, but it seems to me she tries to hide it. Like with those glasses that must weigh five pounds and those dark clothes that definitely aren't Paris.'

'Is she new here?'

'I'd say about four months, transferred from NATO. Word is that she's kinda quietlike and keeps to herself, y'know what I mean?'

'I think so . . . All right, keeper of the mystic keys, get me into a front seat.'

'Actually, it's in the first row, third office on the right. Her name's on the door.'

'You peeked?'

'Damn right. When that door's locked, we patrol the place every night, keep our hands on our sidearms in case there are uninvited stragglers.'

'Ah, the secret-missions types. You should be in the movies, the cleaner ones.'

'You should talk. A full-course dinner with all the wine we could drink for *thirteen* gyrenes? And a nervous owner who kept racing around telling everybody we were his best friends and probably his American relatives, who would be at his place with bazookas the minute he called us, anytime he was in trouble? That's a straight arrow, Hardy Boys scenario?'

'A harmless, innocent invitation by an ardent admirer of the Corps.'

'Your nose is growing longer, Mr Pinocchio.'

'You've torn my ticket. Let me in, please.'

The marine pressed a button on his desk and a loud click was heard in the steel door. 'Enter the Wizard's palace, sir.'

Latham walked inside, into the low, continuous hum of computer equipment. Documents and Research consisted of succeeding rows of offices on both sides of a central aisle, and as in the communications complex, everything was white, antiseptic, with overhead neon tubes crossing the low ceiling like columns of thick, bright circular stalks. He walked to his right, to the third office door; in the centre of the upper panel was a black plastic strip with white lettering. MADAME DE VRIES. Not Mademoiselle, but Madame, and the widow De Vries had several questions to answer regarding one Harry Latham and his brother Drew. He knocked.

'Come in,' said the voice inside. Latham opened the door, greeted by the startled face of Karin de Vries; she was seated at her desk on the left wall. 'Monsieur, I hardly expected you,' she said, in her voice the sound of fear. 'I apologize for my rudeness. I should not have left the way I did.'

'You've got it wrong, lady. I'm the one who should apologize. I spoke to Witkowski—'

'Oh, yes, the colonel—'

'That's what we have to talk about.'

'I should have known,' interrupted the researcher. 'Yes, we'll talk, Monsieur Latham, but not here. Elsewhere.'

'Why? I went through everything you gave me, and it wasn't just good, it was outstanding. I barely know a debit from an asset, but you made so much so clear.'

'Thank you. But you're here for another reason, aren't you?'

'What are you talking about?'

'There is a café off the Gabriel, six blocks east of here, Le Sabre d'Orléans. It is small and not popular. Be there in forty-five minutes. I'll be in a booth at the rear.'

'I don't understand—'

'You will.'

*

Precisely forty-seven minutes later Drew walked into the small, run-down café off the avenue Gabriel, blinking at the lack of light, somewhat surprised at the shabby environs in one of the more expensive real estate sections of the city. He found Karin de Vries, as she had said, in the farthest booth of the establishment. 'This is some joint,' he whispered, sitting down opposite her.

'*L'obstination du Français*,' De Vries explained, 'and there's no need to speak so quietly. No one of substance will hear us.'

'Who's stubborn?'

'The owner. He's been offered a great deal of money for this property, but he refuses to sell. He's rich and it's been in his family for years – long before he was rich. He keeps it to employ relatives – here comes one now; don't be shocked.'

An obviously drunken elderly waiter approached the table, his walk unsteady. 'Do you care to order, we have no food?' he asked in one breath.

'Scotch whisky, please,' replied Latham in French.

'No Scotch today,' said the waiter, belching. 'We have a fine selection of wines, and some Japanese junk they call whisky.'

'White wine, then. Chablis, if you have it.'

'It'll be white.'

'I'll have the same,' said Karin de Vries. The waiter trudged away and she continued. 'Now you can see why it's not popular.'

'It shouldn't exist ... Let's talk. Your husband worked with my brother in East Berlin.'

'Yes.'

'That's all you can say? Just "yes"?'

'The colonel told you. I didn't know he was here in Paris when I requested the transfer. When I found out, I was astonished, and knew this moment between us was inevitable.'

'You wanted the transfer because of *me*?'

'Because you are the brother of Harry Latham, a man both Frederik and I considered a dear, dear friend.'

'You know Harry that well?'

'Freddie worked for him, although the arrangement was off the books.'

'There *are* no books in those areas.'

'What I mean is that not even Harry's people, much less Colonel Witkowski and his army G-2, knew that Harry was my husband's control. There could be no hint of their association in that "area", as you call it, not a scintilla.'

'But Witkowski *told* me they worked together.'

'On the same side, yes, but not as control and runner. I don't think anyone ever suspected that.'

'It was so vital to keep it a secret, even among our own top people?'

'Yes.'

'Why?'

'Because of the kind of work Frederik did for Harry – willingly, enthusiastically. If certain events were traced back to the Americans, there could have been terrible consequences.'

'Neither side was particularly clean, and at times both were pretty damned gruesome. It was a negative quid pro quo, so what?'

'I think it was the killing, that's what I was led to believe.'

'We both killed—'

'Perhaps it was the prominence of many who were assassinated,' Karin de Vries broke in, her eyes wide, almost pleading. 'As I understand, a number were in high positions, Germans favoured by Moscow, leaders who reported directly to the Kremlin. A parallel might be found if mayors of your large cities or the governors of New York State or California were killed by Soviet agents, do you see what I mean?'

'It couldn't have happened at all, it's counterproductive. Moscow would never have allowed it.'

'It happened here and Moscow covered it up. Wisely, I might add.'

'Are you saying my *brother*, your husband's control, ordered him to assassinate such men? That's preposterous! It would make the U-2 fiasco pale by comparison. I don't believe you, lady. Harry's too smart, too knowledgeable to do anything like that; there could have been mass reprisals in the States, everyone one step closer to nuclear war, and nobody wanted that.'

'I did not say your brother ordered my husband to commit such acts.'

'Then what are you saying?'

'They were committed and Harry was Frederik's control.'

'You mean your *husband*—'

'Yes,' interrupted Karin de Vries softly. 'Freddie served your brother well, boring into the Stasi to the point where they threw him parties as a diamond merchant from Amsterdam who was making the apparatchiks rich. Then a pattern developed; times and locations coincided where powerful East Germans beholden to the Kremlin were assassinated. Separately and together, both Harry and I confronted Frederik. He denied everything, of course, and his innocent charm and his quick tongue – the same qualities that made him an extraordinary deep-cover operative – persuaded us both that it was coincidence.'

'There's no such thing as coincidence in this business.'

'We found that out when Frederik was captured a week before the Berlin Wall came down. Under torture, compounded by the injected serums, my husband admitted to the assassinations. Harry was among the first specialists to reach and tear apart the Stasi headquarters, and in his anger over Freddie's death he knew exactly what to look for and when it happened. He found a copy of the transcript and kept it on his person, bringing it to me later.'

'Then your husband was a loose cannon, and neither you nor my brother saw through him?'

'You would have to have known Freddie. There was a

reason behind his intemperance. He had a hatred towards the militant Germans, a deep loathing that did not extend to the tolerant, even penitent citizens of West Germany. You see, his grandparents were executed in the town square by a Waffen SS firing squad in front of the entire village. Their crime: bringing food to the starving Jews held behind an open barbed-wire enclosure in a field by the railroad yard. However – and this is most painful – along with his grandfather and grandmother, seven innocent males, all fathers, were shot as examples for a disobedient citizenry. In the hypocrisy of panic, the De Vries family was stigmatized for a generation. Frederik was brought up by relatives in Brussels, permitted only on rare occasions to see his parents, who eventually committed suicide together. I'm convinced the terrible memory of those years stayed with Freddie until the moment he died.'

Silence. And then the bewildered waiter returned with their glasses of wine, spilling part of one on Drew's trousers. He left, and Latham said, 'Let's get out of here. There's a decent restaurant, a brasserie, around the corner.'

'I know it too, but I would prefer to finish our conversation here.'

'Why? This place is awful.'

'I don't think it's right that we be noticed together.'

'For God's sake, we work in the same place. Incidentally, why haven't I ever seen you at our embassy get-togethers? I'm sure I'd have remembered.'

'Such parties are not a priority with me, Monsieur Latham. I live a very solitary and quite happy life.'

'By yourself?'

'That is my choice.'

Drew shrugged. 'Okay, then. You saw my name on our roster sent to The Hague, and on the basis of my being Harry's brother, you asked for your transfer. *Why?*'

'I told you, I was cleared by NATO for maximum-classified materials. Six months ago I took a secure-channel memorandum from radio traffic to the supreme commander, and being curious – as I was today – I looked at it. It said that one Drew Latham was being transferred to Paris with full Quai d'Orsay credentials, to explore the "German problem". It took no imagination to know what that was, monsieur. It was the "German problem" that killed my husband, and I remembered all too clearly your brother talking about you most affectionately. How he wished you had never tried to follow in his footsteps, for you were too quick-tempered and had no facility with languages.'

'Harry's jealous because Mother always liked me better.'

'You're joking.'

'I certainly am. Actually, I have an idea she thought – still thinks – we're both a little strange.'

'Because of your professions?'

'Hell no, she doesn't know what they are, and Dad's smart enough not to tell her. She's convinced we're somewhere in the ranks of the State Department, travelling all over the world for months at a time, and why aren't we both married so she can spoil her grandchildren.'

'A natural concern, I'd say.'

'Not for two sons in an unnatural profession.'

'However, Harry did allow that you were very strong and quite intelligent.'

'*Quite* intelligent? . . . Jealousy again. I got extra money on my college scholarship because of my prep school hockey – he fell on his ass on a pair of skates.'

'You're joking again.'

'No, not that part, it's real.'

'You had scholarships?'

'We had to. Our father was a PhD in archaeology, and all it brought him were digs from Arizona to the old Iraq. The National Geographic Society and the Explorers' Club paid for the travels but not for the wife and kids. When those movies came out, Harry and I used to laugh and say to hell with the "Lost Ark", where were the kids of Indiana Jones?'

'The frame of reference is beyond me, although I recognize the academic aspect.'

'Our father had tenure, so we weren't broke, but we certainly weren't rich, barely middle-class well-off. We *had* to get scholarships . . . Now, you've heard my life story, and I've heard more than I care to hear about your husband . . . what about *you*? Where are you coming from – out of the woodwork, *Mrs* de Vries?'

'It's not relevant—'

'Yes, you said that before and I don't buy it. Before you go much further in the embassy, *especially* in D and R, you'd better make it clear.'

'You don't believe a word I've told you—'

'I believe the surface, what Witkowski confirmed, but beyond that I'm not sure.'

'Then you can go to the devil, monsieur.' Karin de Vries started sliding across the booth to get up, when the inebriated waiter approached.

'Is there anyone here named Lat'am?' he asked.

'*Latham*? Yes, that's me.'

'There is a call for you on our telephone. That will add thirty francs to your bill.' The waiter wandered away.

'Stay here,' said Drew. 'I told Communications where I'd be.'

'Why should I?'

'Because I want you to, I *really* want you to.' Latham got up and walked rapidly to the antiquated telephone at the end of the distressed bar. He picked up the receiver, which was lying in a pool of stale wine, and spoke. 'This is Latham.'

'Durbane here,' said the voice on the line. 'I'm patching you through on scrambler to Director Sorenson in Washington. You're clear at both ends. Go ahead.'

'*Drew?*'

'Yes, sir—'

'It happened! We just got word about *Harry*. He's alive!'

'*Where?*'

'As near as we can determine, somewhere in the Hausruck Alps. A call came through from the anti-neos in Obernberg saying they were engineering his escape, and to keep our secure lines open from Passau to Burghausen. They refused to identify themselves, but they have to be real.'

'Thank God!' cried Latham in relief.

'Don't be too confident. They say he's got to get through damn near twelve miles of snow in the mountains before they can reach him.'

'You don't know Harry. He'll get there. I may be stronger, but he was always tougher.'

'What are you talking about?'

'Never mind. I'll go back to the embassy and wait.' Latham replaced the phone and returned to the table.

Karin de Vries was not there.

CHAPTER FIVE

The column of figures trudged through the snow as the long shadows of evening spread across the mountain range, the only illumination the headlights of the two huge vehicles and the flashlights of the guards. Harry Latham leapt off the truck, the ache in his head subsiding the nearer they came to the bridge over the gorge above the offshoot of the Salzach River. He could *make* it! Once over the narrow bridge, he would find his way; he had memorized the reverse route and the markings he had made, recalling it all a thousand times during his so-called hospitalization, otherwise known as being held hostage. But he could not remain in the alpine truck, where he had hidden himself, for the vehicles were searched, each piece of equipment matched to an invoice. Instead, he had to join the column of Sonnenkinder, blindly marching off to their uncertain futures throughout Germany and all Europe, singing their songs of blood purity. Aryan righteousness, and death to the ill born. Harry sang with the loudest of them, his fervour acknowledged by grins and bright eyes as they crossed over the bridge. *Only moments now.*

The moment came! The column marched to the right in the snow-swept night, and Harry ducked away, crouching, and scurried to his left during a particularly brief, heavy snowfall. An observant guard saw him and raised his pistol.

'*Nein!*' said the *Reichsführer* of the detail, gripping the soldier's arm and lowering it. '*Verboten. Ist schon gut!*'

The man known in covert operations as Sting trudged through the knee-deep snow untrampled by preceding feet,

84

breathlessly hoping he would see the first of the marks he had made weeks before – *years* ago in his mind – when he was first escorted to the hidden valley. There it was! Two broken limbs of a sapling that would not rejuvenate until spring. The small tree had been on the left, the next marking was on the right, a descending, diagonal right . . . Three hundred yards later, his face hot and flushed, his legs freezing, he saw it! The branch of an alpine spruce he had snapped; it was still angled downward, its remnant dried, devoid of sap. The mountain road between the two alpine villages was less than five miles away, most of it downhill. He would make it. He *had* to!

Finally, his feet in ice-cold agony, his body bent over in pain, he did. He sat down and massaged his legs, his hands scraped by his half-frozen trousers, when a truck appeared on the left. He propelled himself to his feet, staggered into the road, and violently waved his arms in the beams of the headlights. The truck stopped.

'*Hilfe!*' he yelled in German. 'My car went off the road!'

'No explanations, please,' said the bearded driver in accented English. 'I've been waiting for you. I've driven up and down this road for the past three days, hour after hour.'

'Who *are* you?' asked Harry, climbing into the seat.

'Your deliverance, as the British say,' replied the driver, chuckling.

'You *knew* I was coming out?'

'We have a spy in the hidden valley, although we have no idea where it is. She, like everyone else, was taken there blindfolded.'

'How did she *know?*'

'She's a nurse in the hospital down there, a nurse when she isn't ordered to copulate with another Aryan *Bruder* so to produce a new Sonnenkind. She watched you, saw you folding pieces of paper and sewing them into your clothes—'

'But *how?*' interrupted Latham/Lassiter.

'Your rooms have hidden cameras.'

'How did she get word to you?'

'All the Sonnenkinder are permitted, even ordered, to reach parents or relatives to explain their absences with pleasant fictitious stories. Without those explanations, the *Oberführer* fear exposure, as with your American cults, who barricade themselves in other mountains and valleys. She reached her "parents", and with precise codes told us the American would be leaving, the precise day or time she couldn't know, but you were definitely going to escape imminently.'

'The evacuation – and it is just that – was my way out.'

'Whatever, you're here and on your way to Burghausen. From our humble headquarters there you may reach whomever you like. You see, we are the Antinayous.'

'The *who*?'

'The opposite of the one who, under the nom de plume of Caracalla, slaughtered twenty thousand Romans who opposed his despotic rule, according to the historian Dio Cassius.'

'I've heard of Caracalla, Dio Cassius as well, but I'm afraid I don't understand you.'

'Then you are not a serious student of Roman history.'

'No, I'm not.'

'So we'll bring it up-to-date, in another context, in another reversal, *ja*?'

'Whatever you say.'

'Anglicized, we are anti-Nyoss, *ja*?'

'Okay.'

'Substitute "neos" for "nyoss," *h'okay*?'

'Sure.'

'Then what have you got? Anti-neos, *nicht wahr*? Anti-neo-*Nazis*. That's who we are!'

'Why do you have to hide under an obscure name?'

'Why do *they* hide under the secret name of the Brüderschaft?'

'What has one got to do with the other?'

'Secrecy must match secrecy!'

'Why? You're legitimate.'

'We battle our enemy both above the ground and underneath the dirt.'

'I've been there,' said Harry Latham, falling back into the seat. 'And I still don't understand you.'

'Why did you leave?' asked Drew, having gotten Karin de Vries's telephone number from security.

'There wasn't anything more to say,' replied the D and R researcher.

'There was a *hell* of a lot more to say, and you know it.'

'Please check my clearance files, and if anything upsets you, report it.'

'Forget that crap! Harry's *alive*! After three years under cover, he escaped and he's on his way back!'

'*Mon Dieu*. I cannot tell you how happy, how *relieved* I am!'

'You knew all along what my brother was doing, didn't you?'

'Not on the telephone, Drew Latham. Come to my flat on the rue Madeleine. It is twenty-six, apartment five.'

Drew gave the number to Durbane in Communications, grabbed his jacket, and raced out to the Deuxième car, which was now his constant companion. 'Rue Madeleine,' he said. 'Number twenty-six.'

'A nice neighbourhood,' said the driver, starting the unmarked vehicle.

The apartment on rue Madeleine added another dimension to the enigma that was Karin de Vries. Not only was it large, it was tastefully, expensively appointed; the furniture, the drapes, and the paintings were far beyond the salary of an embassy employee.

'My husband was not a poor man,' said the widow, noting Drew's reactions to the decor. 'He not only played the part of a diamond merchant, he actively participated, and with his usual élan.'

'He must have been some kind of fellow.'

'And then something beyond that,' added De Vries without a comment in her voice. 'Please, sit down, Monsieur Latham. May I offer you a drink?'

'Considering the sour wine at the café of your choice, I gratefully accept.'

'I do have Scotch whisky.'

'Then I more than accept, I beg.'

'No need to,' said De Vries, laughing softly and walking to a mirrored bar. 'Freddie taught me to always keep four libations on hand,' she continued, opening an ice bucket, a bottle, and pouring a drink. 'Red wine at room temperature, white wine chilled – one full-bodied, the other dry, and both of good quality – as well as Scotch whisky for the English and bourbon for the Americans.'

'What about the Germans?'

'Beer, the quality unimportant, for he said they'd drink anything. But then, as I told you, he was extremely bigoted.'

'He must have known other Germans.'

'*Natürlich*. He insisted they had a fetish for imitating the British. "Whisky" – which is Scotch – without ice, and although they prefer ice, they deny it.' She brought Drew his glass and, gesturing at a chair, said, 'Sit down, Monsieur Latham, we have several things to discuss.'

'Actually, that's my line,' said Drew, sitting in a soft leather armchair across from the light-green velveteen couch preferred by Karin de Vries. 'You won't join me?' he asked, partially raising his glass.

'Perhaps later – if there is a later.'

'You're one hell of a puzzle, lady.'

'From where you sit I'm sure I appear so. However, looking over at you, I am simplicity itself. It's you who are the puzzle. You and the American intelligence community.'

'I think that remark requires an explanation, Mrs de Vries.'

'Of course it does, and you shall have it. You send a man out under the deepest cover, an extraordinarily talented operative fluent in five or six languages, and you keep his existence so secret here in Europe, *so* secret, he has no protection, no one he can reach as a control, for no one has the authority, much less the responsibility, to advise him.'

'Harry always had the option to pull out,' protested Latham. 'He travelled all over Europe and the Middle East. He could have stopped anywhere, picked up a phone, called Washington, and said, "This is it, I'm finished." He wouldn't have been the first deep cover to have done that.'

'Then you don't know your own brother.'

'What do you mean? For Christ's sake, I grew *up* with him.'

'Professionally?'

'No, not that way. We're in separate branches.'

'Then you truly have no idea what a bloodhound he is.'

'Bloodhound . . . ?'

'As fanatic in his pursuits as the fanatics he was pursuing.'

'He didn't like Nazis, who does?'

'That's not my point, monsieur. When Harry was a control, he had assets in East Germany, paid by the Americans, who fed him information that dictated his orders to his runners, runners like my husband. Your brother had no such advantage this last time. He was alone.'

'He *had* to be. It was the nature of the operation, total isolation. There couldn't be the slightest possible trace. Even I didn't know his cover name. What *is* your point?'

'Harry had no assets over here, but his enemy has assets in Washington.'

'What the hell are you saying?'

'You rightly assumed that I knew about your brother's assignment. Incidentally, his cover name was Lassiter. Alexander Lassiter.'

'*What?*' Astonished, Latham shot forward in the chair. 'Where did you get that information?'

'Since even you didn't know the name he was using, where else? The enemy, of course, a member of the Brotherhood – that's the name they use.'

'This is getting awfully sticky, lady. Another explanation, please.'

'Only partial. Some things you'll have to accept on faith. For my own protection.'

'I haven't got much faith, even less now, so let's start with the partial. Then I'll tell you whether you still have a job or not.'

'Considering my contributions, that's hardly fair—'

'Give it a try,' interrupted Drew sharply.

'Freddie and I kept a flat in Amsterdam, in his name, naturally, an apartment commensurate with his wealth as a young entrepreneur in the diamond trade. Whenever our schedules permitted, we'd be together there, but I was always, shall we say, a far different woman from the one they saw at NATO . . . from the one you see here at the embassy. I dressed fashionably, even extravagantly, and wore a blonde wig and a great deal of jewellery—'

'You were living a double life,' interrupted Latham again, nodding, again impatient.

'It was obviously necessary.'

'Conceded. And?'

'We entertained – not frequently, and only with Freddie's most vital contacts – but I was in evidence as his wife . . . I must stop here and explain something to you, even though you undoubtedly know it. Whenever powerful government policing agencies are duped by externals, they will, of course, get rid of the perpetrators by execution or by inverted compromise, thus causing them to be killed by their own people as double agents, do you agree?'

'I've heard about it, that's as far as I'll go.'

'But the one thing they will not suffer is embarrassment, the admission that they *were* penetrated; those occasions were kept intensely private, even within their own organizations.'

'I've heard about that too.'

'It happened in the Stasi. After Frederik was killed and the

Wall came down, a number of his important East German contacts continuously left messages on our telephone answering machine, pleading for meetings with Freddie. I accepted several, in my role as his wife. Two men, the first being the fourth highest ranking officer in the Stasi, and the other, a code breaker as well as a convicted rapist exonerated by his superiors, had been recruited by the Brotherhood. They came to see Frederik to reconvert their diamonds into currency. As with others, I dined them and filled them with alcohol – laced with powders Freddie always insisted I have in a sugar bowl – and as these two tried to make love to me, each telling me how important he was, they both drunkenly revealed *why* they were so important.'

'My brother Harry,' said Drew in a monotone.

'Yes. Under my prodding, each spoke of an American agent called Lassiter, whom the Brotherhood knew about and were prepared for.'

'How did you know it was *Harry*?'

'The clearest way possible. My first questions were innocuous, but I grew more specific with time – Freddie always claimed that was the best way, especially with alcohol and the powders. Eventually, each man said essentially the same words. They were as follows: "His real name is Harry Latham, Central Intelligence, Clandestine Operations, Project Time – two years plus, Code Sting, all information deleted from computers at Level AA-Zero."'

'*Jesus!* That had to come from the top, the *very* top! AA-Zero doesn't go far down the hall from the director's office . . . That's pretty outrageous, Mrs de Vries.'

'Since I had, and have, no idea what AA-Zero means, I submit it is the truth. Those were the words I heard, the reason I requested the transfer to Paris . . . Do I still have my job, monsieur?'

'It's solid as a rock. Only there's a new wrinkle.'

'Wrinkle? I understand the word, but how do you apply it?'

'You'll remain in D and R, but you're now part of Consular Operations.'

'Why?'

'Among other things, you'll have to sign a sworn affidavit that says you won't divulge the information you've just given me, and it also spells out thirty years in an American prison if you do.'

'And if I refuse to sign such a document?'

'Then you're the enemy.'

'*Good!* I like that. It is precise.'

'Let's be more precise,' said Latham, his eyes locked with Karin de Vries's. 'If you turn, or you *are* turned, there's no appeal. Do you understand?'

'With all my intellect and with all my heart, monsieur.'

'Now it's my turn to ask. Why?'

'It's really quite simple. For several years my marriage was a gift from God, a man I adored loved me as I loved him. Then I saw that man crippled by hatred, not blind hatred, but hate seen clearly with wide-open eyes, focused on a reemerging enemy that had destroyed his family – his parents and their parents before them. That glorious, ebullient young man I married deserved far better than was meted out to him. It's now my turn to fight his enemy, the enemy of all of us.'

'That's good enough for me, Mrs de Vries. Welcome to our side.'

'Then I shall join you in a drink, monsieur. There is a "later" after all.'

The American F-16 jet landed at the airport in Althein. The pilot, an air force colonel cleared by the CIA, requested immediate departure once his 'package' was on board. Harry Latham was driven across the field, assisted into the second cockpit; the canopy was closed, and within minutes the plane was airborne back to England. Three hours after his arrival in the UK, the exhausted deep-cover agent was driven under guard to the American Embassy on Grosvenor Square, his reception committee consisting of three high-ranking members of the Central Intelligence Agency, British MI-6, and France's equivalent, the French Service d'Etranger.

'*Hey*, it's great to have you back, Harry!' said the American.

'Damn fine show,' said the Englishman.

'*Magnifique!*' added the Frenchman.

'Thank you, gentlemen, but can't we postpone the debriefing until I get some sleep?'

'The *valley*,' said the American, 'where the hell is it? That can't wait, Harry.'

'The valley doesn't matter anymore. It's gone, the fires were started two days ago. Everything's destroyed, and everyone's out of there.'

'What the hell are you talking about?' persisted the man from Central Intelligence. 'It's our *key*.'

'My American colleague's quite right, old chap,' pressed the MI-6er.

'*Absolument*,' said the man from the Deuxième. 'We must destroy it!'

'Hold on, just *hold on!*' countered Harry, looking wearily at the intelligence tribunal. 'It may be the key, but the lock isn't there anymore. However, it doesn't matter.' To the astonishment of the others around the table, Latham began ripping apart the lining of his jacket, then proceeded to get up and remove his trousers, turning them inside out, and doing the same with the interior linings of his pockets. Standing in his jacket and shorts, he slowly, carefully, removed dozens of handwritten scraps of paper and piled them across the conference table. 'I brought out everything we need. Names, positions, agencies, and departments, the whole ball of wax, as my brother would phrase it. Incidentally, I'd appreciate—'

'It's been done,' interrupted the CIA station chief, anticipating the request. 'Sorenson at Cons-Op told him you came out. He's in Paris.'

'Thank you . . . If you have a totally secure secretarial pool among you, get all of these typed up using relays – no one person should be aware of what the others are doing. Regarding the coded pieces, I'll put them together later.'

'What *are* they?' asked the Englishman, staring at the scattered pieces of paper, many torn.

'An influential army behind the Brüderschaft, powerful men and women in each of our countries who either for greed or warped beliefs support the neos. I warn you, there are a number of surprises, both in our governments and the private sectors ... Now, if someone will find me a decent hotel and buy me some clothes, I'd like to sleep for a day or two.'

'Harry,' said the man from Central Intelligence, 'put on your trousers before you walk out of here.'

'Good point, Jack. You always were observant.'

Harry Latham lay in bed, the quasi-insulting and therefore caring telephone call from his brother, Drew, over with. They would meet in Paris by the end of the week, or as soon as Harry completed his debriefing, including the deciphering of the information he brought out of Germany. The older brother did not describe his immediate agenda, nor did he have to, the younger sibling understood the unspoken. The only pieces of information the latter offered were the following.

'With you back as a whole person, we can really move into high gear. We've got the ident of a car driven by a couple of scum-buckets ... Incidentally, reach me at my office or the Meurice hotel on the rue de Rivoli.'

'What happened to your flat? The management threw you out for indecent behaviour?'

'No, but someone else's indecent behaviour makes it currently unliveable.'

'Really? The Meurice is pretty high living, little brother.'

'Bonn's paying for it.'

'My goodness, I can't wait to hear. I'll call you when I'm

flying over. By the way, I'm at the Gloucester under the name of Moss, Wendell Moss.'

'Very classy ... Glad you're back, bro.'

'So am I, bro.' Harry had closed his eyes, sleep rapidly enveloping him when there was a soft, steady knocking on his hotel door. Shaking his head in irritation, he flipped off the covers, unsteadily climbed out of the bed, and reached for the hotel-provided bathrobe draped over a chair. He walked, half lurching, to the door. 'Who is it?' he called out.

'It's Catbird from Langley,' came the quiet reply. 'I have to talk to you, Sting.'

'*Oh?*' Bewildered, but knowing the maximum secrecy attached to his field code, Harry opened the door. In the corridor stood a relatively short man with a pleasant, rather pale, forgettable face, dressed in a dark business suit and wearing steel-rimmed glasses. 'What's a catbird?' asked Latham, gesturing for the emissary from Central Intelligence to come inside.

'Our codes changed, yours never did,' replied the stranger, entering the room and offering his hand. Harry took it, still confused. 'I can't tell you how pleased we are that you made it back from a very cold region.'

'What is this, a replay from John le Carré? If it is, he did it better. Sting I can understand, but Catbird's a trifle banal, don't you think? And why weren't you at the embassy? I'm one exhausted deep c, Mr Catbird. I really need my sleep.'

'Yes, I know, and I sincerely apologize. However, there's a level above the embassy, I'm sure you're aware of that.'

'Sure. There's the DCI, the Secretary of State, and the President. So, to repeat, what's a catbird?'

'I'll take up but a few minutes of your time,' said the pleasant-faced man, dismissing Harry's question and removing a pocket watch from his vest. 'This is a family heirloom, and with fading eyes, I find it easier to read. Two minutes, Mr Latham, and I'll be gone.'

'And before you go any further, you'd better show me some very damned authentic identification.'

'Naturally.' The intruder held up the pocket watch in front of Harry's face and spoke clearly, precisely, while pressing the crown. 'Hello, Alexander *Lassiter*. It's your friend, Dr Gerhardt *Kroeger*, and we must talk.'

Harry's eyes suddenly became unfocused, the pupils dilated; briefly, he was staring at nothing. 'Hi, Gerhardt,' he said, 'how's my favourite sawbones?'

'Fine, Alex. How are you, and have you taken your stroll today through our meadows?'

'Hey, come on, Doc, it's night. You want me to walk into a pack of Dobermans? Where's your head?'

'Sorry, Alexander, I've been operating most of the day, and you're quite right, I'm as tired as you ... But tell me, Alex, when in your *thoughts* you met with those people at the American Embassy, what happened?'

'Nothing really. I gave them everything I brought out and for the next few days we'll go over it all.'

'That's good. Anything *else*?'

'My brother called from Paris. They're tracing a car under suspicion. My kid brother's a nice fellow, you'd like him, Gerhardt.'

'I'm sure I would. He's the one who works for Consular Operations, isn't he?'

'That's right ... Why are you asking me these questions?'

Instantly, the pale-faced stranger in the hotel room again held up the pocket watch, pressing the crown twice as Harry Latham's eyes became clear, his focus direct. 'You really do need sleep, Harry,' said the man who called himself Catbird. 'I'm just not getting through to you. Tell you what, I'll try you tomorrow, okay?'

'What ... ?'

'I'll be in touch tomorrow.'

'Why?'

'Don't you remember? Good Lord, you *are* exhausted. The DCI, the Secretary of State ... the *President*, Harry. That's who I've been cleared by, that's what you wanted, *right?*'

'Sure . . . okay. That's what I wanted.'

'Get some sleep, Sting. You deserve it.' Catbird left hurriedly, closing the door behind him as Harry Latham robotically walked back to the bed and fell into it.

'Who's Catbird?' asked Harry. It was morning and the three intelligence officers were seated around the conference table, as they had been the previous day.

'I got your call two hours ago,' said the American station chief: 'I woke up the DCI himself and he never heard of a Catbird. He also thought it was a pretty stupid name – just like you did, Latham.'

'But he was *there*! I saw him, spoke with him. He *was* there!'

'What did you talk about, monsieur?' asked the man from French intelligence.

'I'm not sure – I don't really know, actually. He seemed perfectly normal, asked me a few innocuous questions, and then . . . I just don't remember.'

'May I suggest, Field Officer Latham,' the brigadier from Britain's MI-6 broke in, 'that you have undergone a most stressful – oh, the devil take it – and *unendurable* three years. Isn't it possible, and I say this with respect for your outstanding intellect, that you could be subject to illusionary moments? My *God*, man, I've had operatives working dual personas fantasize and break, having gone through only *half* your stress.'

'I don't break, General. I don't break and I don't fantasize.'

'Let's go back. Monsieur Latham,' said the Frenchman. 'When you first arrived at the Brüderschaft valley, what happened?'

'Oh.' Harry's eyes glanced downward; he felt disoriented for several moments, then everything was clear. 'You mean the accident. *Christ*, it was terrible. A lot of it's a blur, but the first thing I remember is the shouting, it was hysterical. Then I realized that I was stuck under the truck, a heavy piece of metal pressed against my head – I've never *felt* such pain . . .' Latham played out the litany programmed by Dr Gerhardt Kroeger, and when he was finished, he raised his head, his eyes clear. 'I've told you the rest, gentlemen.'

The tribunal looked at one another, each shaking his head very briefly in obvious confusion. Then the American spoke.

'Look, Harry,' he said softly, 'for the next few days we'll go over everything you've brought us, okay? After that, you've earned a long period of rest, *okay*?'

'I'd like to fly to Paris and see my brother—'

'Sure, no sweat, even if he's with Cons-Op, not my favourite branch.'

'I understand he's pretty good at what he does.'

'Hell,' agreed the CIA station chief, 'he was damn good when he played hockey for the Islanders farm team in Manitoba. I was stationed in Canada then, and I tell you, that hulk body-checked much bigger hulks into the walls more often than anyone I ever saw. He could have made it big in New York.'

'Fortunately,' said Harry Latham, 'I talked him out of such a violent profession.'

Drew Latham woke up in the overstuffed bed in his suite at the Meurice on the rue de Rivoli. Blinking his eyes, he looked at the bedside telephone and pressed the buttons for room service. As long as Germany was paying for it, he decided to have a porterhouse steak topped with two poached eggs, and porridge with heavy cream on the side; he was told his order would be delivered in thirty minutes. He stretched in the bed, his left arm annoyed by the automatic beneath the pillow, then closed his eyes for a few last minutes of rest.

A scratch, a metallic slice in the door. Not natural – not at *all* natural! Suddenly there were loud staccato bursts from a jackhammer six storeys below in the street, a repair crew starting unusually early in the morning . . . Unusual – *not* normal! It was barely light! Drew grabbed his weapon and slid off the left side of the bed; he rolled over and over until he was flush with the corner moulding of a far wall. The door opened and an explosive fusillade of bullets ripped apart the bed, shattering the mattress and pillows alike, in concert with the deafening noise from outside the windows. Latham raised his gun and fired five successive rounds into the black-encased figure in the doorframe. The man fell forward; Drew rose as the jackhammer stopped in the street, and he raced to his would-be killer. He was dead, but as the assassin had clutched at his upper body, he had torn down his skintight black sweater. On his chest were tattooed three small lightning bolts. Blitzkrieg. The Brüderschaft.

CHAPTER SIX

Jean-Pierre Villier stoically accepted the criticism levelled at him by the Deuxième Bureau's Claude Moreau. 'It was, indeed, a brave gesture on your part, monsieur, and be assured we are tracing the automobile in question, but please understand, should any harm have come to you, all France would have revolted against us.'

'I think that's rather overstated,' said the actor. 'However, I'm glad I was able to contribute in some small way.'

'In a very considerable way, but we now understand each other, isn't that so? There'll be no more contributions, correct?'

'As you wish, although it was a simple role to play, and there could be further information I might unearth—'

'Jean-Pierre!' exclaimed Giselle Villier. 'You will do no such thing, I won't permit it!'

'The Deuxième Bureau will not permit it, madame,' interrupted Moreau. 'You'll no doubt learn of it later in the day, so I might as well tell you now. Three hours ago a second assassination attempt was made on the American Drew Latham.'

'*My God . . . !*'

'Is he all right?' asked Villier, leaning forward.

'He's fortunate to be alive. To say the least, he's a very observant man and has learned a few of our less advertised rules of Paris.'

'I beg your pardon?'

'Everything was timed to the extremely loud and offensive noise of a street repair crew who started working at an hour when the majority of our visitors had barely gone to bed after experiencing the joys of our city, especially those to be found in the more expensive hotels.'

'It's summer,' said Giselle, shaking her head. 'We have enough trouble because of our manners. The Ministry of Tourism would cut off heads.'

'Our friend Latham somehow instinctively knew that. There was no repair crew, only a single man with a concrete hammer machine below his windows. Perhaps akin to the title of one of your films, Monsieur Villier, *Prelude to a Fatal Kiss*, if I'm not mistaken. It's one of my wife's favourites.'

'It should be banned from television,' said the actor succinctly. 'The kiss was from a vacuous actress who was more concerned with her camera angles than with her lines, which she rarely got right.'

'That's why she was perfect,' rejoined his wife. 'Her insecurity was so apparent, it made your obsession terribly believable – the bewildered male driven mad because he couldn't penetrate the mystery of the woman he thought he loved. You were really very good, my darling.'

'If I was even tolerable, it was because I was trying to get the bitch to *act*.'

'I don't think Monsieur Moreau is here to listen to an actor's complaints, dear.'

'I'm not complaining, merely telling the truth.'

'Nor in an actor's ego—'

'Oh, but I'm fascinated, madame. My wife will hang on every word!'

'Aren't police interrogations confidential beyond official circles?' asked Giselle.

'Naturally – of course, I misspoke.'

'Go ahead and speak, Moreau,' said Jean-Pierre, grinning, 'at least to your wife. You see, *my* wife is a retired attorney, if you haven't already guessed, and the actress in question has long since left the profession, having married an oil baron in the American state of Texas or Oklahoma, I forget which.'

'May we return to the issue at hand, if you please?'

'Of course, madame.'

'If Drew Latham escaped being killed, do you have any information on the failed assassin?'

'Indeed we do. He's dead, shot by Monsieur Latham.'

'Identification?'

'None. Except three very small tattoo marks above his right breast. Lightning bolts, the symbol of the Nazi blitzkrieg. Latham rightly assumed the origins, but he does not know what they stand for. We do . . . Those marks are very selectively issued, and only to a highly trained elite group within the neo-Nazis' larger organization. They number, by our estimate, no more than two hundred here in Europe, South America, and the United States. They're called the Blitzkrieger – they're assassins, trained killers skilled in multiple means of death, chosen for their dedication, their physical prowess, and, above all, their willingness – even their need – to kill.'

'Psychopaths,' said the former attorney. 'Psychopaths recruited by psychopaths.'

'Precisely.'

'Who could well have been recruited by any number of fanatical organizations, or cults, because such groups would permit them to exercise their natural tendencies for violence.'

'I'd have to agree with you, madame.'

'And you haven't told the Americans or the British or God knows who else about this – how would you call it? – this battalion of killers?'

'The highest officials have been informed, of course. None below those levels.'

'Why not? Why not a Drew Latham?'

'We have our reasons. There are leaks in the lower ranks.'

'Then why tell *us*?'

'You are French and you are famous. Celebrity is vulnerable; if word leaked out, well, we'd know—'

'*And?*'

'We appeal to your patriotism.'

'That's fatuous, unless it's an avenue to destroy my husband!'

'Now, just a minute, Giselle—'

'Be quiet, Jean-Pierre, this man from the Deuxième is here for another reason.'

'*What?*'

'You must have been an extraordinary attorney, Madame Villier.'

'Your line of direct inquiry, mixed with obfuscated indirect, is also extraordinarily obvious, monsieur. You demand that my husband be prohibited from doing one thing – even by my lights and knowing his talents, not actually life-threatening – yet in the next breath you reveal highly secret – *extraordinarily* secret – information which if he revealed it might cost him his career *and* his life.'

'As I said,' said Moreau, 'a brilliant attorney.'

'I don't understand a goddamned word either of you are *saying*!' cried the actor.

'You're not supposed to, darling, leave it to me.' Giselle glared at Moreau. 'You took us from one step down to another, didn't you?'

'I cannot deny it.'

'And now that he's vulnerable, knowing what he knows, what do you want us to do? Isn't that the basic question?'

'I imagine it is.'

'Then what *is* it?'

'Close the play, close *Coriolanus*, stating a part of the truth. Your husband has learned so much about this Jodelle that he can't go on, he's filled with remorse, and especially with loathing towards the people who did this to the old man. You'll be protected around the clock.'

'What about my mother and father?' shouted Villier. 'How could I *do* this to them?'

'I spoke with both of them an hour ago, Monsieur Villier. I told them as much as I could, including the rise of the Nazi movement in Germany. They said it would have to be your decision, but they also hoped that you would honour your natural mother and father. What more can I say?'

'So I close the show, and by what I have *not* said in public, I am the man in their gun sights, my dear wife as well. Is that what you're asking?'

'To repeat, you'll never, *ever*, be out of our protection. Streets, rooftops, armoured limousines, agents in restaurants, police in resorts – beyond anything you would ever require for your safety. All we need is a live Blitzkrieger so we can learn where they get their orders. There are drugs as well as other methods that will convince a killer to tell us.'

'You've never captured one?' said Giselle.

'Oh, yes. Several months ago we trapped two, but they hanged themselves in their cells before we could put them under chemicals. Such is the dedication of psychopathic zealots. Death is their profession, even their own.'

In Washington, Wesley Sorenson, director of Consular Operations, studied the secure facsimiles wired from London. 'I can't believe this,' he said. 'It's incredible!'

'That's what I thought,' agreed Sorenson's young chief of staff, standing at the left of the desk. 'But we can hardly dismiss it. Those names came from Sting, the only deep cover ever to have penetrated the Brüderschaft. It's what he was sent out to do and he did it.'

'But, my *God*, man, so many of these people are beyond reproach, and this isn't even the complete list – certain names have been selectively withheld! Two senators, six congressmen, CEOs of four major corporations, as well as a half dozen prominent men and women in the media, faces and voices we see and hear and read every day on television, radio, and the newspapers ... Here, *look*, two anchormen and a woman co-host, and three talk show bullies—'

'The fat one I'd say is a possible,' interrupted the head staffer. 'He attacks anything he thinks is left of Attila the Hun.'

'Not at all, he's too obvious. A third-rate mind, minimally

educated and filled with hate, yes, but not a bona fide Nazi. He's just a buffoon with a glib tongue.'

'The names came from the Brotherhood valley, sir. Nowhere else.'

'Jesus, here's a member of the President's *Cabinet*!'

'That one blew me away, I'll grant you,' said the Cons-Op chief of staff. 'He's down-home corn silk, hardly a political bone in his body . . . On the other hand, such people are accomplished at deception. There were Nazis in Congress during the late thirties, and Communists all over the place in the fifties, if you believe the loyalty investigations.'

'The vast majority were pure bunk, young man,' said Sorenson emphatically.

'I realize that, sir, but there were successful prosecutions.'

'How many? If I remember the statistics, and I *do*, the number of people specifically named by that son-of-a-bitch Hoover and that fraud McCarthy came to nineteen thousand seven hundred. And after the screaming was over, there were exactly *four* convictions! Four out of damned near twenty thousand! That comes to point zero zero zero two plus, and a lot of congressional wind, as well as a great deal of wasted taxpayers' money. Don't bring back those good old days to me, *please*. I was around your age then – not as bright, God knows – but I lost a lot of friends to that insanity.'

'I'm sorry, Mr Sorenson, I didn't mean to—'

'I know, I know,' the director of Cons-Op broke in, 'there's no way you can understand the pain those times caused. And that's what worries me.'

'I don't understand, sir.'

'Could we be starting our own helter-skelter persecutions? Harry Latham is probably the only real genius the CIA has in the field, a super brain who can't be tricked, but this stuff is from another planet . . . Or is it? Christ, it's *crazy!*'

'What is, Mr Sorenson?'

'The ages of all these people, they're pretty much the same – late forties, early fifties, a number in their sixties.'

'So?'

'Years ago, when I first joined the Agency, there were rumours out of Bremerhaven – actually from an old submarine base in the Heligoland Bight – that told of a last-ditch strategy designed by fanatics of the Third Reich who knew they had lost the war. It was called Operation Sonnenkinder, selected children sent out secretly all over Europe and America to families who welcomed them and would bring them up to fill positions of financial power and political influence. Their final objectives were to create a climate that was conducive to . . . the Fourth Reich.'

'That's *wild*, sir!'

'It was also totally disproven. We had a couple of hundred agents, along with Army Intelligence and British MI-6, who tracked down every lead over a period of two years. It all came to nothing. If there ever was such an operation, it was aborted at the start. There wasn't a shred of evidence that it was ever put in motion.'

'But you're wondering now, aren't you, Mr Sorenson?'

'Reluctantly, Paul. Doing my goddamnedest to restrain an imagination that kept me alive in the field. But I'm *not* in the field, I'm not in a situation where I have to anticipate the movements of someone in the next dark street, or over a hill at night. I have to look at the whole landscape in clear daylight, and there's no way I can accept the Sonnenkinder operation.'

'So why don't you reject the premise and put the list of names on a back burner?'

'Because I can't. Because Harry Latham brought it out . . . Set up a meeting tomorrow with the Secretary of State and the DCI over at State or Langley. Since I'm the stepchild, I'll meet wherever they say.'

Drew Latham sat at his desk on the second floor of the American Embassy, swallowing the dregs of his third cup of coffee. The single knock on his office door was followed by its being opened, an anxious Karin de Vries walking inside.

'I heard what happened!' she exclaimed. 'It *had* to be you!'

'Good morning,' said Drew, 'or is it noon? And if you brought your Scotch, you're very welcome.'

'It's all over the papers,' cried the researcher from D and R, crossing to the desk and throwing down the noon edition of *L'Express*, 'A burglar attempted to rob a guest at the Meurice, shot up the room, and was killed by a floor guard!'

'Boy, their public relations people work quickly, don't they? That's real security; it can't get much better.'

'Stop it, Drew! *You* were at the Meurice, you told me so. And when I called the arrondissement police, they said – very awkwardly – that no information was available.'

'Wow, everybody in Paris protects the influx of tourist cash. Actually, they should. This sort of thing never happens except to people like me.'

'Then it *was* you.'

'You said that already. Yes, it was me.'

'Are you all right?'

'I think that's been asked before, but, yes, I am. I'm still scared to death – strike the last two words – but I'm here, breathing, warm, and ambulatory. Do you want to go to lunch, anyplace you want except the last joint you recommended?'

'I have at least forty-five minutes' worth of work to do.'

'I can wait that long. I just got finished with Ambassador Courtland and his diplomatic crony, Ambassador Kreitz of Germany. They're probably still talking, but my stomach couldn't take their interacting, exculpatory bullshit any longer.'

'In some ways, you *are* like your brother. He dislikes authority.'

'Correction, please,' said Latham. 'We both dislike authority when it doesn't know what it's talking about, that's all. Incidentally, he's flying over from London tomorrow or the next day. Would you like to see him?'

'With all my heart. I *adore* Harry!'

'Strike two against my brother.'

'I beg your pardon?'

'He's a nerd.'

'I don't understand.'

'His intellect, it's so far up in the sky, you can't reach it, can't talk to it.'

'Oh, yes, I recall so well. We had such wonderful conversations about the incremental explosions of religiosity from Egypt to Athens to Rome and into the Middle Ages.'

'Strike three against Harry. Where for lunch?'

'Where you suggested yesterday. The brasserie across the Gabriel from the café where we talked.'

'We're likely to be seen together.'

'It doesn't matter now. I spoke to the colonel. He understands completely. As he said, "No sweat."'

'What else did Witkowski say?'

'Well' – De Vries lowered her head and spoke softly – 'he said you weren't your brother.'

'In what way wasn't I?'

'It's not important, Drew.'

'Maybe it is. In what way?'

'Let's say, you aren't the scholar he is.'

'Harry just struck out on fouls . . . Lunch in an hour, okay?'

'I'll make the reservation, they know me.' Karin de Vries walked out of the office, closing the door far more quietly than she had before.

Latham's telephone rang. It was Ambassador Courtland. 'Yes, sir, what is it?'

'Kreitz just left. Drew, and I'm sorry you weren't here to listen to the rest of what he had to say. Your brother hasn't just disturbed a hornet's nest, he's smashed hell out of it.'

'What are you talking about?'

'Kreitz couldn't have said it in front of you anyway, actually, as a matter of security. It's so maximum classified, even I had to get clearance to confirm it.'

'*You?*'

'Given the fact that Heinrich had broken Bonn's seal and

insofar as Harry's your brother and is flying here tomorrow, I guess the intelligence hats felt it was useless to keep me out of the circle.'

'What did Harry do, find Hitler and Martin Bormann in a South American gay bar?'

'I wish it were so insignificant. Your brother brought out lists from his German operation, names of neo-Nazi supporters in the Bonn government and industry, as well as the same in the US, France, and England.'

'Good old bright Harry!' exclaimed Latham. 'He never ever did things halfway, did he? Damn, I'm proud of that elderly gentleman!'

'You don't understand, Drew. Some – no, many – of those names are among the most prominent people in our respective countries, men and women of high profiles and fine reputations. It's all so extraordinary.'

'If Harry brought it out, it's also goddamned authentic. No one on earth could turn my brother.'

'Yes, that's what I've been told.'

'So what's the problem? Go after the bastards! Deep cover isn't simply a matter of weeks or months or even years. It could just as easily be decades, the dream of strategists in every intelligence think tank you can name.'

'It's all so difficult to comprehend—'

'*Don't* comprehend. Go to work!'

'Heinrich Kreitz totally rejects four people on the Bonn list, three men and a woman.'

'What makes him an all-knowing God here?'

'They have Jewish blood; they lost relatives in the camps, specifically Auschwitz and Bergen-Belsen.'

'How does he know that?'

'They're in their sixties now, but each was an early student of his when he first taught in grammar school, each he protected from the Ministry of Aryan Investigation at the risk of his own life.'

'It's possible he was conned. From the two meetings we've had, he strikes me as being very connable.'

109

'That's the academic in him. As with so many, he's both hesitant and loquacious, but neither weakness contradicts his brilliance. He's a perceptive man of enormous experience.'

'The last part could also describe Harry. There's no way he'd bring out false information.'

'I'm told there are some extraordinary names on the Washington list. *Unbelievable* was the word Sorenson used.'

'So was Lindbergh; the *Spirit of St Louis* was on Goering's side until young Charlie figured out that they were the evil people and then fought like hell for us.'

'I don't think that kind of comparison is even called for.'

'Probably not. I'm only trying to illustrate a point.'

'Suppose your brother's right? Even half right, or a quarter right, or even half of that – or even far less than *that*?'

'He brought out the names, Mr Ambassador. No one else did or could, so I suggest you proceed as if they were bona fides until proven otherwise.'

'What you're saying, if I read you, is that they're all guilty until proven innocent.'

'We're not talking law, sir, we're talking about the reemergence of the worst goddamned plague this world has ever seen, including the bubonic! There's no time for legal claptrap. We have to stop them now.'

'We once said that about the Communists, and the reputed Communists, and the vast majority in our own country proved to be nothing of the sort.'

'This is *different*! These neos aren't boring within like the Nazis did in the thirties; they've *had* the power; they remember how they got it. *Fear*. Armed gangs roaming through the streets in blue jeans, streaked faces, and chopped hair; then come the uniforms – even the shovels and the boots of the *Schultsefein*, the first of Hitler's thugs – and everything goes berserk! We have to *stop* them!'

'With only the names we have?' asked Courtland softly. 'Men and women of such high regard that no one would ever suspect them of being remotely part of this insanity. How do we proceed? How do any of us proceed?'

'With people like me, Mr Ambassador. Men and women trained to break through the shells and get to the truth.'

'That has a distinctly unattractive ring to it, Latham. Whose truth?'

'*The* truth, Courtland!'

'I beg your pardon?'

'Forgive me – *Mr* Courtland, or Mr *Ambassador*. The time for diplomatic – even *ethical* – niceties is over! I could have been a riddled corpse in my bed at the Meurice. These bastards play hardball, and the balls are made of concrete exploded from weapons.'

'I think I understand where you're coming from—'

'Try living it, sir. Try picturing your ambassadorial bed blown apart while you're crouched against the wall, wondering if one of those bursts will find your face or your throat or your chest. This is war – undercover war, I grant you, but war nevertheless.'

'Where would you begin?'

'I've got a place to start, but I want Harry's list of names here in France while Moreau and I go after the one we have.'

'The Deuxième's not yet cleared for any conceivable French collaborators.'

'*What?*'

'You heard me. Again, where would you start?'

'With the name of the man who rented the car that our famous, if crazy out-of-his head, actor identified north of the Pont Neuf.'

'Moreau gave it to you?'

'Of course he did. The car on the Montaigne that Bressard smashed into was a bust. It was from Marseilles, but the rental is so convoluted, it would take weeks to process. This man we've got; he goes on at his desk at four o'clock this afternoon. We'll break him if we have to put his testicles in a vice.'

'You can't work with Moreau.'
'What are you talking about? Why *not*?'
'He's on Harry's list.'

CHAPTER SEVEN

Stunned, Drew walked out of his office, down the circular staircase to the embassy's lobby, and out the bronze entrance onto the avenue Gabriel. He turned right and headed for the brasserie where he and Karin de Vries had agreed to have lunch. He was not only stunned, he was furious! Courtland had refused even to discuss the astonishing revelation that Claude Moreau, head of the Deuxième Bureau, was on 'Harry's list.' He just left the extraordinary statement hanging in mid-breath, overriding Latham's protestations with the words 'There's nothing more to say. Play along with Moreau but don't give him a damn thing. Call me tomorrow and tell me what happened.' With those precise instructions, the ambassador had hung up the phone.

Moreau a *neo*? It was about as credible as saying De Gaulle had been a German sympathizer in World War Two! Drew was not a fool; he fully understood and accepted the reality of moles and double agents, but to consign a man with Moreau's record to either category without examination was sheer sophistry. For a field officer to rise in the ranks through years of clandestine operations to head up a branch so specialized as the Deuxième, he would have to pass under the scrutiny of a thousand pairs of eyes, both admiring and envious, the latter determined to derail him with all the damaging input at their command. Yet Moreau had survived the gauntlet, not only survived it but emerged with the epithet 'world class', a phrase Latham doubted another world-class practitioner, one Wesley Sorenson, would use casually.

113

'*Monsieur!*' shouted the voice from a car in the street; the Deuxième vehicle was obviously keeping pace with him. '*Entrez-vous, s'il vous plaît!*'

'I'm only walking a couple of blocks,' shouted Drew, dodging the pedestrians as he made his way to the kerb. 'Like yesterday, remember?' he added in his simplified French.

'I did not like yesterday and I do not like today. Please come inside!' The Deuxième car stopped as Latham reluctantly opened the door and lurched into the front seat.

'You're overreacting, René – or are you Marc? I get confused.'

'I am François, monsieur, and I don't care for confusion. I have my job.'

Suddenly, with ear-shattering explosions, bullets pelted the thick outer safety glass of the side windows and then the windshield as a black sedan raced ahead, weaving through the traffic. '*Christ!*' roared Drew, hugging the front seat, his head below the dashboard. 'You saw that coming, *didn't* you?'

'Only the possibility, monsieur,' replied the driver, breathing heavily, his body arched back in the seat. He had stopped the car, the windshield so pockmarked that vision was nil. 'An automobile drove away from the kerb when you emerged from the embassy. One doesn't give up a parking space on the Gabriel without a good reason, and the men in that car were very angry when I cut them off and yelled for you.'

'I owe you, François,' said Latham rapidly, awkwardly rising, turning, and planting his feet on the floor as people in the street cautiously approached the Deuxième vehicle. 'What now?'

'The police will come any moment, someone will call them—'

'I can't talk to the police.'

'I understand. Where were you going?'

'To a brasserie in the next block, on the other side of the street.'

'I know it. Go there now. Walk with the crowds and be one of them. Look very excited, as everyone else does, when you get outside, then make your way to the brasserie as inconspicuously as you can. Stay there until we come for you or reach you on the phone.'

'What name?'

'You're American – Jones will do. Tell the maître d' that you expect a call. Do you have a weapon?'

'Of course.'

'Be careful. It's unlikely, but be prepared for the unlikely.'

'You don't have to spell it out. What about you?'

'We know what to do. *Hurry!*'

Drew opened the door, closing it quickly and instantly lowering his body, then rising, feigning the panic of those surrounding him. In moments he was indeed one with the crowd. Altering his height frequently, he scurried to the other side of the avenue Gabriel and while glancing around, his eyes darting in every direction, he once again headed for the brasserie and Karin de Vries.

He was far too early. He realized that when he saw the half-empty restaurant, but he had to stay away from his office, away from the embassy. Suddenly both took on images he did not care to think about, not after what had happened less than four hundred feet up the street. Still he *had* to think about them, think hard and deep. 'Reservation in the name of De Vries,' he said in English to the tuxedoed man at the lectern.

'Yes, of course, sir . . . You're a bit early, monsieur.'

'Is that a problem?'

'Not at all. Come, I'll take you to your table. The madame prefers the rear section.'

'My name's Jones. I may be getting a telephone call.'

'I'll bring it to the table—'

'To the table?'

'These days everyone has a telephone, no? How people

115

can drive and walk across the streets in traffic while on the phone amazes me. *Mon Dieu*, no wonder our accident rate is so high!'

'Tell me,' said Latham, thinking quickly as he sat down. 'Could you bring me a telephone now?'

'*Certainement*. Local or long distance, monsieur?'

'Long distance,' replied Drew, frowning in thought.

'The telephone is numbered, and the charges will be listed on your bill.'

'It must be a pain in the neck for you,' said Latham.

'It could be, but we don't tell everyone or advertise the convenience. So many carry around their own phones—'

'You told *me*,' Drew interrupted, looking at the man.

'Well, of course. You are with the *ambassade américaine*, *n'est-ce pas*? You've come in here a number of times, Mr Jones.'

'I guess I have,' agreed Latham, handing the maître d' his telephone credit card. 'I just never made a reservation.'

'*Merci*. May I order you a drink or a bottle of wine?'

'Whisky. Scotch, if you please.' The manager left, the whisky arrived, and Drew settled back in the booth, a tremble developing in his hands, his face flushed.

My God, but for an experienced, observant driver he would have been killed on the Gabriel! Three attempts on his life had been made within a day and a half, the first the night before last, the second that morning at dawn, and now only minutes earlier! He was *marked*, and the posthumous honour of having died in the line of duty held no appeal for him whatsoever. There was no question that the Nazi cancer was spreading throughout Germany and beyond. Where else, who knew? How effective, who could estimate? Harry's list would seem to portend the worst scenario for the NATO countries, and Karin de Vries's disclosure that the Brotherhood had invaded the Agency's top-secret computers for information about Operation Sting certainly supported the Washington penetration. *Christ*, he had told Villier that the regenerated Nazis were expanding everywhere, but it was

116

hyperbole, a hook to enlist the actor's interest because he suspected Villier's background, the Jodelle connection and all it represented, not the least of which were the missing interrogation files. When Villier confirmed his suspicions, he was both elated and horrified, elated that he had zeroed in on a truth, frightened because it *was* the truth.

And now he was a maximum target *because* he had found the truth. In line with his theory that dead intelligence officers served no useful purpose, he would rescind his previous instructions and seek whatever further protection the Deuxième could offer.

The Deuxième – *Moreau*? Was it possible? By asking Moreau for additional personal security, was he signing his own death warrant? Despite all his instincts, and regardless of his convictions about the man, was Harry's list that accurate? He could not *believe* it – it was crazy! Or was it?

The maître d' returned to the table carrying the portable phone. It was barely seven A.M. in Washington, and before the director of Consular Operations began his morning, one Drew Latham needed guidance.

'Press the button marked *Parlez* and dial, monsieur,' said the maître d'. 'Should you require additional calls, touch *Finis*, then again press *Parlez* and dial.' He handed Drew the phone and walked away. Latham touched the button marked *Parlez*, dialled, and within moments an alert voice answered.

'Yes?'

'Paris calling—'

'I thought you might,' Sorenson broke in. 'Has Harry arrived? You can talk, we're on scrambler.'

'He's not due until tomorrow at the earliest.'

'Dammit!'

'Then you know? About the information he brought out, I mean.'

'I do, but I'm surprised *you* do. Brother or no, Harry's not the type who's free with classified data, and I do mean classified to the maximum.'

'Harry didn't tell me anything. It was Courtland.'

117

'The ambassador? I find that incredible. He's a good man, but he's not in this loop.'

'He had to be included. Bonn's ambassador broke the seals, pretty angrily as I understand it, over four possibles in his own government.'

'What the hell is going *on*?' shouted Sorenson. 'This is all supposed to be kept in a deep tank until decisions are made!'

'Somebody jumped the gun,' said Drew. 'The sprinters began running before the starter's pistol was fired.'

'Have you any idea what you're *saying*?'

'Oh, yes, I certainly do.'

'Then, goddammit, tell me! I have a meeting at ten o'clock with the Secretary of State and the DCI—'

'Be careful what you say,' interrupted Latham rapidly.

'What in God's name does *that* mean?'

'The Agency's AA-Zero computers were compromised. The Brüderschaft – that's the name the neos call themselves – knew all about Harry's operation. Code Sting, objectives, even the projected time of his mission – two years plus. It was all picked up from Langley.'

'This is shit-kicking *nuts*!' roared the director of Cons-Op. 'How did you find out?'

'From a woman named De Vries, whose husband was Harry's runner in the old East Berlin. He was killed by the Stasi, and she's on our side. She works at the embassy now, and says she has a few scores to terminate. I believe her.'

'Can you be certain?'

'Nothing's in cement, but I think so.'

'What does Moreau think?'

'Moreau?'

'Yes, of course. Claude Moreau, the Deuxième.'

'I thought you had Harry's list.'

'So?'

'He's on it. I was ordered not to tell him anything.'

Following a short gasp, the silence from Washington was electrifying. Finally, Sorenson spoke quietly, ominously. 'Who gave you that order? Courtland?'

'Presumably relayed from on high . . . Wait a minute. You *have* Harry's list—'

'I have *a* list that was sent to me.'

'Then you've got Moreau's name. Did you miss it?'

'No, because it's not there.'

'*What* . . . ?'

'It was understood that for maximum security, certain names were "selectively withheld".'

'From *you*?'

'Those were the words.'

'They're bullshit!'

'Yes, I know.'

'Can you think of a reason – *any* reason?'

'I'm trying to, believe me . . . Among the upper echelons it's common knowledge that Moreau and I worked closely together—'

'Yes, you mentioned Istanbul—'

'That was our last posting; there were others. We were a good team and whenever it was feasible, the analysts in Washington and Paris paired us.'

'Would that be reason enough to exclude him from your list?'

'Possibly,' replied the director of Cons-Op, now barely audible. 'The argument could be made, but not convincingly. You see, he saved my life in Istanbul.'

'We all try to do that kind of thing if we're in a position to, usually on the assumption that the favour might be returned someday.'

'That's why it's not a convincing argument. Still, a bond is indelibly formed, isn't it?'

'Within limits and depending on the circumstances.'

'Well said.'

'It's axiomatic . . . I'm to reach Moreau this afternoon. There's a lead on a rental car our actor picked up playing secret agent. What should I do?'

'Normally,' began Sorenson, 'even abnormally, I'd consider Claude's name on that list to be ludicrous.'

'Agreed,' interrupted Latham.

'Yet Harry brought it out. The fact that he's your brother notwithstanding—'

'Again axiomatic,' Drew broke in curtly.

'I find it extremely difficult to believe Harry could be fooled, and turned is out of the question.'

'Again – agreed,' mumbled Latham.

'So where are we? If your woman friend is genuine, the Agency's been penetrated, and there's obviously someone in either French intelligence or our own who spotted Moreau's name and by extension doesn't trust me.'

'*That's* ludicrous!' said Drew, raising his voice and instantly lowering it as heads turned at several tables in front of his booth.

'It's a hell of a shock, I'll say that much.'

'I'm going to call Harry in London. Tell him our thoughts.'

'He's sequestered.'

'Not to me. When he was fourteen and I was eight, to get away from me and read one of his goddamned books, he climbed a tree and got stuck. I said I'd rescue him if he promised never to avoid me again – he was kind of a wimp about climbing down, you know what I mean?'

'On such oaths are the secrets of the world nullified. If you reach him, for God's sake, call me back. If you can't – and it sticks in my craw to say it – follow the ambassador's order. Cooperate with Claude, but keep silent.'

Drew pressed the button marked *Finis*, touched the *Parlez*, and dialled. The operator at the Gloucester hotel in London, after repeated rings, observed that Mr Wendell Moss was not in his room. Latham left a simple message. 'Call Paris. Keep calling.' And Karin de Vries arrived, practically racing between the tables.

'Thank God you're here!' she cried, sitting down quickly, her words whispered, intense. 'It's all over the street and the embassy's in an uproar. A French government car was attacked by terrorists below us in the Gabriel!' Karin abruptly stopped, aware of the blank look in Drew's eyes. She frowned in silence, her lips forming the word *you*. He nodded; she continued. 'You've got to get out of Paris, out of *France*! Go back to Washington.'

'Take my word for it – better yet, take your own – I'm no less a target over there than I am here. Maybe an easier one.'

'But three times they've tried to kill you in the space of two days!'

'Try thirty-five hours, I've been counting.'

'You can't stay here, they *know* you.'

'They know me better in Washington. I might even have a welcoming committee I'd rather not meet. Besides, Harry's going to call me and I've got to see him, talk to him. I *have* to.'

'He's the reason you have the phone?'

'He and someone else. Someone in DC I trust – I have to trust. My boss, in fact.' A waiter arrived and De Vries ordered a Chardonnay. The aproned man nodded and was about to leave, when Latham held up the portable phone for him.

'Not yet,' interrupted Karin, reaching over and touching Drew's outstretched arm. The waiter shrugged and left. 'Forgive me, but you may have overlooked a problem or two.'

'That's entirely possible. As you've pointed out, I've been shot at three times in less than two days. Discounting strenuous field training, where they used dyed pellets, that's roughly one half of all the weapons fired at me in my entire career. What did I forget? I still remember my name. Ralph, isn't it?'

'Don't try to be funny.'

'What the hell's left? For your edification, my automatic is on my lap, and if my eyes stray now and then, it's because I'm prepared to use it.'

'There are police all over the Gabriel; no terrorist would chance a kill under the circumstances.'

'You're well versed in the language.'

'I was married to a man who was both shot at and shot more times than he could remember.'

'And I forgot. The Stasi. Sorry. What was your point?'

'Where is Harry calling you?'

'My office or the Meurice.'

'I submit that it would be foolish for you to return to either.'

'You may have half a point.'

'Grant me a full one. I'm right and you know it.'

'Granted,' said Latham reluctantly. 'There are crowds in the streets, a weapon could be inches from me and I'd never know it. And if the CIA's been penetrated, the embassy's child's play. So?'

'Your superior in Washington. How did you explain the attack in the Gabriel? What protection did he advise?'

'He didn't because I didn't tell him. It's one of those things you talk about later ... He's got a bigger problem, *much* bigger than any event I survived.'

'Are you really so charitable, Monsieur Latham?' asked Karin.

'Not at all, Madame de Vries. Things are coming so fast, and the problem we both face is so great, I didn't want his head overburdened.'

'Can you tell me about this problem?'

'I'm afraid I can't.'

'Why not?'

'Because you asked.'

Karin de Vries leaned back against the banquette and raised the wine to her lips. 'You still don't trust me, do you?' she said softly.

'We're talking about my life, lady, and a spreading lethal fungus that scares the hell out of me. It should scare the hell out of the whole civilized world.'

'You're speaking from a distance, Drew. I'm speaking from the immediate, "close up" as you Americans say.'

'It's *war*!' whispered Latham, the whisper guttural, his eyes on fire. 'Don't give me abstractions!'

122

'I gave you my *husband* in this war!' said Karin, bolting forward. 'What more do you want from me? What more for your trust?'

'Why do you want it so badly?'

'For the simplest reason of all, the one I explained to you last night. I watched a beautiful man destroyed by a hatred he could not control. It consumed him and for months, even years, I couldn't understand, and then I did. He was *right*! A putrid cloud of horror was rising over Germany, the East more than the West actually – "one evil monolith for another; they thirst for screeching leaders for they'll never change" was the way Freddie expressed it. And he *was* right!' Emotionally spent, her closed eyes forming tears, De Vries lowered her whisper. 'He was tortured and killed because he had found the truth,' she finished in a monotone.

Found the truth. Drew studied the woman across the table, remembering how elated he had been when he had found the truth about Villier's father, old Jodelle. And then how frightened he was *because* it was the truth. The parallel lines of his and Karin's response to revealed facts could not be falsified. They were beyond lying to themselves, certainly beyond concealing the anger each felt, for it was too genuine.

'Okay, okay,' Latham said, briefly covering her clenched hands with his free left one. 'I'll tell you what I can without specific names, which may come later . . . depending on the circumstances.'

'I accept that. It's part of the drill, isn't it? Beware the chemicals.'

'Yes.' Drew's eyes wandered rapidly, widely, towards the entrance and the surrounding tables, his right hand out of sight. 'The key is Villier's father, his natural father—'

'Villier the *actor*? The newspaper stories . . . the old man who killed himself in the *theatre*?'

'I'll fill you in later, but for now assume the worst. The old man *was* Villier's father, a Résistance fighter found out by the Germans and driven insane in the camps years ago.'

'There was a notice in the early afternoon papers!' said De Vries, unclenching her hands and grabbing his left. 'He's closing the play, the revival of *Coriolanus*.'

'That's stupid!' spat out Latham. 'Did they say *why*?'

'Something about that old man and how disturbed Villier was—'

'*More* than stupid,' broke in Latham. 'It's goddamned grotesque! He's as big a target as I am now!'

'I don't understand.'

'There's no way you could, and in a crazy way it's all tied in with my brother.'

'With *Harry*?'

'Intelligence files about Jodelle – that's Villier's father – were removed from the Agency's archives—'

'As in the AA-Zero computers?' asked Karin, interrupting.

'Every bit as secure, believe me. In those files was the name of a French general who wasn't simply turned by the Nazis, he became one of them, a fanatically devoted convert consumed by the cause of the master race.'

'What can he matter now? A general so many years ago – he's undoubtedly dead.'

'He may be, or he may not be, it's irrelevant. It's what he set in motion, what's going on now. An organization here in France that's brokering millions from all over the world into the neos in Germany. The same thing that brought you to Paris, Karin.'

De Vries again leaned back in the booth, removing her hand from his, her eyes wide, staring at him in bewilderment. 'What has any of this to do with Harry?' she asked.

'My brother brought out a list of names, how many I don't know, of neo sympathizers here in France, the UK, and in my own country. I gather it's explosive, men and women of influence, even political power, that no one would ever suspect of such leanings.'

'How did Harry get these names?'

'I haven't a clue, that's why I've got to see him, *talk* to him!'

'Why? You sound so disturbed.'

'Because one of those names is a man I'm working with, a man in whose hands I'd put my life without thinking twice. How do you like them apples?'

'Disregarding the grammar, I don't understand you.'

'It's idiosyncratic, Madame Linguist. I'm told it stems from an old trick apple growers used, placing their best specimens on top of a barrel they were selling, while underneath there were rotten ones.'

'It still eludes me.'

'Why not? It's probably apocryphal.'

'You sound like your brother, without his clarity.'

'Clarity is what I need from him now.'

'Regarding this man you're working with, of course.'

'Yes. I can't *believe* it, but if Harry's right and I meet with him later this afternoon, which I'm to do, it could be the dumbest decision I could make. Fatally dumb.'

'Put him off. Tell him something important has come up.'

'He'll ask what it is, and at the moment he has every right to know. Among other not-so-incidentals, an alert employee of his saved my life barely a half hour ago on the Gabriel.'

'Perhaps it was meant to appear that way.'

'Yes, that's another possible equation. I can see you've been around, lady.'

'I've been around,' conceded Karin de Vries. 'It's Moreau, Claude Moreau of the Deuxième Bureau, isn't it?'

'Why do you suggest that?'

'D and R gets the logs of entry and departure for every twenty-four hours. Moreau's name was listed twice, the night before last, when the first attack was made on you, and then the next morning, when the German ambassador arrived. The pattern was obvious. Several colleagues remarked that they could not remember when any member, much less the head, of the Deuxième had ever come to the embassy.'

'I won't confirm your suggestion, naturally.'

'You don't have to, and I agree with you completely. To

associate Moreau in any way with the neos strikes me as ludicrous.'

'The exact word I heard from Washington less than ten minutes ago. Still, Harry brought it out. You know my brother. Could he have been fooled?'

'The word *ludicrous* again comes to mind.'

'Turned?'

'*Never!*'

'So, as my extremely experienced boss, who worked with Moreau in the bad days, and who also agrees with us, said, "Where the *hell* are we?"'

'There has to be an explanation.'

'That's why I have to talk to Harry ... Whoa, hold it. You're pretty opinionated about Moreau. Do you know him?'

'I know that East German intelligence was frightened to death of him, as subsequently were the neos, for he recognized the links between the Stasi and the Nazis before anyone else, except possibly your brother. Freddie met him once, a debriefing in Munich, and came back exuberant, claiming Moreau was a genius.'

'So to recap, where are we really?'

'You have an expression in the United States that's uniquely American,' said Karin. '"Between a rock and a hard place." I think it fits, at least until you can talk to Harry, which, for your own safety, you cannot do from either the Meurice or the embassy.'

'They're the only numbers he has,' protested Drew.

'I should like to ask for your trust once more. I have friends here in Paris from the old days in Amsterdam, friends you *can* trust. If you wish, I'll go further and give their names to the colonel.'

'What for? Why?'

'They can hide you, yet you can still operate here in Paris; they're less than forty-five minutes from the city. And I myself can reach Moreau with the most plausible explanation there is – the truth, Drew.'

'Then you *do* know Moreau.'

'Not personally, no, but two Deuxième staff interviewed me before I came to the embassy. The name De Vries will accord me the courtesy of speaking to him personally, believe that.'

'I do. But what's the truth, that he himself is under suspicion?'

'Another truth. Three attempts have been made on your life, and your natural concern aside—'

'Call it by its rightful name,' Latham broke in. 'The word is fear. I was almost killed each time and my nerves are a lot frayed – like in *afraid*.'

'Very well, that's honest; he'll accept it . . . Your fear for your own life aside, you must meet with your brother who's flying over from London – day and time unknown – and you can't risk his life, either, by being in the open. You're going under for a few days and will contact him when you come out. Naturally, I have no idea where you are.'

'There's a large gap. Namely, why are *you* my conduit?'

'Yet another truth that overrides the lie and will be substantiated by Colonel Witkowski, an intelligence rock whom everyone respects. He'll confirm that my husband worked with your brother. Moreau assumes you knew that, and therefore easily understands why you came to me to act as your intermediary.'

'Two more gaps,' Drew pressed quietly, once again nervously glancing around the now-crowded brasserie. 'One, I *didn't* know – Witkowski had to tell me; and two, why didn't I use *him*?'

'Old-timers like Stanley Witkowski, smart, even brilliant veterans of the "bad days", as you called them, know the pecking order better than any of us. To get things done, really accomplished, he has to operate from his niche. He's in a position now to confirm things, not to initiate them. Can you understand that?'

'It's one of the things I've always objected to, but, yes, I can. We put some of our best minds into a pasture-hold mode because either their retirements are coming up or they never quite made enough of a name for themselves to go for the next level of retirement. It's so goddamned dumb, especially in our business, because the quiet ones invariably make it possible for the "names" to succeed. How many deep-cover legends became legends because they were guided by the quiet ones ... Sorry, again I'm rambling; it takes my mind off the possibility that someone in this very Parisian brasserie may get up and take a shot at me.'

'It's quite unlikely,' said De Vries. 'We're close to the embassy; and you've no idea how sensitive the French are to their lack of control over terrorism.'

'So are the British, but people get killed outside of Harrods.'

'Not often, and the English have isolated their primary enemy, the IRA, may they rot in hell. The French are targets for so many others. Whole arrondissements are populated with warring factions from abroad. In the Scandinavian countries, too, the protests grow more violent, to say nothing of the Netherlands – the most peaceful of people, where the Right and the Left clash incessantly.'

'Add Italy, the Mafia corruption of Rome tearing people apart, men fighting in Parliament, bombs going off. And take Spain, where the Catalonians and the Basques bear more than arms, they bear generations of resentment. And there's the Middle East, where Palestinians kill Jews and Jews kill Palestinians, each blaming the other, while in Bosnia-Herzegovina full-fledged massacres take place between people who used to live together, and nobody appears to want to do anything. It's everywhere. Discontent, suspicion, name-calling ... violence. It's as though some terrible grand design is being shaped.'

'What are you saying?' asked De Vries, staring at him.

'They're all meat for the new Nazi grinders, can't you *see* that?'

'I hadn't considered things on such a large scale. It's rather melodramatically far-reaching, isn't it?'

'Think about it. If Harry's list is right, even half right, how long have the discontents everywhere been approached and told that their grievances can be addressed, the grievers crushed once the great new order is in place?'

'That's not the "new order" you Americans have talked about, Drew. Yours is a far more benevolent agenda.'

'Suppose again. Suppose it's all a code for something else, a "new order" going back fifty years. The New Order of the Reich to last a thousand years.'

'That's preposterous!'

'Yes, it is,' agreed Latham, leaning back in the booth and breathing hard. 'I took it to its zenith, because you're right, it couldn't happen. But a large *part* of it could happen, right here in Europe, the Balkans, and the Middle East. Then what's the next step? After the multiple uprisings of people against people, religion against religion, new nations breaking away from the old?'

'I'm trying to follow you, and I'm not stupid. As Harry might say, where is the clarity?'

'Nuclear weapons! Bought and sold on the international markets, and perhaps, with their millions, too many in the hands of the Brotherhood, the new religion, the cure, and maybe, eventually, the refuge for all the discontents the world over, drawn to them, convinced of their invincibility. It happened in the thirties, and not a hell of a lot has changed in terms of those circumstances.'

'You're way beyond me,' said Karin, drinking her wine. 'I fight a spreading disease, as you called it, that killed Freddie. You see an imminent apocalypse I cannot accept. We've passed that stage in civilization.'

'I hope we have, and I hope I'm wrong, and I wish to God I could stop thinking the way I do.'

'You have an extraordinary imagination, very much like Harry's, except his was – is – *sang-froid*. Nothing *is* until analysed without emotion.'

'It's funny you say that; it's the difference between us. My brother was always so cold, so without feeling, I thought, until a young cousin of ours, a girl of sixteen, died of some kind of cancer. We were kids, and I found him bawling his eyes out behind the garage. When I tried to help him as best I could, he yelled at me and said, "Don't you ever tell anyone I cried or I'll put a double hex on you!" Kid stuff, of course.'

'Did you?'

'Of course not, he was my brother.'

'There's something you're not telling me.'

'Good Christ, is this a confessional?'

'Not at all. I simply want to know you better. That's no crime.'

'Okay. I worshipped the guy. He was so smart, so kind to me, running me through exam questions and helping me with my term papers, then in college, even selecting my courses, always telling me I was better than I thought I was, if I would only concentrate. Our dad was always away on one of his digs, so who came up to see me at college, who yelled loudest at the hockey games – Harry, that's who.'

'You love him, don't you?'

'I'd be nothing without him. That's why I damn near threatened him with a hammerlock if he didn't get me into this business. He didn't like it, but there was a bastard organization called Consular Operations being formed that apparently wanted jocks who could think. I fit the description and made it.'

'The colonel said you were a terrific hockey player in Canada. He said you should have gone to New York.'

'It was an interlude, a farm team, and I was pretty well paid, but Harry flew to Manitoba and said I had to grow up. So I did; the rest is what I am. The questions over with?'

'Why are you so hostile?'

'I'm not really. I'm good at what I do, lady, but as you've pointed out ad nauseam, I'm not Harry.'

'You have your own attributes.'

'Oh, hell, yes. Basic martial arts, but no expert, believe

me. All those courses in enemy interrogation and manipulation, psychological and chemical; survival techniques and how to determine which flora and fauna are edible – all that's ingrained.'

'Then what bothers you so?'

'I wish I could tell you, but I don't even know myself. I think it's the absence of authority. There's a rigid chain of command and I can't go around it – not even sure I want to. It's what I said before, the "quiet ones" know more than I do . . . and now I can't trust *them*.'

'Give me your phone, please.'

'It's set for long distance.'

'By pressing F zero one eight you can revert it to Paris and its environs.' De Vries touched the numbers she knew by rote, waited several moments, and spoke. 'I'm arrondissement six, please run a check.' She covered the mouthpiece and looked at Drew. 'A simple intercept run, nothing out of the ordinary.' Suddenly Karin's gaze shot downward to the floor, her face frozen, her chin jammed into her throat. She stood up and screamed. 'Get out! Everyone get *out* of here!' She grabbed Latham's arm, yanking him out of the booth, and kept yelling. '*Everyone!*' she roared in French. 'Leave your tables and go outside! *Les terroristes!*' The mass exodus was chaotic; several windows were smashed as diners fled, clashing with waiters and busboys, racing to find whatever egresses they could as bewildered, furious management personnel tried to stem the stampede, then reluctantly followed. Out on the avenue Gabriel all watched in horror as the rear section of the brasserie was blown apart, the impact of the explosion shattering what was left of the windows, sending fragments of glass flying into the street, embedding themselves into the flesh of faces and through the fabric of clothing into arms, chests, and legs. Pandemonium filled the street as Latham fell over the body of Karin de Vries.

'What did you learn?' shouted Drew, shoving the gun into his belt. 'How did you *know*?'

'There's no *time*! Get up. Follow me!'

CHAPTER EIGHT

They raced down the Gabriel until they reached a deep, shadowed storefront, a *joaillier* whose expensive gems shone more brightly in the relative darkness. Karin yanked him into it; breathless, they both gulped in air before Latham spoke.

'Goddammit, lady, what *happened*? You said that whoever you called was running an intercept check, then you started yelling and all hell broke loose! I want an answer.'

'The check was never made,' replied De Vries, still gasping for breath. 'Instead, someone else came on the phone and yelled, "Three men in dark clothes, they're running up and down the street from place to place. They want your friend *out*!" Before I could ask any questions, I saw two baguettes rolling on the floor towards our booth.'

'Baguettes? Loaves of bread?'

'Shiny small loaves, Drew. Artificial bread. Plastic explosives ten times more powerful than grenades.'

'Oh, my *God* . . .'

'There's a taxi stand at the next corner. Quickly!' Still breathless, they settled into the backseat of a cab as Karin gave the driver an address in the Marais district. 'In an hour I'll return to the embassy—'

'Are you *crazy*?' Latham broke in, snapping his head towards her. 'You've been seen with me, you said so yourself. They'll kill you!'

'Not if I return within a reasonable amount of time – and behave as if I've had a terrible shock – reasonably hysterical, although not out of control.'

'Words,' said Drew sharply, disparagingly.

'No, basic common sense in a tenuous situation that demands my getting back to my normal routine as soon as I can.'

'I repeat, you're a lunatic. Not only were you with me, you were the one who shouted the warning! *You* started the stampede.'

'So would anyone else who'd come in off the Gabriel, seeing all those policemen and the patrol cars, and hearing how terrorists had shot up an automobile. Good Lord, Drew, two loaves of bread – even if they were real – rolling into a booth as a man in a dark sweater and black visored cap raced out, colliding with a waiter, really!'

'You didn't tell me about any man racing outside—'

'In a heavy sweater on a warm spring day, his face hidden and nearly upsetting a waiter carrying a tray!'

'Or about any waiter.'

'Incidentally, no waiter in a Paris brasserie would treat loaves of bread as if they were bocci balls.'

'Okay, okay, you can explain away that part, but not the fact that you were with me.'

'I'll take care of it in a way any Frenchman, terrorist or not, will understand. I'll make several phone calls establishing the fact.'

'What phone calls? About what and to whom?'

'To people at the embassy, D and R first, of course, then the entry desk, and a few others who are known gossips, including Courtland's chief aide and the first attaché's secretary. I'll tell them I was with you at the restaurant that was bombed, that we got out, you disappeared, and I'm frantic.'

'You're simply pointing up the fact that we were together!'

'For quite a different reason that has nothing to do with your work, which I know nothing about because I haven't known *you* that long.'

'*What* reason?'

'We met the other day, were attracted to each other, and obviously are heading towards an affair.'

'That's the nicest thing you've said.'

'Don't take it literally, Monsieur Latham, it's emphatically a cover. The point is that since we can assume the embassy's been penetrated, the word will circulate rapidly.'

'Do you think Paris's branch of the neos will buy it?'

'They have no choice on two levels. If it's a lie, they'll watch me, assuming you'll reach me and they can track you down; if it's the truth, well, I'm really not worth their time. In either case, I'm in a position to help you where I am.'

'For Freddie's sake, I understand,' said Drew, smiling gently as the driver entered the Marais, 'but I still think you're taking a hell of a risk, lady.'

'May I say something about your language, please?'

'Be my guest.'

'Your erratic but inveterate use of the word *lady* has a distinctly condescending connotation.'

'It's not meant that way.'

'Probably not. Even so, it's an unconscious cultural contradiction.'

'I beg your pardon?'

'By employing the word *lady*, you're actually using it in the pejorative sense, as in *girl*, or, worse, *broad*.'

'I apologize.' Latham smiled, again gently. 'I've used that term more times than I can remember with my mother, and I assure you it was never – what did you call it? – pejorative.'

'A mother can accept it as an *en famille* endearment. I'm not your mother.'

'Hell, no. She's a lot prettier and doesn't caterwaul so much.'

'Caterwaul . . . ?' De Vries studied the American's face, seeing the humour in his eyes. She laughed and touched his arm. 'You have the point you conceded to me at the table back in the brasserie. Sometimes I take things too seriously.'

'No sweat. I can see why you and Harry got along. You

analyse, then reevaluate, then analyse again. It all gets to be a bunch of circles, doesn't it?'

'No, it doesn't, because somewhere among those circles there's a tangent that breaks off and leads to something else. Invariably the truth.'

'Would you believe I understand that?'

'Of course you do. Your brother was right years ago, you're much better than you think you are . . . But then, you don't need me to say these things.'

'No, I don't. Right now I want to know where we're going, where *I'm* going.'

'To what you Americans call a sterile house, an intermediate place where your credentials are confirmed before you're sent on to sanctuary.'

'The people you were calling at the restaurant, the brasserie?'

'Yes, but in your case you'll be sent immediately. I'll be your confirmation.'

'Who are thcsc people?'

'It's enough to say that they're on our side, yours and mine.'

'It's not enough for me, lady – sorry, Mrs de Vries.'

'Then you can stop the taxi, get out, be on your own, and be hunted like an animal until they have you in their gun sights.'

'Not necessarily. I may not be Harry, but I've got certain skills that have served me through a scrape or two. Shall I tell the driver to pull over, or will you tell me exactly where we're going and who we're going to see?'

'You need protection right now and you admit you don't know whom you can trust—'

'And you're saying I should trust people I don't *know*?' interrupted Latham. 'You're certifiable.' He leaned forward, speaking to the driver. 'Monsieur, *s'il vous plaît, arrêtez le taxi—*'

'*Non!*' Karin intruded firmly. 'It's not necessary,' she continued in French to the driver, who shrugged and took his foot off the brake. 'All right,' she went on, looking at Drew, 'what do you want to do, where do you want to go? Or would you rather I get out so I have no idea? You can always reach me at the embassy – I'd suggest a pay phone, but I don't have to tell you that. You can't have much money on you, and you shouldn't go to your bank any more than to the office, your flat, or the Meurice, they'll all be covered. I'll give you what I have and we can make further arrangements later . . . For God's sake, *decide*. I have to start my own strategy soon – in minutes for it to be credible!'

'You mean it, don't you? You'd give me money, get out, and let me fade, not knowing where I am.'

'Naturally I mean it. It's not preferable, and I think you're a damn fool, but you're stubborn and there's nothing I can do about that. It's far more important that you stay alive, see Harry, and get on with the business at hand. Every day the new Nazi leadership survives, the deeper they entrench themselves.'

'Then you don't insist on taking me to your old friends from Amsterdam.' Latham did not ask a question.

'How can I? You won't listen to me, so of course not.'

'Then take me to them. You're right, I really don't know who to trust.'

'You're *impossible*, you realize that, I presume!'

'No, I'm not, I'm just very cautious. Did I mention that I've been shot at three times in less than thirty-six hours, and ten minutes ago someone tried to bomb me to the moon? Oh, yes, lady, I'm *very* cautious.'

'You've made the right decision, believe me.'

'I have to. Now, who are these people?'

'Germans, mostly. Men and women who loathe the neos more than any of us do – they see their country being soiled by the so-called inheritors of the Third Reich.'

'They're here in Paris . . . ?'

'And in the UK, the Netherlands, Scandinavia, the Balkans – wherever they believe the Brüderschaft is operating. Each cell is small in number, fifteen to twenty people, but they operate with renowned German efficiency, secretly funded by a group of German industrial leaders and financiers who not only despise the neos but fear what they could do to the nation's image and thus its economy.'

'They sound like the flip side of the Brotherhood.'

'What do you think is tearing the country apart? That's exactly what they are, they *have* to be. Bonn is political; business is practical. The government must appeal for votes from a diverse electorate; the financial establishment must, above all, guard against isolation from world markets because of the spectre of a Nazi revival.'

'These people, your friends – these "cells" – do they have a name, a symbol, something like that?'

'Yes. They call themselves the Antinayous.'

'What kind of name is that?'

'I really don't know, but your brother laughed when Freddie told him. He said it had something to do with ancient Rome and a historian called Dio Cassius, I believe. Harry said it fit the circumstances.'

'Harry's a piece of work,' mumbled Drew. 'Remind me to replace my encyclopaedia . . . Okay, let's meet your friends.'

'They're only two streets away.'

Wesley Sorenson had made up his mind. He had not spent an adult lifetime in the service of his country to be frozen out of essential information by an intelligence bureaucrat who drew an erroneous, insulting conclusion. In short, Wes Sorenson was an angry man and he saw no reason to conceal that anger. He had not sought the directorship of Consular Operations, he had been summoned by a thinking President who saw the need to coordinate the intelligence services so that one branch or another did not frustrate post-Cold War State Department objectives. He had answered the call out of a pleasant retirement, in which, thanks to an affluent family, there was no need of a pension. Still, he had earned it many times over, as, indeed, he had earned the respect and trust of the entire intelligence community. He would make his feelings known at the conference he was about to attend.

He was ushered into the enormous office, where Secretary of State Adam Bollinger sat behind his desk. In front of the Secretary, in one of two captain's chairs, his body turned in greeting, was a large, heavyset black man in his early sixties. His name was Knox Talbot, the director of Central Intelligence, a former ranking intelligence officer in the Vietnam action, and a giant intellect who had made several fortunes in the back-stabbing worlds of commodities and arbitrage. Sorenson liked Talbot, and was constantly bemused by the way he masked his brilliance and self-deprecating humour and a show of wide-eyed innocence. Secretary Bollinger, on the other hand, was a problem for the Cons-Op director. Sorenson acknowledged the Secretary of State's political acumen, even his international stature, but there was a hollowness in the man that disturbed him. It was as if everything he said and did was calculated, contrived, devoid of passionate commitment – a cold man with a bright smile that held surface charm but little warmth.

'Good morning, Wes,' said Bollinger, his smile perfunctory, for this was a meeting of dire consequence, no time for amenities, and he wanted his subordinates to know it.

'Hello there, ye spook of spooks,' added Knox Talbot, smiling. 'It seems we neophytes need a touch of input here.'

'Nothing on our agenda is remotely amusing, Knox,' noted the Secretary, his neutral eyes glancing up from the papers on his desk, directed at Talbot.

'Neither will it help to be uptight, Adam,' rejoined the director of the Central Intelligence Agency. 'Our problems may be immense, but a number might be dismissed with a chuckle.'

'I find that statement close to irresponsible.'

'Find it however you like, but I submit that a lot of what we have from Operation Sting is, to be blunt, *really* irresponsible.'

'Join us, Wesley,' said Bollinger as Sorenson crossed to the chair on Talbot's right and sat down. 'I'll not deny,' continued the Secretary of State, 'that Field Officer Latham's list is appalling, but we must consider the source. I ask you, Knox, is there a more experienced undercover agent in the CIA than Harry Latham?'

'To my knowledge, there isn't,' replied the DCI, 'but that doesn't preclude his being fed disinformation.'

'That assumes his cover was blown to the neos' leadership.'

'I have no knowledge of that,' said Talbot.

'It was,' said Sorenson flatly.

'What?'

'*What?*'

'I spoke with Harry's brother,' said Sorenson. 'He's one of my men, and he learned it through a woman in Paris, the widow of Latham's runner in East Berlin. The neos knew all about Sting. Name, objective, even the presumed length of his mission.'

'That's impossible!' cried Knox Talbot, his sizeable frame lurching forward in the chair, his large head turned towards Sorenson, his black eyes glaring. 'That information is so deep, it couldn't be unearthed.'

'Try your AA-Zero computers.'

'*Inviolate!*'

'Not so, Knox. You've got somebody in the secret chicken coop who's actually a fox.'

'I don't *believe* you.'

'I just gave you chapter and verse, what more do you need?'

'Who the hell could it be?'

'How many people operate the AA-Zeros?'

'Five, with three alternates, each one researched to the day he or she was born. Each cleared total white, which, despite my obvious objection to the phrase, I completely accept. For Christ's sake, they're all among our top brass in high technology!'

'One of them is tarnished, Knox. One of them slipped through your impenetrable nets.'

'I'll put them all under total surveillance.'

'You'll do more than that, Mr Director,' said Adam Bollinger. 'You'll put everyone on Harry Latham's list under surveillance. My *God*, we could have a global conspiracy on our hands.'

'Please, Mr Secretary, we're nowhere near that. Not yet. But I have to ask *you*, Knox, who deleted Claude Moreau's name from the list that was sent to me?'

His astonishment apparent, Talbot winced, then rapidly composed himself. 'I'm sorry, Wes,' he said quietly, 'it came from a reliable source, a senior case officer who worked with you both in Istanbul. He said you two were close, that Moreau saved your life in the Dardanelles while on assignment in Marmara. Our man wasn't sure you could be objective, it's as simple as that. How did you find out?'

'Somebody cleared a list for Ambassador Courtland—'

'We had to,' interrupted Talbot. 'The Germans leaked it and Courtland was put on a diplomatic spit . . . *Moreau's* name was on it?'

'So much for the Agency's oversight.'

'An error, human error, what more can I say? There are two goddamned many machines that spew out data too fast . . . The justification in your case, however, was understandable. A man saves your life, you're damned quick to come to his defence. Perhaps unwittingly, just by sympathetically probing, you could even tip him off that he's under a microscope.'

'Not if you're a professional, Knox,' said the head of Consular Operations curtly, 'and I believe I've attained that status.'

'Christ, you certainly have,' agreed Talbot, nodding his head. 'You'd be sitting in my chair if you'd been willing to accept it.'

'I never wanted it.'

'Again, I apologize. But while we're on the subject, what *do* you think about Moreau's inclusion?'

'I think it's crazy.'

'So are about twenty or twenty-five others in this country alone, and when you consider their staffs and associates, well over a couple of hundred in high places. There's another seventy or so in the UK and France and they could be multiplied tenfold. Among them are men and women we regard as true patriots, and regardless of political affiliations we may not like, people we honour. Is Harry Latham, one of the best and the brightest, a cuckoo bird, a deep cover who lost his marbles?'

'That's hard to imagine—'

'Which is why every man and woman on his list will be backgrounded from the moment they could walk and talk,' announced the Secretary of State emphatically, his thin lips now a straight line. 'Turn over every rock, bring me dossiers that make the Federal Bureau's check look like a hungry salesman's credit search.'

'*Adam*,' protested Knox Talbot, 'it's the Bureau's *territory*, not ours. That's clearly spelled out in the charter.'

'To hell with the charter. If there are Nazis roaming the corridors of government, industry, and the so-called arts, we have to find them, *expose* them!'

'With what authority?' asked Sorenson, studying the face of the Secretary of State.

'With *my* authority, if you like. I'll be responsible.'

'Congress might object,' pressed the director of Cons-Op.

'Screw the Congress, just keep it quiet. Good *God*, you can at least do that, can't you? You're both part of the administration, aren't you? It's called the Executive Branch, gentlemen, and if the Executive, the presidency itself, can root out the Nazi influence in this country, the nation will forever be thankful. Now, go to work, coordinate, and bring me results. Our conference is over. I have an appointment with one of those Sunday morning talk-show producers. I'm going to announce the President's new policy on the Caribbean.'

Outside in the State Department corridor, Knox Talbot turned to Wesley Sorenson. 'Beyond finding out who's compromising our AA-Zero computers, I have no stomach for any of this.'

'I'll resign first,' said the Cons-Op head.

'That's not the way, Wes,' countered the DCI. 'If you go and I go, he'll find a couple of others he can really control. I say we both stay and "coordinate" quietly with the Bureau.'

'Bollinger ruled that out.'

'No, he specifically objected to and overrode the charter of '47 that prohibits you and me from operating domestically. We filtered his words and came to the conclusion that he didn't actually want us to act unconstitutionally. He'll probably thank us later. Hell, the acolytes around Reagan did this all the time.'

'Is Bollinger worth it, Knox?'

'No, he's not, but our organizations are. I've worked with the Bureau's chief. He's not obsessed with his turf – he's no Hoover. He's a decent guy, a former judge who was considered fair, and he has plenty of street smarts. I'll convince him it's all got to be silent and deep but conclusive. And, let's face it, Harry Latham can't be ignored.'

'I still think Moreau's a mistake, a terrible error.'

'There may be others too, but there could also be *other* others who aren't. I hate to say it, but Bollinger's right about that. I'll make contact with the Bureau, you keep Harry Latham alive.'

'I see another problem, Knox,' said Sorenson, frowning. 'Remember the garbage of the fifties, the McCarthy bullshit?'

'*Please*,' answered the black DCI. 'I was a freshman in college and my father was a civil rights lawyer. They called him a Communist, and we had to move from Wilmington to Chicago so my two sisters and I could walk to school. Hell, yes, I remember.'

'Make sure the FBI understands the conceivable similarity. We don't want reputations, even careers, ruined by irresponsible charges – or worse, rumours that won't die. We don't want federal gunslingers; we have to have discreet professionals.'

'I lived through the gunslingers, Wes. It's a priority that they be cut off at the pass. Strictly professional, strictly quiet, that's the mantra.'

'I wish us all good luck,' said the director of Consular Operations, 'but half of my brain, if I have one, tells me we're in dangerous waters.'

The Antinayous' sterile house in Paris's Marais district was staffed by two women and a man ensconced in a comfortable flat above a fashionable dress shop on the rue Delacort. The introductions were quick, Karin de Vries doing most of the talking, making the case for Drew Latham not only immediate but emphatic. The grey-haired woman in charge conferred briefly with her colleagues.

'We'll send him to the Maison Rouge in Carrefour. You'll have everything you need, monsieur. Karin and her departed husband were always with us. Godspeed, Mr Latham. The Brüderschaft must be destroyed.'

The old stone edifice referred to as the Maison Rouge was initially a small economy-class hotel converted into a small economy-class office building. According to the shabby tenant directory, it housed such businesses as an employment agency for manual labour, a plumbing firm, a printer, a private detective agency specializing in 'divorce procedures', as well as a smattering of bookkeepers, typists, janitorial services, and offices for rent, of which there were none. In reality, only the employment agency and the printer were legitimate; the rest were not in the Paris telephone book, ostensibly either out of business or closed for specific dates (altered successively on door signs). In their places were single and double rooms and a number of mini-suites, all complete with unlisted telephones, fax machines, type-writers, television sets, and desktop computers. The building was unattached, and two narrow alleyways led to the rear, where there was a concealed sliding door disguised as a tall, rectangular panoply of basement windowpanes. It was never to be used during daylight hours.

Each guest of the Antinayous was given a concise briefing as to what was expected of him or her, including clothing (wardrobe provided, if necessary), behaviour (not *haut Parisien*), communication between residents (absolutely verboten unless cleared by the 'management'), and the precise scheduling of entries and departures (again cleared by management). Failure to adhere to the regulations would result in immediate expulsion, no appeal possible. The rules were admittedly harsh, but they were for everyone's benefit.

Latham was assigned to a mini-suite on the third floor; he was as impressed by the technical appointments as he was by what Karin had described as 'German efficiency'. After having been thoroughly tutored in the workings of the equipment by a member of the management, he went into the bedroom and lay down, glanced at his watch, and estimated that he could call Karin de Vries at the embassy in a little over an hour. He wished it were sooner; the waiting to find out whether or not her strategy was successful was nerve-racking, although the lie she had concocted was exotic, even humorous considering the circumstances. Her tactic was simple: she had been with him at the bombed-out brasserie; he had disappeared and she was frantic. Why? Because she found him delightful and they were 'heading towards an affair'. It was an appealing prospect and equally out of the question – on second thought, perhaps not terribly appealing, thought Drew. She was a strange woman, justifiably filled with anger and painful memories, her attractiveness diminished by both. She was a child of European angst, the national and racial upheavals that were poisoning the entire continent, and Latham was not prepared to join her crowd. He was uncomfortable when he observed her sharp yet oddly soft, lovely features turn glacial, her wide, stunning eyes become two orbs of ice, when her past consumed her. No, he had enough problems of his own.

Then why was he thinking so about her? She had saved his life, of course . . . but then, she had saved her own as well. *His* life . . . what was the phrase she had used? 'Perhaps it was meant to appear that way.' *No*! He was sick of the circles within circles, where *none* broke off in tangents that led to the irrefutable truth. Where *was* the truth? Harry's list? Karin's concern? Moreau? Sorenson? . . . He had nearly been killed four times and that was enough! He had to rest, then think, but rest first. Rest was a weapon, often more potent than firepower, an old trainer had once told him. So with the exhaustion born of fear and anxiety, Drew closed his eyes. Sleep, fitful as it was, came quickly.

The harsh bell of the Paris phone awakened him; bolting upright, he grabbed it. 'Yes?'

'It is I,' said Karin. 'I'm speaking on the colonel's telephone.'

'It's swept,' interrupted Latham, rubbing the sleep from his eyes with his left hand. 'Is Witkowski there?'

'I thought you might ask that. Here he is.'

'Hello, Drew.'

'The attempts on my life are multiplying, Stosh.'

'So it would appear,' agreed the G-2 veteran. 'You stay deep until things are clearer.'

'How clear do they have to be? They want me *out*, Stanley!'

'Then we have to convince them that temporarily it would not be to their advantage. You have to buy time.'

'How the hell do we do that?'

'I'd have to know more than I do to give you an answer, but basically by making them believe you're more valuable alive than dead.'

'What do you need to know?'

'Everything. Sorenson's your boss, your ultimate control.

I know Wesley, not well, but we're acquainted, so reach him, clear me, and bring me up to speed.'

'I don't have to reach him. It's my life and I'm making an on-scene decision. Take notes, then burn them, Colonel.' Latham started from the beginning, with Harry's disappearance in the Hausruck Alps, his capture and escape from the Brotherhood, then the missing files in Washington that dealt with an unknown French general, followed by the Jodelle connection, his suicide at the theatre, and his son, Jean-Pierre Villier. At this juncture Stanley Witkowski sharply interrupted.

'The *actor*?'

'That's the one. He was enough of a jackass to go out on his own playing a street bum, and come up with information that could be valuable.'

'Then the old man really *was* his father?'

'Confirmed and reconfirmed. He was a member of the Résistance, captured by the Germans, and sent to the camps, where he was driven insane – damn near completely.'

'"Damn near"? What's that mean? Either you are or you're not.'

'A small part of him wasn't. He knew who he was . . . what he was . . . and for nearly fifty years he never tried to make contact with his son.'

'Didn't anyone try to make contact with *him*?'

'Like thousands of others who never returned, he was presumed dead.'

'But he wasn't,' said Witkowski thoughtfully, 'just mentally crippled and no doubt physically a wreck.'

'Barely recognizable, I'm told. Still, he couldn't stop going after a turncoat general who had ordered his family executed and whose name disappeared with the files. Villier confirmed that; he learned it was someone in the Loire Valley, in and around which some forty or fifty retired generals live, usually in modest country houses or larger places owned by others. That was his information, that and a licence plate number of a capo who rousted him for asking questions.'

'About the general?'

'One of four or even five dozen down there. A soldier with the rank of general fifty years ago would have to be somewhere in his middle to late nineties if he's still alive.'

'Actuarially, that's pretty remote,' agreed the colonel. 'Old soldiers, especially those who've weathered combat, rarely last beyond their early eighties – something to do with past traumas catching up with them. The Pentagon did a study a few years ago relative to secure consultancies.'

'That's pretty ghoulish.'

'And necessary where confidential information is imparted and mental stability's on a collision course with declining health. Those old gaffers usually stay by themselves, fading quietly away, as the Big Mac put it. If they don't want to be found, you won't find them.'

'Now you're overdoing it, Stosh.'

'I'm *thinking*, goddammit . . . Jodelle found out something, then killed himself in front of the son he had never acknowledged while screaming that he *was* his son. Why?'

'I figure it's because whatever he learned was too big for him to fight. Just before he shoved the barrel in his mouth and blew his head off, he also screamed that he had failed – both his son and his wife. His defeat was total.'

'I read in the papers that Villier closed *Coriolanus*, no specific reason except how affected he was by the old man's suicide. The article wasn't clear at all; actually it sounded as though he knew things he didn't care to talk about. Naturally, like me, everyone's wondering if Jodelle was telling the truth. Nobody wants to believe it, because Villier's mother was a great star and his father one of the most respected members of the Comédie Française, and they're both still alive. Of course, they can't be reached by the press; they're supposedly on a private island in the Mediterranean. The gossip columns are the Super Bowls of Paris.'

'All of which makes Villier as big a target as I am, a fact I made clear to our employee, Mrs de Vries.'

'It's crazy, Villier should have been controlled, stopped.'

'I've been thinking about that, Stanley. I called Villier a jackass, and to do what he did, he was, but he's not a blind jackass. I have no doubt he'd risk his own life, confident of his actor's disguises and techniques. However, I don't believe for a minute he'd risk the lives of his wife or parents by making himself so public a mark for the neos – to repeat, a target.'

'Are you saying he was programmed?'

'I don't want to even think it because the Deuxième's Moreau was the last knowledgeable official to confront Villier before it was announced that the play was closing.'

'I don't understand,' said Witkowski hesitantly. 'Claude Moreau's the best there is. I really don't follow you, Drew.'

'Fasten your seat belt, Colonel. Harry brought out a list of names.' Latham proceeded to describe the profoundly disturbing information his brother had learned while being held captive by the regenerated Nazis. How alarming and bewildering were the identities of so many powerful people, who were apparently not only sympathetic to the aims of the neo master race, but who were actively working for them.

'It wouldn't be the first time since the pharaohs' legions that nations have been infested by lice in the upper ranks,' Witkowski broke in. 'If Harry Latham brought it out, you can take it to the bank. He's on that rare plateau with Claude Moreau: brains, instinct, talent, and tenacity all coming together. There's nobody in this business better than those two.'

'Moreau's on Harry's list, Stanley,' said Drew quietly. The silence from the swept embassy phone was as electric as it had been with Sorenson when Latham delivered the same information. 'I trust you're still there, Colonel.'

'I wish I weren't,' mumbled Witkowski. 'I can't think of anything to say.'

'How about *bullshit*?'

'That's my first reaction, but there's a secondary one and it's just as strong. His name is Harry Latham.'

'I know that – for all the reasons you mentioned and several dozen you didn't. But even my brother can make a mistake, or accept disinformation until he analyses it. That's why I have to talk to him.'

'Mrs de Vries explained that he's due here in Paris within a day or two, that you left word for him to keep calling you, which now he obviously won't be able to do.'

'I can't even give him a number, it's not on the phone here. But you have it.'

'That number is buried in the underground telephone lines, at least the address is, and it's undoubtedly a false one.'

'So what do we do?'

'It's a leap of faith neither Sorenson nor I would normally approve of, but tell Mrs de Vries where Harry is in London. We'll take it from there and arrange your getting together. Here she is.'

'Drew?' said Karin, now on the phone. 'Is everything at the Maison Rouge all right?'

'Only outstanding, lady – excuse me, how about "my benevolent female friend"?'

'Stop trying to be clever, it doesn't help. The Antinayous can be quite hostile, even with their proven allies.'

'Oh, they're fine, except that everything they say seems to end with an exclamation mark.'

'It's the language, dismiss it. You heard the colonel, how can I reach Harry?'

'He's at the Gloucester, under the name of Wendell Moss.'

'I'll make the arrangements. Stay where you are and try to remain calm.'

'That's not terribly easy. I'm *in* this mess but I'm also outside of it. I can't call the shots, and that bothers me.'

'You're not in a position to "call the shots", my dear. The colonel and I are, and we will act in your best interests, in all our best interests, believe me.'

'Again, I have to, and thanks for the "my dear". A touch of warmth is appreciated right now. It's cold out here.'

'I give it freely. As you do with the word *lady* that you applied to your mother, who is prettier and less cotter-whatever than I am. We are now *en famille*, for few families could be closer than we are, whether we like it or not.'

'You know, I kind of wish you were here.'

'You shouldn't. I'd be a dreadful disappointment, Officer Latham.'

Far below in the embassy's pristine white cellars, a white-coated member of Team C, the afternoon shift, snapped off the override switch that taped everything spoken over every telephone in the embassy; the scramblers did not affect the in-house calls, a fact even the ambassador was not aware of – orders from Washington. The interceptor looked at the clock on the wall; it was seven minutes to four o'clock, seven minutes to the end of his shift, seven minutes to retrieve the tape and surreptitiously replace it with a blank. He could do it. He had to do it. *Sieg Heil!*

CHAPTER NINE

Patient No. 28.
Harry J. Latham, American. CIA Case Officer. Undercover.
Code Name: Sting.
Operation Terminated: May 14, 5:30 P.M. 'Escape.'
Current Status: Day 6, post procedure.
Estimated time span remaining: 3 days minimum,
6 days maximum.

Dr Gerhardt Kroeger studied the computer screen in his new offices on the outskirts of Mettmach. A complete clinic was being built deep in the forests of Vaclabruck; until it was finished he could continue his research but, unfortunately, without human experimentation. Still, there was enough to do in terms of unexplored microsurgery enhanced by the newest laser techniques to occupy him, but currently the progress of Patient No. 28, one Harry Latham, was as vital as anything else. The initial report from London was exhilarating. The subject had responded to interrogation under computerized electronic impulses. Excellent!

Harry Latham replaced the phone in his room at London's Gloucester hotel. A rush of warmth spread over him, sweet memories of things past, hours of comfort and delight in a world that had gone mad. He was a confirmed bachelor, realizing that it was too late to share or impose his likes and dislikes with, or on, another person. But if ever there was a woman who could negate this conclusion, it was Frederik de Vries's wife, Karin. Freddie de V had been the finest runner

151

under his control in the Cold War years, but Harry had spotted his flaw, the flaw that made him extraordinary. Simply put, it was hatred – unmitigated, passionate hatred. Latham had tried constantly to impose a cold neutrality on De Vries's emotions, warning over and over again that his inner self would explode one day and betray him. It was a useless plea, for Freddie was a demonic romantic, riding the blinding white crest of the wave, not understanding the power beneath, preferring the shining armour of a surfing Siegfried to the force of an unseen Neptune below.

His wife, Karin, understood. How often would she and Harry talk in Amsterdam, alone, while Freddie went out playing the outrageous role of a diamond merchant, gulling players of the darkest arts of espionage until they opened up to him ... temporarily. That very image ultimately destroyed him, for his hatred led him to one more kill he shouldn't have made.

It was the end of the minor legend that was Freddie de V. Harry had tried to comfort Karin, but she was beyond consolation. She knew too well what had led to his death, and she swore she would operate differently.

'*Forget* it!' Harry had yelled. 'You're not going to make any difference, can't you understand that?'

'No, I can't,' she had replied. 'To do nothing is to admit that Freddie meant nothing. Can't *you* understand that, my dear Harry?'

He had no answer then. His only impulse was to take this woman, this intellectual companion he felt so deeply for, into his arms and love her. But it was not the time, nor, perhaps, would it ever be. She had lived with her dead Freddie, loved her dead Freddie. Harry Latham had been that man's superior, but he was not his equal.

And now, nearly five years later, she had come back into his life from Paris. Even more remarkably, as the guardian of his brother, Drew, who was marked for execution! Jesus *Christ* ... no, he had to impose his legendary control on himself. Maybe it was the ache in his head that seemed to grow stronger, that allowed his frustration to surface when normally it wouldn't. Regardless, he would fly to Paris in the morning on a diplomatic jet to a private field at De Gaulle Airport, and be met by Karin de Vries in an unmarked embassy vehicle.

He wondered what he would say to her. Would he be foolish enough, when he saw her, to say things he shouldn't say? It didn't much matter . . . The ache in his head was pulsating. He walked into the bathroom, turned on the tap, and took two more aspirin. Glancing at himself in the mirror, he abruptly looked a second time. A pale rash was developing above his left temple, partially obscured by his hairline. His nervous system was making its mark literally. It would go away with a mild antibiotic or a few days of diminished tension; perhaps the sight of Karin de Vries would hasten its disappearance.

There was a knock on the suite's door, probably a maid or a steward looking after his needs; it was early evening, and such were the courtesies of the better London hotels. Early evening, he mused, walking out into the sitting room. Where had the day gone? Gone? *Wasted* was the better word, for he had spent ten hours being interrogated by his tribunal. Ad nauseam, they had questioned him about the information he had brought out of the Brüderschaft valley rather than accepting it and setting the machinery in motion. To make matters even more aggravating, the three-man panel was augmented by several senior intelligence officers from the UK, the US, and France, all querulous, argumentative, and arrogant. Wasn't it conceivable that he had been fed disinformation, erroneous data that could easily be denied on the outside possibility that Alexander Lassiter was a double agent? Of *course* it was conceivable! he had said. Disinformation, misinformation, human or computer error, wishful thinking, fantasizing – *anything* was possible! It was *their* job to confirm or deny, not his. His work was finished; he had delivered the material, it was their function to evaluate it.

Harry reached the door and spoke. 'Who is it?'

'A new old friend, Sting,' came the reply from the corridor.

Catbird! thought Latham, instantly freezing his reaction. The Catbird no one at the Agency had ever heard of. Harry welcomed this strange intruder; he had been too worn out, too wasted to think clearly last night when the CIA impostor had paid him a visit. 'Just a moment,' he said in a louder voice. 'I'm dripping wet from a shower, I'll go put on a robe.' Latham ran first to the bathroom, threw handfuls of water over his hair and face, then dashed into the bedroom, removing his trousers, shoes, socks, and shirt, and grabbed the hotel bathrobe from the closet. He stopped briefly, looking down at the bedside table; he opened the top drawer and pulled out the small automatic supplied by the embassy and shoved it into the terry-cloth pocket. He returned to the door and opened it. 'Catbird, if I remember correctly,' he said, admitting the pale, grey-faced man wearing steel-rimmed glasses.

'Oh, that,' remarked the visitor, smiling pleasantly. 'It was a harmless ruse.'

'A trick? What do you mean? What for?'

'Washington told me you were probably exhausted, more out of the picture than in it, so I decided to cover myself in case you were hyper and felt the need to make phone calls. DC doesn't want my participation known at this point. Later, of course, but not now.'

'So you're not Catbird—'

'I knew that if I used the code name Sting, you'd let me in,' the man interrupted. 'May I sit down? I'll only be a few minutes.'

'Certainly,' replied a bewildered Harry, gesturing aimlessly towards the couch and several chairs. The visitor chose the centre of the couch as Latham sat in an armchair directly across, a coffee table between them. 'Why doesn't Washington want your presence – your participation – known?'

'You're certainly much more alert than you were last

evening,' said the stranger, again pleasantly. 'Heaven knows you weren't traumatic, but you definitely weren't yourself.'

'I was pretty tired—'

'*Tired?*' The visitor raised both his voice and his eyebrows. 'My dear fellow, you practically passed out as we talked. At one point I had to grab your arm to keep you from falling. Don't you remember, I said I'd come back when you were rested?'

'Yes, I vaguely remember, but please answer my question, and while you're at it, show me some identification. Why does Washington want you to be a ghost? I'd think the opposite would be the case.'

'Quite simply, because we don't know who's really secure and who isn't.' The man removed first his pocket watch, placing it on the table, and then a black plastic ID case; he kept it closed and handed it across the coffee table to Latham. 'I'm timing myself so as not to wear you out. Orders again.'

Fingering the small case, Harry had difficulty opening it. 'Where's the clasp?' he asked as his visitor held up the pocket watch and pressed the crown. 'I can't find the—' Latham stopped. His eyes grew unfocused, the pupils dilated; he blinked briefly but repeatedly, then his face sagged, the tense muscles turning flaccid.

'Hello, *Alex*,' said the visitor sharply. 'It's your old saw-bones, *Gerhardt*. How are you, my friend?'

'Fine, Dr Straightface, it's good to hear from you.'

'Our telephone connection's better this evening, isn't it?'

'Telephone? I guess so.'

'Did everything go well today at the embassy?'

'Hell, *no*! Those idiots kept asking questions *they* should find the answers for, not me.'

'Yes, I understand. Men in that other business of yours – the one we never mention – protect themselves at all costs, don't they?'

'It's in every question they ask, every word they say. Frankly it's deplorable.'

'I'm sure it is. So what are your plans, what have the idiots allowed you to do?'

'I'm flying to Paris in the morning. I'll see my brother, and also someone I'm very fond of, Gerhardt. The widow of a man I worked with covering East Berlin. I'm quite excited about seeing her again. She'll meet me at the airport, the diplomatic complex, in an embassy car.'

'Your brother can't meet you, Alex?'

'No ... *Wait!* Alex's brother?'

'Never mind,' said the grey-faced visitor quickly. 'The brother you speak of, where is he?'

'It's off the books. They tried to kill him.'

'Who tried to kill him?'

'You know. *They* did ... we did.'

'Tomorrow morning, the diplomatic complex. That's De Gaulle Airport, right?'

'Yes. Our ETA is ten o'clock.'

'Fine, Alex. Have a splendid reunion with your brother and the woman you find so attractive.'

'Oh, it's more than her looks, Gerhardt. She's extraordinarily intelligent, a scholar actually.'

'I'm sure she is, for my friend Lassiter is a deep man with many facets. We'll talk again, Alex.'

'Where are you going, where *are* you?'

'They're beeping me for the OR. I have to operate.'

'Yes, of course. You'll call again?'

'Certainly.' The visitor wearing steel-rimmed glasses leaned forward over the edge of the coffee table; he continued quietly, firmly, staring into Latham's neutral eyes. 'Remember, old friend, respect the wishes of your guest from Washington. He's under orders. Forget his name, which you just read on his identification. It's authentic, that's all you really care about.'

'Sure. Orders are orders, even when they're stupid.'

Half rising, the 'guest' reached over and took the ID case out of Harry's limp left hand. He opened it, sat back down on the couch, and picked up the pocket watch from the small, low table. He pressed the crown, holding it in place until he saw Latham's eyes coming back into focus, saw him blinking, suddenly aware of his surroundings, his face again firm, the muscles of his chin taut. '*There,*' said the visitor, loudly snapping the ID case shut, 'so now that you know I'm legitimate, photograph and all, just call me Peter.'

'Yes ... authentic. I still don't understand ... Peter. All right, you're a ghost, but why? Who's not secure on the tribunal?'

'Mine not to wonder why or who, I'm just the unseen presence that talks to you ... My word, I think that's a rhyme.'

'A bad one, but never mind. How could any of them be questioned?'

'Maybe they're not, individually, but others were brought in, weren't they?'

'A gaggle of clowns, yes. They didn't want to examine the names I brought out. They just wanted to clear a lot of them before the microscopes are activated – less work and less chance of stepping on the toes of big feet.'

'What do you think of the names?'

'What I think doesn't *matter*, Peter. Naturally, a number of them strike me as preposterous, but I was at the source, a trusted confidant until I escaped. I was a major contributor, a believer in their cause, so why would they feed me dirt?'

'The rumour is that the Nazis, the new Nazis, may have known who you were from the beginning.'

'That's not a "rumour", that'll be their *credo*. What the hell would we do, and how often did we do it, when we found a mole or a turnaround who fled to Mother Russia after looting us? Of course we proclaimed how smart we were, how deep-efficient, and how useless was the information stolen from us – when it wasn't.'

'It's a conundrum, isn't it?'

'What isn't in this business? Right now, for my own sanity, if you like, I have to purge Alexander Lassiter from my psyche. I have to be Harry Latham again; my job is finished. Let others take over.'

'I agree with you, Harry. Also my time's up. Please, remember my orders. We didn't meet tonight ... Don't blame me, blame Washington.'

The visitor walked up the hallway to the elevators. He took the first one available and descended a single floor, then went down the corridor to his own suite, directly below Latham's. Inside, on the desk, was an arrangement of electronic equipment. He crossed to it, pressed several buttons rewinding a tape, and confirmed its accuracy. He picked up the telephone and dialled Mettmach, Germany.

'Wolf's Lair,' said the quiet voice over the line.

'It's Catbird.'

'Introduce your impediment, please.'

'At once.' The man who called himself Peter delicately pulled a thin wire out of his equipment, its tip attached to a razor-sharp alligator clamp, and rotated it around the telephone cord until there was a momentary burst of static on the line. 'The metrometer indicates clearance, how so there?'

'Clear. Go ahead.'

'*Catbird, if I remember correctly,*' began the tape recording. The resident below Harry Latham's suite played it to the finish. '*I agree with you, Harry ... Don't blame me, blame Washington.*'

'What's your assessment?' asked Latham's visitor.

'It's dangerous,' said Gerhardt Kroeger in Germany. 'Like most deep-cover operatives, he's subconsciously crossing over from one identity to another. It's in his own words: "I have to purge Alexander Lassiter from my psyche." He was Lassiter too long, and he's fighting back to be himself. It's not an uncommon occurrence, the dual persona becoming a dual personality.'

'He's accomplished what you wanted him to do in a matter of two days. The list itself was sufficient to put our enemies into a collective state of shock. They don't want to believe his information, they're very vocal about that, but they're also frightened to deny it. I can take him out with a single shot in the hallway. Shall I?'

'It would lend credence to the list of names, but no, not yet. His brother is closing in on the trail of that senile tramp, Jodelle, and it could be catastrophic for us. As much as it tortures me not to follow up my patient's progress, the movement comes first and I must make the sacrifice. Alexander Lassiter will lead us to the other interfering Latham. Kill them both.'

'It won't be difficult. We have Lassiter's itinerary.'

'Follow it, follow them, and leave nothing but corpses. Jodelle's resurrected son, the actor, will be next, then all traces to the Loire Valley will be dust, as it is with the Hausruck.'

Harry Latham and Karin de Vries held each other as close brothers and sisters do after having been parted for a very long time. Their chatter, at first, was garbled, each excitedly telling the other how marvellous it was to be together again. Karin then clutched his arm, steering them both towards the diplomatic lounge, where Harry was processed rapidly, then out to the restricted parking area thick with uniformed guards, a number holding the leashes of various dogs trained to ferret out such items as narcotics and explosive devices. The car was a nondescript black Renault, indistinguishable from several thousand others on the streets of Paris. De Vries climbed behind the wheel while Harry got into the passenger seat.

'We don't rate a driver?' asked Latham.

'Let's say we're not permitted to have one,' replied Karin. 'Your brother is under the protection of the Antinayous, remember them?'

'Most emphatically – from the other night to be precise; they were waiting for me. I pretended not to understand a word my contact said in the truck because it would have involved an explanation that could lead to Freddie, and by extension, you.'

'You needn't have feared. I've been working with them since my last year in The Hague.'

'It's *so* good to see you,' said Harry, his voice filled with emotion, 'to hear you.'

'I feel the same way, old friend. Since I learned the Brüderschaft knew about you, I've been so terribly worried—'

'They *knew* about me?' Latham interrupted sharply, his eyes wide, bulging in astonishment. 'You're not serious!'

'Nobody's told you?'

'How could they? It's not *true*.'

'It is, Harry. I explained to Drew how I found out.'

You?'

'I assumed your brother had passed on the information.'

'Christ, I can't *think*!' Latham brought his hands to his temples, pressing harshly, his eyes tightly closed, the crow's-feet emphasized.

'What is it, Harry?'

'I don't know, there's a dreadful pain—'

'You've been through so much, so long. We'll get you to a doctor.'

'*No*. I'm Alexander Lassiter – I *was* Alexander Lassiter, that's *all* I was to them.'

'I'm afraid not, my dear.' Karin glanced at her old friend, suddenly alarmed. There was a dark red circle on his left temple; it seemed to throb. 'I brought your favourite brandy so we could celebrate, Harry. It's in the glove compartment. Open it and have some. It'll calm you down.'

'They *couldn't* have known,' choked Latham, with trembling fingers opening the glove compartment and pulling out the pint of brandy. 'You don't know what you're *saying*.'

'Perhaps I was wrong,' said De Vries, now frightened. 'Have a drink and relax. We're meeting Drew at an old country inn on the outskirts of Villejuif. The Antinayous wouldn't permit us to meet at the safe house. Calm *down*, Harry.'

'Yes, yes, I will, because, my dear – my dearest Karin – you *are* wrong. My brother will tell you, Gerhardt Kroeger will tell you, I'm Alex Lassiter, I *was* Alex Lassiter!'

'Gerhardt *Kroeger*?' asked a bewildered De Vries. 'Who's Gerhardt Kroeger?'

'A goddamned Nazi . . . also a superb doctor.'

'In fifteen or twenty minutes we'll be at the inn where your brother is waiting for us . . . Let's talk about the old days in Amsterdam, my old friend. Do you remember the night Freddie came home half soused and insisted on playing your American game of Monopoly?'

'Good God, yes. He threw out a handful of diamonds and said we should use them instead of the paper money.'

'And the time you and I drank wine and listened to Mozart until it was almost dawn.'

'Do I?' cried Latham, swallowing brandy and laughing, his eyes, however, not bright with laughter, but dark, glaring. 'Freddie came out of your bedroom and made it plain that he preferred Elvis Presley. We threw pillows at him.'

'And that morning in the café on the Herengracht when you and I told Freddie he could not jump into the canal to make a point about pollution?'

'He was going to do it, my dear – my *dearest* Karin. I swear he was.'

The harmless badinage covered the remaining minutes until De Vries turned into the gravelled parking area of the run-down country inn, country but barely out of the city, flanked by overgrown fields, isolated, and not really inviting. The meeting between the brothers was as warm, although warmer on the younger's part, as the welcoming embrace between Harry and Karin. The difference was in the older brother; there was surface ebullience, but a chill underneath. It was unexpected, not natural.

'Hey, big bro, how did you *do* it?' exclaimed Drew as the

three of them sat in a booth, De Vries on Harry's side. 'I've got a legend for a brother!'

'Because Alexander Lassiter was a person. It's the only way it could be done.'

'Well, you sure pulled it off – at least up to a point, enough to get you there.'

'You're talking about what Karin told you?'

'Well, yes—'

'*Untrue*. Totally false!'

'Harry, I said I could be wrong.'

'You *are* wrong.'

'Okay, Harry, okay.' Drew held up both hands, palms forward. 'So she's wrong, it happens to be what she heard.'

'Bastard sources, illegitimate, no confirmation.'

'We're on your side, bro, you know that.' The younger brother looked at De Vries, his expression questioning, disturbed.

'Alexander Lassiter was *real*,' said Harry emphatically, wincing as he raised his left hand to his temple, rubbing it in circles. 'Ask Gerhardt Kroeger, *he'll* tell you.'

'Who is—'

'Never mind,' Karin broke in, shaking her head, 'he's a fine doctor, your brother explained that to me.'

'How about to me, bro? Who's this Kroeger?'

'You'd really like to know, wouldn't you?'

'Is it a secret, Harry?'

'Lassiter can tell you, I don't think I should.'

'For Christ's sake, what the hell are you talking about? You're Lassiter, Harry *Latham* is Lassiter. Cut the bullshit, Harry.'

'I hurt, oh, God, I hurt. Something's wrong with me.'

'What is it, dear Harry?'

'"Dear Harry"? Do you know how much that means to me? Have you any idea how much I love you, *adore* you, Karin?'

'And I adore you, Harry,' said De Vries, suddenly finding

the older Latham crying and falling into her chest. 'You know I do.'

'I love you so much, so *very* much!' went on the semi-hysterical, babbling Harry as Karin cradled him in her arms. 'But I *hurt* so—'

'Oh, my *God*,' said Drew softly, watching the astonishing sight across the table.

'We have to get him to a doctor,' said De Vries, whispering. 'He began this in the car.'

'You're damned right,' agreed Drew. 'A head doctor. He was in deep cover too long. *Jesus!*'

'Call the embassy, get an ambulance. I'll stay with him.'

The younger Latham got up from the booth just as two men carrying weapons came rushing through the entrance, both in stocking masks. The target and the kill were apparent. 'Get *down!*' he shouted, pulling his gun from his hip holster and firing before the assassins had adjusted to the dim light. He took out the first killer and lunged behind the freestanding bar as the second man raced forward, his automatic weapon on rapid fire. Drew stood up, squeezing the trigger repeatedly, emptying his magazine. The second assassin fell as the few scattered customers ran hysterically out the front door. Latham rushed from behind his worthless barrier. Karin de Vries was on the floor, her left hand still gripping his brother's arm; she had tried to drag him with her. She was alive, her right hand bloodied, but she was alive! But Harry Latham was dead, his head blown apart, a horrible mass of blood and white tissue, what was left of his brain in fragments, half out of his skull. Drew, his mouth stretched in dread, shut his eyes in terror, then forced them open as he plunged his hands into his dead brother's pockets, pulling out his billfold and all other papers that could lead to his identity. *Why?* He was not sure, he just knew he had to do it.

He then pulled the sobbing Karin out from under the booth and, wrapping her hand in a cloth napkin, propelled her away from the terrible scene. He shouted to the management, who had fled into the kitchen, to call the police. He would make the proper inquiries later. It was no time to mourn the brother he loved, nor any moment to stare in remembrance at his corpse. He had to get Karin de Vries to a doctor, and then go back to work. The Brotherhood had to be destroyed, they *had* to be, if it took him the rest of his life, or if it *took* his life. It was a commitment he swore before any and all the gods there might be.

'You *can't* go to your office, don't you understand that?' said Karin, sitting on a gurney in the surgical annexe of the doctor on the embassy's secure listing. 'The word will go out and you're a dead man!'

'Then my office has to be moved to wherever I am,' said Drew, his voice low, insistent. 'I need all the resources we have, *everywhere*, and I'm not settling for anything less. The key is a man named Kroeger, Gerhardt Kroeger, and I'll find the son of a bitch, I've got to! *Who* is he? *Where* is he?'

'He's a doctor, we know that, and he must be German.' De Vries studied the younger Latham brother as she slowly raised and lowered her bandaged right hand following the doctor's instructions. 'For God's sake, Drew, let it out.'

'What?' asked Latham sharply, standing beside her and taking his eyes off her wounded hand.

'You're trying to make believe it didn't happen, and that doesn't make sense. You grieve for Harry as I do – undoubtedly more so – but you're holding it inside, and it's shattering you. Stop pretending to be so coldly efficient. That was Harry, not you.'

'When I saw what they did to him, I told myself that mourning would come later. It's on hold and that's the way it's going to stay.'

'I understand.'

'Do you?'

'I think so. Your rage can't be contained. You want revenge, and that comes first.'

'You used a phrase about Harry before, about the way he approached problems, or crises. You called it *sang-froid*, which I understand means calmness or lack of passion.'

'It does.'

'My French is limited, a fact I'm reminded of a lot, but there's a variation of that phrase—'

'*De sang-froid* – in cold blood,' said Karin, her eyes locked with his.

'Exactly. That's what Harry was really good at. He approached everything in life, not just calmly or coolly, but coldly – ice cold. I was the only exception; when he looked at me there was a warmth in those looks I rarely saw otherwise . . . No, there was one other, our cousin, the one I told you about who died of cancer. She was also special to him, very special. Speaking in the gender sense, could be she was his "Rosebud" until you came along.'

'You refer to Welles's *Citizen Kane*, of course.'

'Sure, it's part of our lexicon now. A symbol from the past that has more meaning for the present than a person realizes.'

'I had no idea he had such feelings towards me.'

'Neither did Kane. In his mind's eye he just saw a thing he loved as a child, and he never found anything else to take its place. That left only his accomplishments.'

'Harry was like that as a child?'

'Child, young man, and man. A straight-A student with an IQ that was off the charts. Bachelor's degree, master's, and PhD before he was twenty-three. He was always driven to be the best there was, and along the way he became fluent in five, or is it six, languages. As I mentioned, he was a piece of work.'

'What an extraordinary life.'

'Hell, I suppose the Freudians would say he was a gifted kid reacting to a distant father – distant geographically as well as emotionally – and a sweet, intuitively bright but nonintellectual mother who was maritally mismatched and decided that being attractive, loving, and gracious was her role in life, so why get into debates she couldn't win.'

'And you?'

'I guess I inherited a few more of my mother's genes than Harry did. Beth's a large woman and was a damn good athlete when she was young. She captained the girls' track team in college, and if she hadn't met my father, she might have tried out for the Olympics.'

'You have a very interesting family,' said Karin, once again studying Drew's face, 'and you're telling me all this for another reason beyond my curiosity, aren't you?'

'You're quick, lady – sorry, I'll try to stop saying that.'

'Don't bother, I'm beginning to find it rather nice ... What's the reason?'

'I want you to know me, where I am and where I came from. At least part of your curiosity should be satisfied.'

'Considering your penchant for reticence, that's an odd thing to say.'

'I realize that. I'm only just putting it together ... Back at the inn, when the firing stopped and the horrible thing was over, I found myself in a panic, rummaging through Harry's pockets, inches from what was left of his skull, his destroyed face, every second hating myself, as though I were committing some despicable act. The strange thing was, I didn't know *why*, I just knew I had to do it. I was being ordered to and I had to obey that order despite the fact that I knew it wouldn't make any difference, wouldn't bring him back.'

'You were protecting your brother in death as you would in life,' said De Vries. 'There's nothing strange in that. You were shielding his name—'

'I think I told myself that,' Latham interrupted, 'but it doesn't hold water. With today's pathology, his identity would be known in a matter of hours ... unless his body were taken, quarantined.'

'After you got the name of the doctor from the embassy—'

'From the colonel, in fact,' Drew clarified.

166

'You called back, asking the doctor for a private telephone. It was a long conversation.'

'Again with Witkowski. He knows whom to reach and how to do these things.'

'What things?'

'Like removing a body and holding it in isolation.'

'Harry?'

'Yes. No one at the scene could have learned who he was after we left. That's when I put it together, somewhere between our getting out of there and my second call to the colonel. *Harry* was giving me those orders, he was telling me what to do.'

'Please be clearer.'

'I'm to become him, I'm taking his place. *I'm* Harry Latham.'

CHAPTER TEN

Colonel Stanley Witkowski moved quickly, calling in old debts from the Cold War years. He reached a deputy chief of the Paris Sûreté, a former intelligence officer who had headed up the French garrison in Berlin, and with whom a frustrated Witkowski, then a major in the US Army G-2, had seen fit to go around regulations and exchange information. ('I thought we were on the same side, Senator!') As a result, the colonel had under his sole control not only the body of the slain Harry Latham, but also those of the two assassins. All three were stored under fictitious names in the morgue on the rue Fontenay. Further, in the interest of both countries, a fact readily accepted by the Sûreté deputy, a blackout was put on the terrorist act in the pursuit of additional information.

For Witkowski understood what Drew Latham only half perceived. The removal of his brother's body would create partial confusion, but along with the blackout, the disappearance of the killers made it total.

In a hotel room at Orly, prepared to take the three-thirty P.M. flight to Munich, the man in the steel-rimmed glasses paced nervously in front of a window, erratically distracted by the planes departing from and arriving at the field. The muted thunder of the jets served only to heighten his anxiety. He kept glaring at the telephone, furious that it did not ring, delivering him the news that would justify his return to Munich, his mission completed. That the assignment could fail was unthinkable. He had reached the Paris branch of the Blitzkrieger, the elite killers of the Brüder-schaft, so highly trained and skilled, so superior in the deadly crafts, they numbered less than two hundred instantly mobile predators operating in Europe, South America, and the United States. Catbird had been officially informed that in the four years since they had been sent to their posts, only three had been taken, two preferring their own deaths to interrogation and one killed in Paris in the line of duty. No details were ever revealed; regarding the Blitzkrieger, secrecy was absolute. Even Catbird had to appeal to the second highest leader of the Brotherhood, the tempestuous General von Schnabe, to be permitted to enlist these élite assassins.

So why didn't the phone ring? Why the delay? The lethal surveillance had been in operation since the arrival of Harry Latham at 10:28 in the morning at De Gaulle Airport and his departure by car at eleven o'clock. It was now past one-thirty in the afternoon! Catbird couldn't stand the lack of communication; he crossed to the bedside telephone and dialled the Blitzkrieger number.

'Avignon Warehouses,' said the female voice on the line in French. 'How may I direct your call?'

'Frozen foods division, if you please. Monsieur Giroux.'

'I'm afraid his line is busy.'

'I'll wait precisely thirty seconds, and if he's not free, I'll cancel my order.'

'I see . . . That won't be necessary, sir, I can ring him now.'

'Catbird?' asked a male voice.

'At least I used the right words. What the hell is going on? Why haven't you *called*?'

'Because there's nothing to report.'

'That's ridiculous! It's been over three hours!'

'We're as disturbed as you are, so don't raise your voice to me. Our last contact was an hour and twelve minutes ago; everything was on schedule. Our two men were following Latham in a Renault driven by a woman. Their last words were "Everything's under control, the mission will be carried out shortly.'"

That was it? An *hour* ago?'

'Yes.'

'Nothing *else*?'

'No. That was the last transmission.'

'Well, where are they?'

'We wish we knew.'

'Where were they *going*?'

'North out of Paris, specifics weren't mentioned.'

'Why *not*?'

'With frequency traffic, it would be stupid. Besides, those two are a prime unit, they've never failed.'

'Is it possible they failed today?'

'It's extremely unlikely.'

'Extremely unlikely is hardly an unequivocal answer. Have you any idea how vital this assignment is?'

'All our assignments are vital, or else they would not be directed to us. May I remind you, we are the solution of last resorts.'

'What can I say to Von Schnabe?'

'Please, Catbird, at this point, what can *we* say to him?' said the leader of the Paris branch of the Blitzkrieger, hanging up the phone.

Thirty minutes passed and the man called Catbird could contain himself no longer. He dialled a number deep in the forests of Vaclabruck, Germany.

'This is information I do not care to hear,' said General Ulrich von Schnabe, the words delivered through a frozen mist. 'The targets were to be eliminated at the earliest opportunity. I approved Dr Kroeger's orders, for you, yourself, told the doctor that there would be no difficulty, as you had the itinerary. On that basis alone I permitted you to contact the Blitzkrieger.'

'What can I say, *Herr General*? There is simply no word, no communication. Nothing.'

'Check with our man at the American Embassy. He may have heard something.'

'I have, sir, from public phones, of course. His last intercept simply confirmed that the Latham brother was under the protection of the Antinayous.'

'Those black-loving, Jew-kissing *scum*. No location, naturally.'

'Naturally.'

'Stay in Paris. Stay in touch with our killer unit and keep me informed of any developments.'

'Now you're the one who's crazy!' cried Karin de Vries. 'They've seen you, they *know* you, you can't possibly be Harry!'

'Sure I can, if they don't see me again, and they won't,' said Drew. 'I'll operate in absentia, from one place to another, keeping in touch with you and the colonel because I don't dare show up at the embassy. As a matter of fact, since we know the embassy's penetrated – hell, we knew it when Little Adolf showed up as my driver the other night – we might be able to find out who it is, or who they are.'

'Just how?'

'A railroad trap.'

'A what?'

'Like in a row of railroad cars filled with passengers, only one of them holds wild dogs.'

'*Please—*'

'I'll call you *as* Harry three or four times asking for papers from my dead brother Drew's files, naming one of Witkowski's couriers to meet me at a given time and place – a crowded place. You process the requests and I'll be wherever it is, but not where anybody can see me. If a legitimate courier shows up – I know them all – and he's not followed, fine. I'll throw away whatever you send. Then later I'll call again, with another request, telling you it's urgent, I'm on to something. That's your cue to hang up and say nothing, relay nothing.'

'And if anyone shows up, you'll know he's a neo, and that my phone was tapped from inside,' Karin interrupted.

'Exactly. If the circumstances are right, maybe I'll be able to take him and turn him over to our chemists.'

'Suppose there's more than one?'

'I said *if*. I'm not about to challenge a crowd of swastikas.'

'To use your own terminology, I see a very large "gap", as you called it. Why would Harry Latham remain here in Paris?'

'Because he *is* Harry Latham. Tenacious to a fault, unrelenting in his pursuits, all the things that Harry was with the added intensely personal burden of his younger brother having been murdered here in Paris.'

'Certainly a convincing motive,' agreed De Vries. 'Yours actually . . . But how will you get the news out? Isn't that a problem?'

'It's touchy,' said Drew, nodding his head and frowning. 'Primarily because the Agency will throw up its collective hands and cry foul. However, it'll be too late if we're off and running, and I have an idea the colonel might come up with something. I'm meeting him later at a café in Montmartre.'

'*You're* meeting with him? What about me? I believe I'm somewhat intrinsic to this strategy.'

'You've been shot, lady. I can't ask you—'

'You don't ask, monsieur,' Karin broke in. 'I'll tell you. I'm going with you. Frederik de Vries's wife is going with you. You lost a brother most horribly, Drew, and I lost a husband . . . most horribly. You will not exclude me.'

The door of the outpatient surgery room opened, and the doctor cleared by the embassy walked in. 'I have reasonably favourable news for you, madame,' said the physician in French, an awkward smile on his face. 'I've studied the postoperative X-rays, and with therapy you should regain at least eighty per cent of the use of your right hand. However, the tip of the middle finger will be lost. Of course, a permanent replacement can be attached.'

'Thank you, Doctor, it is a small price and I'm grateful. I'll come to see you in five days, as you instructed.'

'Pardon, monsieur – your name is Lat'am?'

'It's as close as you people get. Yes.'

'You're to telephone a Monsieur S. in Washington when it's convenient. You may use the phone here. All expenses are billed, naturally.'

'Naturally, but it's not convenient at the moment. If he calls again, please tell him I left before you could give me the message.'

'Is that proper, monsieur?'

'He'll thank you for not adding to his problems and personally approve your charges.'

'I understand,' said the doctor, his smile now appreciative.

'*I* don't,' said Karin, her first words as they walked through the entrance of the medical building and up the concrete pavement towards the parking area.

'Don't what?'

'Understand. Why didn't you want to talk to Sorenson? I'd think you'd want his advice; you said you trusted him.'

'I do. I also know that he basically trusts the system, he's lived with it for decades.'

'So?'

'So he'd have trouble with what I'm going to do. He'd say it's the Agency's turf, the Agency's decision as to what happens next, not mine. Of course, he'd be right.'

'If he's right, why are you doing it? . . . Sorry, don't bother to answer, it was a stupid question.'

'Thank you.' Latham looked at his watch. 'It's nearly six o'clock. How's your hand?'

'I can't say it's terribly pleasant. The local anaesthetic is wearing off, and thank God I couldn't see anything with my hand in that little cloth tent.'

'An hour under the knife means a lot of cutting. Are you sure you want to go with me to Witkowski?'

'My damn hand can fall off and you still won't stop me.'

'But why? You're one exhausted lady and you hurt. I

173

wouldn't keep anything from you, you should know that by now.'

'I do.' They stopped at the car as Drew opened the door; their eyes met. 'I know you won't keep anything from me, and I appreciate that. But perhaps I can add something, once I understand what you're really trying to do. Why don't you explain it to me?'

'All right, I'll try.' Latham shut the door, walked around the Renault, and climbed into the driver's seat. He started the engine, manoeuvred the car into the exit lane, and continued, aware that she was staring at him. 'Who's Gerhardt Kroeger and what hold did he have over Harry?'

'Hold? What hold? He's obviously a Nazi doctor, a skilled one apparently, whom your brother knew in the Hausruck. He probably treated Harry for some sort of severe trauma. One can appreciate even the enemy if he helps you, especially if it's medical.'

'This Kroeger goes beyond normal gratitude,' said Drew, studying the road signs for the one that would lead them to Paris's Montmartre. 'When I asked Harry who Kroeger was, he answered me with these words; they're exact and I don't think I'll ever forget them. "Lassiter can tell you. I don't think I should." That's frightening, lady.'

'Yes, it is – it was. But it was also consistent with his behaviour. The sudden display of emotion, the weeping, the cries for help. That wasn't the Harry we both knew and described to each other, not the cool, analytical man, the dispassionate man we talked about.'

'I disagree,' said Latham quietly. 'Isolate those words, repeat them, and you'll hear the Harry we knew speaking, pondering an option, not prepared to make a decision until he thought it through. "Lassiter can tell you. I don't think I should."' Drew shuddered as he turned the Renault into the main highway towards the centre of Paris. 'Gerhardt Kroeger is more than just a doctor he met in the Brüderschaft valley. I called him a son of a bitch before, but maybe I'm wrong. Maybe he's the one who helped my brother to escape. Whoever he is, he can tell us what happened to Harry when he was there, how he got his hands on that list of names.'

'You're saying that Kroeger may be an ally, not a neo, and that Harry in his psychological confusion is actually *protecting* him?'

'I just don't know, but I do know that he's more than a doctor who treated him for a bad cold, or the arthritis Harry was beginning to complain about. Gerhardt Kroeger was too important to my brother, I sense it; I'm convinced of it. That's why he's the key, and that's why I have to find him.'

'But how?'

'Again, I don't know. Witkowski may have some ideas. Maybe we can enlist the Antinayous, they can spread the word that Harry's still alive. I simply don't *know*. I'm flying blind, but our combined antennas will pick up things . . . Sorry, Madame Linguist, I should have said "antennae", except it sounds silly.'

'I concur. I'm also intrigued by your constant apologies over the things you say and think, backtracking, as though I'm a tutor of sorts.'

'I guess it's because you were closer to Harry than I was in those areas. He was constantly correcting me, mostly in a nice way, but he never stopped.'

'He loved you—'

'Yeah,' Drew interrupted wearily. 'Let's change the subject, okay?'

'Okay. What do you think the colonel will come up with, as you put it?'

'I haven't the vaguest idea, but if he's anything like his dossier, it'll be pretty fine-tuned.'

THE INTERNATIONAL HERALD TRIBUNE
—*Paris Edition*

TERRORIST ATTACK ON US EMBASSY PERSONNEL

The United States Embassy has revealed that yesterday

terrorists in stocking masks assaulted a restaurant in the Villejuif area, where two Americans were having lunch. Mr Drew Latham, an attaché at the American Embassy, was killed. His brother, Mr Harry Latham, a liaison at the embassy, survived and is currently in hiding on orders of his government. The assassins escaped and neither the identity nor the cause of the assailants are clear, for they disappeared. They are described as two men, medium height, and wearing dark business suits. The surviving Mr Latham described both assailants as being severely wounded as a result of his brother's alertness. Mr Drew Latham was armed and fired his weapon repeatedly until he was killed. French authorities, under enormous pressure from the American Embassy, are looking into the matter. Speculations center upon both Iraqi and Syrian—

'For Christ's sake, what's going *on* over there?' yelled the Secretary of State, Adam Bollinger, over the phone to the ambassador to France, Daniel Courtland.

'If I knew, I'd *tell* you. Do you want to replace me? If so, go right ahead, Adam. You bastards put me into a raging fire and I don't know enough French to call for help. I'm career *State*, Mr Secretary, not one of your fucking political appointments – come to think of it, none of your contributors speak the language anyway, most barely speak English.'

'It's no time to be vitriolic, Daniel.'

'It's time to have a chain of command, Bollinger! Drew Latham, one of the very few spooks with an open-minded head on his shoulders, is killed after four previous attempts on his life, and I don't have any answers!'

'His brother's alive,' said the Secretary of State lamely.

'That's just terrific! Where the hell *is* he?'

'I've got open lines to the Agency. As soon as I know, you'll know.'

'You're something else,' said Courtland derisively, letting his breath out. 'Do you really think deep-cover Agency personnel will tell you a goddamned thing? You're sitting behind a desk, but they have to survive. Hell, I learned that when I was posted to Finland, and the KGB was right next door. We're *zeros* in situations like this, Adam. We're told what they want to tell us.'

'That's hardly proper. *We* are the ultimate authority, your chain of command, if you like.'

'Tell that to Drew Latham, who got blown away because we couldn't support him. Even our own embassy is penetrated.'

'I simply can't understand you people.'

'You'd better begin to, Mr Secretary. The Nazis are back.'

Director Wesley Sorenson of Cons-Op sat at his desk, his head forward, resting on his fingers. His sorrow was such that tears slowly emerged from his eyes, the loss so tragic, so unnecessary, that he questioned the essence of his own life. Drew Latham taken out – as *he* might have been so many times – and for what? What changes could the life of a single intelligence officer make when the hoo-haws of international negotiations came together at their fancy hotels and their banquets, their flag-strewn parades in convention halls signifying nothing but ceremonial hypocrisy?

Sorenson felt that it was the end for him. He had nothing more to give; he had seen too much death in the shadows of those parades. If there was a spark of light, it did not come.

And then it did!

'Wes, I trust we're on scrambler,' said the familiar voice on the line.

'*Drew?* My God, is that *you?* Sorenson lurched forward over his desk, the blood drained from his face. 'You're *alive?*'

'I also trust you're alone. I asked your secretary and she gave me an affirmative.'

'Yes, of course ... Let me catch my breath; this is incredible – I don't know what to say, what to think. This *is* you?'

'Last time I checked my pulse it was.'

Silence. The quiet before the storm.

'Then I believe you have some serious explaining to do, young man! Goddammit, I wrote a *sympathy* note to your parents.'

'Mother's a tough lady, she can handle it; and Dad, if he's around, will probably try to figure out which one of us caught the bullets.'

'You're distastefully cavalier—'

'It's better than being the other way, Mr Director,' Latham interrupted. 'There's no time for that now.'

'There'd better be time for an explanation. Then Harry is – he's the one who was killed?'

'Yes. I'm taking his place.'

'You're doing *what*?'

'I just told you.'

'For Christ's sake, *why*? I never cleared anything like this, I wouldn't!'

'I knew that. It's why I went around you and did it myself. If I make any progress, you can take the credit. If I don't, well, it won't matter, will it?'

'To hell with credit, I want to know what you think you're *doing*. This is an intolerable breach of field conduct, and you know it!'

'Not entirely, sir. We all have the leeway of on-scene decisions, you gave us that.'

'Only in the event that proper channels of authority can't be reached in times of crisis. I'm *here* and you can reach me, whether I'm at the office, at home, on a golf course, or in a goddamned whorehouse – if I had any use for one! Why didn't you?'

'I just told you. You'd turn me down, and it'd be wrong because you aren't here, and there's no way I can make you understand because I don't really understand it myself, but I know I'm right. And, if I may, *sir*, knowing something of your service record, I believe you've taken such unilateral actions yourself in the past.'

'Cut the crap, Latham,' said a weary, frustrated Sorenson.

'What've you got and how are you approaching it? Why are you playing Harry?'

Painfully, reluctantly, Drew described the last minutes of his brother's life, the uncharacteristic outbursts of emotion, the tears, the apparent confusion he had in differentiating between his cover and his real identity, and finally, his refusal to amplify on a name, a doctor, that he brought up several times with Karin de Vries and then with Drew himself. 'He mentioned him,' explained Latham, 'as if the man were some sort of secretive figure, to be either exposed or protected.'

'A sinner and a saint?' Sorenson asked.

'Yes, I guess you could say that.'

'It's the Stockholm syndrome, Drew. The captive identifies with the captor. His feelings are a mixed bag of resentment, yet he's still currying favour, until finally, he episodically imagines himself to be the one with power. Quite simply, Harry was burned out; he lived over the edge too long.'

'I understand all that, Wes, including the all-too-familiar Stockholm theory which covers too many bases for me, at least as it applies to Harry. His well-known cold rationality was still there. This Dr Gerhardt Kroeger, that's his name, was somehow important to my brother, sinner or saint notwithstanding. He knows what happened to Harry, maybe even how he got that list of names. It's possible this Kroeger is on our side and slipped them to him.'

'I suppose anything's possible, and right now those names are a national catastrophe waiting to happen. At the moment, the Bureau is mounting a dozen covert operations to microscope everyone on the list over here.'

'Things have gone that far already?'

'In the words of our ubiquitous Secretary of State, who has both ears of the President, if this administration "can root out the Nazi influence in the country, the nation will be forever grateful." It's "damn the torpedoes, full steam ahead."'

179

'My God, that's scary.'

'I agree, but I can also understand why it's happening. Harry Latham was considered the finest, most experienced undercover man in the Agency. It's not easy to dismiss his findings.'

'Not was,' corrected Drew. '*Is*, Wes. Harry's alive; he's got to remain alive until I can smoke out this Gerhardt Kroeger.'

'If he's alive, he's got to reach the Agency, you damn fool!'

'He can't, because he knows, as I told you, that Langley is penetrated, as high up as the AA-Zero computers, and that's practically as close as you can get to Director Talbot.'

'I relayed that information to Knox. He can't believe it.'

'He'd better, it's on the mark.'

'He's working on it, I convinced him,' said Sorenson. 'But your flying solo won't wash, young man. You do that, you become a rogue agent no one will trust.'

'My flying solo is restricted because I have a conduit to Langley.'

'Not me. I won't compromise Consular Operations by going around the Agency. There's enough turf-snipping in this town as it is, and I admire Knox Talbot, I respect him. I will not be a party to it.'

'I knew you wouldn't, so I found someone else. Remember Witkowski, Colonel Stanley Witkowski?'

'Certainly. G-2 Berlin. Met him a number of times, a bright man – that's *right*, he's posted at the embassy now.'

'Chief of Security. He's got all the credentials he needs to satisfy the DCI. Harry worked with Witkowski in Berlin, and he's the natural conduit because my brother trusted him – hell, he had to, the colonel fed him enough G-2 input to prolong his station and probably his life. Stanley will figure out a way to reach Talbot on a sub-rosa channel and ask him to run an in-depth trace on this Kroeger.'

'It makes sense, Witkowski makes sense. What do you want me to do?'

'Absolutely nothing; we can't risk any cross-checks that

might be picked up by neo moles. However, I'd appreciate your standing by when and if I think I'm in over my head and could use some advice.'

'I'm not sure I'm capable of that. It's been a long time.'

'I'll take what you even vaguely remember as gospel, Mr Director . . . Here we go. Harry Latham's alive and well and going out in search of a doctor – saint or sinner or both. Be in touch.'

The line went dead and Wesley Sorenson held the phone in his hand, as if in a daze. The younger Latham's actions were dangerously unorthodox and should be aborted, the Cons-Op director knew that, knew that he should call Knox Talbot and come clean, saying whatever he could say to explain and protect his man, but it wasn't in him to do it. Drew had been right; how often had Case Officer Sorenson worked outside of sanction because he understood that his decisions would be struck down, yet knew that his course of action was the only one to take. Not only knew it, but passionately believed it. He heard his younger self talking as he listened to Drew Latham's words. Slowly, he replaced the phone, the chant of a prayer forming silently on his lips.

Jean-Pierre and Giselle Villier stepped out of the limousine at the hotel L'Hermitage in Monte Carlo; they had flown there from Paris by private jet. The reason for the trip, as described by the press, was to give the celebrated actor some rest after six arduous months performing in *Coriolanus*, culminating in the emotionally draining event that caused him to close the play. This information, however, was all that the media was given, all it would be given, as there would be no further statements and certainly no interviews. And after a few days of pleasant distraction at the Casino de Paris, it was understood that the couple would fly to an undisclosed island in the Mediterranean, perhaps to join his parents.

What the press did not know was that two military Mirage jets flew above and below the private plane from Paris, escorting it to its destination. Further, one of the two uniformed doormen, the assistant manager at the front desk, and assorted minor hotel functionaries were all Deuxième personnel, each cleared by the Bain de Mer, the select organization that ran the affairs of Monte Carlo and was the diplomatic liaison to the royal family of Monaco. In addition, whenever Monsieur and Madame Villier left the hotel for the slow three-block ride to the casino, the bulletproof limousine was flanked by armed men in expensive, well-tailored suits until the luxurious vehicle arrived at the steps of the majestic gambling establishment, where their counterparts took over.

Upon their arrival, the couple was joined in their suite by the chief of the Deuxième Bureau, Claude Moreau.

'As you can see, my friends, everything is covered, including the rooftops, where we have expert marksmen; and below in cars, all windows are constantly under roving telescopes. You have nothing to fear.'

'We are not your "friends", monsieur,' said Giselle Villier coolly. 'And as to these precautions, a single gunshot destroys the facade.'

'Only if a gunshot is permitted, madame, and none will be.'

'What about the casino itself, how can you possibly control the crowds who may recognize me?' asked the actor.

'Actually, they're part of the protection, but only a peripheral part. We know the games you enjoy, and at each such table we will have men and women who follow you, surround you, and block your bodies with theirs. No assassin, and certainly no Blitzkrieger, will attempt to fire unless his shot is clean. Such killers can't afford to.'

'Suppose your assassin is someone at a table?' Giselle interrupted. 'How can you protect my husband?'

'Another astute question, which I fully expect from you, madame,' replied Moreau, 'and I trust my answer will satisfy you. At each table you will observe a man and a woman going around, pausing at each player – curious bystanders

182

trying to decide whether or not to enter the gambling fray. Actually, they will carry in their palms metallic scanners which will pick up the solid steel of even the smallest-calibre weapon.'

'You are thorough,' conceded Giselle.

'We are, I promised you that,' agreed Moreau. 'Please remember, I'll settle for just *one* Blitzkrieger who tries to assault you. My goal is to take him alive. If it does not happen here, with all the publicity we've issued, you're free to fly out and join your husband's parents.'

'On that mythical island?'

'No, monsieur, it's quite real. They're enjoying a lovely vacation on an estate in Corsica.'

'In a way, then,' said Jean-Pierre, 'I hope the hell it does happen here. I never appreciated how lovely it was to be free.'

It did happen, but not in any way Claude Moreau had anticipated.

CHAPTER ELEVEN

The music from the salon floated in diminishing strains the farther one walked from the marble entrance of the Casino de Paris into the interior of the majestic gaming establishment. It was so easy to imagine the glorious early decades of the century, when magnificently adorned horse-drawn carriages, and then enormous motorcars, drew up to the glistening steps and disgorged royalty and the wealthy of Europe in all their finery. The times had changed, the clientele hardly as rarefied now, but the core of opulence remained, defined by the restored elegance of bygone eras.

Jean-Pierre and Giselle walked between the myriad tables towards the exclusive Baccarat Room, the entrance to which required an initial deposit of fifty thousand francs, said fee instantly waived for the celebrated actor and his wife. As they made their way, heads turned, audible gasps were heard, and not a few cries of '*C'est lui!*' overrode the general hum as various guests recognized Villier. The actor smiled and continuously nodded his head in appreciation, but with a distant modesty that conveyed a desire for privacy. While he did so, his entourage of finely dressed couples flanked Jean-Pierre and his wife, permitting only glimpses of the couple. Moreau's theory that no assassin would dare fire a weapon at such an elusive target was being borne out.

Once in the large, restricted room replete with silver stanchions connected by thick red velvet cords around the tables, champagne was ordered. The entourage was filled with ebullient laughter as Jean-Pierre and Giselle sat down, two large stacks of expensive chips placed in front of each, a *contrôle* unobtrusively slipping a receipt for the actor to sign. The game proceeded, far better for Giselle than for Jean-Pierre, who mocked tragedy with every turn of the boot. Their accompanying 'friends' subtly, slowly, silently moved around the table, each with one hand out of sight, in shadow. Moreau again; palm-held metal scanners were at work detecting weapons. Obviously, there were none and the game continued until the actor cried in great good humour. *'C'est finis pour moi! Un autre table, s'il vous plaît!'*

They moved to another table, champagne glasses refilled for everyone, including the Villiers' gambling companions at the previous table, everything put on the actor's account. They settled in for another series of rounds and boots, now tilting to Jean-Pierre's favour. As the laughter grew, fuelled by the chilled Cristal Brut, several members of the entourage sat in the seats of discontinued players. The actor pulled a *double neuf*, and, consistent with his excitable, theatrical reactions, he roared with approval.

Suddenly, at the table they had left, there was a prolonged scream, a hysterical cry of pain. All heads turned; the room erupted with consternation as the men at Jean-Pierre's table rose as one, their attention on the man who was collapsing off his chair, breaking down the velvet cord as he plunged to the floor.

Then there came another sound, more than a scream, far louder than a cry. It was the roar of alarm, shouted by a female voice, as a fashionably dressed woman lunged across the table at another woman sitting beside the actor, a killer with an ice pick she was about to plunge into the dark side of Jean-Pierre's left ribcage, only inches away. The tip drew blood, a complete thrust would have penetrated Villier's heart, but Moreau's agent gripped the assassin's wrist, twisting it counterclockwise. Paralysing her at the throat, she slammed the would-be killer to the floor.

'Are you all right, monsieur?' yelled the Deuxième agent, looking up at the actor as she lay across the immobile assailant.

'A small puncture, mademoiselle – how can I thank you?'
'*Jean-Pierre—*'

'Easy, my dearest, I'm all right,' replied the actor, holding his left side and sitting down, 'but we owe this courageous woman so much. She saved my life!'

'Are you *hurt*, young lady?' shouted Giselle, leaning over her husband's legs and grabbing Moreau's agent's arm.

'I'm fine, Madame Villier. Quite a bit better when you call me a young lady. I'm well beyond that.' Breathlessly, she smiled.

'Aren't we all, my dear ... I must get my husband to a doctor.'

'My associates are taking care of that, madame, believe me.'

Claude Moreau, appearing as if from nowhere, walked into the Baccarat Room, his expression one of both concern and muted exhilaration. 'We have *done* it, monsieur and madame – *you* have done it! We have our Blitzkrieger.'

'My husband has been wounded, you idiot!' shouted Giselle Villier.

'For which I apologize, madame, but it is not serious, and his contribution has been enormous.'

'You promised he'd be safe.'

'In my business, guarantees are not always absolute. However, if I may say it, he has greatly enhanced the quest of his natural father and performed an act for which the Republic of France is eternally grateful.'

'That's gratuitous nonsense!'

'No, it isn't, madame. Whether you accept it or not, the unholy Nazis are coming out of the mud, out of the filth of their own creation. Each rock we can turn over brings us all closer to stamping out the snakes underneath. But your part in this is over. Enjoy your vacation on Corsica. After you see a doctor, our plane is waiting for you in Nice, everything paid for by the Quai d'Orsay.'

'I can do without your money, monsieur,' said Jean-Pierre. 'But I should like to reopen *Coriolanus*.'

'Good heavens, why? You've proved your triumph. You certainly do not need the employment, so why go back to such a gruelling schedule?'

'Because like you, Moreau, I'm pretty good at what I do.'

'We shall discuss it, monsieur. One night's success does not mean the battle is over.'

Grey-haired, sixty-three-year-old Senator Lawrence Roote of Colorado hung up the phone in his Washington office, a disturbed man. Disturbed, bewildered, and angry. Why was he the subject of an FBI investigation he knew nothing about? What did it concern and who called for it? Again, *why*? His assets, admittedly considerable, were in a blind trust by his own choice so as to avoid even a scintilla of legislative compromise; his second marriage was solid, his first wife having been tragically killed in a plane crash; his two sons, one a banker, the other a university dean, were upstanding citizens of their communities, so much so that Roote thought they were at times insufferable; he had served in Korea without incident but with a silver star; and his drinking consisted of two or three martinis before dinner. What was there to investigate?

His conservative views were well known and frequently attacked by the liberal press, which consistently took his words out of context, making him appear like a rabid proselytizer of the far right, which he definitely was not. Among his colleagues on both sides of the aisle, it was common knowledge that he was fair and listened to the opposition without rancour. He simply believed firmly that when government did too much for the people, they did too little for themselves.

Further, his wealth did not come from any inheritance; his family had been dirt poor. Roote had climbed that elusive ladder to success, frequently slipping on the rungs, by holding three jobs through a small, obscure college and the Wharton School of Finance, where several members of the faculty recommended him to corporate recruiters. He chose a young, profitable firm; there was room and time to grow in the executive ranks. However, the smaller company was taken over by a larger corporation, which was in turn absorbed by a conglomerate, whose board of directors recognized Roote's talents and audacity. By the time he was thirty-five, the sign on the door to his suite of offices read Chief Executive Officer. At forty it proclaimed President and CEO. Before fifty, his mergers, acquisitions, and stock options had made him a multimillionaire. At which point, tired of the limiting pursuit of an ever-increasing profit margin and bothered by the direction the country was taking, he turned to politics.

As he sat at his desk, ruminating over his past, he tried to coldly objectify, searching areas where his actions might call into question his ethics or morality. In the early days, overworked and vulnerable, he had had several affairs, but they were discreet and only with women who were his peers, as eager as he was to maintain the discretion. He was a tough negotiator in business, always using the tools of advantage by researching, even creating what his adversaries wanted, but his integrity had never been doubted . . . What in *hell* was the Bureau doing?

It had begun only minutes ago when his secretary buzzed him. 'Yes?'

'A Mr Roger Brooks from Telluride, Colorado, on the line, sir,' said his secretary.

'Who?'

'A Mr Brooks. He said he went to high school with you in Cedaredge.'

'My God, Brooksie! I haven't thought of him in years. I heard he owns a ski resort somewhere.'

'They ski in Telluride, Senator.'

'That was it. Thank you, all-knowing one.'

'Shall I put him through?'

'Sure . . . Hello, Roger, how *are* you?'

'Fine, Larry, it's been a long time.'

'At least thirty years—'

'Well, not quite,' Brooks contradicted gently. 'I headed up your campaign here eight years ago. The last election you didn't really need one.'

'Christ, I'm sorry! Of course, I remember now. Forgive me.'

'No forgiveness required, Larry, you're a busy guy.'

'How about you?'

'Built four additional runs since then, so you could say I'm surviving pretty well. And the summer backpackers are growing faster than we can cut new trails. 'Course the ones from the East want to know why we don't have room service in the woods.'

'That's good, Rog! I'll use it the next time I'm debating one of my distinguished colleagues from New York. They want room service for everyone on welfare.'

'Larry,' said Roger Brooks, his tone of voice altered, serious. 'The reason I'm calling is probably because we went to school together and I ran that campaign down here.'

'I don't understand.'

'I don't either, but I knew I had to call you in spite of the fact that I swore I wouldn't. Frankly, I didn't like the son of a bitch; he talked quietly, like he was my best friend and was telling me the secrets of King Tut's tomb, all the while saying it was for your own good.'

'*Who?*'

'Some guy from the FBI. I made him show me his ID and it was for real. I came damn near throwing him the hell out of here, then I figured I'd better learn what his grief was, if only to let you know.'

'What was it, Roger?'

'Nuts, that's what it was. You know how some of the press paint you, like they did old Barry G. in Arizona? The nuclear freak who'd blow us to hell, the downtrodder of the downtrodden, all that crazy stuff ?'

'Yes, I do. He survived it with honour and so will I. What did the Bureau man want?'

'He wanted to know if I'd ever heard you express

sympathy for – get this – "Fascist causes". If maybe at one time or another you might have indicated that you thought Nazi Germany had certain justifications for what they did that led to the war ... I tell you, Larry, by then my blood was boiling hot, but I kept cool and just told him that he was way off base. I brought up the fact that you were decorated in Korea, and you know what the bastard said?'

'No, I don't, Roger. What did he say?'

'He said, and he said it with kind of a smirk: "But that was against the Communists, wasn't it?" Shit, Larry, he was trying to build a case without a case!'

'The Communists being an anathema to Nazi Germany, is that what you gathered?'

'Hell, yes. And that kid wasn't old enough to know where Korea is, but he was smooth – *Jesus*, was he wrapped tight, and spoke like a benevolent angel. All innocence and sweet talk.'

'They're using their best men,' said Roote softly, staring down at his desk. 'How did the conversation end?'

'Oh, upbeat, let me tell you. He made it clear that his confidential information was obviously wrong, very wrong, and the investigation would stop then and there.'

'Which means it's just begun.' Lawrence Roote picked up a pencil and cracked it with his left hand. 'Thanks, Brooksie, thank you more than I can say.'

'What's going on, Larry?'

'I don't know, I *really* don't know. When I find out, I'll call you.'

Franklyn Wagner, anchorman for MBC News, the most-watched evening news programme in the country, sat in his dressing room rewriting much of the copy he would recite in front of the cameras in forty-five minutes. There was a knock on his door and he casually called out, 'Come in.'

'Hi there, Mr Sincere,' said Emmanuel Chernov, chief producer of network news, walking inside and shutting the door; he crossed to a chair and sat down. 'You got problems

190

with the words again? I hate to repeat myself, but it's probably too late to change the TelePrompTers.'

'And to repeat myself, that won't be necessary. None of this would be necessary if you hired writers who could spell the word *journalism*, or even knew its basic precepts.'

'You print-types, or should I say, you refugees from print who can now afford joints in the Hamptons with swimming pools, always complain.'

'I went to the Hamptons once, Manny,' said the handsome, silver-haired Wagner while continuing to edit the sheets of copy, 'and I'll tell you why I won't go there again. Do you want to hear?'

'Sure.'

'The beaches are filled with people of both sexes, either very thin or very fat, who walk up and down the sand carrying galleys to prove that they're writers. Then at night they gather together in candlelit cafés to extol their unprintable scribblings and exercise their egos at the expense of unwashed publishers.'

'That's pretty heavy, Frank.'

'It's pretty damned accurate. I grew up on a farm in Vancouver where, if the Pacific winds brought in sand, it meant the crops wouldn't grow.'

'That's kind of a leap, isn't it?'

'Perhaps, but I can't stand writers, on television or otherwise, who let the sand pile up between the words . . . *There*, I'm finished. If there aren't any newsbreaks, we'll have a relatively literate broadcast.'

'Nobody can say you're humble, Mr Sincere.'

'I don't pretend to be. And, speaking of humility, to which you're uniquely entitled, why are you here, Manny? I thought you delegated all criticisms and network objections to our executive producer.'

'This goes beyond that, Frank,' said Chernov, his eyes heavy-lidded, sad. 'I had a visitor today, this afternoon, a fellow from the FBI, who, God knows, I couldn't ignore, am I right?'

'So far. What did he want?'

'Your head, I think.'

'I beg your pardon?'

'You're Canadian, right?'

'I am indeed, and proud of it.'

'When you were in that university, the . . . the . . .'

'University of British Columbia.'

'Yeah, that one. Did you protest the Vietnam War?'

'It was a United Nations "action", and, yes, I opposed it vociferously.'

'You refused to serve?'

'We were not obliged to serve, Manny.'

'But you didn't go.'

'I wasn't asked to and if I had been, I wouldn't have.'

'You were a member of the Universal Peace Movement, is that correct?'

'Yes, I was. Most of us, not all, of course, were.'

'Did you know that Germany was one of the sponsors?'

'The *young* people of Germany, student organizations, certainly not the government. Bonn is prohibited from engaging in armed conflicts or even parliamentary discussions of the issues. Their surrender codified neutrality. Good God, despite your title, don't you know anything?'

'I know that a lot of Germans were part of the Universal Peace Movement, and you were a member in pretty obvious good standing. "Universal Peace" could have another meaning, like Hitler's "Peace Through Universal Might and Moral Strength." '

'Are you playing paranoid *Hebrew*, Manny? If so, I should remind you that my wife's mother was Jewish, which is apparently more important than if her father were. Therefore, my children, by extension, are hardly Aryan. Beyond that irrefutable fact, which disqualifies me from being part of the Wehrmacht, the German government had nothing to do with the UPM.'

'Still, the German influence was pretty damned apparent.'

192

'Guilt, Manny, profound guilt was the reason. What the hell are you trying to say?'

'This FBI man, he wanted to know if you had any ties with the new political movements in Germany. After all, Wagner is a German name.'

'I don't *believe* this!'

Clarence 'Clarr' Ogilvie, retired chairman of the board of Global Electronics, drove his restored Duesenberg off the Merritt Parkway at the Greenwich, Connecticut, exit nearest his home, or estate, as the press sarcastically called it. In his family's wealthier days, before the '29 crash, three acres of land with a normal-size pool and no tennis court or stables would have hardly constituted an estate. However, because he had 'come from money', he was somehow an object of scorn, as if he had chosen to be born rich, and his accomplishments were therefore deemed meaningless, merely the products of high-priced public relations which he obviously could afford.

Forgotten, or, to be less charitable, purposefully overlooked, were the years he had spent, twelve to fifteen hours a day, turning an only marginally profitable family company into one of the most successful electronics firms in the country. He had graduated from MIT in the late forties, an advocate of the new technologies, and when he came into the family business, he had instantly recognized that it was a decade behind the times. He let go virtually the entire executive hierarchy, providing all with pensions he hoped he could afford, and replaced them with like-minded, computer-oriented young bulls – and cows – for he hired by talent, not gender.

By the middle fifties the technological advances his teams of long-haired, jean-clad, pot-smoking innovators came up with had caught the attention of the Pentagon – with a shock and a thud. The patience of the sharply pressed 'uniforms' was sorely tried by the despised, ill-kempt 'beards' and 'miniskirts' who casually placed their feet on polished tables or buffed their fingernails during conferences while they patiently explained the new technology. But their products were irresistible and the nation's armed might was substantially increased; the family business went global.

All that was yesterday, thought Clarr Ogilvie as he threaded through the backcountry roads that led to his house. Today was a day he never in his wildest nightmares had thought could come to pass. He realized that he had never been the most popular player in the so-called military-industrial complex but this was beyond the pale.

In short words, he had been labelled a potential enemy of his country, a closet zealot who supported the aims of a growing Fascist – *Nazi* – movement in Germany!

He had driven into New York to see his attorney and good friend, John Saxe, who said over the phone that it was an emergency.

'Did you supply a German firm called Oberfeld with electronic equipment that involved satellite transmissions?'

'Yes, we did. Cleared by FTC, the export boys, and the State Department. No end-user contract was necessary.'

'Did you know who Oberfeld was, Clarr?'

'Only that they paid their bills promptly. I just told you, they were cleared.'

'You never examined their, let's say, their industrial base, their business objectives?'

'We understood their desire to expand electronically, their specifications. Anything else was up to Washington's export controls.'

'That's our out, naturally.'

'What are you talking about, John?'

'They're Nazis, Clarr, the new generation of Nazis.'

'How the hell would *we* know that if Washington *didn't?*'

'That's our defence, of course.'

'Defence against what?'

'Some may claim that you knew what Washington didn't know. That you wilfully, knowingly, supplied a bunch of

Nazi revolutionaries with the latest technological communications equipment.'

'That's *insane!*'

'It may be the case we have to fight.'

'For Christ's sake, *why?*'

'Because you're on a list, Clarr, that's what I've been told. Also, you're not universally loved. Frankly, I'd get rid of that Duesenberg of yours.'

'What? It's a classic!'

'It's a German car.'

'The *hell* it is! The Duesenbergs were American, built mostly in Virginia!'

'Well, the name, you understand.'

'No, I don't understand a goddamned thing!'

Clarence 'Clarr' Ogilvie pulled into his driveway, wondering what he could possibly say to his wife.

The elderly man with the shaved head and the thick tortoiseshell glasses that magnified his eyes stood thirty feet from the line of passengers validating their departures on Lufthansa Flight 7000 to Stuttgart, Germany. As each produced his or her passport, along with an airline ticket, the only pause in the procedure came when the clerks checked passports against an unseen computer screen on the left side of the counter. The bald man had been processed, his boarding pass in his pocket. He watched anxiously as a grey-haired woman approached a clerk and presented her credentials. Moments later he sighed audibly in relief; his wife walked away from the counter. They met three minutes later at a newspaper stand, both studying the displays of magazines, but neither acknowledging the other, except in whispers.

'That's over with,' said the man in German. 'We board in twenty minutes. I'll be among the last, you be there among the first.'

'Aren't you being overly cautious, Rudi? Our passports and the photographs show two people completely different from our true selves, if, indeed, anybody is remotely interested in us.'

'I prefer excessive caution to indifference in these matters. I'll be missed in the morning at the laboratory – I may have been missed already if one of my colleagues has tried to reach me. We are approaching breakneck speed refining the fibre optics that will intercept international satellite trans-missions regardless of frequencies.'

'You know I don't understand such talk—'

'Not *talk*, dear wife, but hard, solid research. We're working in shifts, twenty-four hours a day, and at any moment an associate may wish to check the research in our computers.'

'So let them, dear husband.'

'You are an unscientific fool! *I* have the software, and I've spread a virus throughout the system.'

'You know, your bald head is far less attractive than your waves of full white hair, Rudi. And if I ever permit this much grey in my hair, I'll forgive you if you seek a mistress.'

'You are also impossible, my adorable young wife.'

'*Ach*, so why do we go through this nonsense?'

'I've told you time and time again. The Brüderschaft, there is only the *Brüderschaft*!'

'Politics so bore me.'

'We'll see each other in Stuttgart. By the way, I bought you the diamond necklace you saw at Tiffany's.'

'You're a *darling*! I shall be the envy of every woman in Munich!'

'Vaclabruck, my dear. Munich only on weekends.'

'*Boring!*'

Arnold Argossy, radio and television impresario of the hysteria-prone ultraconservative wing of American political thought, squeezed his enormous frame into the inadequate chair at the studio table. He put on his earphones and looked over at the tinted glass panel, beyond which were his producer and the various technicians who caused the familiar high-pitched, grating voice, so beloved of his constituency, to be heard across the land. The once-staggering number of his listeners had begun to fall off, insulted, perhaps, by his singularly vicious attacks on anything and everything he considered *liberal*! without his offering any coherent alternatives to the programmes he attacked. The gradual decline in his ratings had done nothing to diminish his ego; instead, he held on to his decreasing audience by ever-increasing assaults on Libbo-Commies, Female-Fascists, Embryo-Killers, Homeless-Suckers, and assorted labels that eventually had to turn off even the vast 'patient, stable majority' who began to question his diatribes.

The red light flashed. ON AIR.

'Hello, America, you true, red-blooded sons and daughters of giants who carved a nation out of a land of savages and made it sweet. It's A.A. talking, and this afternoon I want to hear from *you*! The honest, hardworking people of this great land that's been soiled and spoiled by the sex-ridden, religion-bashing, morality-blasting, sick sycophants who run our government while running away with your money. Hear the latest, my friends! There's a bill before Congress that would permit our taxes to pay for obligatory sex education, specifically targeting inner-city youths. Can you *believe* it? *Our* cold cash squandered away on a hot topic, *our* dollars to fund, at the least, a million condoms a day so the rootless offspring of the lazy and the indolent can fornicate at the drop of a – no, I can't say it, for this is a family programme. We spread the morality of our God; we do not pander to the base, savage hungers of Lucifer, the archangel of hell . . . What is the solution to this promiscuous madness? It's so obvious, I can hear you shouting the answer. *Sterilization*, my friends! Benign denial of procreation by *lust*, for lust is not married love. Lust is the nonselective appetite of animals, and no amount of so-called *sexual* education can cure it, it can only cause it to proliferate! . . . Now, *you* know and I know who we're talking about, don't we? Oh, yes? I can hear the liberal chorus shouting *racism*! But I ask you, my friends, is it racist to inaugurate programmes that without the slightest doubt can benefit the very people who are being debased by their promiscuity? I think not. What do you think?'

'*Whippo!*' cried the first caller. 'I got nuthin' against nobody, but I betcha if we paid every black person on welfare twenty-five thousand bucks to go back to Africa and start his own tribe, they'd grab it in a shot. I even figured it out. It'd be cheaper, right?'

'We cannot condone migration through bribery, sir, it's unconstitutional. But in a word, *yowsah!* Next, please.'

'I'm calling from New York City, A.A., lower West Side, and let me tell you, the Cuban-Spic cooking's stinking up the whole apartment house, and I can't read the signs on the stores no more. Can't we get rid of Castro and send 'em back where they belong?'

'We also can't condone ethnic slurs, sir, but disregarding the unfortunate epithet you attached to a nationality, you do have a point. Write your senators and congressmen and ask why we haven't sent in a hit team to assassinate the Commie dictator. What else is left?'

'Double whippo, A.A.! The senators and congressmen, they gotta listen to us, don't they?'

'They certainly do, my friend.'

'Great! . . . Who are they?'

'The post office has that information. Next caller for the Argossy Argonaut, please.'

'Good evening, *mein Herr*, I'm calling from Munich, Germany, where it is evening. We listen to you on the Religion of the World Broadcast, and we thank God they bring you to us. Also, we thank *you* for everything you've done for us!'

'Who the hell is this?' said Argossy, covering the microphone and looking over at the tinted glass panel.

'The RWB is a hell of a good market for us, Arnie,' answered the producer over the earphones. 'We're reaching into Europe on shortwave. Be nice and listen to the guy, it's his nickel and it's a lot of nickels.'

'So how are things in Munich, my new friend?'

'Much better for hearing your voice, Herr Argossy.'

'That's nice to know. I went to your fair city about a year ago and had the best sausage and sauerkraut I ever tasted. They mixed it all together with mashed potatoes and mustard. Terrific.'

'It is you who are terrific, *mein Herr*! You are obviously one of us, one of the new Germany.'

'I'm afraid I don't know what you mean—'

'*Natürlich*, of course you do! We will build the new Reich, the Fourth Reich, and you will be our Minister of Propaganda. You will be far more effective than Goebbels ever was. You are far more persuasive!'

'Who the fuck *is* this?' roared Arnold Argossy.

'Cut the mikes and stop the tape!' yelled the producer. '*Christ*, how many stations did this go over live?'

'Two hundred and twelve,' replied an uninterested technician.

'Holy shit,' said the producer, falling into a chair.

THE WASHINGTON POST

QUIET INVESTIGATIONS ALARMING HILL
FBI Agents Roaming Around Asking Questions

WASHINGTON, DC, Friday – The Post has learned that agents of the Federal Bureau of Investigation have been travelling across the country seeking information about prominent figures of the Senate and the House of Representatives, as well as members of the administration. The nature of these inquiries is not clear and Justice will not elaborate on or even confirm the existence of such interrogations. The rumours, however, persist, given substance by an angry Senator Lawrence Roote of Colorado, whose staff admitted he had demanded an immediate meeting with the Attorney General. After their conference, Roote, too, refused to comment, stating only that there had been a misunderstanding.

Hints that other 'misunderstandings' have spread beyond the nation's capital came last night when the popular and respected anchor of MBC's evening news programme, Franklyn Wagner, set aside two minutes for what he called a 'personal essay'. In his normally well-modulated tones there was an obvious bitterness, if not a controlled fury. He struck out at what he termed 'the hyenas of vigilantism who pounce on long-past but totally legitimate political positions, even names and their origins, to smear the objects of their disaffections.' He recalled the 'mass hysteria of the McCarthy years, when decent men and women were ruined by innuendo and baseless guilt by association,' ending his essay by saying he was 'a grateful guest in this magnificent country' – Wagner is Canadian – but would grab the next plane back to Toronto should he and his family 'be pilloried'.

Bombarded later with questions, he also refused comment, saying only that the instigators knew who they were, and 'that was enough'. MBC stated that their switchboards were overloaded, estimating that the calls were well into the thousands, over eighty per cent supporting Mr Wagner.

The only clue this reporter has been able to unearth is that the inquiries are somehow related to recent events in Germany, where right-wing factions have made significant inroads throughout the Bonn government.

In his still unfinished medical complex, Gerhardt Kroeger paced aimlessly, impetuously, in front of his wife, Greta, who sat in a chair in their quarters deep in the forests of Vaclabruck. 'He's still alive, that we know,' said the surgeon excitedly. 'He's passed the first crisis, and that's a good sign for my procedure but not healthy for the cause.'

'Why so, Gerhardt?' asked the surgical nurse.

'Because we can't find him!'

'So? He will die shortly, no?'

'Yes, of course, but if he has a cranial haemorrhage and dies among the enemy, their doctors will perform an autopsy. They will find my implant, and that we cannot permit!'

'There's not much you can do about it, so why aggravate yourself?'

'Because he must be found. *I* must find him.'

'How?'

'There will come a time in his last days, his last hours, when he'll have to make contact with me. His confusion will be such that he demands instructions, *demands* them.'

'You haven't answered my question.'

'I know. I don't know the answer.' The telephone rang on the table beside the wife's chair. She picked it up.

'Yes? . . . Yes, of course, *Herr Doktor*.' Greta placed her hand over the phone. 'It's Hans Traupman. He says it's an emergency.'

'I would think so, he rarely calls.' Kroeger took the telephone from his wife. 'This must be an emergency, Doctor. I can't remember when you called me last.'

'General von Schnabe was arrested an hour ago in Munich.'

'Good heavens, what for?'

'Subversive activities, inciting to riot, crimes against the state, all the usual legal garbage our forebears refined in a far more conducive environment.'

'But *how*?'

'Apparently your Harry Latham/Lassiter was not the only infiltrator in our valley.'

'Inconceivable! Each and every one of our followers was put through the most rigorous examinations, even to the point of electronic brain scans that would reveal lying, doubts, the smallest hesitation. I myself devised the procedures; they're foolproof.'

'Perhaps one of them had a change of heart after he or she left the valley. Regardless, Von Schnabe was picked up by the police and identified in a lineup where the accuser could not be seen. According to what little we've learned, it may have been a woman, as there apparently were references to sexual abuse. A middle-level police officer was heard laughing about it with his colleagues in the Munich station.'

'I told the general constantly, warned him repeatedly, about his liaisons with female personnel. He always answered, "With all your learning, Kroeger, you don't understand. A general connotes power, and power is the essence of sex. They *want* me."'

'And he wasn't even a general,' said Traupman over the phone. 'Much less a *von*.'

'Really? I thought—'

'You thought what you were meant to think, Gerhardt,' interrupted the doctor from Nuremberg. 'Von Schnabe is a brilliant student of military operations, a devoted partisan of our cause – few among us could have found, created, and managed our valley – those were his enormous strengths. Actually, in medical terms, he was, *is*, a sociopath of the highest intelligence, the sort of person such movements as ours demand, especially in the initial stages. Afterwards, of course, they are replaced. That was the error of the Third Reich; they believed their false titles, lived them out, and overrode the real generals, the Junkers who might have won the war with a properly timed invasion of England. We will not make those mistakes.'

'What do we do now, *Herr Doktor*?'

'We've arranged for Von Schnabe to be shot in his cell tonight. The assassin will use a silenced pistol. It's not difficult; unemployment is high even among the criminal classes. It must be done before his interrogation begins, specifically the Amytals.'

'And Vaclabruck?'

'It's yours to run for now. What concerns us, what concerns our leader in Bonn, is your computerized robot in Paris. When will he *die*, for God's sake?'

'One day, three days at the outside, he can't last more than that.'

'Good.'

'Excuse me, Herr Traupman, but it is all too possible that he will experience a virtual explosion in his occipital lobe.'

'Where your implant resides?'

'Yes.'

'We must find him before that happens. If they discover one robot, they'll believe there are a thousand others!'

'I said as much to my wife.'

'Greta, of course. What does she suggest?'

'She agrees with me,' replied Kroeger as his wife stood up and shook her head violently. 'I must fly to Paris and meet with our people. First with the Blitzkrieger; they're missing something. Then with our plant at the American Embassy; we must refine what he knows about the Antinayous. Finally, our man at the Deuxième Bureau. He vacillates.'

'Be careful with Moreau. He's one of us in his stomach, but he's a Frenchman. We really don't know which side he's on.'

CHAPTER TWELVE

Drew Latham, now his brother Harry, waited in the shadows of the Trocadéro, behind the statue of King Henry the Innocent, his eyes peering through night-vision binoculars. Nearly a hundred yards across the vast concrete pavement were the equally dark spaces between the statues of Louis the Fourteenth and Napoleon the First. It was the rendezvous point of his last request to Karin de Vries that day. The delivery of selected confidential papers he needed from his 'dead brother's' office. It was almost eleven o'clock, the Paris night illuminated by a summer moon, a professional white hunter's moon in the African veldt, and Drew Latham found comfort in that fact.

Two men emerged from a black sedan parked in the long, kerbed entrance to the great facade of monuments. They wore dark business suits and walked towards the rendezvous, each carrying a briefcase ostensibly holding the papers he had 'urgently requested' from his 'brother's' desk. They were neos, for that last request, as coded, had not been transmitted by Karin de Vries. It was proof that her telephone was tapped within the embassy.

Drew ambled into the scattered groups of strollers, many Parisians, the majority foreign tourists holding cameras. Erratic flashes popped everywhere. The lapels of Drew's jacket were turned up, and a black visored cap partially covered his face as he made his way through the crowds, constantly remaining in the company of one group after another until he was within fifty feet of the rendezvous. He studied the two men between the two imposing statues; they were calm, as immobile as the monuments, the immobility only slightly marred by their slowly turning heads. Latham moved with his current group of tourists, instantly, alarmingly, noting that they were Asian and uniformly much shorter than he. Another small crowd of Westerners was coming from the opposite direction; he joined in, ironically realizing by the language that these sightseers were German. Perhaps it was a favourable omen; then it became practically optimistic. As one, the group closed in on the monument to Napoleon, conqueror of conquerors, and by the stridency of the comments there was a certain unmistakable association. *Sieg Nappy!* thought Drew as he kept his eyes on the two false couriers, now less than ten feet away. It was the moment to do something, but Latham was not sure what it was. Then it came to him. *Les rues de Montparnasse.* Pickpockets! The scourge of the seventh arrondissement.

He chose the thinnest, least imposing woman nearest him and suddenly grabbed her shoulder bag. She screamed, '*Ein Dieb!*' In the semidarkness, Drew threw the purse to an unsuspecting man closest to the first false messenger from the embassy, and pummelled a couple into him, then another man and then another, while shouting unintelligible words in ersatz German. In seconds, a minor riot was taking place in front of Napoleon's statue, the screams reaching a rapid crescendo as everyone in the crowd tried to locate the thief and his stolen property in the shadows. The first illegitimate courier was caught up in the melee; he awkwardly struggled against the encompassing crowd, when suddenly Latham stood in front of him.

'*Heil Hitler,*' said Drew quietly in counterpoint to the surrounding hysterical voices as he punched the man in the throat with all his strength. As the neo collapsed, Latham dragged him away, pulling him into the darkness behind the row of statues that overlooked the Eiffel Tower, its majestic spires bathed in floodlights.

He had to get the man out of the Trocadéro! Get him out but avoid the second courier and whatever backups there were in the black sedan. He had come prepared to this rendezvous as he had to the others, with equipment willingly provided by the Antinayous. A medical spray of Arcane that would numb the vocal cords, a wire garrotte that served to immobilize wrists, and a cellular phone with an untraceable number. He exercised the first two, taking a moment off to render his awakening captive back into unconsciousness, then pulled out the phone from his inside pocket. He dialled the colonel's unlisted home number.

'Yes?' came the soft voice over the line.

'Witkowski, it's me. I've got one.'

'Where are you?'

'The Trocadéro, north side, last statue.'

'The situation?'

'I'm not sure. There's another man, and a car, a black four-door parked above. Who's in it, I don't know.'

'Is the place crowded?'

'Half and half.'

'How did you grab your target?'

'Have we got *time* for this?'

'If I'm to operate effectively, we make time. How?'

'A crowd of tourists near the marks. I stole a purse and started a riot.'

'That's good. We'll escalate. I'll call the police and say we believe an American may have been murdered for his money.'

'They were German.'

'That's hardly relevant. The sirens will be there in a few minutes. Get to the south side and work your way to the street. I'll be there soon.'

'*Jesus*, Stanley, the guy's dead weight!'

'You out of shape?'

'Hell, no, but what do I say if I'm stopped?'

'He's a drunken American. Everyone in Paris loves to hear that. Should I repeat it in French – actually it doesn't matter, you'll do better your way – more believable. Get going!'

True to the colonel's words, ninety seconds later the

clamorous *hee-haws* of the Paris police filled the vast complex of the Trocadéro as five patrol cars converged on the entrance. The crowds raced towards the street and the excitement as Latham, his arms supporting a dragging figure, hurried across the concrete to the south side. Once behind the statuary, he lifted the neo over his shoulder in a fireman's carry and raced up the darkness to the street. The Nazi's body slumped beside him. Drew knelt waiting for Witkowski's signal. It came when an embassy car swerved into the kerb, its lights flashing on and off twice, the basic signal to evacuate.

THE NEW YORK TIMES

TOP SECRET GOV'T LABORATORY ROBBED
Rudolph Metz, Scientist, Disappears. Data Missing

BALTIMORE, Saturday – In the hills of outer Rockland, a little known and highly classified scientific compound housing top-secret experiments in microcommunications called in the authorities this morning, initially because the staff could not reach Dr Rudolph Metz, the internationally renowned fiber-optics scientist, on his telephone or on his beeper. Visits to his residence produced no response. The police, under warrant, broke in and found nothing irregular except for a minimal amount of clothing in the closets of a couple as well off as Dr Metz and his wife. Later, the laboratory's technicians reported that the past year's entire research had been deleted from the computers, leaving in its stead a series of 'frostbites' connoting a virus.

Dr Metz, a seventy-three-year-old former wunderkind of German science and a man who continuously extolled and 'thanked the heavenly Father' for his American citizenship, was a strange person, as was his fourth wife, according to neighbors in Rockland. 'They always kept to themselves, except when his wife would suddenly throw grand parties, showing off her jewelry, but nobody really knew them,' said Mrs Bess Thurgold, who lives next door. 'I couldn't relate to him,' added Ben Marshall, an attorney who lives across the street. 'He'd clam up whenever I mentioned anything political, you know what I mean? I mean, here we were, a bunch of people who'd made it – hell, we couldn't afford to live here if we hadn't – but he never had an opinion. Not even about taxes!'

Unattributed speculation, at this juncture, centers on psychiatric distress induced by overwork, marital problems as a result of the disparity of age between his current wife and the oft-married Metz, and even kidnapping by terrorist organizations who could benefit by extracting his knowledge.

Latham and Stanley Witkowski drove the unconscious body of the false courier directly to the colonel's apartment on the rue Diane. Using the delivery entrance, they took the neo up the freight elevator to Witkowski's floor and dragged him into the colonel's suite of rooms.

'This way we're not official, and that's *bardzo dobrze*,' said Witkowski as they splayed the figure of the would-be killer on the couch.

'What?'

'It means that's "very good". Harry would have understood; he spoke Polish.'

'Sorry about that.'

'It's okay. You did all right tonight . . . Now, we just have to get this cat awake and scare the shit out of him until he talks.'

'How do we do that?'

'Do you smoke?'

'Actually, I'm trying to cut down.'

'I'm not your conscience or someone from your support group. Have you got a *butt*?'

'Well, I carry a few – emergencies, you know.'

'Light one and give it to me.' The colonel began slapping the cheeks of the neo; the killer's eyes began to blink as

Witkowski took the lighted cigarette from Latham. There's a bottle of Evian on my bar over there. Bring it to me.'

'Here it is.'

'Hey, *Junge!*' cried Witkowski, pouring the water over the face of their captive, whose eyes sprung wide. 'Keep those baby-blues open, fella, because I'm going to burn your eyeballs out, okay?' The colonel placed the burning cigarette a quarter of an inch above the neo's left eye.

'*Ah-haa!*' screamed the Nazi. 'Please, *nein!*'

'Are you telling me you're not so tough after all? Hell, you burned people, eyes and all, bodies and all. Are you saying you can't take one eyeball – then, of course, maybe the next?' The lighted cigarette touched the outer jell of the neo's eye.

'*Ahhyaa-ayahh!*' The colonel slowly pulled the cigarette away. 'The sight may come back in that one, but only with proper treatment. Now, if I perform the same operation with your other, it will be different. I'll burn through the retina and, God knows, even I couldn't stand the pain, forget about the blindness.' Witkowski moved the cigarette to the right eye, an ash falling into it. 'Here we go, Wehr-macht, see how it feels.'

'*Nein – nein!* Ask me what you will, but do not *do* this!'

Moments later, the colonel continued while the neo held an ice pack over his left eye. 'Now you know what I'm capable of, Herman, or whatever your name is. Just as you bastards were fifty years ago, when I lost a couple of grandparents in Auschwitz. As far as I'm concerned, I'll put you back on those pillows and not only burn your eyes out, but cut off your balls. Then I'll set you free and see how you handle the streets!'

'Cool it, Stosh,' said Latham, gripping Witkowski's shoulder.

'Don't you tell me to cool *anything*, youngster! My people hid Jews and they were gassed for it!'

'Okay, okay, but right now we need information.'

'Right . . . right.' The colonel breathed deeply, then spoke quietly. 'I got carried away . . . you don't know how I *hate* these bastards.'

'I've got a good idea, Stanley. They killed my brother. The interrogation, please.'

'Right. Who are you, where do you come from, and whom do you represent?'

'I am a prisoner of war and I am not required—'

Witkowski struck the neo's mouth with the back of his free hand, the blow savage, his gold army ring drawing blood. 'There's a war, all right, you scum, but it's not declared, and you're not entitled to a damn thing except what I can dream up for you. And let me assure you, it won't be pleasant.' The colonel looked up at Latham. 'There's an old carbine bayonet of mine on the desk over there, I use it to open envelopes. Be a good lad and bring it to me, will you? We'll see how it opens throats, that's really what it was designed for, you know.'

Drew crossed to the desk and returned with the snub-handled blade as Witkowski probed the flesh around the terrified false courier's neck. 'Here you are, Doctor.'

'Funny you should say that,' said the far older G-2 veteran. 'I was thinking of my mother only last night; she always wanted me to become a doctor, a surgeon, to be exact. If she said it once, she said it a thousand times. "You got big strong hands, Stachu. Be a doctor who operates; they make good money." . . . Let's see if I can get the hang of it.' The colonel jabbed his finger into the soft flesh just above the German's breastbone. 'This feels like a good place to start,' he continued, lowering the point of the blade. 'It's kind of Jell-O-like, and you know how that spreads so easily when you put the edge of a spoon into it. Hell, it ought to be a cinch with a knife, and believe me, this is a real *knife*. Okay, let's start the first incision – how do you like that? "Incision".'

'*Nein!*' shrieked the struggling neo as a trickle of blood

rolled down across his neck. 'What do you *want* from me? I know nothing, I do only as I'm ordered!'

'Who gives you the orders?'

'I don't know! I receive a telephone call – a man, sometimes a woman – they use my code number and I must obey.'

'That's not good enough, scumbucket—'

'He's telling the truth, Stosh,' Latham broke in quickly, stopping Witkowski from cutting further. 'The other night, that driver told me the same thing, practically word for word.'

'What were your orders tonight?' pressed the colonel as the Nazi screamed under the increased pressure of the blade. '*Tonight!*' roared Witkowski.

'To kill him, *ja*, to kill the traitor, but to make sure we take the body far away and burn it.'

'*Burn* it?' interrupted Drew.

'*Ja*, and to cut off the head, burning it also, but in another place, far away from the body.'

'"Far away" . . . ?' Drew stared at the trembling, horror-stricken neo.

'I swear it, that's all I know!'

'The hell it is!' shouted the colonel, drawing more blood. 'I've interrogated hundreds like you, slugball, and I *know*. It's always in your eyes, something you haven't said, haven't told us! . . . A kill's no big deal, the rest of it's a little tougher, maybe a lot more dangerous, carrying around a dead body, cutting off a head, and burning everything. That's even a little weird for you psychopaths. What haven't you told us? *Talk*, or it's the last breath of air in your throat!'

'*Nein*, please! He will die shortly, but he cannot die among the enemy! We must reach him first!'

'He's going to *die*?'

'*Ja*, it cannot be stopped. Three days, four days, that's all he has, all we know. We were to take him tonight, kill him before morning, far away, where he will not be found.'

Latham walked away from the couch, half in a daze, trying

to understand the enigma presented by the Nazi revolutionary. Nothing made sense, except one apparently incontrovertible projection.

'I'm sending this ratface over to French intelligence with our entire testimony, every word he said here, which, actually, we've got, thanks to that little machine on my desk,' said Witkowski.

'You know, Stosh,' countered Drew, turning around and looking at the colonel, 'maybe you should put him on a diplomatic jet to Washington, to Langley, no information available, except to the receivers at the CIA.'

'Good Christ, *why*? This is a French problem.'

'Maybe it's more than that, Stanley. Harry's list. Perhaps we should see who at the Agency tries to protect this man, or, conversely, who tries to kill him.'

'You're beyond me, youngster.'

'I'm beyond myself, Colonel. I'm Harry now, and someone expects me to die.'

CHAPTER THIRTEEN

It was three o'clock in the morning in Monte Carlo, the narrow, dimly lit streets beyond the casino deserted except for stragglers from the still-active gambling palace; a few were despondently drunk, several elated, most weary. Claude Moreau made his way down an alley that led to a stone wall overlooking the harbour. He reached the wall, his eyes scanning the scene below; it was a haven for the world's rich, memorialized by the lights of the huge, luxurious yachts and cabin cruisers at their moorings. He felt no sense of envy whatsoever; he was merely an observer appreciating the surface beauty of it all. His civil servant's lack of jealousy came easily, for his job required that he spend infrequent time among the owners of these opulent craft, watching their lifestyles, often delving deeper. It was enough. If one could categorize, in many ways they were a desperate people, forever seeking out new interests, new experiences, new thrills. The constant seeking became their reality, the search without end, leading only to still another search. They had their comforts; they needed them, for the rest was boredom, looking for the next stimulation that would occupy them. What now? What's new?

'*Allô*, monsieur,' said the voice out of the darkness as a figure approached from the shadows. 'Are you the friend of the Brotherhood?'

'Your cause is futile,' said Moreau without turning. 'I've told you people that a hundred times, but if you continue to better my impoverished circumstances, I'll do as you ask.'

'Our Blitzkrieger, the woman at the table in the casino. You took her away. What *happened*?'

'She took her own life, as the other two did in prison months ago. We are French; we did not, upon her arrest, examine her private areas. If we had, we would have found cyanide capsules encased in plastic.'

'*Sehr gut.* She told you nothing?'

'How could she? She never came out of the ladies' room alive.'

'Then we are clear?'

'For now. And I shall expect the usual payment in Zurich for my considerable cooperation. Tomorrow.'

'It will be done.'

The figure walked away in the darkness as Moreau reached into his breast pocket and turned off his recorder. Unwritten contracts meant nothing, unless their violations were recorded.

Basil Marchand, member of the House of Lords, slammed the brass paperweight down on his desk with such force that the glass cover shattered, sending fragments across the room. The man facing him took a step backward while briefly turning his face away.

'How *dare* you?' shouted the elderly gentleman, his hands trembling with rage. 'The men of this family go back to the Crimea and all the wars since, including the Boer, where a newspaper boy named Churchill extolled their bravery under fire. How can you think to imply such a thing to me?'

'Forgive me, Lord Marchand,' said the MI-5 officer calmly, unflinchingly, 'your family has deservedly received recognition for its military contributions throughout this century, but there was an exception, wasn't there? I refer, of course, to your older brother, who was among the founders of the Cliveden set, which held Adolf Hitler in rather high regard.'

'Drummed out of the family!' Marchand broke in furiously as he yanked open a drawer and pulled out a silver-framed scroll. 'Here, you insolent bugger! This is a citation from the King himself for my boat at Dunkirk. I was a lad of sixteen and brought out thirty-eight men who would have been slaughtered or captured. And that was before I was awarded the Military Cross for my service in the Royal Navy!'

'We're aware of your outstanding heroism, Lord March-and—'

'So don't ascribe to me the warped delusions of an older brother I barely knew – and didn't like what I did know,' continued the outraged member of the House of Lords. 'If you've done your research, *you* should know that he left England in 1940 and never returned, no doubt drank himself to death hiding in one of those South Pacific islands.'

'Not quite accurate, I'm afraid,' said the MI-5 visitor. 'Your brother ended up in Berlin with another name, and worked throughout the war in the Reich's Ministry of Information. He married a German woman and, like you, he had three sons—'

'*What* . . . ?' The old man fell slowly back in his chair, his mouth agape, barely breathing. 'We were never told,' he added so quietly he could hardly be heard.

'There was no point, sir. After the war he disappeared with his entire family, presumably to South America, one of those German enclaves in Brazil or Argentina. Since he was not officially listed as a war criminal, no search was instituted, and considering the losses the Marchands sus-tained—'

'Yes,' Lord Marchand interrupted softly, 'my other two brothers and my sister – two pilots and a nurse.'

'Precisely. Our offices decided to bury the whole nasty business.'

'That was kind of you, very kind. I'm sorry I treated you so shabbily.'

'Not to be concerned. As you said, you couldn't know what you'd never been told.'

'Yes, yes, of course . . . But here, now, this afternoon, you damn near accused me – and by extension, the family – of being part of some Fascist movement in Germany. *Why?*'

'It's a rather clumsy technique few of us are comfortable with, but it's effective. I didn't specifically accuse you, sir; if you recall, I phrased my allusion in terms of "how offended the Crown would be to learn" et cetera, et cetera. The immediate answer is always outrage, but there is false outrage and then there is true outrage. It's not difficult to discern which is which, not if you've been around for a while, and I have.'

'What did I do right?'

'I believe, if you were younger, you would have physically assaulted me, thrown me bodily out of your house.'

'Quite true, I would have.'

'It was a genuine reaction on your part, not false at all.'

'Again, I ask *why?*'

'The names of two of your sons are on a list, a highly confidential list of people who silently support the neo-Nazi revolutionaries in Germany.'

'Good God, *how?*'

'Marchands Limited is a textile complex, is that correct?'

'Yes, of course, everyone knows that. With our factories in Scotland, we're the second largest in the UK. Two of my sons run it since I retired; the third, may the Lord have mercy on his soul, is a musician. So what have they done to warrant such an accusation?'

'They've dealt with a firm called Oberfeld, shipped thousands upon thousands of rolls of fabric for identical shirts, blouses, trousers, and slacks to their warehouses in Mannheim.'

'Yes, I've studied the accounts, which I insist on doing. Oberfeld pays its charges on due-date time and is a splendid customer. So?'

'Oberfeld doesn't exist, it's a front for the neo-Nazi movement. As of seven days ago, the name and the warehouse in Mannheim are gone, disappeared, as your brother disappeared fifty years ago.'

216

'What are you *suggesting*?'

'I'll put this as gently as possible, Lord Marchand. Is it possible that the sons of your brother have come back, and with terrible irony have involved your own unwitting sons in a conspiracy to accelerate the Nazi resurgence by supplying uniforms?'

'*Uniforms?*'

'It's the next step, Lord Marchand. Historically, it's standard.'

Knox Talbot disliked playing God, for too many had played God over his race for too long. He was uncomfortable assuming the position, feeling not a little hypocritical, but he had no choice. The Agency's all-powerful top-secret computers had been compromised, software containing the secrets of the globe invaded, including the most sensitive operations the CIA had mounted across the world, among them Harry Latham's torturous three-year odyssey. Harry Latham/Alexander Lassiter . . . code name, *Sting*.

Under the pretext of rotation assignments, he had requested over three dozen personnel records but only eight demanded his attention. The men and women responsible for the AA-Zero computers, for they alone had the keys, the codes, to learn the secrets that could end the lives of deep-cover agents and informers, or conversely render the operations useless. Someone had – no, more than someone, some *two*, for the locked disks required two people to punch in different codes, freeing the software and permitting screen transmission. But which two, and what had they really accomplished? Harry Latham had escaped, at the terrible price of his brother's life, but he was alive and in hiding in Paris. Not only alive, but he had brought out an incriminating list of names that was already alarming the country, or at least the media, which did its damnedest to alarm the country whenever possible. According to the murdered Drew Latham, the Nazis knew about Sting, but *when* did they know? Before or after Harry had uncovered the names? If before, the entire list was suspect, but even that judgement did not wash with the disappearance of Rudolph Metz, a neo-fanatic if there ever was one. The Rockland laboratories had established that Metz had arrogantly used his own ciphers to extract and delete an entire year's research, and the FBI had traced Metz and his wife's escape to Stuttgart, using false passports, via Dulles International Airport and Lufthansa Flight 7000. How many other Metzes were there? Or to reverse the question, how many other innocent Senator Rootes were there? Everything was spiralling out of control, or soon would be, as the investigations continued.

Two out of eight totally 'white', completely cleared specialists in the most demanding of computer operations were moles. How was it possible? Or even *was* it? There was nothing in their personnel records that gave the slightest hint . . . Then suddenly sections of Harry Latham's London debriefing came back to Talbot. He opened a drawer and pulled out the transcript. He found the page.

> *Q (MI-5): The rumour is that the Nazis, the new Nazis, may have known who you were from the beginning.*
>
> *HL: That's not a rumour, that will be their credo. How often did we do the same thing when we found a mole who fled back to Mother Russia after looting us. Of course we proclaimed how smart we were, and how useless was the information stolen from us – when it wasn't.*
>
> *Q (Deuxième): Isn't it conceivable that you were fed disinformation?*
>
> *HL: I was a trusted confidant until I escaped, a major contributor and a believer in their cause. Why would they feed me dirt? But to answer your question, yes, of course it's conceivable. Disinformation, misinformation, human or computer error, wishful thinking, fantasizing – anything's possible. It's your job to confirm or deny. I've brought you the material, now it's your function to evaluate it.*

Knox Talbot studied the agent's statements. It could be argued that Harry Latham himself left the door wide open. Everything was crazy, crazy with probable confirmations and possible contradictions, except the existence of a spreading Nazi virus in Germany. The CIA director put the transcript away and stared at the eight separated records spread in an arc over his desk. He reread the words but found no hints, nothing of substance. He would take each one and try with all his concentration to read *between* the lines until his eyes were bloodshot. Then, thankfully, his telephone buzzed. He touched the button on his console; his secretary spoke.

'Mr Sorenson on line three, sir.'

'Who's on one and two?'

'Two network producers. They want you to appear on programmes discussing the Bureau's domestic interrogations.'

'I'm out to lunch for a month.'

'I understood that, sir. Line three, unless you want me to tell him the same.'

'No, I'll take it . . . Hello, Wes, please don't add to my aggravation.'

'Let's have lunch,' said Wesley Sorenson. 'We have to talk. By ourselves.'

'I'm kind of obvious, old boy, if you hadn't noticed. Unless you want to go to a restaurant in the darker part of town, where you'd be more obvious than me by a couple of nine yards.'

'Then let's eliminate any yards. The zoo in Rock Creek Park. The bird sanctuary; there's a hot dog stand I was introduced to by my grandchildren. Not bad; it has chilli.'

'When?'

'This is priority. Can you make it in twenty minutes?'

'I guess I have to.'

Oliver Mosedale, a fifty-year-old scholar attached to the Foreign Office and a prominent adviser to Britain's foreign secretary, poured himself a brandy as his young housekeeper filled his pipe, packed it down, and brought it to him. 'Thank you, my child,' he said, crossing to a large leather armchair facing a television set. The pipe securely in his mouth, he sat down with a sigh, placed his drink on a side table, reached into his pocket, and fired his pipe with a gold Dunhill lighter. 'The evening was nothing short of an exhausting bore,' Mosedale continued. 'The chef was undoubtedly drunk – I'm sure the *canard à l'orange* was soaked in Gatorade – and those idiots from Treasury would cut our budgets to the point where we couldn't represent Liechtenstein, much less what's left of the British Empire. It's really all quite mad as well as most irritating.'

'You poor ducks,' said the buxom twentyish housekeeper, more than a trace of cockney in her voice. 'You work too hard, that's what you do.'

'Please don't mention ducks, my dear.'

'Wot?'

'It's what I presumably had for dinner.'

'Sorry . . . Here, let me massage your neck, that always relaxes you.' The girl walked behind the chair and leaned over her employer, her generous breasts, made obvious by her décolletage, touching the back of his head, while her hands moved about his neck and shoulders.

'*Marvellous,*' moaned the foreign service officer, drawing out the word as he reached for his brandy, taking sips between draws on his pipe. 'You do that so well, but then, you do everything well, don't you?'

'I try, Ollie darling. As I may have mentioned, I was brought up to respect men of quality, to do their bidding out of admiration. I'm not one of those scruffs who shout all the time about privileged classes, I'm not. My mum always said, "If the good Lord wanted you to live in a castle, you'd have been born in one." And my mum's a wise old bird, she is. She also says that we should take Christian pride in serving our betters, 'cause somewhere in the Bible it says it's better to give than to get, or sompin' like that. 'Course my pa works on the docks and doesn't have mum's refinements—'

'It really isn't necessary that you talk, dear child,' Mosedale interrupted, his brows arched in controlled frustration. 'As a matter of fact, it's time for the BBC news, isn't it?' He glanced at his watch. 'Indeed, it is! I think that's enough of a massage, my sweet. Why not turn on the telly, then go up and bathe. I'll join you in a while, so wait for me, my angel.'

'Sure, Ollie. And I'll wear that nightie you like so much. God knows it's easy to put on, what there is of it.' The housekeeper-cum-concubine went to the television set, snapped it on, and waited for the proper channel to be in focus. She blew Mosedale a kiss and walked provocatively through the arch to the staircase.

The BBC newsreader, his voice and expression neutral, began with the recent events in the Balkans, shifted to the news out of South Africa, briefly touched on the accomplishments of the Royal Academy of Science, then paused and continued with words that caused Oliver Mosedale to sit up and stare at the figure on the screen.

'Reports out of Whitehall have a number of members of Parliament and other government officials in high dudgeon due to what appear to be ongoing inquiries by British intelligence into their private lives. Jeffrey Billows, MP from Manchester, rose on the floor to denounce what he called "police state" tactics, claiming that his neighbours had been questioned about him, including his vicar. Another MP, Angus Ferguson, shouted that not only had his neighbours been interrogated, but that his garbage had been rummaged, and the bookstore he frequents asked what books he purchases. Apparently, even the Foreign Office is not immune, as several high officials have declared they will resign before being subjected to such "utter nonsense", as one put it. Their names are being withheld at the request of the Foreign Secretary.

These events would seem to mirror the news from the United States, where prominent figures in and out of government are experiencing similar invasions of privacy. A story in the Chicago Tribune *headlined the question, "Is the Hunt for Unreconstructed Communists or for Reconstructed Fascists?" We here at BBC will keep you informed as the story develops.*

Now to the painful, all-too-familiar antics of the Royal family . . .'

Mosedale shot out of his chair, turned off the television, and lurched for the telephone on a Queen Anne table against the wall. Frantically, he dialled. 'What the hell is going *on?*' screamed the adviser to the Foreign Secretary.

'You have time, Rute,' said the female voice on the line. 'We were going to call you early in the morning, suggesting you not go to Whitehall. They haven't reached your section yet, but they're close. You have a reservation on British Air for Munich tomorrow at noon, the ticket's in your name. Everything's been cleared.'

'That's not good enough. I want out tonight!'

'Please hold, I'll check the computers.' The interim silence was torture for Mosedale. Finally the voice came back. 'There's a Lufthansa flight to Berlin at eleven-twenty. Can you make it?'

'You're damned right I can.' Oliver Mosedale hung up the phone, walked into the foyer, and shouted at the base of the staircase. '*Angel*, start packing a bag for me! Just a simple change of clothes like you've done before. Quickly!'

A naked 'Angel' appeared at the railing above. 'Where are you going, luv? I'm about to put on the nightie you like to take off. And then it's heaven, isn't it, Ollie?'

'*Shut* up and do as you're told! I've one more call to make, and when I'm finished I expect my suitcase to be down here!' Mosedale ran back to the Queen Anne table, picked up the phone, and again dialled furiously. 'I'm leaving,' he said to the voice which had only grunted.

'My phone indicator tells me that this is *Rute's* number. Is that you, code Switch?'

'You know goddamned well it is. Take care of my affairs here in London.'

'I've already done so, Switch. The house is on the market, the proceeds to be wired to Bern, when and if there's a sale.'

'You'll probably take half—'

'At least, Herr Rute,' the voice on the line interrupted. 'I think it's quite fair. How many thousands have I transferred to Zurich at my own peril?'

'But you're one of us!'

'No, no, you're mistaken. I'm merely a solicitor who accommodates nefarious men who may or may not be traitors to the Crown. How am I to know?'

'You're nothing but a rotten money-changer!'

'Again, you're wrong, Switch. I'm an expediter, no matter how it frequently pains me. And to tell you the truth, you'll be lucky to receive ten pounds for your house. You see, I really don't like you.'

'You've worked for me – for us – for years! How can you *say* that?'

'So easily, I can't tell you. Farewell, code Switch, and for your edification, the one thing that remains constant between us is the confidentiality between client and solicitor. You see, it's my strength.' The English attorney hung up, and Mosedale looked around the huge sitting room, panicked by the thought that he would never see so many mementoes of his life again. Then he stood up straight, his posture rigid, and recalled the words his father had shouted from the upper staircase when war was declared. 'We'll fight for England, but we'll *spare* Herr Hitler! He is far more right than wrong! The inferior races are corrupting our nations. We will win the temporary conflict, establish a unified Europe, and make him the de facto chancellor of the Continent!'

The young woman called Angel slid a suitcase down the staircase, properly – or improperly, as one would have it – clad in her brief nightgown. 'C'mon, luv, what's goin' on here?'

'I may be able to send for you later, but right now I have to leave.'

'Later? What're you talkin' about, Ollie?'

'There's no time for explanations. I must catch a plane.'

'Wot about me? When are you comin' back?'

'Not for a while.'

'Well, isn't that nice and clear! Wot am I supposed to do?'

'Stay here until someone throws you out.'

'Throws me *out?*'

'You heard me.' Mosedale grabbed the suitcase, rushed to the front door, and opened it, stunned by what he saw. The London fog had turned into a downpour, and two men in raincoats stood on the brick steps to his house. Beyond them, in the street, was a black van with a lateral antenna on the roof.

'Under proper authority, your telephone has been monitored, sir,' said the first man. 'I think it's best you come with us.'

'*Ollie*,' cried the scantily clad maid in the foyer. 'Ain't you gonna introduce me to your friends?'

The shouts of children marshalled in groups by parents and camp counsellors mingled with the shrieks of myriad birds behind the wired screens of the huge aviary in the Rock Creek Park Zoo. The summer crowds were boisterous, the exceptions being Washingtonians who had come to the park for peaceful strolls, away from the hectic pace of the nation's capital. When faced with the hordes of tourists, these natives usually cut their interludes short, preferring the quiet of silent monuments. A particularly nasty condor, its wing-spread at least eight feet, suddenly swooped down from a high perch, screeching as its claws gripped the wires of the enormous cage. Children and adults alike backed away instantly; the glaring eyes of the giant bird conveyed hostile satisfaction.

'That's one mother of a predator, isn't it?' said Knox Talbot, standing behind Wesley Sorenson.

'I've never understood the use of the word *mother* too describe enormity,' replied the director of Consular Operations, looking straight ahead.

'Try tenacity. It was the female's unrelenting aggressiveness in protecting her young that got us through the Ice Age.'

'What were we men doing?'

'Pretty much the same as we're doing now. Out hunting while the women protected the caves from far more dangerous beasts than our quarry.'

'You're particularly biased.'

'I'm particularly married, and that conclusion was drawn by my wife. Since we've only been together thirty-six years, why rock the boat at this early stage?'

'Let's get a hot dog. The stand's about fifty yards to the left and we can sit down on a bench. It's usually crowded, so I doubt anyone will notice us.'

'Chilli gives me gas.'

'Try sauerkraut.'

'Worse.'

'Then just mustard.'

'Ever see how hot dogs are made, Wes?'

'Have *you*?'

'I think I own a company that makes 'em.'

Seven minutes later Sorenson and Talbot sat next to each other, not unlike two grandfathers taking a much-needed respite from their rambunctious grandchildren. 'There's something I can't tell you, Knox,' began the Cons-Op director, 'and you're going to be mad as hell later when you find out.'

'Like our removing Moreau's name from Harry Latham's list, the one we sent to you?'

'There's a distinct similarity.'

'Then we're even. What *can* you tell me?'

'First, I can openly tell you that the request comes from a former G-2 specialist who operated in the Berlin sectors during the bad times. His name is Witkowski, Colonel Stanley Witkowski—'

'Currently chief of security, Paris embassy,' Talbot interrupted.

'You know him?'

'Only by reputation. He's a man so bright that he could have been right behind you for my job if he'd gotten the recognition he deserved. But he couldn't; he worked in the silent zone.'

'Right now he's apparently working as a conduit for Harry Latham, who won't risk reaching Langley himself.'

'The AA-Zero computers?'

'Apparently . . . Látham wanted a sub-rosa route to you but he doesn't know you. Remember, you became the DCI with the new administration, almost two years after Harry went deep. So knowing Witkowski from the old days, he used him; and since I've known the colonel from those same days, *he* decided to use me as the sub-rosa.'

'Logical,' said Talbot, nodding his head.

'Maybe logical, Knox, but later, when I can come clean, you'll see it's so ironic, you may even forgive me.'

'What's the sub-rosa?'

'There's a man, a German doctor, who may have enormous influence in the Nazi movement, or, conversely, may be a man with a conscience who's turned against them. We have to learn everything we can about him, and you people are the kings of the hill in that department.'

'So I'm told,' agreed the DCI. 'What's his name?'

'Kroeger, Gerhardt Kroeger. But there's a catch and it's a big one.'

'Do tell.'

'You've got to go underground with this, and I mean deep. His name can't be circulated within the Agency.'

'The AA-Zero computers again?'

'The straight answer to that is yes, but there could also be others beyond the computers. Can you do it?'

'I think so. When I took this job, the job you should have taken, I insisted on bringing along my secretary of twenty years. She's quick and bright to the point that I don't have to finish sentences. She's also British; that apparently gives her a certain authority over us colonials . . . Kroeger, Gerhardt, medicine man, the works. She'll go down to the vaults herself and bring up everything there is.'

'Thank you.'

'You're welcome. I'll call you when I've got the papers. We'll have a few drinks at my place.'

'Fine, I appreciate it.'

'There's something else neither of us has said, isn't there, Wesley?'

'The witch-hunts, naturally. Harry's list is getting out of control.'

'I said the very same thing to myself only moments before your call. Have you heard the latest from the UK?'

'The outcry in Parliament, yes. Even the insidious comparisons to what's happening here. I suppose it couldn't be avoided. *Sua culpa*, Secretary Bollinger, and I hope he knows it.'

'Then you haven't heard. We get this stuff before you, I suppose.'

'What are you talking about?'

'A man named Mosedale, very high up in the Foreign Office.'

'What about him?'

'Faced with various alternatives, he confessed. He's been working for the Brotherhood for the past five years. He was on Harry's list, and he claims there are hundreds, perhaps thousands, like him everywhere.'

'Oh, my *God*. Gasoline tanks on the fires. Everywhere.'

CHAPTER FOURTEEN

Gerhardt Kroeger walked out to the transportation platform at Orly Airport carrying two pieces of luggage, a medical bag, and a medium-size nylon suitcase, both carry-ons. He veered to the left and proceeded down the long concrete walkway until he saw the area designated as PETITE CARGAISON, small cargo. He scanned the constantly moving traffic, then centred in on the few vehicles parked at the kerb in front of the huge sliding metal doors through which precleared cases and cartons of merchandise were wheeled on dollies to those waiting for them. He saw what he hoped to see, a grey van with white lettering on the side. ENTREPÔTS AVIGNON, the Avignon Warehouses, a massive market depot where over a hundred distributors kept their consumer goods prior to delivering them to retail stores throughout Paris. And somewhere within that mazelike complex were the quarters of the Blitzkrieger, the elite assassins of the Brotherhood. The doctor approached a man in a red and white rugby shirt leaning against the side of the vehicle. As he had been ordered to do.

'Has the Malasol arrived, monsieur?' he asked.

'The best caviar from Iranian waters,' replied the muscular man in the rugby shirt, flipping away a cigarette and staring at Kroeger.

'Is it really better than the Russian?' continued Gerhardt.

'Anything's better than Russian.'

'Good. Then you know who I am.'

'No, I don't know who you are, monsieur, and I do not

care to know. Just get in the back with the rest of the fish, and I'll take you to another who does know you.'

The ride to their destination was odious for Gerhardt, both in terms of the overpowering smell of iced fish and the fact that he was forced to sit on a hard-slatted bench while the tight-springed van raced over potholed roads that might have been the remnants of the Maginot line. Finally, after nearly thirty minutes, they stopped, and a harsh voice came over an unseen speaker.

'*Out*, monsieur. And please to remember, you never saw us, and we never saw you, and you never were carried in our truck.' The rear doors of the van opened mechanically. Kroeger grabbed his luggage, bent over so as not to hit his head on the roof, and squat-walked to his exit and fresh air. A youngish man in a dark suit, with close-cropped hair, studied him in silence as the van sped away, its tyres screeching in a hasty retreat.

'What kind of transport was *this*?' exclaimed Gerhardt. 'Do you know who I *am*?'

'Do you know who we are, Herr Kroeger? If so, your question is foolish. Our presence must be the most secret in France.'

'We'll discuss that when I meet your superiors. Take me to them immediately!'

'There's no one superior to me, *Herr Doktor*. I insisted on meeting you myself.'

'But you're – you're . . .'

'So young, sir? . . . Only the young can do what we do. Our reflexes are at the height of their powers, our bodies superbly trained. Old men like you would be disqualified during the first hour of indoctrination.'

'That said and agreed to, *you* should be disqualified within *two* hours for not carrying out your orders!'

'Our unit is the best. May I remind you that they killed one of the targets under the most hostile conditions—'

'Not the *right* one, you imbecile!'

'We'll find the other. It's merely a question of time.'

229

There is no time! We must talk further; you've missed something. Let's go to your headquarters.'

'*No*. We talk here. No one goes to our offices. We've made arrangements for you; the Hotel Lutetia, once the headquarters of the Gestapo. It has changed, but the memories are in the walls. You will be comfortable, *Herr Doktor*.'

'We must talk *now*.'

Then talk, Herr Kroeger. You will go no farther.'

'You're insubordinate, young man. I am now the commandant of Vaclabruck until a replacement for Von Schnabe is named. You'll take your orders from me.'

'I beg to differ, *Herr Doktor*. Since General von Schnabe's removal, we've been instructed to take our orders solely from Bonn, from our leader in Bonn.'

'Who *is*?'

'If I knew, I would have been sworn to secrecy, but since I don't, it doesn't matter. Codes are used, and through them we recognize their absolute authority. All our assignments must be sanctioned by him, and only him.'

'This Harry Latham must be hunted down and killed. There's not a moment to waste!'

'We understand that, Bonn made it clear.'

'Yet you stand there and say to me quite casually that it's "merely a question of time"?'

'It wouldn't help matters to shout, *mein Herr*. Time is measured in seconds, minutes, hours, days, weeks, an—'

'Stop it! This is a crisis and I demand that you accept the fact.'

'I do – we do, sir.'

'So what have you done, what are you doing? And where in hell are your two men? Have you heard from them?'

The young Blitzkrieger, his body rigid but his eyes flickering with insecurity, answered slowly, quietly. 'As I explained to Catbird, Herr Kroeger, there are several possibilities. They escaped but both were wounded, how severely we don't know. If their situations were hopeless, they would have done the honourable thing, as each of us has sworn to do, and taken themselves out with cyanide or gunshots to their heads.'

'You're saying you haven't heard from them.'

'Correct, sir. But we know they escaped in the car.'

'How do you know it?'

'It was in all the papers and on the news broadcasts. Also, we've learned that there is a massive search for them, a manhunt employing the police, the Sûreté, even the Deux-ième Bureau. They've spread out everywhere: towns, vil-lages, even the hills and the forests, questioning every doctor within two hours of Paris.'

'Then your conclusion is dual suicide, yet you said there were several possibilities. What others?'

'That is the strongest, sir, but it is conceivable that they are getting their strength back, minimally recuperating, out of reach of a telephone. As you are aware, we are trained like animals to succour our wounds out of sight until we are strong enough to make contact. We are all schooled in advanced aid to bodily punctures and the setting of broken bones.'

'That's splendid. I'll turn in my licence and send my patients to you.'

'It's not a joke, *mein Herr*, we are simply trained to survive.'

'Any other "possibilities"?'

'You're asking if they were captured, no?'

'Yes.'

'We'd know it if they were. Our informers in the embassy would have picked it up, and the manhunt has been established beyond question. The French government has over a hundred personnel looking for our unit. We've watched them, heard them.'

'You're persuasive. So what else? Where are you? Harry Latham must be found!'

'We believe we're closing in, sir. Latham is under the protection of the Antinayous—'

'We *know* that!' Kroeger broke in angrily. 'But knowing it means nothing if you don't know where they are or where they've hidden him.'

'We may learn the whereabouts of their central headquarters within two hours, *mein Herr*.'

'*What?* . . . Why didn't you say that before?'

'Because I'd prefer to present you with an accomplished fact rather than speculation. I said "we may learn", we haven't yet.'

'How?'

'Telephone contact with the Antinayous was made by the embassy's security chief, whose phone, like the ambassador's, is swept for intercepts. However, there's a sealed log of the calls he's made; our man thinks he can get a look at it and run a handheld photocopier down the list. Once we have the numbers, we can easily bribe someone in the telephone company to unearth the locations. From that point it is a process of elimination.'

'It sounds too simple. It's my understanding that unpublished numbers are well guarded, God knows ours are. I doubt you can walk into the office of a telephone official and put money on his desk.'

'We won't walk into any office. I used the word *unearth* and that's exactly what I mean. We find a worker in the underground trunk lines, for that's where the true locations are in the computers. They have to be, for installations and repairs.'

'You seem to know your business, Herr – what is your name?'

'I have no name, none of us does. I am Number Zero One, Paris. Come, I've arranged transportation for you and we'll stay in constant touch, perhaps within minutes after you reach your hotel.'

Sitting at the desk in his rooms at the Antinayous' Maison Rouge, Drew picked up the telephone and dialled the embassy, asking the switchboard to connect him with Mrs de Vries in Documents and Research.

'This is Harry Latham,' said Drew in response to Karin's greeting. 'Can you talk?'

'Yes, monsieur, there is no one here, but first I have instructions for you. The ambassador summoned me and asked me to deliver them to you when you next called.'

'Go on,' said Latham, now his dead brother Harry, squinting, and listening carefully. Karin was about to send him a message. He picked up a pencil as she spoke.

'You are to make contact with our Courier Number Sixteen at the top of the funicular in Sacré-Coeur at nine-thirty this evening. He has communiqués from Washington for you . . . You understand, *non*?'

'I understand, yes,' replied Drew, knowing that the French *non*, rather than the usual *n'est-ce pas*, meant he was to disregard the information. Witkowski was setting another trap, based on the knowledge that Karin's phone was tapped. 'Anything else?'

'Yes. You were scheduled to meet your brother Drew's friend from London's Cons-Op office at the fountains in the Bois de Boulogne at eight forty-five, correct?'

'Yes, it was cleared.'

'It's cancelled, monsieur. It interferes with the Sacré-Coeur contact.'

'Can you reach him and call it off?'

'We have, *oui* – yes. We'll arrange another meeting.'

'Please do. He can tell me things I want to know about Drew's last weeks, especially the details of the Jodelle business . . . Is that all?'

'For now, yes. Did you have something?'

'Yes. When can I come back to the embassy?'

'We'll let you know. We're convinced it's being watched around the clock.'

'I don't like this hiding out. It's damned inconvenient.'

'You can always return to Washington, you know that.'

'No! This is where *Drew* was killed, this is where his killers are. I'm staying here until we find them.'

'Very well. You'll call tomorrow?'

'Yes, I want more papers from my brother's files. Everything he's got on that actor.'

'Au revoir, monsieur.'

'Bye.' Latham hung up the phone and studied the brief notes he had made, brief because he quickly understood the method of Karin's concealed instructions. The Sacré-Coeur was out and the fountains at the Bois de Boulogne in; the French *non* eliminated the first, the double *oui*-yes confirmed the second. The rest was merely 'fill' to emphasize 'Harry' Latham's insistence on remaining in Paris. Whom he was to meet at the Bois, he had no way of knowing, but he would obviously recognize whoever it was, or if he did not, someone would reach him.

At the end of his shift, the Brotherhood's informer in Communications at the embassy had walked out into the Gabriel, waited, then suddenly crossed the avenue, brushing up against a man on a motorcycle. He slipped the cartridge to the cyclist and the motorcycle shot away down the street, weaving between the traffic. Twenty-six minutes later, at precisely 4:37 in the afternoon, the tape was delivered to the assassins' hidden headquarters at the Avignon Warehouses.

Holding a 5-inch-by-6-inch photograph of Alexander Lassiter/Harry Latham, the Blitzkrieger's Zero One, Paris, for a third time listened to the tape recording of the telephone conversation between Latham and the De Vries woman.

'It would seem our search has ended,' said Zero One, standing above the table and reaching down to shut off the cassette player. 'Who will go to the Sacré-Coeur?' he asked, addressing his colleagues around the conference table.

As one, they all raised their hands.

'Four of you will be sufficient, more could be obvious,' continued the leader. 'Split up and carry the photograph with you, remembering that Latham will no doubt disguise his appearance.'

'What can he do?' asked the Blitzkrieger nearest Zero One. 'Put on a moustache and wear a beard? We know his height, the nature of his build, and his facial structure. Ultimately, he will reach a courier who will be waiting for him, a stationary man or woman we'll certainly spot within the contact area.'

'Don't be so optimistic, Zero Six,' said the young leader. 'Bear in mind that Harry Latham is an experienced deep-cover agent. As we have tricks, so does he. And for God's sake, remember the kill must be made through the head, a coup de grâce shattering the left side of his skull. Don't ask me why, just don't forget it.'

'If you have such serious doubts about us,' interjected an older Blitzkrieger at the far end of the table, his tone of voice in the zone of implied hostility, 'why don't you go yourself?'

'Instructions from Bonn,' answered Zero One coolly. 'I'm to remain here for orders that will arrive at ten o'clock. Would any of you care to take my place in the event we have not found Harry Latham and must deliver the news?'

'Non.' 'Nein.' 'Of course not.' These were the responses of those around the table, some chuckling, others grim.

'However, I will cover the Bois de Boulogne.'

'Why?' asked Zero Seven. 'It's cancelled; you heard the tape.'

'Again, I ask *you*, would any of you *not* care to cover the Boulogne in the event that an emphatic negative was the signal for a positive, or that plans were changed again?'

'You have a point,' said Zero Seven.

'Probably a useless one,' conceded the youthful leader. 'Nevertheless, it will take me no more than fifteen or twenty minutes, then I'll drive back and be here by ten o'clock. If I were in Sacré-Coeur, I'd never make it on time.'

The unit for the Sacré-Coeur selected, Zero One, Paris, returned to his office and sat down at his desk. He was a relieved man, for his mythical instructions from Bonn had not been questioned, nor had anyone insisted that, as their superior, he should lead the assault on Harry Latham and let someone else take the call from Bonn. In truth, he wanted no part of the kill for the simple reason that it might not be successful. Any number of unforeseen contingencies could prevent it, and Zero One, Paris, could not afford another 'miss' on his record, like the driver who had been no match for the late Drew Latham, or the unit sent to take out two Americans, which had missed the vital one and then disappeared, or their female comrade who had not survived Monte Carlo. Should Alexander Lassiter/Harry Latham be properly executed, shattered skull included, he could take the credit, for he had orchestrated the assault. If the trap failed, he wasn't there; others were to be blamed.

For Paris's Zero One understood what the others did not; as their leader he was to carry out the orders. If a Blitzkrieger failed once, he was severely reprimanded; if he failed twice, he was shot, another in training given his or her place. If Sacré-Coeur failed, he knew who would be eliminated – the thirty-year-old Zero Five, for a start; his resentment of his younger superior was surfacing too frequently . . . and he had strenuously objected to the selection of the unit that had disappeared. 'One's a baby who simply likes to kill, and the other's a bull head; he takes too many risks! Let *me* handle it!' Those had been Zero Five's words, spoken in front of Zero Six. Both were heading out to Sacré-Coeur; both would be executed if the kill failed. Zero One, Paris, could not allow another blemish on his record. He *had* to be brought into the inner circle of the Brotherhood; he had to gain the respect of the true leaders of the movement, of the new *Führer* himself, and pay his obeisance with all his heart and soul. For he believed, he truly believed.

He would take his camera out to the Bois de Boulogne, snapping enough night photographs to prove he was there, the proof in the camera itself as it imprinted the date and the time of each picture. It was merely a cover, if he ever needed one, which he doubted.

The telephone rang, startling the young superior Blitz-krieger. He picked it up.

'The code's right,' said the female operator, 'it's Malasol caviar on the line.'

'*Herr Doktor*—'

'You haven't called!' cried Gerhardt Kroeger. 'I've been here over three hours and you haven't *called* me.'

'Only because we are refining the strategy. If my subordinates do not miscalculate, we may achieve the objective, *mein Herr*. I have orchestrated it down to the last detail.'

'Your *subordinates*? Why not *you*?'

'A contradictory piece of information was received, sir, one that may be far more dangerous and possibly equally productive. I have decided to take the risk myself.'

'You're not making sense!'

'Nor can I over the telephone.'

'Why *not*? The enemy hasn't the slightest idea who I am, or that I'm even here, so the hotel's switchboard could hardly be compromised. I demand to know what's happening!'

'There are two situations converging within the hour. Tell Bonn that Zero One, Paris, has used all of his talents to control both, but he cannot be in two places at once. Since he cannot, he's chosen to take the highest risk. That's all I can tell you, *mein Herr*. If I do not survive, think well of me. I must go.'

'Yes . . . yes, of course.'

The young neo-revolutionary slammed down the phone. No matter what happened, he was covered. He would have a long, leisurely dinner at the Au Coin de la Famille, then stroll to the main fountain in the Bois de Boulogne, take useless photographs, and return to the Avignon Warehouses, accepting whatever took place. Either the credit for the kill, or the death of two Blitzkrieger executed for incompetence. He truly believed.

Drew moved about the Bois de Boulogne's glistening fountain, bathed in floodlights from the waters below, and meandered through the evening strollers, looking for a face he knew. He had arrived at the rendezvous shortly before eight-thirty; it was now nearly nine o'clock, and he had seen no one he recognized, nor had anyone approached him. Had he misread Karin's instructions? Had the reversed words presumed an acknowledged reversal on the part of those tapping her phone, and thus were they to be taken literally? No, that made no sense. Karin's Amsterdam years notwithstanding, they did not know each other well enough to play cover-recover games; they had no history of intuitive communication under stress. Latham looked at his watch; it was 9:03. He would circle the area once more, then return to the Maison Rouge.

'*Américain!*' He spun around at the sound. It was Karin, her face crowned by a blonde wig, her right hand bandaged. 'Walk to your left, *quickly*, as if I'd bumped into you. There's a man taking photographs on the right. Meet me on the north path.'

Latham did as he was told, relieved at knowing she was there but concerned by her words. He circled his way in the lackadaisical rhythm of the fountain crowds until he reached the flagstone path to his extreme right. He entered it, walked up the tree-lined tunnel thirty or forty feet, and waited. Two minutes later Karin arrived ... As if by an accident neither anticipated, they fell into each other's arms, holding one another, not long, but long enough.

'I'm sorry,' said De Vries, pushing herself gently away and uselessly brushing her blonde wig with her bandaged right hand.

'I'm not,' Drew interrupted, smiling. 'I think I've wanted to do that for a couple of days now.'

'Do what?'

'Hold you.'

'I was simply pleased to see that you were all right.'

'I'm all right.'

'That's very nice.'

'It was also nice to hold you.' Latham laughed softly. 'Look, lady, you put the idea in my head. You were the one who said your excuse at the embassy was that you found me attractive, et cetera, et cetera.'

'It was not a self-fulfilling wish, Drew. It *was* an excuse, strategically employed.'

'Come on, I'm not Quasimodo, am I?'

'No, you're a rather large, not ungainly fellow who, I'm sure, many women find quite attractive.'

'But not you.'

'My concerns lie elsewhere.'

'You mean I'm not Freddie – "Freddie de V", the incomparable.'

'No one could be Freddie, the good *or* the ugly.'

'Does that mean I'm still in the race?'

'What race?'

'For your affections, maybe, as temporary and as little as they may be.'

'Are you talking about sleeping with me?'

'Hell, that's down the road. Remember, I'm an American from New England. Way down the road, lady.'

'You're also a prevaricator.'

'A what?'

'I won't say a liar, that's too harsh.'

'*What?*'

'You're also a brutal man who smashes other men into whatever it's called in hockey matches. Oh, yes, I've heard. Harry told me.'

'Only when they got in my way. Never gratuitously.'

'Who made those decisions?'

'I did, I guess.'

'My point is made. You're a belligerent individual.'

'What the hell has that got to do with anything?'

'Only, at the moment, I'm grateful that you are.'

'What?'

'The man with the camera, at the other side of this fountain.'

'What about him? People take pictures of Paris at night. Toulouse-Lautrec painted them, today they take photos.'

'No, he's a neo, I feel it, I *know* it.'

'How?'

'The way he stands, the way he's so . . . so aggressive.'

'That's not a lot to go on.'

'Then why is he here? How many people really take pictures at night in the Bois de Boulogne?'

'You've got a point. Where is he?'

'Directly across from us – or he was. On the south path.'

'Stay here.'

'No, I'll go with you.'

'Goddammit, do as I say.'

'You cannot order me!'

'You don't have a gun, and even if you did, you couldn't fire it. Your hand's all wrapped up.'

'I *do* have a weapon, and if you were more alert, you'd know I'm left-handed.'

'What?'

'Let's go.'

Together they raced through the trees until they reached the south path that led to the illuminated fountain. The man taking photographs was still there, ramrod-straight and snapping what seemed to be random shots of the strollers circling the fountain. Silently, Latham approached, his hand gripping the automatic in his belt. 'You get your kicks taking pictures of people who don't know they're being photographed,' said Drew, tapping the man on the shoulder.

The Blitzkrieger whipped around at his touch, staring at Drew in the dim light, his eyes bulging. '*You!*' he cried gutturally. 'But no, *not* the same! Who *are* you?'

240

'I've got one for *you*.' Latham grabbed the man by the throat, hurling him into the trunk of a tree. '*Kroeger!*' he shouted. 'Who's Gerhardt Kroeger?'

The neo recovered quickly, instantly kicking his boot up into Drew's groin; Latham leapt backward, avoiding the blow, and smashed the barrel of his automatic into the Nazi's face. 'You son of a bitch, you were looking for me, *weren't* you?'

'*Nein!*' screamed the neo, blood spreading across his face, partially blinding him. 'You are not the man in the photograph!'

'But someone like me, right? Same kind of face, sort of, *right?*'

'You are *crazy!*' shrieked the Nazi, levelling a lethal chop to Drew's neck; Latham gripped the wrist and twisted it violently counterclockwise. 'I was only taking photographs!' The man fell into the bushes.

'Now that we've established that,' said Drew breathlessly, straddling the neo, then suddenly crashing his knee into the man's ribcage, 'let's talk about Kroeger!' Latham pressed the barrel of the automatic into the flesh between the Nazi's eyes. 'You tell me or you've got a tunnel in your head!'

'I am prepared to die!'

'That's nice, because you're about to. You've got five seconds, Adolf . . . One, two, three . . . four—'

'*Nein!* . . . He's here in Paris. He must find *Sting!*'

'And you thought I was Sting, correct?'

'You are not the same man!'

'You're damned right I'm not. *Sit* up!'

Where it came from, Drew would never know, but before he could adjust, a large pistol was in the neo's right hand. Without any sound preceding it, a loud gunshot suddenly came from behind them; the Nazi's head snapped back, blood flowing from his neck. Karin de Vries had saved Latham's life. She ran down the path to him. 'Are you all right?' she cried.

'Where did he get the *gun*?' asked a shaken, bewildered Drew.

'The same place you got yours,' answered De Vries.

'What?'

'The belt. You grabbed him and told him to sit up; that's when I saw him reaching under his jacket.'

'*Thank* you—'

'Don't thank me, *do* something. People are running away from the fountain. Soon the police will be here.'

'Come on!' ordered Latham, shoving the automatic into his belt and pulling the cellular phone from his inside pocket. 'Into the trees – way into.' Awkwardly, they raced through roughly sixty feet of dark foliage when Drew held up his hand. 'This'll do,' he said, out of breath.

'Where did you get that?' asked Karin, pointing at the barely visible outline of the telephone in Latham's hands.

'The Antinayous,' replied Drew, squinting and touching the buttons in the dim, filtered light from the fountain. 'They're very high-tech.'

'Not when anyone can scan into a mobile phone's frequency, although in emergencies, I suppose—'

'*Stanley*?' said Latham, cutting her off. 'Christ, it happened again! The Bois de Boulogne; a neo was covering the area, sent to take me out.'

'*And*?'

'He's dead, Stosh, Karin shot him when he was about to blow my head off ... But, Stanley, listen to me. He said Kroeger was here in Paris, here to find Sting!'

'What's your situation?'

'We're in the woods off a path, maybe twenty or thirty yards from the body.'

'Now, you listen to me,' said Witkowski harshly. 'If you can do it without running into the police – hell, even if you risk running into them – pick that bastard's pockets clean and get out of there.'

'Like I did with Harry...' Drew's voice dropped to a painful whisper.

'Do it *for* Harry now. If what you say about this Kroeger isn't second-hand nonsense, that corpse is our only link to him.'

'For a moment he thought I was Harry; he's got a photograph, he said.'

'You're wasting time!'

'Suppose the police arrive . . . ?'

'Use your well-known bullshit officialese to talk your way out of it. If that doesn't work, I'll take care of it later, although I'd rather not go by the book on this. Get going!'

'I'll call you later.'

'Make it sooner rather than later.'

'Come on,' said Latham, grabbing Karin's right wrist above the bandage and heading for the path.

'Back *there*?' cried De Vries, stunned.

'Our colonel's orders. We've got to move fast—'

'But the police!'

'I know, so even faster . . . I've got it! You stay on the path, and if the police come, act frightened, which won't take much talent if you're anything like me, and tell them your boyfriend stepped into the woods to take a leak.'

'Not impossible,' conceded Karin, holding on and dodging the trees and the underbrush with Latham. 'More American than French, but not impossible.'

'I'll drag our would-be killer into the woods and sweep him clean. He also has a better watch than mine; I'll take that too.'

They reached the path, the fountain below now practically deserted, only a few morbidly curious observers scattered about the borders. Several kept glancing down the other paths, obviously expecting the police. Drew pulled the corpse feet-first into the brush and went through the pockets, removing everything that was in them. He did not bother to look for the weapon that came within a second of ending his life; it would tell them nothing. Finished, he rushed back to the path and Karin as the shouts came from below.

'Les gendarmes, les gendarmes! De l'autre côté!'

'Où?'

'Où donc?'

Fortunately, in answer to the two police officers' demands of *where* 'on the other side', the remaining civilians pointed in various directions, including several shadowed paths. Frustrated, the policemen split and raced down different paths. It was enough; Latham and De Vries ran across the open fountain and up the north path again until it levelled out, and they found themselves in the splendour of summer gardens surrounding a small man-made pond where white swans paddled majestically under the wash of floodlights. They spotted an empty bench, and with very little breath in either of their lungs, sat down, their spines slumping against the back slats. Karin tore the blonde wig from her head and shoved it into her purse, shaking her hair loose.

'As soon as I can talk, I'll call Witkowski,' said Drew, breathing deeply. 'How's your hand? Does it hurt?'

'You can think of my hand at a time like this?'

'Well, I grabbed it back there because you were still holding the gun in your left and I thought the goddamned thing might go off if I reached for it – your left hand, I mean.'

'I know what you mean. There was no time to put it back in my purse then . . . Call the colonel, please.'

'Okay.' Latham again removed the cellular phone from his pocket and dialled, thankfully seeing the numbers clearly under the pond's floodlights. 'Stanley, we made it,' he said.

'Someone else didn't, lad,' interrupted the colonel. 'And we don't know how the hell it happened.'

'What are you talking about?'

'That neo scumbucket I put on a military jet under a drape to Washington at five o'clock this morning.'

'What about him?'

'He arrived at Andrews Air Force Base at three-thirty A.M., DC time – total darkness, incidentally – and was shot while under military escort to the waiting area.'

'*How?*'

'A damned powerful rifle with an infrared scope on one of the roofs. Naturally, nothing was found.'

'Who was looking?'

'Who knows? As we agreed, I let the word out on a need-to-know basis to Knox Talbot's top senior officers that we had a genuine Nazi, when he was flying in, and all the rest.'

'So?'

'Someone hired a gun.'

'So where are we?'

'Narrowing everything down, that's where we are. We know about the AA computers, now we've got another four or five deputy directors on the list. That's how it's done, youngster, you keep closing the doors until there's only one or two left in a room.'

'What about me, what about Paris?'

'It's a cat-and-mouse, isn't it, lad? This Kroeger wants to find Harry – *you* – as much as you want to find him, isn't that so?'

'Apparently, but why?'

'We'll only know that when we catch him, won't we?'

'You're not very comforting—'

'I don't care to be, get that straight. I want you on your uppers every minute of the day and night.'

'Thanks a lot, Stosh.'

'Bring me whatever you've got—'

'I grabbed everything there *was*,' Latham broke in furiously. 'So don't say "whatever". Except I forgot to take the goddamned *watch*!'

'I like that,' said the colonel. 'I like anger in situations like this. My place, in an hour, and make three changes of vehicles.'

CHAPTER FIFTEEN

The flames shot upward, bright bursts of fire illuminating the darkness. The enormous Vaclabruck complex was nearly completed, including a vast scythed-down field descending from a sloping hill that held fifteen hundred selected disciples of the Brüderschaft from all over the world. The night was cloudless and the torches filled the huge natural arena, both along the surrounding borders as well as in front of the dais, a fifty-foot-long table on the crest of the hill where the leaders sat. The microphone was in the centre lectern, its wires leading to speakers throughout the area, and on top of tall poles behind the imposing table, spotlighted and fluttering in the breezes, were the bloodred and black flags of the Third Reich, with one startling difference. A white lightning bolt shot down across the swastikas. It was the banner of the Fourth Reich.

A series of speakers, all in the military uniforms of Nazi Germany, had spoken, their exhortations bringing the audience to clamorous crescendos of fanatical endorsement. Finally, the next-to-last orator approached the centre of the dais; he gripped the lectern, his fiery gaze sweeping over the serried ranks, and spoke with quiet, echoing authority.

'You have heard it all tonight, the cries of those around the world who need us, *demand* us, *insist* that we take up the sword of global order, purifying the races and eliminating the human and ideological garbage that pollutes the civilized world. And we stand *ready*!'

The applause, pulsated by roars of approval, rocked the ground, reverberating throughout the surrounding forests.

The uniformed man held up his hands for silence; it came quickly, and he continued.

'But to lead us, we must have a *Zeus*, a *Führer* greater than the last – not in thought, for no one could surpass Adolf Hitler in philosophy – but in strength and determination, a leader who will strike down the timid and not be stopped by the cautious strategies of military intellectuals; who will smite the enemies of racial progress, and will attack when he knows the time is right! History has proved that had the Third Reich invaded England when Herr Hitler ordered his armies to do so, we would have a different and far better world than we have today. He was persuaded *not* to by the privileged dilettantes of the Junker corps. Our new leader, our *Zeus*, will never submit to such cowardly interference . . . However, and I know this will be a disappointment, it is not yet the time to reveal his identity, even to you. Instead, he has recorded a message for you, for each and every one of you.'

The next-to-last orator shot his right arm up in the Nazi salute. As he abruptly snapped it back, an amplified voice came from the speakers everywhere. It was a strange voice, mid-deep, sharp, and cutting, each echoing consonant delivered like a swinging axe meeting hard wood. In some ways it evoked the memory of Hitler's diatribes in the sense that the hysterical climaxes came numerously and rapidly, but there the similarity ended. For this speaker was more of this age; the shock value of his screaming apogees was preceded by cold words, spoken slowly, icily, followed by sudden bursts of emotional excess that lent power to his conclusions. His harangues were not diminished by the shrieking one-note delivery of Hitler; instead, they were heightened by contrast, as if he were confiding in his audience, who undoubtedly understood every point he was leading up to, then rewarded their acumen by shouting, affirming the judgements they had already made. The Age of Aquarius was long gone; the age of manipulation had taken its place. The lessons of Madison Avenue were heeded across the world.

'We are at the beginning, and the future is *ours*! But you know that, don't you? You who work tirelessly here in the Fatherland, and you who labour unceasingly in foreign countries – you can see what is happening, can't you? And isn't it *magnificent*? The message we bring is not only accepted, but zealously desired, *desired* in the hearts and minds of people everywhere – and you do see that and *hear* that, and you *know* it! . . . I cannot see you, but I hear you, and I accept your gratitude, although, to be frank, it is misplaced. I am merely *your* voice, the voice of the righteously discontented all over the civilized globe. And you understand that, *don't* you? You understand the agony we face everywhere when inferior people make us *pay* for their inferiority! When industrious men and women are deprived of their hard-earned benefits by those who refuse to work, or are incapable of working, or too demented even to *try*! Are we to suffer for their laziness, their incompetence, or their derangement? If so, the indolent, the incompetent, and the deranged will rule the world! For they will rob us of our moral leadership by *overwhelming* us, draining our coffers in the name of humanity – but no, it is not humanity, my soldiers, for they are *garbage*! . . . But they cannot and will not do that, for the future is *ours*!

'Everywhere our enemies are increasingly confused, bewildered by what is sweeping over them, not sure who is and who is not part of us, in their deepest thoughts applauding our progress, even as they deny those thoughts. Continue the march, my soldiers. The future is *ours*!'

Again, the applause was thunderous, as the strains of the Horst Wessel anthem filled the huge stadium carved out of the forest. And in a prearranged back row, two men, alternately clapping and shouting cries of devotion, turned to each other and spoke softly, both recognizing their partially shaved opposing eyebrows.

'Madness,' said the Frenchman in English.

'Not unlike the newsreels we've seen of Hitler's speeches,' added the Hollander from the Dutch Foreign Service.

'I think you're wrong, monsieur. This *Führer* is far more believable. He doesn't force his judgements on the crowd by constant shouting. He leads them there by asking seemingly reasonable questions. Then suddenly explodes, delivering the answers they want to hear. He understands dynamics – very clever, indeed.'

'Who *is* he, do you think?'

'He could be any one of the far-right wingers in the Bundestag, I imagine. As instructed, I've recorded him so our department can match voiceprints, if the ridiculously small machine in my pocket is sufficient for the task.'

'I haven't been in touch with the office in over a month,' offered the Dutchman.

'Nor I in six weeks,' said the Frenchman.

'We must, however, give our superiors credit. The satellites picked up the clearing of the forest the way the high-altitude planes-revealed the missiles in Cuba nearly thirty years ago. They could not accept the explanation of another wealthy Far Eastern religious retreat despite the official papers. They were right.'

'My people were convinced something was odd when foreign construction workers were recruited.'

'I was a simple carpenter, what about you?'

'An electrician. My father owned a *magasin électrique* in Lyons. I worked there until I went away to university.'

'Now we have to get out of here, and I don't think that's going to be so easy. This compound is nothing short of an old concentration camp – barbed-wire fences, towers with machine guns, and all the rest.'

'Be patient, we'll find a way, monsieur. We'll meet at breakfast, tent six. There has to be a way.'

The two men turned from each other, only to be faced by a semicircle of uniformed men, their tunics emblazoned with the banner of the Fourth Reich, the white lightning bolts descending across the swastikas. 'Have you heard enough, *meine Herren?*' said an officer, standing forward of the guards confronting the two foreigners. 'You think you are so clever, *nicht wahr?* You even converse in English.' The soldier held up a small electronic listening device, common in police and intelligence circles. 'This is a wonderful piece of equipment,' the officer continued. 'One can zero in on, say, two people in a crowd and hear every word being spoken by shutting out the external noises. Remarkable ... You have both been watched since the moment you showed up among our privileged, *invited* guests, enthusiastically claiming to be two of them. Do you think we're so unsophisticated? Did you really believe we had no computerized lists to scrutinize? When you were nowhere, we cross-checked the foreign labour forces. Guess what we found? Never mind, you know, of course. A gruff Dutch carpenter, and a particularly peevish French electrician ... *Mitkommen! Zackig!* We shall talk for a while, your accommodations unfortunately not the finest, but then you'll find peace, your earthly remains in a deep trench along with the other worms and grubs.'

'You people are well versed in such executions, aren't you?'

'I regret to say, Dutchman, that I wasn't alive to participate. But our time will come, my time will come.'

Witkowski, Drew, and Karin sat around the colonel's kitchen table in his apartment on the rue Diane. Spread across the surface were the articles Latham had taken from the pockets of the dead neo. 'Not bad,' said the army G-2 veteran, alternately picking up the objects and studying them. 'I'll tell you this much,' he went on, 'this bastard son of Siegfried didn't expect to find any trouble at the Bois de Boulogne.'

'Why do you say that?' asked Latham, gesturing at his empty whisky glass.

'Get it yourself.' The colonel raised his eyebrows and nodded at the brass dry bar just beyond the archway to the living room. 'In this house I pour the first, the rest is up to you. Except for the ladies – ask the *lady*, you jackass.'

'That's a pejorative term,' said Drew, standing up and looking at Karin, who shook her head.

'A what?'

'Never mind, Colonel, he's childish,' interrupted De Vries. 'But please answer his question. There are no papers, no identification; why is it "not bad"?'

'Actually, it's pretty good. He'd tell you that himself if he'd look at the stuff instead of swilling the sauce.'

'I've had *one* drink, Stosh! A damn well-deserved one, I might add.'

'I know, lad, but you still haven't really looked, have you?'

'Yes, I have. As I put it all on the table. There's a matchbook from a restaurant called Au Coin de la Famille, a dry cleaning pick-up receipt for a store on the avenue Georges Cinq in the name of André – meaningless; a gold money clip with a couple of, I presume, endearing words in German and nothing else; another receipt on a credit card, *that* name and number so obviously false, or so buried, it would take days to trace it to another blind alley. The banks pay; that's all the merchants want and they *get* paid . . . The rest, I grant you, I didn't examine, but then, what I just told you was the result of approximately eight seconds. Anything *else*, Colonel?'

'I told you, Mrs de Vries, he does have merit. I doubt it was even eight seconds – nearer five by my count, because of his wanting a drink so fast.'

'I'm impressed,' conceded Karin, 'but you found other things, other items?'

'Just two. One, another receipt for repairs from a custom boot shop, also in the name of André, and the last a crumpled admission to an amusement park outside of Neuilly-sur-Seine – a *free* admission ticket.'

'I never saw those!' protested Latham, pouring himself a drink at the dry bar.

'What do they tell you?'

'Shoes, especially boots, are extremely personal, Mrs de Vries—'

'Please stop calling me that, sir. Karin will do.'

'All right, Karin. Footwear is, shall we say, idiosyncratic; a custom shop services the particular form and shape of an individual foot. If a person goes to such a store, he's usually been there before, that is, if he's been in Paris for any length of time. Otherwise, he would return to his original boot-maker, you follow me?'

'I do, indeed. And the amusement park?'

'*Why* was he issued a free ticket?' interjected Drew, carrying his drink back to the table and sitting down. 'I really didn't see those, Stosh.'

'I know, *chłopak*, and I wasn't trying to top you, but they were there.'

'So tomorrow morning we hit on a bootmaker, and someone in an amusement park who gives away free tickets – not exactly a French tradition. *Christ*, I'm tired. Let's go home . . . *No*, wait a minute! What about the trap you set at Sacré-Coeur?'

'What trap?' asked an astonished Witkowski.

'*The* trap! Courier Sixteen at the top of the funicular.'

'Never heard of it.' Both men looked at Karin de Vries. '*You?*'

'I did that for Freddie many times,' said Karin, smiling awkwardly. 'He used to say, "Make up something, the more foolish the better, for we're all fools."'

'Just hold it, both of you,' said Witkowski, shaking his head, then looking at Drew. 'Are you positive no one could have followed you here?'

'I'll overlook the insult, and give you my professional reply. No, you son of a bitch, because I knew better than to take three changes of vehicles, which could have been picked up electronically, but you're too antediluvian to know that. Our changes took place underground, on the Metro, not three, but *five*. You got that?'

'Oh, I do like your anger. My sainted Polish mother

always said that there was truth in anger. It was the only thing you could trust.'

'That's fine. Now may I call a taxi and get us both home?'

'No, that's the one thing you can't do, lad. Since no one knows where you are, you'll stay right here, both of you. I've got a guest bedroom and that very nice couch over there . . . I suspect you'll be on the couch, youngster, and I'll thank you not to drink up all of my whisky.'

The frustrated Blitzkrieger unit had returned to headquarters from the 'trap' at Sacré-Coeur only to be met by muted confusion. It served to heighten the elite killers' anger.

'There was *no* one!' spat out the older Paris Five, throwing himself into a chair at the conference table. 'Not a goddamned man or woman who even looked like a contact! We were set up – a foolish and dangerous waste of time.'

'Where's our so brilliant leader, Zero One?' asked another member of the unit, addressing the three remaining Blitzkrieger who had not been sent to Sacré-Coeur. 'He may be in charge between his changes of diapers, but he's got an explanation or two to deliver. If we were set up, we were undoubtedly spotted!'

'He's not here,' replied another neo killer, his elbow on the table, his voice a mixture of weariness and boredom.

'What are you *talking* about?' cried Paris Five, sitting up sharply. 'The ten o'clock call from Bonn. He had to be here for it.'

'He wasn't, and no call came,' said another.

'Could it have come in on his private line?'

'No, it could not and did not,' answered the weary Blitzkrieger whose number was Zero Two, Paris. 'When he didn't show up, I sat in his putrid office from nine-thirty to quarter of eleven. Nothing . . . Zero One may be a devoted favourite of our superiors, but I wish he'd bathe more often. That room is a stink tank.'

'Taking a shower takes him away from his throne, and all its gadgets.'

'He's a mad child in an electronics toy store—'

'Careful,' interrupted yet another. 'Dissension's frowned upon, I remind you.'

'Legitimate criticism isn't,' pressed Paris Five. 'Where *is* One and why isn't he here? I gather you haven't even heard from him.'

'You "gather" correctly, but then, we all understand the friction between you two.'

'Admitted and irrelevant,' said Five, standing up, his lean frame over the table, supported by strong, splayed-out hands. 'However, his behaviour now is unacceptable, and I'll express that to Bonn. Our team is sent out on a false mission filled with jeopardy—'

'We all heard the embassy tape,' the weary Paris Two broke in. 'We agreed it was the priority.'

'We certainly did, I foremost. But instead of leading this priority assault, our first Zero chose the secondary Bois de Boulogne on the pretext that he could not return from the Sacré-Coeur in time for the call from Bonn. There was no call and he's not here. An explanation is definitely required.'

'Perhaps none is available,' said a previously silent Blitzkrieger at the far right end of the table. 'However, there was another call, our informer at the American Embassy.'

As one, the unit from Sacré-Coeur reacted like startled cats. Again Five spoke. 'It's absolutely forbidden for him to contact us directly, especially by telephone.'

'He felt the information warranted his disobedience.'

'What was it?' demanded Three.

'The subterranean, Colonel Witkowski.'

'The coordinator,' added Paris Two quietly. 'His impressive connections in Washington are familiar to our – our people over there.'

'What *was* it?' insisted Five.

'Our man stationed himself in an automobile outside the colonel's apartment on the rue Diane. It was instinct, based on the telephone intercepts of Fredrik de Vries's widow in Documents and Research.'

'*And?*'

'Over an hour ago a man and a woman ran into the building. They were in shadow, and he couldn't really see the man but thought he knew him. The woman he did know. It was the widow De Vries.'

'The *man's* Latham!' exploded Paris Five. 'She's with Harry Latham; it can't be anyone else. Let's *go!*'

'To do what?' asked the sceptical Blitzkrieger, Zero Two.

'To complete the kill that One miscalculated.'

'The circumstances are different, and considering the colonel's background in security, the location is extremely dangerous. In Zero One's absence, I suggest we get clearance from Bonn.'

'I suggest we don't,' Paris Six broke in. 'Sacré-Coeur was enough of a fiasco, why open a window, much less a door? If we bring in the kill, it erases the fiasco.'

'And if you fail?'

'The answer to that is obvious,' replied another from Sacré-Coeur, touching the outline of the shoulder holster under his jacket with his right hand, his left reaching for the collar of his shirt, wherein were sewn three cyanide capsules. 'We may have our differences, our frictions, if you like, but the baseline is our commitment to the Brüderschaft, the emergence of the Fourth Reich. Let no one mistake that commitment.'

'I don't think anyone does,' said Two. 'Then you agree with Paris Six? We go to the rue Diane.'

'Certainly. We'd be idiots not to.'

'We present Bonn with a triple kill our leaders can only applaud,' added the angry, frustrated Paris Five. '*Without* Zero One, who's screwed us up enough. When he returns, he can answer to us as well as to Bonn. I suspect, at best, he'll be recalled.'

'You really want to command this unit, don't you?' asked Two, looking up wearily at the imposing figure of Five.

'Yes,' answered the elder assassin, elder because he had reached the age of thirty. 'I'm the oldest and more experienced. He's a mad teenager who acts and makes decisions before he's thought things out. I should have been given the position three years ago, when we were assigned here.'

'Why weren't you? After all, we're all mad, so madness doesn't count, does it?'

'What the hell are you *saying*?' pressed another Blitzkrieger, sitting up and staring at Zero Two.

'Don't mistake me, I approve of our madness. I'm the son of a diplomat and grew up in five different countries. I saw firsthand what you've only been told. We're right, absolutely *right*. The weak, the mentally and racially inferior, are inserting themselves in governments everywhere; only the blind do not see that. One doesn't have to be a social historian to understand that intellectual levels everywhere are being dragged down, not propelled upward. *That* is why we are right . . . But my question to Paris Five started this. Why was Zero One chosen, my friend?'

'I really don't know.'

'Let me try to explain. Every movement must have its zealots, its shock troops who inhabit that dark area beyond madness that compels them to hurl themselves against impenetrable barricades to make a statement heard across the land. Then they disappear into the background, supplanted – or at least they *should* be supplanted – by superior people. The gravest error the Third Reich made was to permit the shock troops, the thugs, to control the party and thus the nation.'

'You're a thinker, aren't you, Two?'

'The philosophical theories of Nietzsche have always appealed to me, especially his doctrine of perfectibility through self-assertion and the moral glorification of the supreme rulers.'

'You're too educated for me,' said Zero Six, 'but I've heard the words before.'

'Of course you have.' Paris Two smiled. 'Variations have been drummed into us.'

'We're wasting time!' Five broke in, standing erect, his eyes squinting slightly, riveted on Two. 'You *are* a thinker, aren't you? I've never heard you talk so much, especially about such matters. Is there something else beneath your words? Perhaps you believe that you should command our Paris unit.'

'Oh, no, you're very wrong, I'm not qualified. What I may have in my head I lack in practical experience, as well as my youth.'

'But there is something else—'

'Indeed, there is, Number Five,' interrupted Two, their eyes locked. 'When our Reich emerges, I have no intention of fading into an obscure background – any more than you do.'

'We understand each other ... Come, I'll choose the team for the rue Diane – six men. Two of you remain here to expedite emergency procedures should they be necessary.'

The chosen six rose from the table, three of them going to their rooms to change into black sweaters and trousers, the remaining Blitzkrieger studying a large street map of Paris, concentrating on the area of the rue Diane. The three properly dressed killers returned; the team checked their weapons, gathered up the equipment designated by Zero Five, and the telephone rang.

'This situation's now intolerable!' screamed Dr Gerhardt Kroeger. 'I shall report you all for gross incompetence and refusal to keep in communication with a Brüderschaft of the highest level!'

'Then you would be doing yourself a disservice, sir,' said a controlled Zero Five. 'Before the night is over, we'll have the kill you so greatly desire, as well as two additional targets Bonn will be pleased to know you were instrumental in directing us to.'

'I was told that nearly four hours ago! What *happened*? Let me talk to that insulting young man who claims he's your leader.'

'I wish I could, *mein Herr*,' replied Five, choosing his

words carefully. 'Unfortunately, Zero *One*, Paris, has not kept in touch with us. He elected to pursue a secondary source, a highly questionable source, if you'll forgive me, and he hasn't called in to report. In truth, he's over two hours late.'

'A "questionable" source? He said it was the highest risk. Perhaps something happened to him.'

'In the delights of the Bois de Boulogne, sir? Again, highly unlikely.'

'Then what happened at the first location, for God's sake?'

'No more than a trap, *mein Herr*, but my team, Zero *Five's* team, eluded it. However, it led to a third source, an unimpeachable one, that we're going after now. Before the sun comes up you'll have proof of the primary target's death, the prescribed method of execution very much in evidence. I, Zero Five, will have the photographs delivered to you personally at your hotel.'

'Your words relieve me; at least you speak more reasonably than that damned youngster with the eyes of a cobra.'

'He's young, sir, but very accomplished in the physical aspects of our work.'

'Without a head on his shoulders, that sort of talent doesn't mean a thing!'

'I tend to agree, but, please, *mein Herr*, he is my superior, so I never said what I just said.'

'You didn't say it, I did. You merely agreed to a generalization . . . What was your number? Five?'

'Yes, sir.'

'Bring me the photographs and Bonn will be apprised of your worth.'

'You're most kind. We must leave now.'

Stanley Witkowski sat in the darkness, peering down through a window at the street below. His broad, leathery face was set, immobile, as every now and then he brought a pair of infrared binoculars to his eyes. The object of his concentration was a stationary automobile at the far right corner of the block, no more than a hundred feet across from the entrance to his apartment building. What had caught the veteran intelligence officer's attention was the flash of a face in the front seat picked up by a street lamp. Sporadically, the face came into view, then receded in the shadows as if the man were waiting for someone or watching for something on the opposite side. The hollow pressure in the colonel's chest, a pressure he had felt hundreds of times in the past, was a warning to be accepted or rejected with the passing minutes or hours.

Then it happened. The face came into view again, but there was a car phone pressed against the man's right ear. He appeared to be excited, angry, his head angled upward, his gaze directed at the upper floors of the apartment building, Witkowski's building. The observer then thrust the phone away, again in anger or frustration. It was enough for the colonel. He rose from the chair and walked rapidly to his bedroom door and into the living room, shutting the door behind him. He found Drew Latham and Karin de Vries sitting on the couch, to his distinct pleasure at opposite ends; Witkowski hated personal relationships in their work.

'Hello, Stanley,' said Drew. 'You chaperoning? If so, you've nothing to fear. We're discussing the post-Cold War situation, and the lady doesn't like me.'

'I didn't say that,' countered Karin, laughing softly. 'You've done nothing to cause me to really dislike you, and I do admire you.'

'Translation. I've been shot down, Stosh.'

'Let's hope that's figuratively speaking,' said the colonel icily, the tone of his voice bringing Drew up short.

'What are you talking about?'

'You said you weren't followed, youngster.'

'We weren't. How could we have been?'

'I'm not sure, but there's a man in a car down in the street who makes me wonder. He's been on the phone and he

259

keeps looking up here.' Drew quickly rose from the couch and started for Witkowski's bedroom door. 'Turn off the lamp before you go in there, you damn fool,' Witkowski barked. 'You can't allow any light to bleed through that window.' Karin reached over and switched off the single floor lamp above her. 'Good girl,' the intelligence officer went on. 'The eye-red binoculars are on the sill and stay low, away from the glass. It's the sedan across the street at the corner.'

'Right.' Latham disappeared into the bedroom, leaving Witkowski and De Vries alone in the relative darkness, only the spill of the streetlights below providing what illumination there was.

'You're really worried, aren't you?' asked Karin.

I've been around long enough to be worried,' replied the colonel, still standing. 'So have you.'

'It could be a jealous lover, or a husband too intoxicated to go home.'

'It could also be the tooth fairy trying to find the right pillow.'

'I wasn't being facetious, and I don't think it's fair for you to be.'

'I'm sorry. I mean that. To repeat what my old acquaintance – *friend* would be misleading, I'm not in his league – Sorenson said in Washington, "Things are moving too fast and getting far too complicated." He's right. We think we're prepared, but we're not. The Nazi movement is coming out of the dirt like white slugs in a garbage heap, many real, many not, merely specks of light-coloured refuse. Who is and who isn't? And how do we find out without accusing everybody, forcing the innocent to prove they're not guilty?'

'Which would be too late once the accusations are made.'

'You couldn't be more accurate, young lady. I lived through it. We lost dozens of deep- and middle-level agents. Our own *people* blew their covers, sucking up to politicians and so-called investigative journalists, none of whom knew the truth.'

'It must have been very difficult for you—'

'The standard resignations included such phrases as "I don't need this, Captain," or Major, or whatever I was at the time. And "Who the hell are you to ruin my life?" and most terribly, "You clean my slate, you son of a bitch, or I go ballistic and blow your whole operation out of the water." I must have signed fifty or sixty "confidential memorandums" stating that the individuals involved were extraordinary intelligence operatives, an awful lot of them far more flattering than they deserved.'

'Not after what had been done to them, certainly.'

'Maybe not, but a lot of those clowns are in the private sector now, making twenty times what I make due to the mystique of their past employment. Several of the lesser ones, who couldn't decipher a cereal box code, are heading up the security of big corporations.'

'That sounds "nuts", an American expression, I believe.'

'Of course it is. We're *all* nuts. It's not what we do, it's what we *did* – on paper, that is, no matter how ridiculous. Blackmail is the order of the day, from top to bottom, my dear.'

'Why haven't you resigned yourself, Colonel?'

'Why?' Witkowski sat in the nearest chair, his eyes on the bedroom door. 'Let me put it this way, as archaic as it may sound. Because I'm very good at what I do, which doesn't say much for my character – being serpentine and suspicious are not exactly admirable traits – but if they're refined and applied to the work I do, they can be assets. The American entertainer Will Rogers once said, "I never met a man I didn't like." I say, I never met a man in my business I didn't suspect. Perhaps it's the European in me, my heritage. I'm Polish by descent; actually it was my first language.'

'And Poland, which has given more to the arts and sciences than most other countries, has been betrayed more than most countries,' said De Vries, nodding.

'I suppose that's part of it. I guess you could say it's ingrained.'

'Freddie trusted you.'

'I wish I could return the compliment. I never trusted your husband. He was a burning fuse I couldn't control, couldn't stamp out. His death at the hands of the Stasi was inevitable.'

'He was *right*,' said Karin, her voice rising. 'The Stasi and their ilk are now the core of the Nazis.'

'His methods were wrong, his rage misplaced. Both betrayed his cover and he was killed for it. He wouldn't listen to us, to me.'

'I know, I know. He wouldn't listen to me either . . . By then, however, it didn't really matter.'

'I'm not sure I understand.'

'Freddie became violent, not only to me but to anyone who disagreed with him. He was enormously strong – trained by your commando troops in Belgium – and came to think he was invincible. At the end he was as fanatic as his enemies.'

'Then you understand where I come from when I say I never trusted your husband.'

'Naturally. Our last months in Amsterdam were not days I care to relive.'

Suddenly the door to Witkowski's bedroom flung open, Latham in its frame. '*Bingo!*' he shouted. 'You were right, Stanley. That bastard down there in the street is Reynolds, Alan *Reynolds* in Communications!'

'Who?'

'How many times have you gone down to Communications, Stosh?'

'I don't know. Maybe three or four times in the last year.'

'He's the *mole*. I saw his face.'

'Then something's about to happen, and I suggest we take countermeasures.'

'What do we do and where do we start?'

'Mrs de Vries – Karin – would you please go to my bedroom window and let us know what develops?'

262

'On my way,' said Karin, rising from the couch and running into the colonel's room.

'Now what?' asked Drew.

'The obvious,' answered Witkowski. 'Weapons first.'

'I have an automatic with a full clip.' Latham pulled the gun from his belt.

'I'll give you another one with an extra clip.'

'You're expecting the worst, then?'

'I've been expecting it for nearly five years now, and if you haven't, it's no wonder your flat was blown apart.'

'Well, I have this instrument that stops anyone from opening the door.'

'No comment. But if the bastards send two or three after you, Lord love a duck, I'd surely like to ship a couple back to Washington. It'd make up for the one we lost there.' The colonel walked to an imposing Mondrian print on the wall and swivelled it back, revealing a safe. He spun the dial back and forth, opened the large vault, and withdrew two sidearms and an Uzi, which he clipped to his belt. He threw an automatic to Drew, who caught it, followed by a clip of ammunition which Latham missed; it fell to the floor.

'Why didn't you throw them both at once?' said an irritated Drew, bending down to retrieve the clip.

'I wanted to watch your reactions. Not bad. Not good, but not bad.'

'Did you also mark the bottle?'

'Didn't have to. With what's left in your glass, you've had maybe a couple of ounces during the last hour. You're a big fella, like me; you can handle it.'

'Thank you, mother. Now what the hell do we *do*?'

'Most of it's been done. I simply have to activate the externals.' Witkowski walked to the kitchen sink, unscrewed the chromium faucet in the centre, reached into the orifice, and pulled out two wires; each end was capped with a small plastic terminal. He broke the seals and pressed the wires together; five loud beeps filled the adjoining rooms. 'There we are,' said the colonel, replacing the faucet and returning to the living room area.

'Where *are* we, O Wizard?'

'Let's start with the fire escapes; in these old buildings there are two – one in my bedroom, the other over there in the alcove, in what I foolishly call my library. We're on the third floor, the building has seven. By activating the external security devices, the fire escapes between the top of the second floor and the bottom of the fourth are electrified, the voltage sufficient to cause unconsciousness but not death.'

'Suppose whoever the evil people are simply walk up the stairs or take the elevator?'

'Naturally, one has to respect the privacy and civil rights of one's neighbours. There are three other flats on this floor. My apartment is on the left front quadrant, the door twenty feet from the nearest resident on my right. You probably didn't notice, but there is a thick, rather attractive Oriental runner leading to my door.'

'And once you turn on your externals,' interrupted Latham, 'something happens when the bad guys step on the rug, is that it?'

'You're exactly right. Four-hundred-watt floodlights go on, accompanied by a siren that can be heard in the Place de la Concorde.'

'You won't catch anybody that way. They'll run like hell.'

'Not on the fire escape; and if they use the stairs, they'll come right into our welcoming arms.'

'What? How?'

'On the floor below is a miscreant, a Hungarian who deals in, shall we say, misappropriated jewels. He's barely above small-time and does no great harm, and I've befriended him. A phone call or a tap on his door and we wait inside his apartment. Whoever comes racing down these stairs will have bullets in their legs – I trust you're a decent shot, I wouldn't want anyone killed.'

'*Colonel!*' Karin de Vries's voice from the bedroom was

emphatic. 'A van just pulled in front of the car; men are climbing out . . . Four, five, six – six men in dark clothing.'

'They really must want you, youngster,' said Witkowski as he and Drew ran into the bedroom, joining Karin at the window.

'A couple of them are carrying knapsacks,' said Latham.

'One of them is talking to the driver of the car,' added De Vries. 'He's obviously telling him to leave. He's backing away.'

'The others are spreading out, examining the building,' completed the colonel, touching Karin's arm, forcing her to turn to him. 'The young fellow and I are going to leave.' The woman's eyes flashed in alarm. 'Not to worry, we'll be right below. Close the bedroom door and bolt it; it's steel-plate and no one could break it open without a truck or a ten-man battering ram.'

'For Christ's sake, call the police or at least embassy security!' Drew was cool but firm.

'Unless I'm grossly mistaken, my friendly neighbours will reach the police, but not before you and I have a chance to grab one or two of the bastards for ourselves.'

'And you'd lose them if our security was involved,' Karin broke in. 'They'd be forced to cooperate with the police, who'd take everyone into custody.'

'You're very quick,' Witkowski agreed, nodding at her in the dim light from the street. 'You'll hear a loud siren from the hallway, and most likely a great deal of electric static from the fire escape—'

'It's wired. You activated the current.'

'You *knew* about that?' asked Latham, astonished.

'In Amsterdam, Freddie did the same with ours.'

'I taught him,' said the colonel without emphasis. 'Come on, *chłopak*, there's no time to waste.'

Eighty-five seconds later, the irritated Hungarian had been persuaded to accept the price offered by an influential American who had interceded for him in the past and might be helpful in the future. Witkowski and Drew stood by the downstairs neighbour's door, which was open less than an inch. The waiting was interminable, the time elapsed nearly eight minutes. 'Something's wrong,' whispered the colonel. 'It's not reasonable.'

'No one's come up the stairs and there's no static from either fire escape,' said Latham. 'Maybe they're still casing the building.'

'That doesn't make sense either. These old structures are open books, and like books on a shelf, close together . . . *Jesus*, "close together . . ." The *knapsacks*!'

'Where are you talking about?'

'I'm a damn fool, that's what. They've got grappling hooks and ropes! They're crossing from one building to another and scaling down the stone. *Out!* Upstairs as fast as we can. And for God's sake, don't step on the rug!'

Karin sat in the shadows across from the window, her weapon in her hand, listening for the sounds of high-voltage electricity from outside. None came, and it was now nearly ten minutes since the colonel and Latham had left. She began to wonder. Witkowski, by his own admission, was suspicious of everyone and everything to the point of paranoia, and Drew was exhausted. Was it possible all of them were wrong? Had the colonel mistaken a jealous lover or a frightened husband for something sinister? And had the tired Latham seen a face that reminded him of Alan Reynolds in Communications but was someone else's entirely? Were the men in the van, men who moved so quickly they had to be young, merely a group of university students returning from a camping trip or a late night in Paris? She put the gun down on a small table beside the chair, and stretched, her head arched back and yawning. Good heavens, she needed sleep.

And then, like an enormous combination of thunder and lightning, a figure crashed through the window, shattering glass and wood, landing on its feet and releasing a rope.

Karin sprang out of the chair, instinctively rushing backward, her bandaged right hand groping for anything and everything. And then came another silhouetted, daredevil intruder, sliding on his rope until he landed by the bed.

'Who *are* you?' screamed De Vries in German, collecting what thoughts she could, realizing that her gun was on the small table. 'What do you *want* here?'

'You speak German,' said the first invader, 'so you know what we want! Why else would you speak our language?'

'It is second to my own, and few understand my native Walloon.' Karin circled, approaching the table.

'Where is he, Mrs de Vries?' asked the second man by the bed menacingly. 'You won't get out of here, you know. Our comrades will block you; they're on their way up now. They just needed our signal and the window was it.'

'I don't know what you're talking about! Since you know who I am, does it shock you that I'm having an affair with the owner of this flat?'

'It's an empty bed, not even slept in—'
'We had a lovers' quarrel. He drank too much and we fought.' Karin was within arm's reach of her weapon, and neither of the Nazis had bothered to unholster his. 'You've never had such fights with your women? If not, you're children!' She lunged for the gun, grabbed it, and fired into the first neo as the stunned second unstrapped his holster. '*Stop* or you're *dead*!' said De Vries.

As she spoke, the steel-plated bedroom door swung open, crashing into the wall. 'Oh, my God!' roared Witkowski, snapping on the light. 'She's got a live one.'

'I thought it took a truck or a battering ram to get in here,' said Karin, visibly shaken.

'Not if you've got grandchildren who visit you in Paris; they can get real playful. There's a concealed button in the frame.' It was as far as the colonel got. An ear-shattering siren erupted, so loud that within seconds lights were turned on in the nearby buildings.

'They're coming to stop you from leaving!' cried De Vries.

'Let's welcome them, youngster,' said Witkowski. He and Latham ran through the living room to the front door. The colonel opened it, he and Drew standing concealed behind the door itself. Two men rushed in, their automatic weapons on rapid fire, blowing up whatever was in their paths. The colonel and Drew took aim, and shooting three rounds apiece, shattered the arms and hands of the killers. They collapsed, writhing and moaning. 'Cover them!' shouted Witkowski, racing into the kitchen. Seconds later the siren stopped and the hallway lights were out. The colonel returned, giving his orders rapidly as clamouring footsteps, growing fainter, could be heard running down the hallway steps. 'Tie these sons of bitches up and throw them into the guest bathroom along with the live one in my bedroom. We'll give the *gendarmes* the bastard Karin sent to Valhalla.'

'The police will want to know what happened, Stan.'

'Until tomorrow – this morning – that's their problem. I just want to pull some diplomatic strings and get these scum on one of our supersonics to Washington. With no announcement except to Sorenson.'

Suddenly a scream came from the bedroom; it was Karin. Drew raced through the door and saw her, weapon hanging at her side, staring at the still, wide-eyed figure across the bed. 'What *happened*?'

'I'm not sure. He reached for his collar and bit into it. Seconds later he collapsed.'

'Cyanide.' Latham felt the young neo's throat for a pulse. '*Deutschland über Alles*,' he said softly. 'I wonder if this kid's mother and father will be proud. Christ, I hope not.'

CHAPTER SIXTEEN

Their hands and forearms bandaged, their shirt collars ripped off, Zero Five, Paris, sat with Paris Two in the cramped quarters of the jet flying across the Atlantic to Washington. It was unlikely they would be executed, thought Five; the Americans were weak in that area, especially if a prisoner appeared irrational and repentant. He nudged the scholarly Zero Two, who was dozing. 'Wake up,' he said in German.

'*Was ist?*'

'What should we do when we get there? Have you any ideas?'

'A couple,' replied Two, yawning.

'Let's hear them.'

'The Americans are, by nature, given to violence, although their leaders pontificate otherwise. Equally ingrained is a proclivity for seeking out conspiracies, no matter how remote they may be. Our leaders have their mistresses, who cares? Their leaders enjoy a whore, and suddenly they're tied to the overlords of crime. Do such men really need criminals to provide such women for them? It's ludicrous, but the Americans accept it; their hypocritical puritanism rejects natural law. A life of monogamy is simply not the nature of the male animal.'

'What the hell are you saying? You're not answering me.'

'Certainly I am. When we get there we feed both their hypocrisy and their need for conspiracy.'

'How?'

'They believe, or surely must believe by now, that we're

269

an elite branch of the Brüderschaft, and in a way we are, although not in the way they think. What we must do is to pretend we really *are* important. That we have ties to the zealots in Bonn who see us as the true storm troopers, who confide in us because they need us.'

'But they don't. We have no names, only codes that change twice weekly. The Americans will put us under drugs and learn this.'

'These days the truth serums are no more reliable than hypnosis in sophisticated circles; one can usually be programmed to resist them. US intelligence knows that.'

'We haven't been programmed.'

'Why should we be? As you say, we have no names, only codes authorizing us to proceed with our orders. If we're subjected to chemicals and we reveal those useless codes, they can be only more impressed.'

'You're still not answering me. I liked you better when you didn't talk so much and were less erudite. How do we deal with the Americans?'

'First, we acknowledge our importance, our close ties with the leadership both in Europe and in America. Then, with reluctance, we also admit that there's a fair degree of hypocrisy in our actions. Our lifestyles are extravagant – concealed, expensive residences, unlimited funds, the most voluptuous women whenever we want them. The fantasies of every young man are our reality, and the cause that makes this possible is the cause we work for, not necessarily a cause we would die for.'

'Very good, Two, very convincing.'

'It's the foundation. From there we appeal to their appetite for conspiracy. We reemphasize our importance, our influence, the fact that we're constantly consulted and must be in contact with our counterparts all over the world in these days of supersonic travel.'

'Especially the United States, of course,' said Zero Five, Paris.

'Of course. And the information we have – specific names,

and in the absence of names, positions in both government and civilian industry – is truly shocking. Men and women they could not imagine are sympathetic to the Brotherhood of the Watch.'

'That's being done now.'

'We'll escalate the process to new heights. After all, no one's heard it from "the horse's mouth", as the Americans say. If our computers are right, and I expect they are, we're the first of the new Nazi elite to be taken alive. Actually, we're trophies, prisoners of war of the highest order. We might very well be given special privileges if we appear to waver. I'm rather looking forward to the next few days.'

Zeros Four and Seven, near-hysterical escapees from the rue Diane, burst into the Blitzkrieger headquarters at the Avignon warehouse complex, trying to impose some control over their emotions – none too successfully. Their two remaining comrades were in the conference room – one at the table, the other pouring coffee.

'We're *finished*!' cried the impulsive Paris Zero Four, breathlessly throwing himself into a chair. 'All hell broke loose!'

'What *happened*?' The Blitzkrieger pouring coffee dropped the cup.

'It wasn't our fault.' Paris Seven, standing, held his place, and spoke in a loud, defensive voice. 'It was a trap, and Five and Two panicked. They ran inside the flat on rapid fire—'

'Then there were different shots and we heard them fall,' Zero Four broke in, his eyes unfocused. 'They're probably dead.'

'What about the *others*, the two who scaled down the building to the window?'

'We don't know; there was no way we *could* know!'

'What do we do now?' asked Seven. 'Any word from Zero One?'

'Nothing.'

'One of us must assume his position and reach Bonn,' said the elite killer by the coffee.

To a man, the other three shook their heads emphatically. 'We'll be executed,' said Four quietly, matter-of-factly. 'The leaders will demand it, and speaking personally, I will not die for others' mistakes, others' panic. Were I responsible, I would gladly take the cyanide, but I am not, *we* are not!'

'But what can we *do*?' repeated Seven.

The erect Four walked pensively around the table, pausing in front of the Blitzkrieger by the coffee machine. 'You handle our accounts, not so?'

'Yes, I do.'

'How much money do we have?'

'Several million francs.'

'Can you get more quickly?'

'Our requests for funds are not questioned. We place a phone call and they are wired. We justify them later, naturally understanding the consequences if they are for false pretences.'

'The same consequences we face now, am I right?'

'Essentially, yes. Death.'

'Make your call and ask for the maximum you can get. You might drop a hint that we may have the President of France or the head of the Chamber of Deputies in our pockets.'

'That would call for the maximum. The transfer will be immediate, but the funds would not be available to us until the Algerian bank opens ... It's past four now; the bank opens at nine o'clock.'

'Less than five hours,' said Zero Seven, staring at Four. 'What are you thinking of?'

'The obvious. We stay here, we all face execution ... What I'm about to say to you may turn your stomachs, but I submit that we can better serve our cause alive than dead. Especially when our deaths are the result of others' incompetence; we still have much to offer ... I have an elderly uncle outside of Buenos Aires, seventy miles south of the Rio de la Plata. He was one of many who fled the Third Reich when it was being destroyed, but the family still holds that Deutschland to be holy. We have passports; we can fly there and the family will give us sanctuary.'

'It's better than execution,' said Seven.

'Unwarranted execution,' added the Blitzkrieger at the table solemnly.

'But can we be unreachable for five hours?' asked the killer/accounts manager.

'We can if we tear out the phones and leave,' replied Four. 'We'll pack whatever we need, burn what has to be destroyed, and get out of here. A long day and night lie before us. Hurry! Crumple the files and any other papers there are, stuff them into the metal wastebaskets and light them.'

'I'm rather looking forward to it,' said a relieved Zero Seven.

The ultimate believers had found a convenient crack in their sacred covenant, and as the first wastebasket was set on fire, the bookkeeper opened a window to let out the smoke.

Knox Talbot, director of the CIA, opened the front door for Wesley Sorenson. It was early evening, the Virginia sun descending over the fields of Talbot's property. 'Welcome to these humble lodgings, Wes.'

'Humble, like hell,' said the head of Consular Operations, walking inside. 'Do you own half of the state?'

'Only an itty-bitty part. The rest I leave for the white folk.'

'Really, it's very beautiful, Knox.'

'I won't argue,' agreed Talbot, leading them through an extravagantly appointed living room to a huge glass-enclosed sun porch. 'If you like, and if you have time, I'll show you the barn and the stables. I have three daughters who fell in love with horses until they discovered boys.'

'I'll be damned,' exclaimed Sorenson, sitting down. 'I have two daughters who did the same.'

'Did they leave you when they found husbands?'

'Well, they come back now and then.'

'But they left you with the horses.'

'Yea so, my friend. Fortunately, my wife adores them.'

'Mine doesn't. As she frequently points out, growing up on 145th Street in Harlem didn't exactly prepare her for an estate with stables. She allows me to keep them 'cause they draw the kids back, sometimes too often . . . Can I get you a drink?'

'No, thanks. My cardiologist allows me three ounces a day, and I've already had four. Then I'll get home, and it'll be a total of six with my wife.'

'Then to business.' Talbot reached down to a wicker magazine rack and pulled up a black-bordered file folder. 'First, the AA computers,' he said. 'There was nothing, absolutely nothing, I could go on. I'm not questioning Harry Latham and his source, but if they're right, it's so buried, it would take an archaeologist to pull him or her out.'

'They're right, Knox.'

'I don't doubt it, so while I continue to dig, I've replaced the whole unit as a matter of a new rotation policy. Expanding the venues of upper-level personnel is the way I explained it.'

'How did that go down?'

'Not well, but with no discernible objections, which, of course, I was looking for. Naturally, the former team is under a microscope.'

'Naturally,' said Sorenson. 'What about this Kroeger, Gerhardt Kroeger?'

'Far more interesting.' Talbot flipped several pages in the file folder. 'To begin with, he was apparently some kind of genius in the brain surgery field, not only in removing delicate tumours, but in eliminating "subcutaneous pressures" that made mentally sick people well again.'

'*Was?*' asked Wesley Sorenson. 'What do you mean, was?'

'He disappeared. He resigned his post as associate chief of cranial surgery at the Hospital of Nuremberg at the age of

274

forty-three, claiming he was burned out, psychologically unfit to continue operating. He married a prominent surgical nurse named Greta Frisch, and the last anyone heard – the last trace, in fact – was that they emigrated to Sweden.'

'What do the Swedish authorities say?'

'That's what's interesting. They have him entering Sweden, at Göteborg, four years ago, ostensibly on a pleasure trip. The hotel records show that he and his wife spent two days and departed. The trail ends there.'

'He's back,' said the director of Consular Operations. 'In reality, I suppose, he never went away. He found another cause beyond making sick people well.'

'What in hell could that be, Wes?'

'I don't know. Maybe making well people sick. I just don't know.'

Drew Latham opened his eyes, annoyed by the sounds from the street, louder because of the smashed window in the bedroom. Witkowski, along with marine guards, had taken the captured Nazis to the airport under cover, and someone had had to stay in the colonel's room. An open window was too inviting. Slowly, Drew slid over to the other side of the bed and got to his feet, cautiously avoiding fragments of glass. He grabbed his trousers and shirt from a chair, put them on, and walked to the door. He opened it and saw Witkowski and De Vries across the living room at a table in the alcove, having coffee.

'How long have you been up?' he asked of both, not really caring.

'We let you sleep, my dear.'

'There's that "my dear" again. I sincerely believe you do not mean an endearment.'

'It's an expression, Drew,' said Karin. 'You were quite wonderful last night – this morning.'

'Naturally, the colonel was better.'

'Naturally, youngster, but you held your own, by damn. You're a cool customer in the face of the enemy.'

'Would you believe, Mr Super Guy, that I've done it before? Not that I take any pride in it; it's merely a matter of survival.'

'Come,' said De Vries, rising. 'I'll get you some coffee. Here, sit down,' she continued, heading for the kitchen. 'Take the third chair.'

'I'll bet she wouldn't give it to me if it was hers,' said Latham, stumbling across the room. 'So, what happened, Stosh?' he asked, sitting down.

'Everything we wanted, young man. At five o'clock this morning I got our scumbuckets on a jet to DC and nobody will know but Sorenson.'

'What do you mean, *will*? Didn't you speak to Wes?'

'I spoke to his wife. I met her once and nobody could duplicate that half-American, half-British speech. I told her to tell the director that a package was due at Andrews at four-ten in the morning, their time, under the code name Peter Pan Two. She said she'd tell him the moment he got in.'

'That's too loose, Stanley. You should have requested a return confirmation.'

The apartment telephone rang. The colonel got up and walked rapidly across the room; he picked it up. 'Yes?' He listened for six seconds and then hung up. 'That was Sorenson,' he said. They've got a platoon of marines on the ground and on the roofs. Anything else, Mr Intelligence Man?'

'Yes,' replied Latham. 'Do we call off the bootmaker and the amusement park?'

'I shouldn't think so,' answered Karin, bringing Drew his coffee and sitting down. 'Two neos are dead and two on their way to America. Others have fled, an additional two, by my count.'

'Six altogether,' agreed Drew. 'Hardly a platoon,' he added, looking at Witkowski.

'Not even half a squad. How many others are there?'

'Let's try and find out. I'll take the amusement park—'

'*Drew*,' cried De Vries, sharply interrupting.

'You'll take nothing,' added the colonel. 'You haven't much of a short-term memory, youngster. They want you – or I should say Harry – on a slab with rigor mortis, remember?'

'What am I supposed to do, open a trapdoor and hide in the sewers?'

'No, you'll stay right here. I'll send two marines to guard the stairs and a maintenance man to repair the window.'

'Would you mind, I'd like to be useful?'

'You will be. This will be our temporary base camp and you'll be the contact.'

'With whom?'

'With whoever I tell you to reach. I'll be calling you at least once an hour.'

'What about me?' asked Karin apprehensively. 'I can be of value at the embassy.'

'I realize that, specifically in my office with a guard at the door. Sorenson knows who you are and no doubt Knox Talbot as well. If either reaches me on my secure phone, you take the messages, call them to our amnesiac here, and I'll get them from him. Now, if I can only figure out a way to get you there in case there are hostiles in the street.'

'Perhaps I can help you help us both.' De Vries reached down for her purse beside the chair, stood up, and started for the bedroom. 'This will only take a moment or two, but it does require a little prodding and primping.'

'What's she doing?' said Witkowski as Karin went through the door.

'I think I know, but I'll let her surprise you. Maybe then you'll promote her as your assistant.'

'I could do worse. Freddie taught her a lot of tricks.'

'Which you taught him.'

'Only the fire escape; the rest he figured out for himself

277

and he was usually way ahead of us ... all of us, except probably Harry.'

'What happens when she leaves the embassy, Stanley?'

'She won't. There are a lot of staff rooms. I'll throw someone out for a few days and she'll stay there.'

'With a guard, of course.'

The colonel looked over at Latham, his eyes steady. 'You care, don't you?'

'I care,' replied Drew simply.

'Normally, I wouldn't approve, but in this case I'll reduce my objections.'

'I didn't say it'll lead anywhere.'

'No, but if it does, you've got a couple of miles on me. She's in the same business.'

'I beg your pardon?'

'You don't get grandchildren because some quartermaster issued them. I was married for thirteen years to a fine woman, a splendid woman who finally admitted she couldn't accept what I did for a living, and all the complications it involved. For once in my life I pleaded, but to no avail – she saw through those pleas. I was too used to what I did, too primed for it every day. She was very generous though – I had unlimited visitation rights with the children. But, of course, I wasn't around that much to visit them very often.'

'I'm sorry, Stanley. I had no idea.'

'It's not the sort of thing you put in *Stars and Stripes*, now, is it?'

'I guess not, but you obviously get along with your kids. I mean, visiting grandchildren, and all.'

'Hell, yes, they consider me a hoot. Their mother remarried very well, and what in Sam Hill am I going to do with the money I make? I've got more perks than I can handle, so when they all come to Paris, well, you can figure it out.'

They were interrupted by the figure in the bedroom doorway, a very blonde woman in dark glasses, her skirt hiked up above her knees, her blouse unbuttoned to mid-chest. She shifted her weight from leg to leg in mock sensuality. 'What'll the boys in the back room have?' she said, her voice low, imitating the well-worn motion picture cliché.

'Outstanding!' exclaimed the stunned Witkowski.

'And then some.' Drew spoke softly, adding a quiet whistle.

'Will this do, Colonel?'

'It surely will, except I'll have to screen the guards, hopefully find a few gay ones.'

'Worry not, Wizard,' said Latham. 'Beneath the heat is a will of ice.'

'Obviously, I can't fool you, monsieur.' Karin laughed, released her skirt, buttoned her blouse, and started towards the table, when the telephone rang. 'Shall I get it?' she asked. 'I can say I'm the maid – in the proper French, naturally.'

'I'd be obliged,' answered Witkowski. 'Today's the laundry morning; he usually calls around now. Tell him to come up, and press Six on the phone to open the foyer door.'

'*Allô? C'est la résidence du grand colonel.*' De Vries listened for a moment or two, placed her hand over the phone, and looked over at the embassy's chief of security. 'It's Ambassador Courtland. He says he must speak to you immediately.'

Witkowski rose quickly and crossed the room, taking the phone from Karin. 'Good morning, Mr Ambassador.'

'You listen to me, Colonel! I don't know what happened at your place last night or at the Orly Airport annexe field – and I'm not sure I want to know – but if you have any plans for this morning, *scratch* them, and that's an *order!*'

'You heard from the police, then, sir?'

'More than I care to. And more to the point, I heard from the German ambassador, who's fully cooperating with us. Kreitz was alerted several hours ago by the German section of the Quai d'Orsay that there was a fire in a suite of offices at the Avignon Warehouses. Among the debris were remnants of Third Reich memorabilia, along with thousands of charred pages, burned beyond recognition, set on fire in wastebaskets.'

'The papers set the whole place on fire?'

'Apparently a window was left open and the breezes spread the flames, setting off the smoke alarms and the sprinklers. Get over there!'

'Where are the warehouses, sir?'

'How the hell do *I* know? You speak French, ask somebody!'

'I'll check the telephone book. And, Mr Ambassador, I'd prefer not to take my own car, or a taxi. Would you please call – have your secretary call – Transport, and send secure equipment to my apartment on the rue Diane. They know the address.'

'"Secure equipment"? What the dickens is that?'

'An armoured vehicle, sir, with a marine escort.'

'*Christ*, I wish I were in Sweden! Find out what you can, Colonel. And hurry!'

'Tell Transport to hurry, sir.' Witkowski hung up, not, however, before giving the telephone the proverbial 'finger'. He turned to Latham and Karin de Vries. 'Everything's changed, at least for the time being. With any luck we may have found a jackpot. Karin, you stay the way you are. You, youngster, you go to my closet and see if you can find a uniform that fits. We're about the same size, one of 'em will come close.'

'Where are we going?' asked Drew.

'To a group of offices in a warehouse that got torched by neos. A Nazi wastebasket brigade didn't quite work out the way it was intended. Some asshole opened a window.'

The neo-Nazi headquarters were in shambles, the walls scorched, the few curtains burned up to their rods, and the whole mess drenched by the sprinkler system. In an office filled with computerized electronic equipment, undoubtedly used by the leader of the unit, was a huge locked steel cabinet. Smashed open, it revealed an arsenal of weapons, from high-powered rifles, telescopic sights attached, to boxes of hand grenades, miniaturized flame-throwers, garrottes, assorted handguns, and various stilettos – some automated from canes and umbrellas. Everything coincided with Drew Latham's description of elite Nazi killers in Paris. This was their lair.

'Use pincers,' ordered Colonel Witkowski, speaking French and addressing the police while pointing to charred sheets of paper on the floor. 'Get plates of glass and place anything that isn't totally destroyed between them. You never know what we can pick up.'

'The telephones have all been torn from the walls and the receptacles destroyed,' said a French detective.

'The lines haven't, have they?'

'No. I have a technician from the telephone company on his way. He will restore the lines and we can trace their calls.'

'Outgoing, maybe, incoming negative. And if I know these bozos, the ones made here were routed for payment to a little old lady in Marseilles who gets a money order and a bonus once a month.'

'As it is with the drug dealers, no?'

'Yes.'

'Still, there are instructions somewhere, yes?'

'Definitely, but none you can trace. They'll come from a Swiss or Cayman bank, the secret accounts not to be invaded. That's the way things work these days.'

'I investigate domestically, monsieur, in Paris and its environs mainly, not internationally.'

'Then get me someone who does.'

'You would have to appeal to the Quai d'Orsay, the Service d'Etranger. These are beyond my province.'

'I'll find 'em.'

The uniformed Latham and a blonde-wigged Karin de Vries approached, stepping cautiously on the floor, their feet avoiding the charred, windblown pages. 'Have you figured out anything?' asked Drew.

'Not much, but this sure was the core of their operations, whoever they were.'

'Who else but the men who attacked us last night?' said Karin.

'I'll buy that, but where did they go?' agreed Witkowski.

'*Monsieur l'Américain*,' shouted another plainclothes police official, rushing from an outer room. 'Look what I found. It was beneath a pillow on a sitting room chair! It is a letter – the beginning of a letter.'

'Let me have it.' The colonel took the piece of paper. '"*Meine Liebste*", Witkowski began, his eyes squinting. '"*Etwas Entsetzliches ist geschehen.*"'

'Give it to me,' said De Vries, impatient with Witkowski's hesitation. She translated in English. '"My dearest, tonight is most shocking. We must all leave immediately lest our cause be damaged and we are all to be executed for others' failures. No one in Bonn must know, but we are flying to South America, to some place where we will be protected until we can return and fight again. I adore you so . . . I must finish later, someone is coming down the hallway. I will post this at the air—" . . . It stops there, the letters blurred.'

'The airport!' cried Latham. 'Which one? Which airlines fly to South America? We can intercept them!'

'Forget it,' said the colonel. 'It's ten-fifteen in the morning, and there are a couple of dozen airlines that leave between seven and ten and end up in any one of twenty or thirty cities in South America. Those flights are well beyond us. However, there's a positive. Our killers got the hell out of Paris fast, and their scumbucket brothers in Bonn haven't a clue. Until others take their place, we've got some breathing room.'

Gerhardt Kroeger, surgeon and alterer of minds, was about to lose his own. He had called the Avignon Warehouses a dozen times in the past six hours, using the proper codes, only to be told by an operator that all lines to the office he wished to reach were 'not in service at this time. Our computers show manual disconnects.' No amount of protestations on his part could change the situation; it was all too obvious. The Blitzkrieger had shut down. *Why?* What had *happened?* Zero Five, Paris, had been so confident: the photographs of the kill would be delivered to him in the morning. Where *were* they? Where *was* Paris Five?

There was no other option. He had to reach Hans Traupman in Nuremberg. Someone had to have an explanation!

'It's foolish of you to reach me here,' said Traupman. 'I don't have the proper telephone devices.'

'I had no choice. You cannot do this to me, *Bonn* cannot do this to me! I'm ordered to find my creation at whatever the cost, even to the point of employing the so-called incomparable skills of our associates here in Paris—'

'What more can you ask for?' interjected the doctor in Nuremberg arrogantly.

'Something, *anything* that makes sense! I've been treated abominably, given promise after promise with nothing to show for them. Now, at this minute, our associates cannot even be reached!'

'They have special arrangements, as befits confidential consultants.'

'I used them. The operator said her computers show that the phones were disconnected, manually disconnected. What more do you *need*, Hans? The . . . our associates have cut us off, cut us *all* off! Where *are* they?'

Seconds passed before Traupman spoke. 'If what you say is accurate,' he said quietly, 'it's most disturbing. I assume you're at the hotel.'

'I am.'

'Stay there. I'll drive home, reach several others, and call you back. It may take me over an hour.'

'It doesn't matter. Just call me back.'

Nearly two hours passed before the Lutetia phone rang. 'Yes?' said Kroeger, pouncing on it.

'Something very unusual has happened. What you told me

is true . . . more than true, it's catastrophic. The one man in Paris who knows where our associates were located went over and found the police everywhere.'

'Then they *have* disappeared!'

'Worse than that. At four thirty-seven this morning, their "bookkeeper" reached our finance department, and with a plausible, if outrageous, story involving women and young boys and drugs and high French officials, requested an enormous sum of money – to be verified later as proper expenditures, of course.'

'But there is no later, no verification.'

'Obviously. They're cowards and traitors. We'll hunt them to the ends of the earth.'

'Your hunting them doesn't help me. My creation has reached the critical period. What do I do? I must *find* him!'

'We've talked it over. It's not the most favourable course of action, but we think it's the only one you've got. Reach Moreau at the Deuxième Bureau. He knows everything that happens in French intelligence circles.'

'How do I reach him?'

'Do you know what he looks like?'

'I've seen photographs, yes.'

'It must be done on the outside, no phone calls, no messages, a simple meeting in the street, or a café, someplace where no one would suspect an encounter. Say something short, no more than a sentence or two, in a way that only he can hear. The important thing is for you to use the word *brotherhood*.'

'What then?'

'He may dismiss you, but even as he does so he'll tell you where to meet him. It will be a common place, probably crowded, and the hour late.'

'You told me before to be suspicious of him.'

'We've taken that into consideration, but we have a counterattack should he not be the sympathizer he claims to be. To date, we've paid over twenty million francs into his Swiss account, substantiated by written records. He would

284

be destroyed, sent to prison for years, if those records were anonymously leaked to the French government, not to mention the press. He could not deny them. Use it if you have to.'

'I'll head for the Deuxième immediately,' said Kroeger. 'Perhaps tomorrow, Harry Latham.'

CHAPTER SEVENTEEN

In his office at the Deuxième Bureau, Claude Moreau studied the decoded message from his man in Bonn. The content was judgemental, not factual, and not terribly enlightening, but there was a substance to it that could be helpful.

> In yesterday's session, the Bundestag fully addressed the problem of the spreading Nazi revivals throughout Germany, the parties coalescing, united in their denunciations. However, my inside sources, several of whom dine frequently with the leaders of the left and the right factions, report that there is rampant cynicism among both. The liberals don't trust the conservative denouncements, and a small circle of conservatives seem to wink at their own oratory. The leaders of industry, of course, are appalled, fearing the Nazi movement will close markets to them abroad, but are reluctant to support the socialistically inclined left, and do not know whom on the right to trust. Their money flows like spreading inkblots throughout Bonn, without sure direction.

Moreau leaned back in his chair, mentally abstracting the phrase that caught his attention. Not only caught it, but set it on fire. *A small circle of conservatives seem to wink at their own oratory.* Who, specifically, were they? What were the names? And why didn't his man in Bonn include them?

He picked up his console phone, the line to his secretary. 'I want to go on absolute scrambler, no intercepts possible.'

'I'll activate the procedure, sir, and you'll know by the

five-second hum on line three, as usual,' said the female voice in the outer office.

'Thank you, Monique, and since my wife expects me for lunch at L'Escargot in a few minutes, she'll undoubtedly call when I'm not there. Please tell her that I'm delayed but will arrive shortly.'

'It's no problem, sir. Régine and I are good friends.'

'Certainly. You both conspire against me. The scrambler, please.'

The low-toned hum on the line-three telephone completed, Moreau dialled his man in Bonn.

'*Hallo*,' said the man in Germany.

'*Ihr Mann in Frankreich.*'

'Go ahead and talk,' the man in Bonn broke in. 'I'm so clean here, I'm wired into the Saudi Arabian Embassy.'

'*What?*'

'I use their lines, not their receivership. Think of the money I save France. I should be given a bonus.'

'You are a rogue.'

'Why else would you pay me, Paris?'

'I read your communiqué to us. Several things were left out.'

'Such as?'

'Who comprises that "small circle of conservatives who wink at their own oratory". You deliver no names, not even a hint of their affiliations.'

'Naturally. Isn't that part of our very personal agreement? Do you really want the entire Deuxième Bureau to have the information? If so, your bank in Switzerland is entirely too generous to this rogue.'

'Enough!' snapped Moreau. 'You do what you do, and I do what I do, and neither has to know what the other is doing. Is that understood?'

'I imagine it has to be. So what do you want to know?'

'Who are the people leading, or behind, this small circle you describe?'

'Most are nothing but opportunists with little ability who

wish to catch on to a tail that will bring back the old days. Others are followers who march to past drums because they have none of their own—'

'Their leaders?' said Moreau curtly. 'Who are they?'

'That'll cost you, Claude.'

'It will cost *you* if you don't spell them out. Monetarily and otherwise.'

'I believe you. Alas, my presence would barely be missed. You're a tough man, Moreau.'

'And eminently fair,' countered the Deuxième chief. 'You're well paid, both on and off the books, the former far more dangerous for you. I wouldn't have to leave this office, or issue a single order except one: "Quietly release selected top-secret information to our friends in Bonn." Your demise probably wouldn't even make the papers.'

'And if I give you what I have?'

'Then a lovely, productive friendship will continue.'

'It's not much, Claude.'

'I trust that's not a prelude for your withholding anything.'

'Of course it isn't. I'm not a fool.'

'There's a logic in your words. So give me this disappointing, limited information that concerns your "small circle".'

'My informants tell me that every Tuesday night a meeting is held at one or another's house along the Rhine, usually a large house, an estate. Each has docking facilities and all those coming together arrive by boat, never by automobile.'

'A boat's wake is somewhat less identifiable than tyre tracks,' interrupted Moreau, 'or vehicles with licence plates.'

'Understood. Therefore, these meetings are secret and the identities of those attending concealed.'

'The houses, however, are not, are they? Or hadn't that fact occurred to your informants?'

'I was getting to them. For God's sake, give me some credit.'

'I'm impatient. The owners' names, please.'

'It's a mixed bag, Claude. Three are upstanding aristocrats whose families opposed Hitler and paid for it; three, possibly four, are part of the new rich who guard their assets from further government appropriations; and two are men of the cloth – one an old Catholic priest, the other a Lutheran minister who apparently takes his vows of non-ostentation seriously. He's listed as the lessee of the smallest house on the river.'

'The *names*, damn you!'

'I have only six—'

'Where are the others?'

'The unknown three are also renters, and the leasing agents in Switzerland won't reveal anything. That's standard practice among the very rich who want to avoid taxes on outside income.'

'Give me the six, then.'

'Maximilian von Löwenstein, he owns the largest—'

'His father, the general, was executed by the SS in the Wolfsschanze incident, the attempted assassination of Hitler. Next?'

'Albert Richter, once a playboy, now a converted, serious politician.'

'He's still a dilettante, with property in Monaco. His family was about to cut him off unless he changed his ways. It's an act. Next?'

'Günter Jäger, he's the Lutheran minister.'

'I don't know him, at least nothing that comes to mind. Next?'

'Monsignor Heinrich Paltz, he's the priest.'

'An ancient right-wing Catholic who covers his biases with sanctimonious drivel. Next?'

'Friedrich von Schell, he's the third of the rich people we've identified. His estate has more than—'

'He's smart,' interrupted Moreau, 'and he's tough where the unions are concerned. A nineteenth-century Prussian in Armani suits. Next?'

'Ansel Schmidt, very outspoken; an electronics engineer

who made millions in high-technology exports and fights the government at every turn.'

'A pig who went from one firm to another stealing technology until he had it all, and formed his own companies.'

'That's what I have, Claude; it's hardly worth my life.'

'Who are the Swiss rental agencies?'

'The contact is a real estate company here in Bonn. One sends an emissary with a hundred thousand deutsche marks as a sign of serious intent, and they forward it to a bank in Zurich, along with a profile of the would-be lessee. If the money's returned, there's no deal. If it isn't, someone goes to Zurich.'

'Telephone and household bills? I trust you've looked into these with our unknown three.'

'In each case they are sent to personal managers, two in Stuttgart, one in Munich, all coded, no names included.'

'Certainly the Bundestag has a list of addresses.'

'Private residences are closely guarded, as they are in governments everywhere. I could try, but it might be dangerous if I were caught. Frankly, I can't stand pain, even the thought of it.'

'Then you don't *have* the specific addresses?'

'There, I'm afraid, I've failed you. I could describe them from a distance, and from the river, but the residence numbers have been removed, the gates closed, and there are patrols with guard dogs both within and without. There are no mailboxes, of course.'

'It's one of those three, then,' said Moreau softly.

'Who's one of what?' asked the man in Bonn.

'The leader of our "small circle" . . . Put your people on the roads to these houses and order them to identify the vehicles driving through the gates. Then match them with those at the Bundestag.'

'My dear Claude, perhaps I wasn't clear. These estates are patrolled both inside and outside, dozens of cameras mounted throughout the grounds. If I could hire such men, which is unlikely, and they were caught, the trail would lead to me, and, as I mentioned, even the prospect of pain is abhorrent to your obedient servant.'

'I often wonder how you got to where you are.'

'By living well, with the proper finances to ingratiate myself among the powerful, but most important, by not being caught. Does that answer you?'

'God help you if you ever get caught.'

'No, Claude, God help *you*.'

'I won't pursue that.'

'My fee?'

'When mine comes in, yours will follow.'

'Whose side *are* you on, my old friend?'

'No one's and everyone's, but especially my own.' Moreau hung up the phone and looked at the notes he had taken. He circled three names: Albert Richter, Friedrich von Schell, and Ansel Schmidt. One was probably the leader he sought, but each had a reason to be and the wherewithal to build a constituency. At the least, they provided him with the immediate ammunition he needed. He saw that the blue strip on line three was lit; the scrambler was still activated. He picked up the phone and dialled a number in Geneva.

'*L'Université de Genève*,' said the operator four hundred miles away.

'Professor André Benoit, if you please.'

'*Allô?*' said the voice of the university's most prominent scholar of political science.

'It's your confidant from Paris. May we talk?'

'In a moment.' The phone was silent for eight seconds. 'Now we may,' said Professor Benoit, back on the line. 'No doubt you're calling about the problems we've had in Paris. I can tell you now, I know nothing. *Nobody* does! Can you enlighten us?'

'I don't know what you're talking about.'

'Where have you *been*?'

'In Monte Carlo, with the actor and his wife. I got back just this morning.'

'Then you haven't heard?' asked the man in Geneva, astonished.

'About the attacks on the American Latham and his subsequent murder at the country restaurant, no doubt engineered by your psychopathic K Unit here in the city? It was a stupid act.'

'*No!* Zero One, Paris, has disappeared, and early this morning the police reported an assault on the rue Diane—'

'Witkowski's place?' Moreau interrupted. 'I haven't seen the information.'

'They don't have what I know either. The entire K Unit has also disappeared.'

'I never knew where they were posted—'

'None of us did, but they're *gone!*'

'I don't know what to say.'

'Don't say, get on top of things and find out what happened!' demanded Geneva.

'I'm afraid I have more bad news for you and Bonn,' said the Deuxième chief haltingly.

'What could it possibly be?'

'My agents in Germany have come up with names, men who meet every Tuesday night in houses along the Rhine.'

'Oh, my God! What names?'

Claude Moreau gave them to him, slowly spelling out each. 'Tell them to be very, very careful,' he said. 'They're all under intelligence microscopes.'

'Outside of certain reputations, I don't know *any* of them!' exclaimed the professor in Geneva. 'I had no idea—'

'You weren't meant to have any ideas, *Herr Professor*. You follow orders, as I do.'

'Yes, but . . . but . . .'

'Academicians aren't very competent when it comes to practical matters. Just make sure our associates in Bonn get the information.'

'Yes . . . yes, of course, Paris. Oh, my *God!*'

Moreau hung up the phone and leaned back in his chair. Things – *things* – were going his way. They might not be the best, but they were better than anyone else's. If he lost, he and his wife could always retire comfortably somewhere outside of France. On the other hand, he could also be executed by a firing squad. *C'est la vie.*

It was early evening, the setting sun filtered through the windows of Karin de Vries's apartment on the rue Madeleine. 'I went to my flat this afternoon,' said Drew, sitting in the armchair, talking to Karin, across on the couch. 'Of course, I had a marine on either side of me – sworn to secrecy by Witkowski, who could send them back to boot camp – and they kept their hands on their holstered weapons, but still it felt good to be able to walk in the street, you know what I mean?'

'I do, indeed, but I worry about misplaced confidence. Suppose there are others we don't know about?'

'Hell, we know about one, Reynolds, in Communications. I'm told he fled like a rat into the sewers, probably living on a Nazi pension in the Mediterranean, if they didn't decide to shoot him first.'

'If he's in the Mediterranean, I suspect his body is several hundred feet below on the ocean's bottom.'

'Actually, it's a sea.'

'I don't think the definition would matter to him.'

Silence. Finally, Drew spoke. 'Where are we, lady?'

'What do you mean?'

'What do I have to do, go by the numbers?'

'What numbers?'

'Like, "One, two, three, four, what the hell am I marching for?" You've been hiding me all night and all day, but I can't get near you.'

'What are you talking about, Drew?'

'Christ, I'm not even sure how to put it ... I never thought I'd think it, not really, and certainly not say it to someone who may be keeping me from being killed, a subordinate who has an apartment I could never afford.'

'Please be clearer.'

'How can I? I always thought I'd march to my brother's drum; he was so right, so perfect. Then I heard him in that booth before he was killed – you know what I mean – crying out how much he loved you, adored you—'

'*Stop* it, Drew,' said De Vries sharply. 'Are you saying you're imitating your brother in his *delusions*?'

'No, I'm not,' said Latham calmly, quietly, his eyes locked with hers. 'His delusions are not my feelings, Karin. I've grown out of that syndrome; it never did me much good anyway. You came into his life first, mine years later, and the equation, no matter how similar, is worlds apart. I'm not Harry, I could never be him, but I'm me, and I've never known anyone like you . . . How's that for some kind of declaration?'

'Extremely touching, my dear.'

'There's that "my dear" again. Meaning nothing.'

'Don't belittle it, Drew. I have to get rid of my ghosts, and when I do, it would be nice to think that you might be there for me. Perhaps I could become attached to you, for you have qualities I so admire, but a relationship is a remote and distant thing to me now. The past has to be put to rest. Can you understand that?'

'Whether I do or I don't, I'll do my goddamnedest to make it happen.'

The post-noonday crowds filled the street, the office buildings severely depleted as hordes of employees rushed to their favourite cafés and restaurants for luncheon engagements. The Parisian lunch was more than a meal; as often as not, it was a minor event, and God help the employer who expected his hired hands, particularly his manicured executives, to return on time, most especially during the summer weeks.

Which is why Dr Gerhardt Kroeger was becoming more and more agitated, continuously jostled as he was by the departing crowds while he stood holding the folded newspaper in front of his face, his eyes on the entrance of the

Deuxième Bureau's building on his left. He could not afford to miss the figure of Claude Moreau. Time was of the essence, not an hour to be wasted. His creation, Harry Latham, had entered the countdown; he had, at maximum, two days, forty-eight hours, and even this was imprecise. And what added to the surgeon's near-unbearable stress was a detail he had not described to his superiors in the Brüderschaft: prior to a subject's brain finally rejecting the implant, virtually exploding, the area around the surgery became horribly discoloured; an inflamed skin rash the size of a demitasse saucer appeared, directing whoever performed an autopsy to investigate the unusual manifestation. Contrary to general belief, the data stored in an ROM for a solitary purpose and environs could be extracted by equipment foreign to its original controls.

In the wrong hands, the Brotherhood of the Watch could be destroyed, its secrets exposed, its global objectives all too clear. *Mein Gott!* reflected Kroeger. *We are the victims of our own progress!* Then he thought of the proliferation of nuclear weapons and realized the truth of his unoriginal conclusion.

There was Moreau! The broad-shouldered chief of the Deuxième walked out of the building's entrance and turned to his right, hastening his steps on the pavement. He was in a hurry, which meant Kroeger had to practically run to catch up, for the Frenchman was heading in the opposite direction. Parting the bodies in front of him, his apologies half in German, half in French, he closed the distance between himself and Moreau, leaving angry strollers in his wake. Finally, he was within arm's reach. 'Monsieur, *monsieur!*' he cried out. 'You dropped something!'

'*Pardon?*' The Deuxième chief stopped and turned around. 'You must be mistaken, I dropped nothing.'

'I was sure it was you,' continued the surgeon in French. 'A billfold or a notebook. A man picked it up and ran!'

Moreau quickly felt his pockets, his face changing from concern to relief. 'You *are* mistaken,' he said, 'I'm missing nothing, but I'm grateful nevertheless. Pickpockets are numerous in Paris.'

'As they are in Munich, monsieur. I apologize, but the brotherhood I belong to insists we follow the Christian precepts of helping others.'

'I see, a Christian brotherhood, how admirable.' Moreau stared at the man as pedestrians rushed by on both sides. 'The Pont Neuf at nine o'clock tonight,' he added, lowering his voice. 'The north trespass.'

The Paris mist diffused the moon's reflection on the waters of the Seine; a summer rain was imminent. In contrast to the majority of strollers on the bridge who were hurrying to escape the inclement weather, the two figures walked slowly towards each other on the north pedestrian walk. They met at midpoint; Moreau spoke first.

'You made reference to something that might be familiar to me. Would you care to clarify?'

'There's no time for games, monsieur. We both know who we are and what we are. Terrible things have happened.'

'So I understand – things I knew nothing about until this morning. The alarming aspect is that my office was not kept up-to-date. I can't help but wonder why. Have any of your couriers been indiscreet?'

'Certainly not! Our mission now, our *paramount* mission, is to find the American Harry Latham. It's more vital than you can imagine. We know that the embassy, with the aid of the Antinayous, is hiding him somewhere here in Paris. We must find him! Surely American intelligence keeps you informed. Where *is* he?'

'You've just made several leaps beyond my knowledge, monsieur ... what is your name? I do not talk to unidentified men.'

'*Kroeger*, Dr Gerhardt Kroeger, and a call to Bonn will confirm my high station!'

'How impressive. And what "high station" do you occupy, Doctor?'

'I was the surgeon who . . . who saved Harry Latham's life. And now I must find him.'

'Yes, you said that. You're aware, are you not, that his brother Drew was killed by your idiot K Unit?'

'It was the wrong brother.'

'Again, I see. It *was* the K Unit, killers barely out of school, if they ever went to one.'

'I will not tolerate your insults!' cried a frustrated Kroeger. 'Frankly, you're not considered entirely reliable, so I advise you to be direct with me. You know the consequences if you're not.'

'If what you say is true, I'm a rich man for it.'

'Find us Harry Latham!'

'I'll certainly try—'

'Stay up all night, reach every source you have – French, American, British, *everyone*. Find out where they've hidden Harry Latham! I'm at the Lutetia, room eight hundred.'

'The top floor. You must be important.'

'I will not sleep until I hear from you.'

'That's foolish, Doctor. As a physician, you should know that a lack of sleep makes for unstable thinking. But since you're so persuasive, your threats also, be assured I'll do my best to satisfy you.'

'*Sehr gut!*' said Kroeger, reverting to German. 'I will leave now. Do not disappoint me; do not disappoint the Brüderschaft, for you know what will happen.'

'I understand.'

Kroeger walked rapidly away, his figure quickly obscured by the settling mists. And Claude Moreau strolled slowly to find a taxi on the Rive Gauche. He had some thinking to do, among those thoughts the secure communications equipment at the Deuxième Bureau. Too many things had become elliptical.

It was 7:42 A.M. Washington time when Wesley Sorenson

walked into his office at Consular Operations; the only other person there was his secretary. 'All the overnight reports are on your desk, sir,' she said.

'Thanks, Ginny. As I've said repeatedly, I really hope you put in for overtime. No one else gets here before eight-thirty.'

'You're very understanding when the kids are sick, so why push it, Mr Director. Also, it's easier for me; I can collate everything before the troops come in.'

They have come in, in more ways than you know, thought Sorenson. He had been at Andrews Air Force Base at four o'clock in the morning and personally escorted the two neo-Nazis off the jet from Paris, seeing them into a marine van to a safe house in Virginia. Despite his exhaustion, the Cons-Op director would be driven there shortly past noon to, again, personally interrogate the prisoners; it was a craft he knew well.

'Anything urgent?' he asked his secretary.

'Only everything.'

'Nothing changes.'

Sorenson walked into his inner office, crossed to his desk, and sat down. The file folders were labelled: THE PEOPLE'S REPUBLIC OF CHINA, TAIWAN, THE PHILIPPINES, THE MIDDLE EAST, GREECE, THE BALKANS . . . and finally, GERMANY and FRANCE.

Shoving aside the rest, he opened the file from Paris. It was explosive. Using the police reports, it described the assault on Colonel Witkowski's apartment with no mention of the colonel's sending two captives on a military jet to Washington. It spoke of the burned-out headquarters of a neo-Nazi unit in the Avignon warehouse complex. They were reputed to be killers who had disappeared. The final news from Paris was a coded message from Witkowski, decoded in Consular Operations; this was the explosion. *Gerhardt Kroeger in Paris. He's hunting Harry Latham. The target has been alerted.*

Gerhardt Kroeger, surgeon, mystery man, and the key to

many things. No one outside of American intelligence knew about him. In a way, thought Sorenson, it was wrong. The French and the British should be included, but the CIA – Knox Talbot agreeing – could not trust them.

And then at eight in the morning his telephone rang. 'Paris calling,' said his secretary. 'A Mr Moreau from the Deuxième Bureau.'

Sorenson quietly gasped, his face suddenly pale. Moreau had been cut off; he was suspect. The Cons-Op director breathed deeply, picked up the phone, then spoke, his words controlled.

'Hello, Claude, it's good to hear from you, old friend.'

'Apparently, Wesley, it's not proper for me to hear from you, if I may speak plainly.'

'I don't know what you mean.'

'Oh, come, within the last thirty-six hours a great many things have happened that concern us both, but not a word of them has been processed to my office. What kind of cooperation is *that*?'

'I . . . I don't know, Claude.'

'Of course you do. I've been systematically excluded from the operation. *Why?*'

'I can't answer that. I don't control the operation, you know that. I had no idea—'

'*Please*, Wesley. In the field you were an accomplished liar, but not with someone who told lies *with* you. We both know how these things work, don't we? Someone heard something from someone else and the diseased oyster grows, producing a false pearl. But there's time for that later. Assuming that you're still functioning, I may have a chess piece for you.'

'What is it?'

'Who's Gerhardt Kroeger?'

'*What?*'

'You heard me, and it's obvious that you've heard the name before. He's a doctor.'

Kroeger was off limits to the Deuxième. Moreau was out of the loop! Was he fishing?

299

'I'm not sure I have heard it, Claude. Gerhardt ... Kroeger, was it?'

'Now you're positively insulting. Again, I'll let it pass, for my information is too important. Kroeger followed me and stopped me during my evening stroll. In short words, he made it plain that I either directed him to Harry Latham or I was a dead man.'

'I can't believe this! Why would he come to *you*?'

'I asked him the same question and his answer was one I might have expected. I have people in Germany, as I do in most countries. A year ago I negotiated for the life of one man being held by a skinhead crowd in Mannheim. I got him out for roughly six thousand dollars American, a bargain, I'd say. Still, they had the name of the Deuxième, and knew the arrangement could not have been made without my approval.'

'But you never heard of Gerhardt Kroeger before?'

'Not until last night, I just told you that. I went back to my office and searched our records for the past five years; there was nothing. By the way, he's staying at the Hotel Lutetia, room eight hundred, and he expects me to call him.'

'For God's sake, *take* him!'

'Oh, he won't leave, Wesley, I can assure you of that. But why not play with him a bit? He certainly doesn't work solo, and we're looking for bigger fish.'

A wave of relief spread over Sorenson. Claude Moreau was clean! He never would have offered up Gerhardt Kroeger, hotel and room number included, if he were working for the Brotherhood.

'If it makes you feel any better,' said the director of Cons-Op, 'I was excluded myself for a while. Guess why? Because we worked together, specifically Istanbul, where you had the grace to save my ass.'

'You would have done the same for me.'

'That's what I angrily told the Agency, and what I'm going to tell them again, even angrier.'

'One moment, Wesley,' said Moreau slowly. 'Speaking of

Istanbul, do you remember when the *apparatchiks* of the KGB believed you were a double, actually an informer for their superiors in Moscow?'

'Certainly. They lived like the suleimans with the riches of the Topkapi at their disposal. They were frightened to death.'

'So they took you into their confidence, did they not?'

'Naturally, telling me things – anything – to justify their lifestyles. Most of it was rubbish, but not all.'

'But they *did* take you into their confidence, no?'

'Yes.'

'Then, for the moment, let things stay the way they are. I'm still on the outside, not to be trusted. Perhaps I can play with Herr Doktor Kroeger and learn things.'

'Which means you need something first.'

'"Anything", as you said, referring to Istanbul. It doesn't have to be accurate, but it should be relatively acceptable.'

'Like what?'

'Where is Harry Latham?'

There was no Harry Latham. The doubts returned to the former deep-cover intelligence officer. 'Even I don't know that,' said Sorenson.

'I don't mean where he *really* is,' broke in Moreau, 'just where he might be. Something they would believe.'

The doubts receded. 'Well, there's an organization called the Antinayous—'

'They know about it,' interrupted Moreau. 'Those people are untraceable. Something else.'

'They certainly know about Witkowski and the De Vries woman—'

'They certainly do,' agreed the Deuxième chief. 'Give me someplace where, with a little research, they could learn how your people operate.'

'I suppose that would be Marseilles. We follow up on the drug interdictions; too many of our people have been bought or disappeared. Actually, we're fairly obvious if anyone's looking. It's a deterrent.'

'That's good. I'll use it.'

'Claude, I'll be honest, I want to clear you over here! It's insufferable that you're under suspicion.'

'Not yet, my old friend. Remember Istanbul. We've played these games before.'

In Paris, Moreau hung up the phone, once more leaning back in his chair, his eyes on the ceiling, his thoughts bouncing from one fragment of information to another. He was now in the race to the finish. The risks he was taking were gargantuan, but he could not stop. *Revenge*, it was all that mattered.

CHAPTER EIGHTEEN

Since Drew Latham had supposedly departed this world, his Deuxième car had been withdrawn. In its place, Witkowski had ordered embassy Transport to supply security measures: three personnel on eight-hour shifts, and an unmarked vehicle kept available for an unnamed army officer and his lady, at the moment in the rue Madeleine. The colonel made it clear to the marines, who would be on rotation duty, that should they recognize the officer, his identity was to remain secret. If it did not, certain gyrenes would be sent back to Parris Island along with the lowest recruits, their accomplishments stricken from their records.

'You don't have to say that, Colonel,' said a marine sergeant. 'If you'll forgive me, sir, it's goddamned demeaning.'

'Then I apologize.'

'You should, sir,' added a corporal. 'We've been on embassy duty from Beijing to Kuala Lumpur, where real security mattered.'

'Hog damn right!' whispered a second corporal, then louder, 'We're not army – sir. We're marines.'

'Then I *really* apologize, fellas. Forgive this old GI issue. I'm just a fossil.'

'We know who you are, Colonel,' said the sergeant. 'You have nothing to worry about, sir.'

'I thank you.'

As the three departed for the bowels of Transport, Witkowski was struck by a comment from one of the corporals. 'He shoulda been a marine. Hell, I'll follow that son of a bitch down the barrel of a cannon.'

Stanley Witkowski considered for a moment that it was the highest praise he had ever received during his entire career. But now there were other things to think about, not the least of which were Drew Latham and Karin de Vries. The confluence of hours and exhaustion dictated that Latham stay in De Vries's apartment rather than drive out to the Antinayous' sterile house – actually, the Antinayous insisted upon it in the event the target was still being followed. After several days without any untoward occurrence, they would reconsider, but only reconsider. 'He has involved himself in things too public for our purposes,' an abrupt woman at the Maison Rouge had said. 'We admire him, but we cannot tolerate the remotest possibility of being discovered.'

As to Karin staying at the embassy, there simply was no point. As a member of classified D and R who resided outside the embassy, her address was filed only in Security, and anyone requesting it had to be cleared by the colonel himself. Several male attachés had; they were refused. Added to which, the widow De Vries had once shared a piece of information that greatly relieved him.

'I'm not a poor woman, Colonel. I have three automobiles here in Paris in different garages. I change appearances with each change of vehicle.'

'That takes a load off my mind,' said Witkowski. 'Considering the information in your head, it's damned smart thinking.'

'It wasn't mine, sir. General Raichert, the supreme commander of NATO, ordered it in The Hague. There the Americans paid for it, but the circumstances were different. I don't expect it here.'

'You must *not* be poor.'

'I'm committed to what I do, Colonel. The money's not important.'

That conversation had taken place over four months

before, and Witkowski then had no idea how 'committed' the new arrival was. He had no doubts now. The telephone on his private line rang, interrupting the colonel's reverie. 'Yes?'

'It's your wandering angel, Stanley,' said Drew. 'Any word from House Red?'

'There's no room at the inn, at least not for a while. The fact that you're a mark has them worried.'

'I'm wearing a uniform, your uniform, for Christ's sake! By the way, you're a tad bigger in the waist and the ass than I am. The tunic's fine, however.'

'I'm greatly relieved; it'll cover the imperfections when the fashion photographers take your picture . . . You could be disguised by that actor, Villier, and they'd still want you to stay away.'

'I guess I can't really blame them.'

'I don't,' agreed the colonel. 'Will Karin put up with you another day or two until I can find proper lodgings?'

'I don't know, ask her.' Latham's voice became fainter as he held the phone away from his face. 'It's Witkowski. He wants to know if my lease is up.'

'Hello, Colonel,' said Karin. 'I gather the Antinayous are balking.'

'I'm afraid so.'

'It's understandable.'

'Yes, it is, but I haven't come up with a suitable alternative. Can you stand him for another day, perhaps two? I'll arrange something by then.'

'It's not a problem. He tells me he made his bed this morning.'

'*Hell*, yes,' Drew's voice was heard in the background. 'I'm back in Boy Scout camp with lots of cold showers!'

'Pay no attention to him. Colonel. I believe I mentioned he can be quite childish.'

'He wasn't at the Trocadéro or the Meurice or the Bois de Boulogne, Karin. Even I'll give him that.'

'Agreed,' said De Vries, 'but if you have difficulties,

there's a possible solution, at least it worked several times in Amsterdam. Freddie would put on one of several uniforms – American, Dutch, English, it didn't matter – and register at the Amstel for confidential meetings.'

'One of his well-known tricks, then?' asked a wary Witkowski.

'A benign one, Colonel. As Drew told you, your uniform fits him quite well, and I can easily sew tucks in the waist and other places—'

'I'm painfully aware of that other place . . . What then; he's still Latham?'

'With a slight altering of appearance, certainly less so.'

'I beg your pardon?'

'A change of hair colour,' she replied, speaking softly, 'especially around the temples, where it's obvious below his officer's cap, and a pair of thick-rimmed glasses, plain lenses of course, and a false military ID. I can do the hair and supply the glasses if you'll furnish an identification card. He could then register at any crowded hotel, which I'm sure you can arrange.'

'This is hardly in the embassy's purview, Karin.'

'From what I understand of Consular Operations, I submit it's within *its* range of operations.'

'You've got me there, I guess. You must really want him out.'

'It's not the person, Colonel, it's the fact that he's a man, seen here only as an American army officer. I doubt that anyone in the building knows that I work for the embassy, but if anyone does or suspects that I do, it compromises Drew, myself, and our objectives.'

'In simple words, your residence could become another target.'

'Far-fetched, perhaps, but not implausible.'

'Nothing's implausible in this war. I'll need a photograph.'

'I still have Freddie's camera. You'll have a dozen in the morning.'

'I wish I was there to see you dye his hair. That'd be a real hoot.'

De Vries hung up the telephone, walked to a closet in the foyer, opened it, and took out a small suitcase with two combination locks. Latham watched her from the armchair, a drink in his hand. 'I trust that's not holding a quickly assembled automatic weapon,' he said as Karin placed the luggage on the coffee table in front of the couch and sat down.

'Good heavens, no,' she replied, manipulating the combination locks and opening the suitcase. 'In truth, I hope it can help you avoid the necessity of facing such a gun.'

'Hold it. What's in there? I couldn't hear you most of the time when you were talking to Stanley. What's boiling in that awesomely attractive head of yours?'

'This is what Freddie called his "emergency travelling case".'

'Already I'd rather not know. Freddie was violent with you and that makes him unfriendly.'

'There were the other years too, Drew.'

'Thanks for nothing. What's *in* there?'

'Simple methods of disguise, nothing dramatic or mind-boggling. Various pre-glued moustaches, also a couple of chin beards, and numerous eyeglasses ... and some basic washable dyes.' She described the last far more quietly.

'What was that?'

'You can't stay here, my friend,' said Karin, looking at him over the top of the suitcase. 'Now, don't become defensive and take it personally, but the houses and flats here in the Madeleine are like a small upscale neighbourhood in America. People talk, and gossip abounds in the cafés and the bakeries. To use your word, it could reach "unfriendly" ears.'

'I accept that, I understand it, but that's not what I asked you.'

'You'll be registering at a hotel under a different name,

which the colonel will supply, and with a slightly different appearance.'

'*What?*'

'I'm going to dye your hair and your eyebrows with a washable solution. Reddish-blond, I think.'

'What are you *talking* about? I'm no Jean-Pierre Villier!'

'You don't have to be. Just be yourself; no one will recognize you unless he's standing a few feet in front of you and staring straight at you. Now, if you'll please put on the colonel's trousers, I'll pin them and adjust the size.'

'You know, you're crazier than a pissed loon!'

'Can you think of a better solution?'

'Goddammit!' roared Latham, swallowing the remainder of his Scotch. 'No, actually, I can't.'

'On second thought, we'll do the hair first. Please remove your shirt.'

'How about my trousers? I'd feel more natural, more at home that way.'

'You're not at home, Drew.'

'Gotcha, lady!'

Moreau picked up his console phone, pressing a button that would record his conversation, and spoke to the Lutetia switchboard. 'Room eight hundred, if you please.'

'Certainly, sir.'

'*Yes?*' said the muffled, guttural voice on the line.

'*Monsieur le docteur?*' asked the chief of the Deuxième, unsure that he had the right connection. 'It is I, from the Pont Neuf. Is it you?'

'Of course it is. What have you brought me?'

'I have reached deep, Doctor, far deeper than is healthy for me. I've provoked the American CIA into telling me that it is, indeed, hiding Harry Latham.'

'*Where?*'

'Perhaps not here in Paris, perhaps in Marseilles.'

'Perhaps, *perhaps*? That does me no good! Can you be sure?'

'No, but possibly you can.'

'*Me?*'

'You have people in Marseilles, no?'

'Of course. A great deal of finance comes through there.'

'Look for the "Consulars", that's what they're called.'

'We know about them,' said Gerhardt, breathless. 'The bastard intelligence group, Consular Operations. One can spot them at every corner, every café.'

'Take one of them, see what you can learn.'

'Within the hour. Where can I reach you?'

'I'll call you back an hour from now.'

The hour passed, and Moreau called the Lutetia. 'Anything?' he asked a hyper Gerhardt.

'It's insane!' said the doctor. 'The man we spoke with is someone we've paid thousands to so we could collect millions through the network. He said we were crazy; no such man as Harry Latham is on their list or in Marseilles!'

'Then he's still in Paris,' said Moreau, frustration in his voice. 'I'll go back to work.'

'As fast as you can!'

'Ever so,' said the Deuxième chief, hanging up the phone and smiling an enigmatic smile. He waited exactly fourteen minutes and then called back the Lutetia. It was the moment to propel anxiety into high gear.

'Yes?'

'It is I again. Something just came in.'

'For God's sake, what *is* it?'

'Harry Latham.'

'*What?*'

'He called one of my people, a man he had worked with in East Berlin who rightfully believed he should inform me. Apparently Latham is quite intense – isolation can do that, you know – even to the point that he thinks his own embassy is compromised—'

'It's Latham!' interrupted the German. 'The symptoms are predictable.'

'What symptoms? What do you mean?'

'Nothing, nothing at all. As you say, isolation can do strange things to people . . . What did he want?'

'Possibly French protection, is what we gather. My man's to meet him at the Metro station, the Georges Cinq stop at two o'clock this afternoon, towards the rear of the platform.'

'I must be there!' shouted Gerhardt.

'It's not advisable, nor is it the policy of the Bureau to involve the hunted with the hunter, monsieur, when they are not part of our organization.'

'You don't understand. I *must* be with you!'

'Why is that? It could be dangerous.'

'Not to me, *never* to me.'

'Now I don't understand you.'

'You don't have to! Remember the Brotherhood, *it* is what you must obey, and I'm giving you your orders.'

'Then, of course, I must obey, *Herr Doktor*. We meet on the platform at ten minutes to two o'clock. Not before or after, is that understood?'

'I understand.'

Moreau did not hang up the phone; instead, he pressed the disconnect button and touched the digits that connected him to his most trusted subordinate officer. 'Jacques,' he said calmly, 'we have a very important confrontation at two o'clock, just you and me. Meet me downstairs at one-thirty and I'll fill you in. Incidentally, carry your automatic, but fill the magazine with blanks.'

'That's a very strange request, Claude.'

'It's a very strange confrontation,' said Moreau, hanging up the phone.

Drew looked into the mirror, his eyes wide in shock. 'For Christ's sake, I look like a Disney cartoon!' he roared.

'Not really,' said Karin, standing above him over the kitchen sink and taking the mirror from him. 'You're just not used to it, that's all.'

'It's preposterous! I look like the leader of a gay rights parade.'

'Does that bother you?'

'Hell, no, I've got a lot of friends in that crowd, but I'm not one of them.'

'It can be washed out in a shower, so stop complaining. Now, put on the uniform and I'll take some photographs for Colonel Witkowski, then adjust the trousers.'

'What has that son of a bitch got me *into*?'

'Basically, saving your life, can you accept that?'

'Are you always so logical?'

'Logic and the illogically logical saved Freddie's life more times than I can tell you. Please put on the uniform.'

Latham did as he was told, returning two minutes later as a full colonel in the United States Army. 'A uniform becomes you,' said De Vries, observing him, 'especially when you stand up straight.'

'One doesn't have any choice in this coat – excuse me, tunic. It's so damn tight, if you don't arch your spine, you're punctured somewhere and can't breathe. I'd make a lousy soldier. I'd insist on wearing fatigues.'

'Regulations wouldn't permit it.'

'Another reason why I'd make a lousy soldier.'

'Actually, you'd probably be a good one, as long as you were a general.'

'Hardly likely.'

'Hardly.' Karin gestured towards the foyer. 'Come into the hallway, I'm set up. Here are your glasses.' She handed him a pair of heavy tortoiseshells.

'Set up? Glasses?' Drew looked over at the short hall that greeted a visitor from the front door. There was a camera on a tripod aimed at a blank off-white wall. 'You're a photographer too?'

'Not at all. Frequently, however, Freddie needed a new photograph for a different passport. He instructed me how to use this, not that I needed any instructions. It's an instant-picture camera, sized down to passport dimensions ... Put on the glasses and stand against the wall. Take off the hat; I want the full glory of your blond hair evident.'

A few minutes later De Vries had fifteen small Polaroid photographs of a light-haired, bespectacled colonel, looking as grim and uncomfortable as any passport picture. 'Splendid,' she decreed. 'Now let's go back to the couch, where I've got my equipment.'

'Equipment?'

'The trousers, remember?'

'Oh, this is the good part. Should I take them off?'

'Not if you want them to fit. Come along.'

Fifteen minutes later, having suffered only two painful punctures of a straight pin, Latham was ordered back into the guest room to resume his normal appearance. Again he returned, now to find Karin at the alcove table, on which was placed a sewing machine. The trousers, please.'

'You know, you're blowing my mind, lady,' said Drew, handing her the army issue. 'Are you some kind of female deep-cover factotum who works behind the scenes?'

'Let's say I've been there, Monsieur Latham.'

'Yes, it's not the first time you've said that.'

'Accept it, Drew. Besides, it's none of your business.'

'You're right there. It's just, as the layers peel away, I'm not sure whom I'm talking to. I have to accept Freddie, and NATO, and Harry, and the subterranean way you got to Paris, but why do I have the feeling that there's something else that's driving you?'

'It's your imagination because you live in a world of probables and improbables, possibles and impossibles, what's real and what isn't. I've told you everything you have to know about me, isn't that enough?'

'For the moment it has to be,' said Latham, his eyes locked with hers. 'But my instinct says there's something else you won't tell me ... Why don't you laugh more? You're goddamned radiant when you laugh.'

'There hasn't been that much to laugh about, has there?'

'Come on, you know what I mean. A little laughter now and then relieves the tension. Harry once told me that, and we both believed Harry. Years from now, if we run into each other, we'll probably laugh at the Bois de Boulogne. It had its funny moments.'

'A life was taken, Drew. Whether it was the life of a good man or a bad man, I killed him, I cut short the life of a very young person. I've never killed anyone before.'

'If you hadn't, he would have killed me.'

'I know that, I keep telling myself that. But why does the killing have to go on? That was Freddie's life, not *mine*.'

'And it shouldn't have to be yours. But to answer your question logically – logic being a part of your lexicon – if we don't kill when it's necessary, if we don't stop the neos, ten thousand times the killings will take place. Ten thousand, hell, let's start with six million. Yesterday they were Jews and Gypsies and other "undesirables". Tomorrow they could be Republicans and Democrats in my country who can't stomach their bilge. Don't kid yourself, Karin, they get a foothold in Europe, the rest of this discontented world goes down like a row of dominoes, because they're constantly, incessantly, appealing to every zealot who wants "the good old days". No crime in the streets because even the onlookers are shot on sight; executions rampant because there are no appeals; no habeas corpus because it's not necessary; the presumed innocent and the guilty are lumped together, so let's get rid of them both, prison being more expensive than bullets. *That's* the future we're fighting against.'

'You think I don't know that?' said Karin. 'Of course I do, you sermonizing fool! Why do you think I've lived as I have my entire adult life?'

'But the exalted Freddie notwithstanding, there's something else, isn't there?'

'You have no right to probe. May we stop this conversation?'

'For now, sure. But I think I've made clear my feelings for you, returned or not, so it may come up again.'

'*Stop* it!' said De Vries, tears slowly falling from her blinking eyes. 'Do not *do* this to me.'

Latham ran to her, kneeling by her chair. 'I'm sorry, I'm really *sorry*. I didn't mean to hurt you, I wouldn't do that.'

'I know you wouldn't,' said Karin, composing herself and cupping his face with her hands. 'You are a good person, Drew Latham, but don't ask any more questions – they *do* hurt too much. Instead . . . make love to me, make *love* to me! I so need someone like you.'

'I wish you'd eliminate the "someone", and just say "you".'

'Then I say it. You, Drew Latham, make love to me.'

Gently, Drew helped her from the chair, then lifted her up in his arms and carried her into the bedroom.

The rest of the morning was one of sexual excess. Karin de Vries had been too long without a man; she was insatiable. At the last, she threw her right arm over his chest. 'My God,' she cried, 'was that *me*?'

'You're laughing,' said Latham, exhausted. 'Do you know how wonderful you sound when you laugh?'

'It feels wonderful *to* laugh.'

'We can't go back, you know,' said Drew. 'We have something now, we are something now, that we weren't before. And I don't think it's the bed alone.'

'Yes, my darling, and I'm not sure it's wise.'

'Why isn't it?'

'Because I must operate coldly at the embassy, and if you're involved, I don't think I can act coldly.'

'Am I hearing what I want to hear?'

'Yes, you are, you American *naïf*.'

'What does that mean?'

'I believe, in your parlance, that it means I think I'm in love with you.'

'Well, as a good old boy from Mississippi once said, "if that don't beat hens a-wrastlin'!"'

'What?'

'Come here and I'll explain it to you.'

It was twelve minutes to two in the afternoon when Claude Moreau and his most-trusted field officer, Jacques Bergeron, arrived at the Georges Cinq station of the Paris Metro. They walked, separately, to the rear of the platform, each carrying a handheld radio, the frequencies calibrated to each other.

'He's a tall man, quite slender,' said the Deuxième chief into his instrument. 'With a propensity for bending over due to his usually addressing shorter people—'

'I've *got* him!' exclaimed the agent. 'He's leaning against the wall, waiting for the next train to come in.'

'When it does, do as I told you.'

The underground train arrived and came to a hall; the doors opened, disgorging several dozen passengers.

'Now,' said Moreau into his radio. '*Fire.*'

As ordered, Bergeron's blank gunshots reverberated along the platform as the Metro riders raced en masse to the exit. Moreau ran to the panicked Gerhardt Kroeger, grabbing his arm and shouting. 'They're trying to *kill* you! Come with me!'

'*Who's* trying to kill me?' screamed the surgeon, running with Moreau into a prearranged open storage room.

'What's left of your idiotic K Unit, you fool.'

'They've disappeared!'

'To your ears from their mouths. They must have bribed a maid or a maintenance man and placed a tap in your room.'

'*Impossible!*'

'You heard the gunfire. Shall we bring back the train and see where the bullets came from? You were lucky it was crowded.'

'*Ach, mein Gott!*'

'We have to talk, *Herr Doktor*, or we both may be within their gun sights.'

'But what about Harry *Latham*? Where was he?'

'I saw him,' lied Jacques Bergeron, walking behind them, his pistol filled with spent blank shells in his pocket. 'When he heard the gunfire, he got back on the train.'

'We must talk,' said Moreau, staring at Kroeger, and

heading for a large steel door that was partially open, 'otherwise, we all lose.' They walked inside.

The Deuxième chief found the light switch and flipped it on. They were in a medium-size enclosure of dull white cinder block, housing huge antiquated switches and track lights along with unopened crates of new equipment. 'Wait outside, Jacques,' said Moreau to his agent. 'When the police arrive, as they surely will, identify yourself and tell them you were on the train and got off when you heard the gunshots. Close the door, please.'

Alone with the German in the dim grey light of a wire-enclosed ceiling bulb, Moreau sat on one of the crates. 'Make yourself comfortable, Doctor, we'll be here for a while, at least until the police have come and gone.'

'But if they find me in here—'

'They won't, the door locks upon closing. We were most fortunate that some idiot left it open. On the other hand, who'd want to steal anything here? Who could even carry anything?'

'We missed him, we *missed* him!' cried Kroeger, banging his fist on a crate, then sitting on the large wood box, shaking his bruised hand.

'He'll call again,' offered Moreau. 'Perhaps not today, but certainly tomorrow. Remember, we're dealing with a desperate man, an isolated man. But I must ask you, why is it so important that you find Latham?'

'He's . . . he's dangerous.'

'To whom? You? The Brotherhood?'

'Yes . . . to all of us.'

'Why?'

'How much do you know?'

'Everything, naturally. I am the Deuxième Bureau.'

'I mean specifically.'

'Very well. He escaped from your Alpine valley, somehow made his way through the mountain snows until he reached a road, and was picked up by a villager in a truck.'

'A *villager*? Now you're the fool, Herr Moreau. The

Antinayous, *that's* who picked him up. His escape was arranged from inside, a traitor *inside* the valley. We must find that *Hochverräter*!'

'"Traitor", yes, I understand.' Over the years the head of the Deuxième had learned to sense a lie when told by amateurs under stress. The vacuous desperation in the eyes, the words tumbling over one another, often accompanied by spittle forming at the corners of the mouth. As he studied Gerhardt Kroeger, the signs were all there. 'So that's why you must find him? To interrogate him before executing him, so as to learn the identity of your traitor?'

'You must understand, it was a woman, and she has to be someone very high up in the organization. She must be eliminated!'

'Yes, of course, I understand that too.' Beads of perspiration began to form on Kroeger's hairline, and the underground room was cool. 'So that's it, the reason for your K Unit, the reason such an important man as yourself would come to Paris – to learn the identity of a traitor high in the ranks of the Brotherhood.'

'*Precisely.*'

'I see. And there's no other reason?'

'None.' Two rivulets of sweat rolled down the German's forehead, fell over his brows, and continued down his cheeks. 'It's terribly warm in here,' said Kroeger, wiping his face with the back of his right hand.

'I hadn't noticed it. Actually, I thought it was rather cool, but then, such events as this afternoon are not unfamiliar to me, and do not excessively fray my nerves. Off and on, gunfire has been a part of my life.'

'Yes, yes, that's you, not me. I daresay if I brought you into an operating room during a particularly nasty procedure, you'd probably faint.'

'There's no debate, undoubtedly I would. But you see, Doctor, for me to be at my most efficient, I must know everything, and something tells me you *haven't* told me everything.'

'What more can you possibly need?' Kroeger's sweat was more profuse.

'Perhaps you're right, at times I'm overzealous. Then this is how we'll proceed. When Harry Latham calls again, I will *not* phone you at the Lutetia, but instead take him ourselves. Once taken, we'll treat him handsomely, and after a few hours I'll reach you.'

'*Unacceptable!*' cried the surgeon, rising from the crate, his hands trembling. 'I must be there when you find him! I must be alone with him before any interrogation takes place, away from all of you, for I'll be discussing information no one else can overhear. It's vital, and those are your orders from the Brüderschaft!'

'And if, for my own well-being, I don't comply?'

'News of over twenty million francs deposited into your account in Switzerland could find its way to the Quai d'Orsay and the French press.'

'Well, that certainly is a persuasive argument, isn't it?'

'I should hope so.'

'When you say "away from all of you", what do you mean?'

'Just what I say. I carry with me several syringes and various narcotics that will force Harry Latham to reveal to me what we must know. *Natürlich*, no one else may be in the vicinity.'

'You mean in a room by yourselves?'

'Absolutely not. Conversations in a room can be transmitted, as you claim my own hotel room is tapped.'

'Then how can we accommodate you?'

'An automobile of my own choosing, *not* one of yours. I will drive Latham somewhere, administer my chemicals, learn what I must learn, and bring him back to you.'

'No execution?'

'Only if I'm followed.'

'Again, I understand. It seems I have no choice.'

'Time, Moreau, *time*! It's extremely important. He must be found within the next thirty-six hours!'

'*What?* Now I don't understand you at all. Why thirty-six hours? Does the earth stop moving around the sun then? Please explain to me.'

'Very well, it's what you perceived, what I haven't told you . . . Remember, I'm a doctor, some say the finest cranial surgeon in Germany, and I will not dispute that judgement. Harry Latham is insane, a combination of schizophrenia and manic-depressive syndrome. I saved his life in our valley, operating to relieve the pressures that caused his illness. In looking over my notes, I found a horrible realization. Unless given medication within six days after he escaped, he will die! He's reached four and a half of those six days. Now do you see? We must question him before he takes the name of the traitor to his grave.'

'Yes, now I do understand, but, Doctor, are *you* all right?'

'What?'

'You've grown quite pale and your face is drenched with perspiration. Are there pains in your chest, perhaps? I can have an ambulance here in minutes.'

'I don't want an ambulance, I want Harry Latham! And I have no chest pains, no angina, only an intolerance for slow-witted bureaucrats.'

'Would you believe I understand that too? For you're a learned man, a brilliant man, and in addition to my devotion to your cause, I'm honoured to know you . . . Come, we'll leave now, and I shall press my energies to their zenith.'

Out on the Champs-Élysées, Moreau and his field officer saluted as Gerhardt Kroeger climbed into a taxi, then headed for their Deuxième vehicle. 'Hurry!' said the veteran of Istanbul and more posts than one could name. 'That bastard was lying to the point of swallowing his spit! But what was he lying about?'

'What are you going to do, Claude?'

'Sit and think and make several phone calls. One to the eminent scholar Heinrich Kreitz, the German ambassador. He and his government are going to dig out some records for me whether they like it or not.'

CHAPTER NINETEEN

Drew Latham, attaché case in hand, presented himself at the Inter-Continental's front desk. He placed on the counter an American Embassy requisition order for a reservation and a military identification card. They were swiftly picked up and studied by a formally dressed hotel clerk who pulled a card out of his file.

'*Ah, oui*, Colonel Webster, you are a most welcome guest. The embassy requested a mini-suite and would you believe we found one for you. A Spanish couple left early.'

'I'm very grateful.'

'Further,' said the clerk, reading the card, 'you may be having visitors, and we are to call you before giving them your room number, *n'est-ce pas?*'

'Quite correct.'

'Your luggage, monsieur?'

'I left it at the concierge's desk and gave him my name.'

'Excellent. You are a traveller, then.'

'The army has me going from one place to another,' said Drew, signing the register. *Anthony Webster, Col., US Army. Washington, DC, USA*.

'Ah, so interesting.' The clerk spun the registry pad around and withdrew the hotel record.

He raised his eyes and tapped his bell. 'Take *Monsieur le Colonel* to Suite seven hundred and three, and inform the concierge to send up his luggage. The name is Webster.'

'*Oui*,' replied the uniformed bellman. 'Follow me, monsieur. Your luggage will arrive in a few minutes.'

'Thank you.'

The elevator ride to the seventh floor was uneventful except for a middle-aged American couple who were arguing. The woman, hair bluish and neck and wrists replete with jewels, berated her obese husband, who was wearing a wide-brimmed Stetson.

'Lucas, you can at least be pleasant!'

'What's to be pleasant about? Ah cain't git a real limo, jest one of those tiny jobs you can barely put yer ass in, and nobody speaks American till you give 'em a tip, then you'd think they were brought up in Texarkana.'

'That's because you won't learn the money.'

'*You* did?'

'I shop. Do you know what you gave the last taxi driver?'

'Hell, no, Ah jest peeled off some paper.'

'The fare was fifty-five francs, roughly ten dollars. You gave him a hundred, which is nearer twenty dollars.'

'Ah'll be swaggled. Mebbe that's why he kept winkin' at me when you got out, sayin' in perfectly good English that he'd be outside the hotel most of the night and I should look for him.'

'*Really!*' Fortunately, the door to the sixth floor opened and the couple walked out.

'I apologize for my countrymen,' said Drew, lacking for anything else to say as he saw the raised eyebrows of the bellman.

'Don't, *Monsieur le Colonel*. Later tonight it's quite possible the gentleman will be on the pavement looking for that taxi.'

'*Touché.*'

'*D'accord*. This is the Paree of their dreams, *n'est-ce pas*?'

'*C'est vrai*, I'm afraid.'

'It's all harmless . . . Here is your floor, monsieur.'

The suite was small, a bedroom and a separate living area, but it was charming, very European, and what made it rather outstanding was a bottle of Scotch on the small bar. Witkowski must have had pangs of guilt, which were definitely appropriate. Latham hated the goddamned uniform. His chest, his waist, and his rear end were encased in a cloth tube. Why weren't there massive resignations in the armed forces on the basis of clothing alone?

The bellman gone, Drew waited for his suitcase, which held a basic change of civilian clothes, taken from his flat by a blonde-wigged Karin. He removed the suffocating tunic, poured himself a drink, turned on the television set, switching the channels until he found the CNN station, and sat down. The current news was on sports, mainly American baseball, which did not interest him; when the hockey season arrived, it was different.

The doorbell rang; it was a young bellboy with his suitcase. Drew thanked and tipped him, astonished to hear him say, 'This is for you, monsieur.' The wide-eyed youngster gave him a note. 'It is, how do you say, *confidentiel*?'

'That's good enough, thanks very much.'

Call room three hundred and thirty. A friend.

Karin? It was so like her very unpredictable behaviour. They were lovers now – more than lovers. There was something between them that no one could take away. *So* like her!

He picked up the phone, studied the printed instructions, and dialled. 'Hi, I *made* it,' he said, the moment the phone was picked up.

'Hey, man, then it *is* you!' said a male voice on the line.

'*What?* Who are you?'

'C'mon, Bronco, you can't recognize your old roommate from the Manitoba Stars? It's Ben *Lewis*! I saw you in the lobby. At first I thought I was seeing double, but I knew it was you! 'Course, then you took off your hat and I figured I was nuts, until I watched you walk to the elevators.'

'I . . . I really don't know what you're talking about.'

'Get with it, Bronc! Your right foot. Remember when your ankle got sliced by a guy on the Toronto Comets? You healed in a few weeks and came back on the ice, but your

322

right foot was always angled, just slightly, to the left. Nobody who didn't know you would notice, but I did. I *knew* it was you!'

'Okay, okay, Benny, it's me, but you can't say anything to *anybody*. I'm working for the government now and you've got to keep your mouth shut.'

'Hey, I understand, pal. You know, I played for the Rangers for two seasons—'

'I know, Benny, you were terrific.'

'The hell I was, I got cut on the third.'

'It happens.'

'Not if I were you, pal. You had it over all of us.'

'That's history. How did you find me, Ben?'

'The concierge's desk. I asked where the bag was going.'

'They *told* you?'

'Sure, because I said it was mine!'

'Christ, you do bring back memories. We'd go to an expensive restaurant in Montreal, the check would come, and if it was too large, you'd say it belonged to another table, or another one after that, until it was small enough for you to accept it. What are you doing in Paris?'

'I'm in the fast-food business, representing all of the majors; they recruit jocks like you and me 'cause we got big muscle and they hype our reputations. Would you believe my résumé says I was a *star* on the Rangers? What do they know over here? I was a second-rater, but I fill out a jacket.'

'I never filled out one like you did.'

'No, you didn't. You were like a Toronto paper said, "all raw sinew and speed". I wished the hell they'd said that about me.'

'Again, that's history, Ben, but I have to tell you once more. You've got to forget you saw me! It's terribly important that you remember that.'

'Sure, old pal.' The man named Lewis burped, then hiccupped twice.

'*Benny*,' said Latham firmly, 'you're not on the sauce again, *are* you?'

'No,' answered the fast-food international salesman, combining another burp and a hiccup. 'But what the hell, pal, this is Paris.'

'Talk to you later, *pal*,' said Latham, hanging up the phone. No sooner had he done so than it rang again. 'Yes?'

'It's me,' said Karin de Vries. 'Did everything go all right?'

'No, goddammit, someone I knew years ago recognized me.'

'*Who?*'

'An old hockey player from Canada.'

'Is he a problem?'

'I don't think so, but he's a drunk.'

'Then he's a problem. What's his name?'

'Ben – Benjamin Lewis. He's in room three-thirty.'

'We'll get on it . . . How are you, my darling?'

'Wanting you with me, that's how I am.'

'I've decided.'

'Good *God*, what have you decided? Do I want to hear it or not?'

'I hope so. I *do* love you, Drew, and as you said, quite rightly, the bed was but a small part of it.'

'I love you so much, I can't find the words to tell you . . . I can't believe I just said that! I never believed it could happen—'

'Nor did I. I hope we're not wrong.'

'What we feel couldn't be wrong. In a few days we've been through more than most people have in a lifetime. We've been tested, lady, and neither of us blew apart. Instead, we found each other.'

'The European in me might call that inconclusive, but I know what you feel, for I feel it too. I do, and I ache for you.'

'Then come to the hotel, blonde wig and all.'

'Not tonight, my darling. The colonel would court-martial us both. Perhaps tomorrow.'

Within the hour, as it was barely noon in New York, the

324

president of the International Food Services Trade Association on Sixth Avenue received a call from Washington. Thirty minutes later, one of their representatives, a former star of the New York Rangers, currently in Paris, was ordered to Oslo, Norway, to pave the way for new business opportunities. There was only one minor difficulty. The salesman in question was dead drunk on his bed, and it took two of the concierge's assistants to rouse him for the call, help him pack, and put him in a taxi for Orly Airport.

Unfortunately, everything being rather hectic, Benjamin Lewis got in the wrong line, missed the plane, and bought a ticket to Helsinki, as he could not remember Oslo, but knew his employer had named a Scandinavian city, and he had never been to Helsinki. Such is the fate of those interfering with far-flung intelligence operations.

Halfway through the flight, Benny suddenly recalled Oslo, and asked the stewardess if he could step out and flag down another plane. The flight attendant, a gorgeous Finnish blonde, was sympathetic but explained that it would not be a good idea. So Benny asked her for a late dinner in Helsinki. She politely refused.

Wesley Sorenson left Cons-Op headquarters and was driven to the safe house in Fairfax, Virginia, where the two Nazi revolutionaries were being held. As the car passed through the gates into a long, circular drive that led to the imposing front entrance, once the estate of an Argentinean diplomat, the director of Consular Operations tried to remember all the tricks he had used in his field interrogations. The first, of course, was 'Hey, fellas, I'd rather see you alive than dead, which won't be my decision, I hope you understand that. We can't play games here; there's an underground sound-proof room where the wall is pretty well pockmarked from previous executions' . . . et cetera, et cetera. Naturally, there was no such wall, no such room, and usually only the most fanatical prisoners would be taken down the black-draped elevator to an anticipated death. Those that chose to travel

325

that short fifty feet were injected with scopolamine derivatives and were so thankful when they revived that they normally cooperated to a fault.

The large two-man cell was not the prison variety. It was twenty feet long and twelve feet wide, and included two normal-size beds, a sink, a walled toilet, a small refrigerator, and a television set. It was closer to a moderately priced hotel room than to something out of the old Alcatraz or Attica. What the prisoners did not know, but probably suspected, was that concealed cameras were in the walls, covering every foot of space.

'May I come in, gentlemen?' said Sorenson, standing outside the cell door. 'Or should I speak German to make myself clear?'

'We are well versed in English, *mein Herr*,' replied the relaxed Paris Two. 'We have been captured, so what can we say? . . . No, you cannot come in?'

'I take that as an affirmative. Thank you.'

'Your guard and his weapon will remain outside,' said the less cordial Paris Five.

'Regulations, not mine personally.' Sorenson was let into the cell by the intelligence patrol, who stepped back to the opposite wall, removing his sidearm from its holster. 'I think we should talk, talk seriously, gentlemen.'

'What is there to talk about?' asked Paris Two.

'Whether you live or die, I suppose is the primary question,' replied the director of Cons-Op. 'You see, it's not my decision. Downstairs, twenty feet below ground, there's a room . . .' Sorenson described the execution chamber to the discomfort of Paris Five and a cooler reception from Zero Two, who kept staring at the director, a tight smile across his lips.

'Do you think we're so committed as to give you an excuse to kill us?' he said. 'Unless you're predisposed to do so.'

'In this country we regard the taking of a life very seriously. It's never predisposed or accepted lightly.'

'Really?' Paris Two continued. 'Then why is it that

outside of certain Arab states, China, and what's left of selected Russian breakaways, you are the only country in the civilized world to retain the death penalty?'

'The will of the people – in certain states, of course. However, your situation is beyond national policies. You're *international* killers, terrorists operating on behalf of a discredited political party that doesn't dare show itself, for it would be denounced throughout the world.'

'Are you so certain of that?' interrupted Paris Five.

'I would hope so.'

'Then you'd be wrong!'

'What my comrade is saying,' Two broke in, 'is that perhaps we have more support than you think. Look at the extreme Russian nationalists, are they so different from the Third Reich? And your own right-wing fanatics and their brothers, the book-burning religious fundamentalists. Their agendas could have been written by Hitler and Goebbels. No, *mein Herr*, there is far more sympathy for our goals of cleansing than you can conceive of.'

'I would hope not.'

'"Hope is a thing with feathers", as one of your finest writers suggested, is it not so?'

'I don't happen to believe that, but you're a pretty well-read young man, aren't you?'

'I've lived in various countries, and – I would hope – absorbed some of their cultures.'

'You mentioned something about being committed,' said Sorenson. 'You asked me if I thought you were "so committed" as to use that commitment as an excuse to have you executed.'

'I said "to kill us",' corrected Zero Two. 'Execution implies a legal justification.'

'For which, in your case, there's more than ample evidence. I refer to three attempts and the final murdering of Field Officer Latham, for starters.'

'It's war!' cried Paris Five. 'In war, soldiers kill soldiers!'

'I'm not aware of any declaration of hostilities, no national call to arms. Therefore, it's murder, pure and simple ... However, this is all academic and beyond my scope. I can only relay information; the decision is up to my superiors.'

'What sort of information?' asked Two.

'What can you offer in exchange for your lives?'

'Where do you wish to begin – if we have such information?'

'Who are your colleagues in Bonn?'

'That I can tell you honestly, we don't know ... Let me go back, *mein Herr*. We are an elite group who live extraordinary lives, the fantasies of all young men who are superbly trained to follow orders. These orders are issued to us by codes, codes that change constantly.' Paris Two described their lifestyles as he had told Zero Five he would do on the jet to Washington. 'We are the shock troops, the storm troopers, if you wish, and we maintain contacts with our units in every country. No names are ever used, the prefix Zero is Paris – I am Paris, Zero Two – the United States is the prefix Three, the specific names preceding.'

'How do you make contact?'

'By revolving, secure telephone numbers issued by Bonn. Again, our digits are used, no names.'

'Regarding this country, what can you tell me that could convince me to recommend leniency with regard to your executions?'

'*Mein Gott*, where do you want to begin?'

'Anywhere you like.'

'Very well, let's start with the Vice President of the United States.'

'*What?*'

'He's one of us to the core. Then there is the Speaker of the House, German ancestry, naturally, an ageing gentleman who claimed conscientious objectorship during World War Two. Of course, there are others, many others, but their names, or positions, will depend on your recommendation to the execution committee.'

'You could be lying through your teeth.'

'If that's what you think, shoot us.'

'You're *garbage*.'

'As you are in our eyes!' shouted Paris Five. 'But time is on our side, not yours. Sooner or later the world will wake up and see that we're right. The dehumanized blacks commit the vast majority of crimes; the Arabs constitute the largest groups of terrorists, and the Jews are the manipulators of the world, cheating and corrupting all within their reach – everything for themselves, nothing for anyone else!'

'My passionate associate notwithstanding, do you want our information or not?' asked Zero Two. 'I loved my privileged life in Paris, but if it is to stop, why not make it complete?'

'Can you provide any evidence for the outrageous accusations you've made?'

'We can only tell you what we've been told. But please remember, we are the elite of the Brotherhood.'

'*Die Brüderschaft*,' said the director of Consular Operations, disgust in his voice.

'Precisely. That name will sweep across the globe and it will be honoured.'

'Not if I have anything to say about it.'

'But do you, *mein Herr?* You are no more than a small cog in many wheels, as I am. Frankly, I'm bored with the whole thing. Let history take its inevitable course, it's beyond such men as you and me. Also, I'd much rather live than die.'

'I'll confer with my superiors,' said Wesley Sorenson coldly, walking to the cell gate and signalling the guard. When both men had disappeared through the outer door, Paris Two picked up a notepad and, covering his hand, wrote in German, 'He cannot afford to execute us.'

'*Monsieur l'Ambassadeur*,' said Moreau, alone with Heinrich Kreitz in the latter's office at the German Embassy. 'I trust there is no recording made of our conversation. It would not be to the advantage of either of us.'

'There is none,' replied the aged ambassador, his small

stature, pale, lined face, and thin steel-rimmed glasses making him appear more like a weathered gnome than a giant intellect of Europe. 'I have the information you requested—'

'Requested over a secure line, *n'est-ce-pas?*' interrupted the chief of the Deuxième Bureau, seated in front of the desk.

'Naturally, you have my word for it . . . The records go back to what's known of Gerhardt Kroeger's childhood and family, through his university and medical training, to his hospital appointment and his eventual resignation in Nuremberg. It's a remarkable dossier, filled with the triumphs of a brilliant man; and with the possible exception of his abrupt resignation from the medical community, there's nothing to indicate impropriety, much less sympathy with the neo-Nazi movement. I've made a copy for you, of course.' Kreitz leaned forward and placed the sealed manila envelope in front of Moreau, who picked it up, impressed by its thickness and weight.

'Save me some time, if *you've* got the time, sir.'

'There's nothing more important than our combined investigations. Go on.'

'You've read this thoroughly?'

'As if it were a doctoral thesis I had to accept or reject. Very thoroughly.'

'Who were his parents?'

'Sigmund and Elsi Kroeger, and you've just struck the first note that discredits any association with the neo-Nazis. Sigmund Kroeger was officially listed as a deserter from the Luftwaffe in the final months of the war.'

'So were thousands of others.'

'Of the Werhmacht, perhaps, not the Luftwaffe, and very few senior officers. The elder Kroeger was a decorated major, decorated by Goering himself. The military records, ours and yours, show that had the war continued and Kroeger been captured, he would have been court-martialled and shot. By the Third Reich.'

'What happened to him after the war?'

330

'The usual obfuscations. He had flown his Messerschmitt over the Allied lines, parachuted out, and let his plane crash into a field. British troops kept the nearby villagers from killing him and he was given the status of prisoner of war.'

'And after the surrender, he was repatriated?'

'Obfuscations, what can I tell you? He was the son of a factory owner who employed hundreds of people. However, in the final analysis, he *was* a deserter, and no devoted follower of the *Führer*. Hardly the basis for his own son to become one.'

'Yes, I see. What about his wife, Gerhardt's mother?'

'A stolid, upper-middle-class *Hausfrau* who probably detested the war. At any rate, she was never listed as a member of the National Socialist Party and never known to attend the numerous rallies.'

'Not exactly a pro-Nazi influence.'

'That's what I'm trying to tell you.'

'And Kroeger's university and medical schooling, were there any student factions antagonistic to Germany's democratizations, its rejection of the Third Reich, that might have impressed the young Kroeger?'

'None that I can find. His professors, by and large, termed him a man who kept to himself, a born scholar and doctor in training, simply outstanding. His surgical residency was so superb, he was operating months before it was customary.'

'His specialization?'

'The brain. They say he had "golden hands and quick-silver fingers"; that's a direct quote from the renowned Hans Traupman, another giant in the field.'

'Who?'

'Traupman, Hans Traupman, chief of cranial surgery, Nuremberg.'

'Are they friends?'

'Other than a professional association, there's no reference to a specific friendship.'

'Yet he was excessive in his praise of a subordinate.'

'Not all surgeons are ungenerous, Moreau.'

'I suppose not. Were there any conclusions or opinions as to why Kroeger resigned his post and immigrated to Sweden?'

'Other than his own very emotional statement, no. He had been performing extremely delicate, one might say nerve-racking, operations for nearly twenty years. His personal judgement was that he had burned himself out, that a tremble had developed in those "quicksilver" fingers of his, and he would not further risk patients' lives. Most admirable.'

'Most obfuscational,' said Moreau quietly. 'Has anyone followed up on where he is now?'

'Only hearsay, as you'll read. Several former colleagues who've heard from him, none less than four years ago, say he opened a general practice under a Swedish name, north of Göteborg.'

'Who are these "former colleagues"?'

'Their names are in the report. You may reach them yourself, if you wish.'

'I wish.'

'Now, Monsieur Moreau,' said the German ambassador, his short, skeletal body leaning back in the chair, 'I think it's time you were clear with me. When we spoke – on a secure line, as you demanded – you implied that one Gerhardt Kroeger, surgeon, *could* be part of the Nazi movement, but you offered no evidence, to say nothing of proof. Instead, rather outrageously, you said that if my government, through this office, refused to comply with your request to furnish you with a complete dossier on Kroeger, you would complain to the Quai d'Orsay that we were conceivably covering up the identity of a powerful member of the new Nazi core. Again, no evidence, no proof, and once you enter that file into your system, it's quite possible that an innocent doctor somewhere in Sweden will have his very life in jeopardy, for I have no doubt you'll find him. There's your information, Monsieur Moreau. Give me something, if only to assuage my conscience, for, as I say, you *will* find him.'

'We have found him, *Monsieur l'Ambassadeur*. He's here in Paris, less than twenty blocks away. His mission is to find Harry Latham and kill him. But why *he*, why a doctor, a surgeon? That's the question we must answer.'

Out on the street, Moreau went directly to his Deuxième Bureau vehicle, climbed in, nodded to his driver to proceed, and picked up the embassy telephone from its cradle. He dialled an in-house sterile number. 'Jacques?'

'Yes, Claude?'

'Run an in-depth trace on a doctor named Traupman, Hans Traupman, a surgeon in Nuremberg.'

The evening was passing slowly, far too slowly for an agitated Drew Latham. The hotel suite was his personal prison; even the recycled air was beginning to become oppressive. He opened a window, immediately shutting it; the Paris night was humid, the air-conditioning preferable. He had spent too long cooped up like the fugitive he was presumed to be. He had to get *out* as he had yesterday afternoon when he had visited his flat on the rue du Bac, accompanied by his marine escort. It had taken less than an hour, only minutes in the street, but that hour, those minutes, were a brief respite from the suffocating, restricting enclosures of the Antinayous' Maison Rouge, Witkowski's place, even Karin's apartment – no, not Karin's apartment. That had been a release from something else, something he had been running away from for years, and it was splendid and warm and filled with comfort.

But now, *now* he had to feel like a free man again, if only for a while; he had to walk in the streets among people, it was as simple as that, perhaps. He had spoken to Karin two hours earlier while she was still at the embassy, agreeing that in the interests of absolute security, he would not call her in the Madeleine. Certainly not; the last thing he wanted was to make her a fugitive too. She had, however, given him an urgent message from Washington. He was to reach Wesley Sorenson on his very private line, and keep trying until the

Cons-Op director answered; and if by six o'clock DC time they had not made contact, he was to call Sorenson at his home, regardless of the hour.

He had tried repeatedly, knowing the number could not be traced, until eleven o'clock in Paris, six o'clock in Washington. Then he had phoned Wes's home. Mrs Sorenson had answered; the compleat spook's wife had said the proper words. 'My husband's expecting a call from our antiques dealer in Paris. If this is he, Mr Sorenson is tied up until around seven, our time, but if it's not too inconvenient, please try then, as we don't have your apartment number. He's most eager about the tapestry we saw last month.'

'It hasn't been sold, madam,' Drew had said. 'I'll call him shortly past midnight, Paris time, seven o'clock yours. It's the least I can do for such excellent clients.'

What was so important that Sorenson termed it 'urgent'? No matter, there was an hour to waste, and to speculate on a dozen possibilities in the confines of the small hotel suite was more than he could tolerate. Besides, he was wearing the inhibiting uniform that barely allowed him to breathe, his hair was dyed a ridiculous blond, he would wear the glasses Karin had given him, and it was dark out. What could be more secure than the combination of altered appearance and darkness? Finally, he had his thin cellular phone. If Witkowski or anyone with maximum clearance at the embassy needed him in an emergency, they would try that number should they not be able to reach him at the hotel.

He took the elevator down to the lobby, walked past the concierge's desk, feeling foolish as fingers touched caps along with such salutations as '*mon colonel?*' and 'Monsieur le Colonel Webster?' until he went through a revolving door and out onto the rue de Castiglione. God, it felt good to be outside, away from his prison walls! He turned right, away from the street lamps, and proceeded down the sidewalk, breathing the air deeply, his stride firm, almost military, he realized, chuckling to himself.

And then it happened. The phone on his tunic pocket rang, a low, emphatic ring. It so startled him that he fumbled, forgetting the buttons on the army jacket, wanting only the damn noise to stop. At last he ripped the ringing instrument out, pressed the receiver button, and put the phone to his ear. 'Yes, *what*?'

'This is marine unit W, that's *you*, mister! What are you doing outside the hotel?'

'Getting a little air, do you mind?'

'You can bet your ass we do, but it's too late. You're being followed.'

'*What?*'

'We've got a photograph; we can't be sure, but we think it's Reynolds, Alan Reynolds from the comm centre. We've got him in our binoculars, but the light's not so good, and he's wearing a hat with his lapels up.'

'How the hell could he *spot* me? I'm in uniform and my goddamn hair's blond!'

'A uniform can be rented, and blond hair doesn't mean much when it's mostly dark out and someone's wearing an officer's cap . . . Keep walking and laugh a lot when you put the phone back in your pocket. Then turn right into the next narrow street. We've studied the area; we'll get out and be behind you.'

'For Christ's sake, stop him, *take* him! If he's found me, it's more than likely he's zeroed in on Mrs de Vries's place!'

'She's not our priority, whoever she is. *You* are, mister.'

'She's a *big* priority with me, Mr Marine!'

'Start laughing real loud and put the phone away.'

'You got it!' Drew, making a fool of himself on the crowded rue de Castiglione, laughed like a howling hyena, replaced the cellular phone in his pocket, and turned right into the first narrow street only yards ahead. However, instead of walking, he broke into a run, racing to the nearest doorfront on the right and whipped around the stone corner out of sight. The street itself, barely more than a double alleyway, was one of those lower Parisian residential areas where the histories were long and the rents short. The only light came from two street lamps, at opposite ends of the thoroughfare; the rest was bathed in dark shadows. Removing his officer's hat, Latham, inch by inch, peered around the stone. The figure walking cautiously down the narrow street held a gun in his hand, causing Drew to swear silently. He had not thought to carry a weapon – thought, hell, there was no place under the tight-fitting fabric of the uniform to *wear* one!

Then, obviously seeing no one, the man with the gun began running towards the lamplight at the other end; it was all Latham had to observe. At the instant the figure came into view, Drew lashed his right foot out, catching the man in the groin, then sprang forward, throwing Alan Reynolds across the wide alleyway into the wall, Latham's hand gripping the weapon loosened by the traitor's lack of balance.

'You son of a *bitch*!' roared Drew, crashing Reynolds into the stone more aggressively than he had ever body-checked an opponent on the ice. 'Where do you come from, what do you *know*? Where does my *brother* fit in?'

'You're not *him*!' choked the Nazi. 'I suspected as much, but they wouldn't *listen* to me!'

'*I'm* listening, you bastard,' said Latham, the mole's gun pressed against his forehead. '*Talk!*'

'There's nothing to talk about, Latham, they have my report. You and the De Vries woman, the trap you've set.'

Suddenly Reynolds's right hand surged up in the shadows to his collar. He squeezed the cloth and bit into the bulging fabric. '*Ein Volk, ein Reich, ein Führer*!' shrieked Alan Reynolds with his dying breath.

The marine unit, designated W, raced down the dark, narrow street, their weapons bared. 'Are you all *right*?' yelled the sergeant in charge.

'No, I'm not all right!' answered a furious Drew. 'How did this son of a bitch pass muster? How did he get by all those high-tech microscopes and the psychiatrists and the researchers who supposedly can pinpoint the date, hour, and minute of an applicant's conception? It's all *bullshit*! This man wasn't just a neo out for money or a few medals, he was a certifiable fanatic who screamed the Nazi salute as he took his cyanide. He should have been spotted years ago!'

'Can't argue with you there,' said the sergeant. 'We radioed Colonel Witkowski that we'd spotted him, or thought we had. He told us to do whatever we had to do, shoot him in the legs or the arms, but to bring him in alive.'

'Unless the Corps issued you powers I don't think it possesses, that'll be a tad difficult, Sergeant.'

'We'll take the body to the embassy, but first we're getting you back to the Inter-Continental.'

'You'd have to drive around several blocks to drop me off. I can walk quicker.'

'The colonel would fry our asses if we let you do that.'

'And I'll fry them if you don't. I'm not responsible to Witkowski, but if it'll make you feel better, he's the first person I'm going to call.'

Back in his hotel suite, Latham picked up the phone and dialled the colonel's apartment. 'It's me,' he said.

'And the next time you tell my people you'll do what you like because you're not responsible to me, I'll dismiss your protection and do my best to steer you into a Nazi assassination unit.'

'I believe you would.'

'You can take it to the bank!' confirmed the angry colonel.

'I had my reasons, Stanley.'

'What the hell are they?'

'Karin, to begin with. Reynolds filed a report to the neos that claimed I wasn't Harry but the other Latham and that Karin was part of the trap.'

'Pretty goddamned accurate. Did he say what the trap was?'

'The cyanide cut him off—'

'Yes, I gathered that from the sergeant, along with your rather strong opinions of our security checks.'

'I believe I called them bullshit, and that's exactly what they are . . . Get Karin out of her apartment, Stanley. If Reynolds found me, the rue Madeleine isn't far behind. Get her out!'

'Any suggestions?'

'Here at the Inter-Continental, blonde wig and all.'

'That's about the dumbest thing you could say. If Reynolds found you there, who else did he tell, and who told *him*?'

'I'm missing something.'

'You certainly are. There's another Alan Reynolds, another mole, at the embassy, and he's as high up as they come. I'm moving you to the Normandie, on the pretext that Colonel Webster is being transferred back to Washington for evaluation.'

'That's kind of negative, isn't it?'

'Actually, we'll probably imply that you're incompetent. The French love to hear that about Americans.'

'Colonel Webster is outraged. At least I can wash out this blond hair and get rid of the uniform, right?'

'Wrong,' said Witkowski. 'Keep both a while longer. You can't go back to your own name and you've got the proper ID as Webster. It's been leaked, and by keeping it that way we may find the mole here. The circle is tight and we're watching the few who know, and they're *damned* few. Maybe only the marines, Reynolds, and that fruit-juiced salesman Lewis, who's probably going from door to igloo door in some tundra somewhere.'

'If Reynolds leaked it to the right people, measure me for a coffin!'

'Not necessarily. You're guarded, *Colonel*. By the way, did Karin tell you? Wesley Sorenson has been trying to reach you. We didn't give him your cover and he didn't want it, but you're to phone him.'

'It's next on my list. Call me back on my move to the Normandie, and get Karin out of harm's way. How about the Normandie?'

'For a spook, you're not entirely subtle, Latham.'

Drew hung up the phone and glanced at his watch. It was past midnight, past seven o'clock in DC. He picked up the telephone and pressed the numbers for the States.

'Yes?' said the voice of Sorenson.

'It's your antiques dealer from Paris.'

'Thank heavens! Sorry I was tied up, but that's another story, another massive headache, if not a catastrophe.'

'Can you tell me?'

'Not at the moment.'

'Then what was so urgent?'

'Moreau. He's clean.'

'That's nice to hear. Our embassy isn't.'

'I gather that, so judgement-wise it's in your court. If you're strung out and don't know where to turn—'

'Hold it, Wes, I have no problem with Witkowski,' interrupted Latham.

'Nor do I, but we don't know who's tapped in to him.'

'Agreed. Someone is.'

'Then turn to Moreau. He doesn't know you're alive, so before you do, reach me and I'll play the scenario for him.'

'He's still cut out?'

'One of our larger mistakes.'

'Incidentally, Wes, did you ever hear of an Alan Reynolds, embassy comm centre?'

'Can't say as I have.'

'Wish we hadn't. He was a neo.'

'*Was?*'

'He's dead.'

'I suppose that's a blessing.'

'Can't say that it is. We wanted him alive.'

'Things go wrong sometimes. Stay in touch.'

CHAPTER TWENTY

Gerhardt Kroeger laboured over the fax from Bonn, a code book in his left hand, a pencil in his right. Carefully he inserted the proper letters above the coded words of the message. The nearer he came to completing the task, the more excited was his state of mind, excited but controlled, the scientist in him demanding total concentration. Finished at last, elation swept over him. Their informer at the American Embassy had succeeded where the vaunted Blitzkrieger had failed. The mole's information was flawed, but he had found the surviving Latham! His last source remained nameless, but he claimed it was irrefutable, a person he had cultivated over the years, a woman for whom he had done many favours, now living far beyond her means. She would not lie to him for two specific reasons, the first being her current expensive way of life; the second and far more powerful, the threat of exposure. They were the usual components in keeping an inner source on a chain.

Where the informer was in error was his conviction that the Latham who had survived the assassination attempt was not Harry Latham but his brother, Drew Latham, the Consular Operations officer. Kroeger knew that was preposterous; the evidence was overwhelmingly to the contrary, evidence from so many different quarters, it could not have been manufactured. Beyond the police reports, the press, and the government's widespread dragnet for the killers, there was the Deuxième's Moreau and his associate. The latter had *seen* Harry Latham get back on the Metro train after the gunfire. Of all the officials in French intelligence,

340

Moreau was the last who would dare lie to the Brotherhood. Should he do so, he would become a pariah, a man disgraced beyond redemption. Scores of financial transfers to his account in Bern guaranteed it.

My inner source, concluded the message from Bonn, *tells me that Documents and Research mocked up papers for a Colonel Anthony Webster, a military identification card, and an embassy requisition for rooms at the Hotel Inter-Continental on the rue de Castiglione. The same source further states she briefly saw the plastic ID card. The inserted photograph was obviously also mocked, a man with familiar features but with blond hair rather than dark brown, and wearing a uniform and large-framed glasses. Although she has never seen a photograph of Harry Latham, she believes the man in the picture is his brother, Drew Latham, a Consular Operations officer. According to embassy records, authorized by security, the body of Drew Latham was flown back to the family in the United States. However, my own research, including the manifest records of American diplomatic aircraft, shows no such transfer for the date in question. Therefore, in my judgement, the Latham at the Inter-Continental is not Harry Latham but his brother. Together with embassy security and the Dutch woman, De Vries, they have mounted a strategy to entrap a member or members of our Brotherhood. What the nature of the trap is I hope to learn tonight, as I will post myself outside Latham's hotel, and if it takes all night and all day, I will take him and learn. Or I will kill him in the method prescribed.*

Rubbish! thought Kroeger. Brothers frequently have similar features. Why would the Americans lie about the slain Latham? There was no reason to, and every reason *not* to! Harry Latham's list was the key to the global search for the reemerging Nazis everywhere. They needed him, which was why they were going to such lengths to keep him alive, from enlisting the contentious Antinayous to issuing false military identification cards and moving him from hotel to hotel. Harry Latham/Alexander Lassiter was an intelligence tiger; he mourned his brother and wanted revenge at all costs. Little did he know that in roughly twenty-eight hours it wouldn't make any difference to him; he would be dead. But it did to Gerhardt Kroeger. He had to find him and blow his head apart. Now he knew where to go, hoping rather desperately that their informer had already performed the execution – properly.

It was two-ten in the morning and Kroeger put on his jacket and a light raincoat; the raincoat was necessary if only to conceal the large, heavy-calibred pistol that held six Black Talon shells. Each bullet penetrated the flesh and spread on impact like a lethal Roman candle, leaving total destruction in its wake.

'You're being picked up at three o'clock sharp,' said Witkowski.

'Not before?' asked Latham.

'Hell, it's only forty-five minutes. By the time you come down, I want a unit in the lobby and a team in the street. That takes a little organization, proper civilian clothes and all.'

'I approve. What about Karin?'

'She's out of harm's way, as you wanted. Blonde wig and all, as I think you suggested.'

'Where?'

'Not where you are.'

'You're all heart, Stanley.'

'You sound like my mother, God rest her soul.'

'Why can't I wish the same for yours?'

'Because you always want instant gratification, and I won't permit it . . . One of my people will pick up your luggage and attaché case fifteen minutes before you go down. If anyone asks where you're off to, just tell him you can't sleep. Another of your strolls outside. We'll take care of the hotel later.'

'You really believe Reynolds tipped off other neos here in Paris?'

'Frankly, no, because from what we can piece together, his killer platoon is gone – who was he going to reach? No one in Germany could get here in time, and this Kroeger's a doctor, not an assassin. My judgement is that he's here to confirm, not to pull any triggers, assuming he knows how. Reynolds was acting solo because he'd been spotted in the street outside of my place and wanted to make up for it. Killing you would have given him points.'

'We can't be sure he knew he was spotted, Stanley.'

'Really? Then why didn't he show up at the embassy in the morning? Remember, *chłopak*, two neos got away while surviving my externals—'

The fire escapes and the rug, right?' interrupted Drew.

'You're getting brighter. If A equals B and B equals C, then it's a good bet that A equals C. Not a bad rule to go by.'

'Now you sound like Harry.'

'Thanks for the compliment. Get yourself ready.'

Latham packed his suitcase rapidly, which was easy because he had barely unpacked, taking out only his civilian trousers and blazer, an embassy attaché's uniform of the day. Now the waiting began, minutes ticked off within his prison walls. Then his telephone rang; expecting Witkowski, he picked it up. 'Yes, what is it now?'

'What is what? It's Karin, my dear.'

'*Jesus*, where are you?'

'I swore not to tell you—'

'*Bullshit!*'

'No, Drew, it's called protection. The colonel tells me he's moving you – please, I don't care to know where.'

'This is getting ridiculous.'

'Then you don't know our enemy. I just want you to be careful, *very* careful.'

'You heard about tonight?'

'Reynolds? Yes, Witkowski told me, which is why I'm calling you. I can't get through to the colonel; his line's busy, which means he's constantly on the phone to the embassy, but something occurred to me only moments ago, and someone other than me should know about it.'

'What are you talking about?'

'Alan Reynolds frequently came down to D and R on one pretext or another, usually concerning our maps and transportation information.'

'No one thought it was odd?' Latham broke in.

'Not really. It's easier than calling the airlines or tracking train schedules, or, even worse, buying road maps in small-lettered French. Ours are in legible English.'

'But you thought it was strange, right?'

'Only after the colonel told me about tonight, not before, frankly. Many of our people take weekend trips all over France, Switzerland, Italy, and Spain. Especially those whose tours in Paris are limited. No, Drew, it was something else, and that *was* strange.'

'What was it?'

'On two occasions when I went back to Transport, I saw Reynolds walking out of the last aisle before the Transport door. I suppose I thought something like, "Oh, he has a friend in one of the offices and is arranging a lunch or a dinner," or some such thing.'

'And now you're thinking something else?'

'Yes, but I could be quite wrong. All of us in D and R work with degrees of confidential materials, much of it not deserving the designation confidential, but it's common knowledge that those in the last aisle, the farthest from the door, deal solely with maximum-classified information.'

'A pecking order?' asked Latham. 'From the first to the last aisle degrees of confidentiality?'

'Not at all,' replied Karin. 'The offices are simply different. When one is working on highly secret material, he or she moves into the last aisle, where the computers are far more inclusive and the communications set up for instant contact worldwide. I've worked there three times since I arrived here.'

'How many offices in the last aisle?'

'Six on each side of the central corridor.'

'Which side did you see Reynolds in?'

'The left side. I turned my head to the left, I remember that.'

'Both times?'

'Yes.'

'What were the days, the dates, you saw him?'

'Good Lord, I don't know. It was over several weeks, going back a month or two.'

'Try to think, Karin.'

'If I could pinpoint them, I would, Drew. At the time, I simply didn't consider it important.'

'It is. *He* is.'

'Why?'

'Because your instincts are right. Witkowski says there's another Alan Reynolds at the embassy, another mole, someone very high up and very inside.'

'I'll get a calendar and do my best to isolate the weeks, then the days. I'll try like mad to recall what I was working on.'

'Would it help to get into your office at the embassy?'

'That would mean getting into the supercomputer, which is somewhere below our own cellars. It stores everything for five years because our own papers are destroyed.'

'It can be arranged.'

'Even if it can, I haven't the vaguest idea how to operate it.'

'Someone does.'

'It's two-thirty in the morning, my darling.'

'I don't care if it's half past the third moon! Courtland can order in whoever operates it, and if he can't, Wesley Sorenson can, and if *he* can't, the goddamn President can!'

'Getting angry won't help, Drew.'

'How many times do I have to tell you, I'm not Harry.'

'I loved Harry, but he was never you either. Do what you have to do. In your anger, which is probably the only way it can be done.'

Latham depressed the lever, disconnecting the call, then immediately dialled the embassy, demanding to speak to

Ambassador Courtland. 'I don't care what time it is!' he shouted when the operator objected. 'This is a matter of national security, and I'm under direct orders from Washington's Consular Operations.'

'Yes, this is Ambassador Courtland. What can be so urgent at this hour?'

'Is this phone secure, sir?' asked Latham, lowering his voice to a whisper.

'I'll put you on hold and take it in another room. It's constantly swept, and besides, my wife is asleep.' Twenty seconds later Courtland continued on an upstairs telephone. 'All right, who are you and what's this all about?'

'It's Drew Latham, sir—'

'My God, you're *dead*! I don't understand—'

'You don't have to understand, Mr Ambassador. Just find our computer whizzes and order them down to the underground super stuff.'

'That's pretty heavy – my God, you were *killed*!'

'Sometimes we get too complicated, but *please*, do as I ask ... Also, you have the capability. Break into Witkowski's phone and order him to call me.'

'Where are you?'

'He knows. Do it quickly. I'm expected to leave here in fifteen minutes, but I can't until I speak to him.'

'All right, all right, whatever you say ... I guess I should mention that I'm glad you're alive.'

'So am I. Go to it, Mr Ambassador.'

Three minutes later Latham's phone rang. '*Stanley?*'

'What the hell's going on?'

'Get Karin and me to the embassy as soon as possible.' Drew explained in a few emphatic words what De Vries told him about Alan Reynolds.

'A couple of minutes won't change the scenario, young man. Stick to the schedule I've set, and I'll reroute you to the embassy and meet you both there.'

Latham waited; Witkowski's marine, in civilian clothes, arrived and took his suitcase and attaché case. 'Come down in four minutes, sir,' said the man courteously. 'We're prepared.'

'Are you people always so polite in these situations?' asked Latham.

'It doesn't help to be uptight, sir. It blurs your focus.'

'Why do I think I've heard that before?'

'I don't know. See you downstairs.'

Three minutes later, Drew walked out the door and went to the elevators. At that hour the ride down was swift, the lobby practically deserted except for a few late-night revellers, Japanese and Americans, by and large, all of whom disappeared into the bank of elevators. Latham strode across the marble floor, every inch the military man, when suddenly, ear-shattering gunshots exploded, echoing off the walls, emanating from the mezzanine balcony. Drew lunged towards a space between the lobby furniture, his eyes riveted on the two men behind the concierge's desk. He saw the chest and stomach of one literally explode, a monstrous detonation that sent the man's bloody intestines hurling across the lobby; the other raised his hands as his head blew apart, skull tissue flying everywhere. *Madness!* Additional gunfire then filled the huge ornate enclosure, followed by voices, shouting in English with American accents.

'We've got him!' yelled a man, also on the mezzanine level. 'In the legs!'

'He's *alive!*' roared another. 'We've *got* the son of a bitch! He's nuts! He's crying and moaning in German!'

'Take him to the embassy,' said a calmer voice in the lobby, turning to the terrified clerks behind the front desk. 'This is an antiterrorist operation,' he continued. 'It's over now, and you may assure the owners that all expenses for damages will be covered, as well as generous compensation for the families of your personnel who tragically lost their lives. However meaningless it may appear to you now, they died heroes, and a grateful Europe will honour them . . . *Hurry up!*'

The horrified clerks stood frozen behind the marble

counter. The man on the left began to weep as his colleague slowly, as if in a trance, reached for a telephone.

Latham and De Vries embraced under the disapproving eyes of Colonel Stanley Witkowski and Ambassador Daniel Courtland in the latter's office at the American Embassy.

'May we get to the issue – the issues – at hand, if you please?' said the ambassador. 'Dr Gerhardt Kroeger will survive and our two-man computer team will arrive shortly. Actually one of them is here now, and his superior is being flown in from his holiday in the Pyrenees. Will somebody *now* tell me what the hell is going on?'

'Certain intelligence operations are beyond your purview, Mr Ambassador,' replied Witkowski, 'for your own deniability, sir.'

'You know, I really find that phrase rather obscene. Colonel. Since when did civilian intelligence, or military intelligence, or any of the clandestine exercises take precedence over the State Department's ultimate control?'

'That's why Consular Operations was created, sir,' answered Drew. 'The purpose was to coordinate between State, the administration, and the intelligence services.'

'Then I can't say that you have, have you?'

'In crises we can't afford a bureaucratic delay,' said Latham firmly. 'And I don't give a goddamn if it costs me my job. I want the person, the people, who killed my brother. Because they're part of a much larger disease, and it's got to be stopped – *not* by bureaucratic debate, but by individual decision.'

Courtland leaned back in his chair. Finally, he spoke. 'And you, Colonel?'

'I've been a soldier all my life, but here I must reject the chain of command. I can't wait for some Congress to declare war. We *are* at war.'

'And you, Mrs de Vries?'

'I gave you my husband, what more do you want?'

Ambassador Daniel Courtland leaned forward in his chair,

both hands on his forehead, his fingers massaging his flesh. 'I've lived with compromises all my diplomatic life,' he said. 'Maybe it's time to stop.' He raised his head. 'I'll probably be demoted to Tierra del Fuego, but go for it, you rogues. Because you *are* right, there are times when we can't wait.'

The three rogues were taken down to the supercomputer thirty feet below the cellars. It was both enormous and frightening; an entire ten-foot wall was covered by a plate of thick glass with whirling disks behind it, dozens spinning and abruptly stopping, trapping information from the skies.

'Hi, I'm Jack Rowe, one half of your deep, under-the-earth geniuses,' said a pleasant-looking sandy-haired man of less than thirty years. 'My colleague, if he's sober, will be here in a few minutes. He landed at Orly a half hour ago.'

'We didn't expect to find drunks,' exclaimed Witkowski. 'This is serious business!'

'Everything's serious here, Colonel – yes, I know who you are, it's standard operating procedure. You too, Cons-Op guy, *and* the lady who probably could have run NATO if she were a man and wore a uniform. There are no secrets here. They all spew out on the disks.'

'Can we get at them?' said Drew.

'Not until my buddy arrives. You see, he has the other code, which I'm not allowed to have.'

'To save time,' said Karin, 'can you collate the data from my office with specific dates as I recalled them?'

'Don't have to, it's one and the same. You give us the dates, and whatever you recorded on those days will show up on the screen. You couldn't change it or erase it if you wanted to.'

'I don't care to do either.'

'That's a relief. When I got the hurry-up from the Big Man, I figured we maybe had one of those Rose Mary Wood things we read about in history books.'

'*History* books?' Witkowski's brows arched in indignation.

'Well, I was about six or seven when all that stuff happened, Colonel. Maybe *history* is the wrong word.'

'I hope to kiss a pig it was.'

'That's an interesting phrase,' said the young, sandy-haired technician. 'Root linguistic vernaculars are kind of a hobby with me. That's either Irish or Middle European, Slavic probably, where *sus scrofa* – pigs or hogs – were valuable property. To "hope to kiss a pig" implied ownership, a status symbol, actually. And if you supplant the *a* with a *my*, therefore *my pig*, it meant you were either pretty rich or soon expected to be.'

'Is *that* what you do with computers?' asked an astonished Latham.

'You'd be surprised at the mountains of incidental intelligence these Big Birds can hold. I once traced a Latin chant, a religious chant, to a pagan cult in Corsica.'

'That's *very* interesting, young man,' interrupted Witkowski, 'but our concerns here are speed and accuracy.'

'We'll give you both, Colonel.'

'Incidentally,' Witkowski said, 'the phrase I used was Polish.'

'I'm not sure of that,' said Karin. 'I believe it stems from Gaelic roots, Irish in fact.'

'And *I* don't give a damn!' cried Drew. 'Will you please concentrate on the days, the time spans, you can remember, Karin?'

'I already have,' replied De Vries, opening her purse. 'Here they are, Mr Rowe.' She handed the computer expert a torn piece of notebook paper.

'These are all over the place,' said the technician partial to linguistic vernaculars.

'They're in sequence, it's the best I could do.'

'No problem for the biggest bird in France.'

'Why do you call this thing a bird?' asked Latham.

''Cause it flies into the ether of infinite recall.'

'Sorry I asked.'

'But this helps, Mrs de Vries. I'll program my side, so when Joel arrives, he can key in and the sideshow can begin.'

'*Sideshow?*'

'The screen, Colonel, the screen.'

As Rowe inserted the codes that released his side of the massive computer, and typed in the data, the metal door of the subterranean complex opened and another technician, this one perhaps in his early thirties, perhaps older, walked in. What distinguished him from his colleague was a long, neatly bound ponytail, held in place by a small blue ribbon at the nape of his neck.

'Hi,' he said pleasantly, 'I'm Joel Greenberg, the resident general here. How're you doin', Jackman?'

'Waiting for you, Genius Two.'

'Hey, I'm *Numero Uno*, remember?'

'I just replaced you, I got here first,' replied Rowe, still typing.

'You must be the exalted Colonel Witkowski,' said Greenberg, extending his hand to the perplexed chief of security, whose glare did not convey much pleasure at the sight of the slender man in blue jeans and an open-collared bush jacket, so say nothing of the ponytail. 'It's an honour to meet you, sir, and I mean that.'

'At least you're sober,' said the colonel awkwardly.

'I wasn't last night. Wow, did I do a mean flamenco! . . . And you have to be Mrs de Vries. The rumours weren't wrong, ma'am. You're gorgeous, A-plus.'

'I'm also an officer-attaché of the embassy, Mr Greenberg.'

'I'll bet I outrank you, but who's counting . . . I apologize, ma'am, I didn't mean to offend you. I'm just sort of the ebullient type. No offence, okay?'

'Okay,' said Karin, laughing quietly.

'You've got to be our Mr Cons-Op, right?' said Greenberg, shaking hands with Drew, then becoming suddenly serious. 'My heart goes out to you, sir. You lose a parent, it's kind of expected, you know what I mean? You lose a brother – yes, Jackman and I were told the scenario – well, it's something else. Especially the way it happened. I don't know what else to say.'

'You've said it very well; it's appreciated ... Who else down here knows what you just told me?'

'Nobody, only Rowe and myself. We have two pairs of relief. The last left when the Jackman arrived, but none have the codes to invade our super bird. If either of us has an accident or a cardiac arrest, a sub is flown down from NATO.'

'I've never seen you around the embassy,' said Witkowski. 'And I'm *sure* I'd recall having seen you.'

'We're not permitted to fraternize, Colonel. We have a separate entrance and our own very small elevator.'

'That seems rather excessive.'

'Not when you consider what's in Mother Bird. The only people accepted for this job are computer PhD's, male and unattached. That may be sexist, but it's the way things are.'

'Are you armed?' asked Latham. 'Just curiosity.'

'Two weapons. Both Smith and Wesson, nine milli-metres. One in a chest holster and one strapped to the leg. Trained in usage, by the way.'

'May we get to work,' said Karin firmly. 'I believe your partner has inserted the information I need.'

'It won't do us any good until I repeat it,' said Greenberg, heading for his chair on the left of the giant equipment and sitting down, entering his code. 'Print it up for me, Jackman, okay?'

'Transfer in sequence,' answered Rowe. 'It's in your ballpark. Repeat and release on demand-print key.'

'I'm with you.' Joel Greenberg swivelled in his chair and addressed the three intruders. 'As I repeat his data, it'll come out on the printer below the centre screen. That way you won't have to remember everything on the movie.'

'The *movie*?'

'The screen, Colonel, the screen,' said Jack Rowe.

As the computer printouts spewed forth, page by page, date by date, Karin ripped them off and studied them. Twenty minutes passed. When the printouts were finished, she went back over each, circling items in a red pencil.

Finally, she said softly but emphatically, 'I've found it. The two occasions when I went back to Transport. I remember exactly . . . Can you now bring up the names of the D and R personnel on the left side of the centre aisle?' She handed the printouts with the data circled in red to Greenberg.

'Sure,' said the PhD with a ponytail, in concert with his associate. 'Ready, Jack?'

'Go ahead, *Numero Duo*.'

'Asshole.'

The names appeared on the screen before the ten-second delay for the printer. 'You're not going to like this, Mrs de Vries,' said the computer PhD named Rowe. 'Out of the six days you specified, you were on three of them.'

'That's crazy – insane!'

'I'll bring up your data, see if you recall it.'

The screen printed out the information. 'Yes, that's *mine*!' cried Karin, her eyes on the line of green letters as they first appeared. 'But I wasn't there.'

'Big Bird doesn't lie, ma'am,' said Greenberg. 'It wouldn't know how.'

'Try the others, *their* inputs,' insisted Latham.

The bright green letters appeared again on the screen, each from different offices. And again, the very data Karin had recognized was on two others.

'What more can I say? I could not have been in three offices at once. Someone has penetrated your holy computers.'

'That would require such a complex number of codes, including insertions and deletions, that it would take someone with more knowledge than Joel and I have to do it,' said Jack Rowe. 'I hate to say it, Mrs de Vries, but the info on you from Brussels made it clear that you were pretty expert in this department.'

'Why would I implicate *myself*? With three insertions?'

'You've got me there.'

'Run down our top personnel, and I don't care if it takes

until the sun comes up,' said Drew. 'I want to see every résumé from the Big Man on down.'

The minutes passed, the printouts continued, studied by all, until an hour went by, then an hour and a half. 'Holy shit!' exclaimed Greenberg, looking at his screen. 'We may have a probable.'

'Who is it?' asked Witkowski, ice in his voice.

'You're not going to like this, any of you. *I* don't like it.'

'Who *is* it?'

'Read it yourselves,' said Joel, arching his head, his eyes closed as if in disbelief.

'Oh, my *God*,' cried Karin, staring at the centre screen. 'It's Janine Clunes!'

'Correction,' said the colonel. 'Janine Clunes Courtland, the ambassador's wife, his second wife, to be precise. She works in D and R, under her maiden name for obvious reasons.'

'What were her qualifications?' asked the stunned Latham.

'I can bring them up in a couple of minutes,' replied Rowe.

'Don't bother,' said Witkowski. 'I can give you a fairly accurate picture; it isn't often security's told to clear an ambassador's wife. Janine Clunes, University of Chicago, its think tank, PhD and full professorship in computer science before marrying Courtland after his divorce about a year and a half ago.'

'She's brilliant,' added Karin. 'She's also the sweetest, kindest woman in D and R. If she hears somebody has a problem and thinks she can help, she'll go right to her husband. Everyone adores her because, among other reasons, she never takes advantage of her position; to the contrary, she constantly covers for those who may be late, or can't complete their assignments on time. She's always offering to help.'

'A real roving butterfly,' said Drew. '*Christ*, is Courtland now on our list, *Harry's* list?'

'I can't believe that,' answered the colonel. 'I'm not very partial to him, but I can't believe it. He's been too open with us, even gone out on a limb for us. I remind you and Karin that we wouldn't be here without his giving us the go-ahead, because we *shouldn't* be here unless we had clearance from the State Department, DC, the CIA, the National Security Council, and probably the Joint Chiefs.'

'The only people left out are in the White House,' said the irreverent Greenberg. 'But then, what do they know? They're too busy trying to get their free parking spaces back.'

'I remember reading about Courtland's divorce in the *Washington Post*,' interrupted Drew, looking at Stanley Witkowski. 'As I recall, he gave everything to his wife and children, admitting that the constant relocations of a State Department officer were no way to bring up the kids.'

'I can understand that,' said the colonel coldly, returning Latham's look. 'But it doesn't necessarily mean his current wife is the other informer.'

'Of course it doesn't,' broke in Jack Rowe. 'My comrade in computer arms merely said he had a possible, right, Joel?'

'I believe he said "probable", *right*, Joel?' Latham said.

'Okay, Cons-Op, because I happen to believe it. The Big Bird fed us too much not to. Don't tell me Courtland doesn't know about our lady from NATO here, and please don't tell me they haven't talked about her. Her looks, her remoteness, her NATO duty – she's high-quality fodder for the rumour mill. If anyone was a logical candidate for suspicion, I submit it's Mrs de Vries. At least it throws people off the scent for the real mole.'

'What about languages?' said Latham, turning to Karin. 'They'd have to be important.'

'Janine speaks an acceptable French and Italian, but her German is completely fluent—' De Vries stopped, aware of what she just said.

'A "probable",' mused Drew softly. 'Where do we go from here?'

'I've gone,' replied Greenberg. 'I just sent a query to Chicago, asking for in-depth data on Professor Clunes. That stuff is all stored, so it should be coming back in a minute or two.'

'How can you be sure?' asked Karin. 'It's nearly midnight there.'

'*Shhh!*' whispered the computer scientist in mock secrecy. 'Chicago's a government-funded database, like the earthquake equipment, but don't tell anybody. Someone's always there because no one on the taxpayer's payroll wants to find his pants wet for withholding information from a machine like ours.'

'Here it comes!' cried Jack Rowe as the screen lit up from Chicago.

The woman named Janine Clunes held the position of full professor of computer science for a period of three years before her recent marriage to Daniel Courtland, then ambassador to Finland. She was highly regarded by both faculty and students alike for her ability to demystify computerese. She was active in campus politics, a staunch conservative when it was not popular, but her winning personality softened the negative reactions. It was rumoured that she had several affairs while in residence but nothing of consequence or detrimental to her position. It was noted, however, that political events excepted, she was not known to frequent social occasions, living off campus in Evanston, Illinois, an hour's drive from the university.

Her background is quite conformist for the times. She emigrated from Bavaria in the late forties as an infant, her parents deceased, and was brought up by relatives, Mr and Mrs Charles Schneider, in Centralia in the county of Marion, Illinois. Her records show that she was an outstanding student in high school, won a Merit Scholarship to the University of Chicago, and upon completion of her bachelor's degree, master's, and doctorate, was offered a position on the faculty. She made frequent trips as an unpaid political consultant to Washington, DC, where she met Ambassador Court-land. That's about it, Paris. Regards, Chicago.

'That's not "about it",' said Witkowski quietly as he read the bright green letters on the screen. 'She's a *Sonnenkind*.'

'What the hell are you talking about, Stanley?'

'I thought the Sonnenkinder theory was discredited,' said Karin softly, nearly inaudible.

'To most people,' replied the colonel, 'not to me, never has been. Look what's happening now.'

'What's a *Sonnen* – whatever?'

'A concept, Drew. The premise was that before and after the war, the zealots of the Third Reich sent out selected children to chosen "parents" throughout the world, whose mission was to raise the *Kinder* to positions of influence and power so as to pave the way for a Fourth Reich.'

'That's fantasyland, it couldn't happen.'

'Maybe it did after all,' said Witkowski. '*Christ*, the world's gone crazy!' exploded the embassy's chief of security.

'*Hold* it,' said Joel Greenberg at the computer, overriding Witkowski's outburst. 'There's an addendum coming in from Chicago. Catch the movie.' All heads turned to the screen and the bright green letters.

Additional information re Janine Clunes. While cham-pioning conservative causes, she violently opposed the Nazi march through Skokie, Illinois. She went on the parade's rostrum at her own peril and denounced the event as barbarism.

'What do you make of that, Stanley?' asked Drew.

'I'll tell you what I make of it,' interrupted De Vries. 'What better way to support an ultimately horrible agenda than by denying it? You could be right, Colonel. The Sonnenkinder operation may be alive and well.'

'Then tell me, how can I approach the ambassador? What

the hell can I say? He's living with, sleeping with, a daughter of the *Third Reich*?'

'Let me handle this, Stanley,' said Latham. 'I'm the coordinator, right?'

'Who are you going to lay it on, youngster?'

'Who else? A man we both appreciate. Wesley Sorenson.'

'May God have mercy on his soul.'

The telephone rang on Rowe's computer. He picked it up. 'S-Two here, what is it? . . . Yes, sir, right away, sir.' He turned to Witkowski. 'You're to go right up to medical, Colonel. Your "prize" is awake and talking.'

CHAPTER TWENTY-ONE

Gerhardt Kroeger, strapped in a straitjacket, was on the narrow bed, crouched against the wall, his body curled up and pressed into the wood. He was alone in a room at the embassy's infirmary, his wounded legs bandaged underneath his medical pyjamas, his eyes wide, glaring, roving everywhere but focused on nothing. '*Mein Vater war ein Verräter*,' he whispered hoarsely. '*Mein Vater war ein Verräter! . . . Mein Leben ist vorbei, alles vernichtet!*'

Two men watched him through a false mirror in an adjoining office – one, the embassy physician, the other, Colonel Witkowski. 'He's getting real squirrelly,' said the chief of security.

'I don't understand German. What's he saying?' asked the doctor.

'Something about his father being filth, a traitor, and that his life is over, everything destroyed.'

'What do you make of it?'

'Only what I hear. He's a basket case, carrying a ton of guilt that's driving him up the wall he can't climb.'

'Then he's suicidal,' concluded the doctor. 'He stays in the jacket.'

'You're damn right,' agreed the colonel. 'But I'm still going in to try to question him.'

'Be careful, his blood pressure's almost out of sight. Which, I suppose, is natural, considering who he is – or was. When the mighty fall, they crash with a bang.'

'You know who he is – was?'

'Sure. Most anybody who got through medical school would. Especially the head sessions.'

'Enlighten me, Doctor,' said Witkowski, looking at the physician.

'He is, or was, a famous German surgeon – I haven't heard of him for a few years now – but his speciality was brain disorders. It was said at the time that he cured more mentally dysfunctional patients than anyone else in the field. With a scalpel, not drugs, which are overloaded with side effects.'

'So why was this goddamned genius sent to Paris to kill someone when he couldn't hit the side of a barn with buckshot?'

'I wouldn't know, Colonel, and if he said anything about it, I wouldn't understand.'

'Fair enough, but not good enough, Doctor. Let me go inside, please.'

'Sure, but remember, I'll be watching. If I see him reaching an apex – the jacket is wired to blood pressure, heart rate, and oxygen – you're *out*. Understood?'

'I don't take lightly to orders like that where a killer is concerned—'

'You'll take them from me, Witkowski,' the doctor interrupted curtly. 'My job is to keep him alive, perhaps even for your benefit. Do we understand each other?'

'I don't have a choice, do I?'

'No, you don't. I'd advise talking quietly.'

'That advice I don't need from you.'

The colonel sat in a chair in front of the bed; he remained immobile until the unfocused Kroeger realized he was there. '*Guten Abend, Herr Doktor. Sprechen Sie Englisch, mein Herr?*'

'You know perfectly well I do,' said Kroeger, struggling against the constricting jacket. 'Why am I in this undignified attire? I am a doctor, a surgeon of repute, so why am I treated like an *animal*?'

'Because the families of two of your victims at the Hotel Inter-Continental no doubt consider you a vicious animal.

360

Should we let you free to face their wrath? I assure you that death at their hands would be far more painful than execution at ours.'

'They were an error, a *mistake*! A tragic event brought about by *your* hiding an enemy of humanity!'

'An enemy of humanity . . . ? That's a very serious charge. Why is Harry Latham an enemy of humanity?'

'He's insane, a violent schizophrenic who must be relieved of his tortures, or given medication so he can be institutionalized. Hasn't Moreau *told* you?'

'Moreau? The Deuxième Bureau?'

'Of course. I explained everything to him! He did not reach you? Of course he's French, and they keep things to themselves, don't they?'

'Perhaps I overlooked the communication.'

'You see,' said Kroeger, still struggling, but sitting up straight on the bed, 'I treated Harry Latham in Germany – where, it does not matter – I saved his life, but you must bring me to him so I can inject him with the drugs that were in my clothes. It's the only way he can stay alive and serve your purposes!'

'A tempting scenario,' said Witkowski. 'He brought out a list of names, you know, several hundred names—'

'Who knows where he *got* them?' interrupted Gerhardt Kroeger. 'He travelled with the drug-infected scum of Germany. Some could be right, many could be wrong. That's why you must bring me to him in neutral quarters so we can learn the truth.'

'My God, you're desperate enough to cover all the bases, aren't you?'

'*Was ist?*'

'You know goddamned well *was ist, Doktor* . . . Let's talk about something else for a minute, okay?'

'*Was?*'

'Your daddy, your *Vater*, do you mind?'

'I never discuss my father, sir,' said Kroeger, his eyes blank, unfocused, staring at nothing on the wall.

'Oh, I think we should,' insisted the colonel. 'You see, we ran a check on you, the whole you, and we considered your father a hero, an enlightened hero of Germany.'

'*Nein! Ein Verräter!*'

'We don't think so. He wanted to save lives, German, English, and American. He finally saw through the hollow crap of Hitler and his thugs and decided to make a statement at the risk of his life, if not certain death. That's a real hero, Doctor.'

'*Nein!* He betrayed the Fatherland!' Kroeger writhed in the staitjacket, bouncing back and forth on the bed, a man in agony, as tears fell from his eyes. 'Throughout the *Gymnasium*, then through the *Universität*, the schoolboys would come up to me – frequently they beat me. "Your father was a traitor, we all know it!" and "Why did the Americans make him the *Bürgermeister* when none of us wanted him?" *Mein Gott*, such tortures!'

'So you decided to make up for what he never completed, is that it, Herr Kroeger?'

'You have no right to interrogate me this way!' screamed the surgeon, sitting up straight, his eyes wet and red. 'All men, even enemies, have the privacy of their lives!'

'And I respect that,' said Witkowski, his posture straight in the chair. 'But you're an exception, Doctor, because you're too intelligent, too educated to buy the bilge you've been sold, and are now selling. Tell me, do you respect the sanctity of life outside of the womb?'

'Naturally. Breathing life is life.'

'Including Jews, Gypsies, the disabled and mentally impaired, along with homosexuals of either gender?'

'Those are political decisions, beyond the realm of the medical profession.'

'Doctor, you are one son of a bitch. But I'll tell you something. I may just bring you to the Latham you're after, if only to watch him listen to you, then spit in your face . . . "Political decisions?" You make me sick.'

*

Wesley Sorenson stared out his corner office window in Washington, absently noting the morning traffic congestion in the street below. The scene resembled a fish tank maze filled with insects, all trying to reach the next horizontal tube, only to find themselves in yet another tube, leading to still another, none with a finish line. It was a visual metaphor for his thoughts, concluded the director of Consular Operations, swinging his chair around, facing the separate piles of notes on his desk, notes that would be shredded and burned before he left the office at the end of the day. The strands of information were coming in too fast, clogging the alleyways of his mind, each revelation seemingly no less explosive than the one preceding it. The two Germans in custody in Fairfax had implicated the Vice President of the United States, and the Speaker of the House in the spreading hunt for neo-Nazis, with the promise of additional names to follow; the CIA was compromised in its upper levels (how many more agencies were so infected?); a Defense Department communications laboratory had had an entire year's research deleted from its computers by a neo who had disappeared on a Lufthansa flight to Munich; senators, congressmen, powerful businessmen, even newscasters, had been tainted with the Nazi brush with no substantive evidence whatsoever, the allegations dismissed until an influential member of Britain's Foreign Office had been caught, apparently giving the names of other influential figures in the UK's government hierarchy. Finally, Claude Moreau was clean, but the US Embassy in Paris was not – good God, it was far from it if the latest information was accurate! Ambassador Courtland's *wife*?

It was a maelstrom of charges and countercharges, of insidious implications furiously denied, a battleground where blood would be spilled, the innocent mortally wounded, the guilty vanishing from the scene. It was as if the insanity of the crazed McCarthy period had been fused with the Nazi madness of the late thirties, the marching Bunds everywhere, all in lockstep with demonic leaders whose screaming exhortations brought the intellectually unwashed to their feet, their fears and their hatreds – frequently one and the same – finding volcanic outlets for their own inadequacies. The sickness of fanaticism was again spreading across the world; where would it end, if ever?

What concerned Sorenson at the moment, however – concerned, hell, *shocked* him – was the information, followed by a faxed background check, on Courtland's second wife, Janine Clunes. On the surface it would appear inconceivable; he had said as much to Drew Latham over their secure phones only minutes before.

'I can't believe it!'

'That's what Witkowski said until he read the check from Chicago. Then he said something else, only he kind of whispered it. You could barely hear him but the words were clear. "She's a *Sonnenkind*."'

'Do you know what that means, Drew?'

'Karin filled me in. It's wild, Wes, and it could never fly. Infants, kids, sent all over the place—'

'You left out a couple of items,' interrupted Sorenson. '*Selected* kids, pure Aryan blood, parents with combined IQ's over two hundred seventy, none less.'

'You know about it?'

'They were called the products of the Lebensborn. SS officers impregnating blonde-haired, blue-eyed northern European women, those closest to or across the Scandinavian borders whenever possible.'

'That's *nuts*!'

'That was Heinrich Himmler. It was his concept.'

'It *happened*?'

'Not according to every intelligence investigation after the war. The conclusion was that the Lebensborn scheme was abandoned, due to the difficulty of transport and the time it took for medical evaluations.'

'Witkowski doesn't believe it was abandoned.'

Silence. Then Sorenson spoke. 'I was convinced it was,' he said. 'Now I'm not so sure.'

'What do you want us to do – *me* to do?'

'Keep cold and keep silent. If the neos know Kroeger's alive, they'll break everyone's balls to find him. If you've lucked out, nobody on our side will be killed.'

'That's pretty icicle-like, Wes.'

'"Remembrance of things past," if you'll forgive the literary bastardization,' said Sorenson. 'Send a signal out to the Antinayous. Tell them you've got the prize.'

'For Christ's sake, *why*?'

'Because at this point I don't trust anybody, and I'm covering all our flanks. Do as I say. Call me back in an hour, or less, as things develop.'

Things, however, *had* developed for the veteran intelligence officer, now the director of Consular Operations. No one had ever *found* a Sonnenkind. Even those once suspected were totally, angrily, deemed innocent children because of official papers and the perfectly Americanized, loving couples who took in the bereft orphans. But now, courts notwithstanding, a possible Sonnenkind had surfaced! A grown-up woman, once a child of Nazi Germany, now a highly desirable, accomplished academician who had snared a high-level officer of the State Department. It was a Sonnenkinder agenda if one ever existed.

Sorenson picked up his phone and touched the numbers for the private phone of the director of the FBI, a decent man of whom Knox Talbot had said, 'He's okay.'

'Yes?'

'It's Sorenson over at Cons-Op, am I disturbing you?'

'On this line, hell no. What can I do for you?'

'I'll be up front. I'm transgressing into your area, but I don't have a choice.'

'Do any of us at certain times?' asked the FBI director. 'We've never met, but Knox Talbot says you're a friend of his, which gives you a pretty clean slate with me. Where's the transgression?'

'Actually, I haven't gone over the line yet, but I want to, I think I have to.'

'You said you had no choice.'

'I don't believe I do. However, it's got to remain within Cons-Op.'

'Then why call me? Isn't solo better?'

'Not in this case. I need a shortcut.'

'Go ahead, Wes – that's what Knox calls you. I'm Steve.'

'Yes, I know. Steven Rosbician, the paradigm of law enforcement.'

'My troops carry the PR way beyond the goal line. I was a white LA judge who got lucky, 'cause the blacks figured I was fair. Your petition, please.'

'Have you got a unit in Marion County, Illinois?'

'I'm sure we do. Illinois goes way back in our history. What city?'

'Centralia.'

'Close enough. What do you need?'

'Anything you've got on a Mr and Mrs Charles Schneider. They may be dead and I don't have an address, but I have an idea they may have immigrated from Germany in the early to middle thirties.'

'That's not much to go on.'

'I realize that, but in the context of our inquiry and considering the times, the Bureau may have a file on them.'

'If we have one, you'll get it. So where's the transgression? I'm not that long in this job, but I don't see it.'

'Then let me clarify, Steve. I'm going domestic, which is your province, and I can't give you the background for my inquiry. In the old days, J. Edgar, the hound, would have demanded it or slammed down the phone.'

'I'm no goddamned Hoover, and the Bureau has changed considerably. If we can't cooperate with each other, full disclosure or no, where are we?'

'Well, it's kind of spelled out in our charters—'

'More honoured in the breach, I'd suggest,' interrupted Rosbician. 'Give me your secure fax number. Whatever we've got, you'll have within the hour.'

'Thanks very much,' said Sorenson, 'and also, as you suggested, whatever I do from now on, I'll go solo.'

'Why the bullshit?'

'Wait till you face a congressional hearing with six dour faces who don't like you. Then you'll understand.'

'Then I'll go back to a law firm and live a hell of a lot better.'

'I like your perspective, Steve.' Sorenson gave the FBI director the number of his secure fax machine.

Thirty-eight minutes passed before the loud beep of the Cons-Op machine in his office preceded the emergence of a single page of paper from the FBI. Wesley Sorenson retrieved it and read the information.

Karl and Johanna Schneider came to the US on January 12, 1940, expatriates from Germany with relatives in Cicero, Illinois, who vouched for them, stating that the young male Schneider had skills that would easily find him work in the technical field of optometry. Their ages were, respectively, twenty-one and nineteen. The stated reason for their leaving Germany was that Johanna Schneider's grandfather was Jewish, and she was discriminated against by the Aryan Ministerium in Stuttgart.

In March of 1946, Mr Schneider, by then Charles rather than Karl, owned a small optometric factory in Centralia, and petitioned the Immigration Service to allow his niece, one Janine Clunitz, an infant female child, to immigrate, as her parents had died in an automobile crash. The petition was granted and the Schneiders legally adopted the child.

In August of 1991, Mrs Schneider died of heart failure. Mr Schneider, age 76, still resides at 121 Cyprus Street, Centralia, Illinois. He has retired, but goes down to his business twice a week.

The MO for this file is based on long-ago surveillance of German immigrants at the beginning of World War Two. In the opinion of this field officer, it should be terminated.

Thank heavens it wasn't, thought Sorenson. If Charles-Karl Schneider was really a Sonnenkind recipient, a wealth of information might be extracted from him on the assumption that the Sonnenkinder had a network. It would be asinine to assume that it did not have one. The legal and technical paperwork involved in the US immigration procedures were complex to the point of total confusion; a support system was mandatory. It could well be past the time when it should have happened, but a crack in the ice now might release the fouled waters below, exposing dirt that was relevant to the present. Sorenson picked up his phone and pressed the button for his secretary.

'Yes, sir?'

'Book me on an airline that flies into Centralia, Illinois, or whatever's closest. Under an assumed name, of course, which, I trust, you'll tell me.'

'For when, Mr Director?'

'Early this afternoon, if you can. Then get my wife on the phone. I won't be home for dinner.'

Claude Moreau studied the transcript from Nuremberg, Germany, the decoded dossier on one Dr Hans Traupman, chief surgeon in residence at the Nuremberg Hospital.

> Hans Traupman, born April 21, 1922, in Berlin, the son of two physicians, Drs Erich and Marlene Traupman, showed early signs of a high intelligence quotient, according to his initial school years . . .

The dossier went on to describe Traupman's academic achievements, including a brief period in the Hitler Youth movement, ordered by decree, and his duty after medical school in Nuremberg as a young doctor in the *Sanitätstruppe*, the Wehrmacht's medical corps.

> After the conflict, Traupman returned to Nuremberg, where he was trained in residence and specialized in surgeries of the brain. Within ten years, with scores of

operations behind him, he was considered one of the leading cranial surgeons in the country, if not the Free World. As to his personal life, little is known. He was married to an Elke Mueller, said marriage dissolved by divorce after five years and no children. Since that time he has resided in an elegant apartment in Nuremberg's most fashionable section. He is a wealthy man, frequently dining at the most expensive restaurants and known to be an excessive tipper. His guests range from medical colleagues to political figures from Bonn and various celebrities from the motion pictures and television. To summarize, if such a summary is possible, he is a bon vivant with the medical skills to permit his extravagant living.

Moreau picked up his phone and touched the button that put him in direct contact with their man in Nuremberg.

'Yes?' said the voice in Germany.

'It is I.'

'I sent you everything there was.'

'No, you didn't. Dig up everything you can on Elke Mueller.'

'Traupman's former wife? Why? She's history.'

'Because she's the key, you idiot. A divorce after a year or two is understandable, after twenty perfectly acceptable, but not after five. There's a story there. Do as I ask, and send me the material as fast as you can.'

'It's a whole different agenda,' protested the agent in Nuremberg. 'She's living in Munich now, under her maiden name.'

'Mueller, of course. Do you have an address?'

'Naturally.' The Deuxième agent gave it to him.

'Then forget my previous order. I've changed my mind. Alert Munich that I'm flying in. I wish to confront this lady myself.'

'Whatever you say, but I think you're crazy.'

'Everyone's crazy,' said Moreau. 'It's the times we're living in.'

*

Sorenson's plane landed in Mount Vernon, Illinois, roughly thirty miles south of Centralia. Using the false driver's licence and credit card provided by Consular Operations, he rented a car and, following the routes highlighted for him by the rental agency's clerk, drove north to the city. Cons-Op had also given him a street map of Centralia, the address, 121 Cyprus Street, clearly marked, and the directions from the city limits on Highway 51 specific. Twenty minutes later Sorenson drove down the quiet tree-lined street looking for number 121. The street itself was, indeed, central America, but of a different, bygone era. It was upper-middle-class Norman Rockwell, the houses large, with generous front porches, profuse with latticework, even rocking chairs. One could easily imagine the owners sitting in them and drinking afternoon tea with their neighbours.

Then he saw the mailbox, *121*. Only this house was different, not in style or size, but something else, something subtle. What was it? The *windows*, thought the director of Consular Operations. The windows on the second and third floors all had their shades drawn. Even on the ground floor, the large, multipaned bay window, flanked by two stained-glass vertical rectangles, was blocked by venetian blinds. It was as though this particular residence was not terribly receptive to visitors. Wesley wondered if he'd fall into that category, or worse. He parked in front, got out and walked up the concrete path, climbed the steps, and rang the bell.

The door opened, revealing a slender old man with thinning white hair and wearing thick-lensed glasses. 'Yes, please?' he said in a soft, wavering voice with barely a trace of an accent.

'My name is Wesley Sorenson and I'm from Washington, DC, Mr Schneider. We have to talk, either here or in far less comfortable quarters.'

The old man's eyes grew wide, what colour there was in his face leaving it. He started to speak several times but choked on the words. Finally, he became clear. '*Ach*, it has taken you so long, it was so long ago . . . Come in, I've been expecting you for nearly fifty years . . . Come, come, it is too warm out, and the air-conditioning is expensive . . . Nothing matters now anyway.'

'We're not so far apart in years, Mr Schneider,' said Sorenson, walking into a large Victorian foyer and following the Sonnenkind recipient into a shadowed living room, filled with overstuffed furniture. 'Fifty years is not that long for either of us.'

'May I offer you some schnapps? Frankly, I could use one or two, probably more.'

'A short whisky would be sufficient, if you have it. Bourbon would be nice, but it doesn't matter.'

'Oh, but it does, and I do have it. My second daughter is married to a man from one of the Carolinas, and he prefers it . . . Sit, sit, I shall disappear for a minute or two and bring us our libations.'

'Thank you.' The Cons-Op director suddenly wondered whether he should have arranged for a weapon. He had been away from the field too long! The old son of a bitch could be finding one of his own. Instead, Schneider returned, carrying a silver tray, glasses and two bottles on it, without any bulges in his clothing.

'This will make things easier, *nicht wahr*?' he said.

'I'm surprised you expected me at all,' observed Sorenson once their drinks were in front of them, his on a coffee table, the German's on the arm of an easy chair across from him. 'As you say, it was so many years ago.'

'My young wife and I were part of the fanatical youth of Germany at the time. All those torchlit parades, the slogans, the euphoria of being the true master race of the world. It was all quite seductive, and we were seduced. We were assigned our mission by the legendary Heinrich Himmler himself, who thought "long range", as we say today. I honestly believe he thought we would lose the war, but he was totally devoted to the thesis of Aryan superiority. After the war we did as we were ordered by the Odessa. And even then, we still believed.'

'So you petitioned, accepted the immigration of one Janine Clunitz, later Clunes, and adopted her?'

'Yes. She was an extraordinary child, far more intelligent than Johanna and me. Every Tuesday night from the time she was eight or nine, men would come for her and drive her to someplace else where she was – I suppose the word is *indoctrinated*.'

'Where was this place?'

'We never found out. In the beginning she was only given sweets, ice cream, and so on while blindfolded. Later, as she grew older, she simply told us that she was being trained in our "glorious heritage", those were the words she used and, naturally, we knew what they meant.'

'Why are you telling me this now, Mr Schneider?'

'Because I've lived in this country for fifty-two years. I cannot say it is perfect, no nation is, but it is better than what I came from. Do you know who lives across the street from me?'

'How could I?'

'The Goldfarbs, Jake and Naomi. Jews. And they were Johanna's and my best friends. And down the block, the first Negro couple to buy a house here. The Goldfarbs and we gave them a welcoming party, and everyone came. And when a cross was burned on their lawn, we all got together, hunted the hooligans down, and had them prosecuted.'

'Hardly the agenda of the Third Reich.'

'People change, we all change. What can I tell you?'

'How long has it been since you were in contact with Germany?'

'*Mein Gott*, those idiots keep calling twice, three times a year. I tell them I'm an old man and to leave me alone, for I am no longer involved. I must be in their computers or whatever the new technical machines order them to do. They keep track of me; they never let go, never stop threatening me.'

'There are no names?'

'Yes, one. The last caller a month ago was nearly

hysterical, shouting at me that a Herr Traupman might order my execution. "What for?" I asked. "I'll be dead soon anyway and your secret will die with me.'"

Claude Moreau was driven down the Leopoldstrasse by his man in Munich who had reconnoitred the apartment house where Elke Mueller, the former Frau Traupman, lived. To save Moreau's time, the secret Deuxième office in the Königinstrasse had telephoned Madame Mueller, explaining that a high-ranking member of the French government wished to discuss a confidential matter with her which could be to her financial advantage . . . No, the caller had no idea what the confidential matter was, except that it would no way compromise the eminent lady.

The apartment house was grand, the apartment itself grander still, a fulsome mixture of baroque and art deco. Elke Mueller matched her surroundings, a tall, imperious woman in her seventies, her coiffed dark hair streaked with whitish-grey, her face angular, her features aquiline. She was obviously a woman not to be trifled with; it was in her eyes, wide and bright and bordering on the hostile or suspicious, or both.

'My name is Claude Moreau, madame, and I'm with the Quai d'Orsay in Paris,' said the chief of the Deuxième Bureau in German, having been ushered into a sitting room by the uniformed maid.

'It's not necessary to speak *Deutsch*, monsieur. My French is fluent.'

'You greatly relieve me,' lied Moreau, 'for my German is barely adequate.'

'I suspect it's more than that. Sit down across from me and explain this confidential matter if you will. I can't imagine why the government of France has the slightest interest in me.'

'Forgive me, madame, but I suspect that you might.'

'You're impertinent, monsieur.'

'I apologize. I only wish to be clear and speak the truth as I perceive it.'

'Now you're admirable. It's Traupman, isn't it?'

'Then my gentle suspicion was correct, no?'

'It was, of course. There could be no other possible reason.'

'You were married to him—'

'Not for long, as marriages go,' interrupted Elke Mueller swiftly, firmly, 'but far too long for me. So his filthy little chickens are coming home to roost, is that it? . . . Don't look so surprised, Moreau. I read the papers and watch television. I see what's happening.'

'About those "filthy chickens"? May I inquire about them?'

'Why not? I left the incubator coop over thirty years ago.'

'Would it be impertinent of me to ask you to amplify – only what's comfortable for you, naturally.'

'Now you're a liar, monsieur. You'd prefer that I be terribly uncomfortable, even bitterly hysterical, and tell you what a horrible man he was. Well, I can't do that, whether it's true or not. However, I can tell you that when I think of Traupman, which is rarely, I'm filled with disgust.'

'Oh . . . ?'

'Oh, yes, your amplification. Very well, you shall have it . . . I married Hans Traupman rather late. I was thirty-one, he thirty-three, and a very successful surgeon even at that age. I was struck by his medical brilliance and believed there was a good man beneath his rather cold exterior. There were flashes of warmth that excited me, until I soon realized it was all an act. Why he was attracted to me became evident quite rapidly. I was a Mueller from Baden-Baden, the richest landowners in the area, also socially prominent, and gave him access to the circles he so desperately wanted to be a part of. You see, his parents were both doctors, but not really attractive people, and certainly not very successful, their practices relegated to clinics serving the lower economic classes—'

'If I may,' Moreau broke in, 'did he use his position as your husband to further his social ambitions?'

'I just told you that.'

'Then why did he risk a divorce?'

'He didn't have much to say about it. Besides, after five years he had made the inroads he needed, and his skills accomplished the rest. In deference to the Mueller family, I agreed to a so-called amicable divorce – simple incompatibility, neither party charged with anything. It was the biggest mistake I made, and my father, before he died, soundly criticized me for it.'

'May I ask why?'

'You don't know my family, monsieur, and Mueller is a common name in Germany. I will explain for you. The Muellers of Baden-Baden opposed the criminal Hitler and his gangsters. The *Führer* didn't dare touch us because of our holdings and the loyalties our several thousand employees accorded us. The Allies never understood how frightened Hitler was of domestic dissent. Had they understood, they might have developed tactics within Germany that could have shortened the war. Like Traupman, the little thug with a moustache reached far beyond his grasp, mixing with people he had admired from afar, but who never accepted him. My father always claimed Hitler's diatribes were the rantings of a frightened man, driven to eliminate by murder the slightest opposition, as long as there were no consequences. However, Herr Hitler, through conscription, made sure my two brothers were sent to the Russian front, where they were killed, more likely by German bullets than Soviet.'

'Hans Traupman, please?'

'He was the total Nazi,' said Madame Mueller quietly, turning her face towards the afternoon sunlight that streamed through the window. 'It was strange, almost inhuman, but he wanted power, simply power, beyond the rewards of his profession. He would recite the discredited theories of a superior Aryan race as if they were considered infallible, although he had to know they were not. I think it was the bitter resentment of the rejected young man who could not walk among the elite of Germany, in spite of his growing reputation, because he simply was a coarse, unlikeable person.'

'You're leading to something else, I think,' said Moreau.

'Yes, I am. He began to hold meetings at our house in Nuremberg, meetings with people I knew were unreconstructed National Socialists, Hitler fanatics. He soundproofed the cellar, where they met every Tuesday – I was not permitted to attend. There was a great deal of drinking and from our bedroom I could faintly hear shouting and "*Sieg Heils*" and the Horst Wessel song, over and over. This went on for three years, until the fifth year of our marriage, and finally I confronted him – why I did not do so earlier, I simply don't know . . . Affection, no matter how dwindling, does involve protection. I shouted at him, accusing him of dreadful things, of trying to bring back the horrors of the past. And on a Wednesday morning, after one of those terrible nights, he said to me, "It doesn't matter what you think, you rich bitch. We were right then and we're right *now*!" I left the next day. Does that amplify enough for you, Moreau?'

'It certainly does, madame,' replied the head of the Deuxième. 'Can you recall any of the men or women at those meetings?'

'It was more than thirty years ago. No, I cannot.'

'Even one or two of the "unreconstructed Nazis"?'

'Let me think . . . There was a Bohr, a Rudolf Bohr, I believe, and a former, very young colonel in the Wehrmacht named Von Schteifel, I think. Other than those two, my memory leaves me. I remember them only because they were frequent visitors for lunch or dinner, where no politics were discussed, but I saw them through my bedroom window getting out of their cars.'

'You have been of enormous help, madame,' said Moreau, getting up from his chair. 'I'll not disturb you any longer.'

'*Stop* them,' whispered Elke Mueller harshly. 'They'll be the death of Germany!'

'We'll remember your words,' said Claude Moreau, walking into the foyer.

At the Deuxième headquarters in the Königinstrasse, Moreau exercised his privileges and ordered Paris to reach Wesley Sorenson immediately.

Sorenson was on the plane back to Washington when his Sky-Pager buzzed. He got out of his seat, walked up to the telephone on the first-class bulkhead, inserted his card, and reached his office.

'Hold on, Mr Director,' said the operator in Consular Operations. 'I'll call Munich and patch you through.'

'*Allô*, Wesley?'

'Yes, Claude?'

'It's *Traupman!*'

'Traupman's *the key!*'

They had spoken simultaneously. 'I'll be in my office in roughly an hour,' said Sorenson. 'I'll call you back.'

'We've both been busy, *mon ami.*'

'You can bet your French ass!'

CHAPTER TWENTY-TWO

Drew lay beside Karin in the bed in her room at the Bristol Hotel, their being together a reluctant concession on the part of Witkowski. They had made love, and were now experiencing the comfortable afterglow of lovers who know they belong with each other.

'Where the hell are we?' sad Latham, having lighted one of his infrequent cigarettes. The smoke curled above them.

'It's in Sorenson's hands now. You have no control.'

'That's what I don't like. He's in Washington and we're in Paris and that goddamned Kroeger is on another planet.'

'Drugs could extract information from him.'

'The embassy doctor says we can't do anything in that area until he stabilizes from the gunshot wounds. The colonel's as mad as I've ever seen him, but he can't override the medicine man. I'm not exactly sanguine either; every twenty-four hours we lose makes the bastards harder to find.'

'Are you so sure of that? The neos have been entrenching themselves for over fifty years. What difference can a single day make?'

'I don't know, maybe another Harry Latham. Let's say I'm impatient.'

'I can understand. Is there any strategy where Janine is concerned?'

'You know as much as I do. Sorenson said to keep cold and silent, and let the Antinayous know we have Kroeger. We've done both and left word at Wesley's office that his instructions were carried out. Signed, Paris.'

'Does he really believe the Antis have been infiltrated?'

'He told me he was covering all our flanks; it can't do any harm. We've got Kroeger and nobody can get near him. If anyone tries, we know we've got an exposed flank.'

'Could Janine be an asset there?'

'That's Wesley's job. I wouldn't know how to get near it.'

'I wonder if Courtland told her about Kroeger.'

'He had to say something after we got him up at three o'clock in the morning.'

'He could have said anything, not necessarily the truth. All ambassadors are schooled in what and what not to tell their immediate families. Most of the time for their own protection.'

'There's a flaw in that argument, Karin. He put his own wife in D and R, a hornet's nest of classified information.'

'His marriage is relatively recent, and if what we believe is true, Janine wanted to be put there. It wouldn't be very difficult for a new wife to persuade her husband. Heaven knows she had the qualifications, and no doubt she put it in terms of wanting to make a patriotic contribution.'

'True, or at least I have to take your word for it, Eve and the apple being your foundation—'

'Male chauvinist,' interrupted De Vries, laughing and gently jabbing his thigh.

'The apple wasn't our idea, lady.'

'You're being pejorative again.'

'I wonder how Wes is going to handle it,' said Latham, grabbing her hand and holding it while extinguishing his cigarette.

'Why not call him?'

'His secretary said he wouldn't be back until tomorrow, which means he went somewhere. He mentioned that he had another problem, a heavy one, so perhaps he went after it.'

'I'd think Janine Courtland would take precedence.'

'Maybe she did. We'll know tomorrow – actually today. The sun's coming up.'

'Let it come up, my dearest. We're not allowed near the embassy, so let's consider this our holiday, yours and mine.'

'I like that idea,' said Drew, turning to her, their bodies touching. And the telephone rang. 'Some holiday,' added Latham, reaching for the abusively intruding phone. 'Yes?'

'It's one-something in the morning here,' said the voice of Wesley Sorenson. 'Sorry if I woke you, but I got your hotel number from Witkowski and wanted to keep you up to speed.'

'What happened?'

'Your computer whizzes were on the mark. Everything panned out. Janine Clunitz is a Sonnenkind.'

'Janine who?'

'Clunitz is her real name – the Clunes is anglicized. She was brought up by the Schneiders in Centralia, Illinois.'

'Yes, we read that. But how can you be sure?'

'I flew out there this afternoon. Old Schneider confirmed it.'

'What the hell do we do *now*?'

'Not "we", me,' replied the director of Consular Operations. 'The State Department is recalling Courtland for thirty-six hours for an emergency meeting with several other European ambassadors, the subject to await their arrival.'

'State *agreed* to this?'

'State doesn't know about it. It's a Four Zero directive, issued back-channel through this office to avoid any traffic interception.'

'I trust that makes sense.'

'Who gives a damn? We'll pick him up at the airport and he'll be in my office before Secretary Bollinger orders his eggs Benedict.'

'Wow, I think I hear an old case-officer talking.'

'Could be.'

'How are you going to handle Courtland?'

'I'm trusting he's as bright as his service record says he is. I recorded Schneider – with his permission – and had him vocally confirm a very complete deposition. I'll present Courtland with everything, and hope he sees the light.'

'He may not, Wes.'

'I'm prepared for that. Schneider's ready to be flown to Washington. He really doesn't like where he came from – his words, incidentally.'

'Congratulations, my honcho.'

'Thanks, Drew, not bad, if I do say so ... Also, there's something else.'

'What?'

'Contact Moreau. I spoke to him a few minutes ago and he expects your call this morning – your time.'

'I'm not comfortable going around Witkowski, Wes.'

'You won't be, he knows everything. I reached him too. It'd be stupid to freeze him out; we need his expertise.'

'What's with Moreau?'

'He and I went in different directions but came back with the same information. We've found our tunnel to the Brotherhood. It's a man, a doctor in Nuremberg, where the trials took place.'

'Ironic. What goes around comes around.'

'Talk to you later, after you speak to Moreau.'

Latham hung up the phone and turned to Karin. 'Our holiday's been cut a tad short, but we've still got an hour or so.'

She held out her arms, her bandaged right hand lower than her left.

The night was dark and still, as, one by one, ten minutes apart, the speedboats swung into the long dock in the Rhine River. A dim red light on the highest pylon was their point of arrival, the erratic moon not helpful, for the sky was overcast. The operators of these swift craft, however, were familiar with the waterways and the estates they frequented. Engines were cut a hundred or so feet from the dock, the river tides gently ushering the boats towards their slips, where a two-man crew caught the thrown ropes and pulled them silently into their resting places. And, one by one, the men attending the conference walked up the dock and onto a flagstone path that led to the mansion on the river.

The arrivals greeted one another on a huge candlelit veranda where coffee, drinks, and canapés were served. The conversation was innocuous – golf scores and tennis competitions, nothing of relevance; that would change abruptly. An hour and twenty minutes later the group was complete, the servants dismissed, and the formal meeting began. The nine leaders of Die Brüderschaft der Wacht sat in a semicircle facing a lectern. Dr Hans Traupman rose from his chair and walked to it.

'*Sieg Heil!*' he shouted, thrusting his right arm forward in the Nazi salute.

'*Sieg Heil!*' roared the leaders in unison, rising as one and shooting out their arms.

'Sit, if you please,' said the doctor from Nuremberg. Everyone did so, their posture straight, their concentration absolute. Traupman continued. 'We have glorious news to report. Across the globe, enemies of the Fourth Reich are in disarray, they tremble in fear and confusion. It is now time for another stage, an assault that will plunge them further into bewilderment and panic, while our disciples – yes, our *disciples* – are prepared to move cautiously but firmly into positions of influence everywhere . . . Our action will require sacrifices from many in the field, risk of imprisonment, even death, but our resolve is strong, our cause mighty, for the future *is ours*. I shall turn the meeting over to the man we've chosen to be the *Führer* of the Brüderschaft, the Zeus who will guide our movement to fulfilment, for he is a man without compromise and with a will of steel. It's an honour to ask Günter Jäger to address you.'

Again, as one, the small congregation rose, and once more their arms shot forward. '*Sieg Heil!*' they shouted. '*Sieg Heil*, Günter Jäger!'

A slender, blond-haired man nearly six feet in height and

dressed in a black suit, his neck encased in a pure white clerical collar, rose from a centre chair and approached the lectern. His posture was erect, his walk a stride, his head that of a sculptured Mars. It was his eyes, however, that demanded attention. They were grey-green and penetrating, at once cold, yet strangely alight with flashes of warmth as his gaze settled on individuals, which it did as those eyes roamed from chair to chair, each recipient bathed in the glory of his stare.

'I am the one who is honoured,' he began quietly, permitting himself a gentle smile. 'As you all know, I'm a defrocked father of my own church, for it finds my positions impolitic, but I have found a flock far greater than any in Christendom. You represent that flock, those millions who believe in our cause.' Jäger stopped and inserted his right forefinger between his clerical collar and his neck, adding in self-deprecating humour, 'I often wish the elders of my misguided church had made my banishment public, for this white coil around my throat is suffocating. But, of course, they can't; it would be bad politics. They conceal more infelicitous sins than the scriptures enumerate; they know it and I know it, so an accommodation was made.'

Softly, knowing laughter came from the audience. Günter Jäger continued. 'As Herr Doktor Traupman has told you, we are about to enter our next phase of disorientation among our enemies. It will be devastating, an unseen army attacking the most vital source of life on earth . . . Water, gentlemen.'

The response was now bewilderment; the congregation talked among themselves. 'How is this to be accomplished, my defrocked brother?' asked the old Catholic priest, Monsignor Heinrich Paltz.

'If your church knew who and what you are, Father, we'd be joined at the hip.'

Laughter again. 'I can substantiate our theories back to the book of Genesis!' the monsignor broke in. 'Cain was obviously a Negro, the mark of Cain was his skin and it was black! And in Leviticus and Deuteronomy, both spoke of the inferior tribes who rejected the words of the prophets!'

'Let's not get into a scholarly debate. Father, for we might both lose. The prophets, by and large, were Jews.'

'So were the tribes!'

'*Similia similibus*, my friend. That was two thousand years ago, and we are here now, two thousand years later. But you asked how this operation can be accomplished. May I explain?'

'Please do, Herr Jäger,' said Albert Richter, a dilettante turned politician, but with property and another way of life in Monaco.

'The *reservoirs*, gentlemen, the main water reserves for London, Paris, and Washington. As we convene, plans are being developed to drop tons of toxic chemicals into those central reservoirs from aircraft at night. Once they are dispersed, thousands upon thousands of people will die. Corpses will pile up in the streets, the governments of each nation will be blamed, for it is their responsibility to protect their resources. In London, Paris, and Washington, it will be nothing less than a catastrophic plague, leaving the citizenry terrified, outraged. As political figures fall, our people will take their places, claiming to have the answers, the solutions. Weeks, perhaps months, later, once the crises have been reduced through specific antitoxins introduced into the water in a similar manner, we shall have made considerable inroads within governments and their militaries. When relative calm has been restored, our disciples will be given the credit, for they alone will know and will order the chemical theriacs or counterpoisons.'

'When will this take place?' asked Maximilian von Löwenstein, son of the general and Wolfsschanze traitor executed by the SS but whose loyal mother was a mistress of Joseph Goebbels's, a devoted courtesan of the Reich who loathed her husband. 'My mother constantly spoke of the

384

extravagant promises emanating from the Chancellory without specifics. She felt they were most unfortunate and weakened the *Führer*.'

'And *our* history books will extol the contributions your mother made to the Third Reich; how she exposed her treacherous husband among them. However, in the current situation, tactics are being studied, including the pay-loads of radar-eluding, low-flying aircraft. Everything is in place within two hundred kilometres of the targets, our specialists on the scene. According to the latest projections, Operation Water Lightning will occur between three and five weeks of this date, each national catastrophe taking place at the same moment, in the darkest hours of night on both sides of the Atlantic. It is now determined that it will be at four-thirty A.M. Paris time, three-thirty London, and ten-thirty P.M. of the previous evening in Washington. They are the most accommodating hours of darkness. That is as specific as I can be at this juncture.'

'It's more than sufficient, *mein Führer*, our Zeus!' exclaimed Ansel Schmidt, multimillionaire electronics tycoon who had stolen the majority of his high technology from other firms.

'I see a problem,' said a heavyset man whose enormously large legs dwarfed his chair, his face balloonlike, devoid of lines despite his age. 'As you know, I'm a chemical engineer by training before branching out. Our enemies are not fools; water samples are constantly analysed. The sabotage will be revealed, and treatments prescribed. How do we handle that?'

'German inventiveness is the simplest answer,' replied Günter Jäger, smiling. 'As several generations ago our laboratories created Zyklon B, which rid the world of millions of Jews and other undesirables, our people have developed another lethal formula employing soluble compounds of seemingly incompatible elements, made compatible by isogonic bombardment prior to mixture.' Here Jäger stopped and shrugged, continuing to smile. 'I am a man of the cloth, *our* cloth, and do not pretend to be a master of the subject, but we have the finest chemists, a number of whom were recruited from your own laboratories, Herr Waller.'

'"Isogonic bombardment?"' said the obese man, a thick-lipped smile slowly spreading across his large face. 'A simple variation of isometric fusion, semetrizing the hostile elements, forcing compatibility, like a coating on aspirin. It could take days, weeks, to break down the compounds, let alone isolate them for specific counteractants . . . Absolutely ingenious, Herr Jäger – *mein Führer* – I salute you, salute your talent for bringing together other brilliant talents.'

'You're too kind, but I would not know my way around a laboratory.'

'Laboratories are for cooks, the visions must come first! Yours was in "attacking the most vital source of life on earth. Water . . . "'

'The rich and even the less affluent will buy their Evians and Pellegrinos in the markets,' countered a short man of medium build and close-cropped dark hair. 'The lower classes will be ordered to boil water for the prescribed twelve minutes for purification.'

'The accepted twelve minutes will be insufficient, Herr Richter,' interrupted the new *Führer*. 'Replace that number with thirty-seven, then tell me how many can or will comply. Granted, the bottom rungs of the social ladder will be affected most severely, then again, that is not antithetical to our cleansing purposes, is it? Whole ghettos will be wiped out, saving us time later.'

'I see an even greater advantage,' said Von Löwenstein, son of a Riech's courtesan. 'Depending on the success of Water Lightning, those same compounds could be dropped into selected reservoirs throughout Europe, the Mediterranean, and Africa.'

'Israel first!' shouted the senile Monsignor Paltz. 'The Jews killed our Christ!' A number of the congregation looked at one another, then up at Günter Jäger.

'Surely, my brother priest,' said the Brotherhood's Zeus,

'but we must never raise our voices about such solutions, no matter how justified our anger, must we?'

'I simply wanted the logic of my demand made clear.'

'It is, Father, it is.'

On this same evening, at a long-forgotten airstrip ten miles west of the legendary Lakenheath in England, a small group of men and women studied blueprints and a map under the glare of a single floodlight. Behind them, in the distance, was a partially camouflaged vintage 727 jet, circa the middle 1970s. It stood by the bordering woods, its cloth covering pulled up to permit entry into the forward cabin. The language the group spoke was English, several with British accents, the rest with German.

'I tell you it's impossible,' said a German male. 'The payload capacity is more than adequate, but the altitude is unacceptable. We'd shatter windows for kilometres from the target and be caught on radar the moment we ascended. It's a harebrained scheme, any other pilot would have told you that. Insanity coupled with suicide.'

'In theory it could work,' observed an Englishwoman, 'a single low pass as in a final landing approach, then rapid acceleration in the sweep away, staying below three hundred metres, thus avoiding the grids until over the Channel. But I see your point. The risk is enormous, and the slightest malfunction definitely suicidal.'

'And the reservoirs here are relatively isolated,' added another German. 'But Paris is treacherous.'

'Are we back to land vehicles, then?' asked an elderly Briton.

'Ruled out,' answered the pilot. 'It would take too many large ones to be feasible, and it eliminates the spreading effect, requiring weeks for the poisons to enter the major sluice flows.'

'Then where are we?'

'I believe it's obvious,' said a young neo-Nazi who had been at the rear of the group; he now walked forward, arrogantly brushing aside the aircraft blueprints. 'At least to anyone who kept his eyes open during our training in the Hausruck.'

'That's a gratuitously harsh remark,' objected the Englishwoman. 'My eyesight's quite splendid, thank you.'

'Then what did you see, what did *all* of you see, frequently swooping and circling down from the sky?'

'The glider,' replied the second German. 'A rather small glider.'

'What did you have in mind, *mein junger Mann*?' asked the pilot. 'A squadron of such aircraft, say fifty or a hundred, colliding above the water reserves?'

'No, *Herr Flugzeugführer*. Replace them with aircraft that already exist! Two giant military transport gliders, each capable of carrying twice or three times the tonnage of that excessively heavy relic across the field.'

'What are you talking about? Where are such aircraft?'

'At the aerodrome in Konstanz, under heavy coverings, there are some twenty such machines. They have been there since the war.'

'Since the *war*?' cried the stunned German pilot. 'I really don't understand you, *junger Mann*!'

'Then your studies of the Third Reich's collapse fail you, sir. During the final years of that war, we Germans – who were the experts in gliding equipment – developed the massive *Gigant*, the Messerschmitt ME 323, which evolved from the ME 321, both the largest transport gliders in the air. They were initially created to aid the supply lines to the Russian front in full expectation for use in the invasion of England, their construction of wood and cloth eluding radar.'

'They're still *there*?' asked the elderly Briton.

'As is much of your Royal Navy and the American destroyers – "in mothballs", I believe is the phrase. I've had airmen check them out for me. With minor modifications they can be operable.'

'How do you propose to get them airborne?' said the second German.

'Two aircraft carrier jets can easily lift them off from short fields, assisted by disposable booster rockets under their wings. The Luftwaffe proved it can be done. They did it.'

There was a brief silence, broken by the older Briton. 'The young man's idea has merit,' he said. 'During the invasion of Normandy, scores of such gliders, many carrying jeeps, small tanks, and personnel, were released behind your lines and wreaked havoc. Good show, chap, really *very* good.'

'I agree,' said the German pilot pensively, his eyes squinting. 'I take back my sarcasm, young fellow.'

'Further, if I may, sir,' continued the delighted younger neo, 'the carrier jets could drop off both gliders from an altitude of, say, three thousand metres above the reservoirs, then rapidly ascend to forty thousand, sweeping across the Channel before the radar operators could piece anything together.'

'What about the gliders themselves?' asked a sceptical British neo. 'Unless the mission is specifically one of no return, they have to land somewhere – or crash somewhere.'

'I'll answer that,' replied the pilot. 'Open fields or pastures close by the water reserves should be the designated landing sites, and once on the ground, the gliders will be blown up while our flyers race away in pre-positioned vehicles.'

'*Jawohl.*' The second German held up his hand in the spill of the floodlight. 'This strategy could well change many things,' he said with quiet authority. 'We'll confer with our aircraft engineers as to the modifications of these gliders. I must return to London and call Bonn. What is your name, young man?'

'Von Löwenstein, sir. Maximilian von Löwenstein the Third.'

'You, your father, and your grandmother have erased the treachery on your family's escutcheon caused by your grandfather. Walk with pride, my boy.'

'I've prepared myself for these moments all my life, sir.'
'So be it. You've prepared yourself brilliantly.'

'*Mon Dieu!*' exclaimed Claude Moreau as he embraced Latham. They stood by a stone wall overlooking the Seine, a blonde-wigged Karin de Vries several feet to their left. 'You are *alive* and that is the most important thing, but what has that madman Witkowski *done* to you?'

'Actually, I'm afraid it was my idea, monsieur,' said Karin, approaching both men.

'You are the De Vries woman, madame?' asked Moreau, removing a visored walking cap.

'I am, sir.'

'The photographs I've seen say you are not. But then, if this yellow-haired gargoyle is Drew Latham, I suppose anything is possible.'

'The hair is not my own, it's a wig, Monsieur Moreau.'

'*Certainement.* However, madame, I must admit it is not in concert with such a lovely face. It is, how can I say it, somewhat more blatant?'

'Now I understand why it's reported that the head of the Deuxième is one of the most charming men in Paris.'

'A lovely sentiment, but please don't tell my wife.'

'Would anybody mind,' interrupted Drew. '*I'm* the one he's happy to see.'

'You are, indeed, my friend, but I mourn the loss of your brother.'

'I do too, so let's get on with the reason we're here. I want the sons of bitches who killed him . . . among other things.'

'We all do, among other things. There's an outdoor café up the street; it's usually crowded and no one will notice us. I know the owner. Why don't we stroll up there and get a table far from the entrance? Actually, I've arranged it.'

'An excellent idea, Monsieur Moreau,' said Karin, taking Latham's arm.

'Please, madame,' continued the chief of the Deuxième Bureau, putting on his cap as they started walking. 'My name is Claude, and I suspect we'll be together until the finish, if there is one. Therefore, the "monsieur" is hardly necessary, but you don't have to tell my adorable wife.'

'I'd love to meet her.'

'Not in that blonde wig, my dear.'

The owner of the sidewalk café greeted Moreau quietly behind a row of flower boxes and escorted the three of them to the farthest table from the latticed entrance. It abutted the bordering shoulder-high row of flowers, more in shadows than in light, a single flickering candle in the centre of the chequered tablecloth.

'I thought Colonel Witkowski might be with us,' said De Vries.

'So did I,' agreed Latham. 'How come he isn't? Sorenson made it clear that we needed his expertise.'

'It was his decision,' explained Moreau. 'He is a large, imposing man known by sight to many in Paris.'

'Then why didn't we meet somewhere else?' asked Drew. 'Say a hotel room?'

'Again, the colonel. You see, by extension his presence *is* here. Parked at the kerb in front is an unmarked American embassy car. The driver will remain behind the wheel, and his two marine companions in civilian clothes are roaming among the strollers beyond our garden wall.'

'He's running a test, then,' said De Vries, making a statement, not posing a question.

'Exactly. It is why our mutual friend here is still posing as a soldier, a most contradictory role. Witkowski wants to make certain that there are no other leaks, but if there are, he intends to take a prisoner and learn the source.'

'That would be Stanley,' Latham again agreed. 'The only chance he's taking is with my life.'

'You're perfectly safe,' said the Deuxième chief. 'I have the utmost regard for your aggressive marines . . . Karin,' he added, seeing her bandaged hand, 'your hand . . . the colonel told me you'd been wounded. I'm so sorry!'

'It's healing well, thank you, and later a small prosthesis

will complete the cosmetics. I'm seeing the doctor tomorrow, after which I shall be wearing a fashionable pair of gloves, I expect.'

'A Deuxième vehicle is at your disposal, of course.'

'Stosh already made the arrangements,' said Drew. 'I insisted on that because I want everything on the embassy record. I'll be damned if she pays a *sou* for her medical bills.'

'My darling, it doesn't matter—'

'It does to me!'

'Ah, "*mon chou*". So that's the way it is. I'm so happy for both of you.'

'It slipped out, monsieur. *Je regrette.*'

'Do not, please. Despite my profession, I'm a *romantique au coeur*. Also, Colonel Witkowski did mention, most confidentially, a possible liaison between you. It's far better not to be alone in these situations, loneliness is a terrible detriment when under stress.'

'Well said, monsieur ... *mon ami*, Claude.'

'*Merci.*'

'One question,' interrupted Latham. 'I can understand Stanley's not being here, but what about you? Aren't you pretty well known in Paris?'

'Hardly at all,' replied Moreau. 'My photograph has never appeared in the newspapers or on television – that is the policy of the Deuxième Bureau. Even my office door does not have a *Le Directeur* sign on the glass. I am not saying that our enemies do not have snapshots of me, they obviously do, but my presence is not significant. I am neither a tall man nor do I dress extravagantly, I'm really quite ordinary. As you Americans say, I hardly stand out in a crowd, and I have a large collection of hats; witness the idiotic cap I'm wearing. They're all I need.'

'Except in the case of your enemies,' said Drew.

'That is a risk we all take, is it not, my friend? And now let me bring you up to the moment. As you may or may not know, Ambassador Courtland will be on the Concorde for Washington tomorrow morning—'

'Sorenson said he was bringing him back for thirty-six hours,' Drew broke in, 'the explanation being some trumped-up State Department business that State doesn't know about.'

'Precisely. In the meantime, Mrs Courtland is under our surveillance; believe me, it's absolute. Every move she makes outside the embassy will be watched, and even within the embassy every telephone number she calls will be instantly transmitted to my office, courtesy of the colonel—'

'You can't tap her conversations?' interrupted Latham.

'The risk is too great, there isn't time to reprogram the phones. She's undoubtedly aware of such tactics and will run tests of her own. Should she confirm an intercept, she will know she's under surveillance.'

'In the same way you confirmed that my own telephone was compromised, Drew.'

'The meetings at specific locations.' Latham nodded. 'All right, you've got her under a scope. Suppose nothing happens.'

'Then nothing happens,' said Moreau. 'But that would strike me as most unusual. Remember, beneath her charming exterior there is a zealot, a trained believer in a fanatical cause. Here she is, an hour from the borders of the holy Reich of her passions, and she has risen so high in her life's work, her ego will demand a certain satisfaction. Acclamation says it better, for the Sonnenkinder must have extraordinary egos. The temptation will be equally extraordinary. In my judgement, with the ambassador away, she'll make a move and we'll learn something more.'

'I hope you're right.' Latham frowned as a waiter approached the table carrying glasses and two bottles of wine on a tray.

'The owner here always brings me his newest acquisitions of wine for my approval,' interjected the chief of the Deuxième Bureau quietly as the waiter uncorked the bottles. 'If you'd prefer something else; please tell me.'

'No, that's fine.' Drew glanced at Karin, and both nodded.

'May I ask,' began De Vries after the waiter had left, 'should Drew be right and nothing happen, is it possible we might force Janine to make a move?'

'In what way?' asked the Frenchman. '*A votre santé*,' he added softly, raising his glass. 'To all of us . . . How, my dear Karin?'

'I'm not sure. The Antinayous, perhaps. I know them and they know me; more to the point, they held my husband in great esteem.'

'Go on,' said Latham, his eyes fixed on her. 'Keeping in mind that Sorenson didn't exactly give them a clean bill of health.'

'That's rubbish.'

'It may be, but old Wesley has instincts few people are born with – except perhaps Claude here, and probably Witkowski.'

'You're too generous where I am concerned, but I can vouch for my friend Sorenson. Brilliant only half describes his talents.'

'He says the same about you. He also told me you saved his life in Istanbul.'

'While saving my own, he should have added. But back to the Antinayous, Karin. How would we use them to urge the ambassador's wife into an indiscreet act?'

'Again, I'm not sure, but their knowledge of the neos is extensive. They've unearthed names, codes, methods of contact; their files contain a thousand secrets they will not share. However, this might be an exception.'

'Why?' asked Drew.

'I must join him,' added Moreau. 'From everything we've learned about the Antinayous, they, indeed, share nothing. They are an independent intelligence organization wholly unto themselves, responsible to no one but themselves. Why would they change the rules now and open their files to outsiders?'

'Not "files", only appropriately selected information,

perhaps simply a method of contact using an emergency code recognized by the Sonnenkinder, if there is one.'

'You're not hearing us, lady,' said Latham, leaning forward and gently covering her bandaged hand. 'Why would they do it?'

'Because we have something they don't know about. We have an authentic, highly visible Sonnenkind right here in Paris. I myself will negotiate.'

'*Wow*,' whispered Drew, leaning back in his chair. 'That's powerful bait.'

'It's not unreasonable,' said the chief of the Deuxième Bureau, studying De Vries. 'But won't they demand some proof?'

'Yes, they will, and I think you can provide it.'

'In what way?'

'Forgive me, darling,' said Karin, glancing at Latham, 'but the Antinayous are somewhat more comfortable with the Deuxième than they are with the Central Intelligence Agency. It's a European thing, and not necessarily justified.' She turned back to Moreau. 'A short note on your stationery – date, time, and secrecy classification registered by your security equipment – stating that I'm permitted to describe an ongoing surveillance operation on a confirmed high-ranking Sonnenkind here in Paris, without giving a name until authorized by you. That should be sufficient. If they're willing to cooperate, we'll go on scrambler and I'll call you on a private line.'

'At the moment I cannot think of a flaw,' said Moreau admiringly.

'I can,' objected Drew. 'Suppose Sorenson's right? Suppose a neo or two has infiltrated the Antinayous? She's dead meat and I won't allow it.'

'Oh, *please*,' said De Vries. 'The three Antinayous we met together I've known since I came to Paris, and two of them were Freddie's contacts.'

'What about the third?'

'For heaven's sake, darling, he's a priest!'

Suddenly there was shouting from the pavement beyond the row of flower boxes. The owner rushed to the table and spoke harshly to Moreau. 'There is trouble!' he exclaimed. 'You must leave; get up and follow me!' The three of them rose and walked behind the owner, no more than ten feet, where he pressed a concealed button and the last flower box opened. '*Run*,' he cried, 'into the street!'

'The wine was excellent,' said the Deuxième chief as he and Latham held Karin's arms and raced through the opening.

Suddenly all three turned, their attention drawn by the panicked screaming crowd in front of the outdoor café. Then each understood. Karin gasped, Moreau briefly closed his eyes in pain, and Latham swore in fury. The light of a street lamp penetrated the windshield of the unmarked embassy car, illuminating the driver behind the wheel. He was arched back in the seat, a stream of blood rolling down his face from his forehead.

CHAPTER TWENTY-THREE

'*Christ*, they're everywhere, and we can't see them!' roared Drew, hammering his clenched fist down on the hotel desk. 'How did they *find* me?'

Claude Moreau had been standing silently by a window, looking out. 'Not you, my friend,' he said quietly, 'not Colonel Webster and his uniform, but me.'

'You? I thought you said hardly anybody in Paris knew who you were,' Latham broke in abrasively. 'That you were so ordinary and had a collection of goddamn hats!'

'It had nothing to do with recognizing me, they knew where I'd be.'

'How, Claude?' asked De Vries, sitting on the bed in her room at the Bristol Hotel, where they had decided to retreat, each entering separately.

'Your embassy is not the only place that's been infested.' Moreau turned from the window, his expression a mixture of sadness and anger. 'My own office has been compromised.'

'You mean the sacrosanct Deuxième Bureau actually has a mole or two?'

'Please, Drew,' said Karin, shaking her head, conveying the fact that Moreau was deeply disturbed.

'I did not say the Bureau, monsieur.' The Deuxième chief locked eyes with Latham and spoke coldly. 'I said my own office.'

'I don't understand.' Drew lowered his voice, the sarcasm now absent.

'There's no way you could, for you do not know our system. As *le directeur*, my whereabouts must be known at all times in case there are emergencies. Outside of Jacques, who helps me plan my days, I give them to only one person, a subordinate who works closely with me, one whom I trust completely. This person wears a beeper and can be reached any time of day or night.'

'Who is he?' Karin sat forward on the bed.

'Not he, I must reluctantly say, but *she*. Monique d'Agoste, my secretary of over six years, but more than a secretary, a confidential assistant. She was the only one who knew about the café – until she told someone else.'

'You never had the slightest doubts about her?' continued Karin.

'Did you about Janine Clunes?' asked Drew.

'No, but then, she was the ambassador's wife.'

'And Monique is unquestionably *my* wife's closest friend. In fact, my wife suggested her to me. They went to university together and Monique was trained at the Service d'Etranger, where she worked during a disastrous marriage. All those years, they were like schoolgirls together . . . and now it's all so clear.' Moreau stopped and crossed to the desk where Latham sat. He picked up the phone and dialled. 'All those years,' repeated the chief of the Deuxième, waiting for the call to be completed. 'So amiable, so caring . . . No, you were not the targets, my friends, *I* was. The decision was made, my time was up. I was found out.'

'What are you *talking* about?' pressed Latham from the chair.

'I regret that I cannot tell even you that.' Moreau held up his hand and spoke French into the phone. 'Go to Madame d'Agoste's residence in the Saint Germain at once and take her into custody. Bring along a female officer and have the prisoner immediately stripsearched for possible self-adminis-tered poison . . . I will answer no questions, just do as I say!' The Frenchman hung up the phone and wearily sat down on the small love seat against the wall. 'The maddening sorrow of it all,' he mused softly.

'That's two different things, Claude,' said Drew. 'You

can't be mad and sorry at the same time; at least one's got to outweigh the other where your life is concerned.'

'You can't just leave things suspended, *mon ami*,' added De Vries. 'Considering everything we've been through, I submit we deserve some sort of explanation, vague though it may be.'

'I keep wondering how long she planned this, how much she learned, how much she revealed—'

'To *whom*, for God's sake?' demanded Latham.

'To those who report to the Brüderschaft.'

'Come on, Claude,' Drew went on. 'Give us something!'

'Very well.' Moreau leaned back in the chair, massaging his eyes with the fingers of his left hand. 'For three years I've played a dangerous game, filling my pockets with millions of francs, which will be mine *only* if I fail and their cause succeeds.'

'You became a *double*?' De Vries broke in, startled, and rising from the bed. 'Like Freddie?'

'A double *agent*?' Latham got out of his chair.

'Like Freddie,' continued the Deuxième chief, looking at Karin. 'They were convinced I was a convenient and powerful informer, but it was a strategy that could not be entered into the Bureau's records.'

'On the assumption, no matter how remote, that you were "infested",' De Vries completed emphatically.

'Yes. My great weakness was that I could not find a safety net. There was no one, *no one* in official Paris I felt I could trust. Bureaucrats come and go, the more influential ones into private business, and politicians are sworn companions of the wind. I had to act alone, without authorization, a highly questionable "solo", as the term goes.'

'My God!' exclaimed Drew. 'Why did you put yourself in that position?'

'That part I cannot tell you. It goes back a long time and must remain a forgotten event . . . except to me.'

'If it's forgotten, can it be so important, *mon ami*?'

'It is for me.'

'*D'accord.*'

'*Merci.*'

'Let me try to piece this together,' said Latham, pacing aimlessly in front of the window. 'You did say "millions", am I right?'

'Indeed, yes.'

'Did you spend any of it?'

'A great deal, moving in circles a *directeur's* salary could not permit, always getting closer, paying others who could be bought, learning more and more.'

'A real solo operation. What's for who and what's for you and who's to tell.'

'Unfortunately, that's quite accurate.'

'But you told us,' interrupted Karin. 'That has to mean something.'

'You are not French, my dear. Instead, you are part of the secret movements, the covert operations no country cares to reveal, but which for the average citizen are filled with corruption.'

'I don't think you're corrupt,' stated Drew emphatically.

'I don't think so either,' agreed Moreau, 'but we both could be wrong. I have a wife and children, and before I subject them to the calumny of a disgraced husband and father – to say nothing of an unsanctioned firing squad or years in prison – I will flee with my millions and live comfortably wherever I wish in the world. Remember, I am an experienced intelligence officer with talons everywhere. No, my friends, I've thought this out. I will survive, even if I fail. I owe it to my family.'

'And if you do not fail?' said Karin.

'Then every remaining *sou* will be turned over to the Quai d'Orsay, along with a complete accounting of every franc used in my solo operation.'

'Then you're not going to fail,' said Latham. '*We're* not going to fail. Among other things, I haven't got any millions, I've got only a brother whose face was blown away, and Karin has a husband who was tortured to death. I don't know what your problem is, Moreau, and you won't tell us, but I have to assume it's as important to you as ours is to us.'

'You may assume that.'

'So I think we should go to work.'

'With what, *mon ami?*'

'With our heads, our imaginations. It's all we've got.'

'I like your phraseology,' said the Deuxième chief. 'It is, indeed, all we have.'

'In death, his brother lives after him,' said Karin, crossing to Drew and taking his hand.

'Let's go back to Traupman and Kroeger and the second Mrs Courtland,' said Latham, releasing Karin's hand and sitting down at the desk, impatiently opening a drawer and removing several pages of hotel stationery. 'A connection's going to be made, it has to be. But *how?* The first assumption is your secretary, Claude, your Monique – whatever her name.'

'Entirely possible. We can get her internal telephone calls; they'll show us whom she reached.'

'Also the calls she made at home—'

'*Certainement.* I can do that in minutes.'

'Put 'em all together and confront her with them. Tell her she's expendable – put a gun to her head if you have to. If Sorenson's right, this Traupman has to know what's going on, and *she's* the bitch who can tell him! Then we move on to that all-too-waffling scholar, Heinrich Kreitz, ambassador from Germany, and I don't give a damn if we put him into a tank until he sends out the alarms to Bonn.'

'You move swiftly, my friend; you cut through diplomatic imperatives. It's attractive, but it could backfire on you.'

'*Fuck it!* I'm impatient!'

The telephone rang. Moreau picked it up, identified himself, and listened. The muscles in his strong face fell; his flesh went pale. '*Merci,*' he said, hanging up. 'Another failure,' he added, closing his eyes. 'Monique d'Agoste was beaten to death. Obviously, that's how the information of my whereabouts was extracted from her . . . Where is our *God*?'

Vice President Howard Keller was five feet eight inches tall, but he gave the impression of being a much larger man. Many had remarked on this fact, but few had rendered a satisfactory explanation. Perhaps the closest was that of an ageing New York choreographer who had observed the Vice President during one of those White House cultural evenings. He had whispered to a dancer, 'Watch him. He's simply walking to a microphone to introduce someone, but watch him. He breaks the space in front of him, parting the air with his body. Truman did that; it's a gift. A rooster in the barnyard.'

Gift or rooster notwithstanding, Keller was a politician to be reckoned with, a Washington insider to the core, having spent four terms as a congressman and twelve years as a senator, rising to chair the powerful Finance Committee. He had weathered the Beltway's slings and deadly arrows, accepting the nomination for Vice President despite the fact that he was older and far wiser than his party's nominee for President. He did so because he knew he could deliver the states to guarantee the election, which for him was a national priority. Beyond this, he was genuinely fond of the President, admiring his courage as well as his brains, although the latter had a hell of a lot more to absorb about Washington than was evidenced so far.

At the moment, however, such considerations were far distant concerns as he sat behind his large, cluttered desk and gazed at Consular Operations' Wesley Sorenson. 'I've heard of gorillashit before, but this makes King Kong look like an organ grinder's pet,' he said calmly.

'I realize that, Mr Vice President—'

'Cut the crap, Wes, we go back too long for that,' Keller interrupted. 'I'm the one who tried to promote your name for the DCI spot, remember? The only person who shot me down was you; the whole damn Senate would have been behind me.'

'I never wanted the job, Howard.'

'So you took on a tougher one. A small bastard operation that's supposed to coordinate between State, the CIA, and the administration, to say nothing of the gung-ho uniforms at the Pentagon. You're a lunatic, Wes. You of all people know that's an impossible job.'

'Granted, I thought it would be more in the area of advise and consent – no, don't say it, that's the Congress's job.'

'Thank you for saving my breath . . . Now, to add to the antics of the asylum you're in, two Nazis tell you I'm with them, part of their new Fascist uprising. It'd be hysterically funny except for the quicksand. It was Hitler who said if you told a large enough lie long enough, it would be believed . . . This is large enough, outrageous enough, Wes.'

'For Christ's sake, Howard, I'd never let it circulate!'

'Maybe you won't be able to stop it. Sooner or later your two skinheads will have to be interrogated by others, among them administration haters who'll grab a brass ring even if it's lead.'

'I won't let it go that far. I'll shoot the bastards first.'

'That's not the American way, is it?' asked Keller, chuckling.

'If it isn't, I'm pretty un-American. I've done it before.'

'That was in the field, and you were much younger.'

'Well, if it's any consolation, they also implicated the Speaker of the House, and he's in the other party.'

'My God, how convenient. A direct line of succession to the presidency. The man himself, then the VP, followed by the Speaker. Your Nazis know our Constitution.'

'One of them is pretty well educated, I'll say that.'

'The *Speaker* . . . ? That sweet, kindly old Baptist whose only real sin is praying while he makes deals he doesn't like because it's the only way to get legislation through? How the hell did they arrive at *him*?'

'They said he was of German ancestry and claimed conscientious objector status during World War Two.'

'He also volunteered as a noncombatant medic and was severely wounded while saving soldiers' lives. Now your Nazis aren't too bright. If they did their research properly, they'd have learned he's been wearing a brace for his back ever since they brought him out of Omaha Beach, praying for kids he left behind while damn near dying himself. It's part of his Silver Star citation. Some Hitler goon!'

'Listen to me, Howard,' said Sorenson, leaning forward in his chair. 'I came to you because I thought you should know, not because I thought there was an iota of credence to the accusation. Surely, you realize that.'

'I would hope so, and considering what's happening all over this country, "forewarned is forearmed" takes on new significance.'

'Not just here. In London and Paris they're crawling through cellars and peeking under beds, looking for Nazis.'

'Unfortunately they've found a few – unfortunate in the sense that even a very few inflame the nostrils of the hunters.' Keller reached for a newspaper on his desk; it was folded so a front-page article on the lower right could be read. 'Look at this,' the Vice President added. 'It's today's Houston paper.'

'*Goddammit!*' muttered Sorenson, taking the newspaper and reading, the short headline striking him instantly.

NAZIS ON HOSPITAL STAFF?

Patients' Complaints Cite Abusive Language

HOUSTON, July 14 – Based on statements, written and oral, the specific names withheld by the Board of Trustees, the Meridian Hospital has begun an investigation of its staff. The complaints center around numerous remarks by doctors and nurses which were reported to be blatantly anti-Semitic, as well as insulting to African-Americans and Catholics. Meridian is a non-sectarian institution, but it is common knowledge that its clientele

404

are predominately Protestant, a large percentage Episcopalian. It is also no secret that among the wealthier country clubs the hospital is referred to as the 'WASP watering hole', a play on words, as the Meridian has an active and highly confidential alcoholic rehabilitation annex located twenty miles south of the city.

This newspaper has received copies of twelve letters sent by former patients to the hospital's administration office, but in fairness, and until the situation is clearer, we withhold publication to protect people whose names appear.

'At least they didn't identify anyone,' said Sorenson, slamming the folded paper down on the desk.

'How long do you think that'll last? They sell papers, remember?'

'It's *sickening*.'

'It's spreading, Wes. In Milwaukee there was massive sabotage done to a brewery two days ago because the beer and the owner's name were German.'

'I read about it. I couldn't finish my breakfast.'

'How far did you read?'

'About what I did just now. Why?'

'The name was German, but the family's Jewish.'

'Revolting.'

'And in San Francisco a city councilman named Schwinn resigned because of threats to his family. Reason: he said in a speech that he had no objection to gays, many were his friends, but he felt they were having an impact on the public funding of the arts far beyond their representative numbers. His logic may be questionable – without gays the arts would be considerably diminished – but he had a political point and he was entitled to it . . . He was called a Nazi and his kids were harassed going to school.'

'Sweet Jesus, it's happening all over again, isn't it, Howard? Just switch labels and the snarling dogs are barking at heels, any heels.'

'Tell me about it,' said Keller. 'I've got a lot of enemies in this town, and they're not all in the opposing party. Say our two neos are subpoenaed by the Senate and state with Germanic authority that, of course, I'm one of them, the Speaker of the House also. Do you think either of us will survive?'

'They're outrageous liars. Certainly you will.'

'Ah, but the seeds are planted, Wes. Our records will be scrutinized by hostile zealots, extracting out of context hundreds of remarks we've made that, put together, support the outrage . . . You just mentioned the name Jesus. Did you know that the old KGB built an entire dossier on Christ, basing its conclusions solely on the New Testament, and concluding that He was the consummate Marxist, a true Communist?'

'I not only know it, I read it,' replied the director of Cons-Op, smiling. 'It was damned convincing, except I'd say it showed Him to be more of a Socialist-reformer, hardly a Communist. There was never any reference to His advocating a single political authority.'

'"Render unto Caesar", Wes?'

'It's a grey area, I'd have to go back and reread.' Both men laughed softly; Sorenson went on. 'But I see what you mean. Like statistics, anything can mean anything when it's selectively extracted from a body of work.'

'So what do we do?' asked the Vice President.

'I shoot the sons of bitches, what else?'

'No, others will simply take their place. No, you make assholes out of them. You *demand* a Senate hearing, a full-fledged circus, and make them laughingstocks.'

'You've got to be kidding.'

'Not at all. It could be the remedy for the madness that's infected this country, the UK, and France – and God knows where else.'

'Howard, that's crazy! Their appearance on television alone would fuel the fires of vigilantism!'

'Not if it's done correctly. As they have an agenda, so must we.'

'What sort of an agenda? You're beyond me.'

'You bring in the clowns,' said Keller.

'The *clowns*? What clowns?'

'It'll take a little digging, but you bring in both the pro and the con – witnesses who support the allegations and those who vehemently oppose them. The latter will be easy to find; the Speaker and I have basically honourable records and we'll have reasonable men and women to speak for us from the White House on down. But the "pros", our clowns, that'll be a bit more difficult, but they're the key.'

'Key to what?'

'To the door behind which lunacy thrives unfettered. You've got to find a fair number of crazies who at first appear perfectly sane and even courteous but underneath are fanatics. They should be unwavering zealots, devoted to their cause, but who, when stripped under cross-examination, break and reveal themselves.'

'That seems awfully dangerous,' said the director of Cons-Op, frowning. 'Suppose they don't break?'

'You're not a lawyer, Wes. I am, and I assure you it's the oldest trick in trial law – in the hands of the right attorney. Good Lord, even plays and films have caught on to it because it's damn good melodrama.'

'I'm beginning to see. *The Caine Mutiny* and Captain Queeg—'

'And just about every Perry Mason show that was ever written,' completed Keller.

'But those were fictions, Howard. Entertainments. We're talking about *reality*, and the neos exist!'

'So did the "Commies" and the "Pinkos" and the "fellow travellers", and we damn near lost sight of the quiet professional Soviet spies because we were chasing illuminated ducks in a hundred galleries while Moscow laughed at us.'

'I'd have to agree with you there, but I'm not sure the analogy fits. The Cold War was real, I'm a product of it. How can lawyers deny what's happening now? Not the false

407

ducks in a gallery, like you and the Speaker, but the real vultures like that scientist Metz, or the British assistant to the foreign secretary, Mosedale . . . And there's another, but it's too soon to go into it.'

'I'm not suggesting for a minute that the hunt for the real vultures slow down. I'd just like to puncture the ballooning mania where everybody's a potential Nazi and nobody's a false duck. Furthermore, I believe you agree with me.'

'I do. I just don't know how a Senate hearing can do it. I see only a force-eighteen storm over the waters.'

'Let me explain from recent events, first stating that I served in the military. If the attorney, that fellow Sullivan, who advised Oliver North, had, instead, been a lawyer for the Senate committee, Mr North would still be sitting in a stockade rather than be contemplating his next run for public office. Pure and simple, he was a liar who broke his oath as a soldier, a disgrace to his uniform and his country who coated his illegalities in self-serving, sanctimonious bromides that shifted his guilt to some higher power – read that as God – who had nothing to do with what he did.'

'You're saying a lawyer could have short-circuited him?'

'I just suggested one, and I can think of at least a dozen others. During those days my colleagues and I would sit in one of our offices, enjoying a few drinks while watching the hearings on television. The running joke was which of our legal brethren could bring the lying bastard to his knees – crying, of course – and we were a mix of both parties. We came up with a fiery senator from the Midwest, a former prosecutor who annoyed the hell out of us but who was a thundering advocate.'

'You think he could have done it?'

'Without question. You see, he was also a marine and he'd won the Congressional Medal of Honor. We figured we'd have him in his dress blues with the purple ribbon and the gold medal around his neck and let him loose.'

'Would he have done it?'

'I remember his words. "The little whiner isn't worth it.

I'm working like hell to get industry into my state." But yes, I think he would have liked to.'

'I'll do some quiet checking around in the files,' said Sorenson, standing up. 'I still have grave doubts, however. Pandora's boxes aren't attractive to me, it's a legacy from my years in the field. Come to think of it, I'm about to open one in less than an hour.'

'Care to tell me about it?'

'Not now, Howard, but maybe later. It's possible I'll need your intercession with the President, if only to keep our Secretary of State in line.'

'The trouble's in the diplomatic area, then?'

'To the top of an embassy.'

'Bollinger's a pain in the ass, but they like him in Europe. They think he's an intellectual. They don't realize that his thoughtful pauses are filled more with how-can-we-spin-this-to-our-advantage than with real solutions.'

'I'd have to say I agree. I've always found him to be lacking in deep commitments.'

'You're wrong, Wes. He's got one really deep commitment: himself. And fortunately for us, another to the President, which naturally reverberates back to himself.'

'Does the President know this?'

'Of course he does, he's a very bright man, even brilliant. It's a quid pro quo. I think it's fair to say that our man in the Oval Office has needed a master spin doctor every now and then.'

'No question about it, but as you say, he's bright, he's learning.'

'If I could only get him to kick more ass around this town, he'd learn faster. It's much easier that way.'

'Thanks for your time, Howard— Mr Vice President, I'll be in touch.'

'Don't be a stranger, Mr Director. We dinosaurs have to guide the young two-legged creatures stumbling out of the water.'

'I wonder if we're capable.'

'If not us, who, then? The Adam Bollingers of this world? The witch-hunters?'

'Talk to you soon, Howard.'

Three thousand miles away in Paris it was midafternoon, the sun warm and bright, the sky clear, a perfect day for strolling along the boulevards, or walking through the Tuileries Gardens, or catching the breezes from the Seine, watching the boats glide over the water and under the myriad bridges. Paris in summer was an unmatched blessing.

For Janine Clunes Courtland the day itself was not only a blessing, but a symbol of triumph. She was free for a day or two, free from the middle-class morality of a boring husband who still mooned over another wife, repeating her name frequently in his sleep. For a moment or two she considered how lovely, how fulfilling it would be to have an assignation with someone, a lover who could satisfy her as had the many virile young students in Chicago, carefully selected, and the reason she lived an hour away from the university. There was an attaché at the German Embassy, an attractive man in his early thirties who had flirted with her somewhat obviously; she could phone him and he would come running to wherever she suggested, she knew that. But it could not be, delightful and tempting as the thought was; her free time had to be put to more immediate, less selfish, interests. She had excused herself from D and R for the length of time her husband, the ambassador, would be away, for there were domestic chores far more easily accomplished in his absence. No one argued, naturally, and, naturally, she let Daniel's chief aide know she was scouting the shops for various new fabrics for their quarters ... No, she could not accept an embassy limousine; it was an exercise in personal taste and should not be charged to the State Department.

How easily the words came. Then, why shouldn't they? She had been trained since she was nine years old for her life's work. She did, however, permit the aide to call her a taxi.

Janine had been given the address and the contact code for a member of the Brotherhood before she left Washington. It was a bootmaker's shop in the Champs-Élysées, the name 'André' to be used twice in a brief conversation, such as 'André says you're the best bootmaker in Paris, and André is almost never wrong.' She gave the taxi driver the address and sat back, contemplating what information she would send to Germany . . . The truth, of course, but phrased in such a way that the leadership would not only admire her extraordinary accomplishments but see the wisdom of bringing her to Bonn. After all, the ambassadorship to France was one of the most important diplomatic posts in Europe, at the moment so sensitive that the State Department had reached into its corps of experienced professionals rather than accept a raw political appointee. And she was that professional's wife. She had been told that the recently divorced foreign service officer was soon to emerge as a star of the department. The rest was easy; Daniel Courtland was lonely and depressed, in search of the comfort she provided.

The taxi arrived at the bootmaker's shop, yet it was more than a shop, rather, a small leather emporium. Glistening boots, saddles, and various riding accoutrements filled the tasteful front windows. Janine Clunitz got out and dismissed the taxi.

Thirty yards behind the departing cab, the Deuxième vehicle pulled into a no-parking space. The driver picked up the ultrahigh-frequency phone and was immediately connected to Moreau's office. 'Yes,' said Moreau himself, as no secretary had been chosen to replace the murdered Monique d'Agoste, whose death was kept secret under the pretext of illness.

'Madame Courtland just entered the Saddle and Bootery in the Champs-Élysées.'

'Purveyor to wealthy equestrians,' said the Deuxième chief. 'Strange, there was nothing in the ambassador's dossier that mentioned a fondness for horses.'

'The store is also famous for their boots, sir. Very durable and quite comfortable, I'm told.'

'Courtland in boots, durable or not?'

'Perhaps the madame.'

'If she's partial to such footwear, I suspect she'd march right in to Charles Jourdan or the Ferragamo shop in Saint-Honoré.'

'We're reporting only what is happening, monsieur. Shall I send my colleague in to reconnoitre?'

'A good idea. Tell him to examine the merchandise, inquire as to prices, that sort of thing. If the madame is being fitted, he can leave quickly.'

'Yes, sir.'

In a Peugeot sedan that had circled the wide boulevard of the Champs-Élysées and parked in a space across from the Saddle and Bootery, a man in an expensive pinstriped business suit also picked up his car phone. However, instead of calling a number in Paris, he dialled the code for Germany – Bonn, Germany. In a matter of seconds the call was completed.

'*Guten Tag,*' said the voice on the line.

'It is I, again from Paris,' said the well-dressed man in the Peugeot.

'Was it necessary to *kill* the marine driver last night?'

'I had no choice, *mein Herr*. He recognized me from the Blitzkrieger headquarters in the Avignon warehouse complex. If you recall, you wanted everything I could learn about their disappearance, and since I was the only one who knew where they operated, you yourself ordered me there.'

'Yes, yes, I remember. But why kill the marine?'

'He drove the colonel and the other two, the army officer and the blonde woman, out to the warehouse. He saw me then, and again last night. He shouted at me to stop; what was I to *do*?'

'Very well, then I congratulate you, I imagine.'

'You *imagine, mein Herr*? Had they captured me, they

would have filled me with drugs and learned why I was *there*! That I had killed Moreau's secretary and learned where he was.'

'Then I truly congratulate you,' said the voice in Germany. 'We'll get Moreau; he's far too dangerous to us now. It's simply a matter of time until you succeed, am I right?'

'I'm confident of it, but that's not why I'm calling you.'

'Then what is it?'

'I've been following an unmarked Deuxième automobile; it was parked for hours in front of the American Embassy. Unusual, I think you'd agree.'

'I do. So?'

'They have under surveillance the ambassador's wife, Frau Courtland. She just entered an expensive leather shop called the Saddle and Bootery—'

'My *God*!' interrupted the man in Bonn. 'The André conduit!'

'I beg your pardon—'

'Stay on the line, I'll be back to you shortly.' The minutes passed as the man in the Peugeot tapped the fingers of his left hand against the steering wheel, the telephone at his right ear. Finally, the voice from Germany came back on the line. 'Listen to me carefully, Paris,' said the man emphatically. 'They've found her out.'

'Found who, *mein Herr*?'

'*Never mind*. Just hear your orders and follow them ... Kill the woman as soon as it is humanly possible! *Kill* her!'

CHAPTER TWENTY-FOUR

Daniel Rutherford Courtland, ambassador to the Quai d'Orsay, Paris, stared silently at the pages of the transcript in his hands, reading and rereading them until his eyes were strained. Finally, tears ran down his cheeks; he brushed them away and sat upright in the chair in front of Wesley Sorenson's desk.

'I'm sorry, Mr Ambassador,' said the director of Consular Operations. 'This pains me no end, but you had to be told.'

'I understand.'

'If you have any doubts whatsoever, Karl Schneider is prepared to fly here and speak to you privately.'

'I've heard your taped interview, what more do I need?'

'May I suggest that you speak to him on the telephone? A deposition may be false, another voice can be used. He's in the phone book and you can ask for the number from an ordinary operator . . . Of course, we could have orchestrated both to substantiate our conclusions, but I doubt even we could alter the telephone information system so quickly.'

'You want me to do it, don't you?'

'Frankly, yes.' Sorenson picked up a phone and placed it in front of Courtland. 'This is my private line, a regular telephone, and not connected to my console. You'll have to take my word for that. Here's the area code.'

'I take your word for it.' Courtland picked up the phone, dialled the area code for Centralia, Illinois, as written on the note placed in front of him, and gave the operator the information. He pressed the disconnect, released it, and dialled again.

414

'Yes, hello,' said the accented voice in Centralia.

'My name is Daniel Courtland—'

'*Ach*, he told me you might call! I am very nervous, you understand?'

'Yes, I understand, I'm nervous too. May I ask you a question?'

'Certainly, sir.'

'What is my wife's favourite colour?'

'*Red*, always red. Or lighter – rose or pink.'

'And what is her favourite dish when dining out?'

'That veal plate – an Italian name. "Piccata", I think.'

'She has a favourite type of shampoo, can you tell me what it is?'

'*Mein Gott*, I had to order it from our pharmacy and send it to her at the university. A liquid soap with an ingredient called ketoconzole.'

'Thank you, Mr Schneider. This is painful for both of us.'

'Far more for me, sir. She was such a lovely child, and so brilliant. The ways of the world are beyond my comprehension.'

'Mine too, Mr Schneider. Thank you, and good-bye.' Courtland hung up the phone and sank back in the chair. 'He might have faked the first two, but not the last.'

'What do you mean?'

'The shampoo. It can only be ordered by prescription; it's a preventative remedy for seborrhoeic dermatitis, a condition she episodically suffers from. She's never wanted anyone to know, so I have to buy it under my own name – as did Mr Schneider.'

'Are you convinced?'

'I wish I could yell *foul* and go back to Paris with a clean slate, but that's not possible, is it?'

'No, it's not.'

'It's all so crazy. Before Janine, I had a terrific marriage, *I* thought. Great wife, wonderful kids, but State kept bouncing me around. South Africa, Kuala Lumpur, Morocco,

Geneva, all as a chief attaché, then came Finland, a real ambassadorship.'

'You'd been tested. Good Lord, man, they plucked you out of the chief-attaché pool and made you the ambassador to France, a post usually reserved for the high rollers in political contributions.'

'Only because I could put out the brushfires,' said Courtland. 'The d'Orsay was becoming more and more anti-American, and I could paste over the anti-French stereotypes coming out of Washington. I guess I'm good at that.'

'Obviously, you are.'

'And it cost me my family.'

'How did Janine Clunes come into your life?'

'You know, that's a hell of an interesting question. I'm not really sure. I had the normal postpartums after the divorce, the living alone in an apartment, not a house, the wife and the kids back in Iowa, sort of on my own, scratching around for diversions. It was a kind of limbo. But State kept calling me, saying I should put in an appearance at this party or that reception. And then one evening, at the British Embassy, this lovely lady, so alive and so intelligent, seemed attracted to me. She held my arm as we went from group to group, where very nice things were said about me, but they were diplomats I knew, and I didn't take them seriously. She did, however, and she fed what ego I had left . . . I'm sure you can figure out the rest.'

'It's not difficult.'

'No, it's not. What's difficult is now. What am I going to do? I suppose I should be filled with anger, furious at her betrayal, ready to behave like a howling animal lunging for the kill, but I don't feel any of those things. I just feel empty, burned out. I'll resign, of course, it would be asinine to continue. If a ranking foreign service officer can be duped this way, he should run, not walk, to the nearest plumbing school.'

'I think you can serve yourself and your country in a better way,' said Sorenson.

'How? Come back and fix the pipes?'

'No, by doing the most difficult thing of all. Return to Paris as if we'd never met, never had this conversation.'

Stunned, Courtland stared in silence at the director of Consular Operations. 'Besides being impossible,' he said finally, 'that's inhuman. I could never do it.'

'You're a consummate diplomat, Mr Ambassador. You never would have landed in Paris if you weren't.'

'But what you're asking me to do is beyond diplomacy, it goes to the core of subjectivity, hardly a diplomat's ally. There's no way I could conceal my contempt. Those feelings I claim not to have now would come rushing to the surface the instant I saw her. What you ask is simply unreasonable.'

'Let me tell you what's unreasonable, Mr Ambassador,' Sorenson interrupted, his tone harsher than before. 'It's exactly what you said. That a man of your intelligence and vast experience, a foreign service officer who knows his way around embassies all over the world and is on constant alert to the danger of internal and external espionage, could be deceived into marrying a confirmed Sonnenkind, a *Nazi*. And let me tell you what's even *more* unreasonable. These people have been in hiding for anywhere from thirty to fifty years. Their time has come and they're crawling out of the cracks in the walls, but we don't know who they are or where they are, only that they're there. They've sent out a list of hundreds of men and women in high places who may or may not be part of their global movement. I don't have to tell you the climate of fear and confusion that's spreading across this country and the countries of our closest allies, you can see for yourself. Pretty damn soon there'll be hysteria – who is and who isn't?'

'I'm not disputing anything you say, but how will my going back to Paris as an innocent husband change things?'

'Knowledge, Mr Ambassador. We have to learn how these

Sonnenkinder operate, who they contact, how they reach their counterparts in the new generation of Nazis. You see, there has to be an infrastructure, a chain of command leading to a hierarchy, and the current Mrs Courtland, the brilliant wife of the ambassador to France, isn't small potatoes.'

'You really think Janine can unwittingly help you?'

'She's the best shot we've got – let's be honest, she's the *only* shot. Even if we found another Sonnenkind, her rank, the circumstances, and the fact that she's within minutes by jet of the borders of Germany makes her a prime candidate. If she contacts the hierarchy, or they contact her, she can take us right to those hidden leaders behind the movement. We *must* find those leaders and expose them. As someone said, it's the only way to rip out the cancer . . . Help us, Daniel, *please* help us.'

Again there was silence on Courtland's part. He shifted his weight in the chair, and, uncharacteristically for a diplomat, he seemed uncertain what to do with his hands. He fidgeted, ran his fingers through his greying hair, and massaged his chin several times. At last, he spoke. 'I've seen what those bastards do, and I loathe them . . . I can't guarantee I'll pull it off, but I'll try.'

Janine Clunes Courtland approached the exquisite leather counter of the Saddle and Bootery and asked to speak with the manager. Shortly, a small, slender man wearing an expensive yellowish toupee that flowed back over his skull and covered the nape of his neck appeared. He was dressed in a riding outfit, complete with jodhpurs and boots. 'Yes, madame, how may I help you?' he said in French, glancing beyond her to several well-dressed customers, some standing, others seated.

'You have a lovely shop,' replied the ambassador's wife, her speech betraying her origins.

'Ah, an American,' enthused the manager.

'Is it so obvious?'

'Oh, no, madame, your French is excellent.'

'My friend, André, constantly tutors me, but sometimes I think André is too gentle. Yes, he must be firmer with me.'

'André?' asked the short man in the jodhpurs, looking hard at Janine.

'Yes, he said you might know him.'

'It's such a common name, is it not, madame? For instance, a customer named André left a pair of boots here and they were repaired the day before yesterday.'

'I believe André may have mentioned it.'

'Please come with me.' The manager walked to his right behind the counter, emerged through a green velvet curtain that covered a narrow entrance, and beckoned his new client. Together they went into a deserted office. 'I presume you are who I – presume you are?'

'Not by my identity, monsieur.'

'Of course not, madame.'

'A man in Washington instructed me. He said I should also use the name Catbird.'

'That is sufficient, it's an alternate code changed every few weeks. Again, follow me. We'll go out the back entrance and you will be driven a short distance outside of Paris to an amusement park. Pay your way into the south entrance, second booth, and protest, stating that a courtesy ticket should have been provided by "André". Do you understand?'

'South entrance, second booth, protest in the name of André. Yes, I have it.'

'A moment, please.' The manager reached down and pressed a button on a desk intercom. 'Gustav, we have a delivery for Monsieur André. Go to the vehicle immediately, if you please.'

Outside, in the small alleyway parking area, Janine climbed into the first backseat of a van as the driver jumped in behind the wheel and started the engine. 'There will be no conversation between us, please,' he said as he drove out of the alley into the street.

The manager returned to the deserted office, again

reached for the intercom, pressed a second button, and spoke. 'I'm leaving early today, Simone. It's slow and I'm exhausted. Lock up at six, and I'll see you in the morning.' He went out to his motorbike in the parking area behind the row of shops. He jammed his foot on the ignition pedal; the motor erupted and he sped down the alleyway.

Inside the leather boutique the telephone rang. A clerk at the counter picked it up. '*La Selle et les Bottes*,' he said.

'*Monsieur Rambeau!*' yelled the man on the line. '*Immédiatement!*'

'I'm sorry,' answered the clerk, offended by the arrogance of the caller. 'Monsieur Rambeau has left for the day.'

'Where *is* he?'

'How the hell would I know? I'm not his mother *or* his lover.'

'This is *important!*' screamed the man on the phone.

'No, you're not important, I am. I sell the merchandise, you merely interrupt, and there are customers in the store. Go to the devil.' The clerk hung up the phone and smiled at a young woman who wore a Givenchy cocktail dress obviously designed for her obviously expensive body. She oiled her way across the parquet floor and spoke in the half-whispered voice of a well-kept mistress.

'I have a message for André,' she intoned seductively. 'André will wish to hear it.'

'I am desolate, mademoiselle,' said the clerk, his eyes straying to her swelling décolletage. 'But all messages for Monsieur André are delivered to the manager alone, and he has left for the day.'

'What am I to do, then?' cooed the courtesan.

'Well, you could give the message to me, mademoiselle. I am a confidant of Monsieur Rambeau's, the manager.'

'I don't know that I should. It's very confidential.'

'But I just explained, I am a close confidant, a *confidential* associate of Monsieur Rambeau's. Perhaps you would rather tell me over an aperitif at the café next door.'

'Oh, no, my friend watches me wherever I go, and the

limousine is right outside. Just tell him that he's to call Berlin.'

'*Berlin?*'

'What do I know? I gave you the message.' The Givenchy-dressed young woman, buttocks swivelling, walked out of the store.

'Berlin?' said the clerk to himself. It was crazy, Rambeau hated Germans. When they came into the shop, he treated them with contempt and doubled the prices.

The Deuxième agent walked calmly out of the leather store, then rushed up the pavement to the unmarked car. He opened the door, quickly climbed in beside the driver, and swore. 'Dammit, she wasn't there!'

'What are you talking about? She didn't come outside.'

'I assume that.'

'Then where is she?'

'How the hell do I know? Probably in another arrondissement across the city.'

'She made contact with someone and they left by another exit.'

'My God, you're smart!'

'Why bite my head off?'

'Because we both should have known better. Places like this have delivery entrances; when I went in, you should have driven around and found it, then waited.'

'We're not psychic, my friend, at least I'm not.'

'No, we're stupid. How many times have we done this sort of thing? One of us follows a subject, the other covers the rear.'

'You're too hard on us,' protested the driver. 'This is the Champs-Élysées, not the Montmartre, and the woman is the wife of an ambassador, not a killer we're stalking.'

'I hope Director Moreau sees it that way. For reasons he will not explain, he seems almost obsessed with this particular ambassador's wife.'

'I'd better call him.'

'Please do. I forgot the number.'

The fashionably dressed man in the Peugeot several hundred feet across the wide boulevard was more than impatient, he was deeply troubled. Nearly an hour had passed and Frau Courtland had not emerged from the leather shop. He could accept the time; women were notoriously sluggish shoppers, especially the wealthy ones. What troubled him was the fact that the Deuxième vehicle had sped away, *sped* away, thirty-odd minutes ago, apparently prompted by the second Deuxième agent's running to the car and conferring with his colleague, the driver. What had happened? Something, certainly, but what? He had been torn between following the official automobile and waiting longer for the ambassador's wife. Remembering his orders, and the intensity with which they were delivered, he had decided to wait. 'Kill the woman as soon as it's humanly possible!' His control in Bonn had been apoplectic; the assassination was to be immediate. The meaning was clear: dire consequences would result if there was a delay.

As the assassin of record, he dared not fail. From being the monitor of the Blitzkrieger unit, he had suddenly been thrust into its deadly line of work. Not that he wasn't a trained killer, he was; he had come from the Stasi, one of the first to switch alliances from hard-core Communist to committed Fascist. Labels, merely labels that were meaningless to men like him. He craved the access and the power to live beyond the laws, the exhilaration of knowing he was not accountable to the dictates of small-minded officials. Such bureaucrats, no matter their positions, had been terrified of the Stasi, just as the ministers of the Third Reich had been petrified of the Gestapo. That knowledge, then and now, was truly exhilarating. Yet to remain in their enviable positions, such men as he *were* accountable to the structures that nurtured them.

Kill the woman as soon as it's humanly possible! Kill her!

A bullet in the head at close range in the crowded Champs-Élysées was an attractive option. Perhaps a collision, followed by a small-calibre gunshot, easily drowned out by the traffic, yes, it was feasible. Then, grabbing her purse, a trophy to be sent to Bonn, and disappearing among the crowds of afternoon strollers, time elapsed, no more than two or three seconds. It would work; it *had* worked four years earlier in West Berlin when he had taken out a British MI-6 officer who had made one too many sorties behind the Wall.

The man in the Peugeot unlocked the glove compartment, withdrew a short-barrelled .22 revolver, and shoved it into his jacket pocket. He started the engine, swung into the street, and circled at the first break in the traffic. He pulled into the kerb as a blue Ferrari lurched away from the space; the entrance to the expensive leather shop was diagonally to the left, in full view, no more than ten metres away. He could be out of the car and within feet of the woman in seconds, the moment he saw her, but not spotting her between the bodies of the erratic strollers was too great a risk. He got out of the Peugeot and made his way to the elaborate front windows of the Saddle and Bootery. He studied the extravagant items behind the glass, constantly aware of those leaving the entrance only several arm's lengths away.

Eighteen minutes passed and the fashionably dressed assassin's patience was coming to an end. Suddenly the pleasant face of a clerk looked at him through the window, from behind the banquette of the tasteful display. The killer shrugged amiably and smiled. Seconds later the youngish man came out of the entrance and spoke.

'I noticed you've been looking over our merchandise for quite a while, monsieur. Perhaps I could help you?'

'In truth, I'm waiting for someone who is quite late. We're to meet here.'

'One of our clients, no doubt. Why not come inside, out of the sun? My word, it's broiling.'

423

'Thank you.' The former Stasi officer followed the clerk through the door. 'I believe I'll look over your boots,' he continued in perfect French.

'There are none better in Paris, sir. If you need assistance, please call me.'

The German glanced around the store, at first not believing his eyes. He then slowly studied the women individually; there were seven, either standing in newly purchased equestrian finery or sitting in chairs being fitted for riding boots. She was not *there*!

That was why the Deuxième official had raced back to the Bureau's automobile! He had learned what the assassin of record had just found out nearly an hour later. The ambassador's wife had escaped the surveillance! Where had she gone? Who had made it possible for her to leave unseen? Obviously someone in the shop.

'*Monsieur?*' The killer, standing over a row of polished boots, beckoned the clerk. 'A moment, please.'

'Yes, sir,' replied the employee, approaching with a smile. 'You've found something to your taste?'

'Not exactly, but I must ask you a question. I was not entirely direct with you outside, for which I apologize. You see, I'm with the Quai d'Orsay, assigned to escort an important American woman, protect her from the vagaries of Paris, if you like. As I mentioned, she was late, but she cannot be *this* late. The only answer is that she came inside before I arrived, then left, and I missed her.'

'What does she look like?'

'Medium height and quite attractive, in her early forties, perhaps. She has light brown hair, neither blonde nor brunette, and, I'm told, was wearing a summer dress, white and pink, I think, and obviously very expensive.'

'Monsieur, look around you. You could be describing half the women shoppers here!'

'Tell me,' said the assassin in the pinstriped suit, 'could she have left another way, through a rear exit, perhaps?'

'That would be most unusual. For what reason?'

'I don't *know*,' answered the would-be killer, his tone of voice conveying his anxiety. 'I merely asked if it was possible.'

'Let me think,' said the clerk, frowning and looking around the store. 'There was a woman in a pink dress, but I did not notice her later, as I was with the Countess Levoisier, a lovely but most demanding client.'

Again the assassin was torn. His control had called the Saddle and Bootery the 'André conduit'. If he pursued his questioning too far, word of his carelessness might be sent back to Bonn. On the other hand, if the ambassador's wife was in the back of the store or had been taken somewhere else, he had to know. Frau Courtland had left the embassy unprotected, not in a customary limousine driven by an armed escort. The circumstances were optimum and might not be repeated for days. For *days*! And the kill was not to be delayed. 'If I may,' he said to the accommodating clerk, 'since this is official business and the government would be most appreciative, could you tell me if "André" is on the premises?'

'Good Lord, that name again! "André" is very popular today, but there is no André here. However, when messages come for him, whoever he is, the manager, Monsieur Rambeau, accepts them. He's left for the day, I'm afraid.'

'"Very popular . . . today?"' repeated the killer, stunned.

'Frankly,' said the clerk, lowering his voice, 'we think the mysterious André is Rambeau's lover.'

'You said very popular . . . *today*—'

'Oh, yes. Barely minutes ago, an adorable young lady with a body one could *kill* for gave me a message for André.'

'What was it? Remember, I'm an official of the government.'

'I doubt the government would be remotely interested. It's really quite harmless, even amusing, if I've figured it out correctly.'

'Figured what out?'

'Cities, probably countries, as well – destinations – they're the substitutes.'

'Substitutes for what?'

'Hotels most likely. "Call London" could mean the Kensington or the d'Angleterre; "call Madrid", the Esmeralda; "call Saint-Tropez", the Saint-Pères; do you see what I mean?'

'I haven't the faintest idea.'

'Rendezvous for lovers, monsieur. Hotel rooms where strangers of either persuasion can meet without alarming those they live with.'

'The *message*, please!'

'This one's really quite simple. The hotel Abbaye Saint-Germain.'

'What . . . ?'

'The English for *Allemagne*, Germain – Germany.'

'*What*?'

'That was the message for André, monsieur. "Call Berlin."'

In shock, the assassin studied the soft face of the clerk. Then, without a word, he raced out of the store.

CHAPTER TWENTY-FIVE

Karin de Vries moved in with Drew at the Hotel Norman-die. 'We just want to save the State Department money, Stosh, and as a taxpayer, I insist upon it!'

'You're so full of bullshit, you could be a yellow *torero*. Stick with the uniform and the blonde hair for another day; we've got you watched like a Derby racehorse. I'll explain to the hotel brass that you're a couple of computer freaks we can't stand but have been ordered to use.' The colloquy had ended testily; Stanley Witkowski did not like being out-flanked.

It was late afternoon and Latham was seated at the desk, reading the transcript of his older brother's debriefing in London after his escape from the Brüderschaft valley. Karin had suggested he request it; there were too many mounting questions about Harry Latham's list. 'It's right here,' said Drew, underlining words on a page. 'Harry never claimed the names were written in cement . . . Listen to this. ". . . I brought out the material, it's your job to evaluate it."'

'Then he had doubts himself?' asked Karin, sitting on the couch in the suite's living room and lowering the newspaper in her hand.

'No, not really, but he allowed for the outside possibility, not a probability. When it was suggested that he might have been "fed dirt", he was mad as hell. Here. ". . . Why *would* they? I was a major contributor to their cause. They *believed* me!"'

'The same kind of anger he showed to me when I told him about the Brotherhood having a file on him.'

'He pounced on both of us for that. And right after, when I asked him who Kroeger was, he said the words that'll stay with me for the rest of my life . . . "I don't think I should tell you that, Alexander Lassiter can." He was two people, one moment himself, the next Lassiter. That's *heavy*.'

'I know, my darling, but it's over, he's at peace.'

'I hope so, I really hope so. I'm not religious, as a matter of fact, I don't like most religions. The violence done in their various names is about as God-like as Genghis Khan. But if death is the proverbial Big Sleep, I'll settle for that, and so will Harry.'

'You never went to church as a child?'

'Sure. Mother's an Indiana Presbyterian corrupted by academic New England, and therefore felt that Harry and I should attend regularly until we were sixteen. I made it to twelve, but Harry quit when he was ten.'

'Didn't she protest?'

'Beth was never any good at conflicts, except where track and field events were concerned. There, she was a tiger.'

'What about your father?'

'Another piece of work.' Drew leaned back in the chair, smiling. 'One Sunday, Mom had the flu and told Dad to drive us to church, forgetting that he had never been there. Naturally, he got lost, and Harry and I weren't about to help him. Finally, he stopped the car and said, "Go on in there. It's all pretty much the same, so hear it from somebody else." Only it wasn't our church.'

'Well, it was at least *a* church.'

'Not exactly. It was a synagogue.' They both laughed as the telephone rang. Latham picked it up. 'Yes?'

'It is I, Moreau.'

'Any word on your secretary? I mean, on who might have killed her?'

'Absolutely nothing. My wife is distraught; she's making the arrangements. I shall never forgive myself for what I believed.'

'Get out from under the hairshirt,' said Drew. 'It doesn't help.'

'I know. Fortunately, I have other things to occupy me. Our ambassador's wife made her first move. About an hour ago she stopped at an expensive leather shop on the Champs-Élysées, dismissed her taxi, and then disappeared.'

'A leather shop?'

'Riding equipment, saddles, boots – they're rather famous for their boots.'

'A *bootmaker*?'

'Yes, you could say that—'

'*That* was one of the items we found on the neo who tried to blow my head off!' interrupted Latham. 'A repair receipt in the name of André.'

'Where is this receipt?'

'Witkowski's got it.'

'I'll send someone over to pick it up.'

'I thought you didn't like sending Deuxième people to the embassy.'

'It's only annoying when questions are asked.'

'Then don't bother. Stanley's having a car brought over to take Karin to the doctor. I'll tell him to give the receipt to the marine escort – *wait* a minute!' Drew snapped his head up in sudden thought, his eyes creased as a person's do when trying desperately to remember something. 'You said Courtland's wife disappeared . . . ?'

'She went in and never came out. My people think she was taken somewhere else; they found a delivery entrance in the rear with a small parking area. Why?'

'It's probably a losing long shot, Claude, but there was something else on our Bois de Boulogne Nazi. A free pass for an amusement park on the outskirts of the city.'

'A strange item for such a man—'

'That's what we thought,' Latham broke in. 'We were going to check it out, along with the bootmaker's, when that arsenal at the Avignon Warehouses went up in smoke. It sidetracked us.'

'You think she might have been driven there?'

'As I say, it's a long shot, but as we both agree, a free pass to a fun house is a pretty strange ticket for a Nazi killer to keep buried in his wallet.'

'It's certainly worth a try,' Moreau said.

'I'll reach Witkowski; he'll be sending the car for Karin soon. When it gets here, I'll have the receipts and the pass. In the meantime, you order up one of your fancy vehicles and wait for me at the side entrance of the hotel.'

'It is done. Have you a weapon?'

'Two. I didn't give Stanley's sergeant Alan Reynolds's automatic last night. He was so pissed off at me for going out, I thought he'd wear gloves, shoot me, and say Reynolds did it.'

'Good thinking. One of my people probably would have. *A bientôt.*'

'Make it soon.' Drew hung up the phone and looked over at Karin, who was now standing in front of the couch, her expression none too pleasant. 'I'm calling our colonel, want to say hello?'

'No, I want to go with you.'

'Come *on*, lady, you're going to the doctor's. You think you fooled me last night, but you didn't. You got up and went to the bathroom, and you were there a hell of a long time. I turned on the light and saw the blood around your pillow. Later I found the bandage in the wastebasket. Your hand was bleeding.'

'It was nothing—'

'Let the doctor tell me that. And if it's true, why is your right arm bent at the elbow so your hand is across your chest, somewhat ignoring gravity? Are you in the middle of a benediction, or would you rather not have the bandage soiled again?'

'You're very observant, you bastard.'

'It hurts, doesn't it?'

'Only in spasms, and only now and then. You're probably responsible.'

'That's the nicest thing you've said in quite a while.' Latham got up from the desk; they crossed to each other and embraced. 'My God, I'm glad I found you!'

'It's a two-way street, my darling.'

'I wish I could say things better, say the things I feel. I haven't had much practice, not in a genuine way – I guess that's a dumb thing to say.'

'Not at all. You're a grown man, not a monk. Kiss me.' They kissed, long and sensuously, searching their swelling arousal. Quite naturally, the telephone rang. 'Answer it, Officer Latham,' said Karin, gently disengaging herself and looking up into his eyes. 'Someone's rightfully trying to stop us. There's work to do.'

'Did that uniform make me a general?' said Drew, now in civilian clothes. 'If so, whoever it is, the son of a bitch is going to do fifty years in Leavenworth.' He walked to the desk and picked up the telephone. 'Yes?'

'If you were *really* under my command,' said Colonel Stanley Witkowski harshly, 'you'd be spending the rest of your life in Leavenworth for dereliction of duty!'

'Exactly my thoughts, but in the reverse. Only I've lost my rank temporarily.'

'Shut up. Moreau just reached me and asked if I'd talked to you about the amusement park.'

'I was just going to call you. I had an acid attack—'

'*Thank* you,' whispered De Vries.

'Cut the crap!' the colonel continued over the line. 'The car's on the way for Karin, and the sergeant has what you need. I think I should be with you boys, but Sorenson wants me to stick around. We're trying to figure out how to make Courtland's homecoming as easy as possible.'

'How did he take the news?'

'How would you if Karin turned out to be a neo?'

'Don't even think it.'

'Courtland did better than that. He was shattered but convinced. Wesley's an old-timer, like me. He doesn't pull a

431

put-around unless he has sufficient background confirmation to make it irresistible.'

'You speak a funny language, but I understand you.'

'The bottom line is that the ambassador's going along with us. He's going to play his part.'

'Better you should get the actor Villier. That's going to be one hell of a "homecoming" bed tomorrow night.'

'That's what we're working on. Courtland's frightened to be alone with her. We're orchestrating a series of late-night emergencies.'

'Not bad. With the cumulative jet lag, it might work.'

'It has to. How's your friend?'

'She continually lies to me. Her hand hurts and she won't admit it.'

'A real soldier.'

'A real idiot.'

'Our car will be there in ten minutes. Wait till the marines are inside, then take her out.'

'Will do.'

'Have a good hunt.'

'I don't want a useless one.'

Latham, in grey trousers and a blazer, climbed into the backseat of the armoured Deuxième car beside Moreau and handed him the bootmaker's receipt and the pass for the amusement park.

'This is my associate – Jacques Bergeron – Jacques will do,' said the head of the Deuxième, gesturing at the man in the front passenger seat. Amenities were exchanged. 'And I believe you've met our driver,' added Moreau as the agent behind the wheel angled his head around.

'*Bonjour*, monsieur.' It was the driver who had saved his life on the avenue Gabriel, the man who insisted he get in the car only seconds before a fusillade of bullets pocked the windshield.

'Your name's François,' said Drew, 'and I'll never forget it *or* you. I wouldn't be alive if it weren't—'

'Yes, yes,' Moreau interrupted, cutting Latham off. 'We've all read the report and François has been sufficiently commended. He took the rest of the day off to calm his nerves.'

'*C'est merde*,' said the driver under his breath as he started the car. 'Is it the park we determined, Monsieur Director?' he continued courteously in English.

'Yes, beyond Issy-les-Moulineaux. How long will it take?'

'Once we reach the rue de Vaugirard, not long. Perhaps twenty minutes or so. It's the traffic until then.'

'Don't overburden yourself with city regulations, François. It would be advantageous if you did not run over or crash into someone, but short of that, get us there as quickly as possible.'

What followed belonged on the crassest television show, wherein automobiles replaced characters and became roaring machines hell-bent on self-destruction. The Deuxième vehicle not only weaved perilously in and around the cars in front, but twice François swung up on relatively empty pavements to avoid minor congestions, scattering what pedestrians there were, who ran for their lives.

'We're going to get arrested!' said an astonished Latham.

'It might be attempted, but we haven't got time for that,' disagreed Moreau. 'Our automobile is equipped with an engine superior to any police car in Paris. We could even put in use the siren, but it startles people and could actually cause accidents, which we cannot afford.'

'This guy's nuts!'

'Among François's talents is an extraordinary ability as a driver. I suspect that before he came to us he was what you Americans call "the wheels" in bank robberies – that sort of thing.'

'I saw that a couple of days ago on the Gabriel.'

'So don't complain.'

Thirty-two minutes later, the foreheads of Drew, Jacques, and even Moreau dripping with sweat from the wild drive, they reached Le Parc de Joie, a tawdry alternative to Euro

Disney, popular because it was French and inexpensive. In fact, it was a poor distant relation to Disney's spectacle, more carnival than park, with grotesque, outsize cartoon figures above the various rides and sideshows, the dirt paths littered with debris. The screams of delight from the crowds of children, however, defined the equality with its grandiose American competition.

'There are two entrances, Monsieur Director,' said the driver. 'One north and one south.'

'You know this place, François?'

'Yes, sir. I've taken my two daughters here several times. This is the north entrance.'

'Shall we use the pass and see what happens?' asked Drew.

'No,' replied the Deuxième chief. 'That can come later if we think it will be helpful . . . Jacques, you and François go in together, two fathers looking for your wives and children. Monsieur Latham and I will go in separately through different gates. Where would you suggest we meet, François?'

'There is a carousel in the centre of the park. It's usually crowded and the noise from the excited children and the calliope makes it ideal.'

'You both have studied the photograph of Madame Courtland, no?'

'Certainly.'

'Then split up inside and walk around, looking for her. Monsieur Latham and I will do the same, and we'll meet at the carousel in half an hour. If either of you see her, use your radios and we'll move up the rendezvous.'

'I don't *have* a radio,' complained Drew.

'You do now,' said Moreau, reaching into his pocket.

Madame Courtland had been ushered into a small building at the south end of the seven-acre amusement park. The anteroom was a slovenly mess, garish old posters tacked on the walls in no particular order and without concern for symmetry. Two desks and a long, rickety buffet table were piled high with assorted multicoloured flyers, many stained by coffee rings and cigarette ashes, while three employees laboured over a mimeograph machine and several stencils. Two were overly madeup women in belly dancer costumes and a young male in a strangely ambiguous outfit – soiled orange tights and a blue blouse – his gender revealed by a scraggly beard. There were four small windows on the upper-front walls, too high for those outside to look through, and the clattering of an ancient air-conditioner seemed to be in syncopation with the mimeograph.

Janine Clunes Courtland was appalled. The Saddle and Bootery was a palace compared to this dump, she thought. Yet this dump, this foul-smelling office, was obviously superior in status to the exquisite leather boutique in the Champs-Élysées. Her doubts were partially put to rest with the sight of a tall, middle-aged man who seemingly appeared out of nowhere, but in reality from a narrow door in the left wall. He was dressed informally, the soft blue jeans and tan suede jacket the best to be found in Saint-Honoré, and the ascot around his throat the most expensive Hermès had to offer. He signalled her to follow him.

Through the narrow door, they walked down an equally narrow but dark corridor until they reached another door, this on the right. The tall man in the extravagant sports clothes pressed a series of digits on a square electronic panel and opened the door. Again, she followed him, entering an office that was as different from the first as the Hotel Ritz was from a soup kitchen.

The walls and furniture were made of the finest wood and leather, the paintings authentic works of the Impressionist masters, the recessed, mirror-panelled bar complete with glasses and decanters of Baccarat crystal. It was the lair of a very important man.

'*Willkommen*, Frau Courtland,' the man said in a voice warm and ingratiating. 'I am André,' he added in English.

'You know who I am?'

'Certainly, you used my name twice and the code of the

month, Catbird. We've been expecting your contact for many weeks now. Please, sit down.'

'Thank you.' Janine sat down in front of the desk as the park's manager lowered himself in a chair next to her, not behind his desk. 'The time wasn't right until now.'

'We assumed that. You're a brilliant woman and your coded messages to Berlin have been received regularly. Through your information regarding the financial watchdogs in Paris and Washington, our accounts have swelled. We are all eternally grateful.'

'I've always wondered, Herr André, why Berlin? Why not Bonn?'

'Bonn is such a small city, *nicht wahr*? Berlin is and will remain a mass of confusion. So many interests, so much chaos – the crumbling Wall, the influx of immigrants; it's far easier to conceal things in Berlin. After all, the funds remain in Switzerland, and when they are needed in Germany, the transfers are in successive increments, hardly noticeable in a city of such high finance that millions are sent by computer every hour of the day.'

'My work, then, is appreciated?' asked the ambassador's wife.

'Extraordinarily so. How could you think otherwise?'

'I don't. I just think it's time, after all these years of accomplishment, that I be brought to Bonn and recognized. I'm now in a position to render even more extraordinary service. I am the whore-wife of one of the most important ambassadors in Europe. Whatever our enemies plan against us, I will know. I would like to hear from our *Führer* that the daily risks I take will be rewarded. Is that so much to ask?'

'No, it isn't *gnädige* Frau. Yet I am André, not an ambassador, of course, but perhaps the most vital conduit in Europe, and I take these things on faith. Why can't you?'

'Because I've never even *seen* the Fatherland! Can't you understand that? All my life, since I was a child, I've trained and worked myself into states of exhaustion for one cause only. A cause I could never mention, never confide to *anyone*.

I became the best at what I do and could not tell even my closest friends why I drove myself. I *deserve* recognition!'

The man called André studied the woman across from him. 'Yes, you do, Frau Courtland. You of all people do. I'll call Bonn tonight . . . Now, to more mundane matters, when will the ambassador return to Paris?'

'Tomorrow.'

Drew dodged the hordes of parents and their offspring, in the main mothers chasing after their children, who were chasing other children, laughing or screaming uncontrollably as they raced from one entertainment to the next. He kept shifting his concentration, studying every woman who appeared to be anywhere from early to late middle age, which was just about every female in the amusement park. Sporadically, he raised the radio in his hand, as if expecting the short beeper signal to burst forth, telling him someone had seen something – seen Janine Clunes Courtland. No sound came; he continued walking through the crisscrossing dirt paths, passing the large, malformed figures whose garish grins tempted the onlookers to pay their money and enter.

Claude Moreau chose the quieter sections on the premise that the ambassador's wife would instinctively avoid the more raucous areas, and where her next contact, if there was one, would more likely be situated. Therefore he roamed around the animal cages and the stalls of fortune-tellers and souvenir hawkers, where T-shirts and insignia caps lay in rows under canopies. The chief of the Deuxième kept peering beyond the wares into the shadowed interiors, hoping to see men or a woman who did not belong there. Eighteen minutes passed, and the results were negative.

Moreau's most-trusted subordinate, Jacques Bergeron, was annoyingly caught up in a rush towards a reopened Ferris wheel, which had had a temporary power failure, stranding a number of riders fifty feet in the air. As a result, the crowd racing to the gate included parents who were convinced they had sacrificed their children to the avarice of the park's owners, who were too cheap to pay their electric bill. At one point Jacques collided with a young child and was struck in the face by a mother's purse; reeling, he fell to the ground and was trampled. He lay there, his arms covering his head until the enthusiastic-cum-hysterical onslaught passed him by. He, too, had seen no one resembling Madame Courtland.

François, the driver who frankly was delighted with the English term 'Wheels', sauntered past the ramshackle structures at the south entrance, where the signs were small and subdued, announcing the offices of first aid, complaints, lost and found, management (barely legible), and one larger billboard proclaiming the office of group parties. Suddenly François heard the words, spoken by an obese woman addressing her companion, a gaunt, pinch-faced female. 'What the hell is someone like that coming here for? That pink dress could feed my family for a year!' said the heavy woman.

'They call it slumming, Charlotte. They think they're better than we are, so they have to prove it.'

'It's shit, that's what it is. Did you see those la-di-da white shoes? Five thousand francs if a *sou!*'

François had no doubt whom they were talking about! The unit in the Champs-Élysées had described the ambassador's wife as wearing a pale pink and white summer dress, obviously from one of the better fashion houses. The driver watched the two women, casually walking closer to them as they strolled down the wide dirt thoroughfare.

'I'll tell you what I think,' said the thin woman with the perpetual pout. 'I'll bet my good-for-nothing husband that she's one of the owners of this stinking money trap. The rich do that, you know. They buy up places like this because they're cheap to run and the cash registers ring night and day.'

'You're probably right. After all, she went into the manager's office. *Damn* the filthy rich!'

François dropped behind, then turned and strolled back to

the row of shacks that served as offices. He spotted the small sign that read Management; the building was perhaps twenty feet wide, separated from those on either side by narrow paths that looked more like ditches. The front windows were unusually high, and below there was a door that seemed out of place. It appeared to be much thicker or heavier than the wood surrounding it. François removed the handheld radio from his jacket pocket, pressed the transmit button, and brought the instrument to his ear.

Then abruptly, without warning, he heard two familiar voices, *very* familiar, and then a third, one he had been listening to for years.

'*Papa, Papa!*'

'*Notre père! C'est lui!*'

'François, what are you *doing* here?'

The sight of his wife and two daughters sent the wide-eyed driver into shock. Finding his voice while awkwardly embracing the two young girls, he spoke. 'My God, Yvonne! What are *you* doing here?'

'You called saying you'd be late and probably not home for dinner, so we decided to come here for a little fun.'

'*Papa*, can you come on the carousel with us? *Please, Papa!*'

'My darlings, *Papa* is at work . . .'

'At work?' exclaimed the wife. 'Why would the Deuxième come here?'

'*Shh!*' The perplexed François turned briefly away and spoke rapidly into the radio. 'The subject is over here, near the south entrance. Meet me there. I have complications, as you may have heard . . . Come, Yvonne; you too, children, away from here!'

'Good Lord, you weren't joking,' said the wife as the family rushed down the dirt road towards the south entrance.

'No, I wasn't joking, my dear. Now, for all our sakes, please get into the car and go home. I'll explain later.'

'*Non, Papa!* We just got here!'

'It is "Yes, Papa," or the next time you come here, you'll be in the Sorbonne!'

What François had not noticed was a young man dressed in torn orange tights and a ragged blue blouse, only his unkempt beard declaring him a male. He was standing to the left of the heavy door, smoking a cigarette, his attention drawn to the noisy and obviously unexpected family reunion. Especially noticeable was the handheld radio into which the man spoke, and even more startling, the question posed by the woman. '. . . Why would the Deuxième come here?' The *Deuxième?*

The young man crushed his cigarette under his foot and raced inside.

The elegant proprietor, who called himself André, broke off his conversation with Frau Courtland, politely excusing himself as he got out of the chair and crossed to the ringing telephone on his desk. 'Yes?' he said, then listened silently for no more than ten seconds. 'Prepare the car!' he ordered, replacing the phone and turning to the ambassador's wife. 'Were you escorted here, madame?'

'I was driven from the Saddle and Bootery, yes.'

'I mean, are you under the protection of French or American officials? Are you being followed?'

'Good heavens, no! The embassy has no idea where I am.'

'Someone does. You must leave immediately. Come with me. There is an underground tunnel from here to the parking area; the steps are back here. *Quickly!*'

Ten minutes later, a breathless André was back in his well-appointed office; he sat behind the desk and relaxed, sighing audibly. His telephone rang again; he answered it. 'Yes?'

'Go to scrambler,' instructed the voice from Germany. 'Immediately!'

'Very well,' said a concerned André, opening a drawer and flipping a switch inside. 'Go ahead.'

'You have a most inefficient organization!'

'We don't think so. What troubles you?'

'It's taken me nearly an hour to find out how to reach you, and only then after threatening half of our intelligence branches!'

'I'd say that was most appropriate. I think you should reevaluate.'

'Fool!'

'Now, *I* find that most offensive.'

'You'll be far less offended when I tell you why.'

'Enlighten me, please.'

'Ambassador Daniel Courtland's wife is coming to see you—'

'Come and gone, *mein Herr*,' interrupted André in self-satisfaction. 'Thus eluding those who followed her here.'

'*Followed* her?'

'Presumably.'

'*How?*'

'I have no idea, but they put on quite a show, even to the point of employing the name of the Deuxième in a most unusual manner. Naturally, I rushed her away sight unseen and within the next half hour she'll be safely in the American Embassy.'

'*Idiot!*' screamed the man in Germany. 'She was not to return to the embassy. She was to be killed!'

CHAPTER TWENTY-SIX

Moreau, his chief aide Jacques Bergeron, and Latham converged on François within moments of each other. Together they walked fifty yards west of the south entrance, where the Deuxième chief held up his hand; the area was less crowded, the shabby tents on the right used for the employees' toilets and dressing rooms. 'We can talk here,' said Moreau, looking at the driver. '*Mon Dieu*, my friend, such misfortune! Your wife and children!'

'I shall have to invent a very convincing explanation.'

'The children won't speak to you for a week, François,' said Jacques, grinning sheepishly. 'You know that, don't you?'

'We have other things to discuss,' François broke in defensively. 'I overheard two women, too harridans talking . . .' The driver described the conversation he had surreptitiously listened to, ending with the words, 'She's in there, in the management's office.'

'Jacques,' said Moreau. 'Scout the building in your most professional manner. I'd suggest the inebriated mode; remove your jacket and tie, we'll hold them.'

'I'll be back in three or four minutes.' The agent took off his coat and tie, pulled out a section of his shirt, letting it hang over his belt, and started weaving back and forth towards the south entrance and beyond.

'Jacques does this very well,' observed Moreau, looking at his subordinate admiringly. 'Especially for a man who never touches whisky and can barely tolerate a glass of wine.'

'Maybe he tolerated too much of both before,' said Drew.

'No,' said the head of the Deuxième Bureau, 'it's his stomach. Something to do with acidity. He can be very embarrassing when we dine with the ministers of the Chamber of Deputies, who control our purse strings. They think he's a prissy bureaucrat.'

'What are we going to do if Courtland's wife stays inside?' asked Latham.

'I'm not sure,' replied Moreau. 'On the one hand, we know she's come here, which validates your assumption that this is a Brüderschaft contact, yet on the other, do we want whoever they are to know that we know it? Is it better to be patient and keep this place, this poor excuse for an office, under constant surveillance and learn who goes where, or do we force the issue by assaulting it?'

'I go for the second,' answered Latham. 'We're wasting time if we don't. Pull the bitch out and take her contacts.'

'A tempting shortcut, Drew, but a dangerous one, and conceivably counterproductive. If, as we both now believe, this crude shambles of an amusement park is a vital link to the Brotherhood, do we take it out, leaving a shocking void, or do we let it stand and learn more?'

'I say we take it out.'

'Sending alarms to the neo-Nazis throughout Europe? There are other ways, my friend. We can tap into their phones, their fax machines, their ultra high-frequency radio transmissions, if they exist. We could be giving up a golden prize for a stuffed donkey. Courtland's wife can be watched, this park kept under surveillance twenty-four hours a day. We must think about our actions very carefully.'

'You're so goddamned French! . . . You talk too much.'

'Fortunately or unfortunately, it is my heritage, our Gallic scepticism.'

'And you're probably right. I just wish you weren't. I'm impatient.'

'You had a brother most brutally murdered, Drew. I did not. Were I in your place, I'd feel the same way.'

'I wonder if Harry would.'

'That's an odd thing to say.' Moreau studied Latham's face, noting the distant, briefly unfocused look in the American's eyes.

'*De sang-froid*,' said Drew softly.

'I beg your pardon.'

'Nothing, nothing at all.' Latham blinked several times, the reality of the moment returned. 'What do you think Jacques will find?'

'The ambassador's wife, if he can,' replied François, the wild driver. 'I hope he does, for the sooner I get home, the better. My daughters were crying their eyes out when they left with Yvonne . . . Sorry, Monsieur Director, I don't mean to allow personal matters to interfere – which, of course, they will not. In truth, they are inconsequential.'

'No need to apologize, François. A man who has no life outside the Deuxième is a man lacking in perspective, in itself a dangerous condition.'

'*Alors!*' said the driver, looking up the dirt thoroughfare.

'What is it?' asked Moreau.

'That fellow in the funny costume, the orange stockings and the blue shirt!'

'What about him?' said Drew.

'He's looking for someone. He keeps running back and forth – he's coming this way, past the entrance.'

'Separate!' ordered the chief of the Deuxième.

The three men peeled off in different directions as the young, bearded man in the orange tights raced by, intermittently stopping and glancing around. François walked between two of the employees' tents, his back to the path. A minute later a pounding orange blur ran feverishly, returning to the ramshackle office labelled Management. Moreau and Latham joined François by the narrow space between the tents. 'He sure was looking for someone,' said Drew. 'Was it you?'

'I see no reason why,' answered the driver, frowning, 'but I seem to remember a speck, a splash of orange, when I turned away from my wife and children and called all of you.'

'Your radio, perhaps,' said Moreau. 'But, as you say, there was no reason for you to be singled out . . . I believe there's a rather common explanation. Such places as these small amusement parks are havens for eluding taxes. Everything is cash money, and they print the tickets themselves. Someone probably assumed you were from the Department of Taxation, clocking the sales. Not at all unusual; those investigators are subject to bribery.'

'*Mes amis!*' Jacques, minus his inebriated mode, rushed up to them, taking his jacket and tie from François. 'If Madame Courtland went into the manager's office, she is still inside. There's no other exit.'

'We'll wait,' said Moreau. 'Again, we'll separate but stay in the area, one of us at all times watching the door. We'll rotate, twenty minutes a turn. I'll be first, and remember, keep your radios where you can hear the signal.'

'I'll take over from you,' said Drew, looking at his watch.

'And I from you, monsieur,' added Jacques.

'I'll follow him,' completed François.

Two hours passed, each man having spent double duty at his post, when the chief of the Deuxième ordered them to meet at the tents west of the south entrance. 'Jacques,' said Moreau, 'are you certain there was no door on either side or at the rear of the building?'

'Not even a window, Claude. Except for those in front, there's not a single window.'

'It's beginning to get dark,' offered François. 'Perhaps she's waiting for it to become darker still, then she'll leave when the late-afternoon crowds head home.'

'A possibility, but again, *why*?'

'She got away from your unit on the Champs-Élysées,' said Latham, his eyebrows raised questioningly.

'There was no way she could have known she was under surveillance, monsieur,' objected Jacques.

'Maybe somebody told her.'

'That adds an entirely different dimension, Drew. One we have no evidence of.'

'I'm searching, that's all. It's possible she's just paranoid – possible, hell, such a person would have to be . . . Let me ask all of you. Who did you see going out of that door? I saw the weirdo in the orange tights; he met with someone in a clown costume, who was waiting for him.'

'I saw two hideously made-up women who looked like they came from an impoverished sheikh's harem,' said Jacques.

'Could either of them have been Courtland's wife?' asked Moreau quickly.

'Negative. The same thought struck me, so I reverted to the drunken exercise and literally bumped into both. They were washed out hags, one had terrible breath.'

'You see how accomplished he is,' said the Deuxième chief to Latham. 'And you, François?'

'There was only a tall man, in large dark glasses, about our American's size, dressed in casual but expensive clothing. I suspect he was the owner, as he checked the door to see if it was locked.'

'Then, if Madame Courtland has not emerged, and the office is locked up for the night, we're all saying she's still in there, not so?'

'Definitely,' replied Drew. 'She couldn't be in there for any number of reasons, including a pristine phone call while the ambassador's in Washington . . . Which of you is the best second-storey man?'

'Second storey?' asked François.

'He means opening locked doors and illegally entering places,' clarified Moreau.

'What has that to do with two storeys?' asked the perplexed driver.

'Never mind, the answer is Jacques.'

'You're *really* talented,' said Latham.

'If François was a getaway driver, I suspect my friend

Jacques was probably a jewel thief before seeing the light and joining our organization,' Moreau said.

'That also is *merde*, monsieur,' said Jacques, grinning. '*Monsieur le Directeur* has strange ways of complimenting us. However, the Bureau sent me to a locksmith's training school for a month. With the proper tools, all locks are vulnerable, for the principles are the same, with the exception of the most recently developed computerized ones.'

'That dilapidated hovel looks as computerized as an outdoor toilet. Go to work, Jacques, we'll be across from you on the other side.' The locksmith-trained Deuxième agent walked rapidly back to the crude building as the others followed, staying in the growing shadows on the left of the dirt thoroughfare. Within moments Claude Moreau's judgement was proven grossly wrong; a clamour of bells and sirens suddenly erupted, echoing throughout the park. Guards in various dress, some uniformed, others in outrageous apparel – clowns, half-naked sword swallowers, dwarfs, and tiger-skinned Africans – converged on the violated structure with the aggressiveness of a Mongol assault. Jacques fled the scene, gesturing to his companions to *evacuate*! They did so, running as fast as they could.

'What *happened*?' shouted Latham once they were in the Deuxième vehicle and speeding away.

'Beyond the tumblers, which were easy to penetrate,' answered the breathless Jacques, 'there had to be an electronic scanner that determined the weight and the density of the instrument that caused the tumblers to fall into place.'

'What the hell does *that* mean?'

'You find it every day with the newest automobiles, monsieur. The small black chip in the ignition key; without it you cannot start the motor. In the most expensive cars, if you try, sirens will go off.'

'So much for your outhouse, Claude.'

'What can I say? I was wrong, but it told us something,

did it not? Le Parc de Joie is every bit the vital Brüderschaft drop we believed it was.'

'But now they know it's been penetrated.'

'Not so, Drew. We have backups for such emergencies, in cooperation with the police and the Sûreté.'

'What?'

'There are scores of felons every week, many first-time offenders whose distressed circumstances called for their actions but who are basically decent human beings. Jean Valjean in *Les Misérables* is the perfect example.'

'Christ, you talk too much. What are you trying to say?'

'We have lists of such would-be criminals serving mandatory sentences of, say, six months to a year. In exchange for taking the blame for one more felony – such as attempting to rob an amusement park – their sentences are reduced and in some cases their records expunged.'

'Shall I get to work on it?' asked Jacques from the front seat, reaching for the car phone.

'Please do.' As his subordinate officer dialled and began speaking, Moreau explained. 'Within fifteen or twenty minutes the police will call the park's security, stating that they caught a car racing away and the two men inside were known burglars. Is the scenario clear?'

'I think so. Naturally, they'll ask if there was a robbery and, if so, what was stolen, and is there anyone who might identify the perpetrators?'

'Precisely. Adding, of course, that the police, in their gratitude for any witnesses, would be happy to drive them to and from the station where the prisoners are being held.'

'Said invitation rapidly declined,' added Latham, nodding his head in the rushing, darkening shadows of the backseat.

'Not always, *man ami*,' contradicted Moreau. 'Which is why we must have our false culprits. Every now and then the objects of our disaffections are too curious, too nervous about their own situations, and accept the invitation. However, they invariably have the same request – demand, actually.'

'Let me guess,' said Drew. 'They'll go to the lineup on the condition that they can see the suspects but the suspects can't see them.'

'As I've mentioned, you're very astute.'

'If I couldn't figure that one out, I should have retired the day I finished training. But the concept of – what did you call them? – "false culprits" is a beaut. For God's sake, don't leak the idea to Washington, the "Gates" will multiply. Watergate and Iran-gate will be Puppy Chow compared to CIA-gate and State-gate. The real heavies will figure out they can put in doubles for themselves, including the President himself.'

'Frankly, we over here could not understand why they didn't.'

'Keep that speculation to yourselves, we've got enough troubles.'

'Claude,' interrupted Jacques, turning around in the seat. 'You'll like this. Our perpetrators are a couple of underpaid bookkeepers who tried to rob a butcher chain that was selling poor meat at premium prices.'

'Their premise was correct: Steal from thieves.'

'Unfortunately, the thieves altered their supplies overnight and our bookkeepers were caught on video tape opening a safe.'

'They were hardly suited to their new endeavours.'

'The *gendarmes* were happy to oblige. The chief of detectives has been buying meat from the chain for years.'

'His taste buds weren't very acute. When will they activate?'

'As we speak.'

'*Bien*. Drop off Monsieur Latham at the Normandie and me at the office. Then, for God's sake, have François go home.'

'It is no problem for me to stay with you, Monsieur Director,' said the driver. 'In case there is an emergency.'

'No, François, you will not avoid your domestic responsibilities. Your lovely wife would never forgive you.'

'It's not her forgiveness that concerns me, sir. Children are far more brutal.'

'I lived through it and so can you. It builds character.'

'You're all heart,' said Drew quietly into Moreau's ear. 'What are you going to do at the office?'

'Follow up on this afternoon, tonight. I'll keep you informed. Also, *mon ami*, you have a relatively domestic concern of your own. The enchanting Karin has been to the doctor. Her wound, remember?'

'*Jesus*, I forgot!'

'I would advise not telling her that.'

'You're wrong, Moreau. She'd understand.'

Karin, in a hotel bathrobe, was pacing back and forth in front of the large casement window when Latham opened the door. 'My God, you've been gone a long time!' she cried, running to him, both embracing. 'Are you all *right*?'

'Hey, lady, it was an amusement park, not the battle of Bastogne. Of course I'm all right; we never even thought to look at our weapons.'

'That took nearly four hours? What happened?'

He told her, then asked, 'How about you? What did the doctor say?'

'I'm sorry, darling, it's why I never should have gotten involved with you. I thought such feelings were gone, but they're obviously not. When I care about someone, I care very deeply.'

'That's terrific, but you haven't answered my question.'

'Look!' De Vries proudly held up her right hand, the bandage less than half its previous size, not much more than a small nozzle. 'He fitted me for a prosthesis about two centimetres long – less than an inch. It will slip over my finger, with a nail attached, and be practically unnoticeable.'

'That's great, but how does it feel? You were bleeding last night.'

'The doctor said I must have been quite excited, and

clutched something. Do you have any welts on your back, my darling?'

'Another piece of work.' Drew again pulled her into his arms. Their lips met, the kiss slowly broken off by Karin.

'I want to talk,' she said.

'About what? I told you what happened.'

'About your safety. The Maison Rouge called—'

'They knew where to *find* you? Here at the *Normandie?*'

'They frequently know things before many of us learn about them ourselves.'

'Then they're being fed information they goddamned well shouldn't have!'

'I believe you're right, but then, we know which side the Antinayous are on.'

'Not necessarily. Sorenson cut them off.'

'He was the most feared deep-cover intelligence officer during the Cold War. He suspects everybody.'

'How do you know that? The deep-cover bit?'

'Partially from you, but mainly from Freddie.'

'*Freddie . . . ?*'

'Of course. The sub-networks protect themselves, Drew. Information circulates. Whom can you count on, whom can you trust? Survival's the ultimate answer, isn't it?'

'What did the Maison Rouge call about?'

'Their informers in Bonn and Berlin say that two teams of trained Blitzkrieger are being sent to Paris to find and kill the Latham brother who survived the assault at the inn in Villejuif. The man they believe to be Harry Latham.'

'That's nothing new, for God's sake.'

'They say that the number of assassins is between eight and twelve. Not one or two or even three, but a small army is coming after you.'

Silence, and then Latham spoke. 'I guess that's really impressive, isn't it? I mean, I'm popular beyond my wildest dreams, and I'm not even the guy they want.'

'I'd have to agree with you.'

'But why? That's the question, isn't it? Why do they want

Harry so badly? His list is out and with the confusion and dissension it's causing, they've got to know it's to their benefit, so *why?*'

'Would it have something to do with Dr Kroeger?'

'That cat's in space without an oxygen helmet. He tells one lie after another, forgetting the lies he told before.'

'I wasn't aware of that. In what sense?'

'He told Moreau, who he believes is one of them, that he had to find Harry in order to learn the identity of the female traitor in the Brüderschaft valley—'

'*What* traitor?' De Vries interrupted.

'We don't know and neither did Harry. When he was in London and we talked on the phone, he mentioned something about a nurse who had alerted the Antinayous that he was coming out, but the man who drove the truck that picked him up didn't elaborate.'

'If that was Kroeger's lie, it may not have been a lie.'

'Except that he told Witkowski something entirely *different.* He insisted he had to find Harry before the medication he was on wore off and Harry died. Stanley didn't believe him for a moment and that's why he wanted to shoot him to the moon with chemicals – to see if he could learn the truth.'

'Which the embassy doctor wouldn't permit,' said Karin softly. 'Now I understand why Witkowski was so upset with him.'

'Which is also why that medical saint is going to be overruled if I have to get Sorenson to blackmail the President.'

'Really? Is he . . . blackmailable?'

'Everybody is, especially presidents. It's called political genocide, depending upon which party you belong to.'

'May we get back to another subject, please?'

'What subject?' Latham walked to the desk and the telephone. 'I want to fry a doctor who'd rather prolong the life of a slug than prevent the killing of decent people on our side.'

'Which could be *you,* Drew.'

'I suppose so.' Latham picked up the phone.

'*Stop* it and listen to me!' cried De Vries. 'Hang up and *listen*.'

'Okay, okay.' Drew replaced the phone and slowly turned, facing her. 'What is it?'

'I'm going to be brutally honest with you, my darling – because you're a man I love.'

'For the moment? Or can I count on a month or two?'

'That's not only gratuitously unfair, it's also demeaning.'

'I apologize. Only I'd rather hear *the* man, not *a* man.'

'And *I* loved another, no matter how misguided I was, and I will not apologize for that.'

'Two points for the lady. Go on, be brutally honest.'

'You're a bright, even brilliant man in your own way. I've seen that, watched you, applauded your ability to make quick decisions, as well as your physical prowess – which certainly outstripped my husband's and Harry's. But you are *not* Freddie and you are *not* Harry, both of whom lived with the spectre of death every morning they woke up and every night when they prowled the streets for black rendezvous. It's a world you don't know, Drew, a horrid, convoluted world you've never been steeped in – exposed to, yes, but you are not a veteran of its nightmares.'

'Get to the point, I want to make a phone call.'

'Please, I *beg* you, give all the information you have, all the conclusions your imagination has produced, to those who *have* been in that world ... Moreau, Witkowski, your superior, Sorenson. They will avenge your brother's death; they're equipped to do it.'

'And I'm not?'

'My *God*, there's a band of killers coming after you! People with resources and contacts we know nothing about. They'll be programmed with names, with unlimited funds to corrupt those names, and all it takes is *one* to betray you. *That's* why the Antinayous called me. Frankly, they think your situation is hopeless unless you disappear.'

453

'Then we're back to our original question, aren't we? Why all this firepower against Harry Latham? *Why?*'

'Let others find out, my darling. Let's you and I take ourselves out of this horrible game.'

'You and I . . . ?'

'Does that answer your earlier question?'

'It's so tempting, I could cry like a baby, but it can't work, Karin. I may not have the experience of the others, but I have something they don't have. It's called rage, and along with whatever minor talents I do possess, it makes me the leader of the pack. I'm sorry, I'm really sorry, but that's the way it has to be.'

'I'm appealing to your sense of survival – *our* survival – not your courage, which needs no further proof.'

'Courage hasn't a damn thing to do with it! I never pretended to be brave, I don't *like* bravery, it gets idiots killed. I'm talking about a man who happened to be my brother, a man without whom I would have been a high school or a college dropout, by this time a hockey bum with a swollen face, broken legs, and not a dollar to my name. Jean-Pierre Villier told me he owed as much or more than I did to a father he never knew. I disagree. I owe more to Harry because I *did* know him.'

'I see.' Karin was silent as their eyes met, each levelled at the other's. 'Then we'll see it through together.'

'Hell, I'm not asking you to do that!'

'I wouldn't have it any other way. I ask only one thing, Drew. Don't let your rage kill you. I don't think I could stand losing the only other man I ever loved the same way I lost the first.'

'You can take it to the bank. I have too much to live for . . . Now, may I make that phone call? It's shortly past noon in Washington and I'd like to catch Sorenson before he goes to lunch.'

'You may spoil it for him.'

'I'm sure I will. He doesn't approve of what I'm doing, but he hasn't blown the whistle on me for a damn good reason.'

'What's that?'

'He'd do the same thing himself.'

In Washington, Wesley Sorenson was both annoyed and frustrated. Vice President Howard Keller had faxed him a background list of a hundred and eleven senators and congressmen of both parties who would react in outrage over their former colleague's inclusion as a Nazi, and were perfectly willing to testify. Added to these was another list of potential adversaries, ranging from rejected but still-powerful fundamentalist leaders to fanatical members of the lunatic fringe, both of which would reject the Second Coming of Christ as a political manipulation if it served them. At the bottom of the fax, in his own handwriting, was the Vice President's summation.

The above clowns are in place, ready, willing, and personally eager to destroy anyone who even vaguely disagrees with them. I've got the lawyers. Along with our good guys, we'll make muleshit out of the whole passel of assholes! Let's bring it to the Senate and expose these crap-artist witch-hunters for what they are.

However, Sorenson wasn't ready to go that flagrantly public. Much might be gained, but a great deal could be lost. The Sonnenkinder *did* exist, where they were and how high they were still undetermined. The easiest thing for the hunted to do was to become one of the 'good guys'. He would call Howard Keller and try to make his position clear. And then his telephone rang, the red line that came directly into his office.

'Yes?'

'It's your rogue agent, boss.'

'I wish I weren't – your boss, I mean.'

'Stay with me, we're making progress.'

'How?'

'Bonn and Berlin are sending out a couple of semi-brigades to find me – find Harry, that is – and eliminate me.'

'That's *progress*?'

'One step always leads to another, doesn't it?'

'If I were you, and I speak from experience, I'd get the hell out of Paris.'

'Would you have done that, Wes?'

'Probably not, but it doesn't matter what I'd have done. The times are different, Latham, ours were easier. We knew who our enemies were, you don't.'

'Then help me find out. Tell that humanitarian doctor at the embassy to plug all the Amytals we've got into Kroeger so we might learn something.'

'He said it could kill him.'

'So kill the son of a bitch. Give us a break! Why are they going to the max to kill Harry?'

'We have certain codes of medical ethics—'

'To hell with them, I've got my life too! I'm no advocate of capital punishment because, among other things, it can't be administered fairly – when was the last time a rich white guy with a high-priced law firm behind him was sent to the electric chair? – but if there ever was an exception to my stand, it's Kroeger. I saw that bastard blow apart two innocent hotel clerks with Black Talon bullets simply because they were there! And, furthermore, our benevolent physician at the embassy didn't say the injections *would* kill him, only that they *could*. Those are better odds than Kroeger gave those two men in the hotel.'

'You're developing a rather good sense of advocacy debate . . . Say I went along with you, got State to go along, what do you think you might learn from Kroeger?'

'For God's sake, I don't *know*. But maybe something, anything that could explain the neos' obsession with taking out Harry.'

'I grant you it's an enigma.'

'It's more than that, Wes, it's the key to a lot more than we can understand.'

'Including Harry's list perhaps?'

'Possibly. I read the transcript from his debriefing in London. There's no question that he believed it was authentic, but he allowed for outside disinformation – more in the area of *misinformation*, I grant you, but he considered it.'

'Human error, mistaken names, not dirt,' said Sorenson quietly. 'Yes, I remember reading that. If I recall correctly, he was angry at the implication that he was duped, and insisted it was up to the spiders in counterintelligence to ultimately evaluate the material.'

'He wasn't that precise, but that's what he was saying.'

'And you think Kroeger might fill in some gaps?'

'Let's put it this way, I can't think of anybody else. Kroeger was Harry's doctor, and strangely enough – probably because Kroeger treated him decently – he had some kind of hold over my brother. At least Harry didn't hate him.'

'Your brother was too professional to let hatred surface, much less interfere.'

'I realize that, and I admit it's a fine, very thin line, but I have an idea Harry respected him – maybe *respect* is the wrong word – but there was a definite attachment. I can't explain it because I can't understand it.'

'Perhaps you just said it. The doctor treated him decently, the captor giving attention to the captive.'

'The Stockholm syndrome again? Please spare me, there are too many flaws in that theory, especially where Harry's concerned.'

'Heaven knows you knew him better than anyone else . . . Very well, Drew, I'll give the order and I won't even bother Adam Bollinger over at State. He's already given us carte blanche, although for all the wrong motives.'

'Motives? Not reasons?'

'Reasoning is secondary to Bollinger. Motives come first. Stay well, stay alive, and be terribly careful.'

In the embassy's infirmary, actually a modern clinic of six rooms with state-of-the-art medical equipment, Gerhardt Kroeger was strapped to the table. A single transparent tube combining the flows from two plastic pouches above his head was inserted into his left arm, the needle penetrating the antecubital vein. He had been tranquillized prior to the procedure, a passive patient who had no idea what was in store for him.

'If he dies,' said the embassy doctor, his eyes on the electrocardiogram screen, 'you pricks take the fall. I'm here to save lives, not execute them.'

'Tell that to the families of the men he shot to death without knowing who they were,' replied Drew.

Stanley Witkowski elbowed Latham aside. 'Let me know when he's reaching comatose,' he ordered the physician.

Drew stepped back, standing beside Karin as they all watched, both fascinated and repulsed by what was taking place.

'He's entering the mode of least resistance,' said the doctor. '*Now*,' he added severely. 'And orders or no orders, I'm shutting the IV off in two minutes! *Christ*, a minute after that, and he's dead! . . . I don't need this job, fellas. I can pay off the government for medical school in three or four years, but I can't erase this for all the bread in the Treasury Department.'

'Then stand aside, youngster, and let me go to work.' Witkowski bent over Kroeger's body, speaking at first softly into his left ear, asking the usual questions about his identity and his position in the neo-Nazi movement. They were answered briefly, succinctly, in a monotone, and then the colonel raised his voice; it became gradually threatening until it began to echo off the walls. 'Now we've reached the nucleus, *Doktor!* Why do you want Harry Latham *killed*?'

Kroeger writhed on the table, straining to break the straps as he coughed and spat out grey phlegm. The embassy physician grabbed Witkowski's arm; the colonel shook it off violently. 'You've got thirty seconds,' said the doctor.

'*Tell* me, you tenth-rate Hitler, or you die *now*! I have no use for you, you son of a bitch! Tell me or go join your

Oberführer in hell. It's now or you're gone! *Oblivion, Herr Doktor!*'

'Now you must stop,' said the embassy's physician, again grabbing the colonel's arm.

'Get the fuck away from me, pissant! ... Did you hear that, Kroeger? I don't give a goddamn if you live or die! *Tell* me! Why do you have to kill Harry Latham? *Tell* me!'

'It's his *brain!*' shrieked Gerhardt Kroeger, thrashing on the table with such force he broke one of the leather straps. 'His *brain!*' the Nazi repeated, then fell into unconsciousness.

'That's all you get, Witkowski,' said the doctor firmly, shutting off the valves of the combined intravenous injections. 'His heart rate is up to a hundred and forty. Another five points, he's finished.'

'Let me tell you something, medicine man,' said the veteran G-2 colonel, 'do you know what the heart rate is of the two hotel employees this scuzball blew across the lobby? It's zero, Doctor, and I don't think that's very nice.'

The three of them sat at a table in an outdoor café on the rue de Varenne, Drew still in civilian clothes, Karin holding his hand underneath. Witkowski kept shaking his head, his bewilderment obvious. 'What the hell did the son of a bitch mean when he kept saying "his brain"?'

'The first thought that comes to mind,' said Latham reluctantly, 'is brainwashing, which I find hard to believe.'

'I agree,' said De Vries. 'I knew that side of Harry, his obsession with control, if you like, and I can't imagine his being mentally warped. He had too many defences.'

'So where are we?' asked the colonel.

'An autopsy?' suggested Karin.

'What could it tell us, that he was poisoned?' answered Witkowski. 'We can assume that, or something like it. Besides, all autopsies are assigned by the courts and must be registered with the Ministry of Health with accompanying medical records. We can't take the chance. Remember, Harry's not Harry now.'

'Then it's back to the beginning,' said Drew. 'And I don't even know where that is.'

In the morgue on the rue Fontenay, the attendant whose duty it was to check on the corpses in their refrigerated, temporary tombs, went down the line, sliding out each body to ascertain that the bloodless corpses were properly identified, and not moved due to overcrowding. He reached number one hundred and one, a special case as determined by a red check mark signifying no removal, and opened it.

He gasped, not certain that what he saw made any sense at all. The skull of the near faceless corpse had a huge, gaping hole, as if a postmortem explosion had taken place, the fragments of skin and tissue spread out like an opening strawberry, the fluid grey and diseased-looking. Quickly, the attendant closed the vault, not caring even to breathe the gaseous residue. Let someone else find it.

CHAPTER TWENTY-SEVEN

Claude Moreau issued an irreversible order at eight-thirty in the morning. Latham and De Vries were again under the protection of the Deuxième. American security might offer suggestions as to their safety, but the Deuxième alone would make all final decisions. Unless, of course, the two decided to remain confined to their embassy, which under international law was American territory and therefore beyond the Deuxième's jurisdiction. When Drew roared his objections, Moreau's answer was succinct.

'I cannot permit the citizens of Paris to risk their lives being caught in the crossfire of those trying to kill you,' said the Frenchman, sitting across from Drew and Karin in the suite at the Hotel Normandie.

'That's bullshit!' yelled Latham, putting his morning coffee down with such force that half of it spilled onto the rug. 'Nobody's going to start a war in the streets. It's the last thing they'd do!'

'Perhaps, perhaps not. So why don't you both move into the embassy, and the question becomes irrelevant? I'd have no objections whatsoever, and the citizens of Paris would be free of harm.'

'You know I've got to move around!' Drew rose from the couch angrily, his undersize hotel bathrobe constricting him.

'Then move with my people or stay off the streets. That's final, *mon ami* . . . Oh, and one other thing. Wherever you go, whatever you do, will be cleared by me.'

'You not only talk too much, you're *impossible*!'

'Speaking of the impossible,' continued the Deuxième

chief, 'Ambassador Courtland is arriving on the Concorde at five o'clock this afternoon. His wife will be meeting him at the airport. I don't know that any amount of training prepares a man for the charade he will have to perform.'

'If Courtland can't handle it, he should take himself out,' said Drew, pouring coffee for himself and returning to the couch with his cup.

Moreau raised his eyebrows at Latham's curt tone. 'Perhaps you're right, *mon ami*. One way or the other we'll have our answer before nightfall, *n'est-ce pas?* . . . Now, as to the rest of the day, I want you to familiarize yourselves with the Bureau's protection procedures. They're quite different from my friend Witkowski's operation, but then, the colonel does not have the resources we have.'

'Incidentally,' Drew broke in, 'have you run all this by Witkowski? Does he agree with your off-the-wall "orders"?'

'He not only agrees, he's filled with relief. I think you should know that he's extremely fond of both of you – perhaps the edge goes to the lovely Karin – and he's aware that my resources are far greater than his. Also, he and Wesley Sorenson have their hands full orchestrating the reunion of the ambassador and his wife, a most delicate situation that calls for constant monitoring. What more can I say?'

'You've said it,' said Latham without enthusiasm. 'What do you want us to do?'

'To begin with, meet and familiarize yourselves with our escorts. They all speak fluent English, and the leader, in fact, is your aid-in-survival in the Gabriel—'

'François, the driver?'

'Who else? The others will be around you night and day. There will always be two in the hotel corridor when you are here. Then, perhaps, I thought you might be interested in our various surveillances on Le Parc de Joie and Madame Courtland. Everything's in place.'

'I'll get dressed,' said Drew, again rising and taking his coffee with him as he headed for the bedroom door.

'Don't forget to shave, darling. Your dark stubble is rather apparent in contrast to your hair.'

'That's another thing,' mumbled Latham. 'I want to wash that stuff out just as soon as possible,' he added clearly, walking into the room and closing the door behind him.

'*Bien*,' said Moreau, continuing in French. 'We may talk now, madame.'

'Yes, I knew this was coming. A few moments ago your eyes were like two rifles aimed at me.'

'Shall we speak German?'

'No need to. He can't hear anything in there and French, when spoken rapidly, escapes his ear anyway. Where do we begin?'

'With the obvious,' replied the chief of the Deuxième matter-of-factly. 'When do you intend to tell him? Or do you?'

'I see,' said Karin, drawing out the two words. 'And if I could speak for both of us, I might ask the same of you, mightn't I?'

'You refer to my own secret, not so? The reason why I take the risks I do to destroy the fanatical German wherever I can find him.'

'Yes, I do.'

'Very well. You won't be in a position to spread the information, thus harming my family, so why not? ... I had a sister, Marie, quite a bit younger than I, and as our father had died, she looked upon me as taking his place, and certainly I adored her. She was so alive, so filled with the innocence of blossoming youth, and to add to that crown of spring flowers, she was a dancer – perhaps not a prima ballerina, but certainly an accomplished member of the corps de ballet. However, during the angriest years of the Cold War, solely to avenge themselves on me, the East German Stasi destroyed that glorious child. They kidnapped her and rapidly turned her into a drug addict, forcing her into prostitution to support her induced habit. She collapsed and died on the Unter den Linden at the age of twenty-six, begging for food or money, as she could no longer sell her body . . . That is my secret, Karin. It's not very pretty, is it?'

'It's *horrible*,' said De Vries. 'And you were helpless to do anything about it, about her?'

'I did not know. Our mother had passed away, and I was in deep cover in the Mediterranean sector for thirteen months. When I returned to Paris, I found in my long-suspended mail four photographs, courtesy of the East Berlin Polizei, by way of the Stasi. They showed what was left in death of my child sister.'

'I could cry, and I mean that, Claude, I'm not merely saying it.'

'I'm sure you do, my dear, for you have an equally agonizing story to tell, is it not so?'

'How did you find out?'

'I'll explain later. First, I must ask you again. When will you tell our American friend? Or don't you intend to do so?'

'I can't right now—'

'Then you are merely *using* him,' interrupted Moreau.

'Yes, I *am*,' exclaimed De Vries. 'That's the way it started but not the way it's turned out. Think what you will of me, but I do love him – I've *come* to love him. It's a far greater shock to me than anyone else. He has so many qualities of the Freddie I married – too many, in fact, and that frightens me. He's warm and searching and angry; he's a good man who's trying to find his focus, or his compass, or whatever you want to call it. He's as lost as we all are, but he's determined to find answers. Freddie was like that at the beginning. Before he changed and became an obsessed animal.'

'We both heard Drew several minutes ago talking about Courtland. I was appalled at his coldness. Is this the Freddie syndrome?'

'No, not at all. Drew is becoming the brother he's impersonating. He has to be Harry.'

'Then how far down the road does he become Freddie? The animal?'

'He can't, he *can't*. He's too decent for that.'

'Then tell him the truth.'

'What *is* truth?'

'Start with honesty, Karin.'

'What's honesty any longer?'

'Your husband's alive. Frederik de Vries is alive, but nobody knows where he is or who he is.'

The Deuxième escort consisted of the driver of reckless abandon, François, and two guards whose names were spoken so rapidly that Latham dubbed them 'Monsieur Frick' and 'Monsieur Frack'.

'Are your daughters speaking to you, François?' asked Drew from the backseat as he and Monsieur Frack flanked Karin.

'Not a word,' replied the driver. 'My wife was quite harsh with them, explaining that they should respect their father.'

'Did it do any good?'

'None. They marched to their room and closed the door, on which they hung a sign reading Private.'

'Is this something I should know about?' said De Vries.

'Only the obvious conclusion that children of the female species can be notoriously cruel to their saintly fathers,' answered Latham.

'I think I'll let that pass.'

Twenty minutes later they arrived at the Deuxième Bureau, a nondescript stone building with an underground parking area that was entered only after the scrutiny of armed guards. Frick and Frack took Drew and Karin up in a steel-encased electronic elevator that required an inordinately long series of codes to operate. They reached the fifth floor and were escorted to Moreau's office, less of an office actually than a large living room, the venetian blinds half closed. What comforts existed were shockingly intruded upon by an array of computers and various other high-tech equipment.

'You know how to make all of this stuff work?' asked Drew, sweeping his hand around the room.

'What I don't know, my newly appointed secretary does, and what she doesn't, my associate Jacques does. And if we really get in trouble, I'll simply call up my new friend, Madame de Vries.'

'*Mon Dieu*,' exclaimed Karin, 'this is a technologist's dream! Look over there, you're in instant contact with a dozen relaying satellites, and *there*, telecommunications to every remote section of the world that has receiving equipment, which you obviously have in place or it wouldn't be here.'

'I have a little trouble with that one,' said Moreau. 'Perhaps you could help.'

'The frequencies revolve constantly, even mini-second by mini-second,' said De Vries. 'The Americans are working on it.'

'They were, but a computer scientist named Rudolph Metz gave them a little trouble when he fled the United States and disappeared into Germany. He spread an eliminating virus throughout the entire system; they're still trying to recover.'

'Whoever perfects it will have the secrets of the globe,' said Karin.

'Then let us hope the Brüderschaft require the equipment Metz left behind,' added the chief of the Deuxième Bureau. 'Yet this is futile speculation. We have other things to show you, or more appropriately, for you to listen to. As promised, and with Witkowski's help at the embassy, we've invaded the ambassador's private telephone, a telephone that searches all channels and will operate only on one that is supposedly intercept-free. Le Parc de Joie was far simpler; we simply jammed their lines on a pretext of a fire at the phone company. It was widely reported and caused thousands of complaints, but the ruse was accepted ... Actually, we did start a fire, more smoke than flames, but it worked.'

'Did we learn anything?' asked Latham.

'Listen for yourselves,' replied Moreau, walking to a console on the left wall. 'This tape is from the ambassador's constantly swept telephone in his private office within the upstairs quarters. We've edited it so only the pertinent information is heard. Who cares to listen to innocuous courtesies?'

'Are you sure they're innocuous?'

'My dear Drew, you may listen to the master tape anytime you care to; it's digitally marked.'

'Sorry, go ahead.'

'Madame Courtland has just reached the Saddle and Bootery on the Champs-Élysées.' The tape began.

'I must talk to André at Le Parc de Joie. It's urgent, an emergency!'

'And who speaks?'

'One who knows the code André and was driven to the amusement park in your own vehicle yesterday.'

'I was told of this. Stay on the line, I'll be back to you in a few moments.' *Silence.* 'You are to be at the Louvre at one o'clock this afternoon. In the Ancient Egypt exhibition gallery on the second floor. You will recognize each other and he will direct you to follow him. If by any chance you are interrupted, he is known as Louis, Count of Strasbourg. You are old acquaintances. Is this understood?'

'It is.'

'Good-bye.'

'This next tape is between the store manager and André at Le Parc de Joie,' said Moreau. 'In fact, he *is* the Count of Strasbourg.'

'A real count?' asked Latham.

'Since there are so many, let's say he's more real than most. It's a rather ingenious cover and quite authentic. He's the surviving male of an old distinguished family in Alsace-Lorraine who came upon hard times after the war; the family broke apart, you see.'

'From a count to a carnival owner?' continued Drew. 'That's some drop. What broke up the family?'

'In German the Alsace region is known as Elsass-Lothringen. One side fought for Germany, the other for France.'

'So this Louis, the Count of Strasbourg's half, went with the Nazis,' said Latham, nodding his head.

'No, not at all,' disagreed Moreau, his eyes alive with surprise. 'That's what makes his cover ingenious. He was only a child, but his "half", as you put it, fought valiantly for France. Unfortunately, the German contingent squirrelled the fortune away into Swiss and North African banks, and left the nobler part nearly penniless.'

'Yet he works for the neos?' interrupted Karin. 'He *is* a Nazi.'

'Obviously.'

'I don't get it,' said Drew. 'Why would he do it?'

'He was reached,' answered De Vries, looking at Moreau. 'He was corrupted by the side of the family that had the money.'

'To run a fifth-rate and pretty damned *filthy* amusement park?'

'With promises of a great deal more,' added the Deuxième's chief. 'He is one man at Le Parc de Joie, very much another in the salons of Paris.'

'I'd think he'd be laughed at,' said Latham, 'not allowed anywhere near those salons.'

'Because he runs a "carnival"?'

'Well, yes.'

'Quite wrong, *mon ami*. We French admire practicality, especially the humbling practicality of the dethroned rich, who find ways of rebuilding their resources. You do the same in America, and you're even more blatant about it. A multimillionaire entrepreneur loses his companies, or his hotels, or his various enterprises, loses everything. Then he regains his fortunes, and you make him a hero. We're not so different, Drew. The overlord becomes the vilified underdog, then with a burst of energy reclaims his throne. We applaud him, regardless of the moralities involved. As to what the count hopes to gain from the Nazis, who really knows?'

'Let's hear the tape.'

'You may, of course, but it merely confirms Strasbourg's orders to have Madame Courtland at the Louvre at one o'clock this afternoon.'

Washington, DC. It was shortly past five o'clock in the morning, but Wesley Sorenson could not sleep. Slowly, quietly, he got out of the twin bed next to his wife's, and walked softly across the master bedroom towards his dressing room.

'What are you doing, Wes?' said his wife sleepily. 'You went to the bathroom barely a half hour ago.'

'You heard me?'

'Only most of the night. What is it? Have you got a medical problem you haven't told me about?'

'It's not medical.'

'Then I mustn't ask, must I?'

'Something's wrong, Kate, something I'm not seeing.'

'That's hard to believe.'

'Why? It's the story of my life, looking for the missing pieces.'

'Are you going to look for them in the dark, my dear?'

'It's late morning in Paris, not dark at all. Go back to sleep.'

'I shall. It'll be quieter.'

Sorenson plunged his face into a sink of cold water – practices of the field returning – put on his bathrobe, and walked downstairs to the kitchen. He pressed the button on the automatic coffeemaker, programmed by their house-keeper after the previous night's dinner, waited until nearly a cup was filled, poured it, and trudged into his study beyond the living room. He sat down at his eight-foot-long desk, sipped coffee, and opened a lower drawer for a pack of his 'absolutely forbidden' cigarettes – practices of the field returning. Gratefully inhaling the pacifying smoke, he picked up the phone on his elaborate console, checked for intercepts, and dialled Moreau's private line in Paris.

'It's Wes, Claude,' said Sorenson after hearing the brief, curt *'Oui?'* over the phone.

'It's my morning for Americans, Wesley. Your cantankerous Drew Latham just left with the lovely, if enigmatic, Karin de Vries.'

'Where's the enigma?'

'I'm not sure yet, but when I learn, so will you. However, we're making progress. Your incredible discovery, Janine Clunitz, is leading us right along. Our Sonnenkind is behaving predictably within her sphere of unpredictability.' Moreau described the events of the morning in Paris as they pertained to the ambassador's wife. 'She's to meet with Strasbourg at the Louvre early this afternoon. We'll have them covered, naturally.'

'The Alsace Strasbourgs are a hell of a story, if I remember correctly.'

'You do, and the count takes it several steps further.'

'Elsass-Lothringen?' asked the director of Cons-Op.

'No, those are the additional steps, but we'll climb them later, my friend. The ambassador, his schedule remains, no?'

'His schedule remains, yes, and we're lucky if he doesn't fall apart and strangle the bitch.'

'We're prepared for him here, I assure you . . . Now, what about you, *mon ami?* What is happening on your side of the Pond?'

'Only the most unholy mess you can imagine. You know those two Nazi killers – what are they called?'

'I presume you're talking about the two Witkowski sent to Andrews Air Force Base.'

'They're the ones. They spewed out garbage that could bring down the administration if it was released publicly.'

'What are you *saying*?'

'They say they have direct and specific evidence linking the

470

Vice President and the Speaker of the House to the neo-Nazi movement in Germany.'

'That's utterly preposterous! Where is this so-called evidence?'

'The inference was that they could pick up a phone, call Berlin, and the documentation would be forwarded immediately, presumably by fax.'

'It's a bluff, Wesley, surely, you know that.'

'Certainly, but a bluff that could include false documents. The Vice President is furious. He wants a full Senate hearing and has gone so far as to line up a slew of enraged senators and congressmen of both parties to refute the allegations.'

'That might be an imprudent course of action,' said Moreau, 'considering the climate over there, the witch-hunts.'

'That's what I have to make clear to him. All I can think of is what impact even the phoniest of "official evidence" would have on our frenzy-feeding media. Government letterheads, especially intelligence letterheads, and most especially *German* intelligence letterheads, can be copied in seconds. Good God, can you imagine, they'd be flashed across television screens all over the country?'

'The accused are condemned before they've been heard,' agreed the chief of the Deuxième Bureau. 'Wait a minute, Wesley—' Moreau interrupted himself. 'For such events to take place, the two assassins would need the cooperation of the neo-Nazi hierarchy, not so?'

'Yes. So?'

'*Impossible!* The Paris unit of the Blitzkrieger is in disgrace! They're considered traitors and would receive no assistance from the hierarchy whatsoever because they're too dangerous to the Nazi movement. They're cut off, abandoned ... Who else over there knows about your two prisoners?'

'Well, we're damned shorthanded here, so I used the marines and a couple of Knox Talbot's men to pick them up at Andrews. Also a CIA safe house in Virginia to keep them under wraps.'

'A CIA safe house? The *penetrated* CIA?'

'I didn't have much choice, Claude. We don't own any.'

'I understand that. Still, those two men are major liabilities for the neos.'

'So you've said. *And?*'

'Check on those prisoners, Wesley, but give no advance notice that you're doing so.'

'Why?'

'I'm not sure. Call it the instincts we both developed in Istanbul.'

'On my way,' said Sorenson, disconnecting the line to Paris and touching the speed-dial numbers for Cons-Op transportation. 'I need a car at my residence in half an hour.'

Thirty-six minutes later, shaven and dressed, the director of Consular Operations instructed his driver to take him to the safe house in Virginia. Immediately upon receiving the order, the driver picked up the interceptor-proof UHF radio phone to give the destination to the CIA dispatcher.

'Don't bother with that,' said Sorenson from the backseat. 'It's too early for a reception committee.'

'But it's standard procedure, sir.'

'Have a heart, young fella, the sun's barely up.'

'Yes, sir.' The driver replaced the radio phone in its cradle, his expression conveying his judgement that the old man was a pretty nice guy for a bigshot. A half hour later they reached the winding country road cut out of the woods that led to the concrete gatehouse flanked by an electrified hurricane fence. The gate remained closed as a voice came from a speaker built into the concrete below a thick, tinted bulletproof window outside the limousine's left rear door.

'Please identify yourself and state your business.'

'Wesley Sorenson, director of Consular Operations,' answered the head of Cons-Op, lowering the car's window, 'and my business is max-classified.'

472

'I recognize you, sir,' said the blurred figure beyond the dark glass, 'but you're not on the morning's roster.'

'If you'll check the Permanent Entries log, you'll find my name.'

'One moment, sir . . . Driver, release the vehicle's trunk.' There was an internal snap, followed by the glare of a roving searchlight at the rear of the limousine. 'Sorry, Mr Director,' continued the disembodied voice, 'I should have checked, but the Permanents usually come later in the day.'

'No need to apologize,' said Sorenson. 'I probably should have called the DCI, but it's a little early for him too.'

'Yes, sir . . . Driver, you may leave the vehicle and close the trunk now.' The driver did so, returned to his seat behind the wheel, and the heavy steel gate opened. A quarter of a mile beyond, they entered the circular drive that fronted the marble steps of the former Argentinean ambassador's estate. The limousine came to a stop as the large entrance door swung back and a heavyset, middle-aged army major emerged in the early morning light, the shoulder patch on his beribboned uniform proclaiming a Ranger battalion. He walked rapidly down the steps and opened the door for Sorenson.

'Major James Duncan, Officer of the Watch, Mr Director,' he announced pleasantly. 'Good morning, sir.'

'Good morning, Major,' said the chief of Cons-Op, climbing out of the backseat. 'Sorry I didn't make it a point to call and tell you I'd be arriving so early.'

'We're used to it, Mr Sorenson.'

'The front gate wasn't.'

'I don't know why not. They had a bigger surprise at three o'clock this morning.'

'Oh?' The veteran intelligence officer's antenna picked up a negative signal. 'An unannounced visitor?' he asked as they walked up the steps to the open door.

'No, not really. His name was added to the Perm-Ent log around midnight. That list is pretty long and he didn't like the delay; the deep-c Agency types can be touchy. Hell, I

473

suppose I would be, too, if I worked all day and was called out here during a night's sleep. I mean, this isn't exactly 'Nam with an impending firefight.'

'No, but there are always emergencies, aren't there?' observed Sorenson, knowing better than to probe further.

'Not many at that hour, sir,' said Major Duncan, leading the Cons-Op director to the security counter, behind which sat a tired-looking female officer. 'How may we assist you, sir? If you'll give the information to Lieutenant Russell, she'll call for an escort.'

'I wish to see the two prisoners housed in Section E, Isolated.' The lieutenant and the major looked at each other, as if startled. 'Did I say something wrong?'

'No, Director Sorenson,' replied Lieutenant Russell, her dark-circled eyes roaming over the keys of a computer as she typed. 'Merely coincidence, sir.'

'What do you mean?'

'That's who Deputy Director Connally had to meet with at three o'clock this morning,' answered Major James Duncan.

'Did he say why?'

'Pretty much the same words you used at the gate, sir. The conference was so maximum-classified that our own guard had to remain outside Section E after opening the cell.'

The signal was complete. 'Major, take me there at once. *No* one had clearance to interrogate those men but me!'

'I beg your pardon, sir,' interrupted the lieutenant. 'Deputy Director Connally had full clearance. It was spelled out in an inter-Agency order signed by Director Talbot.'

'Get Talbot on the phone for me! If you don't have his private number, I'll get it for you.'

'Hello?' said the guttural, sleepy voice of Knox Talbot over the line.

'Knox, it's Wesley—'

'Who the hell bombed whom? Do you know what time it is?'

'Do *you* know who a Deputy Director Connally is?'

'No, I don't because there isn't one.'

'What about an inter-Agency order, signed by *you*, that cleared him to meet with the neos?'

'There was no such order, so I couldn't have signed it. Where *are* you?'

'Where the goddamned hell do you *think*?'

'Here in Virginia?'

'I only hope my next call is less unsettling, because if it isn't, you've got some serious housecleaning to do.'

'The AA computers?'

'Try something less sophisticated, try something very human.' Sorenson slammed down the phone. 'Let's go, Major!'

The two Blitzkrieger were in their beds, lying on their sides. When the cell doors clanked open, neither moved. The director of Consular Operations crossed to each and threw back the blankets. Both men were dead, their eyes shocked open at the moment of death, blood still trickling from their closed mouths, the back of their heads blown away, soiling the wall.

The syncopated sound of the jazz combo below floated up to the private dining room; it meshed with the vibrant noise outside on Bourbon Street in New Orleans's French Quarter.

Around the large table sat six men and three women, all but one dressed with relative formality – conservative suits and ties, and severe business apparel for the women. Again, except for one, they were white, clean-cut, and looked as though they had been plucked, much younger, from Ivy League yearbooks of decades ago, when quotas meant something. They ranged in age from their forties to their early seventies, and to an individual, each possessed an aura of wary superiority, as if constantly in the presence of annoying inferiors.

Among this group were the mayors of two major East

Coast cities, three frontline congressmen, one prominent senator, one president of an octopuslike computer corporation, and a most fashionably dressed woman, who was the leading spokesperson of the Christians for a Moral Government. They sat properly upright in their chairs, their sceptical eyes on the man at the head of the table, a large heavyset figure with swarthy skin, wearing a white safari jacket, unbuttoned to mid-chest, and large tinted glasses that blocked out his eyes. His baptismal name was Mario Marchetti; his sobriquet in the FBI files was the Don of Pontchartrain. He spoke.

'Let us understand each other,' be began, his voice deep and soft, the words measured. 'We have what historians might call a concordat, an agreement between entities that do not necessarily concur on all things but find a common agenda that allows them to coexist. Do you follow me?'

There were affirmative murmurs and the slight nodding of heads, until the senator interrupted. 'That's a mighty fancy way of putting it, Mr Marchetti. Wouldn't it be simpler to say we both want something, and each can help the other?'

'Your record in the Senate, sir, hardly reflects such straightforward talk. But yes, you're quite correct. Each entity can give assistance to the other.'

'Since I've never met you before,' said the expensively dressed woman from the Christian far right, 'how exactly can *you* help *us*? Even as I speak, I find the question somewhat demeaning.'

'Get off your fucking high horse,' said the Don of Pontchartrain quietly.

'*What*?' The reaction around the table was more one of stunned silence than of anger or shock.

'You heard me,' continued Marchetti. 'You came to *me*, I didn't go looking for you, lady. Do you want to bring her highness here up to speed, Mr Computer Factory?'

All eyes glanced at the CEO of one of America's preeminent computer companies – most briefly.

'It was a meticulously researched decision,' replied the slender man in the conservative grey suit. 'It was mandatory that we stop the progress being made by an inquisitive executive of mine, a black man we hired – obviously – for cosmetic purposes. He began to question our duplicate shipments to Munich – destination the Hausruck – and even went so far as to trace the receivership, which, naturally, was convoluted. We couldn't fire him, of course, so I flew thousands of miles and met with Mr Marchetti.'

'Who did his *own* research,' broke in the Don of Pontchartrain gently with a friendly smile. 'I mean, why whack a highly intelligent black guy with a lot of letters after his name? It didn't make sense. So before the gentleman went into the arms of Jesus, I had my associates do a little investigating – like in breaking-and-entering his office at home . . . Good heavens, Mr Computer Factory, he was on to you, or close to it. His notes, which he kept locked in his desk, spelled everything out. You were shipping very sophisticated equipment, at virtual cost, to people no one ever heard of and which was picked up by people nobody knew. That was extremely sloppy, sir. If not downright unprofessional. The gentleman we speak of was about to alert the authorities in Washington . . . However, we took care of your problem and you found a partner of sorts – "of sorts" being the operative phrase.'

'I fail to see the connection,' pressed the fashionably dressed Christian woman as if addressing a warted frog.

'You fail once, lady, it's your fault. Twice, it's mine. Don't fail again.'

'*Really!*'

'Please don't insult the both of us,' continued Marchetti calmly. 'Our *compares* in Germany didn't learn where the shipments were going – a plus for your side – but they discovered *who* picked them up.'

'I think enough has been said,' interrupted the mayor of a large northeastern city. 'You have no idea how crime and the minorities are constantly intermingled. Drastic measures are called for.'

'*Basta!*' For the first time the Don raised his voice. 'Try education, *real* education! I'm a "Wop", a "Guinea", a dirty "Greaseball", and not too long ago we couldn't even apply for jobs, except for laying bricks and making gardens grow. Then came the smart ones, the Gianninis and the Fermis – the heritage of the Da Vincis, the Galileos, yes, even the Machiavellis. But you wouldn't accept us . . . Don't tell me about the minorities, Mr Mayor-of-Quick-Solutions, like in blowing up the ghettos. I know history, you don't.'

'Where is this *getting* us?' asked another frustrated mayor from a large city in Pennsylvania.

'I'll tell you where right now,' said Marchetti. 'I don't like you and you don't like me. You consider me dirt, and I think you're assholes, but we *can* work together.'

'Considering your objectionable outburst,' said another woman, prim, and with her streaked hair pulled back into a stern bun, 'I don't believe that is conceivable.'

'Let me explain, dear lady.' The Don of Pontchartrain leaned forward over the table, the separation of his jacket further revealing his hairy chest, his deep voice again quiet and soft. 'You want a country and its government – that's okay with me, I couldn't care less. What *I* want are the profits that come from controlling the country, the government. Quid pro quo. I leave you alone, you leave me alone. I do some dirty work for you – which I've done before and am prepared to do in the future – and you throw massive government contracts to those I tell you. It's as simple as that. Is it a problem?'

'Not that I can see,' said the senator. 'I'm sure such precedents exist. One accommodates for the good of all.'

'Naturally,' agreed the Mafioso. 'Take Mussolini and Hitler, Il Duce and the *Führer*, they were worlds apart, but they fuelled the global profits of war. Unfortunately, they were both paranoid, filled with delusions of invincibility. We are not, for war is not on our agenda. We seek something else.'

'How would you describe that, Mr Marchetti?' asked the youngest man at the table, a crew-cut blond wearing the blazer of a prominent Massachusetts university. 'I'm a political science major, completing my doctorate – a little late, I'm afraid.'

'Very simple, Mr Alphabet, and not what you learn in school,' answered the Don. 'Politics is influence and successful politics is power, and political power is fundamentally money – what goes where and to whom. The so-called people, who picked up the tab, don't give a pig's fart where it goes, because they'd rather watch a game show on television or read a supermarket tabloid. If you want to know the truth, we're a nation of idiots ... That's why you assholes may take over after all.'

'Your language is offensive in the extreme,' added the young doctoral candidate. 'May I remind you that there are ladies present?'

'Funny, I can't see any. Also, let me remind you that this isn't a finishing school and I'm not an etiquette consultant ... What I am is a supplier of last resorts. Should you need something accomplished – and the circumstances are such that you feel you can't use your own extensive resources – you come to me. The deed is done, I take the risk, and nothing can be traced to you – as it might have been in the case of our Mr Computer Factory and his overly curious black executive. *Capisce?*'

'However, as you've just pointed out,' said the third woman, an elderly, gaunt lady with dark, glaring eyes, magnified by thick-lensed glasses, 'we have our own extensive resources. Why use yours?'

'*Va bene!*' exclaimed Marchetti, spreading his hands expansively. 'Then *don't*, and I wish you well. I simply want you to know I'm here for you if the necessity arises. That's why I invited our computer *gigante* – and his friend in the

Congress – to bring you here, so as to clarify our concordat. On my private jets, of course.'

'His *friend* . . . ?' asked the Pennsylvania mayor.

'I,' replied a slightly embarrassed but unapologetic member of the House Subcommittee on Intelligence. 'Orders relayed from the Berlin cell. There may be a very loose cannon at the CIA who must be put under total surveillance and dealt with, if required. To use one of our people is too great a risk. Mr Marchetti has undertaken the task.'

'So it seems we have a La Rochefoucauld marriage – of sorts,' said the seventy-plus old woman with the magnificent glaring eyes. 'Minor though it may be, it is one of convenience.'

'In my own inadequate way, that's what I've been trying to tell you, dear lady.'

'Yes, well, you've told it very well, and, as always, actions speak volumes more than words . . . You have your concordat, Mr Marchetti, and I believe my associates will agree with me when I say that I'd like to leave here as soon as possible.'

'The limousines are downstairs waiting for you, as are the Lears at the private airport.'

'The congressmen and I will leave by the delivery entrance and drive in separate cars,' said the senator.

'As you arrived, sir,' agreed the Don of Pontchartrain, rising with the others. 'I thank you all from the depths of my Sicilian heart. The conference has been a success, our concordat in place.'

One by one, in varying degrees of discomfort, the American Nazis left the ornate dining room in New Orleans. The don reached under the table, snapping off a hidden switch. It stopped the operation of the roving video cameras concealed in the velour-covered walls. His name, voice, and image would be excised from the tapes, the name of another, perhaps an enemy, inserted.

'Assholes,' said Marchetti softly to himself. 'Our family will either be the richest in America or heroes of the Republic.'

CHAPTER TWENTY-EIGHT

The artifacts of ancient Egypt, spectacularly large and delicately small, are among the Louvre's most fascinating exhibitions. The concealed shafts of illumination provide highlights and unearthly shadows, as if centuries past were given life for the present observer. Yet within that life there is the constant reminder of mortality; these men and women lived, they breathed, they made love and bore children for whom they had to provide, usually from the generosity of the Nile. And then they died, rulers and slaves, their legacy both majestic and dreary; neither particularly good nor evil, they simply were.

It was within this ethereal scene that the two Deuxième agents held the tools of their profession, waiting for the meeting between Louis, Count of Strasbourg, and Janine Courtland, wife of the American ambassador. These tools consisted of a miniaturized 8 mm camcorder with a voice beam capable of picking up quiet conversations twenty feet away, and a breast pocket voice-activated recorder for close encounters. The agent with the camcorder, his earplug in place, positioned himself between two huge sarcophagi, the video recorder held level, the Deuxième officer leaning over it, concealing it, as though he were a scholar deciphering an ancient inscription. His colleague wandered about the room among the sparse crowds, sparse because it was summer lunchtime in Paris; both men kept in contact with small lapel radios.

Janine Courtland arrived first. She looked nervously about the exhibition room, squinting into the dimly lit areas.

Finding no one, she walked aimlessly around the exhibits, at one point standing next to the bent-over 'scholar' studying a sarcophagus inscription, then ambling over to a glass-encased display of ancient Egyptian gold. Finally, André – Louis, the Count of Strasbourg – strode through the main archway, resplendent in the most up-to-date gentleman's afternoon attire, completed by a blue silk paisley ascot. He spotted the ambassador's wife, studied the room slowly, cautiously, and, satisfied, approached her. The first Deuxième agent angled his camcorder, activated the voice beam, and started the all-but-silent shooting mechanism. He listened as he watched through the lens, his left arm covering the instrument.

'*You are entirely mistaken, Monsieur André,*' began Janine Clunitz Courtland softly. '*I spoke quite casually and convincingly to the embassy's head of security. He was shocked when I suggested that he had had me followed.*'

'*What else would he say?*' asked Strasbourg coolly.

'*I've lied too long and too often – all my life in fact – not to know a liar. I told him I stopped at a shop and that one of the clerks came up to me and said my two or three escorts were waiting on the pavement for me, and should he ask them inside to get out of the noonday sun.*'

'*A well-phrased story, madame, I grant you that,*' said the man called André more warmly. '*You people are, indeed, superbly trained.*'

'*You'll grant me? I'll grant myself, thank you. We've all spent our lives honing our skills for one purpose only.*'

'*Admirable,*' conceded Strasbourg. '*Did your embassy security suggest who your "escorts" were?*'

'*I led him to the suggestion, naturally; that, too, is part of our training. I asked him if it was possible that the French had me followed. His answer was ingenuous and probably correct. He replied that should the Paris authorities spot the attractive well-known wife of France's most powerful foreign ambassador shopping alone, they might easily order quiet protection.*'

'*I imagine that's logical, unless your chief of security is as well trained as you are.*'

'Rubbish! Now, you listen to me. My husband is arriving on the Concorde in a few hours, and we'll spend a day or two in a connubial reunion, but I still insist on going to Germany to meet our superiors. I have a plan. According to the official records, I have a surviving great-aunt in Stuttgart; she's close to ninety and I'd like to see her before it's too late—'

'The scenario's perfect,' interrupted Strasbourg, gesturing for Janine to follow him into the darkest shadows of the exhibition room. 'The ambassador can hardly object, so here's what we'll do, and Bonn will certainly approve.'

Peering through the lens, the Deuxième officer angled the camcorder, following the couple into the dimly lit area in the corner. Suddenly, he gasped, watching in horror as the count reached into his jacket pocket and slowly pulled out a syringe, the hypodermic needle encased in a plastic cover. With his other hand in shadows, Strasbourg removed the casing, baring the needle.

'Stop him!' the agent whispered harshly into his lapel radio. '*Interfere!* My God, he's going to kill her. He's got a needle!'

'*Monsieur le Comte!*' cried the second Deuxième officer, breaking through the bodies and stunning both Strasbourg and the ambassador's wife. 'I couldn't believe my eyes, but it *is* you, sir! I was the small boy who used to play in your family's orchards years ago. How good it is to see you again! I'm an attorney in Paris now.'

'Yes, yes, of course,' said the frustrated, angry Strasbourg, dropping the syringe on the dark floor in the noise of the intrusion and crushing it under his foot. 'An attorney, how fortunate . . . I'm sorry, this is an awkward time. I'll look you up.' With those words, Louis, the Count of Strasbourg, rushed back through the small crowd and out of the exhibition room.

'I regret the intrusion, madame!' said the second Deuxième man, his apologetic gaze conveying the impression that he had awkwardly bumbled into a lovers' assignation.

'It's of no matter,' stammered Janine Courtland, turning and walking rapidly away.

It was shortly past five o'clock when Latham and Karin de Vries returned for a second time from the Deuxième Bureau. They had been summoned by Moreau after the Louvre tapes, both video and audio, had been duplicated and prepared for scrutiny. Their escorts, Monsieur Frick and Monsieur Frack, were following in separate elevators, five minutes apart, to make certain no curious strangers in the lobby showed undue interest in the American or the Belgian employee of the embassy.

'What is it between you two?' asked Drew as they walked down the hallway to their Normandie suite.

'What are you talking about?'

'You and Moreau. This morning you were like two old friends, closer than ham and cheese. The rest of the day you hardly spoke.'

'I wasn't aware of it. If it appeared that way, I'm sure it's my fault. I was intensely interested in everything that happened. The Louvre operation was brilliant, wasn't it?'

'It was smart and smooth, especially the short-circuiting of Strasbourg, but then, the Deuxième has been around for a while.'

'Those two agents reacted beautifully, surely you agree.'

'I'd be stupid to disagree,' Latham approached the door of the suite, held up his hand for them both to stop, and took out a pack of matches from his pocket.

'I thought you were drastically cutting down on cigarettes. Do you mean that you can't wait till we're inside to light one?'

'I am cutting down, and this hasn't anything to do with cigarettes.' Drew struck a match and moved it back and forth around the door lock. There was a sudden tiny flare of light, swiftly extinguished. 'We're fine,' said Latham, inserting his key. 'No invaders.'

'What?'

'That was your real hair, not your wig.'

'*What?*'

'I found it in the bed.'

'Would you mind—'

'Very simple and damn near foolproof.' Latham opened the door, admitting Karin; he followed her and closed the door. 'Harry taught me that one,' he continued. 'A strand of hair, especially dark hair, is for all intents and purposes invisible to the naked eye. You stick one in a lock, protruding on the outside, and if anyone enters, the hair's gone. Yours was still where I left it, therefore no one's been inside since we left here.'

'I'm impressed.'

'With Harry. So was I.' Drew quickly removed his jacket, threw it on a chair, and turned to De Vries. 'Okay, lady, what's going on?'

'*Really*, I don't understand you.'

'Something happened between you and Claude and I'd like to know what it is. The only time you were alone with him was when he first came over early this morning to lay down the law to us and I went in to get dressed.'

'Oh, *that*,' said Karin casually, her eyes not casual at all. 'I imagine I did overstep – challenged his authority is a better way of putting it.'

'Challenged his authority . . . ?'

'Yes, I told him he had no right placing such restrictions on an officer of American Consular Operations. He said he had every right to do whatever he thought best outside the embassy, and I said, how would he like it if the Deuxième or the Service d'Etranger were told they couldn't move around Washington, and then he said—'

'All right, all right,' Latham broke in, 'I get the picture.'

'Good Lord, Drew, I was acting on your behalf!'

'Okay, I accept that. I saw how angry he was when I told him to pound sand. The French really get ticked off when their almighty authority is questioned.'

'I suspect that most people with responsibility, be they

486

French, German, English, or American, resent it when their authority is challenged.'

'What about Belgians, or is it Flemish? I'll never get the two straight.'

'No, we're too civilized, we listen to reason,' replied De Vries, smiling. They both laughed softly; the argument was over. 'I'll apologize to Claude in the morning and explain that I was simply overwrought ... Tell me. Drew, do you really think Strasbourg was going to kill Janine with that needle?'

'Sure. Her cover was blown, a Sonnenkind exposed – the neos have no choice. And it certainly makes Moreau's job rougher. Now he not only has to keep the surveillance in place, he has to be prepared for an outright attack on her life. What bothers you? You agreed with us an hour ago.'

'I don't know. It all seems so bizarre. The Louvre, the crowds of tourists. I'm sorry, I'm just exhausted.'

'Are you telegraphing me something? Should I send out for a pound of Spanish fly?'

'I said exhausted, not out of my mind.' They fell into each other's arms and kissed, long and arduously. The telephone rang. 'I truly believe,' said Karin, 'that the phone is our natural enemy.'

'I'll tear it out of the wall.'

'No, you won't, you'll answer it.'

'The lady was trained by the Inquisition.' Latham crossed to the desk and picked up the phone. 'Yes?'

'It is I,' said Moreau. 'Has Wesley called you?'

'No, should he?'

'He will, but at the moment he is extremely preoccupied, and our friend Witkowski is all but ready to fly to Washington and personally destroy the CIA complex in Langley, Virginia.'

'Well, Stanley was G-2, and never had much affection for the Company. What happened?'

'The two Blitzkrieger the colonel sent to Washington

487

under the tightest circumstances were found dead in the safe house, bullets in their heads.'

'Holy *shit*! In a *safe house*?'

'As Wesley said to me, "Where are you, James Jesus Angleton, when you might have done some good?" They're running photographs of every single man in every section of Central Intelligence under the eyes of everybody in that house in Virginia.'

'It won't get them anywhere. I've got temporarily blond hair and glasses that nullify the approach. Tell them to look for someone in the lower to middle levels who once toyed with college or community theatres.'

'Another Ames?'

'Certainly not a Jean-Pierre Villier. An amateur, a nerd with a big head and bigger payoffs. Someone who could have been privy to classified data.'

'*You* tell Wesley, I've got enough on my mind. Ambassador Courtland will be arriving in half an hour, and I have to keep his wife alive.'

'What's the problem? She's in an armoured embassy vehicle.'

'So were you when you were nearly killed the other night. *Au revoir*.' The line went dead.

'What is it?' asked Karin.

'The two neos Stanley sent to DC were shot in a safe house – a *safe house*, for Christ's sake!'

'You said it last night,' said De Vries quietly. 'They're everywhere but we can't see them . . . What makes people do their bidding? The killings, the betrayals, it's all so insane. *Why?*'

'The experts say there are three types of motivation. The first is money, lots of it, way beyond their normal circumstances, and in this group are the gamblers, the luxury-lovers and the psychotic show-offs. Then there are the zealots who identify with a fanatical cause that makes them feel superior insofar as the cause is absolute and puts everyone else down – as in a master race. The third, oddly enough, are what the analysts call the most dangerous. They're the malcontents who are convinced they've been shafted by the system, their talents unrewarded.'

'Why are they the most dangerous?'

'Because they become fixtures, sitting at their desks for years, doing their usually unimportant jobs just adequately enough not to be fired.'

'If they're unimportant, why are they dangerous?'

'Because they learn the very system they despise. Where the secrets are, how to access them, or even how to intercept them on their way from one section to another. You see, nobody pays much attention to fixtures, they're simply there, reading dull bureaucratic reports or researching material about as classified as a telephone directory. If they applied themselves as assiduously to their jobs as they do to analysing the system, some of them might go further legitimately, but not many. The psych men say they're generally lazy, like students who'd rather go into an exam with crib notes on their sleeves than study for it.'

'"Assiduously"? You're beginning to sound like Harry.'

'Would you believe I got through "See Jack run. See Jill run"?'

'I never doubted it. Any day now I expect you to extemporize on the terza rima of Dante's *Divina Commedia*.'

'The pizza guy from Brooklyn, right?'

'You really can be adorable, do you know that?'

There was a knock on the hotel suite's door. 'Now, who the hell is that?' said Latham, walking across the room. 'Yes, what is it?'

'The Deuxième,' replied the voice of Monsieur Frack.

'Oh, sure.' Drew opened the door, suddenly facing a gun levelled at his head. He whipped his hand up, simultaneously lashing his right foot out, crashing it into the agent's groin. The man fell back into the hallway; Drew pounced on him, wrenching the weapon from his grip as Monsieur Frick came running down the corridor, shouting.

'*Stop*, monsieur! Please *stop*! This was only an exercise.'

'*What?*' screamed Latham, about to pistol-whip his would-be killer, who was holding his crotch in agony.

'If the monsieur will please listen,' choked Frack on the floor. 'You are never to open the door until you are certain it is one of us!'

'You said you were the Deuxième!' exclaimed Drew, getting up. 'How many Deuxième are there up here?'

'That is the point, sir,' said Frick, looking painfully down at his writhing colleague. '*Monsieur le Directeur* gave you a list of identifying codes that are changed every two hours. You were to ask for the one assigned to this time period.'

'Codes? *What* codes?'

'You never looked at it, my dear,' replied Karin, standing in the doorway and holding up a page of paper. 'You gave it to me and said you'd read it later.'

'Oh . . . ?'

'You must never assume that it is one of us until we are identified!' cried the guard on the floor, embarrassed by the appearance of De Vries, and briefly removing his hands from the assaulted area, but only briefly.

'For God's sake, come in, all of you,' said Karin. 'The very least you can do, Monsieur Latham, is to offer our friends a drink.'

'Sure,' agreed Drew, helping his presumed assailant to his feet as two hotel guests appeared, coming out of a room up the hallway. Seeing them, Latham added clearly enough to be heard, '*Poor fellow!* It must have been his last two drinks.'

Inside the room, the door closed, the wounded agent collapsed on the couch. 'You are *très rapide*, Monsieur Lat'am,' he said, his voice returning, 'and very, very strong.'

'If we were on the ice, you would have been dog meat,' said Drew, breathlessly, falling into the couch beside his victim.

'Ice . . . ?'

'It's difficult to translate,' explained Karin quickly by the dry bar. 'What he means is, do you care for ice in your whisky?'

'*Qui, merci*. But more whisky than the ice, *s'il vous plaît.*'
'*Naturellement.*'

Ambassador Daniel Courtland, as ordered by the government of France, was escorted off the Concorde from a ramp in the forward section before the aircraft reached its gate. The idling jet engines were deafening as Courtland, flanked by a marine guard detail, was taken to the waiting American Embassy limousine on the tarmac. He steeled himself for the ensuing minutes, understanding that they would be the most difficult of his life. To be embraced by the consummate enemy, an enemy trained since childhood to deceive someone like himself, was almost worse than losing the woman he loved.

The limousine door was opened for him and he fell into the arms of his adoring, consummate enemy. 'It was only three days, but I *missed* you so!' cried Janine Clunitz Courtland.

'And I you, dear. I'll make it up to you, to both of us.'

'You must, you *must*! The fact that you were thousands of miles away from me made me ill, positively ill!'

'It's over with, Janine, but you must get used to Washington's demands. I have to go where I am needed.' They kissed violently, viciously, and Courtland could taste the poison in her mouth.

'Then you must take me *with* you – I *love* you so!'

'We'll work it out . . . Now, please, my dear, we can't embarrass the two marines in front, can we?'

'I can. I could rip your trousers off and do wonderful things for you.'

'Later, dear, later. Remember, I *am* the ambassador to France.'

'And I'm one of the leading authorities in computer science, and I say the hell with them both!' Dr Janine Courtland grabbed her husband's unaroused crotch.

The limousine raced down the avenue Gabriel to the embassy's front entrance; it was the quickest route to the elevators that would take them up to their living quarters. The huge vehicle came to a stop as two additional marine guards came out to assist the ambassador and his wife.

Suddenly, seemingly out of nowhere, three nondescript cars without licence plates roared to the kerb, surrounding the limousine as Courtland and his wife walked out onto the pavement. Doors opened and figures in black stocking masks leapt out, their automatic weapons on rapid fire, spraying deadly bullets everywhere. Almost simultaneously, additional gunfire erupted from two automobiles that had obviously been following the embassy car. The crowds in the Gabriel raced for cover. Four masked terrorists fell; one marine collapsed, grabbing his stomach; Ambassador Courtland plunged across the pavement, one hand reaching for his right leg, the other for his shoulder. And Janine Clunitz, Sonnenkind, was dead, her skull shattered, her chest spewing blood. A number of the masked killers – who knew how many? – raced away, soon to discard their head coverings and join the evening strollers of Paris.

'*Merde, merde, merde!*' roared Claude Moreau, emerging from around one of the Deuxième vehicles that had been protecting the Americans. 'We did everything and we did *nothing*! . . . Take all the bodies inside and say nothing to *anyone*. I am disgraced and I should be! . . . See to the ambassador, he's alive. *Quickly!*'

Among the Americans rushing out of the embassy to lend assistance was Stanley Witkowski. He ran up to Moreau, grabbed him by the shoulders as the police sirens grew louder, and shouted, 'Listen to me, Frenchie! You're going to do and say exactly what I tell you, or I'm declaring war on you and the CIA! Is that *clear?*'

'Stanley,' said the Deuxième chief, no spirit in him, 'I have failed miserably. Do what you will.'

'No, you haven't failed, you fucking idiot, because you couldn't have controlled this! These goddamned killers were willing to die tonight, and four did! *Nobody* can control fanatics like them. *You* can't, *we* can't, no one can because they don't give a shit about their lives. We can't obliterate their fanatical commitments, but we can *outthink* them, and you above all people know that!'

'What are you saying, Colonel?'

'Come inside with me, and I'll ream your tight ass with a blowtorch if you refuse to do what I want you to.'

'May I ask in what sphere?'

'Sure you can. You're going to lie through your teeth to your government, to the press, to any son of a bitch who wants to listen to you.'

'So my grave is dug deeper?'

'No, it's your only way out of it.'

CHAPTER TWENTY-NINE

Dr Hans Traupman manoeuvred his short speedboat into the modest dock of the small cottage on the riverfront. No lights were necessary, as the summer moon was bright, glistening off the waters. And there were no dockhands to assist Traupman in securing his craft; they would be an added expense the defrocked Lutheran minister could ill afford. Günter Jäger, as his new friends in the Bundestag knew, watched his deutsche marks; it was rumoured that his rent was minimal for the converted boathouse, now a cottage on the banks of the Rhine. The former estate beyond had been demolished in anticipation of a new mansion to be built in the near future. In truth, a new estate *would* be built, but more than a mansion, a magnificent fortress with all of the most modern technology to ensure the isolation and the safety of the new *Führer*. That day would come soon, when the Brüderschaft controlled the Bundestag. The mountains of Berchtesgaden would be replaced by the waters of the mighty Rhine, for Günter Jäger preferred the constantly moving river to the stationary snow-capped alps.

Günter *Jäger* . . . Adolf *Hitler*! *Heil* Hitler . . . *Heil* Jäger! Even the syllabic rhythm fitted the man. More and more, Jäger assumed the less public trappings of his predecessor: the absolute chain of command; the select few designated as his personal aides and through whom all appointments were made; his disdain for physical contact save for abrupt handshakes; his apparently genuine affection for young children, but not infants, and, finally, his asexuality. Women

494

could be admired aesthetically, but not in a lascivious manner; even off-colour remarks were unacceptable in his presence. Many ascribed this puritanical streak to his previous ecclesiastical duties, but Traupman, a physician to the brain, did not. Instead, he suspected a far darker explanation. Observing Jäger in the presence of women, he thought he discerned brief flashes of hatred in the new *Führer's* eyes when a woman was provocatively dressed or used her physical charms to flatter men. No, Günter Jäger was not driven by a sense of purity, he was – like his predecessor – pathologically obsessed by a *fear* of women, by how much their wiles could destroy. But the surgeon quite wisely decided to keep his speculations to himself. The new Germany was everything, and if it took a charismatic figure with a flaw or two to bring it about, so be it.

The doctor had asked for a private audience this night, for events were taking place in the field that Jäger might not be aware of. His aides were intensely loyal, but none cared to be the bearer of disturbing news. Traupman, however, knew he was on safe ground, for he had literally plucked the mesmerizing orator from his enraged church and pushed him into the front ranks of the Brotherhood. In the final analysis, if there was one man left who could push him back, it was the celebrated surgeon.

He secured his boat, and awkwardly, painfully, climbed up on the dock only to be greeted by a heavyset guard who emerged from the shadows of a riverbank tree. 'Come, *Herr Doktor*,' called out the man. 'The *Führer* is waiting for you.'

'In the house, of course?'

'No, sir. In the garden. Follow me, please.'

'The garden? A cabbage patch is now a garden?'

'I myself planted a great many flowers and our staff cleared the riverbank. They placed flagstones where there were only reeds and debris.'

'You're not exaggerating,' said Traupman as they approached a small clearing on the edge of the Rhine, where two lanterns were suspended from tree branches, the wicks now being lighted by another aide. Around the short flagstone patio were several pieces of outdoor furniture, three upright lawn chairs and a white wrought-iron table. It was a pastoral enclave for private meditation or confidential meetings. And seated in the far chair, his blond hair catching the irregular light of the lanterns, was Güinter Jäger, the new *Führer*. At the sight of his old friend, he rose and held out his arms, immediately lowering his left and extending his right hand.

'How good of you to come, Hans.'

'I requested the meeting, Günter.'

'Drivel. You don't need to request anything of me, you simply say what you want. Sit down, sit down. Can I get you something, a drink perhaps?'

'No, thank you. I want to get back to Nuremberg as soon as I can. The unintercepted messages keep my telephone ringing.'

'Unintercepted? . . . Oh, yes, the scramblers.'

'Exactly. You have the same.'

'Do I?'

'Different channels perhaps, but whatever I learn you should know also.'

'That said and agreed to, what is so urgent, my good doctor?'

'How much do you know of the recent events in Paris?'

'Everything, I trust.'

'Gerhardt Kroeger?'

'Shot to death by the Americans in that mess at the Hotel Inter-Continental. Good riddance; he never should have gone to Paris.'

'He felt he had a mission to complete.'

'What mission?'

'The death of Harry Latham, the CIA officer who penetrated the valley and was exposed by Kroeger.'

'We'll find him, not that it matters,' said Jäger. 'The valley no longer exists.'

'But you're convinced Gerhardt Kroeger is dead.'

496

'It was in the report forwarded to Bonn intelligence by our embassy. In those circles, it's common knowledge, although they're burying it because they don't care to throw a spotlight on us.'

'A report, if I'm not mistaken, that originated at the American Embassy.'

'Presumably. They knew Kroeger was one of us – how could they *not* know? The stupid pig started shooting up the place believing he could kill this Latham. However, the Americans didn't learn anything, he died on his way to their embassy.'

'I see,' said Hans Traupman, shifting his body in the chair, only sporadically glancing at Günter Jäger as if he were pained to engage his new *Führer*'s eyes. 'And our Sonnenkind, Janine Clunitz, wife of the American ambassador?'

'We hardly needed our penetrators to learn what happened, Hans. It was in all the newspapers in Europe and America and everywhere else, confirmed by witnesses. She narrowly escaped an ambush by Israeli extremists out to kill Courtland over what they called an "Arabist" State Department. He was wounded and, unfortunately, our Sonnenkind Clunitz survived. She'll be dead in a day or so, I've been assured of that.'

'Finally, Günter – *mein Führer*—'

'I told you before, Hans, between us that's not required.'

'I require it of myself. You are far more than the gangster from Munich ever was. You are highly educated, historically grounded, and ideologically positioned by what is happening, not only in Germany, but in all countries. The ill born, the unworthy, and the mediocre are assuming positions of power in governments everywhere, and you understand that this destructive trend must stop. You can bring this about . . . *mein Führer*.'

'Thank you, Hans, but you were saying? "Finally" – what?'

'This man Latham, the deep-cover Central Intelligence

officer who penetrated the valley and was exposed by Gerhardt Kroeger—'

'What about him?' interrupted Jäger.

'He's still alive. He's better than we thought.'

'He's only a man, Hans. Flesh and blood and with a heart muscle that can be stopped, punctured with a bullet or a knife. I've authorized two units of Blitzkrieger to fly to Paris and accomplish the task. They won't fail. They dare not fail.'

'And the woman he lives with?'

'The De Vries whore?' asked the new *Führer*. 'She must be killed with him – or before him, preferably. Her sudden death will unnerve him, cause him to be more vulnerable; he'll make mistakes . . . Is all this what you've come to tell me, Hans?'

'No, Günter,' said Traupman, getting up from the chair and pacing between the shadows and the glare of the two lanterns. 'I've come to tell you the truth, as I've perceived the truth through my own sources.'

'Your *own* sources?'

'No different from yours, I assure you, but I'm an old man whose training is in the nuts and bolts of surgery, and all too frequently patients skirt around their symptoms, frightened by my diagnoses if they were totally honest. Eventually, you learn to understand a degree of self-deceiving falsity.'

'Please be clearer.'

'I shall, and I'll support what I say by my own inquiries . . . Gerhardt Kroeger did not die. I suspect he's alive and a prisoner in the American Embassy.'

'*What?*' Jäger shot forward in his chair.

'I sent one of our people to the Hotel Inter-Continental, with official French identification, of course, to interrogate the surviving clerks. They all speak English, and they said they distinctly heard two of the guards on the balcony shouting that the "maniac" had been shot in the legs, but was still alive. They took him away and put him into an ambulance. I repeat, still *alive*.'

'My *God*!'

'Next, I had our people examine the so-called witnesses to the assault on the American Embassy, where the ambassador was severely wounded and his wife supposedly survived. These witnesses could not understand the subsequent reports on television and in the newspapers. They told our people that the woman's upper chest and face were flowing with blood . . . "How could she have lived?" they asked.'

'So our people did their work. She's gone.'

'Then why are they keeping it quiet? *Why?*'

'That godforsaken *Latham*, that's why!' cried Jäger, the hated returning to his ice-cold eyes. 'He's trying to fool us, to pull us into a trap.'

'You *know* him?'

'Of course not. I know men *like* him. All corrupted by whores.'

'Do you know *her*?'

'Good God, no. But since the legions of the pharaohs, the whores have always corrupted armies. They follow in their covered caravans, sapping the soldiers of their strength for a few minutes of unholy pleasure! *Whores!*'

'As accurate as that judgement may be, Günter, and I do not dispute it, it's not particularly relevant to what I'm saying.'

'Then what *are* you saying, Hans? You tell me that things are not as they've been reported and I reply that you may be correct, that our enemies are attempting to entrap us as we lay traps for them. There's nothing new in this – except that we're winning. Assess the circumstances, my friend. The Americans, the French, and the British are finding us everywhere and nowhere. In Washington, senators and congressmen are suspect; in Paris we have twenty-seven members of the Chamber of Deputies shaping laws to our benefit, and the head of the Deuxième in our pocket. London is ludicrous; they find an ineffectual adviser in the Foreign Office and overlook the first associate to the foreign secretary, who's so furious over the black immigration that he could have written *Mein Kampf*!' Jäger stopped briefly as he rose from his chair and stood on the flagstone patio, looking over a flowered hedgerow at the calming waters of the Rhine. 'Yet for all of that, our work in the lesser areas is even more impressive. An American politician once said, "All politics is local," and he was right. Adolf Hitler understood that; it's what gave him the Reichstag. You pit one race against another, one ethnic group against another, one economic class against another seemingly *drained* by it, you provoke chaos, wherein lies a vacuum. He did it from one city to another – Munich, Stuttgart, Nuremberg, Mannheim; troopers everywhere spreading rumours, sowing discontent. Finally, he rushed into and took the *political* Berlin; he could not have done that without the erratic but consuming support of the outlying areas.'

'*Bravo*, Günter,' cried Traupman, applauding. 'You see the landscape so clearly, so perceptively.'

'Then what bothers you so?'

'Things you may not know—'

'Such *as*?'

'Two Blitzkrieger were taken alive in Paris and flown to Washington.'

'I was not *told* of this,' said Jäger, his words frozen in ice.

'It's true, but it's of no significance now. They were shot in a safe house in Virginia by our Penetrator Three at the Central Intelligence Agency.'

'He's a *moron*, a clerk! We give him twenty thousand American dollars a year to tell us what the *other* departments are researching.'

'He now wants two hundred thousand for carrying out an order he believes would have been issued to him if he were higher on the ladder.'

'Kill him!'

'That's not a good idea, Günter. Not until we learn whom he may have spoken to about us. As you pointed out, he's a moron; he's also a braggart.'

'That *swine!*' roared Jäger, turning from the glare of the lantern, his face in shadows.

'A swine who did us a considerable service,' added the doctor. 'We'll live with him for a while, even elevate him. The time will come when we can deal him other cards and he'll become a grateful slave.'

'*Ach*, my dear Hans, you are so good for me. Your mind is like your steady surgical hand. If my predecessor had had more men like you around him, he would still be giving orders to the British Parliament.'

'In that spirit, I hope you will listen to me now, Günter.' Traupman took several steps across the patio; the two men were face-to-face in the flickering shadows.

'When haven't I listened to you, my old friend and mentor? You are my Albert Speer, the precise analytical mind of an architect replaced by the precise analytical mind of a surgeon. Hitler made the mistake of ultimately disregarding Speer for the likes of Goering and Bormann. I shall never make such a mistake. What is it, Hans?'

'You were correct when you said we were winning the battle of nerves with our enemies. You were also accurate when you stated that in certain localities, especially in the United States, our Sonnenkinder have performed admirably, creating schisms and discontent.'

'I'm impressed with my own assessments,' interrupted Jäger, smiling.

'That's the point, Günter, they are merely assessments based on current information ... However, the situation could change, and change rapidly. Right now could be the pinnacle of our strategic success.'

'Why the pinnacle?'

'Because too many traps are being set for us that we can't know about. We may never be in such an advantageous position again.'

Then what you're really saying is "Invade England now, *mein Führer*, do not wait,"' interrupted Jäger once more.

'Water Lightning, of course,' said Traupman. 'It must be

501

moved up. Six Messerschmitt ME 323 *Gigant* gliders have been retrieved and are being reconditioned. We have to strike as soon as possible, and set the panic in motion. The water reservoirs of Washington, London, and Paris must be poisoned the moment our flying personnel have been trained. Once the governments are in a state of paralysis, our people everywhere are prepared to move into positions of influence, even power.'

The woman on the stretcher was carried out of the American Embassy in full view of the strollers on the avenue Gabriel. A sheet and a light cotton blanket covered her body; her long dark hair was swept back over the small white pillow, and her face was concealed beneath an oxygen mask below grey silk blinders that protected her eyes from the Paris sun. The rumours spread quickly, aided by several embassy attachés who circulated through the gathering crowd, answering questions softly.

'It's the ambassador's wife,' said a woman in French. 'I just heard it from an American. Poor dear, she was hurt last evening during that terrible shooting.'

'Crime here has become intolerable,' said a bespectacled slender man. 'We should bring back the guillotine!'

'Where are they taking her?' asked another woman, wincing in pity.

'The Hertford Hospital in the Levallois-Perret.'

'Really? It's called an English hospital, isn't it?'

'They say their equipment is the most advanced for her wounds.'

'Who said so?' broke in an indignant Frenchman.

'That strapping young man over there – where is he? Well, he was there and that's what he said.'

'How badly is she hurt?' asked a teenage girl, her right hand gripping the arm of a young male student, his canvas shoulder bag filled with books.

'I heard one of the Americans say it was extremely painful

but not life-threatening,' answered yet another French-woman, a secretary or a minor executive who carried a large, thick brown envelope under her arm. 'A punctured lung that makes it difficult for her to breathe. She was wearing an oxygen mask. Such a shame!'

'It's such a shame that the Americans are so meddlesome,' said the student. 'She has trouble breathing and one of us who may be seriously ill is shoved aside to make her life more pleasant.'

'Antoine, how can you *say* that?'

'Very easily. I'm a history major.'

'You're a thankless dog!' cried an elderly man with a small Croix de Guerre emblem in his lapel. 'I fought with the Americans and marched into Paris with them. They saved our city!'

'All by themselves, old soldier? I don't think so . . . Come, Mignon, let's get out of here.'

'Antoine, really! Your radicalism isn't only passé, it's boring.'

'Little fuck-up,' said the ageing soldier to anyone who would listen. '"Fuck-up", it's a term I learned from the Americans.'

Upstairs in the embassy, in Stanley Witkowski's office, Claude Moreau was slumped disconsolately in a chair in front of the colonel's desk. 'Fortunately,' he said in a weary voice, 'I do not need money, but I shall never be able to spend what I have in Paris, or even France.'

'What are you talking about?' asked Stanley, lighting a Cuban cigar, his expression one of self-satisfaction.

'If you don't know, Colonel, you should be granted what the American military calls a Section Eight.'

'Why? I've got all my marbles and I'm doing what I'm pretty damned good at.'

'For God's sake, Stanley, I've lied to my own Bureau, to the hastily summoned committee of the Chamber of Deputies, to the *press*, to the *President* himself! I've literally

503

sworn that Madame Courtland survived, that she didn't die, that she received excellent treatment from your clinic!'

'Well, you weren't under oath, Claude.'

'*Merde!* You are crazy!'

'The hell I am. I got her covered body inside and downstairs before anybody could tell the bitch was dead.'

'But will it *work*, Stanley?'

'It has so far . . . Look, Claude, I'm only trying to produce confusion. The Latham the neos are after is the one they killed, but they don't know that. So they're coming after the other, and we're waiting for them. The ambassador's bitch is no less important to them, maybe even more important because they figured out we know who and what she is. After all, the Count of Strasbourg wasn't about to give her a tetanus shot. With luck, along with your minor fibs, our little charade outside will pay off—'

'Minor *fibs*?' choked Moreau, interrupting. 'Have you any idea what I've *done*? I lied to the President of France! I'll never be trusted again!'

'Hell, extend your rationale a touch. You did it for his own good. You had reason to believe his office was bugged.'

'*Preposterous*. It's the Deuxième's responsibility to see that it's not!'

'Guess you can't use that one,' allowed Witkowski. 'How about your running clearance checks on his top aides?'

'We did that most thoroughly months ago. However, your equivocation about extending my rationale may have merit.'

'For your President's own good,' the colonel broke in, drawing heavily and happily on his cigar.

'Yes, exactly. What he doesn't know he can't be held responsible for, and we *are* dealing with psychopaths, with fanatical assassins.'

'I don't get the connection, Claude, but it's a start. Incidentally, thanks for the additional personnel at the hospital. Except for two sergeants and a captain, my marines aren't exactly fluent in French.'

'Your captain was an exchange student, and one of the sergeants has French parents; he knew our language before English. Your other sergeant's use of French mainly consists of obscenities and how to procure specific services.'

'Good! The neos are obscene, so he's perfect.'

'How is our stenographer, the reincarnated Madame Courtland, holding up?'

'She's a loaded gun,' said the colonel.

'I hope not.'

'What I mean is she's a Jewish lady from New York and hates the Nazis. Her grandparents were gassed at Bergen-Belsen.'

'Strange, isn't it? Drew Latham used the phrase "What goes around, comes around." Apparently it's quite true in human terms.'

'What's really true is that when some neo son of a bitch comes after the new Mrs Courtland, and one of them will, we'll nail him and break him!'

'I told you before, Stanley, I have my doubts that anyone will come. The neos are not fools. They'll sense a trap.'

'I've considered that, but my money's on human nature. When the stakes get this high – and a live Sonnenkind puts 'em up there – all bets are covered. The bastards can't afford not to.'

'I hope you're right, Stanley . . . How is our argumentative colleague, Drew Latham, accepting the scenario?'

'Pretty well. We've selectively leaked his cover as Colonel Webster around the embassy, even to the Antinayous, who apparently knew it anyway. Now you do the same. Also, we're moving the De Vries woman here to the embassy with complete marine security at her quarters.'

'I'm surprised she agreed so readily,' said Moreau. 'She's capable of many artifices, but I truly believe she cares for the man, and given her background would not voluntarily leave him under the circumstances.'

'She doesn't know about it yet,' said Witkowski. 'We're moving her tonight.'

It was early evening, the Parisian days growing shorter, and Karin de Vries sat in an armchair by the window, the dull, soft light of a floor lamp careening off her long dark hair, creating soft shadows across her attractive face. 'Have you any idea what you're doing?' she asked, glaring at Latham, who once again was half dressed in the army uniform, the tunic draped over the desk chair.

'Sure,' he replied. 'I'm bait.'

'You're *dead*, for God's sake!'

'The hell I am. At least the odds are on my side. I wouldn't take them otherwise.'

'*Why?* Because the colonel said so? . . . Don't you understand, Drew, that when it comes down to "*mission completed*", you are merely factor X or Y, expendable for the competition? Witkowski may be your friend, but don't fool yourself, he's a professional. The operation comes first! Why do you think he insists that you wear that damned *uniform?*'

'Hey, I know that, or at least I figured it was part of the equation. But they're sending over a chest protector and a larger jacket, or whatever you call it; it's not like I'm being sent out naked. Also, don't tell Stanley how often I *don't* wear his lousy outfit, he'll sulk . . . I wonder what kind of chest protector he'll send?'

'Assassins don't aim for the body, my dear, they aim for the head with telescopic sights.'

'I keep forgetting, you know all about that stuff.'

'Fortunately, I do, which is why I want you to tell our mutual friend, Stanley, to go to the devil!'

'I can't do that.'

'Why *not?* He can send out a decoy on the streets. It would be so simple! But not you.'

'Somebody else? Maybe somebody who's got a brother who's a farmer in Idaho, or an automobile mechanic in Jersey City? . . . I couldn't live with that.'

'And I can't live without *you!*' shouted Karin, lunging out of the chair and into his arms. 'I never, *never* thought I'd ever say that to anyone else in the world, but I mean it with all my heart, Drew Latham. Only God knows why, but it's as if you're the extension of the young man I married years ago, without the ugliness, without the hatred. Don't despise me for saying this, my darling, I simply have to.'

'I could never despise you,' said Drew quietly, holding her. 'We need each other for different reasons, and we don't have to analyse them for years.' He tilted her head back and looked into her eyes. 'How about when we're kind of old and sitting in our rocking chairs, looking out over the water?'

'Or the mountains. I love mountains.'

'We'll discuss it.' There was a rapid knocking on the hotel door. 'Oh, hell,' said Drew, releasing her, 'where's that time-code sheet?'

'I tacked it on the hallway wall. You can't miss it.'

'I got it. What time is it?'

'Seven-thirty is good enough. The shift changes at eight.'

'Who *is* it?'

'*Bonney rabitte*,' said the voice of Frack behind the door.

'This is infantile,' said Latham, opening it.

'It is time, monsieur.'

'Yes, I know. Give me a couple of minutes, okay?'

'*Certainement*,' said Frack as Drew closed the door and turned to Karin.

'You're leaving, my friend.'

'What?'

'You heard me. You're being transferred to the embassy.'

'What? . . . *Why?*'

'You're an employee of the American Embassy, and it has been determined that your work in classified communications is reason enough to remove you from harm as well as from possible compromise.'

'What are you *saying?*'

'I've got to go solo, Karin.'

'I won't *let* you! You *need* me!'

'Sorry. You either go calmly or Messieurs Frick and Frack give you a needle and take you their way.'

'How *can* you, Drew?'

'Easy. I want you alive so we can sit in those rocking chairs in Colorado, looking up at the mountains. How about that?'

'You *bastard*!'

'Never said I was perfect. Just perfect for you.'

The Deuxième agents escorted Karin down the elevator, assuring her that her belongings would be removed from the hotel and delivered to the embassy within the hour. Reluctantly, she accepted her circumstances; the elevator door opened and they walked out into the lobby. Instantly, two other Deuxième personnel came forward; the four agents nodded at each other, and Messieurs Frick and Frack turned, walking rapidly back to the bank of elevators.

'Stay between us, please, madame,' said a stocky, bearded man who placed himself on Karin de Vries's right. 'The car is just outside to the left of the entrance beyond the lights of the canopy.'

'I trust you realize this is not of my choosing.'

'Director Moreau does not confide in us about every assignment, madame,' said the second clean-shaven Deuxième officer. 'We are simply to make sure you get from here to the American Embassy.'

'I could have taken a taxi.'

'Personally,' said the bearded agent, smiling, 'with no offence, I'm glad it was not permitted. My wife and I were to have dinner with her parents. Can you believe after fourteen years and three grandchildren they're still not certain I'm the right husband for their daughter?'

'What does their daughter say?'

'*Ah*, she is again with child, madame.'

'I believe that says enough, monsieur.' Karin smiled weakly as the trio approached the glass doors. Outside on the pavement, they quickly swung left from under the canopy, away from the wash of the dual strands of lights beneath the deep-red canvas. In the relative darkness and through a profusion of evening pedestrians on the rue de l'Echelle, the two Deuxième agents rushed De Vries thirty feet down the street to the armoured Bureau vehicle waiting in the No Parking zone. The bearded escort opened the kerbside door for Karin, smiling and gesturing for her to enter.

At that instant there was an audible spit; the agent's left temple blew apart, blood shooting out where the bullet exited the man's skull. Simultaneously, the second Deuxième escort arched backward, eyes wide, mouth gaping, a guttural cry emerging from his throat as a long-bladed knife was yanked out of his back. Both men slumped to the pavement; De Vries started to scream, but a strong hand was clamped over her mouth and she was shoved violently inside the automobile, her attacker following, slamming her into the backseat. Barely seconds later, the opposite door opened and a breathless second killer jumped in, gripping a blood-streaked knife in his right hand, the dripping blade as deep red as the hotel's canopy.

'*Los schnell!*' he cried.

The car leapt forward into the street, in moments settling into the flow of the traffic. The first killer spoke as he removed his spiderlike hand from Karin's face. 'Screaming will do you no good,' he said, 'but if you try, you'll have scars on both cheeks.'

'*Willkommen, Frau de Vries,*' said the driver, partially turning his head around while shoving a curled-up corpse across the seat. 'It seems you're determined to be with your husband. It will certainly happen if you refuse to cooperate with us.'

'You killed those two men,' whispered Karin, her mouth raw, unable to find her voice.

'We are the saviours of the new Germany,' said the driver. 'We do what we have to do.'

'How did you find me?'

'Quite simple. You have enemies where you think you have friends.'

'The Americans?'

'They're there, yes. Also the British and the French.'

'What are you going to do with me?'

'That depends on you. You can either join your once-celebrated husband, Frederik de Vries, or you can join us. We know you're for sale.'

'I simply want to find my once-celebrated husband, you know that too.'

'You make no sense, Frau de Vries.'

Silence.

CHAPTER THIRTY

The loud radio blocking out much of the abrasive sound of the street traffic outside, Latham tried on the bulletproof jacket, pulling the enlarged army officer's tunic over it, surprised at how relatively comfortable it was. He kept glancing at the telephone on the desk, wondering why Karin had not called him; she had said she would once she settled into her quarters at the embassy. She had left over two hours before, her luggage following shortly. Shaking his head unconsciously while chuckling, he imagined her meeting Witkowski, the colonel being soundly berated, even yelled at, over the decision to let him go solo. Poor Stosh, his tough exterior notwithstanding, he was not prepared for a righteous onslaught by the future wife of his Consular Operations officer. Drew actually felt sorry for the colonel; in a way he could not win except by official decree, which was basically unsatisfying. Karin had love on her side, an emotion both Stanley and Ambassador Courtland had experienced, and lost, courtesy of their government careers.

Latham crossed to the body-length mirror in the hallway and observed his image. The underlining chest protector made him appear more imposing than he was, reminding him of his days on the ice under a green and white uniform in Canada, where body checks and slap shots were as important as life and death – how totally ridiculous in afterthought . . . *Long enough!* he said to himself as he walked back to the desk and the telephone. He picked it up and started to dial, then there was a knock at the door. He

511

slammed down the phone, walked to the door, examining the code sheet, and said, 'Who is it?'

'Witkowski,' answered the voice on the other side.

'What's your code?'

'To hell with that, it's *me*.'

'You're supposed to say, "Good King Wenceslas", you asshole!'

'Open the door before I blow the lock off with my forty-five.'

'That has to be you, cretin, because you probably don't know that a brass lock can richochet a bullet into your stomach.'

'Not if you fire around the rim, you maggot. *Open!*'

In contrast to the shouted insults, a sober, serious Witkowski and Claude Moreau stood in the doorframe, their expressions pained. 'We must talk,' said the chief of the Deuxième Bureau as he and the colonel walked inside. 'Something terrible has happened.'

'*Karin!*' exploded Drew. 'She hasn't called – she said she would call at least an hour ago! Where *is* she?'

'We're not sure, but the facts are unsettling,' answered Moreau.

'*What* facts?'

'Two of Claude's men were killed on the pavement outside,' replied Witkowski. 'One with a bullet in his head, the other with a knife. The Bureau's car is gone, the driver presumed dead also.'

'They were taking her to the embassy!' roared Latham. 'She was under *protection*!'

'She was kidnapped,' said Moreau quietly, his eyes locked with Drew's.

'They'll *kill* her!' screamed Latham, spinning around and pounding his fist against the wall.

'I deplore the possibility,' countered the Deuxième chief, 'but I mourn the death of my colleagues, for at least two *are* dead, most probably a third. As for Karin, we have no evidence she has been dealt the same fate, and in my judgement, she's very much alive.'

'How can you *say* that?' asked Drew, snapping his head towards Moreau.

'Because she's more valuable to them as a hostage than as a corpse. They want the man known as Harry Latham, and that's *you*.'

'So?'

'They'll use her to draw out Harry Latham, for what reason none of us know, but they want your brother and you are now he.'

'What do we do?'

'We wait, *chłopak*,' said Colonel Witkowski, standing erect and speaking softly. 'As we both know, it's the toughest part of our job. If they wanted to kill Karin to make another example, her body would have been left with the other two. It wasn't. We wait.'

'All right, all *right*!' exclaimed Drew, lunging across the room, stopped by the desk, his hand on the edge. 'But if that's the way it's got to be, I want the names of everyone, *everyone* who was told who I am and where I am. The *leaks*, I want to know where *every* leak was planted!'

'What good would it do, *mon ami*? Such leaks are like stones thrown into a pond; the ripples spread across the waters.'

'I have to *have* them, that's why!'

'Very well, I'll give you the names of the people we reached, and Stanley will have to provide those at the embassy.'

'Start writing,' ordered Latham, rushing around the desk, opening the drawer, and pulling out sheets of hotel stationery. 'Everything you've got.'

'We've fed them two hundred and thirty-six names along with corresponding photographs,' said Knox Talbot, director of the Central Intelligence Agency, over the phone to Wesley Sorenson.

513

'Any responses yet?'

'Nothing concrete, but a number of possibles. We're lucky insofar as seven personnel at the safe house actually saw "Deputy Director Connally", unlucky that only four were close enough to give descriptions in any detail.'

'What about the possibles?' asked the director of Consular Operations.

'Very inconclusive. Damned if one of the witnesses didn't pick out your photograph among eight others.'

'If they were all around my age, that tells us something.'

'They weren't. We made it clear that whoever the impostor was would drastically change his appearance, that his hair would most likely not be his own, his eye colour possibly altered with contact lenses, all the usual devices.'

'Except one, Knox. He could look older, but not younger, not without appearing grotesque.'

'That's the strange thing, Wes. To a man and one woman, they pretty much said the same. That this "Connally" was so ordinary as to be almost nondescript – I'm cutting through the verbiage, of course.'

'Of course. What about his clothing?'

'Right out of the old Agency guidelines. Dark suit, white shirt, preppy striped tie, laced brown shoes. Oh, and a light raincoat, the short, hang-loose variety. The woman who was at the security counter said it was like one an officer friend of hers wore, a London Fog.'

'Face?'

'Again bland, very ordinary. No moustache, no chin beard, just pale skin and no outstanding features, but wearing fairly thick glasses, too thick, I'd say.'

'How many possibles are there?'

'Eliminating the obvious, such as yourself, twenty-four.'

'Without eliminating anyone, how many?'

'Fifty-one.'

'May I see them?'

'The twenty-four are on their way over to you. I'll send

the other twenty-seven posthaste. Or should I remove yours? I mean, you don't even work here.'

'Why did you include it?'

'A perverse sense of humour, I guess. As I frequently tell our administration colleague, Adam Bollinger, a laugh now and then can put things into perspective.'

'Granted, my friend, I'm just not feeling very humorous. Have you heard the word from Paris?'

'Not for the last twenty-some hours.'

'Hear it now. Karin de Vries has disappeared. She was abducted by the neos.'

'Oh, my God!'

'Apparently He's not around when you need Him.'

'What does Witkowski say?'

'He's worried about Latham. He said Drew behaved like he was under control, but he's convinced it was an act.'

'How so?'

'Because he demanded to know where the leaks were made that blew his cover.'

'A reasonable request, I'd say. He's the bait.'

'You're not listening, Knox. I said "demanded", and Stanley made it clear that Latham delivered it on a give-me-or-I'm-out basis.'

'I still don't see why that makes him a loose cannon.'

'We've both been married a long time to remember. He's in *love*, old boy. It came a bit late maybe, but probably for the first time. His lady was taken from him, and he's at the height of his professional prowess, which includes a multitude of lethal capabilities. At his age, one frequently has delusions of invincibility. He wants her back.'

'I read you, Wes. What can we do?'

'He's got to do something first, something that gives us an excuse to sandbag him.'

'Sandbag . . . ?'

'Short of putting him in a locked room with sponge-rubber walls, at least getting him out of Paris. He's no good to anybody if the bait becomes the hunter.'

'I understood he was being watched, under guard.'

'So was his brother, Harry, and he escaped from the Brotherhood valley. Don't underestimate the Latham genes. On the other hand, Witkowski and Moreau aren't exactly pikers in counterinsurgency.'

'I'm not sure what that means in this context, but I assume it's reassuring.'

'I hope to hell it is,' said Sorenson.

Under the glare of the desk lamp, Drew studied the names. On Witkowski's list of possible leaks there were seven names, including the Antinayous, and on Moreau's nine, three of them members of the Chamber of Deputies at the Quai d'Orsay, whom the Deuxième chief thought were radically to the right of the political mainstream, in a word, Fascists. On Stanley's list were several rumour-mongering attachés, 'floaters', as he called them, who spent more time sucking up to influential French businessmen than at their jobs; two secretaries whose absences suggested alcohol problems; and a Father Manfried Neuman at the Antinayous' Maison Rouge. Moreau's list, beyond the Quai d'Orsay, were the usual paid informers whose allegiances were exclusively to money, ideology and morality nonexistent.

Working from the viewpoint of reducing the numbers, Latham eliminated Moreau's informers – he had no entrée into their ranks – as well as two of the deputies; the third he had met at diplomatic functions. He would call that man, listening hard. Witkowski's list was easier, for he knew five of them by sight and name, casual embassy acquaintances. The remaining two, both women, both suspected of having a drinking problem, he could reach out of the blue, as it were. What he needed were telephone numbers.

'Stanley, I'm so glad you're working late, because you left out something with your seven candidates.'

'What the hell are you talking about?' said the angry

Witkowski. 'Those are the ones we used for observable leaks.'

'*We?* Who else? Who did the circulation duty?'

'My secretary who came with me from the old G-2, a former sergeant whom I made a first lieutenant before her discharge.'

'Her? *She?*'

'Service-oriented, son. Her husband was a gunny until he retired after his thirtieth, and he was only fifty-three. Kids are all army brats.'

'What does he do now?'

'Plays golf, goes to museums, and still takes French lessons. He can't get the hang of the lingo.'

'Then I don't need her telephone number, but I want all the rest. Their residences, including the Antinayous' Maison Rouge.'

'I can figure where you're coming from. Let me punch up my computer.'

Claude Moreau was somewhat more difficult. He was at home, arguing with a son over politics. 'The youth today, they understand nothing!'

'Neither do I, but I need telephone numbers, unless you want me to benevolently usher your guards into a long night's sleep.'

'How *dare* you say such a thing?'

'Easily. I can do it.'

'*Mon Dieu*, Stanley is right, you are impossible! Very well, I'll give you a phone at the Bureau. Call it in five minutes and you'll be given the numbers you want.'

'Not want, Claude. Need.'

Eleven minutes later, Latham had matched the telephone numbers with every name on both lists. He started calling, using essentially the same words with each.

'*This is Colonel Webster, and I believe you know my true identity. What disturbs me is that others have learned it and we've traced the leak to you. What have you got to say for yourself, before you've got nothing left to say?*'

Every response was a variation on the same theme. Explosive negatives, down to the point of each one offering to have their phone calls checked, both at their offices and their homes; a number volunteered to take lie-detector tests. Those over with, only a holier-than-thou Antinayou at the Maison Rouge was left.

'Father Neuman, please.'

'He's conducting vespers and cannot be disturbed.'

'Disturb him. This is a matter of extreme urgency, directly related to your secrecy.'

'*Mein Gott*, I don't know what to do. The father is an ardent priest. Can't you call back in, say, twenty minutes or so?'

'By that time the Red House may be blown up with no one surviving.'

'*Ach!* I will reach him!'

When Father Manfried Neuman finally came on the line, he snapped, 'What is this foolishness? I'm in the middle of the Lord's work and you take me away from His supplicants.'

'My temporary name is Colonel Webster, but you know who I am, Father.'

'Of course I do! So do many others.'

'Really? That comes as something of a shock. I assumed it was highly privileged information, airtight, in fact.'

'Well, I presume others know. Now, what's this about a bomb here?'

'Maybe I'm the bomber if you don't answer my questions. I stayed there, remember, and right now I'm pretty desperate.'

'How can you behave this way? The Antinayous took care of you, we gave you sanctuary in your hour of need.'

'And refused to take me back when the need was still there.'

'That was a collective decision based on our own security requirements.'

'Not good enough, Father. We're against the same people, aren't we?'

'Do not trifle with us, Herr Latham. I am a man of God and abhor violence, but there are others here who are not of my persuasion.'

'Is that a threat, *padre*?'

'Take it as you will, my son. We know where you are and our vehicles constantly roam the city.'

'Tell me, do you know where Karin de Vries is?'

'*Frau* de Vries . . . ? Our colleague?'

'She's gone. They took her.'

'*No!* That's *wrong* . . . !'

'You just blew it, Bible freak. What's *right?* . . . I guess we're not on the same side after all.'

'*Untrue!* I've given up *everything*—'

'You'll give up the last thing you've got to give unless you tell me whom you spoke to about me,' broke in Latham. '*Now!*'

'As the Lord God is my witness, only to our informant at the embassy . . . and one other.'

'First, the informant. *Who?*'

'A secretary, a woman named Cranston in need of Christ's help.'

'How do you know her?'

'We speak, we meet, and the flesh is weak, my son. I'm not perfect, may God forgive me.'

'The *other?* Who is it?'

'It is a confidence so deep, it would be a sacrilege to violate it.'

'So would exposing the Maison Rouge, along with a couple of grenades that would light up the entrance.'

'You *wouldn't.*'

'The hell I wouldn't. I'm a Four Zero officer of Consular Operations, and among my bag of tricks are a few the Blitzkrieger never thought of. *Give!*'

'Another priest, a former priest. He's an old man now, but when he was a young scholar, he was a talented crypt-analyst for the branch of French intelligence that became the Deuxième Bureau. The secret services still hold him in high regard, and frequently confide in him, seeking his help. His name is Lavolette, Antoine Lavolette.'

'You said he's a former priest, so why is it such a sacrilege to give me his name?'

'Because, damn you, I go to him for religious counselling, *not* politics! I have a problem, not unlike his own years ago, but mine is far more unforgivable, for it is a compulsion and not confined to one woman. I'm an imperfect man and unworthy of my holy church. What more can I tell you?'

'Maybe a lot more, I'll let you know. By the way, *padre*, why did you say it was "wrong" for Karin to be kidnapped?'

'Because it was stupid, it's as simple as that!' spat out the priest.

'Whose side *are* you on, for Christ's sake?'

'Must you use the Lord's name in such a manner?'

'Depends on whose Lord you're talking about. Now, cut the sideshow. Why was it wrong and stupid to kidnap her?'

'Speaking selfishly, it could very well compromise our operation here. If their objective was to kill her, then *kill* her and leave her to God! But to abduct her with no proof of death is to open the floodgates – everyone will be searching for her, as you are searching for her now. Our very headquarters could be revealed – just as you threatened to do with your grenades and your bombs. I ask you in the name of all that is holy and good not to expose us or reveal our whereabouts.'

'You've given me two names, so I'll do my damnedest not to, but Karin de Vries comes first, and that's all I can promise.' Latham hung up the phone, immediately tempted to reach Moreau and ask some pointed questions about the former Father Antoine Lavolette, retired crypt-analyst extraordinary. Then he thought otherwise; the head of the Deuxième was a control freak, especially where one Drew Latham was concerned. Undoubtedly, Moreau would interfere, calling the retired priest himself and usurping the initiative. No, that wasn't the way. This Lavolette had to be cornered, surprised, forced by shock into revealing whatever he knew, or whatever he did not know he knew by disclosing another name or names. The same could be said for the Cranston woman, Phyllis Cranston, errant secretary to a middle-level attaché who was on Witkowski's list of 'floaters', probably the reason she kept her job.

First, there was the primary task of getting out of the hotel. Every hour, every minute, he spent there was an hour and a minute lost in his hunt for Karin.

Karin had said his blond hair was the product of a minor bleach rinse coupled with a 'tint colouring', whatever that was, but she insisted that with a harsh shampoo plus a tube of something that turned grey hair darker, he could return to his normal hair colour, or something close to it. She had put the magic tube in the medicine chest, he had moved it to a bedroom drawer so *she* would not remove it. It was still there.

A half hour later, the bathroom a steaming mess, a naked Latham kept throwing water on the basin mirror to clear it. His hair was now a strange dark brown with specks of auburn, but it was *not* blond. He had sent one hockey puck right through a goalie's legs!

Now there were Messieurs Frick and Frack to consider, or, more accurately, whoever relieved them for the current shift. And it was another shift, as Karin had mentioned. He knew each of the guards, but he knew Frick and Frack better than the others, and he doubted the pair would have related the details of their embarrassment over a missed code word. A lone American disarming an officer of the Deuxième, ripping his weapon away, and punishing his groin to the point of agony? *Mon Dieu, fermez la bouche!*

Drew pulled his other uniform out of the closet and his bureau drawers. It was the all but prescribed dress of the male embassy attaché: grey flannels, dark blazer, white shirt, and a conservative tie – regimental stripes preferable, subdued paisleys permitted for informal evening functions.

He was mildly pleased that the supposedly bulletproof vest was accommodated, snug but not inhibiting. Fully clothed, his suitcase packed, he opened the hotel door and walked out into the corridor, standing in place, waiting for the obvious. It came immediately with the appearance of the guard by the elevators, his colleague simultaneously emerging from the shadow at the opposite end of the hallway.

'*S'il vous plaît*,' he began in even more awkward French than he was capable of, '*voulez-vous venir ici—*'

'*En anglais, monsieur!*' cried the man from the elevators. 'We can understand.'

'Oh, thanks a lot, I appreciate that. If one of you would help me out, I just got a telephone message and I wrote out the words as best I could. It's an address, I think, but the fellow couldn't speak English.'

'You go, Pierre,' said the guard at the opposite end in French. 'I'll stay here.'

'Very well,' replied the man walking down from the bank of elevators. 'Don't they teach any other language but English in America?'

'Did the Romans learn French?'

'They didn't have to, there's your answer.' The first guard entered Latham's suite as Drew followed and closed the door. 'Where is the message, monsieur?'

'Over at the desk,' said Latham, walking behind the Frenchman. 'It's the paper with the writing on it. Right in the centre, I turned it around so you could read it.'

The guard picked up the sheet of paper with the strange words spelled out phonetically. As he did so, Latham raised both arms, hands angled downward, two hammers that crashed into the man's shoulder blades, rendering him instantly unconscious. It was a stunning blow, painful but not injurious. Drew dragged the body into the bedroom, where he had stripped the bed and ripped the sheets into long lengths of narrow cloth. Ninety seconds later the guard was strapped facedown on top of the mattress, arms and legs lashed to the bedposts, his mouth immobilized by a thin strip of cloth, allowing breath to enter and leave.

Picking up a handful of torn sheets, Latham raced out of the bedroom, closing the door. He dropped the strips of cloth on a chair and opened the hallway door. He walked out calmly and addressed the second guard, who was barely seen in the far shadows. 'Your friend Pierre says he must talk to you at once, before he calls that fellow, what's his name? Montreaux or Moneau?'

'*Monsieur le Directeur?*'

'Yeah, that's the guy. He says what I wrote down is *encredeebal*.'

'Get out of my way!' yelled the second guard, running up the corridor and rushing into the suite. '*Where . . . ?*' His question was stopped by an aikido chop to his neck, followed by a two-fingered prong to the space below his ribcage, the combination leaving the guard temporarily breathless and unconscious, but again without harm. Drew pulled him over to the couch and performed the same exercise he had with the first Deuxième officer, only with necessary variations. He laid the man prone on the pillow, legs and arms stretched and tied to the sofa's feet, mouth gagged, but his head angled, with no loss of air. Latham's final gesture was to yank out the telephones in both rooms. He was now free to begin the hunt.

CHAPTER THIRTY-ONE

He walked up the steps of Phyllis Cranston's apartment house in the rue Pavée, entered the lobby, and pressed the bell for her flat. There was no answer, so he kept ringing, thinking she might be in a stupor, if Witkowski's opinion was justified. He was about to give up, when an obese, elderly woman came out of the locked hallway, noticed the button he was pressing, and spoke in French.

'You looking for the Butterfly?'

'I'm not sure I understand you.'

'*Ah, Américain*. Your French is terrible,' she added in English. 'I was the sorriest woman in Paris when your aerodromes left France.'

'You know Miss Cranston?'

'Who here does not? She's a sweet thing and once was very pretty, as I was. Why should I tell you anything else?'

'Because I have to speak with her, it's urgent.'

'Because you're "horny", as you Americans call it? Let me tell you, monsieur, she may have the malady, but she is no whore!'

'I'm not looking for a whore, madame. I'm trying to find someone who can give me information I need very quickly, and that person is Phyllis Cranston.'

'*Hmm*,' mused the old woman, studying Drew. 'You are not looking to take advantage of her because of her malady? If you are, you should know that her friends in this building protect her. She is, as I said, sweet and kind and helps out people who need help. We are not poor here, but many of us are close to being so, what with the taxes and the high prices. The Butterfly is free with her American money and never asks for repayment. On her days off she cares for children so their mothers can work. You will not harm her, not *here*.'

'I don't want to harm her, and I'm not looking for a Mother Teresa. I told you, I want to find her because she may have information I need.'

'Do not mention *catholique* to me, monsieur. I am a Catholic, but we told that filthy priest to stay away from her!'

Bingo, thought Latham.

'A priest?'

'He took advantage of her, he *still* takes advantage of her!'

'How?'

'He comes late at night, and the absolution he's looking for is between his two legs!'

'She accepts him?'

'She feels she has no choice. He's her confessor.'

'Son of a *bitch*! Listen to me, I *have* to find her. I've spoken to that priest and he gave me her name. Not for the reason you might think, only because he may have said things to her he shouldn't have said.'

'And who are you?'

'Someone who, believe it or not, is fighting France's battle as much as I am my own country's. The Nazis, madame, the goddamned Nazis are beginning to march again all over Europe! I know that sounds melodramatic, but it's true.'

'I was a small child and saw them execute people in the streets,' said the old woman, whispering, her lined face pinched. 'They can do it again?'

'They're a long way from it, but we've got to stop them *now*.'

'How is our Butterfly involved?'

'She was given information she may have innocently imparted to others. Or perhaps not innocently. That's as honest as I can be. If she's not here, where is she?'

'I was about to tell you to go to Les Trois Couronnes, a

café down the street, but it is past midnight, and you need not go there. She's right behind you, being helped up the steps by her neighbour, Monsieur du Bois. As is quite apparent, her malady is that she drinks too much wine. There are things she has to forget, monsieur, and she does it with wine.'

'Do you know what they are?'

'It is not my business to know, and what I know I keep to myself. We take care of our Butterfly, here.'

'Will you accompany me to her flat so you can see for yourselves, both you and Monsieur du Bois, that I mean no harm to her? That I merely want to ask her a few questions?'

'You will not be alone with her, I can assure you of that. There'll be no priests in fancy street clothing.'

Phyllis Cranston was a diminutive woman of forty-five or fifty, her figure compact, even athletic. Although unsteady on her feet, each foot was planted firmly, defiantly, both admitting and denying her state of drunkenness.

'So who's going to make some *coffee*!' she demanded in a solidly nasal midwestern American accent as she fell back in a chair at the far end of her flat, her companion, Du Bois, at her side.

'I've got it on the stove, Butterfly, don't you worry,' said the old woman from the lobby.

'Just who is this creep?' asked Cranston, gesturing at Latham.

'An American, *mon chou*, who knows that dirty priest we told you to stay away from.'

'That pig forgives old broads like me, because we're the only women he can get! Is this bastard one of them? Did he come here to get his rocks off?'

'I'm the last person you could imagine being a priest,' said Drew softly, calmly. 'And as to sexual satisfaction, I'm very much committed to a lady who takes care of those needs and whom I expect to stay with for the rest of my life, with or without religious sanction.'

'Boy, you sound like a real square! Where are you from, baby?'

'Connecticut, originally. Where are you from? Indiana or Ohio, or maybe northern Missouri?'

'Hey, you're pretty much on target, macho-boy. I'm a Saint Louis girl, born and brought up in the parochial system – what a drag, right?'

'I wouldn't know.'

'But how did you know I was from that part of the good old USA?'

'Your accent. I'm trained to spot such things.'

'No kidding? . . . Hey, thanks for the java, Eloise.' The embassy secretary accepted the mug of coffee and took several sips, shaking her head after each. 'I guess you figure I'm a real loser, don't you?' she continued, looking at Latham, then suddenly sitting up, staring at him. 'Wait a minute, I *know* you! You're the Cons-Op officer!'

'That's right, Phyllis.'

'What the hell are you *doing* here?'

'Father Manfried Neuman, he gave me your name.'

'That *prick*! So you could *fire* me?'

'I see no reason to fire you, Phyllis—'

'Then why are you here?'

'Father Neuman, that's why. He told you who a Colonel Webster was, didn't he? That he was a deep-cover American intelligence officer from the embassy who was going underground with a new identity, a new appearance. He told you that, didn't he?'

'Oh, for Christ's sake, he was so full of shit, you couldn't find an outhouse big enough. He did that all the time, especially when he got so excited I thought he'd tear my bottom apart. It was like he was playin' God, telling secrets only God would know, and then when he came off, exploded, he'd grab my face and say God would condemn me to the fires of hell if I ever repeated what he said.'

'Why are you telling me now?'

'*Why?*' Phyllis Cranston drank a large portion of her

527

coffee. She answered simply. 'Because my friends here explained to me that I was a damn fool. I'm a good person, Mr Whatever-your-name-is – and I have a problem which is confined to these few streets. So go to hell.'

'Beyond the obvious, what is your problem, Phyllis?'

'I will answer that for you, Monsieur *Américain*,' said the old lady. 'This bilingual child of French parents lost her husband and three children in the American Midwest floods of '91. The raging river by their house destroyed everything. Only she survived, clinging to the rocks until rescued. Why do you think she looks after the children here whenever she can?'

'I have to ask her one more question, the only question, really.'

'What is it, Mr Latham – that is your name, isn't it?' said Phyllis Cranston, sitting up, now more exhausted than drunk.

'After Father Neuman told you who I was – whom did *you* tell?'

'I'm trying to remember . . . Yeah, in the peak of a hangover, I told Bobby Durbane in the comm centre, and a lower-pool stenographer I hardly know, not even her name.'

'Thank you,' said Latham. 'And good night, Phyllis.'

Drew walked down the steps of the apartment house in the rue Pavée; a bewildered man. He had no idea who the pool stenographer could be, but her status hardly suggested much influence. Robert Durbane, however, was a shock. Bobby Durbane, the grey fox of the comm centre, the veteran expert of ethereal communications, the man who only days earlier had Drew on his mysterious grids and sent out embassy vehicles to rescue him from a neo assault? It was beyond understanding. Durbane was the quiet man, the ascetic, the intellectual who pored over his esoteric crossword puzzles and double acrostics, who was so generous to his crew that he frequently took the midnight-to-dawn shifts so his subordinates could get some rest from the daily bombardments.

Or was there another Robert Durbane, a far more secretive one? A man who chose the deserted, early morning hours so he could send his own messages through the ether to others who precalibrated his unknown frequencies and read his codes. And why had the armed embassy cars with all their firepower arrived barely a minute after the Nazi limousine had swung around the street, spraying their bullets everywhere, killing a neo named C-*Zwölf*? Had *Bobby Durbane* orchestrated the would-be massacre by alerting the Nazis first? These were questions that had to be answered; the unknown embassy pool stenographer had to be tracked down as well. Both could wait until morning; now it was time for Father Neuman's adviser, Antoine Lavolette, retired priest and former intelligence cryptographer.

The address was easily gotten from the telephone book. Latham found a vacant taxi two blocks east. It was nearly one o'clock in the morning, just the hour, he decided, to confront the elderly Father Lavolette, defrocked man of God, who possessed secrets that might have to be prised out of him.

The house in the quai de Grenelle was a substantial three-storey structure of white stone and freshly painted strips of green wood, bringing to mind a Mondrian canvas. The owner also had to be substantial, at least in income, for the neighbourhood rivalled the avenue Montaigne in upscale opulence; it was not for the marginally rich, only the rich. The former cryptographer and retired man of the cloth had done very well for himself in the material world.

Drew walked up the short flight of steps to the enamelled green door, the shining brass of the bell plate and the knob casement glistening in the wash of the street lamps. He rang the bell and waited; it was twenty-six minutes after one o'clock in the morning. At 1:29 the door was opened by a startled woman in a bathrobe; she was perhaps in her late thirties, her light brown hair mussed from sleep.

'My God, what do you want at this hour?' she blurted out in French. 'The household is asleep!'

'*Vous parlez anglais?*' asked Latham, holding out his black-bordered embassy identification, a document that was both reassuring and intimidating.

'Un peu,' replied the apparent housekeeper nervously.

'I must see Monsieur Lavolette. It's a matter of great importance and cannot wait until morning.'

'You stay outside. I'll get my husband.'

'He's Monsieur Lavolette?'

'No, he is the *patron*'s chauffeur . . . among other things. He also speaks *anglais* more better. Outside!'

The door was slammed shut, forcing Drew out on the small brick porch. The only comforting fact was that the woman turned on the carriage lights that flanked the entrance. Moments later the door opened again, revealing a large, heavyset man, also in a bathrobe, broad of face and with a chest and shoulders that qualified him as a potential linebacker who would not need much padding. Beyond his menacing size, Latham's eyes were drawn to the bulge in his right bathrobe pocket; the black steel of an automatic's handle was clearly visible through the gap at the top.

'What business do you have with the *patron*, monsieur?' asked the man in a surprisingly gentle voice.

'Government business,' answered Drew, again holding out his identification. 'It can be relayed only to Monsieur Lavolette himself.' The chauffeur took the ID and studied it in the foyer's light.

'The American government?'

'My branch is intelligence, I work with the Deuxième.'

'*Ahh*, the Deuxième, the Service d'Etranger, the secret corps of the Sûreté, and now the Americans. When will you leave the *patron* alone?'

'He's a man of great experience and wisdom, and there are always urgent matters.'

'He's also an old man who needs his sleep, especially since

his wife passed away. He spends exhausting hours in his chapel speaking to her and God.'

'Still, I *have* to see him. He'd want me to; a friend of his could be in terrible trouble over an event that concerns the governments of France and the United States.'

'You people always scream "emergency", and when your conditions are met, you sit on the information for weeks, months, even years.'

'How do you know that?'

'Because I worked for you people for years, and that's all I'll say about it. Tell me, why should I believe you?'

'Because, goddammit, I'm here! At one-thirty in the morning.'

'Why not eight-thirty, or nine-thirty, so the *patron* can sleep?' The question was asked innocently; there was no threat whatsoever in the chauffeur's voice.

'Come on, man, you're busting my chops! Has it occurred to you that I'd rather be home with my wife and three children?'

The lie was interrupted by a loud whirring sound. Instinctively, the huge man turned as the door swung open farther, exposing the foyer and a long hallway. At the end of the hall was a small brass-webbed door; in seconds a miniature elevator descended into view. '*Hugo!*' cried the frail voice of the white-haired figure inside. 'What is it, Hugo? I heard the bell and then people arguing in English.'

'It would be better if you kept your door closed, *patron*. You would not be awakened.'

'Come, come, you overprotect me. Now help me out of this damn thing, I wasn't really sleeping anyway.'

'But Anna said you didn't eat well and then spent two hours on your knees in the chapel.'

'All to good purpose, my son,' said the former Father Antoine Lavolette. Helped from the elevator chair, he cautiously stepped into the hallway. He was a reed of a man in his red-checked bathrobe, over six feet in height but thin to the point of emaciation. His face had the chiselled features of a Gothic saint – an aquiline nose, severe eyebrows, and wide-open eyes. 'I truly believe God is hearing my prayers. I said to Him that since He created everything, He was responsible for my feelings about my wife. I even scolded Him, pointing out that neither His Son nor the Holy Scriptures ever said anything forbidding a priest to marry.'

'I'm certain He heard you, *patron*.'

'If He didn't, I shall loudly complain about my constantly painful kneecaps, if I ever greet Him. I wonder if our Lord God has knees that must bend. But, of course, He does, we're made in His image – that may have been a big mistake.' The old man stopped in front of Latham, who was now standing in the hallway. 'Well, well, whom do we have here? Are you the intruder who breaks into the tent of night?'

'I am, sir. My name is Latham, and I'm with the American Embassy, an officer with the United States Consular Operations. Your chauffeur is still holding my identification in his hand.'

'For heaven's sake, give it back to him, Hugo, you're finished with all that nonsense,' instructed the former priest, suddenly shaken, his head trembling.

'Nonsense, sir?' said Drew.

'My friend Hugo was among the Praetorian guards recruited from the Foreign Legion and sent to Command Saigon when he was a young man. You left him behind, but he got himself out.'

'He speaks English very well.'

'He should, he was a special activities officer under the direction of the Americans.'

'I never heard of any Praetorian guard or of French officers in Saigon.'

'*Praetorian* was a euphemism for suicide squads, and there were many things you never heard of in that action. The Americans paid them ten times what they could make in the Legion; they brought back information from behind the lines. You people forget so easily. French was a language far better known than English among the ruling cadres in Southeast Asia . . . Now, why are you here?'

'Father Manfried Neuman.'

'I see,' said Lavolette, staring at Latham, their eyes level, for the former priest was as tall as Drew. 'Escort us into the library, Hugo, and relieve Monsieur Latham of his weapon, which you will keep in your possession until we're finished.'

'*Oui, patron.*' The chauffeur held out Latham's identification while simultaneously signalling with the fingers of his right hand that Drew give him his gun. Noting that Hugo's stare centred on the slight bulge on the left side of his jacket, Latham reached in slowly and removed his automatic. '*Merci, monsieur,*' said the chauffeur, taking the gun and handing Drew his ID card case. He took his *patron's* elbow and led them through an archway into a book-lined room profuse with heavy leather chairs and marble tables.

'Make yourself comfortable, Monsieur Latham,' said Lavolette, sitting in an upright chair, gesturing for Drew to sit across from him. 'Would you care for something to drink? I know I would. Conversations at this hour require a touch of the grape, I believe.'

'I'll have whatever you have.'

'From the same bottle, of course,' said the former priest, smiling. 'Two Courvoisiers, Hugo.'

'Good choice,' said Latham, looking around the elegant, high-ceilinged library. 'This is a lovely room,' he said.

'Being an avid reader, it suits my purpose,' agreed Lavolette. 'Guests are frequently astonished when they ask me if I've read every volume, and I answer, "Usually two or three times."'

'That's a lot of reading.'

'When you reach my age, Monsieur Latham, you'll find that words are far more permanent than the fleeting images on television.'

'Some people say one picture is worth a thousand words.'

'One photograph out of ten thousand, perhaps, I will not

deny that. However, one exhausts the familiar, doesn't one, even a painting.'

'I wouldn't know. I haven't thought that much about it.'

'No, you probably haven't had time. At your age I never did.' Their snifters of brandy arrived, the liqueur in each precisely an inch from the bottom. 'Thank you, Hugo,' continued the retired cryptologist and former priest, 'and if you'd close the doors and wait in the foyer, I'd be most pleased.'

'*Oui, patron,*' said the chauffeur, leaving the room and pulling shut the heavy double doors.

'All right, Drew Latham, how much do you know about me?' asked Lavolette sharply.

'That you left the priesthood for marriage, and when you were quite young you were a cryptographer for French intelligence. Other than that, virtually nothing. Except, of course, Manfried Neuman. He told me you're helping him with his problem.'

'No one can help him but a trained behavioural psychiatrist, which I've implored him to seek.'

'He says you're giving him religious counselling because you had the same problem.'

'That is the *merde* of the bull, as you Americans say. I fell in love with one woman and stayed faithful to her for forty years. Neuman has the impulse to fornicate with many women, selectivity being merely a result of time and place and maximum opportunity. I've begged him repeatedly to seek help before he destroys himself . . . You came here at this hour to tell me *that*?'

'You know I didn't. You know why I'm here because I saw your expression when I said who I was. You tried to hide your reaction, but it was as if you'd been punched in the stomach. Neuman told you about me and you told somebody else. *Who*?'

'You don't understand, none of you can ever understand,' choked Lavolette, breathing deeply.

'Understand *what*?'

'They have us all with ropes around our necks, not just *our* necks – that would be easy to dispense with – but *others*, so many others!'

'Neuman told you who a Colonel Webster was, didn't he? That he was a man named Latham!'

'Not willingly. I extracted it from him, for I knew the situation. I *had* to.'

'*Why?*'

'Please, I'm an old man and have very little time. Do not make my life any more complicated than it is.'

'Let me tell you, Father, your gorilla out there may have my weapon, but my hands are as good as any gun. What the hell did you *do*?'

'Listen to me, my son.' Lavolette drank his brandy in two swallows, the tremble in his hand returning. 'My wife was German. I met her when the Holy See posted me to the Church of the Blessed Sacrament in Mannheim after the war. She was married with two children and an abusive husband, a former Wehrmacht officer who ran an insurance company. We fell in love, desperately in love, and I left the Church so we could be together for the rest of our lives. She divorced her husband in a Swiss court, but by German law he kept the children . . . They grew up and had children of their own, and then their children began to have children. There are sixteen in the two families that are my dear wife's bloodline, and she was devoted to them, as I was to be.'

'She kept in touch with them, then?'

'Oh, yes. We had moved to France, where I started my businesses, aided in no small measure by my former colleagues in the services, and as the years went by, the children frequently came to visit us, both here in Paris and during the summers at our house in Nice. I came to love them as my own.'

'I'm surprised their father even let them see their mother,' said Drew.

'I don't think he cared one way or the other, except for the expenses, which I was happy to provide. He remarried and had three more children with his second wife. The first two children, my wife's, were more an impediment, I believe, reminding him of a meddling priest who had broken his vows and upset a German businessman's life. A Wehrmacht officer's life . . . Now do you begin to understand?'

'My *God*,' whispered Latham, his eyes once again locked with those of Lavolette. 'It's a trade-off. He's still a Nazi.'

'Exactly, except that he is no longer a factor, he passed away several years ago. However, he left survivors, tokens readily accepted by the movement.'

'His own children and their children, perfect inroads to a former priest, once highly regarded and still in the confidence of French intelligence. A trade-off, and I'm the chess piece.'

'Your life, Mr Latham, for the lives of sixteen innocent men, women, and children, pawns, indeed, in a deadly game they know nothing about. What would you have done in my place?'

'Probably what you did,' acknowledged Drew. 'Now, what *did* you do? Whom did you reach?'

'They could all be killed, you understand that?'

'Not if it's done right, and I'll do my best to do it right. Nobody knows I came here, that's on your side. *Tell* me!'

'There's a man. I loathe to say it, another clergyman, but not of my Church. A Lutheran minister and rather young, late thirties or early forties, I'd say. He is their leader here in Paris, the main contact to the Nazi hierarchy both in Bonn and Berlin. His name is Reverend Wilhelm Koenig, his place of worship is Neuilly-sur-Seine, it's the only Lutheran church in the district.'

'You've met him?'

'Never. When there are papers to be delivered to him, I send a parishioner in the interest of our Christian Alliance Association, either someone very old or very young whose only concern is the francs they make. Naturally, I questioned a few and learned his approximate age and description.'

'What does he look like?'

'He's quite short and very athletic, very muscular. He has a gymnasium, where there are various machines and weights to lift, in the basement of his parish hall. He meets messengers there, without his collar, and always sitting on one of those stationary bicycles, or a torso vehicle, apparently to conceal his lack of height.'

'You are assuming that, of course.'

'I worked for French intelligence, monsieur, but I didn't need its training to learn that. I sent a devout twelve-year-old to deliver a packet to him, and Koenig was so excited, he got off whatever machine he was on, and the boy said to me, "I don't think he's as big as me, Father, but, my God, he's all muscle."'

'He shouldn't be hard to spot, then,' said Latham, finishing his brandy and getting up from the chair. 'Does Koenig have a code name?'

'Yes, known to no more than five people in all France. It is Heracles, a son of Zeus in Greek mythology.'

'Thank you, Monsieur Lavolette, and I'll try to protect your wife's people in Germany. But as I told someone else tonight, that's all I can promise. There's another who comes first.'

'Go with God, my son. Many think I've lost my privilege to say that, but I'm convinced He hasn't lost faith in me. Sometimes this is a terrible world, and we must all act with the free will He decreed for us.'

'I've got a few problems with that scenario, *Father* Lavolette, but I won't burden you with them.'

'Thank you for not doing so. Hugo will return your weapon and see you out.'

'I have a last request, if I may?'

'That depends on what it is, doesn't it?'

'A length of cord or wire, ten feet long should be enough.'

'What for?'

'I'm not sure yet. I just think I should have it.'

'You field people were always so esoteric.'

'It goes with the territory,' said Drew quietly. 'When we

don't know what's ahead, we try to imagine the possibilities. There aren't so many.'

'Hugo will find you what you need. Tell him to look in the pantry.'

It was ten past three in the morning when Drew reached the Lutheran parish in Neuilly-sur-Seine. He dismissed the taxi and approached the church, which was attached to a rectory by a short, closed-in colonnade. All was dark, but the clear night sky, illuminated by a bright Paris moon, sharply defined the two separate structures. Latham spent nearly twenty minutes walking around the area, studying each ground-floor window and door, focusing on the private quarters of the rectory where the neo leader lived. The church could be broken into easily, but not the private quarters; they were wired to the hilt, metallic alarm strips showing everywhere.

To trigger the alarm might shock the Nazi, but it would also be the most negative sort of warning. Drew had the address and number of the parish. He pulled the portable phone issued by Witkowski from a jacket pocket, and then his slim notebook from another. He considered his words, read the number, then dialled.

'*Allô allô!*' said the high-pitched male voice on the second ring.

'I'll speak English, for I'm a Sonnenkind born and brought up in America—'

'*What?*'

'I flew over for a conference in Berlin and was instructed to contact Heracles before I returned to New York. My plane was delayed by weather or else I would have reached you hours ago, and my flight to the States is in three hours. We must meet. *Now.*'

'Berlin ... "Heracles" ...? Who *are* you?'

'I don't like repeating myself. I am a Sonnenkind, the *Führer* of the Sonnenkinder in America, and I demand respect from you. I have information you must be given.'

538

'Where are you?'

'Ten metres from your front door.'

'*Mein Gott!* I've heard nothing of this!'

'There wasn't time; the usual channels could not be used, for you've been compromised.'

'I cannot *believe* this!'

'Believe, or I'll use this phone to reach Berlin, even Bonn, and other instructions will be issued that will remove Heracles from his post. Come down and meet me within thirty seconds or I call Berlin.'

'No! Wait! I'm coming!'

Well before a minute had passed, the lights on the upper floors were turned on, followed by the lights below. The front door opened and the Reverend Wilhelm Koenig, in pyjamas and draped in a blue shawl, appeared. Drew studied him from the shadows of the lawn. He was, indeed, a small man, but with massive shoulders and thick legs, not unlike a bull mastiff, the legs severely bowed. And like a huge bulldog, his large, pinched face was set in defiance, as if prepared to attack.

Latham walked out of the darkness of the lawn into the light of the entrance. 'Please, come here, Heracles. We'll talk outside.'

'Why do you not come in? There's a chill in the air; it's far more comfortable inside.'

'I'm not cold at all,' said Drew. 'As a matter of fact, it's rather warm and humid.'

'Then our air-conditioning would be preferable, would it not?'

'My instructions were not to have any conversations within your rectory; the assumption was obvious.'

'That I'd tape whatever we said, incriminating *myself*?' cried Koenig in a harsh whisper, stepping outside. 'Are you *verrückt*?'

'Another more reasonable assumption could be made.'

'Such as?'

'The house is wired by the French.'

'Impossible! We have devices perpetually in operation that would reveal any invasion.'

'New technology is born every day, Reverend. Come on, humour our superiors in Berlin even if they're wrong. Frankly, we both must.'

'Very well.' Koenig started to walk down the single porch step, when Drew stopped him.

'Hold it.'

'What?'

'Turn off the lights and close the door. Neither of us wants a cruising police car to stop, do we?'

'You have a point.'

'Who else is in the house?'

'My assistant, whose rooms are in the attic, and my two hounds who remain in the kitchen until I summon them.'

'Can you turn off the upstairs lights from down there?'

'The hallway, yes, not the bedroom.'

'Turn them off too.'

'You're excessively cautious, Herr Sonnenkind.'

'A product of my training, Herr Demeter.'

The minister went inside; seconds later the main lights, both upstairs and downstairs, were extinguished, when suddenly Koenig shouted, '*Hunde! Aufrug!*' When the neo leader returned to the darkened doorway, the moonlight revealed two additional figures, one on either side of him. They were low to the ground, large-headed, barrel-chested, and each poised on four slightly bowed legs. The reverend's dogs were not unlike the reverend himself; they were pit bulls. 'These are my friends, Donner and Blitzen; the parishioners' children like the names. They are completely harmless unless I give them a specific command, which, of course, I cannot repeat because they would tear you to pieces.'

'Berlin wouldn't like that.'

'Then don't give me any reason to use it,' continued Koenig, walking out on the lawn, his guards waddling beside him. 'And please, no comments about owners looking like their pets, or vice versa. I hear that all the time.'

'I can't imagine why. You're somewhat taller.'

'You're not amusing, Sonnenkind,' said the Nazi, looking up at Drew and throwing his wide blue shawl over his shoulder, concealing his left hand. It was not difficult to know what Koenig held under the cloth. 'What is this information from Berlin? I'll reconfirm it, of course.'

'Not from this house, you won't,' contradicted Latham firmly. 'Go down the street, or even better, into another district, and call all you want to, but not from here. You're in enough trouble, don't compound it. That's a bit of friendly advice.'

'They're *serious*, then? They believe that with all of my precautions, I am compromised?'

'They certainly do, Heracles.'

'On what *basis*?'

'First, they want to know if you have the woman.'

'De Vries?'

'I think that was the name, I'm not sure; the connection was terrible. I'm to reach Berlin within the hour.'

'How would they even know about her? We haven't filed our report! We're waiting for results.'

'I assume they have moles in French intelligence, the Sûreté, organizations like that ... Look, Koenig, I don't care to know anything that's not in my orbit, I have enough problems of my own back in the States. Just give me the answers I can relay to our superiors. Have you got whoever this woman is?'

'Of course we do.'

'You haven't killed her.' A statement, not a question.

'Not yet. In a few hours we will if she doesn't produce results. We'll drop her body off at the steps of the American Embassy.'

'What results? And don't give me a bunch of complicated facts – just sketch it out so they'll be satisfied. Believe me, it's in your interest.'

'All right. At the first light our unit will reach her lover, this Latham, telling him that if he ever wants to see her alive, he'll come to a rendezvous, a park or a monument, someplace where several of our expert snipers can conceal themselves. When he arrives, a barrage of gunfire will kill them both.'

'Where is this rendezvous?'

'That's the unit's decision, not mine. I have no idea.'

'Where is she being held now?'

'Why would that concern Berlin?' The neo-Nazi suddenly squinted, staring questioningly at Drew. 'They've never wanted such tactical information before.'

'How the hell do *I* know?' At the raising of his voice, the deadly pit bulls growled. 'I'm simply repeating what they told me to ask!' Latham, in his anxiety, could feel the perspiration rolling down his face. *Control*, goddammit, *control!* Only a few more moments!

'All right. Why not?' said the short pit bull on two legs. 'What's in motion can't be derailed by men who are five hundred miles away. She's in a flat on the rue Lacoste, number twenty-three.'

'What flat?'

'The unit never told me. It was for rent and they don't even have a telephone. Naturally, by this morning they'll disappear, and a landlord will have several months' rent and no tenants.'

Step one, thought Drew. *Step two* was to get rid of the goddamn dogs and have Koenig to himself. 'That seems to me all that Berlin can demand,' he said.

'Now, what is the information I'm to be given?' asked the Lutheran neo.

'Orders more than information,' said Latham. 'You're to temporarily close down all activities, neither issuing nor accepting instructions from anyone. When the time is right, Berlin will reach you and tell you to resume operations. Furthermore, should you care to confirm your orders from me, do so at the lowest levels, preferably through Spain or Portugal.'

'This is *insane!*' choked the diminutive prelate as the two dogs growled and snapped their teeth simultaneously. '*Halten!*' he yelled, quieting the animals. 'I am the most secure man in France!'

'They told me to tell you that's what someone called André thought, and now he's finished.'

'*André?*'

'You heard me – and I don't know who he is or what it means.'

'*Mein Gott.* André!' The Nazi's voice grew weak, confusion and fear in his expression. 'He was so *getarnt!*'

'Sorry, I'm not with you, the cells in America don't want all of us to know German. They figured it was a trip point.'

'He was beyond unearthing.'

'I guess he wasn't. Berlin said something about his going back to Strasbourg, wherever the hell that is.'

'*Strasbourg?* Then you *know.*'

'Not a damn thing, and I don't want to. I just want to get to Heathrow and a plane to Chicago.'

'What am I to *do?*'

'I told you before, Heracles. In the morning you call your relays in Spain or Portugal – from a phone far away from here – confirm my orders, and do as Berlin says. How much clearer can I *be?*'

'Everything is so confusing—'

'Confusing, hell,' said Latham, starting to take Koenig's elbow, when the pit bulls snarled. 'Come on, tell your hounds to get inside and I'll follow you. If nothing else, you owe me a drink.'

'Oh, certainly ... *Rein*,' ordered Koenig as the two pit bulls raced through the open door. 'There we are, Herr Sonnenkind, come inside.'

'Not yet,' said Drew, suddenly slamming the door closed and yanking the neo outside, stripping the blue shawl off his shoulders, revealing the small automatic in his left hand.

Before the confused Koenig could react, Latham gripped the weapon, twisting it violently counterclockwise, expecting either the Nazi's wrist to snap or the gun to fall free; it loosened as Koenig's fingers spread in agony. Drew grabbed it and flung it into the dark grass.

What followed was nothing short of a life-and-death struggle between two human animals, pit bulls, perhaps, each possessing an agenda that consumed him, one ideological, the other intensely personal. Koenig was a hissing, attacking cat, thrusts and claws deadly; Latham was the larger, snarling wolf, fangs bared, constantly lunging for the throat – in the present case, any appendage he could grab on to, hold, and immobilize. In the end, the wolf's size and marginally superior strength prevailed. Both animals, bloodied and exhausted, knew who had won the battle. Koenig lay on the ground, one arm broken, the other sprained, the thigh muscles of both legs partially paralysed. Latham, his hands scraped and bleeding, his chest and stomach pummelled almost to the point of vomiting, stood over the Nazi and spat in the direction of his face.

Drew knelt down, pulling the length of coiled cord provided by Hugo out of his belt, and proceeded to tie up the neo leader, legs and arms connected behind Koenig's spine; with each struggle the lines grew tighter. Finally, Latham tore the blue shawl in strips, as he had done with the sheets at the Normandie hotel, and gagged the ersatz minister of God. Glancing at his watch, he dragged Koenig into the bushes, chopped him into unconsciousness, yanked out his telephone, and dialled Stanley Witkowski.

CHAPTER THIRTY-TWO

'You son of a *bitch*!' roared the colonel. 'Moreau wants your ass in front of a firing squad, and I can't say as I blame him one bit!'

'His two men got loose, then?'

'What did you think you were *doing*? What *are* you doing?'

'If you'll calm down for a moment or two, I'll fill you in.'

'Me calm down? Oh, I've got a *lot* to be calm about. Courtland's to be ordered to the Quai d'Orsay in the morning to take the whacks for you; you're being declared persona non grata and thrown out of the country; a formal protest is being lodged against me by a foreign government, and you tell me to be *calm*?'

'Moreau's behind all this?'

'It's not Tinker Bell.'

'Then we can control it.'

'Are you *listening* to me? You assaulted two Deuxième agents, blindsided them, and held them hostage by roping them up without communication for hours, thereby disrupting a major *French* intelligence investigation!'

'Yes, but, Stanley, I made progress, the kind of progress Moreau wants more than anything else.'

'What . . . ?'

'Send a marine unit out to a Lutheran church in Neuilly-sur-Seine.' Latham gave Witkowski the address and described the bound Koenig in the bushes. 'He's the high honcho of the neo movement in Paris, higher, I think, than Strasbourg, at least his cover's better.'

545

'How did you find him?'

'There's no time for that now. Call Moreau and have the marines take Koenig to the Deuxième Bureau. Tell Claude from me it's a bona fide.'

'He'll want more than a roughed-up Lutheran minister. *Jesus*, you could be a nut and he'd be drummed out of his job, facing all kinds of lawsuits!'

'No way. Koenig's code name is Heracles, something out of mythology.'

'Greek mythology?' interrupted the colonel. 'Heracles is a son of Zeus, known for feats of strength.'

'That's nice,' said Drew pleasantly. 'Now, get things moving, which shouldn't take you more than a minute or two. Then I want you to meet me—'

'Meet you? I may blow your brains out!'

'Postpone it, Stanley. I know where they've got Karin.'

'*What?*'

'Twenty-three rue Lacoste, flat unknown, but just recently rented.'

'You sprung this from the padre?'

'Actually, it wasn't difficult. He was frightened.'

'He was what . . . ?'

'No *time*, Stosh! It's got to be just you and me. If they even sense a conversion, or see a strange car or two parking on the street at this hour, they'll kill her. They intend to do just that in an hour or so anyway if they don't reach me and pull me out.'

'I'll meet you a hundred yards east of the building, between streetlights, the darkest storefront or alley.'

'Thank you, Stanley, I mean that. I know when a solo operation has to be added to, and there's no one better than you.'

'I don't have a choice. There's no way you could come up with a code like Heracles unless it was real.'

Karin de Vries sat in the straight chair, her hands tied behind her, a slender, broad-shouldered neo killer sitting in front of her, his legs straddling the seat of a wooden kitchen chair, his arms across the back, a pistol casually in his right hand, a pistol with a large cylinder attached to the barrel. A silencer.

'Why do you think your husband is alive, Frau de Vries?' asked the Nazi in German. 'More to the point, if by an impossible stretch of the imagination he is, why should we know anything about him? Really, my good woman, he was executed by the Stasi, that's common knowledge.'

'It may be common knowledge, but it's a lie. If you live with a man for eight years, you know his voice when you hear it, no matter how garbled or incoherent.'

'That's fascinating. You heard his voice?'

'Twice.'

'The Stasi files say otherwise, most graphically, I might add.'

'That's the problem,' said Karin icily. 'It was too graphic.'

'You're not making sense.'

'Even the most vicious of the Gestapo did not describe in detail the torture and execution of prisoners. It wasn't in their interest.'

'That was before my time.'

'Mine also, but there are records. Perhaps you should read them.'

'I don't need instructions from you, madame ... These voices, how did you hear them?'

'How else? The telephone, of course.'

'The *telephone*? He *called* you?'

'Not using his name, but with a diatribe of invective I was subjected to frequently during the last year of our marriage, before he was presumably executed by the Stasi.'

'Of course you challenged this person on the telephone, did you not?'

'That's only made his screams become more manic. My husband's a very sick man, Herr Nazi.'

'I take the appellation as a compliment,' said the neo,

grinning and twirling the pistol in his hand. 'Why do you say your husband's sick, or, to put it another way, why do you tell me?'

'Because I think he's one of you.'

'One of *us*?' asked the German incredulously. '"Freddie de V," the Amsterdam provocateur, the consummate enemy of the movement? Forgive me, Frau de Vries, but now you've *lost* your senses! How could such a thing happen?'

'He fell in love with hate, and you people are the personification of hatred.'

'You're beyond me.'

'I'm beyond myself, for I'm no psychologist, but I know I'm right. His sense of hate had nowhere else to go, but he couldn't live without it. You did something to him – as to what, I have a theory, but obviously no evidence. You channelled him, channelled his hatred, turning him against everything he believed in—'

'I've heard enough of this foolishness. You are truly a madwoman!'

'No, I'm quite sane. I even think I know how you did it.'

'Did *what*?'

'Turned him against his friends, your enemies.'

'And just how did we perform this miracle?'

'You made him dependent on you. During the final months, his mood swings became more extreme . . . He was away much of the time, as I was, but when we were together, he was another man, depressed one minute, violent the next. There were days when he was like a child, a little boy who wanted a toy so badly that when he didn't get it, he ran out of the apartment and was gone for hours. Then he'd come back, contrite, begging forgiveness for his outbursts.'

'*Madame*,' cried the neo, 'I haven't the slightest idea what you're talking about!'

'Drugs, Herr Nazi, I'm talking about drugs. I believe you supply Frederik with narcotics, that's why he's dependent on you. No doubt you're holding him in a mountain retreat somewhere, feeding his habit or habits, extracting information from him with every move that's made against you. He is a treasure house of secrets, even secrets he's forgotten.'

'You are insane. If we had such a man, there are other drugs that could produce those secrets in a matter of minutes. Why should we spend time and money prolonging his life?'

'Because the Amytals and the scopolamine derivatives cannot produce secrets that are no longer remembered.'

'So what good is such a source?'

'Situations change, circumstances vary. You run into an obstacle, be it a man or a strategy, you face him with it, and memories come back. Identities can be revealed, once-familiar tactics explained.'

'My God, you've read too much fiction.'

'Our world – yours, and not too long ago, mine – is largely based on fictitious hypotheticals.'

'Enough! You're too academic for me ... However, a question, Frau de Vries. Given a fictitious hypothetical, as you call it, say you're correct and we have your husband under the conditions you describe. Why do you want to find him? Do you seek a reunion?'

'That is the last thing I wish for, Nazi.'

'Then why?'

'You could say I want to satisfy my morbid curiosity. What makes a man become another human being from the one you knew? How can he live with himself? ... Or, you might say, if it was in my power, I'd like to see him dead.'

'Those are serious words,' said the neo, leaning back in the chair, his pistol mockingly pointed at his head. '*Boom!* You would do that if you could?'

'Probably.'

'But of course! You've found another, haven't you? An officer of American intelligence, a very accomplished deep-cover operative for the Central Intelligence Agency named Harry Latham.'

Karin froze, her expression immobile. 'That is irrelevant, *he* is irrelevant.'

'We don't think so, madame. You are lovers, we've established that.'

'Establish what you like, it doesn't change the reality. Why are you interested in ... Harry Latham?'

'You know why as well as I do.' The neo grinned, placing both heels on the floor as he straddled the chair, a laughing cavalier on horseback. 'He knows too much about us. He penetrated our former headquarters in the Hausruck and saw things, learned things, he should not have seen or learned. But it's merely a question of an hour, perhaps two, and he will no longer be a thorn to our superiors. We will follow orders down to the letter, including a coup de grâce in the left side of his skull. You see how wonderfully specific we are? We're not hypothetical at all, and certainly not fictitious. We are the reality, you're the fiction. You can do nothing to stop us.'

'Why his skull, the left side of his skull?' asked De Vries in a monotone, mesmerized by the Nazi's words.

'We wondered about that, but then one of our younger recruits, a very educated fellow, supplied the answer. It goes back to the seventeen hundreds, when condemned soldiers were executed by a single officer. If the condemned man had shown valour in battle, he was shot on the right side of his head; if he had no redeeming qualities, he was shot on the left side – *sinistra* in Italian, where the custom began, sinister in English. Harry Latham is filth, need I say more?'

'That strikes me as a barbaric ritual,' said Karin, barely audibly as she stared at the lean, muscular assassin.

'Rituals, dear lady, are the basis of all discipline. The further back they go, the more ingrained they are, the more to be worshipped.'

There was a brief sound of static from an adjoining room, followed by a muffled male voice speaking in German. The voice stopped and moments later another neo appeared in the doorway, this one younger than De Vries's interrogator, but no less lean and muscular. 'That was Berlin on the radio,' he said. 'The Paris authorities are in the dark, they've traced nothing, so we're to proceed on schedule.'

'It was a useless communication. How could they trace anything?'

'Well, there were the bodies outside the Normandie hotel—'

'And a Deuxième vehicle at the bottom of the Seine. So what?'

'They said to make sure that everything – well, you know what I mean – the Château de Vincennes, north of the Bois.'

'Yes, I know what you mean and what Berlin means. Anything else?'

'It will begin to be light in an hour.'

'Helmut is in place, no?'

'He is, and with the words he's to say.'

'Tell him to make the call in twenty minutes.'

'But it will still be dark.'

'I'm aware of that. Better for us to be in place and reconnoitre, no?'

'As always, you're brilliant, sir.'

'I'm aware of that too. *Go!*' The second neo disappeared and the interrogator turned to Karin. 'I'm afraid I must tape your mouth, Frau de Vries, quite extensively. Then I will untie the ropes and you will accompany us.'

'Where are we going, other than to my death?'

'Do not be so pessimistic. Killing you is not a priority with us.'

'And Hitler protected the Jews.'

'*Ach*, you really can be amusing.'

Latham made contact with Witkowski roughly eighty yards east of 23 rue Lacoste, in a dark, narrow alleyway. 'Good spot,' said Drew.

'There wasn't any other. I don't know who pays the electric bills for the City of Lights, but they've got to be horrendous.'

'Speaking of lights, that's the only way we'll be able to centre in on the flat.'

'Wrong,' said the colonel. 'It's on the fifth floor, west corner.'

'You're kidding.'

'I don't kid when I'm carrying two automatics with custom-made silencers, four clips of ammunition, and a cut-down version of a MAC-10 under this raincoat.'

'How did you find out?'

'Thank Moreau, who still wants your ass, but he received your package.'

'Koenig?'

'That's right. Funny thing is, the Sûreté had the good prelate in their files.'

'As a *neo*?'

'No, his predilection for choirboys. Five anonymous complaints had been registered.'

'What about the flat?'

'Claude ran a trace on the owner of the building, the rest was easy. Nobody wants to mess with an agency that can bring down the bureaus of taxation and public health on his head.'

'Stanley, you are a wonder.'

'I'm not, Moreau is, and part of the deal is that you apologize to his men, buy them very expensive gifts, and take them to a very, *very* expensive dinner at the Tour d'Argent. With their families.'

'That's two months' salary!'

'I accepted for you ... Now, let's figure out how we do this without any backup.'

'First we get inside, then climb the stairs,' replied Latham. 'Very quietly and carefully.'

'They'll have patrols on the staircases. Better an elevator. We'll be two drunks singing something like "Auprès de Ma Blonde", loud but not too loud.'

'Not bad, Stosh.'

'I was around when you were sending away for code rings

from cereal boxes. We take the elevator to the sixth or seventh floor and walk down. But you're right about being quiet and careful, I'll give you that.'

'Thanks for the compliment. I'll put it on my résumé.'

'If you get out of this, you may need one quicker than you think. I have an idea Wesley Sorenson would like to see you stationed in a Mongolian outpost. Now let's go. Stay close to the buildings; from the fifth floor, their line of sight is negative.'

Latham and Witkowski, one behind the other, scrambled up the Lacoste, successively ducking into doorways until they reached Number 23. The entrance was at ground level; they entered the hallway, tested the locked foyer door, then studied the list of flats and occupants. 'I know how to do this,' said the colonel, his hand reaching to press the button for an apartment on the ninth floor. When a startled, sleepy female voice responded on the speaker, he answered in fluent French. 'My name is Capitaine Louis d'Ambert of the Sûreté. You may call my office to confirm my identity, but time is of the essence. There is a dangerous person in this building who could bring harm to the tenants. We must gain entrance and arrest him. Here, let me give you the number of my Sûreté office so you can verify my authority.'

'Don't bother!' said the woman. 'Crime these days, it's everywhere – criminals, murderers, in our own buildings!' The buzzer sounded and Drew and Witkowski were inside.

The elevator was on the left; the panel above it showed the car was on the fourth floor. Latham pushed the button; the inner machinery cranked instantly. As the door slid open, a light on the panel inside indicated that someone on the fifth floor had pressed the red button, indicating descent.

'We've got the priority,' said Stanley. 'Press the second floor.'

'It's the *neos*,' whispered Drew. 'It's *got* to be them!'

'At this hour, I figure you're right,' agreed the colonel. 'So we'll get off, walk down the stairs, stay way back in the hallway, and see if our instincts still have merit.'

They did. Racing back to the ground floor, they crouched at the end of the tiled foyer and watched as the elevator door opened and Karin de Vries, her face taped, came into view, accompanied by three men, all dressed in ordinary civilian clothing.

'*Halt!*' shouted Witkowski, lunging out of the shadows, Latham at his side, their weapons levelled. The farthest neo spun around, reaching for his shoulder holster. The colonel fired a silenced automatic; the man spun again, grabbing his arm and falling to the ground. 'This was easier than I thought, *chłopak*,' continued Witkowski, 'these super Aryans aren't as smart as they think they are.'

'*Nein!*' shrieked the obvious leader of the trio, grabbing Karin and shielding himself with her, then yanking out a pistol. 'You make one move, this woman *dies*!' he shouted, the gun at De Vries's right temple.

'Then I must have shown valour in battle,' said Karin coldly, stripping the tape off her face.

'*Was?*'

'You made it plain that you had to administer the coup de grâce on *Harry* Latham at the *left* side of his skull. Your weapon is on my right.'

'*Halt's Maul!*'

'I'm only glad that you don't consider me filth, that I'm not a coward. My execution at least will be honourable.'

'Be *quiet!*' The neo leader dragged her, heels scraping, towards the door. 'Drop your firearms!' he screamed.

'Drop it, Stanley,' said Drew.

'Naturally,' said the colonel.

And then a voice came from the staircase, an angry voice speaking French. 'What is all this *commotion?*' cried an elderly woman in a nightshirt, walking down the steps. 'I pay good rent to get a night's sleep after working in the bakery all day and I have to put up with *this?*'

With the sudden interruption, Karin sprang out of her captor's arms as Witkowski pulled his second automatic from under his raincoat. When De Vries ducked, he fired two shots, one into the neo's forehead, the other into his throat.

'*Mon Dieu!*' screamed the woman on the staircase, racing up the steps.

Latham ran to Karin, holding her fiercely, his arms two clamps of enormous strength. 'I'm all right, my darling, I'm all right!' she said, seeing the tears that streamed down his face. 'My poor dear,' she went on, 'it's over, Drew.'

'The *hell* it is!' yelled the colonel, holding the two live neos under his gun. The Nazi he had wounded was getting up from the floor. 'Here,' said Stanley, picking up his and Latham's weapons and handing one to De Vries. 'Cover this scumbucket who can walk, and I'll shove the other sleaze after us. You, *chłopak*, use your fancy telephone and call Durbane at the embassy! Get us wheels back there!'

'I can't do that, Stosh.'

'Why the hell *not*?'

'He may be one of them.'

It was midnight Washington time, and Wesley Sorenson studied the materials sent over by Knox Talbot from the CIA files. He had been studying them for hours, all fifty-one dossiers, looking for that relevant piece of information that would separate one suspect from the others. His concentration had been interrupted by Claude Moreau's frantic phone call from Paris, describing Latham's outrageous behaviour.

'He may be on to something, Claude,' Wesley said soothingly.

'If he was, he should have told us, not acted alone. I will not tolerate this!'

'Give him time—'

'Absolutely *no*. He's out of Paris, out of France!'

'I'll see what I can do.'

'He's already done it, *mon ami*.'

Later, after an awkward conversation with an equally furious Witkowski, Moreau had called back at five o'clock in the morning Paris time. The storm-tossed horizon began to brighten. Drew had delivered a bona fide neo in the guise of a Protestant minister.

'I must admit, he's somewhat validating his existence,' the Frenchman had said.

'Then you'll let him stay in Paris?'

'On a very tight leash, Wesley.'

Returning to the selected possibles among the material sent over by the CIA, the Cons-Op chief proceeded to weed out the obvious negatives much as Knox had done. From the remaining twenty-four, he pared further based on the time-honoured principles of motive and opportunity, plus an element Sorenson called 'why cubed', or why to the third power; beyond the first and second motives, another was invariably hidden. Finally, as a result of an adult life-time of searching for the elusive, there were three probables, to be expanded if none proved accurate. Each suspect had what he termed a 'neutral' face, physiognomies that lacked the definition of sharp features, the sort political cartoonists emphasize. Second, none held a position of influence or high profile, either of which would disqualify the risk-taking. However, each was part of, or had access to, teams of examiners, either as couriers or researchers. Third, each lived beyond his apparent means.

Peter Mason Payne. Recruitment development as per division's requirements. Married with two children; residence a $400,000 house in Vienna, Virginia, complete with a recently added pool, estimated cost, $60,000. Automobiles: Cadillac Brougham and a Range Rover.

Bruce N.M.I. Withers. Office procurement validation, one of many. Divorced, one daughter, limited visiting rights. Former wife living on Maryland's Eastern Shore, $600,000 house reportedly purchased by her parents. Subject's residence, condominium in Fairfax's high-rent district. Automobile: Jaguar SJ6.

Roland Vasquez-Ramirez. Third-level researcher and coordinator, of whom there were four, with the upper two levels. Married, no children. Residence, upscale garden apartment complex in Arlington. Wife, a bottom-rung attorney at the Justice Department. Known frequenters of expensive restaurants, clothes custom-made. Automobiles: Porsche and Lexus.

Those were the essential facts, none provably relevant until one studied the inter-Agency relationships. Peter Mason Payne sought recruits as specific abilities were required. Perforce, he had to question the various divisions and legitimately ask for examples of subject matter to gain a clearer picture. Bruce Withers's job was to justify the enormous expenditures for office equipment, including complex electronics. Quite correctly, he had to observe, even operate, certain machines himself, in order to ask a superior to sign off on huge purchase orders. Roland Vasquez-Ramirez coordinated the flow of information among three levels of researchers. Granted, there were extraordinary restrictions, sealed envelopes, et al., and a man violating them would not only lose his job but conceivably be prosecuted. Nevertheless, those restrictions often innocently violated in the interest of expedience, would not stop an enemy of the state who did so with an absence of innocence.

All three men fitted the composite of the neo mole. They had the motives to maintain their lifestyles, opportunities due to the access their positions permitted ... what was lacking was the abstract 'why cubed'. What drove any of them to go beyond all that and become a traitor? A Nazi who had killed two captured Nazis. And then he thought he might have found it, but only *might have*. Each candidate was essentially a messenger, a liaison between superiors; none had real authority himself. Payne studied résumés of applicants, and those he advanced soon made far more money than he did. Withers could only recommend extraordinary purchases, purchases that made those demanding them even more efficient – and how many were on the receiving end of kickbacks while he got nothing? SOP. And Vasquez-Ramirez was *really* a messenger, collating sealed envelopes A, B, and C, secrets for others to evaluate, while he stayed out of the loop. And each had been at his innocuous job, his decisions easily overruled, for a number of years with little chance of advancement. Such men were hotbeds of resentment.

There wasn't time to intellectualize any longer, to analyse further. Either he was right, considered Sorenson, or he was wrong, which meant going back to the drawing board. As he had taught Drew Latham in the early stages of his training, sometimes a frontal assault was best, especially if it was totally unexpected. He wondered if Drew had used the strategy in trapping the neo minister. If not specifically, concluded Wesley, certainly a variation. With the constraints of time, there wasn't much alternative. He reached for the telephone.

'Peter Mason Payne, if you please?'

'This is Pete Payne, who's this?'

'Kearns at the Agency,' answered Sorenson, using the name of a relatively well-known deputy director. 'We've never met, Pete, and I'm sorry to bother you at this hour—'

'No trouble, Mr Kearns, I'm watching television in my den. My wife went to bed; she said it was rotten and she was right.'

'Then you don't mind breaking away for a few minutes?'

'Not at all. What can I do for you, sir?'

'It's a little touchy, Pete, but the reason I'm calling you now is that you may be asked upstairs in the morning, and it's possible you might want to consider your answers.'

'*What* answers? What *questions*?' Peter Mason Payne might not be the killer mole, thought Wesley, but he was taking something from somebody. It was in the gasp that had preceded his words.

'We've had severe problems in recruitment, so we're holding evaluation meetings, have been holding them damn near around the clock. Several of your recommendations have been sorely underqualified, costing the Company a lot of wasted man-hours.'

'Then it was the résumés, or the applicants were rehearsed for interviews, Mr Kearns. I never advanced anyone I didn't believe could do the job, and I never took money under the table for a recommendation!'

'I see.' *So that was it*, mused Sorenson. *The denial was too quick, the inference had not even been made.* 'But I didn't suggest that, did I, Peter?'

'No, but I've heard the rumours – wealthy families wanting their kids in the Agency for a couple of years because it looks good when they go after other jobs . . . I'm not saying it's not *possible* a few slipped through, due, as I say, to false information and rehearsed interview responses, but you'd have to look to other recruiters for those things. *They* could supply that information, *I* never did!'

Thank God you've been kept out of the field, Mr Payne, thought the Cons-Op director, *you'd last eleven seconds*. However, Peter Payne had just led him to the conclusive question. 'Then maybe one of the others is trying to lay something on you. You see, the parents of one of our underqualified say they met with a recruiter in the early morning hours the night before last to make their final payment.'

'For Christ's sake, not *me*!'

'Where were you, Pete?'

'Hell, that's easy.' The relief in Payne's voice was, well, painful. 'My wife and I were up the street at Congressman Erlich's home for a late-night neighbourhood barbecue – late because the House stayed in session. We were there until around two-thirty in the morning, and frankly, Mr Kearns, none of us cared to get into a car and drive anywhere.'

Candidate Rejected

'Mr Bruce Withers, please?'

'No one else lives here, pal. Who are you?'

Sorenson repeated the Deputy Director Kearns introduction, now zeroing in on the constant and considerable overruns on office procurements.

'High technology's expensive, Mr Director. There's nothing I can do about that, and, frankly, it's not in my province to make those decisions.'

'But it is your province to make recommendations, isn't it?'

'Somebody has to do the initial spec work, and that's what I do.'

'Say there's a competitive bid for a more powerful computer in the range of a hundred thousand dollars. Your word means a great deal, doesn't it?'

'Not if my bosses know a megabyte from their elbows.'

'But most of them don't, do they?'

'Some do, some don't.'

'So with those who don't, your recommendation is probably accepted, wouldn't you say that?'

'Probably. I do my homework.'

'And there could be instances when the selection of a certain company could benefit you, couldn't it?'

'Stop with those kind of questions! What are you trying to pin on me?'

'A payoff was made the other night, early morning to be precise, by a Seattle firm with lobbyists here in Washington. We'd like to know if it was you.'

'This is *bullshit*,' cried Withers, almost breathless. 'Excuse me, Mr Director, but I'm deeply offended. I've been at this lousy job for seven years now because I know high tech better than anyone else, and it's *nowheresville*! I can't be replaced, so I don't go up, or even down, which has to tell you something.'

'I don't mean to offend you, Bruce, I just want to know where you were at three o'clock in the morning the night before last.'

'You don't have any right to ask that.'

'I think I do. That's when the payoff was made.'

'Listen, Mr Kearns, I'm a divorced man and I have to find my pleasures where I can, if you understand me.'

'I believe I do. Where were you?'

560

'With a married woman whose husband is out of the country. Her husband's a general.'

'Will she back you up?'

'I can't give you her name.'

'We'll find out, you know that.'

'Yeah, I guess you will . . . All right, we spent this evening here, and she just left. The general's on an inspection tour in the Far East and calls her around one o'clock – God forbid he should upset a military schedule for a lonely wife. It's the story of her marriage.'

'Very touching, Bruce. What's her name?'

'It takes her twenty, twenty-five minutes to get home.'

'Her name, please?'

'Anita Griswald, General Andrew Griswald's wife.'

'"Mad Andy" Griswald? The scourge of Vietnam's Songchow? He's pretty old, isn't he?'

'For the army, definitely. Anita's his fourth wife. She's much younger, and the Pentagon's keeping him on loose duty until they can get rid of him next year, which, I gather, they'd like to do as soon as possible.'

'Why did she ever marry him?'

'She was broke and had three kids. Enough questions, Mr Director.'

Candidate Still Open

'Mr Vasquez-Ramirez, if you please?'

'Just a moment,' said a female voice, slightly accented with Hispanic inflections. 'My husband is on the other telephone, but he will be finished quickly. Who shall I say is calling?'

'Deputy Director Kearns, Central Intelligence Agency, Counsellor.'

'You know I am a lawyer? . . . Oh, but of course you do.'

'I apologize for calling so late, but it's urgent.'

'It would have to be, señor. My husband works long hours for you, sometimes until late in the evenings. I wish you paid him accordingly, if I may be so bold to suggest. Please hold.'

Silence. *There were no records of Vasquez-Ramirez working*

late hours. Forty-five seconds later, 'Rollie' Ramirez came on the line. 'Mr Kearns, what's so urgent?'

'Leaks in your department, Mr Vasquez-Ramirez.'

'Please, we've met, sir. *Rollie* or *Ramirez* is sufficient.'

'It saves time, I'll say that.'

'Do you have a cold, Mr Kearns? You don't sound like yourself.'

'It's the flu, Ramirez. I can hardly breathe.'

'Rum, hot tea, and lemon will relieve you . . . Now, what are these leaks and how can I assist you?'

'They've been traced to your section.'

'In which there are four of us,' broke in the Hispanic. 'Why call me?'

'I'll call the others; you're first on the list.'

'Because my skin is not as pale as the others?'

'Oh, cut that out!'

'No, I don't "cut it out", for it's the truth. The spic is the first you go after.'

'Now you're insulting both me *and* you. Money was made by revealing maximum-classified information from your section two nights ago, a great deal of money, and we've got the people who paid it. At this moment it's merely a question of *who* got paid! So don't give me any crap about racism. I'm looking for a leak, not a *spic*!'

'Let me tell you this, *Americano*. My people do not pay for information, it is freely delivered. Yes, there have been times when I've steamed open the sealed envelopes, but only when they've been marked "Caribbean Basin". Why have I done this? Let me explain. I was a sixteen-year-old soldier at the Bay of Pigs and spent five years in Castro's filthy prisons until I was exchanged for medicine. This great *Estados Unidos* talks and talks but does nothing to liberate my *Cuba*!'

'How did you get into the Agency?'

'The easiest way possible, *amigo*. It took six years, but I became a scholar, with three degrees, way overqualified for what you offered me, but I accepted what you offered me, truly believing you would see my qualifications and put me into a position where I could make a difference. You never did, for I was the spic and you gravitated to the white boys and the blacks – oh, there were unqualified blacks chosen over me! You had to clean your racist slate, and they were the answer.'

'I think you're being unfair.'

'Think what you like, I'll be out of this house in twenty seconds and you'll never find me!'

'*Please*, don't do that! You're not what or whom I'm after. I'm after *Nazis*, not you!'

'What the hell are you talking about?'

'It's too complicated,' said Sorenson calmly. 'Stay on your job and do what you're doing. You'll get no grief from me, and I'll make sure your superior qualifications are brought to the attention of those who should know about them.'

'How can I count on that?'

'Because I'm a fake, I'm not with the Company. I'm the director of an outside agency that frequently coordinates with the CIA at the highest levels.'

'Circles within circles,' said Vasquez-Ramirez. 'When will it ever end?'

'Probably never,' replied Sorenson. 'Certainly not until people trust one another – which will be never.'

Candidate Possible

CHAPTER THIRTY-THREE

Suddenly it occurred to the director of Consular Operations that he should follow his immediate instincts. Peter Mason Payne was out, Roland Vasquez-Ramirez barely a possible, but the craw in his throat was Bruce Withers, the man with a quick tongue and an all-too-believable saga of a destitute widow or divorcée with three children who had latched on to an over-age general of the army, with all the retirement benefits that implied. It would be easy for Withers to reach the general's wife by car telephone, if she really had spent the evening with him, or at her home . . . *It'll take her twenty – twenty-five minutes.* More than enough time for the lonely general's wife to be given instructions. The answer might be found somewhere else. On the Eastern Shore of Maryland, perhaps, with the former wife of Bruce N.M.I. Withers.

Again Sorenson picked up his phone, hoping that Withers's name would be listed because of his teenage daughter. It was, with an alternative name, McGraw. McGraw-Withers.

'Yes . . . hello,' whispered the sleepy voice on the line.

'Forgive me, Miss McGraw, for calling you at this hour, but there is an emergency.'

'Who *are* you?'

'Deputy Director Kearns of the Central Intelligence Agency. It concerns your former husband, Bruce Withers.'

'Whom did he shaft now?' asked the barely awake ex-Mrs Withers.

'Perhaps the United States government, Miss McGraw.'

'Thanks for the Miss – I earned it. Of course, he shafted

the government, why should it be any different? He'd flash his CIA badge around, not saying much, but implying he was Mr Super Spook himself, all the while fleecing somebody.'

'He used the Agency to gain favours?'

'*Please*, Mr Whoever-you-are, my family has connections all over Washington. When we found out he was sleeping with every secretary and bimbo tramp who worked for a defence contractor, my father said we should get rid of him, and we did.'

'He still has visitation rights to your child.'

'Under the closest supervision, I can assure you.'

'Because you fear violation?'

'Good God, no. Kimberly is probably the only person in this world that bastard can relate to.'

'Why do you say that?'

'Because children don't threaten him. Her hugs erase the terrible thing inside of him.'

'What is that terrible thing, Miss McGraw?'

'He's the bigot of the world! He hates so many people, I can't begin to tell you. Blacks, or as he says, those lousy niggers, and "Wops", and "Slopes", – that's Asians – the Spanish-speaking, the Jew bastards, anyone who isn't pure white and Christian, and he's definitely *not* Christian. He wants them all eliminated. That's his credo.'

Candidate Accepted

It was four o'clock in the afternoon Paris time, the hour noted by the low, echoing chimes of a mantel clock in Ambassador Daniel Courtland's living quarters at the American Embassy. The ambassador, coatless, the bandages across his chest and left shoulder visible beneath his open blue Oxford shirt, sat at an antique table that served as a desk, talking quietly on the telephone. Across the large, ornate room, Drew Latham and Karin de Vries were sitting opposite each other in brocaded armchairs, also speaking softly.

'How's the hand?' asked Drew.

'It's fine; it's my feet, they still hurt,' answered Karin, laughing quietly.

'I told you to take off your shoes.'

'Then the soles of both feet would be scraped, my dear. How long did we walk from the Lacoste until you reached Claude to send transportation? Nearly forty minutes, I think.'

'I couldn't call Durbane. Even now we don't know where he stands, and Moreau was busy with our Nazi minister.'

'We saw three separate police cars. I'm sure any one of them would have accommodated us.'

'No, Witkowski was right about that. There were five of us, which would have meant two of those small cars or a wagon. Then there was the problem of convincing them to take us to the embassy and not to a police station, a request they'd damn well refuse considering one of the neos was wounded. Even Claude was grateful that we waited for him. As he put it, "There are already too many cooks in the kitchen." We didn't need police reports or the Sûreté.'

'And the Deuxième found no one at the Château de Vincennes?'

'Nobody with a weapon, and they swept the park clean.'

'It's surprising,' said De Vries, frowning. 'I was sure that's where the killing would take place.'

'You're sure and I can confirm it, straight from Koenig's mouth. It's the scenario he described.'

'I wonder what happened.'

'It's pretty obvious. They never got the final go-ahead, so the kill was aborted.'

'Do you realize we're talking about our own lives?'

'I'm trying to keep it clinical.'

'You're devastatingly effective.'

The doorbell of the main entrance to the living quarters rang. Latham rose from the chair and glanced at Courtland, who nodded, still on the phone. Drew crossed to the door, opened it, and admitted Stanley Witkowski. 'Any progress?' asked Drew.

'We think so,' replied the colonel. 'I'll wait till the ambassador's off the horn. He has to hear it. Did either of you get any rest?'

'I did, Stanley,' answered Karin from the chair. 'Ambassador Courtland was kind enough to let us use the guest rooms. I fell right to sleep, but my friend here couldn't stay off the phone.'

'Only after you swore it was sterile,' added Drew.

'No phone up here could be tapped by Swie'ty Piotr himself, as my dear departed mother used to call him. Whom did you reach, *chłopak*?'

'Back and forth with Sorenson. He's made progress too.'

'Any word on the Virginia assassin?'

'He's nailed him. That son of a bitch can't go to the toilet without being heard.'

Daniel Courtland hung up the telephone, awkwardly turning in his chair, wincing in pain as he greeted Witkowski. 'Hello, Colonel, what happened at the hospital?'

'It's in the hands of British MI-5, sir. A pulmonologist named Woodward from the Royal College of Surgeons showed up, claiming the Foreign Office had asked him to fly over and examine Mrs Courtland – at your request. They're looking into it.'

'I made no such request,' said the ambassador. 'I don't know any Dr Woodward, much less the Royal College of Surgeons.'

'We know that,' said Witkowski. 'Our French-American unit at the hospital stopped him just before he was about to inject the false Mrs Courtland with strychnine.'

'A brave woman. What's her name?'

'Moskowitz, sir. From New York. Her late husband was a French rabbi. She volunteered for the assignment.'

'Then we must volunteer compensation. Perhaps a month's vacation, all expenses paid.'

'I'll forward the offer, sir . . . And how are you feeling?'

'I'll be fine. Just a little torn skin, nothing serious. I was a lucky man.'

'You weren't the target, Mr Ambassador.'

'Yes, I understand that,' said Courtland quickly. 'So let's all get current, okay?'

'Mrs de Vries just told me how much they appreciate your inviting them to stay up here.'

'Considering what they've been through, they're quarantined up here for the duration if need be. I assume your full security's in place.'

'Practically a complete platoon of marines, sir. They hear a footstep or a sneeze, their weapons are drawn.'

'Good. Sit down, fellas, we have to recap. You go first, Stanley. Where are we?'

'Let's start back at the hospital,' began Witkowski, lowering himself into a chair next to Karin. 'It was a foul-up, but the British lung doctor, this Woodward, *was* cleared by the Quai d'Orsay as one of Mrs Courtland's physicians, only the clearance came too late. He'd already arrived.'

'That strikes me as pretty sloppy for the neos,' said Courtland.

'Paris is an hour ahead of London, sir,' offered Latham, sitting down. 'It's a common mistake, although you're right, it was sloppy.'

'Perhaps it wasn't,' said De Vries, and all eyes turned to her. 'Is it possible we have a friend in the English neo ranks? What better way to draw attention to such a killer than by withholding clearance when it's necessary and sending it suspiciously late?'

'That's overcomplicated, Karin,' the colonel disagreed, 'and leaves too much room for error. The link in the chain's too weak; a mole would be traced immediately.'

'Complications are our business, Stosh, and errors are what we look for.'

'Is that a lesson from on high?'

'Come on,' persisted Drew, 'she could be right.'

'Indeed, she could be; unfortunately we can't know at this juncture.'

'Why not? We can put out a trace too. Who at the Quai

d'Orsay gave Woodward clearance at the hospital even if it was late?'

'That's why we can't know. It came from the office of an Anatole Blanchot, a member of the Chamber of Deputies. Moreau followed it up.'

'*And?*'

'There's nothing. This Blanchot never heard of a Dr Woodward and there's no record of a telephone call made from his office to the Hertford Hospital. As a matter of fact, the only time Blanchot ever called London was over a year ago on his home phone to place a bet at Ladbroke's for the Irish Sweepstakes.'

'The neos just picked a name, then.'

'That's what it looks like.'

'Son of a bitch!'

'Amen, *chłopak*.'

'I thought you said some progress was made.'

'It was, but not with Woodward.'

'Then *where*?' Courtland broke in.

'I'm referring to Officer Latham's package delivered to the Deuxième in the early hours of the morning, sir.'

'The Lutheran minister?' asked Karin.

'Without knowing it, Koenig's a songbird,' said Witkowski.

'What's the tune?' Drew leaned forward in his chair.

'It's an aria called "Der Meistersinger Traupman". We've heard it before.'

'The surgeon from Nuremberg?' pressed Latham. 'The big-wheel Nazi that Sorenson unearthed from—' He stopped, looking helplessly at the ambassador.

'Yes, Drew,' said Courtland quietly, 'from my wife's legal guardian in Centralia, Illinois . . . I spoke with Mr Schneider myself. He's an old man now with many painful memories and regrets, and whatever he says, I believe he speaks the truth.'

'He's certainly telling the truth about Traupman,' said the colonel. 'Moreau met with Traupman's former wife in

Munich only a few days ago. She confirmed it in double swastikas.'

'I'm aware of that also.' The ambassador spoke again softly, nodding his head. 'Traupman was instrumental in implementing Operation Sonnenkinder all over the free world.'

'What did Claude learn about Traupman from the Lutheran priest?' asked Karin.

'Basically that Koenig and others like him in the upper levels are frightened of him, and curry favours whenever and wherever they can. Moreau understood that Traupman was a major player, but now he thinks he's something else. He thinks Traupman has some kind of hold over the neo movement, a grip that keeps everyone where he wants them.'

'The Nazi *Rasputin*?' continued De Vries. 'The untouchable figure behind the imperial throne, controlling that throne?'

'We know there's a new *Führer*,' said Witkowski, 'we just have no idea who he is.'

'But if this new Hitler is the throne—'

'*That* is where I must stop you, Karin,' Daniel Courtland interrupted, suddenly rising, slowly, painfully, from his chair behind the antique table.

'I'm sorry, Mr Ambassador—'

'No, no, my dear, the apologies are mine, so ordered by my government.'

'What the hell are you *doing*?'

'Cool it, Drew, just *cool* it,' ordered Courtland. 'It may interest you to know that I've been on the phone with Wesley Sorenson, who has temporarily assumed the authority of certain covert activities. I'm to neither hear nor be a party to any further conversation on this subject. However, when I have left the room, you, Officer Latham, are to call him on this scrambled telephone and hear what he has to say . . . Now, if you'll excuse me, I shall retire to the library, where there is a well-stocked bar. Later, if you care to indulge in some innocuous chitchat, please join me.' The ambassador limped across the room and out an inner door, closing it firmly behind him.

Drew leapt out of the chair and raced to the phone. Barely sitting down, he began pressing the numbered buttons. 'Wes, it's me. Why the voodoo?'

'Has Ambassador Daniel Rutherford Courtland in Paris left the room?'

'Yeah, sure, what is it?'

'In the event this conversation is compromised, I, Wesley Theodore Sorenson, director of Consular Operations, take full responsibility for this action under Article Seventy-three of the Clandestine Activities Statutes as they apply to unilateral, individual decisions in the field—'

'*Hey*, goddammit, that's *my* line!'

'Shut up!'

'What *is* it, Wes?'

'Mount a team, fly to Nuremberg, and take Dr Hans Traupman. Kidnap the bastard and bring him to Paris.'

CHAPTER THIRTY-FOUR

Robert Durbane sat at the desk in his office next to the sealed-off Communications Center, a troubled man. It was more than a feeling, for feelings were abstract, based on anything from an upset stomach to an early morning argument with one's wife. His stomach was perfectly normal and his wife of twenty-four years was still his best friend; the last time they had argued was when their daughter married a rock musician. She was for it; he was not. He lost. The marriage was not only successful, but his long-haired son-in-law 'hit' something called 'the charts', and made more money performing for a month in Las Vegas than Bobby Durbane would make in half a century. And what really rankled the father-in-law was that his daughter's husband was a nice young man who drank nothing stronger than white wine, didn't do drugs, had a master's degree in medieval literature, and completed crossword puzzles faster than Bobby. It was not a logical world.

So why was he so uncomfortable? he mused. It probably started with Colonel Witkowski's requisition for a computer printout of all telephone and radio calls made from the comm centre during the past seven days. It was then compounded by the subtle yet still fairly obvious behaviour of Drew Latham, a man he considered to be a friend. Drew was avoiding him, and it was not like the Cons-Op officer. Durbane had left two messages for Latham, one at his rue du Bac apartment, which was still in the process of being restored, and one at the embassy message centre. Neither had been returned, and Bobby knew that Drew was in the embassy, *had* been there all day, sequestered in the ambassador's upstairs quarters. Durbane understood that calamitous events had taken place, that Courtland's wife was so severely wounded during the terrorist attack the night before last that she was not expected to live, but withal, it was not Latham's way to ignore messages from his friend 'the egghead' who filled in those 'detestable crossword puzzles'. Especially considering Bobby had saved his life several nights before.

Something was wrong; something had happened that Durbane could not understand, and there was only one way to find out what it was. He picked up his telephone, a phone that could access any other in the embassy regardless of restrictions, and pressed the numbers for Courtland's living quarters.

'Yes?'

'Mr Ambassador, it's Robert Durbane in the comm centre.'

'Hello ... Bobby,' said Courtland hesitantly. 'How are you?'

'I think it's my place to ask you that, sir.' *Something was wrong. The usually unflappable State Department man was uncomfortable.* 'I refer to your wife, of course. I hear she was taken to a hospital.'

'They're doing everything possible, and that's all I can ask. Other than your well-known courtesy, which I appreciate, is there anything else?'

'Yes, sir. I know no one's supposed to know Drew Latham is alive, but I work closely with Colonel Witkowski. Therefore, I also know that Drew is up there, and I'd like very much to talk to him.'

'Oh ... you rather startle me, Mr Durbane. Hold on, please.'

The line went on hold, the silence unnerving, as if a decision was being made. Finally, Drew's voice came on the phone. 'Hello, Bobby?'

'I left a couple of messages for you. You didn't call me back.'

'I didn't write either. Besides having been shot and gone on to a far better world, I've been up to my ass in confusion, plus a few other less attractive things.'

'I can imagine. However, I think we should talk.'

'Really? About what?'

'That's what I'd like to find out.'

'Is this double acrostics? I'm no good at those, you know that.'

'I know I want to talk to you, and not on the phone. May I?'

'Wait a minute.' Again the silence was pervasive, but shorter than the previous one. 'All right,' said Latham, back on the line. 'There's an elevator I never knew about that stops on your floor. I'll be on it, escorted by three armed marines, and you're to clear the corridor. We'll be there in five minutes.'

'It's gone this far?' asked Durbane quietly. '*Me*? I'm suddenly a danger zone?'

'We'll talk, Bobby.'

Seven minutes and twenty-eight seconds later, Drew sat in the single chair in front of Durbane's desk, his office having been swept by the marine contingent, and no weapons found.

'What the hell *is* this?' said the comm centre's chief of operations. 'What in God's name have I *done* to warrant these Gestapo tactics?'

'You may have used the right word, Bobby. *Gestapo*, as in the Nazi lexicon.'

'What are you *saying*?'

'Do you know a woman named Phyllis Cranston?'

'Certainly. She's the secretary to what's-his-name, the third or fourth attaché below the ambassador's chargé d'affaires. So what?'

'Did she tell you who a Colonel Webster was and where he was staying?'

'As a matter of fact she did, but she didn't have to.'

'What do you mean?'

'Who do you think set up the communications between the embassy and the wandering Colonel Webster? Two, or was it three changes of hotels. Between your movements and Mrs de Vries's, even Witkowski couldn't keep it all straight.'

'Then everything was kept under wraps?'

'I believe the overused phrase, "maximum classified", was affixed to the equally abused "order of the day". Why do you think I was so harsh with Cranston?'

'I didn't know you were.'

'I demanded to know how *she* knew. I even threatened her with exposure, which wasn't easy for me because my mother was an alcoholic. It's a rotten disease.'

'What did she tell you?'

'She fell apart, crying and mumbling some religious claptrap. She'd been on a binge the night before and her defences were nowhere.'

'You must know her pretty well.'

'You want it straight, Drew?'

'That's why I'm here, Bobby.'

'My wife and I went to one of those embassy receptions, and Martha – she's my wife – saw Phyllis hanging around the bar and lapping up the booze. *I* figured, how else could a normal person get through one of those functions without an edge on, hell, I've done it myself. But Martha knew better; she'd lived through my mother's last years with us. She told me to try to help her, that she needed help due to "low self-esteem" and phrases like that. So I tried and obviously failed.'

'Then you never mentioned to anyone else who I was or what hotel I was at?'

'Good God, no. Even when that prick Cranston works for came sniffing around about your staff and resources, I told him I hadn't the vaguest idea who was taking over for you. I was grateful that Phyllis had gotten my message about keeping her mouth shut.'

'Why was he sniffing around?'

'That part sounded legitimate,' replied Durbane. 'Hell,

everyone knows Consular Operations doesn't oversee the embassy's kitchen menus. He said he'd been approached by a French developer and asked to invest in some hot real estate. He thought your staff might check out the guy's legitimacy. It's par for his course, Drew. Cranston says he spends more time lunching with Paris businessmen than with those who could do us some good over here.'

'Why didn't he go to Witkowski?'

'I didn't have to ask him to know why. This isn't a security matter; he can't use an arm of the embassy for a personal financial transaction.'

'What am I, a little toe?'

'No, you're more like a roving outer eye, overlooking the inner operations of a major consular post, which could be interpreted as advising personnel regarding their behaviour, financial and otherwise. At least that's what your official curriculum vitae suggests.'

'Someone should rewrite it,' said Latham.

'Why? It's deliciously obscure.'

Drew leaned back in his chair, arching his neck, his eyes briefly on the white ceiling, and sighing audibly. 'I owe you an apology, Bobby, and I truly mean that. When I learned from Phyllis Cranston that you were one of the two people she told about who and where I was, I jumped – no, slid – into the wrong conclusion. I thought it was bolstered by what happened the other night when the neos damn near killed me in the embassy car with that son of a bitch . . . what did he call himself? . . . C-*Zwölf*. The timing seemed – well, it seemed off centre.'

'It was,' agreed Durbane, 'and there was a good reason why the Nazis got there before we did—'

'That was it. How come?'

'C-*Zwölf*. We discovered it the next morning and included it in the report. Your German driver gave the high frequency calibrations of our backup interior radio to his friends miles away and left the switch on transmit. They heard everything you said from the time you left the embassy. When you called me for two backups, they moved quickly.'

'Christ, it was so simple, and I never thought to look down at the radio casing!'

'If you had, you would have seen a small red dot in the centre of the panel, signifying transmission.'

'Goddammit!'

'For heaven's sake, don't blame yourself. You'd been through a terrible evening; it was the wee hours of the morning and you were exhausted.'

'I hate to tell you, Bobby, but that's never an excuse. When you get to that point, you punch in all the adrenaline you've got, because that's when you're vulnerable . . . It's strange though, isn't it? The neos centred in on Phyllis Cranston.'

'Why is it strange? She's unstable, and instability is milk and honey to those wanting to penetrate.'

'And her boss?'

'I don't see the connection.'

'It's there, my friend, oh, Lord, it's there.'

'If it is,' said Durbane, staring at Latham's unfocused eyes, 'it's made with a pair of pliers. Concentrate on the two of them; hit the alcoholic and squeeze the greedy, ambitious superior. One or the other will break without your spreading yourself around.'

'Thanks to you, Bobby, the first didn't. Now let's go after the second. Reach Phyllis's boss and tell him you've talked to one of my people who's covering for me. Say my assistant agreed to check with a few bankers if he'll give you the name of this developer.'

'I don't understand—'

'If he doesn't give you a name, we'll know he can't. If he does, we'll know who's behind him, who's programming him.'

'I can do that right now,' said Durbane, picking up his phone and dialling the attaché's office. 'Phyllis, it's me, Bobby. Let me speak to the pinstriped idiot – and, Phyl, it has *nothing* to do with you . . . Hello, Bancroft, it's Durbane in the comm centre. I just spoke to Latham's head investigator, and although he's busy as hell, he figures he can make a couple of calls for you to some banking types. What's the name of this real estate broker who wants you to invest? . . . I see, yes, I see. Yes, I'll tell him that. I'll get back to you.' Durbane hung up while writing on a notepad. 'The name's Vaultherin, Picon Vaultherin, with a company of the same name. Bancroft said to tell your office that his consortium has exclusive rights to roughly twenty square miles of choice property in the Loire Valley.'

'Isn't that interesting,' said Drew, turning his head and gazing at the wall.

'There's been talk for years that a lot of those old châteaus are falling apart and nobody can afford to put them back together. Also, that developers are foaming at the mouth to buy up land and build dozens of mini estates at enormous profit. I might put in a few dollars myself, or at least steer my son-in-law to look into it.'

'Your son-in-law?' asked Latham, turning back to the comm centre chief.

'Never mind, it's too embarrassing. You wouldn't know who he is any more than I would if he weren't married to my daughter.'

'I'll leave it alone.'

'Please do. How do you want to move on this Vaultherin?'

'I'll take it to Witkowski, who'll give it to Moreau at the Deuxième. We need a background check on Vaultherin . . . and also a sweep of those exclusive rights in the Loire Valley.'

'What's one got to do with the other?'

'I don't know, I'd just like to explore it. Someone may have made a mistake . . . And remember, Bobby, I never came down here. I couldn't, I'm dead.'

It was nine-thirty in the evening, the embassy kitchen having delivered an excellent dinner for Karin and Drew to the ambassador's living quarters. The stewards had set the dining room table, complete with candles and two bottles of outstanding wine – one red at room temperature (for Latham's thick, rare *bifteck*) – and the other a chilled Chardonnay (De Vries's filet of sole almondine). Daniel Courtland, however, had not joined them, on orders of his government, for it was understood that Colonel Stanley Witkowski would appear and projected strategies be discussed that the ambassador could not be privy to. Deniability was again the order of the day.

'Why do I get the idea that this is my final meal before being executed?' said Drew, finishing his last slice of blood-rare beef and drinking from his third glass of Pommard wine.

'It will be if you continue to eat like that,' replied Karin. 'You've just consumed enough cholesterol to clog the arteries of a dinosaur.'

'Who can tell anymore? They keep switching. Margarine's good, butter is terrible . . . butter is better, margarine's worse. I'm waiting for a new medical analysis that says nicotine is a cure for cancer.'

'Moderation and variety are the answer, my darling.'

'I don't like fish. Beth could never cook fish right. It always smelled like fish.'

'Harry liked fish. He told me your mother broiled it beautifully, with sprinkles of dill.'

'Harry and Mom were in a conspiracy against Dad and me. He and I would go out and get a hamburger.'

'Drew,' began Karin, letting the moment pass, 'have you reached your parents to tell them the truth about you and Harry?'

'Not yet, it's not the time.'

'That's terribly cruel. You're their surviving child and you were with him when he was killed. You can't overlook them; they must be heartbroken.'

'Beth I could trust, not my father. Let's say he's pretty outspoken and not too fond of the authorities. He's spent his

579

life fighting campus politics and various countries' restrictions on archaeological explorations. It's not unlike him to demand an accountability, and I can't give him any.'

'He sounds not unlike his two sons, I'd suggest.'

'Maybe. That's why the time isn't right.' The doorbell of the ambassador's living quarters rang. Instantly, a steward came out of the upstairs kitchen. 'We're expecting Colonel Witkowski,' said Latham. 'Let him in, please.'

'Yes, sir.'

Twelve seconds later the embassy's head of security walked into the dining room, his eyes disapproving as he glanced around the table. 'What the hell *is* this?' he asked curtly. 'You guys suddenly part of the diplomatic crowd?'

'I, personally, am representing the nation of Oz,' replied Drew, grinning. 'If the candlelight is too bright, we'll have the Munchkin slaves extinguish a few.'

'Pay no attention to him, Stanley,' said Karin, 'he's had three glasses of wine. If you'd like something, I'm sure we can get it for you.'

'No, thanks.' Witkowski sat down. 'I had a damn good steak sent up to my office while waiting for Moreau to come through.'

'Too much cholesterol,' said Latham. 'Haven't you heard about that?'

'Not recently, but I've heard from Moreau.'

'What's he got?' asked Drew, abruptly serious.

'This Vaultherin is relatively clean on the surface, but there are questions. He's made a fortune out of the new construction around Paris, making a lot of his investors very rich too.'

'So? Others have done the same.'

'But none with the same background. He's a young, arrogant buccaneer in financial circles.'

'Again, what's new?'

'His grandfather was a member of the Milice—'

'The what . . . ?'

'The French pro-Nazi police during the war,' answered

580

Karin, 'formed under the Germans as a counterpart to the Résistance. They were middle-level henchmen without whom the Nazis couldn't control the occupied country. They were filth.'

'What's the bottom line, Stanley?'

'Vaultherin's major investors come from Germany. They're buying up everything they can purchase.'

'What about the Loire Valley?'

'They damn near own it, at least large chunks along the river.'

'Have you got a breakdown of the properties?'

'Yes, I have,' said the colonel, removing a folded piece of paper from his inside jacket pocket and handing it to Drew. 'I'm not sure what they can tell us, most are owned by families that go back for generations. Those that aren't are either government appropriated because nobody paid the taxes, and therefore they've become landmarks, or they were recently bought by movie stars and other celebrities until their accountants told them what they were costing. Most of those are up for sale.'

'Are there any generals on the list?'

'As you can see, fifteen or twenty by name, but that's only because they purchased their plots of five or six acres and pay taxes on them. There are at least a dozen others, generals and admirals, who've been awarded "domiciles for life" due to their military contributions to the Republic of France.'

'That's wild.'

'We do the same, *chłopak*. We've got a few thousand top brass living in fancy houses within the perimeters of military bases after their retirements. It's not unusual, or even unfair if you think about it. They spend their lives making a fraction of what they could in the private sector, and if they aren't headline-makers sought by various boards of directors, they couldn't afford to live in Scarsdale, New York.'

'I never thought of it that way.'

'Try, Officer Latham. I'll complete my thirty-five years

eighteen months from now, and while I can give my children and grandchildren a hell of a time in Paris, if you think one of my kids could come to me and borrow fifty thousand bucks for an operation, forget it. Sure, I'd do it, but I'd be wiped out.'

'Okay, Stanley, I see where you're coming from,' said Latham, studying the list. 'Tell me, Stosh, these landmark acquisitions, why aren't the inhabitants named?'

'Quai d'Orsay regulations. Same as in our country. There are crazies out there who hold grudges against commanders. Remember the Vietnam vet who tried to kill Westmoreland by firing through a window?'

'Can we get those names?'

'Moreau probably can.'

'Have him do that.'

'I'll call him in the morning . . . Now, can we talk about the operation we've been given, namely the heisting of Dr Hans Traupman in Nuremberg?'

'Five men, no more,' said Drew, putting down Witkowski's list on the dining room table. 'Each fluent in German and each with Ranger training, none of them married or with children.'

'I anticipated you. I dug up two from NATO, with you and me that makes four, and there's a candidate from Marseilles who may qualify.'

'*Stop* it!' cried Karin. '*I* am the fifth man – far better, for I'm a woman.'

'In your dreams, lady. It's a good bet that Traupman is as heavily guarded as if he wore the Hope diamond around his neck like a *mezuzah*.'

'Moreau's looking into that,' said the colonel. 'Frankly, he'd like to take over the operation himself, but the Quai d'Orsay, as well as French foreign intelligence, would blow him away if he tried. But there's nothing on the books that says he can't give us assistance. Within twenty-four hours he expects a report on Traupman's daily routine and security.'

'I'm going with you, Drew,' said De Vries calmly. 'There's no way you can stop me, so don't try.'

'For Christ's sake, *why*?'

'For all the reasons you know very well, and one you do not.'

'What . . . ?'

'As you said about Harry and your parents, I'll tell you when the time is right.'

'What kind of answer is that?'

'For the moment, the only one you'll get.'

'You think I'll settle for that?'

'You have to, it's a gift from you to me. If you refuse, and as much as it pains me, I'll leave and you'll never see me again.'

'It means that much to you? This reason I don't know about means *that* much?'

'Yes.'

'Karin, you're driving me up the wall!'

'I don't mean to, my darling, but some things we must all simply accept. This you must.'

'I should have the words to tell you I don't buy this crap!' said Latham, swallowing, as he stared at her. 'I just don't have them.'

'Listen to me, *chłopak*,' Witkowski interrupted, studying them both. 'I'm not crazy about the idea, but there's a positive side. A woman sometimes makes quiet inroads where men can't.'

'What the hell are you *proposing*?'

'Obviously not what you think. But as long as she's made up her mind, she could be useful.'

'That's the coldest, most insensitive thing I've ever heard you say, *Colonel*! The assignment is everything, the individual *nothing*?'

'There's a middle ground where both are vital.'

'She could be *killed*!'

'So could we all. I think she has as much right to that

option as you do. You lost a brother, she lost a husband. Who are you to play Solomon?'

It was twenty minutes to five in Washington, those hectic minutes before the rush-hour traffic fills the streets, when secretaries, clerks, and typists mildly harass their bosses into giving their final instructions for the day so that personnel can get to garages, parking lots, and bus stops before the crowds. Wesley Sorenson had left the office, already in his limousine but not on his way home; his wife knew how to handle emergencies, filtering the false ones and reaching him in the car for those she considered genuine. After nearly forty-five years she had developed instincts as perceptive as his, and he was grateful for that.

Instead of home, the director of Consular Operations was on his way to a rendezvous with Knox Talbot in Langley, Virginia. The head of the CIA had alerted him an hour earlier; the snare for Bruce Withers, high-tech purchasing agent, bigot, and prime suspect in the safe-house killings, might have been sprung. Talbot had ordered an in-house tap on Withers's phone, and at 2:13 in the afternoon a call had come to him from a woman who identified herself only as Suzy. Knox had played the recording for Wesley over their secure telephones.

'Hi, hon, it's Suzy. Sorry to bother you at work, sweetie, but I ran into Sidney, who says he's got that old set of wheels for you.'

'The silver Aston-Martin, DB-Three?'

'If that's the one you want, he tracked it down.'

'Hey, I can smell it! That's the "Goldfinger" car.'

'He doesn't want to bring it into the lot, so you're to meet him at your watering hole in Woodbridge around five-thirty.'

'You and I and a few younger strong-arms will follow him, Wes,' Talbot had said.

'Sure, Knox, but why? The man's a Fascist, a thief, and a late-blooming yuppie, but what's his buying a fancy English car got to do with anything?'

'I remembered I own a custom-made auto parts company

in Idaho – or is it Ohio? – so I made a call to the fellow who runs it for me. He said that anybody who's an automobile freak knows damn well that the "Goldfinger" car is the Aston-Martin DB-*Four*, not a Three. He even went so far as to say that he could understand if someone said DB-Five, because there wasn't that much difference in the design, but never a DB-Three.'

'I can't tell a Chevrolet from a Pontiac, if they make them any longer, that is.'

'A car freak can, especially if he's going to pay over a hundred thousand for it. Meet me in the south parking lot. That's where Withers's Jaguar is.'

The limousine entered the huge Langley complex, the driver wending his way to the south lot. They were stopped by a man in a dark suit, holding up a badge. Sorenson lowered his window. 'Yes, what is it?'

'I recognized the car, sir. If you'll get out and follow me, I'll bring you to the DCI. There's a change of vehicles, somewhat less obvious than a limo.'

'That makes sense.'

The change of vehicles meant riding in a nondescript sedan of dubious ownership. Wesley climbed into the backseat alongside Knox Talbot. 'Don't let appearances fool you,' said the DCI. 'This iron mother has an engine that could probably win the Indy 500.'

'I'll take your word for it, but then, what choice do I have?'

'None. Besides, in addition to the two gentlemen in front, there's a second car behind us with four other gentlemen armed to their bicuspids.'

'Are you expecting the invasion of Normandy?'

'I got mine in Korea, so I don't know that much about ancient history. I only know we should expect anything from these bastards.'

'I'm on your side—'

'There he *is*,' the driver broke in. 'He's heading straight for the Jag.'

'Go slow, man,' said Talbot. 'Go with the flow, just don't lose him.'

'No way, Mr Director. I'd love to nail that son of a bitch.'

'Why is that, young man?'

'He hit on my girl, my fiancée. She's in the steno pool. He got her in a corner and tried to feel her up.'

'I understand,' said Talbot, leaning into Sorenson's shoulder and whispering, 'I *love* it when there's true motivation, don't you? It's what I try to instil in my companies.'

After nearly an hour's drive, the Jaguar pulled into a shabby motel on the outskirts of Woodbridge. On the far left of a row of cabins was a miniature barnlike structure with a red neon sign proclaiming COCKTAILS, TV, ROOMS AVAILABLE. 'The Waldorf of the quickie afternoon trade, no doubt,' observed Wesley as Bruce Withers got out of his car and went into the bar. 'I'd suggest you swing around and park way to the right of the door,' he continued, speaking to the driver, 'next to that low-slung silver bug.'

'That's the Aston, DB-Four,' said Talbot, "the Gold-finger" car.'

'Yes, I remember seeing it now – a good film. But why would anyone pay a hundred thousand dollars for it? The damn thing can't be very comfortable.'

'According to my manager, it's a classic, and it's well over a hundred thousand by now. Probably nearer two.'

'Then where would a Bruce Withers get anywhere near that kind of money?'

'How much is it worth to the neo movement to get rid of two captured Nazis whose tongues could be loosened?'

'I see what you mean.' Sorenson again addressed the front seat as the driver pulled alongside the British sports car. 'How about one of you fellows going inside and taking a look around?'

'Yes, sir,' replied the agent passenger, 'as soon as our backup parks . . . There, he's in place.'

'May I suggest that you loosen or remove your tie. I don't

586

think this place sees too many men in business suits – going into the cabins, perhaps, but not in there.'

The man next to the driver turned around. His tie was gone and his shirt collar unbuttoned. 'Also my coat, sir,' he said, taking off his jacket. 'It's a hot day.' The agent got out of the car, his erect posture suddenly turning to a slouch as he walked to the door under the neon sign.

Inside the dimly lit bar, the clientele was a Saroyanesque mixture: several truck drivers, men from a construction crew, two or three collegiate types, a white-haired man whose wrinkled, blotched face was once aristocratic and whose threadbare clothes still showed their original quality, and a quartet of ageing local hookers. Bruce Withers had been greeted by the burly bartender.

'Hi, Mr W.,' the man had said. 'You want a cabin?'

'Not today, Hank, I'm meeting someone. I don't see him—'

'Nobody's asked for you. Maybe he's late.'

'No, he's here; his car's outside.'

'He's probably in the can. Take a booth, and when he comes out, I'll send him over.'

'Thanks, and make me a double of the usual. I'm celebrating.'

'Coming right up.'

Withers sat in the high-backed booth at the rear of the bar. His outsize martini arrived and he sipped it, tempted to go to the front window and look again at the Aston-Martin automobile. It was the real thing! He couldn't wait to tool around the roads in it, couldn't wait to show it off to Anita Griswald – especially couldn't wait for his daughter Kimberly to see it! It was a hell of a lot more exciting than anything his former snotty in-laws or his bitch ex-wife could chauffeur her around in! His enjoyable reverie was cut short by a heavyset man in a chequered shirt who suddenly appeared and slid into the booth opposite him. 'Good afternoon, Mr Withers. I'm sure you saw the DB-Four. Nice set of wheels, aren't they?'

'Who the hell are you? You're not Sidney, you're twice his size.'

'Sidney was unavailable, so I'm taking his place.'

'We've never met. How did you know it was me?'

'A photograph.'

'A *what*?'

'It's trivial.'

'I've been here at least five minutes. Why did you wait?'

'Just checking,' said the intruder, continually glancing at the front door.

'Checking what?'

'It's nothing really. To be honest with you, I'm a bearer of great news and considerable riches.'

'Oh?'

'In my pocket are four untraceable bearer bonds, each in the amount of fifty thousand dollars, for a total of two hundred thousand. Along with these is an invitation to visit Germany, all expenses paid, of course. We understand that you haven't taken your summer holiday; perhaps now you can schedule it.'

'My God, I'm *speechless*! This is *great*. Then my contribution *was* appreciated, I knew it would be! I took a hell of a risk, you all know that, don't you?'

'The proof is in the fact that I'm here, isn't it?'

'I can't wait to get to Berlin, because you're right, *we're* right! This country's going to hell in a handbasket. Talk about ethnic cleansing, we'll need fifty *years* of it—'

'Hold it!' whispered the stranger harshly, his eyes again on the door. 'The fellow who came in after you, the one in the white shirt.'

'I didn't notice. What about him?'

'He had a couple of swallows of beer, paid with a deuce, and just left.'

'So?'

'Wait here, I'll be right back.' The man slid out of the

booth, walked rapidly around the bar to the far end of the filthy front window, and peered outside. Instantly, he moved away from the glass and returned to the booth, his expression grim, his eyes narrowed. 'You stupid fool, you were followed!' he said, sitting down.

'What are you *talking* about?'

'You heard me, you idiot! There are three men out there talking to the white shirt, and believe me, they're not patrons of this dump. They've got federal government written all over their faces.'

'*Jesus!* A deputy director named Kearns called me last night asking dumb questions, but I set him straight.'

'Kearns of the CIA?'

'That's where I work, remember?'

'All too well.' The stranger leaned forward over the table, his left hand on it, his right underneath. 'You're a liability to those who expect me to do my job, Mr Withers.'

'Just give me the money and I'll get out of here through the back door, where they make deliveries.'

'What will you do then?'

'Wait in an empty cabin until they leave, bribe one of the hookers to swear she was with me if it's necessary, and head home. It's clean, I've done it before. Call me later about the Aston-Martin. Come *on*!'

'I don't think so.' There was a burst of raucous laughter from the bar, accompanied by four muted spits under the table. Bruce Withers lurched back in the seat, his upper body pinned to the banquette, his eyes wide as blood trickled down the corner of his mouth. The stranger in the chequered shirt sidled out of the booth and walked calmly towards the rear delivery entrance while slipping the silenced pistol under his belt. He opened the door and Mario Marchetti's henchman disappeared. The Don of Pontchartrain was living up to his concordat.

Nine minutes and twenty-seven seconds passed until the shouts, joined by female screams, erupted from inside the motel bar. An overly madeup woman raced out the door screeching, 'For Christ's sake, somebody call the *police*! A guy was shot to death in there!'

The agents of the CIA, accompanied by their director and Wesley Sorenson, ran inside. Everyone in the bar was ordered to remain where they were and not try to make any phone calls. A frustrated, dejected Knox Talbot, Sorenson at his side, came out into the diminishing sunlight. The Aston Martin, DB-Four, was gone.

CHAPTER THIRTY-FIVE

The subject, Dr Hans Traupman (residence above), is in the company of bodyguards around the clock, three-man units on eight-hour shifts who are heavily armed, even when escorting the surgeon into an operating room, where they remain throughout surgery. When Traupman goes to restaurants or attends the theatre, concerts, or events of any kind, his guards are frequently doubled, flanking him in seats or chairs and often roaming the area in a most professional manner, scanning the sections. When at Traupman's home, the bodyguards continuously patrol the elevators, the hallways, and the exterior of his luxury apartment house. This is in addition to multiple alarms and backups. In rare visits to public rest rooms, two guards enter with him, the third remaining outside to courteously prohibit others from going in until Traupman reappears. The vehicle he's driven in is an armour-plated Mercedes limousine, the windows bulletproof, gas jets on all sides to immobilize carjackers and activated from the dashboard. When travelling, he is flown in his private jet, which is kept in an alarmed, sealed-off hangar at an airstrip south of Nuremberg. Digital cameras, operating day and night, record all activity inside and out.

The only deviation from this security routine is when Traupman flies to Bonn and takes his motorboat out on the Rhine during those nights when he is presumably attending clandestine meetings of the neo-Nazi movement. (See previous report.) Apparently none of the members is permitted to have a crew or a captain, which accounts for the size and manoeuvrability of the craft. It is a small boat with a 125 hp motor and inflatable pontoons, starboard and port. However, even here he has a large degree of security by way of revolving cameras that send images and sound back to his guards at the marina, where there is the standard helicopter prepared for immediate emergency takeoff. (Here, unobserved conclusions may be drawn: There is a radar instrument that transmits river-map coordinates, and, as with his Mercedes, gas jets on the gunwales designed to deter or kill unwanted boarders, the man at the helm protected by a simple mask, which was observed.)

Good luck, Claude. You really owe me for this one. I had to talk my way out of the Bonn marina by saying I was going to buy an American Chris-Craft. Fortunately, I left the name of a Spanish undercover pig who operates here and owes me money.

Drew Latham, laughing quietly at the last paragraph, put Moreau's report down on the antique table-desk and looked over at Witkowski and Karin, who were sitting on the couch. 'Is there any contingency that son of a bitch hasn't thought of?' he asked.

'It's pretty complete,' replied the colonel.

'I wouldn't know,' said De Vries. 'I haven't read it.'

'Read it now and weep.' Drew got up and brought the report to Karin, then sat in one of the brocaded armchairs across from both of them. De Vries began reading as Latham continued. 'I'll be damned if I know where to begin,' he said. 'That bastard's really covered, right down to the men's room.'

'It looks rough on paper, but up close we might spot gaps.'

'We damn well better. According to this, it'd be a lot easier to take him out than to take him.'

'It always is.'

'Diversion,' said De Vries, looking up from Moreau's report. 'It's the only thing I can think of. Divert the attention of the guards somehow.'

'That's axiomatic,' said Witkowski. 'Going further,

immobilize a couple and run an assault. The question is how, and how disciplined are his gunslingers.'

'As you say, Stosh, we won't know until we get there.'

'Speaking of which, the two men from NATO are downstairs in my office. They arrived on the three o'clock flight from Brussels, with new passports and papers that say they're salesmen for an aircraft company.'

'Good cover,' said Latham. 'Those salesmen are all over Europe.'

'We had to go around some dicey corners to clear everything. It took all morning and part of the afternoon to complete their "authenticity". They're actually on the company's payroll.'

'Was all that necessary?' asked Karin.

'Indeed it was, young lady. Any references to their real names would reveal the service records of two Special Forces commandos who operated behind the lines in Desert Storm. Each is as handy with a knife as he is with his hands, to say nothing of garrottes and marksmanship.'

'You're saying they're killers.'

'Only when necessary, Karin. Frankly, they're two nice kids, kind of shy actually, who've been trained to react properly in given situations.'

'That's a euphemism for they'll beat your head against a rock if you're a bad guy,' explained Latham. 'You're satisfied with them, Stosh?'

'Very definitely.'

'And they both speak fluent French and German?' added De Vries.

'Absolutely. The first is a Captain Christian Dietz, thirty-two, graduate of Denison University, and a career army officer. Parents and grandparents were German, the latter part of the German underground during the Third Reich. His father and mother were sent to the US as children.'

'The other?' said Drew.

'A lieutenant named Anthony, Gerald Anthony. He's a little more interesting,' said the colonel. 'He has dual master's degrees in French and German literature, was going for his PhD while teaching at a small college in Pennsylvania, when he decided, in his own words, that he couldn't take campus politics. I thought I'd ask them up here,' continued Witkowski. 'We'd sort of get to know each other quietly, informally.'

'That's a good idea, Stanley,' said Karin. 'I'll have the kitchen prepare some hors d'oeuvres and coffee, perhaps drinks.'

'No,' countered Drew. 'No hors d'oeuvres, no coffee, and definitely no drinks. This is a cold paramilitary operation, let's keep it that way.'

'Isn't that a bit *too* cold?'

'He's right, young lady, although I never thought I'd hear him say it. I was wrong, the time for that kind of informality comes later. After you see the slack, or lack of it, in their ropes.'

De Vries looked at him questioningly.

'They're still being evaluated,' explained Latham. 'Interviewed for the job – how do they behave, what have they got to offer? Two Special Forces officers who've operated behind enemy lines in any war should have input.'

'I wasn't aware that we had such a pool of candidates.'

'We don't, but they don't know that. Call for them to come up, Stanley.'

Captain Christian Dietz, except for his relatively short stature, could have walked out of a poster for the Hitler Youth. Blond, blue-eyed, and with a body to be envied by an Olympic champion, he carried himself like the experienced commando he was. Lieutenant Gerald Anthony, on the other hand, was equally muscular but much taller and dark-haired, a reed-thin man who evoked the image of an upright bullwhip, ready to coil and lash out lethally at any given instant. Contradictorily, both their faces were utterly devoid of malice, their eyes without a trace of hostility. And to complete the incongruity, they were, as Witkowski had mentioned, basically shy men, hesitant to expound on their past activities or their citations.

'We were at the right place at the right time,' said Dietz without comment.

'Our intelligence was excellent,' added Anthony. 'Without it, we'd have been roasted over an Iraqi fire, that is, if they'd ever learned how to make one in the sand.'

'You worked together, then?' asked Drew.

'Our radio code was Alpha-Delta.'

'Delta-Alpha,' Dietz corrected Gerald Anthony.

'Both were used,' said Anthony, grinning at his friend.

'Okay,' agreed the captain, smiling modestly.

'You've read the Traupman report,' Latham went on. 'Any suggestions?'

'A restaurant,' said Lieutenant Anthony.

'The river,' said Captain Dietz simultaneously. 'I say we wait in Nuremberg and follow him to Bonn, using the river.'

'Why a restaurant?' asked Karin, addressing Anthony.

'It's easy to create a diversion—'

'I said that,' interrupted De Vries.

' . . . by starting a fire,' continued the lieutenant, 'or by spotting the bodyguards and immobilizing them by force or with instant sedatives in their water or food. Frankly, I think a fire is more effective. All those flambé dishes; it's so simple to switch sauces and the whole place is filled with flames that are short-lived but distract everyone while we take the subject.'

'And the river?' interjected Witkowski.

'You can cork the gas jets on the gunwales – we've done it before. Saddam Hussein's patrols all had them. Then you blow out the cameras with high-powered pellets, as if the electrical systems had malfunctioned. The key is doing it by scuba, out of camera range, and before the boat gets near shore. You climb on board and get out of the area.'

'Let's go back,' said Latham. 'Lieutenant, why do you think a restaurant in Nuremberg is more efficient than the river in Bonn?'

'Saves time, to begin with, and there's too much room for error on the water, sir. Visibility is poor, gas jets could be missed, as well as the transmitting cameras – even one. The emergency helicopter has powerful searchlights and the motorboat is easily identifiable. As I understand it, the enemy would prefer that the subject be killed by strafing or bombing than be taken alive.'

'Good point,' said the colonel. 'And you, Captain, why do you think a restaurant is a poor choice?'

'Again, too much room for error, sir,' Dietz said. 'A panicked crowd is meat and potatoes to security units. The moment a fire diversion is activated, they'll race to the subject to protect him, and there's no way to sedate the guards who aren't at surrounding tables, even if you know who they are.'

'So you disagree with your associate,' said Karin.

'It's not the first time, ma'am. We usually work it out.'

'But you're his superior,' Witkowski interrupted brusquely.

'We don't pay much attention to rank,' said the lieutenant. 'Not in combat anyway. In a month or two I'll be a captain and then we'll have to split lunch and dinner checks. I won't be able to insist he pays anymore.'

'The Thin Man eats like an ox,' grumbled Captain Christian Dietz softly.

'I've got a hell of an idea,' Latham suddenly broke in. 'It's damn near close to the yardarm, whatever that is. Let's have a drink.'

'But I thought you said—'

'Forget what I said, *General* de Vries.'

The five members of Operation N-2 flew into Nuremberg on three different flights. Drew on board with Lieutenant Anthony, Karin with Captain Dietz, and Witkowski by himself. Claude Moreau had made the arrangements: Latham and De Vries had adjoining rooms at the same hotel; Witkowski, Anthony, and Dietz were in different hotels across the city. Their rendezvous was the next morning at Nuremberg's main library, between the stacks of volumes devoted to the once-imperial city's history. They were shown to a conference room as three doctoral candidates and their professor from Columbia University in New York, along with their female German guide. No papers were required, as Moreau's agents had cleared the way.

'I had no idea this was such a beautiful place!' exclaimed Gerald Anthony, the only former PhD candidate from America. 'I got up early and walked around. It's so medieval – the eleventh-century walls, the old royal palace, the Carthusian monastery. Whenever I thought about Nuremberg, all I conjured up were the World War Two trials, beer, and chemical plants.'

'How could you be a student of the German arts and not have studied the birthplace of Hans Sachs and Albrecht Dürer?' said Karin as they all sat around the thick, round, glistening table.

'Well, Sachs was primarily a musician and playwright, and Dürer an engraver and a painter. I concentrated on Germanic literature and the frequently terrible influences—'

'Do you two academics *mind*?' Latham interrupted as Witkowski chuckled. 'We have other things on the current agenda.'

'Sorry, Drew,' said Karin. 'It's just so refreshing to – never mind.'

'I can finish your comment, but I won't,' Latham broke in. 'Who wants to go first?'

'I got up early too,' replied Captain Dietz. 'But not being so aesthetically inclined, I studied Traupman's residence. The Deuxième report said it all. His gorillas prowl around that complex like a wolf pack. They go in, they go out, they circle the building and come back; one disappears, another appears. There's no way to penetrate and live to tell about it.'

'We never seriously considered taking him in his apartment,' said the colonel. 'The Deuxième's men here in Nuremberg are our observers. They'll keep us informed by phone codes when he leaves his residence. One of them should be here pretty soon. You wasted your time, Captain.'

'Not necessarily, sir. One of the guards is a heavy drinker; he's a big, beefy guy and doesn't show it, but he swigs from a flask whenever he's in shadows. Another's got a rash in his crotch and on his stomach – crabs maybe, or poison oak or ivy – he literally runs into dark areas and scratches the hell out of himself.'

'What's your point?' asked De Vries.

'Several, ma'am. Having that information, we could position ourselves to take one or the other or both, and once having taken them, use what we've learned to extract information from them.'

'You employed these tactics in Desert Storm?' Witkowski was obviously impressed.

'It was mostly food there, Colonel. A lot of those Iraqis hadn't eaten in days.'

'I want to know how he enters and leaves his limousine,' said Drew. 'He's got to walk out of the apartment house and into his car, then at the hospital he has to get out of the limo and into the hospital. Whether aboveground or in underground parking lots, he's got to be exposed, if only briefly. Those may be our best opportunities.'

'The compressed times and locations could also work against us, sir,' offered Lieutenant Anthony. 'If we consider them, so will his bodyguards.'

'We have dart guns, silencers, and the element of surprise,' said Latham. 'They've worked more often than not.'

'Go easy,' admonished Witkowski, 'one miss and we're out of business. If they even get a whiff of what we're doing here, they'll pack Herr Doktor Traupman off to a bunker in the Black Forest. I'd say we've got one shot and it had better work. So we wait, we study, and make sure it's our *best* shot.'

'It's the waiting that bothers me, Stosh.'

'The prospect of failure bothers me a lot more,' said the colonel. Suddenly a low, trilling sound erupted from Witkowski's jacket. He reached in and pulled out a small portable phone supplied by the German branch of the Deuxième. 'Yes?'

'Sorry I'm late for breakfast' were the English words spoken in a pronounced French accent over the line. 'I'm only a short distance from the café and should be there in a few minutes.'

'We'll reorder your eggs, they're cold by now.'

'Thank you very much. Cold poached eggs are no eggs at all.'

The colonel turned to his colleagues around the table. 'One of Moreau's men will be here in a couple of minutes. Karin, would you mind going to the desk and bringing him here?'

'Not at all. What's his name and cover?'

'Ahrendt, associate professor, University of Nuremberg.'

'I'm on my way.' De Vries rose from her chair, walked to the door, and left the room.

'That lady is *something*,' said the young commando, Lieutenant Anthony. 'I mean, she's really into history and the arts—'

'We know,' Latham broke in dryly.

The man Karin returned with looked like an average German bank teller, medium height, well dressed in well-pressed off-the-rack clothing of medium cost. Everything about him was medium, which meant he was a superior operative for the spiderlike Deuxième.

'No names are required, gentlemen,' he said, smiling sweetly. 'Even false names – they get so confusing, don't they? However, for convenience sake, just call me Karl, it's such a common name.'

'Sit down, Karl,' said Drew, gesturing at an empty chair. 'I don't have to tell you how much we appreciate your assistance.'

'I only hope and pray it will be helpful.'

'The praying makes me nervous,' interrupted Drew. 'You don't sound terribly confident.'

'You've embarked on an extremely difficult task.'

'We also have extremely competent assistance,' said Witkowski. 'Can you add anything to the report?'

'Quite a bit. Let me start with what we've achieved since the report was sent to Paris. Traupman funnels the majority of his personal business through the office of the hospital's immensely wealthy chairman, a politically and socially connected man – it's an ego trip for Traupman, as if the chairman were at his beck and call.'

'That's a little weird, considering who Traupman is,' said Gerald Anthony, the scholar.

'Not really, Gerry,' Christian Dietz disagreed. 'It's like the secretary of defense ordering up an aircraft by way of the Oval Office. He may be a big man on campus, but there's no one bigger than the President. It's actually very German.'

'Exactly.' The man who called himself Karl nodded. 'And since those instructions are recorded so as to avoid error or blame – also very German – we compromised a hospital clerk into relaying Traupman's instructions to us.'

'Wasn't that dangerous?'

'Not if he was convinced by a uniform that it was Polizei security.'

'You fellows are good,' said Dietz.

'We'd better be or we're dead,' said Karl. 'At any rate, Traupman has made a reservation for six at the garden terrace of the Gartenhof restaurant for eight-thirty this evening.'

'Let's try it.' Lieutenant Anthony was emphatic.

'On the other hand, our man at the airstrip informed us that Traupman has ordered his plane to be ready at five o'clock tomorrow afternoon. Destination Bonn.'

'A neo meeting on the Rhine,' said Dietz. 'The water's best, I *know* it.'

'Easy, Chris,' countered the lieutenant. 'We screwed up on the north beach in Kuwait, remember?'

'We didn't screw up, buddy, the cowboy SEALs did. They were so hyped, they plugged up the engine returns . . . Anyway, we saved their asses by crawling over the sides and—'

'*History*,' Lieutenant Anthony interrupted. 'They got the medals and they deserved them. Two of them got wasted, I hope you remember that too.'

'It shouldn't have happened,' said Dietz quietly.

'But it did,' added Anthony, even quieter.

'So we have two opportunities,' said Latham firmly. 'Tonight at the restaurant, and tomorrow on the Rhine. What do you think, Karl?'

'Both are equally treacherous. I wish you well, my friends.'

In the discarded, obsolete airfield north of Lakenheath, in the cutdown meadows of County Suffolk, the two huge reconditioned Messerschmitt ME 323 gliders had been assembled. It remained only for the powerful jets to sweep down, their engines cut at ten thousand feet so their descents would make minimal noise. Water Lightning would take place within one hundred hours.

In the flattest expanse of bank land between the Dalecarlia reservoir and the Potomac River, two other mammoth reassembled ME 323 gliders – having first been stripped and shipped across the Atlantic – remained on the ground. The huge reservoir, fed by plentiful underground aquifers, was at the end of the final strip of MacArthur Boulevard, and supplied water to all of Arlington, Falls Church, Georgetown, and the District of Columbia, including the ghettos and the White House itself. At the appointed moment, timed down to a fraction of a minute, two Thunderbird jets would swoop down, their engines briefly cut, and with tailhooks would snare the dual pole wires, yanking the

601

gliders airborne. Due to the stress factors, the liftoffs would be assisted by disposable self-propulsion rockets underneath the gliders' wings. They would be activated at the instant of impact. The tactic had been tested in the fields of Mettmach, Germany, the new quarters of the Brüderschaft. Properly executed, it was successful. It would be properly executed here, and the entire capital of the United States would be poisoned, paralysed. Time zero: one hundred hours.

Forty-odd kilometres north of Paris in the Beauvais countryside are the waterworks that supply sections of the city, including the arrondissements that house much of the government – the entire Quai d'Orsay, the presidential palace, the military security barracks, and a host of lesser departments and agencies. Approximately twenty kilometres east of the vast waterworks is flat farmland, and within this massive acreage are scattered three private airfields catering to the rich who disdain the inconveniences of the Orly and De Gaulle airports. At the field farthest to the east stand two huge freshly repainted gliders. The explanation for the curious is properly exotic. They belong to the Saudi royal family for sport over the desert, and since they were built and paid for in France, who cared to know any more? Several jets – how many no one knew – would arrive sometime soon to haul them away on their journey to Riyadh. The control tower was told that they would be airborne in approximately one hundred hours. *Peu d'importance?*

The garden terrace of the Gartenhof restaurant belonged to an older, far more graceful era, when string quartets accompanied fine dinners superbly served and all dishes were carried by hands encased in pure white gloves. The problem was that it *was* a garden, outside on a terrace, profuse with flower boxes overlooking the ancient streets of

Nuremberg, within sight of the hallowed Albrecht Dürer house.

Gerald Anthony, Lieutenant, Special Forces, late of Desert Storm, was furious. He had prepared them all for the mission, for his speciality, a conflagration that would erupt suddenly, distracting everyone, especially the bodyguards seated near Traupman's table who could be sufficiently immobilized during the chaos so as to be useless to their employer. However, the warm breezes winding between the buildings from the Regnitz River were constant, too dangerous for the strategy; only the glass globes around the candles prevented them from being extinguished. A brief, startling burst of fire was all that was needed to spirit Traupman away, but the possibility of the flames spreading throughout the area, conceivably killing or maiming innocent people in the crowded enclosure, was not acceptable. Equally important, the panic engendered by such an expanding breeze-driven fire could easily work against them, clogging the only entrance with hysterical patrons. If even one guard recovered just enough to draw a weapon, the mission could fail with a single gunshot.

In successive glances, each member of the N-2 unit studied Hans Traupman and his guests surreptitiously. The celebrated surgeon was the leader of the peacocks; all that was missing were brightly coloured feathers spreading from half a dozen shoulders, Traupman's the fieriest. He was a thin, medium-size man with animated gestures accompanied by sudden facial expressions, exaggerated to make an inevitably humorous point, although his ageing features resulted in semi-grotesquery. He was not an attractive man, but despite his constant search for approval, if not applause, he was completely in charge – the wealthy host whose abrupt silences caused the others to wait for his next words.

Latham, his appearance altered by horn-rimmed glasses, pasted-on full eyebrows and a moustache, glanced at Karin, equally unrecognizable in the dim candlelight with her pale face unmadeup and her hair sternly pulled back into a hostile bun. She did not return his gaze. Instead, she seemed mesmerized by something or someone at Traupman's table.

Lieutenant Anthony looked across the table at Drew and Colonel Witkowski. Reluctantly, imperceptibly, he shook his head. His superiors, in like manner, did the same. Karin de Vries suddenly spoke in German, her tone frivolous, insouciant, very much unlike her. 'I believe I see an old friend who's going to powder her nose, and so will I.' She got up from the table and walked across the terrace, following another woman.

'What did she say?' asked Drew.

'The ladies' room,' replied Dietz.

'Oh, that's all.'

'I doubt it,' said the equally fluent Anthony.

'What do you mean?' pressed Latham.

'The woman she's tailing is obviously Traupman's date for the evening,' explained Witkowski.

'Is Karin *crazy?*' exploded Latham, whispering intensely. 'What does she think she's *doing?*'

'We'll know when she comes back, *chłopak.*'

'I don't like it!'

'You don't have a choice,' said the colonel.

Twelve frustrating minutes later, De Vries returned to the table. 'To use the American vernacular,' she said in English quietly, 'my new young friend hates the "stinking pervert". She's twenty-six years old and Traupman takes her out to show her off, pays her money, and demands kinky sex when they return to his apartment.'

'How did you *learn* that?' asked Drew.

'It was in her eyes ... I lived in Amsterdam, remember? She's a cocaine addict and desperately needed a dose to get through the evening. I found her giving herself one – also supplied by the good doctor.'

'He's such a beautiful man,' said Captain Christian Dietz contemptuously. 'One day the story will be told how many Iraqis were supplied a daily diet of that crap. Hussein made it part of the military diet! ... Can this lead us to something?'

'Only if we can get into his apartment,' answered Karin, 'which could give us an enormous advantage.'

'How so?' asked Witkowski.

'He makes videotapes of his sexual encounters.'

'*Sick!*' spat out Lieutenant Anthony.

'Sicker than you think,' said De Vries. 'She told me he has a whole library, everything from alpha to zed, including little girls and boys. He claims he needs them to get properly excited.'

'They could be awesome artillery,' interjected the colonel.

'Embarrassment and public disgrace,' said Latham. 'The most powerful weapons ever invented by man.'

'I think we can *do* it,' said Dietz.

'I thought you said we couldn't,' whispered Anthony.

'I can change my mind, can't I?'

'Sure, but your first assessments are usually right, Ringo.'

'*Ringo?*'

'He likes that movie, forget it, sir ... *How*, Chris?'

'First, Mrs de Vries, since you learned about the tapes, I can only assume you made subtle inquiries about the apartment itself. Am I correct?'

'Of course you are. The three guards divide their duties, alternating to give each other breaks, I gather. One remains outside the door at a table with an intercom while the other two, as you described before, Captain, patrol the hallways, the lobby, and the exterior of the building.'

'What about the elevators?' asked Witkowski.

'They don't really matter. Traupman has the penthouse, which is the entire top floor, and to reach it my disturbed young friend says you either enter a code, which is the normal procedure, or you're cleared by the building's own security desk after they've ascertained that you're expected.'

'Then you're talking about two barriers,' said Drew. 'Traupman's guards *and* the apartment building's in-house security.'

'Try three,' interrupted Karin. 'The guard outside the penthouse door has to punch in a series of numbers for the door to open. If he punches in the wrong ones, all hell breaks loose. Sirens, bells, that sort of thing.'

'The girl told you that?' said Lieutenant Anthony.

'She didn't have to, Gerald, it's standard procedure. My husband and I had a variation of that system in Amsterdam.'

'You did?'

'It's a complicated story, Lieutenant,' Latham broke in curtly. 'No time for it now . . . So if we manage somehow – which is highly doubtful – to bypass the guards and the elevator-programmed security desk, we're stymied and probably shot outside the penthouse. It's not exactly an attractive scenario.'

'Do you concede that we could possibly overcome the first two obstacles?' Witkowski asked.

'*I* do,' replied Dietz. 'The drunk and the scratchy-crotch, Gerry and I can take care of. The inside desk could probably be handled by a couple of very official types showing *very* official IDs.' The captain settled his gaze on Latham and Witkowski. '*If* they're really experienced at this kind of exercise, which the lieutenant and I went through twice in Desert Storm,' he added.

'Say we do,' said an increasingly irritated Drew, 'how is anyone going to handle the penthouse robot?'

'There you've got me, sir.'

'Perhaps not me,' interrupted Karin, getting up from the table. 'If things work out, I'll be quite a while,' she continued, speaking softly, enigmatically. 'Please order me a double espresso, it may be an exhausting night.' With those words, De Vries took the long way out of the garden restaurant towards the entrance, and in case anyone was watching her, she doubled back along the walls beyond the crowded tables to the ladies' room.

A full five minutes later the young blonde woman sitting beside Dr Hans Traupman had a mild sneezing fit, the sympathetic conversation at the table ascribing it to Nurem-berg's summer pollen and the breeze. She left the table.

Eighteen minutes later, Karin de Vries returned to her American scholars. 'Here are the conditions,' she said. 'And neither she nor I will accept any less.'

'You met the girl in the ladies' room.' Witkowski did not ask a question, he made a statement.

'She understood that if I left the table and walked towards the entrance, she was to make some excuse and meet me there in three or four minutes.'

'What are the conditions and how does she earn them?' asked Latham.

'Second question first,' said Karin. 'Once inside with Traupman, give her an hour and she'll deactivate the alarm and release the lock on the door.'

'She can be our first woman president,' said Captain Dietz.

'She asks far less. She wants, and I agree with her, a permanent visa to the United States and enough money to see her through rehabilitation, as well as sufficient funds to live in relative comfort for three years. She doesn't dare stay here in Germany, and after three years, while polishing her English, she believes she'll be able to find work.'

'She's got it and then some,' said Drew. 'She could have demanded a lot more.'

'In all honesty, my dear, she may very well, later. She's a survivor, not a saint, and she *is* an addict. That's her reality.'

'Then it'll be someone else's problem,' the colonel interrupted.

'Traupman just signalled for the check,' said Lieutenant Anthony.

'Then, as your German guide, I shall also, in several minutes.' De Vries leaned down over her chair as if to retrieve her purse or a fallen napkin. Three tables away the blonde woman did the same, picking up a gold cigarette lighter that had slipped from her fingers. Their eyes met; Karin blinked twice, Traupman's escort once.

The night's agenda was set.

CHAPTER THIRTY-SIX

The apartment complex – *house* did not do it justice – was one of those cold steel and tinted-glass structures that made a person long for stone walls, spires, arches, and even flying buttresses. It was not so much the work of an architect as it was the product of a robotic computer, the aesthetics found in vast wasted space and stress tolerances. However, it was imposing, the front windows literally two storeys high, the lobby made of white marble, in the centre of which was a large reflecting pool with a cascading fountain illuminated by underwater floodlights. As each floor ascended, the inside corridors were bordered by an interior, fifty-four-inch wall of speckled granite that permitted all but the shortest people to observe the opulence below. The effect was less of beauty than of triumphant engineering.

On the left of the white-marbled lobby was the untinted, sliding glass window of the security office, behind the glass a uniformed apartment guard whose job it was to admit visitors who identified themselves over the entrance inter-com after ascertaining their welcome by those in residence. Further, in the interest of privacy and safety, the security desk had at a guard's fingertips the alarms for *Fire*, *Forced Entry*, and *Police*; the last, stationed approximately a half mile away, could be at the building in no more than sixty seconds. The complex was eleven storeys high, the penthouse occupying the entire eleventh floor.

The exterior, as might be expected, was in keeping with the establishment's prices. A circular drive led from tall hedgerow to hedgerow, between which was a landscaper's semi-annuity: sculptured foliage, flowering gardens, five concrete goldfish ponds – aerated naturally, and with flagstone paths for those who cared to stroll outside amid nature's beauty. In the rear of the complex, in sight of the medieval Neutergraben Wall, was an Olympic-size swimming pool, complete with cabanas and an outside bar for the summer months. Everything considered, Dr Hans Traupman, the Rasputin of the neo-Nazi movement, lived very well.

'This is like breaking into Leavenworth without an army pass,' whispered Latham behind the greenery of sculptured bushes in front of the entrance. Alongside him was Captain Christian Dietz, who had previously reconnoitred the area. 'Every access back by the pool is electronically sealed – you touch a screen with a human hand and the sirens go off. I know those fibres. They're heat sensitized.'

'I'm aware of that, sir,' said the Ranger from Desert Storm. 'It's why I told you the only way was to take out the two roving bodyguards, get past the house security, and reach the eleventh floor.'

'Can you and Anthony really get rid of the guards?'

'That's not the problem . . . sir. Gerry will take the big guy with the flask, and I'll deep-six the scratch merchant. The problem, as I see it, is whether you and the colonel can talk yourselves through the apartment security.'

'Witkowski was on the phone with a couple of the Deuxième agents. He says it's under control.'

'How?'

'Two or three names from the Polizei. They'll make calls to the in-house security guard and pave the way. Top secret and all the rest of that mumbo-jumbo.'

'The Deuxième works with the Nuremberg *police*?'

'They may, but that's not what I said. I said "names", not people. I presume they'll be important names whether they're real people or not . . . What the hell, Chris, it's well after midnight, who's going to check? When the Allies stormed Normandy, no one dared wake up Hitler's chief aides, much less the man himself.'

'Is the colonel's German really good? I've heard him speak only a little bit of it.'

'He's totally fluent.'

'He's got to be authoritative—'

'Can you doubt it? Witkowski doesn't speak, he barks.'

'Look – he just struck a cupped match from the bushes on our right flank. Something's happening.'

'He and the lieutenant are nearer. Can you see what it is?'

'Yes,' replied Captain Dietz, peering through the foliage. 'It's the big Kraut with the juice. Gerry's scrambling around to the far right; he'll take him in the shadows halfway down the building's path.'

'Are you fellas always so confident?'

'Why not? It's simply a job and we're trained to do it.'

'Has it occurred to you that in hand-to-hand the other guy might be tougher?'

'Oh, sure, that's why we specialize in the dirtiest tricks on record. Don't you? A friend of mine at the Paris embassy saw you play hockey in Toronto or Manitoba or someplace; he said you were the mother ship of body-check techniques.'

'This subject is over,' ordered Latham. 'What happens if whisky-boy doesn't come back? Will the other guard be waiting for him?'

'They're German, they go by the clock. Any deviation is unacceptable. If one soldier is derelict, another can't be influenced by the dereliction. He continues the march, the watch. There, *see*! Gerry's got him.'

'*What?*'

'You weren't looking. Gerry struck a match and arched it to his left. Mission accomplished . . . Now I'll crawl straight forward while you join the colonel on the flank, sir.'

'Yes, I know that—'

'It'll be a while, maybe as long as twenty minutes or so, but be patient, it *will* happen.'

'From your mouth to God's ear.'

'Yeah, Gerry said you'd probably say something like that. See you later, Mr Cons-Op.' The Special Forces captain wormed his way towards the canopied entrance of the condominium complex as Drew crawled between the stalks of the flowers of the English-style garden to the hedgerow where Stanley Witkowski lay prone.

'Those sons of bitches are *outstanding*!' pronounced the colonel, a pair of infrared binoculars at his eyes. 'They've got ice water in their veins!'

'Well, it's simply a job they're trained to do, and they do it well,' said Drew, hugging the ground.

'From your mouth to God's ear, *chłopak*,' erupted Witkowski. 'Here goes the *other* one . . . hell, they're magnificent! Go for the kill, nothing less!'

'I don't think we want kills, Stanley. We'd rather have captives.'

'I'll take either one. I just want to get in there.'

'Can we do it?'

'The setup's in place, but we won't know until we try. If there's a problem, we blast ourselves in.'

'The guard will alert the police the moment he sees a weapon.'

'There are eleven storeys, where do they start?'

'Good point. Let's go!'

'Not yet. The captain's target hasn't arrived yet.'

'I thought you just said "here he goes".'

'Into position, not for Maggie's drawers.'

'For *what*?'

'It's a marine term. You can't score until the bull's-eye appears.'

'Will you *please* speak English?'

'The second of the two guards hasn't come out.'

'*Thank* you.'

Six minutes passed and Witkowski spoke. 'Here he comes, right on schedule. Bless the *Ein, Zwei, Drei*!' Thirty seconds later a match was struck and thrown to the striker's left. 'He's out,' said the colonel. 'Come on, and stand up straight.

Remember, you're a member of the Nuremberg police. Just stay behind me and don't open your mouth.'

'What could I say? "*O, Tannenbaum, mein Tannenbaum*"?'

'Here we go.' Both men raced across the circular drive, and upon reaching the broad canopy fronting the thick glass doors of the entrance, they stopped. Catching their breath and standing erect, they approached the outside panel that was the intercom to the security desk.

'*Guten Abend*,' said the colonel, continuing in German, 'we're the detective detail called in to check the external emergency relay equipment for Dr Traupman's residence.'

'*Ach*, yes, your two superiors called an hour ago, but as I told them both, the doctor is entertaining tonight—'

'And I trust they told *you* that we will not disturb the doctor,' Witkowski interrupted curtly. 'In fact, neither he nor his personal escorts are to be disturbed, those are the commandant's orders, and I for one would not care to be a party to disobeying those instructions. The external equipment is in the storage room across the floor from Dr Traupman's door. He will not even know we've been here – that is the way the chief of Nuremberg's police wishes it to be. But then, I'm sure he made it clear to you.'

'What happened anyway? To the . . . equipment?'

'Probably an accident, someone moving furniture or cartons into the storage room and severing a wire. We won't know until we examine the panels, which we're responsible for . . . Frankly, I wouldn't know if I fell over the malfunction, my colleague's the expert.'

'I didn't even know there was such equipment,' said the apartment guard.

'There's a lot you're not aware of, my friend. Between you and me, the doctor has direct lines to all high-ranking officials in the police and the government, even to Bonn.'

'I knew he was a great surgeon, but I had no idea—'

'Let's say he's extremely generous with our superiors, yours and mine,' Witkowski again interrupted, his voice now friendly. 'So, for all our sakes, let's not rock the boat. We're wasting time, let us in, please.'

'Certainly, but you'll still have to sign the register.'

'And possibly lose our jobs? Yours as well?'

'Forget it. I'll insert the elevator codes for the eleventh floor, that's the penthouse. Do you need the key for the storage room?'

'No, thanks. Traupman gave one to our commandant and he gave it to us.'

'You erase all my doubts. Come inside.'

'Naturally, we'll show you our identification cards, but again, for all our sakes, remember you never saw us.'

'Naturally. This is a good job, and I certainly don't want the police on my back.'

The elevator was around the corner and out of sight from the surgeon's penthouse entrance on the eleventh floor. Latham and the colonel inched their way along the wall; Drew peered around the edge of marbleized concrete. The guard at the desk was in shirtsleeves and reading a paperback book while tapping his fingers to the rhythm of the soft music coming from a small portable radio. He was at least fifty feet away, the imposing console in front of him his direct link to several receivers that could cause the aborting of Operation N-2. Latham checked his watch and whispered to Witkowski.

'It's not a pleasant situation, Stosh,' he said.

'Didn't expect it to be, *chłopak*,' said the veteran G-2 officer, reaching into his jacket pocket and taking out five marbles. 'Karin was right, you know. Diversion's everything.'

'We're past the hour when Traupman's girlfriend said she'd deactivate the alarm. She's got to be sweating it out in there.'

'I know that. Use the darts and aim for his neck area. Keep firing until you hit his throat.'

'*What?*'

'He'll get up and walk down here, believe me.'

'What are you going to do?'

'Watch.' Witkowski rolled a marble out on the marble floor; it clattered until it hit the opposite wall and stopped. He then threw another out in the opposite direction; it, too, spun to a stop. 'What's happening?' he whispered to Drew.

'Your scenario. He's getting up and coming towards us.'

'The closer he gets, the better shot you have.' The colonel threw two marbles down the corridor to his right; they clattered, marble against marble; the bodyguard raced forward, weapon in hand. He rounded the corner and Latham fired three narcotic darts; the first missed, ricocheting off the wall, the second and third struck the neo-Nazi on the right side of his neck. The man gasped, grabbed his throat, and uttered a low, prolonged cry as he slowly collapsed.

'Take out the two darts, find the other, and let's get him back to the desk,' said Witkowski. 'The drug wears off in half an hour.' They carried the neo to the desk, placing him in the chair, his upper body slumped over the top. Drew went to the penthouse door, took a deep, prayerful breath, and opened it. There was no alarm, only darkness and silence until a weak female voice spoke – unfortunately in German.

'*Schnell. Beeilen Sie sich!*'

'Hold it!' said Latham, but the command was unnecessary, as the colonel was at his side. 'What's she saying, and can we turn on a light?'

'Yes,' replied the woman. 'I speak *Englisch* little, not good.' With those words she snapped on the foyer light. The blonde girl was fully dressed, her purse and overnight case in hand. Witkowski stepped forward. 'We go now, *ja?*'

'Let's not get ahead of ourselves, Fräulein,' said the colonel in German. 'Business comes first.'

'I have been *promised*!' she cried. 'A visa, a passport – protection for me to go to America!'

'You'll get it all, miss. But short of carrying Traupman out of here, where are the tapes?'

'I have fifteen – the most grotesque of the lot – in my bag here. As to taking the *Herr Doktor* out of the apartment house, it is impossible. The service entrance is locked with an alarm from eight o'clock in the evening until eight in the morning. There is no other way, and television cameras record everything.'

The colonel translated for Drew, who replied, 'Maybe we can get Traupman past the security desk. What the hell, his guards are gone.' Witkowski again translated, now for the German woman.

'That is foolishness leading to the death of us all!' she countered emphatically. 'You don't understand this place. The owners are the richest in Nuremberg, and what with the kidnappings of the wealthy throughout Germany these days, a resident himself must inform the desk that he is leaving the premises.'

'So I'll use the phone and be Traupman, so what? Where is he, incidentally?'

'Asleep in the bedroom; he's an old man and easily exhausted by the wine . . . and other methods. But you really *don't* understand. The rich all over Europe travel with guards and bulletproof automobiles. You may have gotten in here, and I congratulate you on doing so, but if you think you can leave with the doctor, you're mad!'

'We'll sedate him, just as we did the guard outside the door.'

'Even more foolish. His limousine must be called up from the garage before he leaves the building, and only his bodyguards have the combination for the key vault—'

'*Key* vault?'

'Automobiles can be stolen or tampered with – you *really* don't understand.'

'What the hell are you two talking about?' Drew broke in. 'Stop with the German!'

'We're screwed,' said the colonel. 'The Deuxième report didn't go far enough. How about armoured vehicles under the canopy before he goes outside, and combination vaults in the garage for the keys?'

'The whole damn country's paranoid!'

'*Nein*, *mein Herr*,' said Traupman's woman for the evening. 'I understand a little of what you say. Not entire Deutschland – parts, sections where the rich live. They are frightened.'

'How about the *Nazis*? Is anyone frightened of them, lady?'

'They are garbage, *mein Herr*! No decent person supports them.'

'What the hell do you think Traupman is?'

'A bad man, a senile old man—'

'He's a goddamned *Nazi*!'

It was as though the young woman had been struck in the face. She winced and shook her head. 'I have no . . . no knowing of such a thing. His *Freunde . . . in der Medizin*, they have respect. Many are *berühmt*. So famous.'

'That's his cover,' said Witkowski in German. 'He's one of the leaders of the movement, that's why we want him.'

'I can't do any more than I am doing, sir! I'm sorry, but I cannot. You have the tapes, that's all I promised. Now you must make it possible for me to leave Germany, for if what you say is true, I will be marked by the Nazi pigs.'

'We honour our agreements, miss.' The colonel turned to Latham and spoke in English. 'We're out of here, *chłopak*. We can't take the bastard without jeopardizing the whole operation. We'll fly to Bonn in an hour or so on a Deuxième plane and wait for the son of a bitch there.'

'Do you think he'll still go to Bonn tomorrow?' asked Drew.

'I don't think he has a choice. Also, I'm counting on a German chain of command, which is a lot more rigid than ours. Blame is to be avoided at all costs, which is pretty much the same as ours, actually.'

'Clarification, please?'

'Each of Traupman's bodyguards has been drugged.

They'll come to in twenty or thirty minutes, scared shitless no doubt, and immediately check on the penthouse.'

'Where they'll find Traupman peacefully asleep,' interrupted Latham. 'But what about the tapes, Stosh?'

Witkowski looked at the young blonde woman and asked the same question. Traupman's lady of the evening opened her purse and pulled out a key. 'This is one of the two keys to the steel cabinet that holds the rest of the tapes,' she answered in German. 'The other is in the Nuremberg National Bank.'

'Will he miss the key?'

'I don't believe he'll even think about it. He keeps it in the second drawer of his bureau, beneath his underwear.'

'Then I ask this only because I must. Did he tape your activities this evening?'

'Certainly not, it would be too embarrassing. After I met with your associate in the ladies' room, I saw, as they say, my way out. I always carry an eyedropper filled with a sleep-inducing narcotic in the event the evening becomes too repulsive.'

'Yet you're an addict yourself, aren't you?'

'It would be ridiculous to deny it. I have sufficient dosages to last me three days. After that I have been promised to be put on private subsistence in America . . . I did not choose to become an addict, sir, I was led into it, as it was for so many of my sisters in East Berlin. We all became high-priced official hostesses and consequently addicts so we could survive.'

'We're *out* of here,' yelled Witkowski. 'These kids are victims!'

'Then let's go, Colonel-mine,' said Latham. 'Captain Dietz will get his chance on the Rhine after all.'

One by one, the disoriented bodyguards converged in the hallway outside Traupman's door. Each of their accounts of what happened was different, yet each was the same, the variations due to self-serving excuses, for none really *knew* what had happened. That they had been attacked was a given, but none was seriously injured.

'We'd better go inside and see if there's damage,' said the man whose breath was born in a distillery.

'Nobody could *get* inside!' protested the guard who manned the hallway desk. 'There would be a crowd up here if anyone had tried. The alarm simultaneously alerts the lobby security *and* the police.'

'Still, we were assaulted and drugged,' insisted the bodyguard whose hands roamed around his stomach and private parts, scratching furiously.

'I hope to God you're seeing a doctor,' said the whisky-prone man. 'I don't want to catch what you've got.'

'Then don't have a picnic on the banks of the Regnitz with a slut who makes love in the weeds. The *bitch*! . . . We must go inside, if only to learn whether we have to get the hell out of Nuremberg.'

'I'll deactivate the alarm and free the door,' said the desk guard, bending over unsteadily and touching a series of numbers on his console. 'There, it's unlocked.'

'You go first,' instructed the riverbank lover.

Four minutes later the threesome returned to the hallway, perplexed, uncertain, each in his own way stunned.

'I don't know what to think,' said the large man. 'The doctor is sleeping peacefully, nothing was upset, no papers in his study disturbed—'

'And no young woman!' interrupted the scratch merchant. 'You think . . . ?'

'I *know*,' pronounced the guard whose skin was driving him crazy. 'I tried to tell the doctor subtly, you understand, that she was not good for him. She lives with a hot-tempered policeman who's separated from his wife, and, God knows, *he* can't afford her habit.'

'The police . . . the alarms . . . she could have done it all with her boyfriend's help,' said the hallway guard, sitting down at his desk and picking up the phone from his console. 'There's one way to find out,' he continued. 'We'll call her apartment.' Reading from a list of prominent numbers encased in plastic, he dialled. A full minute passed and he replaced the phone. 'There's no answer. They've either left the city or are out somewhere establishing an alibi.'

'For *what*?' asked the guard, nervously drinking from his flask, unnerved because it was now empty.

'I don't know.'

'Then none of us knows ... anything.' The bodyguard was adamant. 'The doctor is fine, the whore left of her own volition – Heinrich can verify that – and everything is normal, *right*?'

'Why not?' agreed the guard named Heinrich at the desk. 'Even Herr Doktor Traupman would find it acceptable. He'd rather not see those women in the morning.'

'So then, my comrades, nothing happened,' said the man, glancing at his empty flask. 'I will continue my watch, stopping in the garage and my automobile for replenishment.'

The floodlights shining down on the docks of the marina on the Rhine River in Bonn were in full force. All but one would be extinguished when the small powerboat left its slip in a matter of minutes. A half mile away, in darkness, was another craft, its hull and deck painted a deep hunter green, its engine off, bobbing up and down in the gentle river currents; its inhabitants were in wet suits, scuba tanks strapped to their backs. There were six of them, the sixth person, a captain, an agent of the Deuxième. Of the five prepared to go underwater, only Karin de Vries had to vociferously justify her inclusion.

'I've probably had more experience with scuba equipment than you have, Officer Latham.'

'I doubt that,' Drew had replied. 'I was trained at the Scripps Institute in San Diego, and you don't get any better than that.'

'And I learned with Frederik in the Black Sea, four weeks

of preparation – our cover was a sporting husband and wife. If Stanley's memory is intact, he might recall the exercise.'

'I do, young lady,' Witkowski had said. 'We paid for the whole operation . . . Freddie de V brought back a couple of hundred underwater shots of the Soviet vessels in and around Sevastopol. Tonnage, displacement, the whole enchilada.'

'I took at least a third of those photographs,' added Karin defiantly.'

'All right,' Latham had conceded, 'but if we get out of this alive, you're going to have to learn that you don't wear the pants in the family.'

'And you'll not get into mine unless you change your attitude . . . Did you just ask me to marry you?'

'I've asked you before – not in so many words, but plain enough – what's new?'

'Put a cap on it, you two,' ordered Witkowski. 'Here comes Dietz.'

The commando captain approached and squatted in front of them. 'I've gone over the strategy with our skipper and he can find no holes. Now, let me go over it again with you people.'

Captain Christian Dietz's plan, if not a masterpiece of confusion, was certainly designed to elude penetration during the moments of hostile activity. Trailing the dark green motorboat, hauled by a rope, was a black PVC life raft with a 250 hp engine, capable of making 40 knots an hour. In addition, rolled up at the bow was a black tarpaulin that could be released over the entire raft, engine included. The strategy was simplicity itself – if everything worked according to schedule.

A mile or so out of its slip, Traupman's small boat would be attacked by the underwater N-2 unit, its gas jets plugged by liquid-steel caps that would harden in seconds. Then from all sides the roving television cameras were to be shorted out by silent pellets exploded from pistols as powerful as .357 Magnums. The unit would then board

Traupman's boat, rip out all other communications equipment, sedate the doctor, and deliver him to the black PVC raft with the Deuxième captain, who would roll out the black tarpaulin. Traupman's boat would then be set on automatic pilot upriver, while the unit returned to their painted dark green motorboat to head into shore near Traupman's destination.

The first two exercises worked. Under the guidance of Lieutenant Anthony and Captain Dietz, Latham, Witkowski, and Karin surfaced beside the speeding boat, grabbing whatever ribs they could find and shoving the steel caps into the small circular gas holes marked by small red circles. The craft slowed down; it was heading into shore. As one, all five climbed on board, facing a terrified Traupman.

'*Was ist los?*' he screamed, reaching for his radio. It was instantly torn out by Latham, while Karin walked up to the Nazi, ripped open his jacket, and inserted a needle into the flesh beneath his shirt. 'I will have you *shot* . . . !' were the last words Traupman spoke before falling to the deck.

'Get him into the raft!' yelled Witkowski as the black PVC pulled alongside and the Nazi's body was lowered over the gunwale. 'Now, full speed out of here!'

'I'll circle the boat and put it on auto, north-northwest!' cried Christian Dietz.

'What the hell is *that*?'

'Not to worry, Cons-Op,' replied Lieutenant Gerald Anthony. 'It's straight up the Rhine, curves included. We studied the maps.'

'Traupman was headed towards that yellow light on a dock over on the left,' said Karin.

'Are you thinking what I'm thinking?' said Drew.

'I hope so, for I will *not* be denied.'

'Then over the sides and swim to our own boat, if we can see it.'

'I anchored it, Cons-Op,' said Anthony. 'It's right over there – no more than a hundred feet away. Once we're on board, I'll steer it into shore under a bunch of trees.'

'How would you like to be a colonel, Lieutenant?'

'I'd *love* it!' cried Captain Dietz, returning from making sure Traupman was under black cover in the motorized raft and was on his way to the opposite side of the Rhine. 'Let *him* pay for *my* dinners . . . Let's get out of here! We've got to send this hunk of wood upriver.'

The suggestion came none too soon, for within minutes, as Traupman's empty boat reached the centre of the Rhine, the marina helicopter descended, as if to provide rescue equipment. Instead, a continuous fusillade of machine gun rounds sprayed the craft, circling twice, and finally blowing it apart with cannon fire. It sank.

'That's hardball,' said Latham to Karin and their three colleagues as they sat on the banks of the Rhine.

'I say we go back to that dock, wait and see who else arrives, and find out how hard,' said Witkowski.

CHAPTER THIRTY-SEVEN

They removed the scuba equipment from their backs, leaving the black wet suits and coarse rubber foot coverings intact. Assorted weapons and miniaturized walkie-talkies were taken out of Captain Dietz's waterproof duffel bag and distributed. The semi-commando unit then crawled along the riverbank to within sight of the dock with the dull yellow light. Slowly, at approximately ten-minute intervals, the small, sleek boats drifted into the slips from various directions until the majority were filled. Suddenly, the yellow light was extinguished.

'I think the class is assembled,' whispered Latham to Witkowski. Karin was on the colonel's left, the two commandos on Drew's right.

'Gerry and I will reconnoitre,' said Dietz as he and the lieutenant elbowed forward, the blades of their long knives erratically reflecting the moonlight.

'I'll go with you,' said Latham.

'That's definitely not a good idea ... sir,' protested Anthony. 'We work better alone – sir.'

'Cut the "sir" crap, please. I'm not army, but I'm running this operation.'

'What he means, Mr Cons-Op,' explained the captain, 'is that he and I have signals we recognize when we've studied an area. Like the low rustle of a breeze through the trees, or the gulp of a frog, anything that's indigenous.'

'You're kidding.'

'Not for a second,' replied the lieutenant, 'it's basic to the work.'

'Also,' continued Dietz, 'if this estate here is what all the reports suggest, there'll be patrols roaming around.'

'Like Traupman's place?' Witkowski interjected.

'That was chocolate cake, sir – I'd studied it before.'

'All right, go ahead,' said Drew. 'Leave your radios on transmit and call us when we can move forward – and be careful.'

'That's even more basic to the work,' said Anthony, glancing hesitantly over at Karin de Vries, and lowering his whisper to the point where Latham could barely hear him. 'Our orders in Nuremberg were to immobilize, not neutralize. From what we saw that chopper do out there on the river, I don't think that rule can apply here.'

'It doesn't, Lieutenant. This is the core of the Nazi movement, so consider yourself at war. If it's at all possible, we have to learn who's in there, that's the most important thing we can do. So if you have to use those knives, use them well.'

The following minutes were akin to the sound track of some ghoulish film noir, the images far more powerful, for they were imagined, not seen. Karin and Witkowski kept a single radio between them, Drew held his in front of his eyes. What all three heard caused each to wince, the colonel less so than Latham and De Vries. As the two commandos crept forward through the dense, tangled foliage of the riverbank, there were rushes of leaves and footsteps and sudden muted screams cut off by the horrible expulsions of air and liquid, the skewering of blades through flesh. Then more footsteps, racing, growing fainter, coughing grunts accompanied by cracking spits that had to be silenced pistol shots. More running feet, snaps of broken twigs, louder now, the range diminishing. Then silence – total, frightening – suddenly broken by a burst of static and the sound once again of footsteps, but on a hard surface. Karin, Drew, and Witkowski looked at one another, their intense eyes conveying their fears of the worst. Then voices, all speaking German, pleading, supplications – in *German*! Crashes of

625

metal and glass followed, now accompanied by moans and the exploding cry of a voice in *English*.

'My God, don't kill me!'

'*Christ!*' exploded Witkowski. 'They've been captured. You stay here, I'm going after them!'

'Hold it, Stanley,' ordered Drew, gripping the colonel's shoulder with the strong hand of a former, younger hockey champion. 'Stay where you are, I *mean* that!'

'I'll be damned if I will! Those boys are in trouble!'

'If they are, you'll only get killed, and we all had that option, isn't that what you said?'

'This is *different*! I've got a full automatic with clips enough to fire two hundred rounds.'

'I feel the same way you do, Stosh, but that's not why we're here, is it?'

'You big son of a bitch,' said the colonel quietly, lowering himself to the ground, 'you really could be an officer.'

'Not in any army I ever heard of, I can't stand the uniforms.'

'All right, *chłopak*, what do we do?'

'We wait – that's another thing you told me – waiting's the hardest part.'

'So it is.'

It was not, however, as the breathless voice of Captain Christian Dietz came softly over the radio. 'Beach One to Beach Two. We've taken out four patrols by necessity, roped and taped two others who gave no resistance. We then followed the lines and captured the security centre in a subcellar below the carriage house sixty or seventy yards east of the estate. Of the three operators here, one is dead, shot while attempting to set off an auxiliary alarm, another roped and taped, the third – a good-ol'-boy redneck who married a German girl while in the army – is still crying and singing "God Bless America."'

'You guys are fantastic!' exclaimed Drew. 'What's happening at the big house? Did you get a chance to see?'

'Only a couple of glimpses through the windows once we

took out the lawn patrols. Between twenty and thirty men and some blond-haired priest at the lectern who wasn't offering any prayers, just fire and brimstone. By the looks of things, he's the chief rabbi around here.'

'A *priest*?'

'Well, he's in a dark suit with a white collar around his neck. What else could he be?'

'There was a priest or a minister in Paris – how tall is he?'

'Not your size, but pretty close. I'd say five eleven or six feet.'

'Oh, my *God*!' intruded the panicked voice of Karin de Vries, her whole body trembling.

'*What?*'

'A *priest* . . . with blond *hair*!' Shuddering, she covered the radio and whispered to Latham and Witkowski. 'We must get over to one of those windows.'

'What is it?' asked Drew as the colonel stared at De Vries. 'What's the *matter*?'

'Do as I *say*!'

'Do it,' said Witkowski, his eyes still on Karin.

'Beach Two to Beach One, what's the scene like at the estate?'

'I don't think we missed anyone, but I can't guarantee it. You know, a guy could've been taking a leak somewhere in the bushes—'

'Then when he came out he'd find a few corpses, wouldn't he?'

'If so, he might have opted for getting the hell out of here and reaching some neos in Bonn.'

'I think you're better than that,' said Drew. 'We're moving forward.'

'Just calm down, Cons-Op. Wait'll we position ourselves between the house and the river. I'll let you know when to come out.'

'I'll accept that, Captain. You're the experts.'

'You better believe it . . . sir,' said the voice of Lieutenant

Anthony. 'And please keep Mrs de Vries on your river flank in case there's a firefight.'

'Naturally.' Latham covered the radio and spoke to Karin over Witkowski's head. 'You know, that kid's beginning to annoy me.'

'He's okay,' said Witkowski.

'He's twelve years old.'

'*Please*, the windows!' Karin urged.

'When we get the word, young lady.' Unobtrusively, the colonel reached for De Vries's trembling hand and gripped it. 'Easy, girl,' he whispered. 'Control, remember?'

'You *know* . . . ?'

'I don't know anything. Just a few unanswered questions from the past.'

'Beach Two,' came Dietz's quiet voice over the radio. 'You're clean, but stay low. There could be infrared trips waist-high until you reach the upper terrace.'

'I thought you short-circuited the system,' Witkowski broke in.

'The cameras and the fences, Colonel. They may be enough, but the trips could be wired underground and independent.'

'Understood, Captain, we'll stay close to the ground.'

The trio crawled forward, Latham in the lead, the waves of the Rhine lapping over the path Drew created on the riverbank. Mud sticking to their wet suits, their weapons held directly over their heads, they reached the border of the estate's sloping lawn. Coming side by side, each nodded to the other as they proceeded up through the grass to the first, lower patio overlooking the dock. Atop the ascending hill of manicured lawn was a second patio-terrace, beyond which was the rear of the river mansion, a wall of sliding glass doors indicating an enormous interior, a ballroom or a banquet hall judging by the dimly lit chandeliers.

'I've seen this place before!' whispered Drew.

'You've *been* here?' asked Witkowski.

'No. Pictures, photographs of it.'

'Where?'

'In one of those architectural magazines, I don't recall which, but I remember the descending terraces and the row of glass doors . . . *Karin!* What are you *doing?*'

'I have to look inside.' As if in a trance, De Vries stood up and began walking like a robot across the grass towards the wall of huge glass panels. 'I must!'

'*Stop* her!' said the colonel. 'Good Christ, stop her!'

Latham shot forward, grabbing Karin around the waist and pulling her to the ground, rolling over and over to the right, away from the wash of light. 'What's *wrong* with you? Do you want to get yourself killed?'

'I have to look *inside*! You can't stop me.'

'All right, all *right*, I agree with you, we all agree with you, but let's be halfway bright about it.'

Suddenly the two Special Forces commandos were on their knees, flanking them, Witkowski scrambling up from the terrace patio. 'That wasn't too smart, Mrs de Vries,' said Captain Dietz angrily. 'You don't know who may be standing by one of those glass doors, and there's a fair amount of moonlight tonight.'

'I'm sorry, truly sorry, but it's important to me, *so* important. You mentioned a priest, a blond priest . . . I must look at him!'

'Oh, my . . . *God!*' whispered Drew, staring at Karin, seeing the panic in her eyes, the trembling of her head. 'This is what you wouldn't tell me—'

'Ease off, *chłopak!*' ordered the colonel, interrupting and gripping Latham's left arm.

'You,' said Drew, turning his head and looking hard at the lined, stern face of the G-2 veteran. 'You know what this is all about, don't you, Stosh?'

'I may or I may not. However, I'm not the issue. Stay with her, young fella, she may need all the support you can provide.'

'Follow us,' said Lieutenant Anthony. 'We swing to the right and reach the corner, then sidestep our way to the first door. We slip-tripped the latch and opened it an inch or two, enough to hear what's going on beyond the drape.'

Half a minute later the five-member unit was huddled by the corner of the estate's ground floor, at the edge of the upper terrace. Witkowski tapped Latham's shoulder. 'Go with her,' he whispered. 'Keep your hands free and quick. There may be nothing, but be prepared for anything.'

Drew gently pushed Karin forward, holding her shoulders, until they reached the first sliding glass door. She peered around the edge of the inside drape and saw the man at the spotlighted lectern, heard the blond priest exhorting the crowd into hysterical shouts of *Sieg Heil, Günter Jäger!* Her mouth agape, her eyes wild, she started to scream. Latham clamped his hand over her mouth while the roars of *Sieg Heil* filled the ballroom, and spun her around back to the corner of the mansion.

'It's he!' choked De Vries. 'It's *Frederik!*'

'Get her back to the boat,' the colonel fairly yelled. 'We'll finish up here.'

'What's to finish? *Kill* the son of a bitch!'

'Now you're not acting like an officer, lad. There's always a follow-up.'

'And we're following up, Colonel,' said Captain Christian Dietz, gesturing at his lieutenant, who held a miniaturized video camcorder in his hands and was recording the frenzied event taking place inside.

'Get her *out* of here!' repeated Witkowski.

The ride back across the river was made mostly in silence, in deference to the shock sustained by Karin. For a long time she preferred to stand alone at the bow, staring in the moonlight at the opposite shoreline. Halfway across she turned and looked pleadingly at Latham, who got up from the gunwale and walked over to her.

'Can I help?' he asked quietly.

'You already have, but can you *forgive* me?'

'For God's sake, for *what*?'

'I lost control, I could have killed us all. Stanley warned me about losing control.'

'You had every reason to . . . So this was your secret, that your husband was alive and—'

'No, *no*,' interrupted Karin. 'Or I should say, yes, but not this way, not what we saw tonight. I was sure he was alive and I believed he had turned and was part of the Nazi movement – willingly or unwillingly – but nothing like this!'

'What did you think?'

'So many things, so many possible explanations. Before East Berlin fell, I left him, telling him that we were finished unless he put his very odd life back together. His drinking was never a problem, for alcohol only made him pleasant, expansive, and full of fun. Then he changed, drastically, and became horribly abusive, striking me and throwing me into walls. He wouldn't admit it, but he had gravitated to drugs, which was antithetical to everything he believed.'

'What do you mean?'

'He believed in himself, *liked* himself. Drinking sporadically was a now-and-then enjoyment, not an addiction. If it had been, your brother wouldn't have tolerated him – for both personal and professional reasons.'

'I'll grant you that,' said Drew. 'Harry liked good wine and a fine brandy, but he had no use for anyone who drank himself into a stupor. Neither do I, as a matter of fact.'

'That's my point, neither did Freddie. Anything that altered who he was for any length of time was abhorrent to him. Yet he changed, as I say, drastically. He became an enigma, a monster one minute, contrite the next. Then one night in Amsterdam, having convinced myself that Harry was right, that Frederik was dead, I got an obscene phone call. It was the sort adolescents make showing off in front of their friends, disguising their voices by pitching them high or low and speaking through paper. There were the usual sexual demands and insults, so I started to hang up, when a particular phrase or series of words were used that stunned me. I'd heard them before – from *Freddie!* I shouted, "My

God, is that you, Freddie?" . . . I can still hear the agonizing scream that followed, and I knew I'd been right and Harry was wrong.'

'What we saw tonight was a variation of that monster,' Drew said. 'I wonder if he's still on drugs.'

'I have no idea. Perhaps a psychiatrist should be brought in to watch the tape Lieutenant Anthony made.'

'I can't wait to see it myself. That tape could be a gold mine . . . Karin, what does Witkowski know?'

'Again, I have no idea. All he said to me was that there were unanswered questions from the past. I don't know what he meant.'

'Let's ask him.' Latham turned and addressed the colonel, who was sitting on the starboard gunwale with the two commandos. 'Stan, can you come here a minute?'

'Sure.' The colonel walked across the deck and stood between Drew and Karin.

'Stosh, you knew more about tonight than you told either of us, didn't you?'

'No, I didn't *know*, I merely assumed the possibility. One of Freddie de V's favourite personas when he went under-cover was that of a priest, and, Lord knows, he was blonder than Marilyn Monroe when he didn't dye his hair. When the captain described a blond priest around six feet tall, I was next to you, Karin, and watched you go ballistic. Suddenly memories came back to me.'

'That doesn't answer why you could even imagine it might be her husband up there,' said Latham.

'Well, now you're going back a few years. When G-2 got word of Frederik de Vries's death at the hands of the Stasi, there were a few gaps we couldn't fill, such as why they recorded his "interrogations" and death in such detail. It wasn't normal, not normal at all. Usually that stuff was buried, deep; the lessons of the concentration camps were learned.'

'That's what first struck me,' said Karin. 'Harry, too, but be ascribed it to the mentality of Stasi fanatics who knew they were about to lose their power, lose everything. I couldn't go along with that because Frederik talked about the Stasi so frequently, how brutal they could be, how manipulative, yet how basically insecure they were. Insecure men don't condemn themselves with their own words.'

'What did my brother say when you told him that?'

'I never did. You see, Harry wasn't just Frederik's control, he was very fond of him. I didn't have the heart to tell him about our difficulties. There was no point, Freddie was dead – for the record.'

'There were a couple of other things too,' said the colonel softly, 'things you couldn't know, Karin. In his last three penetrations, the information De Vries brought out was patently false. By that time we ourselves had compromised quite a few Stasi who knew they were soon going to be unemployed *and* indictable, so they were happy to cooperate. Several brought out proof that contradicted De Vries's findings.'

'Why didn't you call him on it?' asked Drew. 'Pull him out and put him on the grill?'

'It was a lousy, fogged-up area,' replied Witkowski, shaking his head in the shadows. 'Had he been duped, outsmarted? Was it burnout? He had been outstanding in the past, so were these simply lapses as a result of overwork? You figure, we couldn't.'

'You mentioned a "couple of things", Stanley,' said Karin. 'What were they?'

'Only one really, but it was confirmed by two of our turnarounds who didn't know each other, and *we* confirmed that. The Stasi was an octopus with a hundred eyes and a thousand tentacles; in a sense it ran the underside of the country . . . Your husband was flown twice to Munich and met with General Ulrich von Schnabe, later established to be one of the leaders of the neo-Nazi movement. He was assassinated while in prison by one of his own people before he could be interrogated.'

'So the seed was planted and a poison flower called

Günter Jäger bloomed,' said Karin, arching her head back in disbelief. '*How?* In the name of sanity, *how?*'

'Maybe the tape will tell us something.' Latham gently shoved the colonel away and put his arm around her shoulders, then turned to Witkowski. 'Use your fancy phone and call Moreau's people here in Bonn. Tell them to get us a triple suite at the Königshof Hotel, one with a VCR that has duplicating equipment.'

'*Jawohl, mein Herr!*' said the colonel, smiling appreciatively in the erratic darkness of the moonlight. 'You sound like a real commander, *chłopak.*'

'But *how?*' cried Karin de Vries suddenly, her pained face appealing to the rushing night clouds in the sky. 'How could one man become such *another?*'

'We'll find out,' said Drew, holding her.

The words, alternately muted and roared in German, took on a strange cadence of their own, an erratic flow of sound, both numbing and electrifying, a mixture of sermon and threat. The images on the screen were equally hypnotic despite the constant movement of the small camcorder that could not be held steady, or the frequent intrusions of a drape that kept blocking the lens. The blond priest spoke to an all-male audience of thirty-six men, a number, by the looks of their clothes, non-German, but each was expensively dressed, some less formal than others, yachting outfits and Dior jogging gear juxtaposed with business suits. They sat in mostly rapt attention, a few eyes straying in conceivable embarrassment when the fiery priest's harangue became too violent, yet all rose as one during the frequent *Sieg Heils*. And the intense priest with the bright blond hair and piercing eyes was, indeed, mesmerizing.

Before placing the tape in the VCR, Lieutenant Anthony had stood in front of the unit in the large suite at the Königshof Hotel and made an announcement. 'The camera has a zoom lens and a high-impedance microphone, so you'll hear everything, and I tried to get close-ups of everyone in the place for identification purposes. Since Mr Latham doesn't speak German, Chris and I ordered up an English typewriter and did our best to translate what this Günter Jäger said – the text isn't word perfect, but it's clear enough.'

'That was very thoughtful of you, Gerry,' said Drew, sitting between Witkowski and Karin.

'It was more than that. It was very damned important,' interrupted Captain Dietz, kneeling in front of the television set and inserting the tape. 'I'm still shook up,' he added, enigmatically. 'Okay, it's magic time.' The screen was suddenly filled with sound and images, or, perhaps, sound and fury, as the poet wrote. Latham followed the English text.

'*My friends, my soldiers, you true heroes of the Fourth Reich!*' began the man who called himself Günter Jäger. '*I bring you magnificent news! A tidal wave of destruction is about to descend on the capitals of our enemies. Zero hour has been determined, and it is now precisely fifty-three hours away. Everything we have worked for, strived for, sacrificed for, has come to fruition. The end is not yet in sight, but the end of the beginning is upon us! It will be the omega, the final solution, of an international paralysis! As you who have come here tonight from across the borders and the seas are well aware, our enemies are in a state of chaos, so many accusing so many others of being part of our great cause. They curse us on the surface, but millions silently applaud us, for they want what we can provide! Rid the halls of power of the conniving Jews, who want everything for themselves and the loathsome Israel, deport the screeching inferior blacks, squash the Socialists who would tax us into productive oblivion and use our taxes to promulgate the unproductive – in a word, restructure! The world must take a lesson from the Romans before they grew indolent and let the blood of slaves infect their veins. We must be strong and completely intolerant of inferiority! One kills a deformed dog, why not the product of inferior parents? ... Now to our tidal wave – most of you know its name, some of you do not. Its code name is Water Lightning, and that's precisely what it is. As lightning strikes and kills, so will be the water struck by it. In fifty-three hours the water reserves of London, Paris, and Washington will be polluted with such extraordinary toxicity that hundreds of thousands will die. The governments will be paralysed, for it will take days, perhaps weeks, before the toxins are analysed, and weeks after that before countermeasures are in place. By that time—'*

'I've heard *enough*!' said Latham. 'Shut the goddamned thing off and make immediate duplicates. I don't know how you do it, but wire that tape to London, Paris, and Washington! Also, fax this transcript to the number I give you. I'll get on the phone to everyone I can think of. *Christ*, all we've got is two days!'

CHAPTER THIRTY-EIGHT

Wesley Sorenson listened as Latham spoke over the phone from Bonn; the director's eyes were steady, intense, as beads of sweat formed at his white hairline. 'The "water reserves", the *reservoirs*,' he said, barely audible with fear. 'It's the province of the Army Corps of Engineers.'

'It's the province of everyone at the Pentagon, Langley, the FBI, and the police around every water supply source in Washington, Wes!'

'They're fenced, guarded—'

'Double, triple, and quadruple all the patrols,' insisted Drew. 'This maniac wouldn't have promised what he did unless he thought he could deliver, not with that crowd. I'm betting there was more money in there than in half of Europe. They're hungry for power, salivating for it, and I suspect he's got unlimited resources to pay the Nazi god. *Jesus*, barely two days!'

'How are the identities of that crowd going?'

'How the hell do I know? You're the first call I've made. We're wiring the tapes – the President of Germany gave us carte blanche through satellite feeds at the government studios – to French, British, and American intelligence, in our case all questions and releases to be directed to you.'

'There can't *be* any public releases! The climate here and across the country is poisonous; it could get worse than the McCarthy period. There've been several riots, and a march on the state capital in Trenton. The crowds began shouting *Nazi* at the mention of politicians, bureaucrats, union leaders, and corporate executives even distantly associated with those openly being investigated. And this is only the beginning.'

'Wait a minute,' said Latham's voice over the line, '*wait* a minute! Hundreds of those initial names were brought out of the Brüderschaft valley by Harry, weren't they?'

'Of course.'

'And according to the MI-6 transcripts, my brother made it clear that not only should the *names* be examined but everyone around them.'

'Naturally, it's standard.'

'And then after those names were circulated, the order to kill Harry came from the Nazi high command, right?'

'Obviously.'

'Why? . . . *Why*, Wes? They've hunted me like a starving wolf pack in search of a sheep.'

'I've never understood that.'

'Maybe I'm beginning to. It pains me to say it, but suppose Harry *was* fed false names. Purposely, to create the very climate you just described.'

'What I know of your brother, I don't think he'd buy them.'

'Suppose he didn't have a choice?'

'He didn't lose his mind. Of course he had a choice.'

'Suppose he *did* – lose his mind, I mean. Gerhardt Kroeger is a brain surgeon, and he risked his life in Paris to kill Harry. In one scenario he – I – was to be decapitated; in another, a coup de grâce was to be administered that would blow his head away . . . the *left* side of his head.'

'I'd say an autopsy is called for,' said the director of Consular Operations, then added, 'when it's feasible. At the moment, we'd all better move as fast as we can to stop whatever it is that's going to kill hundreds of thousands of people in Paris, London, and Washington.'

'Jäger spelled it out, Wes. Toxicity in the reservoirs.'

'I'm no expert in waterworks, but I know something about them. Good Lord, at one time or another we've all considered them in terms of tactical sabotage, and, conversely, we all rejected them.'

'Why?'

'The task is simply too massive. To have any effect on the water of large cities would entail a supply line of heavy-duty trucks at least three or four miles long, a sight that could hardly be concealed. Then there's the obstacle of entry into the reservoirs, which for such a number of vehicles is virtually impossible. Those fences are like prison barricades, they're equipped with lateral sectional alarms; if penetration is made, a signal is sent to the water tower's security and immediate inspections are made.'

'I'd say you were quite an expert, Mr Director.'

'Rubbish, that information could be and probably is learned by the Boy Scouts, and certainly by any civil engineer on a government payroll.'

'So you've ruled out the ground, what about the air?'

'Just as impossible. There'd have to be at least two squadrons of low-flying cargo aircraft, pinpoint-targeting their materials nearest the water towers for sluice entry. In all likelihood they'd crash into one another, and even if they didn't, they'd be like prolonged deafening thunder across the area, not to mention being tracked by radar.'

'Wow, you really did consider this kind of sabotage, didn't you?'

'You know as well as I do, Drew, various options are basic to the games we play.'

'This isn't a game, Wes. That bastard meant what he said. He's figured out a way. He's going to do it.'

'Then we'd all better get to work, hadn't we? I'll stay in contact with MI-5 and the Quai d'Orsay. You concentrate on the identities of everyone in that estate on the Rhine. Coordinate with Claude, MI-6, and German intelligence. We want every one of those fanatics in cells by tomorrow. And zero in on the non-Germans first; don't let them leave the country.'

*

The government computers of four nations spun their disks furiously for the next twenty-one hours as isolated photographs were wired to the intelligence agencies of Germany, France, England, and America. Of the thirty-six men who roared *Sieg Heil, Günter Jäger*, seventeen were German, seven American, four British, and five French; three were unidentified and presumably had already boarded flights out of the country. All were secretly placed under arrest and held incommunicado in isolated prison cells, no explanations given, no telephone calls permitted. In cases where the individuals were prominent, sudden business trips and prolonged conferences were the stories told their households, issued in the names of their companies.

'This is *outrageous*!' roared the owner of a German chemical factory.

'So are you,' replied the German police officer.

There remained only Günter Jäger, kept oblivious of the events of the last twenty-one hours, alone with his staff in his modest compound on the banks of the Rhine. It was a multilateral command decision, as none of the neo-Nazis taken prisoner could provide any specifics regarding Water Lightning. The strategies they offered up in hopes of better treatment and leniency were totally impractical and therefore false. Even the hysterical Hans Traupman, having been shown the lurid tapes of his sexual experiments, could provide nothing of substance.

'Do you think I would withhold anything from you? My *God*, I'm a surgeon, I know when an operation has failed. We're finished!'

Only Günter Jäger had the answers, and it was the considered opinion of the behavioural scientists who had studied the tape that he would take his own life before revealing them.

'His condition is one of manic-depressive, controlled paranoia, which simply means he's constantly living on the edge. One shove and he's into the abyss of complete madness.'

Karin de Vries agreed.

Therefore, the new *Führer*'s every means of communication was monitored: telephone, radio frequencies, deliveries, even the possibility of carrier pigeons. Agents with powerful electronic listening devices were in the bushes, in trees, and among the ruins of the former demolished estate, the 'ears' beamed to every area of the river cottage and its grounds. All waited for Jäger to make contact with anyone or anything that would give them a clue about Water Lightning. None came, and the hours passed.

In London, Paris, and Washington, the waterworks were virtually under siege. Platoons of armed soldiers patrolled every foot of the areas, roads leading to the reservoirs were blockaded, detours put in place. In the brick water towers of Washington, the operations and security systems were manned by experts of the Army Corps of Engineers, the most experienced personnel flown in from all over the country.

'No son-of-a-bitch Nazi will get near this place,' said the brigadier general in command of the Dalecarlia reservoir. 'It's the same in London and Paris, we've conferred down to the last possibility. I think the French went a little ape though. They've got bazooka and flamethrower units every hundred yards, and they don't even drink water.'

In Bonn, because there was no evidence that Water Lightning would affect the city, the government placed all its resources at the disposal of the allies, *its* allies now, for no one on earth loathed the reappearance of the Nazi more than the German leadership. However, they did not consider history or its plague of repetition. For during the darkest hours of the night of Water Lightning, trucks ostensibly carrying everything from linen supplies to kitchen equipment to cleaning services drove slowly, unobtrusively, into the parking areas of the Bundestag. In reality, within those trucks were stored large tanks of high octane, highly explosive fuel attached to pumps capable of spraying an entire football or soccer field. It was a symbol Günter Jäger could not resist, a personal symbol he shared with no one but his committed disciples who would perform the task. They would torch the Bundestag, burning it to the ground.

'*Reichstag revisited*,' he wrote in his private journal.

'Nothing's happening!' exclaimed Karin in the suite at the Königshof Hotel. It was one o'clock in the morning in Bonn; Witkowski and the two commandos from Desert Storm, exhausted from nearly two days' lack of rest, were asleep in the other rooms. 'We're not getting anywhere!'

'We've all agreed,' said Latham, his eyelids like lead shields he had to constantly prise open, 'if nothing comes down by six o'clock this morning, we take him and put him on the rack.'

There won't *be* a rack, Drew! Freddie never went into an operation without the means to kill himself if he was caught. He always said to me that it wasn't heroic at all, it was only his fear of torture. If he was exposed, he knew he'd eventually be executed, so why not avoid the pain . . . It was one of the reasons I couldn't believe the Stasi file.'

'You mean a cyanide capsule in a collar and all the rest of that crap?'

'It's *real*, you've seen it! Your brother Harry armed himself with the same pill!'

'He never would have used it.' Latham's head fell forward over his chest, then his entire body lurched slowly back on the couch.

'Hundreds of thousands of lives are at stake, Drew! You said it yourself – he's found a way to do it!' Her plea was not heard; Latham was asleep. 'There's another way to stop him,' said De Vries, whispering as she raced into their bedroom, yanked a blanket off the bed, and returned, covering Latham. She then returned to the bedroom and picked up the phone.

A telephone rang, disorienting Drew, who fell off the couch, reaching for what was not there. He rose to his feet unsteadily; the ringing stopped and thirty seconds later a nearly dressed Witkowski burst out of the bedroom. 'Goddammit, she's *done* it!' shouted the colonel.

'Done what . . . ?' asked Latham, back on the couch and shaking his head.

'Gone after De Vries herself.'

'*What?*'

'Karin used our codes and got clearance to pass through the Jäger security.'

'When?'

'A few minutes ago. The officer of the watch wanted to know whether to log her entry by code or by name.'

'We're out of here! . . . Where's my weapon? It was right here on the table. My God, she took it!'

'Put on a jacket and a raincoat,' said the colonel. 'It's been raining for the last hour.'

'A car from German intelligence is on its way,' announced Captain Dietz, rushing out of the third-bedroom door followed by his lieutenant, both fully dressed, their automatics holstered. 'I picked up the phone and heard,' he explained. 'We've got to hurry, it'll take at least ten minutes to get there.'

'Call the security chief and order them to stop her, or go in after her!' said Lieutenant Anthony.

'*No,*' snapped Witkowski. 'Jäger's a mad dog. If he thinks he's cornered, he'll go wild, killing everything in front of him. You heard the psychiatrists. Whatever the hell she thinks she's doing, she's better off doing it alone until we get there.'

'And when we get there,' said Drew quietly, yanking a jacket and a raincoat off a chair, '*we're* going in. Each of you has a second weapon. One of you give me his.'

Identifying herself as a member of the N-2 unit, her name and code verified by the German intelligence officer in charge of the Jäger compound's surveillance team, Karin de Vries was given an overview as well as specific instructions.

'I have nine men strategically placed throughout the grounds with their equipment,' said the officer, crouched in the pouring rain behind a half-demolished wall of the old estate. 'Each is camouflaged and hidden in the foliage, several actually up in trees, and the rain, though extremely uncomfortable, is advantageous for us. Günter Jäger's two patrols stray barely twenty-five metres beyond the boat-house cottage. You say that you must reach the door without being seen, and it's vital to our situation that you are *not* seen – so listen to what I tell you. Follow this old flagstone path until you reach the remnants of a burned-down gazebo where there's a croquet field rebuilt for Jäger's relaxation. On the opposite side is a spreading pine tree; roughly fifteen feet above the first branches is one of my men with clear sightlines to the cottage. He has a penlight he will cup in his hand: two flashes mean a guard is walking around, three mean everything's clear. When you see the three flashes, run across the centre of the croquet course, where there is another flagstone path that curves to the left. Enter it and stop after approximately forty paces, at where the curve is the sharpest. Look to your right; there'll be another man in the brush, another penlight. He has a direct line of sight to a side door which is straight ahead at the end of the path, you can't miss it.'

'A side door?' Karin had interrupted, brushing the rain off her face under her black canvas hat.

'Jäger's living quarters,' answered the German intelligence officer. 'Bedroom, bath, office, and an addition on the north wall that contains a small personal chapel with its own altar. It's said he spends hours there in meditation. The side door is his private entrance, the closest to the riverbank and forbidden to everyone else. The front door is at the far left, the old boathouse's original entrance; it's the one the guards and visitors use.'

'In other words, he's basically separated from the rest of the household when he's in his quarters.'

'Definitely. Director Moreau was particularly interested

in the arrangement as I described it to him. He reached me after you called him in Paris, and together we devised the plan to accommodate you with the minimum of risk.'

'What did he tell you, if I may ask?'

'That you knew Günter Jäger years ago and that you were a highly trained strategist who might accomplish what others could not. I along with most senior officers in our profession accept Moreau's judgements as those of an expert. He also mentioned that you would be armed and capable of protecting yourself.'

'I hope he's right on both counts,' said Karin softly.

'Oh?' The German officer stared at De Vries. 'Your superiors approve of your tactics, of course.'

'Naturally. Would the celebrated Moreau himself have reached you on my behalf if they did not?'

'No, he wouldn't . . . Your raincoat will soon be soaked. I can't offer you a new one, but I have an extra umbrella. You're welcome to it.'

'Thank you, I'm grateful. Are you in touch with your personnel by radio?'

'Yes, but I'm sorry, I can't let you have one. The risk is too great.'

'I understand. Just let them know I'm on my way.'

'Good luck and be very, very careful, madame. Remember, we can lead you to the door, but we cannot do anything else for you. Even if you cried out, we could not respond.'

'Yes, I know. One life compared to so many thousands.' With those words Karin snapped open the umbrella and started down the flagstone path through the deluge. Constantly wiping the rain from her eyes, she reached the once-elegant gazebo, its skeletal outlines of burned wood and coiled screening somehow akin to a wartime photograph illustrating the lesson that war was an equalizer, touching the rich and the poor alike. And then beyond, as if to purposely contradict the lesson, there was a perfectly kept croquet field, the lawn manicured, the wickets and the brightly painted poles intact.

She raised her head, squinting under the brim of her canvas hat, studying the enormous pine tree with different, less imposing trees on either side. Suddenly there were the barely visible flashes. *Two* of them! A guard was on patrol. Karin lowered herself to the ground, peering into drenched darkness, waiting for another signal. It came quickly: three flashes, repeated twice. The way was clear!

She raced across the croquet course, her flat shoes sinking into the swollen, wet grass until she felt the hard surface of the second flagstone path. Without hesitating, she raced down it, keeping in mind the approximate forty paces and the sharp curve; she found it too late, plunging headlong into the overgrown foliage as the flagstones turned abruptly left. There was no visibility, no way she could have known. She got painfully, awkwardly, to her feet and picked up the umbrella; it was broken, useless. On her knees, she looked to her right, as instructed. There was nothing but downpour and darkness, yet she dared not move until the signal came. Finally, it did: three flashes. Karin walked slowly, cautiously, to the end of the flagstone path; she was at the edge of the woods and saw the lair of her once and now-despised husband, *Führer* of the Fourth Reich. There were lights on at the far left side of the structure, darkness everywhere else.

The former boathouse was much longer, though not necessarily larger, than she had envisioned, for it was one level. The German intelligence officer had said there was an addition on the right that housed the isolated living quarters of the man called Günter Jäger. Additions had been made on the left as well, she thought, observing the lighter, newer wood, twenty-five or thirty feet long, and considering the width to the river side, enough for two, three, or four added rooms for the staff. The officer had been correct in one area: the front door was on the far left, at the end of the gravel drive, symmetrically unbalanced, as if temporary, but removed from Jäger's quarters. And directly ahead of her, the short dock and the great river beyond, was the porticoed side door of Günter Jäger's suite of rooms; a dim red light was affixed to the interior roof of the small porch. Karin took several deep breaths, hoping to control the pounding in her chest, removed Drew Latham's automatic from her raincoat pocket, and started across the grass towards the porch with the dim red light. One of them would live, the other die. It was the end of their godforsaken marriage. But first there was Water Lightning, Günter Jäger's omega for the paralyses of London, Paris, and Washington. Frederik de Vries, once the most brilliant of agents provocateurs, had figured out a way to do it. She knew it!

Karin reached the short porch with the eerie red light; she walked up the single step, holding on to one of the two columns that supported the overhang, the heavy rain pounding a steady tattoo on the roof. Suddenly, she gasped, fear and confusion spreading over her. The door was ajar, open no more than three inches, beyond the slit was only black darkness. She approached it, Latham's automatic in her left hand, and pushed the door back. Again only darkness, and except for the now-torrential rain, silence. She walked inside.

'I knew you'd come, my dear wife,' said the unseen figure, his voice echoing off the unseen walls. 'Close the door, please.'

'*Frederik!*'

'Not Freddie any longer, I see. You only called me Frederik when you were angry with me, Karin. Are you angry with me now?'

'What have you *done*? Where are you?'

'It's best we talk in the dark, at least for a while.'

'You knew I'd come here . . . ?'

'That door's been open since you and your *lover* flew into Bonn.'

'Then you understand they know who you are—'

'That's totally irrelevant,' interrupted De Vries/Jäger firmly. 'Nothing can stop us now.'

'You won't get away.'

'Of course I will. It's already been arranged.'

'*How?* They know who you are, they won't let you!'

'Because they're out there in four acres of tangled shrubbery and ruins, their listening devices waiting for me to reach others here in Germany and in England, France, and America? So they can accuse others, arrest others, because I talked with them? I tell you, dear wife, the temptation to place calls to the Presidents of France and the United States, *and* the Queen of England, was nearly irresistible. Can you imagine the utter bewilderment in the intelligence communities?'

'Why didn't you?'

'Because the sublime would become the ridiculous – and we're deadly serious.'

'Why, Frederik, *why?* What happened to the man who, above all, loathed the Nazis?'

'That's not quite right,' said the new *Führer* curtly. 'I loathed the Communists first, for they were stupid. They squandered their power everywhere, trying to live up to the Marxist doctrine of equality when no such equality exists. They gave authority to uneducated peasants and crude, ugly louts. There was nothing grand about them at all.'

'You never spoke in those terms before.'

'Of course I did! You just never listened carefully enough . . . But that, too, is irrelevant, for I found my calling, the calling of a truly superior human being. I saw a void and I filled it, admittedly with the help of a surgeon of great stature and perception who realized that I was the man they needed.'

'Hans Traupman,' said Karin in the darkness, immediately angry with herself for saying the name.

'He's no longer with us, thanks to your team of blunderers. Did you people really think you could hijack his boat and speed away with him? All four cameras blacked out in *succession*, the radio suddenly malfunctioning, the boat itself heading upriver? Honestly, such amateurism. Traupman gave his life for our cause, and he wouldn't want it any other way, for our cause is everything.'

Günter Jäger knew a great deal, but he did not know everything, considered Karin de Vries. He thought Traupman had died on his boat. 'What cause, Frederik? The cause of the Nazis? The monsters who executed your grandparents and forced your father and mother to live as pariahs, until they finally took their own lives?'

'I have learned many things since you abandoned me, wife.'

'*I* abandoned *you* . . . ?'

'I traded my execution for diamonds, all the diamonds I had left in Amsterdam. But who was going to hire me after the Wall fell? What good is a deep-cover espionage agent when there's nothing to penetrate? Where would my lifestyle go? The unlimited expense accounts, the limousines, the extravagant resorts? Remember the Black Sea and Sevastopol? My *God*, we had fun, and I stole two hundred thousand, American, for the operation!'

'I was talking about the "cause", Frederik, what about the *cause*?'

'I've come to believe in it with all my being. In the beginning, others wrote my speeches for the movement. Now I write them all, *compose* them all, for they are like short heroic operas, bringing those who see and listen to their feet, their voices ringing with my praises, honouring me, holding me in adoration as I hold them enthralled!'

'How did it start . . . Freddie?'

'Freddie – that's better. Would you really like to know?'

'Didn't I always want to hear about your missions? Remember how we sometimes laughed?'

'Yes, that part of you was all right, not like the bitch whore you were most of the time.'

'*What* . . . ?' Immediately Karin lowered her voice. 'I'm sorry, Freddie, truly sorry. You went to East Berlin, that's the last word we had of you, any of us. Until we read that you'd been executed.'

'I wrote that report myself, you know. Rather sensational, wasn't it?'

649

'It certainly was graphic.'

'Fine writing's like great speaking, and great speaking's like fine writing. You've got to create instant images to capture the minds of those reading or listening. Capture them immediately with fire and lightning!'

'East Berlin . . . ?'

'Yes, that's where it began. Certain of the Stasi had ties with Munich, especially with a provisional general of the Nazi movement. They recognized my abilities, and my God, why not? I'd made fools of them too often! After the official leaders I dealt with retrieved my diamonds in Amsterdam and set me free, several came to me and said they might have work for me. East Germany was collapsing, the entire Soviet Union soon to follow – everyone knew it. They flew me to Munich and I met with this general, Von Schnabe. He was an imposing man, even perhaps a visionary, but he was basically a martinet, a harsh bureaucrat. He lacked the fire to be a leader. However, he had a concept, a concept he was progressively turning into reality. It could ultimately change the face of Germany.'

'Change the face of *Germany*?' said Karin incredulously. 'How could an obscure, unknown general of a despised radical movement be capable of such a thing?'

'By infiltrating the Bundestag, and infiltration was something I knew a great deal about.'

'That doesn't answer my question . . . Freddie.'

'Freddie – I like that. We had good times for a number of years, my wife.' Günter Jäger's voice still seemed to come from nowhere and everywhere in the darkness of the room, the source further obscured by the pounding rain against the shaded windows and the roof. 'To answer your question. To infiltrate the Bundestag, the right people simply have to be elected. The general, with the help of Hans Traupman, scoured the country for talented but discontented men, placed them in distressed economic districts, fed them "solutions", and funded their campaigns beyond anything their opponents could match. Would you believe we have over a hundred members in the Bundestag at this moment?'

'You were one of those men . . . my husband?'

'I was the most extraordinary, my wife! I was given a new name, a new biography, a completely new life. I became Günter Jäger, a parish clergyman from a small village in Kuhhorst, moved by the church authorities to Strasslach, outside Munich. I left the church, fighting for what I called the disenfranchised middle class, the burghers who were the backbone of the nation. I won my seat in a landslide, as they say, and while I was campaigning, Hans Traupman watched me, and made his decision. I was the man the movement needed. I tell you, whore-wife, it is fantastic! They've made me emperor, king, the ruler of all we espouse, the *Führer* of the *Fourth Reich*!'

'And you accept it, Freddie?'

'Why not? It's the extension of everything I practised in the past. The persuasiveness I exhibited while burrowing into the enemy camps, the speeches I gave solidifying my false commitments, all those dinner parties and symposiums – it was all training for my greatest achievements.'

'But you once considered *these* people your enemies.'

'No longer. They're *right*. The world has changed and it's changed for the worse. Even the Communists with their iron fists were better than what we have now. You take away the discipline of a strong state and what's left is the rabble, screaming at one another, slaughtering one another, no better than animals in a jungle. Well, we'll get rid of the animals and restructure the state, selecting and rewarding only the purest to serve it. The dawn of a great new day is upon us, my wife, and as soon as it is understood, the truth of its force and the force of its truth will sweep across the world.'

'The world will point to and remember the brutality of the Nazis, won't it . . . Freddie?'

'Perhaps for a while, but that will pass when the world sees the results of a cleansed state under strong, benign leadership. The democracies constantly extol the righteousness of the ballot box, but they could not be more in error! Ballots are fought for in the gutter, for that's where the majority of votes are. And bless the Americans, they don't even understand their own Constitution as it was conceived two hundred years ago. Originally, only the landowners, the men who had proved themselves successful and therefore superior, were to be permitted to vote. That was the consensus of the Constitutional Convention, did you know that?'

'Yes, it was an agrarian society, but I'm surprised you know it. History was never one of your strong suits, my husband.'

'All that's changed. If you could see these shelves . . . they're lined with books, new ones brought in every day. I read five or six a week.'

'Let me see them, let me see *you*. I've missed you, Freddie.'

'Soon, my wife, soon. There's a certain comfort in the darkness for I "see" you as I prefer to remember you. The lovely, vivacious woman who took such pride in her husband, who brought me secrets from NATO, a number of which I'm convinced saved my life.'

'You were on NATO's side, how could I do otherwise?'

'Now I'm on a greater side. Would you help me now?'

'It depends, my husband. I can't deny that you're extremely convincing. Having heard your own words, I'm very excited for you. You were always an extraordinary man, even those who disapproved of you said as much—'

'Such as my friend, my former friend, Harry *Latham*, who is now your *lover*!'

'You're wrong, Freddie. Harry Latham is not my lover.'

'*Liar!* He was always fawning on you, waiting for you to show up, asking me when you would.'

'I will repeat my statement to you, and we lived together too long for you not to know when I'm telling the truth. It's your profession, after all, and you've heard me tell a hundred lies on your behalf . . . Harry Latham is not my lover. Shall I repeat it again?'

'No.' The single word echoed off the unseen walls. 'Then who is he?'

'Someone who's assumed Harry's name.'

'Why?'

'Because you want your friend Harry killed, and Harry doesn't care to be killed. How *could* you, Frederik? Harry loved you as a – a younger brother.'

'It was not of my doing,' said the disembodied voice of Günter Jäger quietly. 'Harry penetrated our headquarters in the Alps. He was part of an experiment. I had no choice but to agree.'

'What kind of experiment?'

'A medical thing. I never fully understood it. Traupman, however, was very enthusiastic, and I could not go against Hans. He was my mentor, the man who put me where I am today.'

'And where are you, Freddie? Are you really the new Adolf Hitler?'

'It's odd that you mention him. I've read and reread *Mein Kampf*, and all the biographies I could get my hands on. Have you any idea how parallel our lives are, at least our lives before we joined the movement? He was an artist, and in my own way, I'm an artist too. He was unemployed, as I was about to be. He was rejected by the Austrian Artists League, as well as the Architectural Academy, for a supposed lack of talent – an ex-corporal with nowhere to go. In my case, the same. Who employs someone like me? And we were both penniless; in his case he had nothing, and I sold all my diamonds to save my life . . . Then someone in the twenties saw a street-corner radical screaming passionately, convincingly, against the injustices of social conditions, and years later someone else watched the oratory of a superb, former agent provocateur who had fooled even them. Such men are valuable.'

'Are you saying that both you and Adolf Hitler *backed* into your awesome positions?'

'I'd put it another way, my wife. We didn't find our causes, our causes found us.'

'That's obscene!'

'Not at all. The convert's convictions are always the strongest, for they must be arrived at.'

'To bring all this about will result in an *enormous* loss of life—'

'Initially, yes, but it will pass quickly, be forgotten quickly, and the world will be a far better place. There'll be no massive war, no nuclear confrontations – our progress will be gradual but sure, for much of it is in place already. In a matter of months, governments will change, new laws will be created that benefit the strongest, the purest, and within a few years the useless *garbage*, the dregs of society who suck us dry, will be swept away.'

'It's not necessary to deliver a speech to me ... Freddie.'

'It's all *true*! Can't you *see* that?'

'I can't even see you, and you do excite me when you talk like this, like the extraordinary man I know you are. Please, turn on a light.'

'I have a small problem with that.'

'Why? Have you changed so much in five years?'

'No, but I'm wearing glasses and you're not.'

'I wear them only when my eyes are tired, you know that.'

'Yes, but mine are different. I can see in the dark, and I see the gun in your hand. It reminded me that you were left-handed. Do you remember when you decided you should play golf with me and I bought you a set of clubs, only they were the wrong kind?'

'Yes, of course, I remember, they were for right-handed players ... I carry the gun because you taught me never to go to a meeting at night, even with you, without a weapon. You said neither of us could know if you'd been followed.'

'I was right, I was protecting you. Did your friends outside know you had a gun?'

'I didn't see anyone. I came alone, without authority.'

'Now you're lying, at least in part, but it doesn't matter. Drop the gun on the floor!' Karin did so, and De Vries/Jäger turned on a light, a reflector lamp that shone down on a small chapel altar, heightening the gold crucifix on a purple cloth. The new *Führer* sat on a prayer stool on the right, in a white silk shirt, opened at the collar, his bright blond hair glistening, his handsome, sharp-featured face at its most flattering angle. 'How do I look after five years, wife?'

'As beautiful as ever, but you know that.'

'It's an attribute I cannot deny, and one Herr Hitler never possessed. Did you know he was a rather small, pinch-faced man who wore elevator shoes? My looks are a great help to me, but I wear them in brilliant humility, and pretend to be icelike when women make a point of them. Physical vanity does not become a national leader.'

'Others care. I believed they're awed by it. I was . . . I still am.'

'When did you people suspect that "Günter Jäger" was the new neo-Nazi leader?'

'When one of the Sonnenkinder broke under questioning. With the addition of drugs, I suspect.'

'That couldn't be, I never revealed myself to any of them!'

'Obviously, you did, whether you realized it or not. You said you had meetings, gave speeches—'

'Only to those of us in the Bundestag! All the rest were recorded.'

'Then someone sold you out . . . Freddie. I heard something about a Catholic priest who went to confession and taxed the conscience of his confessor.'

'My God, that senile idiot Paltz. Time and again I said he should be excluded, but no, Traupman claimed he had a large following among the working class. I'll have him shot.'

Karin briefly breathed easier. She had struck the chord she so needed to strike. The name of Paltz came to her from the identifications made from the tape, and the fact that Monsignor Paltz was an old man vociferously disliked by the

Catholic hierarchy in Germany, another fact established by a call to the bishop of Bonn. The bishop had not minced words. 'He's a misguided bigot who should be retired. I've said as much to Rome.' Karin waited until her unwanted husband calmed down.

'Freddie,' she began quietly, in control. 'This Paltz, whoever he is, this priest, said that something dreadful will happen to the cities of London, Paris, and Washington. Disasters of such magnitude that hundreds of thousands will be killed. Is it true . . . Freddie?'

The pitch-black silence from the *Führer* was electric, exaggerated by the pounding rain. Finally Günter Jäger spoke, his voice strained, harsh, sounding like the strings of a taut cello about to snap.

'So that's why you're here, slut-wife. They sent you on the distinctly outside chance that I might reveal the nature of our shock wave.'

'I came on my own. They don't *know* I'm here.'

'It's possible, for you were never a good liar. However, the irony is sweet. I said before that nothing could stop us, and that happens to be the truth. You see, like all great leaders, I delegate responsibility, especially in areas where I lack expertise. I'm given the outlines of a plan or a strategy, in particular the final results, but not the technical aspects, nor even the names of the personnel refining them. I wouldn't know whom to call should I want them myself.'

'We know it concerns the three cities' water, the reservoirs or waterworks, whatever they're called.'

'Really? I'm sure Monsignor Paltz was very technical in his disclosures. Ask him.'

'It can't work, Frederik! Call it off. Everyone involved will be caught. There are troops by the hundreds prepared to fire at anyone or *anything* that gets near the water. They'll be captured and you'll be exposed!'

'Exposed?' asked Jäger calmly. 'By whom? A senile old man who isn't even sure what year it is, much less the month or the day? Don't be ridiculous.'

'*Frederik*, there is a tape of last night's meeting. Everyone who was there has been arrested and kept in isolation! It's *over*, Freddie! For God's sake, call off Water Lightning!'

'Water . . . *Lightning*? My God, you're telling the truth, it's in your voice, your eyes.' Günter Jäger rose from the prayer stool, his face and his body like a Siegfried under an operatic spotlight. 'Still, my whore-wife, it changes nothing, for no one can stop the shock wave. In less than an hour I'll be on a jet to a country that applauds my work, *our* work, and watch as my disciples throughout the Western world move into positions of power.'

'You'll never get away!'

'Now you're naive, dear wife,' said Jäger, walking to the centre of the altar and pressing a button under the gold crucifix. Abruptly, with his touch, a square on the floor opened, revealing the splashing waters of the river below. 'Down there is a two-man submarine, courtesy of a boat-works whose chairman is one of us. It will take me up to Königswinter, where my plane waits for me. The rest is history reborn.'

'And I?'

'Have you any idea how long it's been since I've had a woman?' said Jäger quietly under the altar spotlight. 'How many years I've had to assume the mantle of rigid monastic discipline, while implying that others who succumbed to such temptations were vulnerable to compromise and corruption?'

'Please, Frederik, I'm not interested in your posturings.'

'You should be, *wife*! For over four years I've lived like this, proving that *I*, and *only* I, was the incorruptible supreme leader. I frowned on women who wore indiscreet clothing and would not even permit lewd anecdotes or jokes in my presence.'

'It all must have been unbearable for you,' said Karin, her gaze straying about the shadowed room. 'Whenever you returned from one of your forays into the Eastern bloc, you invariably carried an excess of condoms and various telephone numbers, women's names opposite them.'

'You searched my clothes?'

'They usually had to be sent to the cleaners.'

'You have an answer for everything, you always did.'

'I answer honestly, what first comes to mind as my memory tells me ... Let's return to me, Frederik. What happens to me? Are you going to kill me?'

'I'd rather not, my wife, for that's what you still are, legally and in the eyes of God. After all, my courtesy submarine accommodates two people. You could be my consort, my companion, eventually, perhaps, the empress to the emperor, not unlike Fräulein Eva Braun to Adolf Hitler.'

'Eva Braun committed suicide with her "emperor", accomplished by cyanide and a gunshot. It does not appeal to me.'

'You will not accommodate me, wife?'

'I will not accommodate you.'

'You will in another way,' said Günter Jäger, barely audible as he unbuttoned his white silk shirt and removed it, then began unbuckling his belt.

Karin suddenly lunged to her left, her body in midair as she tried desperately to reach Latham's automatic that she had dropped on the floor. Jäger raced forward, lashing out his right leg, the toe of his boot crashing into her midsection with such force that she collapsed in the foetal position, moaning in pain.

'You'll accommodate me now, wife,' said the new *Führer*, taking off his trousers leg by leg and folding them, matching the creases and laying them over the prayer stool.

CHAPTER THIRTY-NINE

'When did she go in?' asked Latham, raising his voice to be heard in the downpour.

'Roughly twenty minutes ago,' answered the bilingual German officer as the intelligence vehicle, its headlights off, backed out of the compound.

'Christ, she's been in there *that* long? And you let her inside without a wire, without any way to *reach* you?'

'She understood, sir. I made it plain that I could not give her a radio and her very words were "I understand."'

'Don't you think you should have checked with us before letting her pass?' Witkowski fairly shouted in German.

'*Mein Gott, nein!*' replied the officer angrily. 'The great Director Moreau himself reached me and we devised the least dangerous way to get her past the patrols.'

'Moreau? I'll strangle the son of a bitch!' exploded Latham.

'To more fully answer your question, *mein Herr*,' said the German intelligence officer, 'the *Fräulein* has not been in the cottage that long; my forward scout reported by radio that she entered it only twelve minutes ago. Here, see, I wrote the exact time in my notebook with my waterproof ink. I am extremely efficient, we Germans is – are.'

'Then why do all my rich friends have so much trouble getting their Mercedes fixed?'

'Undoubtedly the American mechanics, sir.'

'Oh, shut up!'

'I think it's time for me and the Thin Man,' interrupted Captain Christian Dietz, standing only feet away in the rain,

Lieutenant Anthony at his side. 'We'll replay that big estate downriver and take out the guards.' The captain stepped forward and switched to German, addressing the officer. '*Mein Oberführer*,' he began, 'how many patrols are there, and is there a routeing? I speak to you in *Deutsch*, for I don't care to risk any misunderstanding.'

'My English is as good as your German, sir.'

'But it's a little more hesitant. And your grammar—'

'I shall not pay my tutor next week,' broke in the officer, smiling. 'To reach my next grade, I must have afternoon tea with Englishmen from Oxford.'

'*Abfall!* You'll never understand them. I don't. They talk like they've got raw oysters in their mouths!'

'*Ja*, so I've heard.'

'What are they *talking* about?' yelled Drew.

'They're getting acquainted,' answered Witkowski. 'It's called gaining trust.'

'It's called wasting time!'

'The little things, *chłopak*. Listen to a man in his own language for even a minute, you learn when he's uncertain. Dietz merely wants to make sure there are no ambiguities, no hesitations.'

'Tell them to hurry up!'

'I don't have to, they've about concluded.'

'There are only three patrols,' continued the officer in German to the commando captain, 'but there is a problem. As one guard returns to the door on the far left of the drive, another comes out a short time later, but only *after* the current guard returns. And I must tell you, we've identified two, and they are pathological killers, always with an arsenal of weapons and grenades.'

'I see. It's a relay. The baton is passed to the next man by his presence.'

'Precisely.'

'So we have to figure out a way to get the others outside.'

'*Ja*, but how?'

'Leave it to us. We'll manage.' He turned to Latham and

Witkowski. 'They're crazies in there,' said Dietz, 'which doesn't surprise us. "Pathological killers" as our buddy here explained. These types would rather kill than eat; the shrinks have a word for it, but we can't give a damn about that now. We're going in.'

'And this time I'm going *with* you!' said Drew emphatically. 'Don't even *think* about making any objections.'

'Gotcha, boss man,' agreed the lieutenant, 'only do us all a favour, sir.'

'What's that?'

'Don't play Errol Flynn, like in those old movies. It's not like that.'

'Tell me about it, junior.'

'Give us the precise layout beyond here,' said Witkowski, turning to the German officer.

'You follow the flagstone path to a destroyed gazebo . . .'

Ten seconds later, the quartet started forward from behind the half-destroyed wall of the old estate, the commandos in front, Drew on the radio. They reached the croquet field and waited for the penlight signal from the tree. It came: three flashes, barely seen in the horrendous downpour.

'Let's *go*,' said Latham, 'it's clear!'

'*No!*' whispered Dietz, his strong right arm blocking Latham. 'We want the patrol.'

'Karin's *in* there!' cried Drew.

'A few seconds can't matter,' said Lieutenant Anthony as he and his captain raced forward. 'Stay there!' he added as the two of them scrambled across the croquet course and into the drenching darkness. No signal came; there was nothing. And then it was there, two flashes: a guard was on patrol. Suddenly, from the distance, came a shout, a howl, abrupt, short-lived. And then another and another after that. Then, again, came the muted flashes from the tree, three dim bursts of light; the area was clear. Latham and Witkowski rushed across the croquet field and down the flagstone path, the colonel's flashlight illuminating the way.

They reached the abrupt left turn and raced to the end of the path above the old boathouse. Far on the left, the commandos were having trouble subduing two guards who had run out of the house.

'Go help them,' ordered Drew, looking at the side porch with the red light as described by the officer of German intelligence. 'This is my trick.'

'*Chłopak* ... !'

'Get the hell *out* of here, Stosh, they need help. This is *mine!*' Latham walked down the sloping hill of grass, an automatic in his hand. He walked up on the short porch, beneath the dim red light, and over the pounding rain on the roof, he heard the screams inside. Karin's screams! His personal galaxy blew apart into a thousand infinities. He hurled his body against the door, shattering it, hinges flying, sending the entire panel across the obscenely spotlighted glare of the altar with its glistening gold crucifix. On the floor, stripped to his shorts, was the blond *Führer*, his body on top of a screaming, kicking, struggling Karin, who thrashed her legs in fury and tried to free her hands from his grip. Drew fired his automatic, blowing a hole in the roof. Jäger, in shock, spun off his abused wife, his face and body spastic; he was stunned into silence.

'Get up, you Nazi slug,' said Latham, his voice icelike, deadly with pure hatred.

'You're not *Harry!*' said Jäger suddenly, rising slowly, hypnotically to his feet. 'You look something like him ... but you are not *he.*'

'I'm surprised you can tell in this light.' Drew moved out of the glare. 'Are you all right?' he asked Karin.

'Give or take a few bruises.'

'I want to kill him.' Latham spoke calmly, coldly. 'In light of everything, I have to kill him.' He raised his automatic, levelling it at Jäger's head.

'*No!*' cried Karin. 'I feel the same way, but you can't, we *can't!* ... Water Lightning, Drew. He claims we cannot stop it, that he doesn't know the details, but he's lied all his life.'

'*Drew* . . . ?' interrupted Günter Jäger, a malevolent grin of relief spreading across his face. 'Drew *Latham*, Harry's brutish younger brother. What did he used to call him? "My kid brother, the jock", that was it. I had to ask him what it meant. So Hans Traupman was wrong, the Blitzkrieger did kill Harry, only his brother took his place. *Mein Gott*, we've been hunting the wrong man! Harry Latham is dead after all, and no one was the wiser for it.'

'What do you mean, the wiser for it?' asked Drew. 'Remember, the gun's in my hand, and considering my unstable state, I could easily blow your head off. I repeat, what did you mean?'

'Ask Dr Traupman. Oh, I forgot, he's no longer with us! And even the Polizei, including the ones who are on our side, can't cover every frequency from the marina or know our emergency codes. As the British say, "Sorry, chap, can't help you."'

'He said Harry was part of an experiment,' Karin broke in quickly as Latham again raised his weapon, 'a medical experiment'.

'Sorenson and I came pretty much to that conclusion. We can find out; Harry's body is still in a morgue . . . Okay, glamour boy, start walking out the door.'

'My clothes,' protested Jäger, 'surely you'll permit me to put on my clothes? It's pouring with rain.'

'Would you believe it if I told you I really don't care if you get wet? Also, I don't know what you've got in your clothes, say, in the collars. My friend here will carry them out with us.'

'Friend? Don't you mean your *whore-lover*!' screamed the new *Führer*.

'You son of a *bitch*!' Latham swung the barrel of the automatic into Jäger's head, when suddenly the Nazi thrust his left arm up, blocking the pistol-whip, his right fist crashing into Drew's chest with such force that he was propelled backward off his feet. Jäger then pounced on the automatic, wrenching it out of Drew's grip, and stood up, firing twice as Drew rolled first to his right, then to his left, both feet on the sides of the German's legs, where he locked Jäger's right ankle, smashing his foot in the Nazi's knee with all the desperate strength he could summon. Jäger screamed in pain as he arched back, firing twice more, the bullets piercing the walls. Karin lunged across the floor, grabbing Drew's automatic, which her husband had earlier forced her to drop. She rose and shouted.

'*Stop* it, Frederik! I'll *kill* you!'

'You couldn't, wife!' screamed Günter Jäger, fending off Latham's blows, trying to angle his gun into Drew's chest as Latham pinned his wrist to the floor beside the square hole and the waves of the river below. 'You *adore* me! Everyone adores me, they *worship* me!' The Nazi thrust his right arm behind him, beyond Drew's reach. He arced his hand to his left, then his right; it was free, he could shoot.

Karin fired.

The commandos raced through the open door, Witkowski at their heels. They stopped abruptly, staring at the scene in front of them under the spectral wash of the reflector lamp shining on the misplaced altar. For a few seconds the only sounds were those of the downpour beyond the door, and the heavy breathing of the five individuals of the N-2 unit.

'I assume you had to do it, *chłopak*,' said the colonel finally, staring at Jäger's body, his shattered forehead.

'He didn't, *I* did!' cried Karin.

'It was my fault, Stanley, I caused it,' Latham corrected her, gazing at the veteran G-2 officer, the death of Günter Jäger an acknowledged defeat of immense proportions. 'I lost control and he grabbed the advantage. He was about to kill me with my own gun.'

'Your own *gun*?'

'I took a swing at him with it. I shouldn't have, I know better.'

'It wasn't his fault at all, Stanley!' Karin exclaimed. 'Even if the circumstances were different, I would have shot him!

He tried to rape me, and if Drew hadn't shown up, he would have succeeded and left me dead. He said as much.'

'Then that'll be our report,' said the colonel. 'Things don't always work out, and I wouldn't care to attend Officer Latham's funeral. Did you learn anything, Karin?'

'Primarily how he got to where he was – the deal with the Stasi, his new identity, his oratorical talents discovered by Hans Traupman. About Water Lightning, he claimed no one could stop it, not even him, because he didn't know the technical details or the specific personnel involved. Then, again, he was a consummate liar.'

'*Goddammit!*' yelled Latham. 'I'm a pissant *fool!*'

'I don't know, lad. If I'd found someone attempting such an obscene act on a good friend, I don't think I'd have behaved much differently . . . Come on, we'll tear this whole place apart and see if we can find anything.'

'What about the German detail out there?' asked Christian Dietz. 'They could help us, maybe.'

'I don't think so, Captain,' said Karin quickly. 'Frederik made it clear that the Polizei, even those whose sympathies were with the Nazis, could not monitor every radio frequency. That could mean the neos have infiltrated the authorities as they have the Bundestag. I suggest we do the search ourselves.'

'It'll be a long night,' added Lieutenant Anthony. 'Let's get started.'

'What about the other two guards?' asked Drew. 'Or the first, for that matter?'

'They're bound and fast asleep,' answered Dietz. 'We'll check them now and then, and when we're finished, we'll turn them over to whomever you say.'

'You fellows ransack the rest of the house, we'll concentrate on the living quarters,' ordered the colonel. 'There are three rooms and a bath here, an office, a bedroom, and this unholy holy place. One for each of us.'

'What are we looking for, sir?' said Gerald Anthony.

'Anything that could possibly pertain to Water Lightning

– and anything else that has numbers or names . . . And one of you find a sheet and cover the corpse.'

They left nothing to chance, and as the summer dawn broke over the eastern Rhine, cartons, discovered in the supply room, were filled with materials and brought to the chapel. Most of the contents were probably worthless, but there were experts with far more experience than anyone in the N-2 unit to make that determination. Except, perhaps, Karin de Vries.

'*Flugzeug . . . gebaut* – there's nothing else, the writing's ripped away,' said Karin, studying a torn scrap of paper in her late husbands's handwriting. '"Aircraft made", that's all it says.'

'Anything that connects it to Water Lightning?' asked Witkowski, taping up several other boxes.

'No, not on the surface.'

'Then why spend time on it?'

'Because he wrote it in an excited state, the *l*'s and the *b*'s look alike, the rest is slurred, but the impressions are hard. I know that handwriting; he'd leave lists for me, things I should buy or make sure were available before he went undercover. He'd be on a high, his adrenaline flowing.'

'If you're suggesting what I think you are, I'm afraid it doesn't make sense,' said Drew, standing beside the square hole in the floor that led to the miniature submarine below in the river. 'There's no linkage to Water Lightning. Sorenson, who I learned is something of an expert on reservoirs, ruled out aircraft.'

'He was right,' said the colonel, pressing the tape on the last of the three cartons. 'Sheer numbers and altitudes would make it impossible. It'd be a strategy designed to fail.'

'Wes mentioned that reservoirs and other water sources were frequently considered for sabotage. I never knew that.'

'Because it's never been done except in desert warfare, where oases have been poisoned. First, there are humanitarian concerns – the victors have to live with the vanquished after hostilities cease. And second, the logistics are damn near insurmountable.'

'They've figured out a way, Stanley, I'm convinced of that.'

'What can we do beyond what we've done?' said Karin. 'There's less than twenty-four hours left.'

'Get this stuff over to London and pull in every analyst in MI-5, MI-6, and the Secret Service. Tell them to put everything under multiple microscopes, the more the better.'

'We can have it there in forty-five minutes,' said Witkowski, taking out his portable phone and dialling.

'I want the fastest way back to Paris, to meet with whoever's in charge of guarding the water sources, wherever they are.'

'Why not find out *where* they are and land closest to them?' asked De Vries. 'Claude can do that.'

'If he lives that long after I see him!' Latham spat out. 'He got you in here. You called him and he got you *in* here without telling us!'

'He had every good reason to do as I begged him – *begged* him.'

'With terrific results, I might add,' said Drew. 'You were damn near raped and killed, and the mighty Günter Jäger is dead under a sheet, no longer able to do us any good.'

'For that I'll never forgive myself. Not for killing him – he had to be killed or you would have died – but the fact that I caused it all.'

'What were you *thinking* of?' continued Latham angrily. 'That you were going to fire up his coals and he'd spew out everything?'

'Something like that, but far more than that. Harry would have understood.'

'Make *me* understand!'

'Frederik, for all his flaws, was once devoted to his parents and grandparents. Like many children who lose that love through separation or death, he was passionate about them.

If I could fire up the coals of *those* memories, it was conceivable that he might break, even briefly.'

'She's right, *chłopak*,' the colonel interrupted quietly as he replaced his telephone in his pocket. 'The psychiatrists who saw the tape said he was unstable to the max. I understood that to mean he could go one way or the other under extreme stress. She tried with a courage I've rarely seen; it didn't work, but it might have. Risks like that are taken every day in our ungodly profession, more often than not by brave people who never get credit, even for losing.'

'That was years ago, Stosh, not today.'

'I submit, Officer Latham, that today is the forerunner of our worst projections. You wouldn't be here now, on the banks of the Rhine, if you didn't believe that.'

'Okay, Stanley, I believe it. I'd just like to have better control over my troops – they are called "troops", aren't they?'

'Not in your case, but everything's clear in Paris. Moreau has two German jets at the airport, one heading to London, the other down into France, destination to be determined while airborne.'

Captain Dietz and Lieutenant Anthony walked into the chapel from the door to the rest of the house. 'There's nothing left out there but pots and pans and furniture,' said the captain. 'If there's a paper trail, it's in those boxes.'

'Where to now, boss man?' asked the lieutenant.

Latham turned to Witkowski. 'I know you won't like this, Stanley, but I want you to take these cartons to London. They're the best and you're the best, and no one can crack the whip better than you. Nobody gets any rest, any sleep, everyone just keeps working, reading, trying to find any clues. Karin and our two new friends will fly down into France with me.'

'You're right, I don't like it, *chłopak*, but logic's on your side, I'll not deny it. But, Drew, I'll need help, I'm not exactly on the Joint Chiefs of Staff, you know. I need more clout behind me than *I've* got.'

'How about Sorenson, or Talbot of the CIA, or the President of the United States?'

'I'd love to settle for the last one. Can you do it?'

'You're damn right I can – Sorenson can. Call German intelligence and have a car here in five minutes.'

'It never went away, just down the road. Come on, boys, each of us takes one of these.'

As the two commandos crossed the room to retrieve the boxes, Lieutenant Gerald Anthony spotted a crushed fragment of paper on the floor at the foot of the altar. Sheer instinct made him scoop it up; he unfolded it. There were only a few words in illegible German. Nevertheless, he shoved it into his pocket.

The jet to London, its engines muted but incessantly roaring, approached the coast of England. Witkowski was continuously on the international phone, first with Wesley Sorenson, then Knox Talbot, the director of Central Intelligence, Claude Moreau of the Deuxième, and, finally, to his amazement, the President of the United States.

'Witkowski,' said the Commander in Chief, 'you're now in control of the London operation. This has been fully agreed to by the Prime Minister. You say jump, they'll ask how high.'

'Yes, sir. That's what I wanted to hear. It can be a little awkward for an army colonel to give orders, especially to high-ranking civilians. They resent that kind of thing.'

'There'll be no resentment, only gratitude, believe me. Incidentally, you're cleared at the White House switchboard to reach me whenever you call. I'd appreciate a report every hour or so, if it's convenient.'

'I'll try to do that, sir.'

'Good luck, Colonel. Several hundred thousand people are counting on all of you, even though they don't know it.'

'I understand, sir, but if I may, shouldn't the people be informed of the possibilities?'

'And have panic in the streets, the highways at a standstill, public transportation bursting at the seams as people start racing out of Washington? If an alarm is issued that the entire city's water supply may be poisoned by terrorists, what's next? Contaminated food, Legionnaires' disease in all the air-conditioning units, germ warfare?'

'I hadn't thought of that, sir.'

'And you can add wholesale destruction of property, the looting and roving gangs that would follow, rampant hostilities out of control. Also, our experts tell us that the main reservoir is armed to the teeth, every conceivable penetration prepared for. They don't believe anything like Water Lightning can happen.'

'I hope they're right, Mr President.'

'They'd better be, Colonel.'

Twenty minutes out of the airport in Bonn, Latham received a call from Claude Moreau. 'Please do not waste time berating me, Drew. We can debate my decision later, argue the risk I took.'

'You can bet your ass we will. So what have you got?'

'You'll be landing at a private airport in the Beauvais district; it's twelve miles away from Paris's major reservoir. You'll be met by my second-in-command, Jacques Bergeron – you remember him, I trust.'

'I remember him. So?'

'He'll take you to the water tower and the military commander in charge of the defences. He'll answer any questions you have and give you a tour of the fortifications.'

'The problem is, I really don't know a goddamn thing about reservoirs other than what Sorenson told me and Witkowski confirmed.'

'Well, at least you've been prepared by experts.'

'*Experts?* They're not even engineers.'

'All of us become experts and engineers when the sabotage of utilities may be on the table.'

'What are *you* doing?'

'Overseeing an army of agents, soldiers, and police who

are searching every square foot of territory within ten miles of the waterworks. Looking for what, we don't know, but a few of our analysts have suggested missile launchers or rockets.'

'That's not a bad idea—'

'Others say it's insane,' the Deuxième director interrupted. 'They say that to use launchers with the accuracy required would entail a couple of tons of equipment with enough electrical power to light up a small town, or blow it out. Also, they'd need launching sites, and we've photographed every inch of ground via aircraft and satellites.'

'Underground pads?'

'That's what we're afraid of, but we have over two thousand "deputies" spreading out all over the place, asking if any unusual construction equipment has been sighted. Have you any idea how much concrete goes in a single pad? Or the electrical wiring required from a power station?'

'You're keeping busy, I'll say that.'

'Not busy enough, *mon ami*. I know you're convinced that the pigs have figured out a way, and I agree with you. Frankly, it was the reason I let Karin convince *me* – but let's *not* go into that. I have a gnawing feeling that we're missing something, something rather obvious, but still it eludes me.'

'How about something as simple as bazooka-type rocket launchers with canisters?'

'Among the first things we thought of, but using such weapons would require many hundreds, all positioned with clear sightlines. You can't walk twenty paces in the woods around the water without colliding with a soldier. A dozen rocket launchers, much less hundreds, would be spotted instantly.'

'Could it all be a hoax?' asked Drew.

'A hoax on whom? We both saw that tape. *Führer* Günter Jäger was not speaking to us, not threatening us, he was declaiming to his sworn constituency, some of the wealthiest men in Europe and America. No, *mon ami*, he believes he can do it. And so we must keep thinking. Perhaps the

London analysts will find something, God willing. Incidentally, you were right to send those materials to the British.'

'I'm surprised to hear you say that.'

'You shouldn't be. Not only are they very professional, but the UK was never occupied. I grant you that the majority of the people reading through the material were probably not around during that war, but the scar of occupation remains on the national psyche. The French can never be totally objective.'

'That's quite an admission.'

'It is the truth, as I see it.'

They landed in Beauvais at 6:47 in the morning, the private airfield awash with the blinding early sun. The N-2 unit disembarked and was taken directly to the airport's lounge, where clean, dry clothes awaited them. They changed quickly into the lightweight military fatigues, Karin the last to finish. When she emerged from the ladies' room in the pale blue army coveralls, Drew remarked. 'You look better than you should,' he said. 'Now roll or bunch your hair up and shove it under the beret.'

'It'll be uncomfortable.'

'So's a bullet, and if anyone in that German detail at Jäger's place was on his side, word will be sent down to take out the female. Come on, let's go. We're down to seventeen-plus hours. How long will it take us to get to the – what-do-you-call-it, Jacques?'

'The water tower complex at the reservoir,' replied the Deuxième agent as they walked out to the waiting car in the parking lot. 'It's eighteen kilometres from here – twelve miles American – so it won't be longer than ten minutes. François is our driver, you remember François, don't you?'

'From that carnival? The man with two bawling daughters he sent home?'

'The same.'

'My blood pressure remembers him very well, especially when he drove up on sidewalks.'

'He's quite clever behind the wheel.'

'Another word is *maniacal*.'

'The director sent up several hundred aerial photographs for you to look at, to see if you might spot something we've missed.'

'Not likely. While I was in college I got my pilot's licence – props only – and did about thirty hours solo, but without a radio I could never find my way back to an airport. Everything looked the same.'

'I can commiserate. I spent two years as a pilot officer in the Armée de l'Air and it was the same for me.'

'No kidding? The French air force?'

'Yes, but I did not especially like heights, so I resigned and studied languages. The mystique of a military pilot fluent in different tongues still exists. The Deuxième picked me up.'

They reached the Bureau's vehicle; it was the same non-descript car, with an engine designed for Le Mans or Daytona, that Latham remembered so well. François was effusive in his greeting. 'Have your daughters forgiven you?' asked Drew.

'Never!' he exclaimed. 'Le Parc de Joic is closed down and they blame me for it!'

'Maybe someone will buy it and reopen. Let's go, old friend, we're in a hurry.'

The N-2 unit piled in and François took off – literally, it might have seemed, by the expressions of Karin and the two commandos in the backseat. De Vries's eyes were wide open, and the faces of the two behind-the-lines veterans of Desert Storm were white with fear as François screeched, side-slipping around curves and pressing the accelerator to the floor on straightaways until the speedometer read over a hundred and fifty kilometres an hour.

'What the hell is this freak *doing*?' asked Captain Dietz. 'Is this a suicide run, because if it is, I want out!'

'Not to worry!' yelled Drew, turning his head between François and Jacques, trying to be heard over the roar of the engine. 'He was a racing car driver before he went to the Deuxième.'

'He should have gone to a permanent traffic court,' cried Lieutenant Anthony. 'He's crazy!'

'He's good,' answered Latham. 'Watch!'

'I'd rather not,' mumbled Karin.

The Deuxième sedan screamed to a stop in the parking area of an enormous brick structure that was the water-works of the Beauvais reservoir. As the unit got shakily out of the car, a contingent of two platoons of French soldiers converged on the vehicle, their weapons drawn. '*Arrêtez!*' shouted Jacques Bergeron. 'We are the Deuxième, here is my official identification.'

An officer approached, studied the shield and the plastic card. 'Of course, we knew it was you, monsieur,' he said in French, 'but we do not know your guests.'

'They are with me, that's all you have to know.'

'Naturally.'

'Alert your commander and tell him I'm bringing the N-2 unit inside.'

'Right away, sir,' said the officer, unclipping a walkie-talkie from his belt and announcing the new arrivals. 'Proceed, sir, the commander of the watch is waiting for you. He says to please hurry.'

'Thank you.' Jacques, Latham, Karin, and the two commandos proceeded in front of a row of rifles at port arms to the entrance of the waterworks. Inside, the four new-comers were startled by what they saw. It was like the bowels of an ancient castle, devoid of ornamentation, dark and reeking of dampness. Everything was very, very old brick, the walls reaching up to high ceilings; in the centre, flanked by two wide stone staircases, the huge open area rose to the top of the structure. 'Come,' said Jacques Bergeron in English, 'the elevator is down this hallway to the right.' The unit followed the Frenchman as Lieutenant Anthony spoke.

'This place must have been built over three hundred years ago.'

'With an elevator?' interrupted Dietz, grinning.

'That came much later,' replied Bergeron, 'but your colleague is correct. This plant, with crude but serviceable viaducts, was built by the Beauvais dynasty for the purpose of capturing the water and sending it out to their fields and gardens. That was in the early sixteen hundreds.'

The enormous old square elevator was the sort found in warehouses or freight depots where heavy equipment must be sent from one floor to another. It creaked and stuttered its way up, metal abrasively rubbing against metal, until it reached the top floor. Jacques opened the heavy vertical panel with such obvious effort that Captain Dietz helped him shove it up. Instantly revealed was the imposing figure of a general in the uniform of the army of France. He spoke quickly, urgently, to the Deuxième officer. Jacques frowned, then nodded, muttered a few words in French, and walked rapidly away with the soldier.

'What did they say?' asked Drew, turning to Karin as the four of them walked out of the elevator. 'They rattled too fast for me, but I got something about "terrible news".'

'Basically, that was it,' answered De Vries, squinting in the dim light at the two Frenchmen down the darker brick hallway. 'The general said he had terrible news and had to speak with Jacques privately.'

Suddenly there was a desperate cry. *'Mon Dieu, non! Pas vrai!'* It was followed by the mournful wail of a damaged man in pain. As one, the N-2 unit rushed into the shadowed corridor.

'What *happened*?' asked Karin in French.

'I will answer so our friend, Drew, will understand,' said Bergeron, slouched, his back against the brick, tears falling down his cheeks. 'Claude was assassinated twenty minutes ago in the Deuxième underground parking area.'

'Oh, my *God*!' cried De Vries, stepping forward and gripping Jacques's arm.

'How could it *happen*?' roared Latham. 'That place is tighter than a drum – with your own *people*!'

'The Nazis,' whispered the Deuxième agent, his words choked. 'They're everywhere.'

CHAPTER FORTY

The large rectangular window looked out over the vast expanse of the Beauvais reservoir. They were in the huge office complex belonging to the manager of the waterworks and his staff, who had been temporarily displaced by the military commander overseeing the fortifications. The general was nonetheless intelligent and sensitive enough to seek the advice of the civilian manager and decline to use his desk. Jacques Bergeron had been on the telephone to Paris for over fifteen minutes, intermittently catching his breath and checking his tears.

The general had spread a map and a stack of photographs over an enormous table in front of the window, and, using a pointer, was describing in detail his defences. However, the old soldier was aware that his audience of four was not totally attentive, eyes darting and ears listening to the Deuxième officer at the desk. Finally, Jacques hung up the phone, rose from the chair, and walked to the table.

'I'm afraid it is far worse than we imagined,' he said quietly, breathing deeply to find his own control. 'In a macabre way, perhaps it's best that Claude was cut down where he was if it had to be. For if he had survived, he would have found his beloved wife shot to death at their home.'

'*Goddammit!*' shouted Drew, then lowered his voice to a guttural murmur. 'No quarter,' he said, 'no quarter at all for those sons of bitches! We see, we kill; we find, we kill.'

'There is something else, and I consider it totally irrelevant, for Claude Moreau was my mentor, my instructor-father in so many things, but it is a fact. By the order of the President of France, I am the temporary director of the Deuxième and must return to Paris.'

'I know you never wanted it this way, Jacques,' said Latham, 'but congratulations. You wouldn't have been chosen if you weren't the best. Your mentor trained you well.'

'It doesn't matter. Regardless of what happens in the next sixteen hours, I will resign and find other work.'

'*Why?*' asked Karin. 'You could be made the permanent director. Who else is there?'

'You're very kind, but I know myself. I am a follower, a very good follower, but I am not a leader. One must be honest with oneself.'

'I *hate* what's happened,' said Latham, 'but we've got to go back to work. You owe it to Claude and I owe it to Harry. Start from the beginning, General,' he went on. 'We temporarily lost you.'

'I must return to Paris.' repeated Bergeron. 'I don't want to, but those are my orders – orders from the President – and I must obey them. Orders must be obeyed.'

'Then do so,' said Karin gently. 'We'll do our best, Jacques.'

'Right. You go down to Paris and stay in touch with London and Washington,' said Latham firmly. 'But, Jacques – keep us informed.'

'*Au revoir, mes amis.*' The Deuxième officer turned and walked disconsolately out of the room.

'Where were we, General?' asked Drew, leaning over the table, Dietz and Anthony on either side, Karin across from them.

'These are the armed personnel I've dispersed throughout the area,' began the old soldier, pointing at the huge map of the reservoir and its surrounding woods. 'From long years of experience, including in Southeast Asia, where the enemy's guerrilla forces presented similar concerns for penetration, I cannot think of any additional defences we haven't considered. A squadron of fighter planes is on an alert at an air base

678

thirty kilometres from here, and they are fully armed. We have over twelve hundred troops throughout the woods and the roads, all units in constant contact with one another, as well as twenty antiaircraft emplacements with instant trajectory guidances. Seventeen bomb squads have been working without rest, studying the banks, searching for time-set explosives. There is also a patrol boat with chemical-analysis equipment crisscrossing the areas nearest the major flows. At the first signs of toxicity, the sluice gates will send signals, the valves on alert for alternative sources from other districts.'

'If that's necessary,' asked Drew, 'how long will it take for the alternative sources to start flowing?'

'According to the manager, who will be back shortly, the longest time on record was four hours and seven minutes in the middle thirties – due to machinery failure. However, the first major problem is a drastic lowering of water pressure everywhere, followed by initial massive impurities from the unused flows.'

'Impurities?' Karin broke in.

'Nothing like toxic poisoning; some dirt or mud, or pipe residue. Perhaps enough to cause upset stomachs, vomiting, diarrhoea, but not fatal. The potential *real* danger is with the underground hydrants; the pressure might preclude their use in case of fires.'

'Then the potential crisis has geometric proportions,' said De Vries. 'Because if Water Lightning somehow, some way *does* succeed, and your solutions are activated, the pressure still goes down and fires could be set all over Paris. Günter Jäger used the phrase "fire and lightning" – *fire* and lightning. It could be significant. If I remember my history, Hitler's last order to his evacuating commanders was "Burn Paris down!"'

'All too true, madame, but I ask you, and I'll ask you again after we take a tour of our defences, can you really believe this Water Lightning can succeed?'

'I don't want to, General.'

'What about London and Washington?' said Latham. 'Moreau . . . Moreau told me you were in touch with both.'

'You see the bald man at the desk over there with the red telephone?' The old soldier gestured at an army major across the room, a red telephone at his ear. 'He is not only my most trusted adjutant, he is my son. The baldness comes from his mother's side, poor fellow.'

'Your *son*?'

'*Oui*, Monsieur Latham,' replied the general, smiling. 'When the Socialists took over the Quai d'Orsay, many of us in the military practised nepotism for our own protection until we discovered that they weren't such bad fellows.'

'How very Gallic,' said Karin.

'Again, too true, madame. *La famille est éternelle*. However, my hairless son is an exceptional officer, for which I thank my side of the family – we are extremely astute. He is also on the telephone with either London or Washington right now. The lines are constantly open, a single button changes the capital.' The major hung up the phone and the general called out. '*Adjutant-Major*, is there anything new?'

'*Non, mon général*,' answered the stern-faced, bald major, turning to reply to his father. 'And I would appreciate it if you would not continue to ask the same question. I will inform you when there is anything unexpected or a suggested change in our strategies.'

'He's also impudent,' said the general softly, 'again his mother's influence.'

'My name's Latham,' said Drew, interrupting.

'I know who you are, sir. My name is Gaston.' The major rose from his desk and extended his hand to each member of the N-2 unit. The hands were shaken awkwardly, as if the command had been shifted from father to son. 'I must tell you that the general has deployed extraordinary defences, as only a man with his experience in incursion and infiltration can, and we are all grateful. He has been through such campaigns and we have not, at least I haven't, but as technology has changed, so the rules have changed. London and Washington have upgraded their fortifications, as we have, employing the newest electronics.'

'Like what specifically?' asked Drew.

'Infrared sensor beams throughout the woods as well as webs of spun plastic matting along the roads that, when penetrated, activate clouds of vapour immobilizing everyone in the vicinity – naturally, our troops have masks. In addition, radar and radio signals that flare out over the trees on all sides, capable of intercepting missiles as far away as two hundred kilometres; they trigger our own heat-seeking countermissiles—'

'Like the Patriots in D-Storm,' Captain Dietz interrupted.

'When they worked,' said the lieutenant, barely audible.

'Precisely,' agreed the major, in his enthusiasm not hearing the subordinate officer.

'What about the reservoir itself?' inquired Karin.

'What about it, madame? To anticipate you, if there are scores of huge drums filled with toxins, and attached to pre-set explosives to blow them apart, our divers have not found them. They've searched, I assure you, and considering the sheer mass of metal required, the underwater sonar would have. Finally, even in normal times the reservoir is constantly under observation, the perimeters fenced, penetration instantly known. How could it happen?'

'It obviously couldn't, I'm just trying to think of everything. You've undoubtedly done so already.'

'This is not *necessarily* so,' disagreed the old general. 'You are all accomplished intelligence personnel, and you know the enemy, you've been dealing with him. Once – before Dien Bien Phu – a spy whose cover was as an accountant, which he actually was in Lyons, told me that the anti-government forces could afford far greater firepower than Paris acknowledged. Paris scoffed and we lost a country.'

'I don't see the relevance,' said Karin.

'Perhaps there is none, but you may see something we've missed.'

'That's what Moreau said to me,' interjected Drew.

'I know. We talked. So let us get into an open truck and each of you – all of you – see for yourselves. Dissect us, pick us apart, as you Americans say, find our flaws, if they exist.'

The 'tour' throughout the forests, the fields, and the adjacent roads was not only exhausting in the roofless truck that seemed to gravitate to every ditch and minor gully, but it took over three hours. Everyone made notes, in the main affirmative; only the two commandos were negative, in terms of underbrush incursion.

'I could send fifty men on their bellies through a sector of this foliage, taking out the soldiers and putting on their uniforms,' exclaimed Captain Dietz. 'This is nuts!'

'And once you get into the uniforms,' added Lieutenant Anthony, 'you can waste away your flanks and create a big, wide boulevard.'

'The roads are protected by plastic webs, they set off alarms!'

'You freeze 'em with cold nitro sprays, General,' said Dietz. 'They close down electrical impulses.'

'*Mon Dieu* . . .'

'Let's face it, guys,' said Latham when they were back at the waterworks, 'your theories may have merit, but you're thinking too small. There wouldn't *be* fifty men, there'd have to be five hundred to be effective. See what I mean?'

'The general asked for criticisms, Mr Latham,' replied Captain Dietz. 'Not solutions.'

'Let's look at the photographs,' said Drew, approaching the table and seeing that they had been spread out in rows in some sort of precise order.

'I have arranged them from top to bottom as determined by the farthest distance from the reservoir to the nearest,' explained the general's son. 'All were taken by infrared cameras at relatively low altitudes according to aerial radar, and where suspicious images occurred, they were repeated frequently, no more than a few hundred feet above the objects.'

'What are these?' asked Dietz, pointing at several dark circles.

'Farm silos,' replied the major. 'To make certain, we had them examined by the local police.'

'And those?' said Karin, her index finger on a series of three photographs depicting long, dark rectangular images with muted lights on one side. 'They look dangerously like missile sites.'

'Railroad stations. You're seeing the lamps under the overhang, next to the tracks,' answered Gaston.

'And these?' Latham used the pointer and touched a photograph that showed the outlines of two large aeroplanes on what appeared to be a field off the major runway of a private airport.

'Aircraft purchased by Saudi Arabia, awaiting transport to Riyadh. We checked the Ministry of Export and found everything to be in order.'

'They bought *French*, not American?' said Gerald Anthony.

'Many do, Lieutenant. Our aircraft industry is superb. Our Mirages are considered to be among the finest fighter planes in the world. Also, one saves millions of francs by having them flown from Beauvais instead of, say, Seattle, Washington.'

'I'll grant you that, Major.'

And so it went for the rest of the morning, every photograph scrutinized with magnifiers, a hundred questions asked and answered. Everything led to nowhere.

'What *is* it?' exclaimed Latham. 'What is it they've got that we don't *see*?'

In the restricted cavernous hall in the bowels of British intelligence, the most experienced analysts and cryptographers of MI-5, MI-6, and Her Majesty's Secret Service pored over the cartons of material from Günter Jäger's house on the Rhine. Suddenly there was a firm, controlled voice that rose above the hum of nearby machines.

'I've *got* something,' said a woman in front of one of the endless computers around the huge room. 'I'm not sure what it means, but it was buried in the deep code.'

'Explain, please.' The MI-6 director in charge rushed to her station, the silent Witkowski at his side.

'"Daedalus will fly, nothing can stop him." Those are the decoded words.'

'What the devil do they mean?'

'Something about the sky, sir. In Greek mythology, Daedalus escaped from Crete with feathered wings attached to his arms by wax, but his son, Icarus, flew too high and the sun melted *his* wax. He fell to his death into the sea.'

'What in blazes has that got to do with Water Lightning?'

'Frankly, I don't know, sir, but there are three gradations of codes, A, B, and C, C being the most complex.'

'Yes, I'm aware of that, Mrs Graham.'

'Well, this was in the C classification, which is equivalent to our top secret, which means it's the most restricted of the ciphers. Others in the neo movement might intercept it, but it's doubtful they would break it. The message was meant for very few eyes.'

'Any idea where it came from?' asked the American colonel. 'Is there a date, a time?'

'Fortunately, to both questions, yes. It was a fax from here, from London, and the time was forty-two hours ago.'

'Well done! Can you trace it?'

'I have. It's one of yours, sir. MI-6, Duro-Division, German section.'

'*Shit!* Sorry, old girl. There are over sixty officers in that section – just a moment! Each has to enter a two-digit marker, the machine won't transmit without it. It has to *be* there!'

'It is, sir. It's Officer Meyer Gold, chief of the section.'

'*Meyer*? That's impossible! He's a Jew, to begin with, and lost both sets of grandparents in the camps. He requested the German section for just that reason.'

'Perhaps he's not actually Jewish, sir.'

'Then why did we all attend his son's bar mitzvah last year?'

'Then the only other explanation is that someone else used his marker.'

'The manual makes clear that each individual keeps his marker to himself.'

'I'm afraid I can't help you any further,' said the clear-eyed, grey-haired Mrs Graham, returning to her stack of materials.

'I may – or I may not,' said another analyst several stations away, a black West Indian officer, a Rhodes scholar from the Bahamas.

'What is it, Vernal?' asked the MI-6 director, walking quickly to the Bahamian's table.

'Another Code C entry. The name Daedalus appears, only with no marker, no London, and it was sent thirty-seven hours ago from Washington.'

'What's the communication?'

'"Daedalus in position, countdown begun." And then it ends, and I'll say it in German. *"Ein Volk, ein Reich, ein Führer Jäger."* How about that?'

'Did you trace the fax?' asked Witkowski.

'Naturally. The American State Department, the office of Jacob Weinstein, undersecretary for Middle Eastern affairs. He's a highly regarded negotiator.'

'Good God, they're using well-respected Jewish personnel for their covers.'

'That shouldn't surprise us,' said the Bahamian. 'The only thing that could top it would be to use us blacks.'

'You've got a point,' agreed the American. 'But colour doesn't come over a fax.'

'Names do, sir, and the fact that Daedalus appears twice in two top-secret ciphers nine hours apart has to mean something.'

'They've already told us. The countdown's begun and they're too damned confident of its success to suit my skin.' The MI-6 officer walked to the centre of the large room and clapped his hands. 'Listen up, everyone!' he cried. 'Listen up, if you please.' The room went silent except for the soft humming of the computers. 'We seem to have found a significant piece of information related to this bloody Water Lightning. It's the name "Daedalus". Have any of you run across it?'

'Yes, rather,' replied a slender middle-aged man with a chin beard and wearing wire-rimmed glasses, quite professorial in appearance. 'About an hour past. I considered it to be the code name for a Nazi agent or agents, Sonnenkinder, no doubt, and saw no relevance to Water Lightning. You see, Daedalus was the builder of the great labyrinth of Crete, and as we all recognize, *labyrinthine* connotes circuitous thought, concealed avenues, that sort of thing—'

'Yes, yes, Dr Upjohn,' interrupted the impatient MI-6 director, 'but in this case it may refer to the mythological flight he took with his son.'

'Oh, Icarus? No, I doubt that. As the legend has it, Icarus was a headstrong moron. Sorry, old man, but my interpretation is far more academically valid. Where in heaven's name does Water Lightning fit in? It simply doesn't, don't you see?'

'*Please*, Professor, just dig the damn thing out, will you?'

'Very well,' said the wounded academic, his voice resounding with superiority. 'It's here somewhere in the reject pile. It was a facsimile, I believe. Yes, here it is.'

'Read it, please. From the top, old fellow.'

'Its point of origin was Paris, and it was sent yesterday at 11:17 A.M. The message is as follows. "Messieurs Daedalus in splendid condition, prepared to strike in the name of our glorious future!" Obviously, either he or they are misguided zealots with functions to perform following this Water Lightning. Quite possibly assassins.'

'Or something else,' said the grey-haired Mrs Graham.

'Such as, dear lady?' asked Professor Upjohn patronizingly.

'Oh, stop it, Hubert, you're not in a Cambridge classroom now,' she snapped. 'We're all searching.'

'You obviously have an idea,' said Witkowski with sincerity. 'What is it?'

'I don't really know, I'm merely struck by the French plural. "Messieurs", not "monsieur"; not one but more than one. That's the first time Water Lightning – if it *is* Water Lightning – has been described in such a way.'

'The French are inordinately precise,' offered Dr Hubert Upjohn acidly. 'They cheat so frequently, it's in their nature.'

'Poppycock,' said Mrs Graham, 'we've both had our share of subterfuge. I submit to you the battles of Plassy, as well as Henry the Second's marriage to Eleanor of Aquitaine.'

'May we please *stop* this all-too-unenlightening colloquy,' said the MI-6 director, turning to an aide. 'Gather up the materials, call Beauvais and Washington, and fax everything to them. Someone's got to make sense out of this.'

'Yes, sir.'

'Quickly,' added the American colonel.

At the Dalecarlia reservoir in Georgetown, analysts from Central Intelligence, G-2, and the National Security Agency studied the faxes from London. A deputy director of the CIA threw up his hands.

'There's *nothing* we're not prepared for! I don't give a damn if the attacks come from every point on the compass, we'll blow them away. Like London and Paris, we've got the grounds covered, and our heat-seeking rockets will knock any missiles out of the air. What the hell's left?'

'Then why are they so confident?' asked a lieutenant colonel from G-2.

'Because they're fanatics,' answered a young intellectual from the National Security Agency. 'They must believe what they're instructed to believe, that's drummed into them. It's called the Nietzsche imperative.'

'It's called *crap*!' said the brigadier general in charge of Dalecarlia. 'Aren't those bastards in the real world?'

'Not really,' replied the NSA analyst. 'They have their own world, sir. Its parameters are those of total commitment, nothing else matters or can interfere.'

'You're saying they're fruitcakes!'

'They're fruitcakes, General, but they're not stupid fruitcakes. I agree with that Consular Operations officer in Beauvais. They think they've found a way, and I can't dismiss the possibility that they have.'

Beauvais, France. Zero hour minus three. It was exactly one-thirty A.M. Everyone's eyes continuously darted to wall clocks and watches, the tension growing as the minutes ticked by and four-thirty grew nearer.

'Let's go back to the photographs, okay?' said Latham.

'We've been over them and *over* them,' replied Karin. 'Every question we've asked has been answered, Drew. What else is there?'

'I don't know, I just want to look again.'

'At what, monsieur?' asked the major.

'Well ... those silos, for example. You said the local police had investigated them. Were they qualified? Silos can be packed with feed or hay and there can be something else entirely underneath.'

'They were told what to look for, and one of my officers accompanied them,' said the general. 'The ground-level contents were studied.'

'The more I think about missiles, the more plausible they seem.'

'We are as prepared as we can be,' said the general's son. 'Mobile units with launchers for heat-seeking rockets surround the reservoir, I've told you that, monsieur.'

'Then let's go back over the stuff from London. For *Christ's* sake, what's a Daedalus or Daedaluses?'

'I can explain it again, sir,' offered Lieutenant Anthony. 'You see, according to the myth, Daedalus, who was both an artist and an architect, studied the birds on Crete, mostly sea gulls, I guess, and figured that if man could attach feathers to his arms, feathers being close to air in density, and in motion almost as light as air—'

'*Please*, Gerry, if I hear that one more time, I'm going to burn every Bulfinch I come across for the rest of my life!'

'We keep returning to *air*, don't we?' said De Vries. 'Missiles, rockets, Daedalus or Daedaluses.'

'Speaking of air,' the balding major interrupted with a touch of irritation, 'no missile or rocket or plane can penetrate our airspace without being detected far in advance and getting shot down either by antiaircraft cannon fire or by our own missiles. And as we've all agreed, to carry out the objective of Water Lightning, there would have to be several very large cargo aircraft or dozens of smaller ones, sweeping down from nearby fields to achieve the element of surprise.'

'Have you checked the airports in Paris?' pressed Latham.

'Why do you think all the airlines' schedules are delayed?'

'I didn't know they were.'

'They are, causing a great deal of anger among their passengers. It is the same at Heathrow and Gatwick in England, and Dulles and National in Washington. We can't say why without risking riots and far worse, but every aircraft is being inspected before it's given clearance to enter a runway.'

'I didn't realize that. Sorry. But then why are the neos so goddamned sure they've figured it *out*?'

'That is beyond me, monsieur.'

London. Zero hour minus two and eight minutes. It was 1:22 A.M., Greenwich Mean Time, and the MI-6 director in Vauxhall Cross was on the phone to Washington. 'Any developments over there?'

'Not a wrinkle,' answered an angry American voice. 'I'm beginning to think this whole frigging exercise is a pile of shit! Somebody's laughing his ass off in Germantown.'

'I'm inclined to agree, old man, but you saw that tape and the materials we sent you. I'd say they were pretty convincing.'

'I'd say they're a bunch of paranoid freaks, playing out some kind of *Götterdämmerung* that guy Wagner wouldn't touch, or is it *Vagner*?'

'We'll know soon enough, Yank. Keep steady.'

'I'll try to keep from falling asleep.'

Washington DC. Zero hour minus forty-two minutes. It was 9:48 P.M., the July sky overcast, the rain imminent, and the brigadier general in charge of the Dalecarlia reservoir was pacing back and forth across the floor of the water-works office. 'London doesn't know anything, Paris is a bust, and we're sitting on our duffs, wondering whether we've been conned! This is one fucking *joke* that's costing the taxpayers millions, and we'll be blamed for it! *God*, I hate this job. If it's not too late, I'll go back to school and become a dentist!'

Zero hour minus twelve minutes. It was 4:18 in Paris, 3:18 in London, 10:18 in Washington, DC. Miles away from the reservoirs of the three cities, and synchronized down to minutes, six powerful jets went airborne, instantly sweeping away from their targets.

'*Activités inconnues!*' said the radar specialist in Beauvais.

'*Unidentified aircraft!*' said the specialist in London.

'*Two blips, unknown!*' said the specialist in Washington. 'Not in sync with Dulles or National communications.'

Then, although separated by small and large distances, each spoke seconds later.

'*Superflu,*' corrected Paris.

'*False alarm,*' corrected London.

'*Forget it,*' corrected Washington. 'They're headed the other way. Probably rich kids with their private jets who forget flight plans. Hope they're sober.'

Zero hour minus six minutes. In the dark skies over the

outskirts of Beauvais, Georgetown, and North London, the jets continued their manoeuvres, sweeping away from the three targets, climbing at incredible accelerations, each millisecond counted off by the computers. The precomputed flight patterns were instantly activated. The jets turned, their engines cut back to minimum, and as rapidly as they had ascended, they descended with equal speed, entering air corridors chosen for their minimum populations, and that would lead them to the fields where their tailhooks would lash out and down, snaring the heavy steel cables that would pull the massive Messerschmitt ME 323 gliders aloft.

There was one final command that each flight leader was prepared to issue when deceleration was complete. He would give it over a determined radio frequency to each glider, *his* signal to deliver it being a red light on his computerized panel. It would come in one minute and seven seconds, give or take seconds, due to airspeeds and head winds or tailwinds. Everything now was sheer distance.

Beauvais. Zero hour minus four minutes. Drew stared out the huge window overlooking the reservoir, while Karin sat at the desk with the major on a second red telephone, both linked to London and Washington. The two commandos stood with the general behind the radar specialist and his screen.

Suddenly Latham turned from the window and spoke in a loud voice. '*Lieutenant*, what did you say about that Daedalus's wings?'

'They were made of feathers—'

'Yes, I know, but after that, something *about* the feathers? What *was* it?'

'Just feathers, sir. Some people – mostly poets – liken their density to air, the way they kind of float in the wind, born to the air, as it were, which is why they're on birds.'

'And birds swoop down silently, it's how the predators catch their quarry.'

'What are you talking about, Drew?' asked De Vries, the

red phone still at her ear, as was the major's. He looked up at the Cons-Op officer.

'They *glide*, Karin, they glide!'

'So, monsieur?'

'Gliders, goddammit! That may be it! They're using *gliders*!'

'They would have to be extremely large,' said the general, 'or dozens of them, perhaps more, far more.'

'And they would have been picked up by the radar, monsieur,' added the major. 'Especially the airborne radar.'

'They were, in the photographs! Those two aircraft for Saudi Arabia – how many times have end-user clearances been manipulated? But they *wouldn't* be picked up by your heat-seeking missiles. There are no engines, no *heat*! Probably very little metal either.'

'*Mon Dieu!*' exclaimed the general, his eyes wide, intense, as if sudden memories consumed him. '*Gliders!* The Germans were the experts, the final authority. In the early forties they developed the prototype for all the cargo gliders the world over, far more advanced than the British Airspeed-Horsing or the American WACOs. Actually, we all stole their designs. The Messerschmitt factories turned out the *Gigant*, a huge bird from hell that could silently float over borders and battlefield, delivering its deadly merchandise.'

'Could there be any left, *mon père?*' asked the major.

'Why not? All of us, on both sides, have kept our fleets – sea and air – in "mothballs", as the Americans say.'

'Could they be made operational after so many years?' pressed Karin.

'The enemy notwithstanding,' answered the old soldier, 'the Messerschmitt companies built for the ages. Undoubtedly, certain equipment would have to be replaced or upgraded, but again, why not?'

'Still, they would appear on the screen,' insisted the radar specialist.

'But how strong? How strong an image would you get on that screen of yours with a flying object that has little or no metal, no motors, the struts made of replaced bamboo, maybe, which in the Far East they use for scaffolds – they claim it's stronger and safer than steel.'

'My English is adequate, sir, but you speak so *rapidement*—'

'Someone tell him what I just said, just asked.'

The major did so, and the radar specialist replied, never taking his eyes off the screen. 'It would be less strong than that of a conventional aircraft, that is true.'

'I mean, even clouds can produce some image, can't they?'

'Yes, but one can tell the difference.'

'And people who own boats carry radar reflectors on board in case they get in trouble and want the radars to pick them up.'

'Again, quite normal.'

'So radar is basically interpretive, isn't it?'

'As are medical X-rays. One doctor will see one thing, another something else. Then there are experts, and I am one of them with radar, monsieur.'

'Good for you. Could you possibly be distracted?'

'By *what*? You become insulting, if I am permitted to say so.'

'You're permitted, and, honestly, I don't mean to insult you—'

'*Wait!*' said Karin, searching her pockets feverishly, finally yanking out a torn piece of paper. 'This was in a carton from, I think, Jäger's outer living room. I kept it because I didn't understand it, it was only a partial sentence. It has just two words in German, "Aircraft made" . . . the rest was ripped away.'

'Good God almighty,' muttered Gerald Anthony, reaching into the breast pocket of his French military fatigues and pulling up a scrap of a wrinkled note. 'I did the same damn thing. I found this in Jäger's chapel, at the foot of an altar that shouldn't be there. Since then I've looked at it every once in a while, trying to figure out the handwriting. I did, and it fits with Mrs de Vries's information. These are the words: "*Aus Stoff und Holz*", that's "of cloth and wood".'

"'Aircraft made of cloth and wood,'" said De Vries.

'Gliders,' added Latham quietly. '*Gliders.*'

'*Arrêtez!*' cried the radar specialist, breaking off the conversation. 'The aircraft have reentered our space! They are within forty kilometres of the water!'

'Prepare to activate the missiles!' shouted the general's son into a third telephone.

London. Zero hour minus three minutes ten seconds. 'Unidentified aircraft reappearing on screen! Direction, Code Intolerable!'

Washington, DC. Zero hour minus two minutes forty-nine seconds. 'Son of a bitch! The unknowns are back and heading our way!'

Beauvais. Zero hour minus two minutes twenty-eight seconds. 'Scramble military aircraft everywhere!' roared Latham. 'Get that to London and Washington!'

'But the *missiles*,' cried the general's son.

'Blast them off!'

'Then why the fighter planes?'

'For what the missiles don't get! Inform London and Washington. *Do* it!'

'It is done.'

In the dark skies above Beauvais, London, and Washington, the computerized neo-Nazi jets swept down towards their respective fields, their tail hooks released for the final approach.

'Fire rockets!'

'Fire rockets!'

'Fire rockets!'

Below, in three separate stretches of cut grass, there were instant explosions of ballistic fire below the wings of all six

694

Messerschmitt cargo gliders. Each reached a prereleased ground thrust of four hundred miles an hour as the jets raced above them, their hooks grappling the cables, the huge gliders instantaneously matching the acceleration of their lifting crafts. Within seconds all were airborne, and at barely a hundred feet the underside rockets were released into the fields. Unencumbered, the gliders above London, Beauvais, and Georgetown were pulled to the prescribed, computerized altitude of twenty-seven hundred feet. The cables were snapped, the gliders free to begin their circling descents to the targets.

Suddenly, at higher altitudes, the skies were lit up like compressed bolts of lightning as the jets were blown out of the air, each exploding in erratic splashes of fire. Yet below, each glider pilot, aided by his own computers, knew his mission well. *Ein Volk, ein Reich, ein Führer!*

Beauvais. Zero hour. 'We've *got* them!' yelled the general as the splotches of white appeared on the radar screen. 'They're utterly destroyed. We've beat Water Lightning!'

'London and Washington agree!' shouted the major. 'The results were the same. We have won!'

'No, you *haven't*!' roared Drew. 'Look at the radar grids! Those explosions took place thousands of feet above the initial entry level. *Look* at them! Tell London and Washington to do the same ... Now look below at those far less visible, skeletonlike images. *Look.* They're the gliders!'

'Oh, my *God*!' said Captain Dietz.

'Jee*zus*!' exclaimed Lieutenant Anthony.

'What do you estimate the altitude, Mr Radar?'

'I can more than estimate, monsieur. Those "images" are between eighteen and nineteen hundred feet. They rotate in slow, descending, wide circles of between three and four hundred feet—'

'Why would they *do* that, Radar Man?'

'One must presume for accuracy.'

'How about the time to touch down? Can you give us a figure?'

'The winds change, so here I will estimate. Between four and six minutes.'

'That's four or six hours in jet time. *Major*, alert London and DC and tell them to get their fighter planes to circle the perimeters of the reservoirs starting at fifteen hundred feet! Yours too. *Now!*'

'If they are there, we will shoot them out of existence,' said the general's son, picking up his red telephone.

'Are you *crazy*?' screamed Latham. 'Those aircraft are loaded with poison, probably liquid, and the casings will self-destruct instantly when they hit water or land. Manoeuvre the fighters so their jet streams blow the gliders off course, into unpopulated areas, fields or woods, but for Christ's sake, *not* where there are people. So instruct Washington and London!'

'Yes, of course. Understood, monsieur. I have both on a combined line.'

The next few minutes were like waiting for mass slaughter, everyone present a part of that mass. All eyes were on the radar screen, when suddenly the skeletal images veered in different directions, violently to the left and the right, away from the target zone, the Beauvais reservoir.

'Check London,' said Drew, 'check Washington.'

'They're on the line now,' replied the major. 'They're experiencing precisely what we have experienced. The gliders have been blown away from the water reserves, and are being forced to land in isolated areas.'

'Everything was computerized down to minutes, wasn't it?' said Latham breathlessly, his face pale. 'Bless high technology, it microwaves a corned beef sandwich and melts the plastic container. Now, perhaps, we *have* won, but only a battle, not the war.'

'*You've* won, Drew.' Karin de Vries walked towards him, placing her arms on his shoulders. 'Harry would have been so proud.'

'We're not finished, Karin. Harry was killed from within, and so was Moreau. Each was betrayed. So was I, but I was lucky. Someone has a telescope that looks into the core of our operations. And that someone knows more about the Nazi movement and the legacy of a mad general in the Loire Valley than all of us put together . . . The strange thing is, I suddenly think I know who it is.'

CHAPTER FORTY-ONE

Beauvais. Zero hour plus twenty minutes. The general's son arranged for an army vehicle to drive Latham, Karin, and the two commandos down to Paris. And, as insignificant things keep occurring during cataclysmic events, their luggage had arrived from the Königshof Hotel in Bonn. It was in the back of a van that provided their transportation to the City of Lights, a city that until twenty-one minutes before would have been a city in panic.

'We'll stay at the same hotel,' said Drew as all bade good-bye to their French colleagues in the Beauvais water-works and started for the door and the ancient elevator. 'And you two,' he continued, addressing Captain Dietz and Lieutenant Anthony, 'you can tear Paris apart, all expenses paid.'

'With what?' asked the captain. 'I don't think we have two hundred francs between us, and our credit cards, along with any other means of identification, are up in Brussels.'

'In about four hours, a grateful government of France will supply you with hard cash, say fifty thousand francs apiece. How about it, think it's initially enough? More to come, of course.'

'You're nuts,' said Anthony.

'No, I'm not, I'm mad. Mad as hell.'

'*Monsieur, Monsieur Lat'am!*' exclaimed one of the numerous military aides, rushing out of the waterworks office into the dark stone hallway. 'You are wanted on the *téléphone*. It is urgent, monsieur!'

'Wait here,' said Drew. 'If it's who I think it is, the conversation will be courteous but over quickly.' Latham

698

returned with the aide and picked up a phone nearest the door. 'Cons-Op here.' The gruff voice on the line told him it was not the man he had expected.

'Well done, *chłopak*!' fairly shouted Colonel Witkowski from London. 'Harry would have been proud of you.'

'I've heard that twice too often, Stanley, but thank you. It was a team effort, same as in hockey.'

'You can't really buy that horseshit.'

'Oh, but I do, Stosh. And it started with Harry, when he said to that tribunal in London, "I brought out the data, it's your job to evaluate it." We didn't do it right.'

'I'll let that pass until we're not on a phone.'

'Good idea. The thread's there and we missed it.'

'Later,' interrupted Witkowski. 'What do you think about Bonn?'

'What do you mean? What about Bonn?'

'Haven't you been told?'

'Told what?'

'The whole damn Bundestag is in flames! There are over a hundred fire engines from all over the place trying to put it out. Didn't Moreau call you?'

'Moreau's dead, Stanley.'

'*What?*'

'Killed in his own impenetrable underground parking lot.'

'Jesus Christ, I didn't *know*!'

'How could you? You're in London, undercover, I presume.'

'When did it happen?'

'Hours ago.'

'Still, the Deuxième is *your* alternate control. You should have been told about Bonn.'

'I guess somebody forgot. It was a crazy night.'

'What *is* it, Drew? You're not yourself.'

'Who could be after tonight . . . You asked me what I thought about the Bundestag fire, so I'll tell you. That son of a bitch Jäger was writing his own memoirs. I've got to go,

Stosh, there's someone I have to see before the fires go out. Talk to you in Paris.'

The foursome had adjoining suites at the Hotel Plaza-Athénée, where the early sun broke through the drapes of the tall windows. It was 6:37 in the morning, Karin de Vries deep in sleep as Latham crawled silently out of the bed. He had hung up his civilian clothes before disrobing; he put them on and walked through the door into the huge communal sitting room where the two commandos were waiting, both in their innocuous jackets and trousers.

'One of you has to stay here, I told you that,' said Drew. 'Remember?'

'We flipped for it,' replied Dietz, 'and you're stuck with the Thin Man, although I think it's a bad option. I'm the superior officer, for God's sake.'

'And your job may be rougher than ours. The embassy marine unit is outside, but they can't enter the hotel without tipping off the neos, if there are any. *If* there are, you've got only your own firepower and a radio to get our men up to the second floor very damn fast.'

'You really think the neos have gone so deep?' asked the lieutenant.

'My brother was killed while under maximum security; Claude Moreau was executed within his own secret environs. What do you think?'

'I think we should get going,' said Anthony. 'Watch that lady, Captain. She's very special – in an academic way, of course.'

'Please don't break my heart,' said Drew as he and the lieutenant gathered up their weapons. 'The car's in back, we go through the cellar.'

'Monsieur *Lat'am*!' The guard at the underground parking area of the Deuxième Bureau recognized the name on the clearance log and was close to tears. 'Is it not a terrible *tragédie*? And right here, where it could never happen!'

'What do the police say?' asked Drew, studying the face of the man.

'They are as bewildered as we are! Our magnificent director, may he be at peace with the almighty, was shot inside the gates yesterday morning, his body found at the far end. Everyone in the building was questioned by the Sûreté, their whereabouts examined; it went on for hours, the new director like a furious tiger, monsieur!'

'Were your exit logs checked?'

'*Certainement!* All personnel who had left were taken into custody, I understand. They say there is nothing to enlighten anyone.'

'Are most of the people here now? I know it's early.'

'Almost everyone, monsieur. I'm told that there are conferences on every floor. See, behind you, three other automobiles await entrance. Everything is *tohu-bohu!*'

'What?'

'In chaos,' said Lieutenant Anthony softly. 'Pandemonium, sir.'

'Thank you, guard.' Latham pressed the accelerator of the rented car and sped through the open gate into the cavernous shadows of the underground parking area. 'Keep your hand on your weapon, Lieutenant,' he said as he swung the automobile into an open space.

'It's already on it, boss man.'

'You know, that's an irritating title.'

'I don't know why, you earned it . . . You think a stray neo or two could still be down here?'

'If I could call the hotel and talk to your buddy, I'd give you a better guess.'

'Why don't you? You've got the cellular.'

'Because I don't want to wake up Karin. She'd barrel-ass down here, and that's the last thing we need.'

'Then I guess I ought to tell you,' said Anthony.

'Tell me *what?*'

'A few hours ago, when we checked into that fancy hotel and you phoned Deuxième security to say where we were,

Dietz monitored every telephone there with a little device we carry that picks up intercepts. There weren't any, so he pulled the plug on your bedroom phone—'

'He *what*?'

'We both agreed you two needed sleep. I mean, look at the facts, we're younger than you guys, and we're obviously in better shape—'

'Will you two *Boy Scouts* stop trying to help us across the street!' exclaimed Drew, yanking the cellular phone out of his inner breast pocket and dialling. 'I'm still running this opera, remember?'

'If an important call came through, we would have woken you up. Is that so hard to take?'

'Suite two-ten and eleven,' said Latham to the hotel switchboard; it was instantly picked up.

'Yes?'

'Dietz, it's Latham. What's the status?'

'We think you were on the mark, Cons-Op,' replied the captain, his voice low. 'A couple of minutes ago the embassy gyrenes radioed me from the street. A heavy-metal vehicle pulled around the east corner and two gum-balls got out and walked around to the front, separately. They just entered—'

'Are they *neos*?'

'We don't know yet, but the desk is cooperating – *hold* it! The hotel override is lit up.' The seconds seemed like minutes to Drew until Dietz came back on the line. 'Unless all statistics lie, you *were* on the mark. They pressed the button for the second floor.'

'Get the marines in!'

'You think I won't?'

Suddenly a loud, echoing horn erupted behind Latham. 'I think you took someone's parking space,' said the lieutenant.

'Tell them to shove it!'

'Hey, why don't we just move?'

'Then you hold the phone. *Christ*, the neos just went into the hotel! The second floor!' Drew backed out of the space.

'There's no one on the line. The captain is a devious field guy; if they come to the door, they'll wish they hadn't.'

'Is the line dead?' asked Latham, swinging into another space.

'He hung up, if that's what you mean.'

'Get him back!'

'That's not a good idea, sir. He's got work to do.'

'*Shit!*' exploded Drew. 'Now I *know* I'm right.'

They were joined in the elevator by five other men and two women, all speaking near hysterical French. Latham kept staring at one face after another, the blur of pinched features, squinting and then bulging eyes, strained voices, and pronounced throat veins became a cartoonlike montage of screaming animals, each trying to outstretch the other. Without thinking, Drew reached over a shoulder and pressed the floor he vaguely remembered having pressed before on Moreau's instructions. Two stops were made prior to the button Latham had punched; he and the lieutenant were alone as they ascended to the top floor.

'What were they saying?' asked Drew. 'I caught some of it, not much.'

'They don't know what the hell is going on, but if you want to know the bottom line, they're all concerned about their jobs.'

'I suppose that's natural. When this kind of thing happens, nobody's above suspicion; and when that happens, the clean sweepers come out of the government woodwork.'

'You mean a lot of babies get thrown out with the bathwater?'

'That's exactly what I mean.' The elevator stopped, the door opened, and both men walked out into the anteroom, whose various doors led to the corridors and offices of the clandestine operations agency. Latham approached the middle-aged receptionist and spoke. '*Je m'appelle Drew—*'

'I know who you are, sir,' said the woman pleasantly in English. 'You were here to see *Monsieur le Directeur* several days ago. We are all still in shock, I'm afraid.'

'So am I. He was my friend.'

'I'll inform our new director that you're here. He came straight down from Beauvais—'

'I'd rather you didn't,' interrupted Latham.

'I beg your pardon?'

'Considering what's happened, he's got to be busy with so many problems, he doesn't need any interference from me. My coming here is inconsequential; I left some articles in the Deuxième car. Is the agent named François inside? I believe he drove the director down from Beauvais.'

'Yes, he is. Shall I ring his office?'

'Why bother? He'd probably call Jacques – forgive me, your new director – and I really don't want to interrupt him. Certainly not over a pair of shoes.'

'Shoes . . . ?'

'French, you see. The best, and quite expensive but worth every franc.'

'*Naturellement.*' The receptionist pressed a button on her desk; a buzzer from a door on the far right erupted and there was the click of a lock. 'His office is down that hallway, the third on the left.'

'Thank you. Excuse me, this is my associate, Major Anthony, United States Army, Special Forces.' The lieutenant snapped his head towards Drew in surprise as Latham continued. 'He'll remain here, if you don't mind. He speaks fluent French . . . and probably Urdu, for all I know.'

'*Bonjour, madame. Mon plaisir.*'

'*Je vous en prie, Major.*'

Drew opened the anteroom door and walked into the narrow grey corridor, moving rapidly to the third door on the left. He knocked once, opening the door quickly, startling François, who was asleep, his head on the desk. He shot up, lurching back into his chair. '*Qu'est-ce que se passe?*'

'Hello there, *Wheelman*,' said Latham, shutting the door. 'Catching a little nap? I envy you, I'm tired as hell.'

'Monsieur Lat'am, what are you *doing* here?'

'I have an idea you may know, François.'

'*Mon Dieu*, know what?'

'You were close to Claude Moreau, weren't you? He knew your wife, her name, Yvonne . . . your two daughters.'

'*Oui*, on a less-than-familiar basis, monsieur. We all know one another, our families as well, but from a distance.'

'And you're pretty tight with Jacques Bergeron too, Moreau's top gun.'

'Tight?'

'You and Jacques, Jacques and you, chief driver and chief aide, always together with your boss, the intrepid trio bound by years of working together. Regular "Mousquetaires". So ordinary, so usual, so easy to accept because you see them every day.'

'You talk in riddles, monsieur!'

'Hell, yes. Because it is a riddle, a riddle based in utter simplicity. Who would question the sight of the three of you or the grief of the two who escaped being killed? A couple of hours ago, when I called here to tell Jacques where we were staying, guess who I got?'

'I do not have to guess. You spoke to me, Monsieur Lat'am.'

'Everyone goes up a big notch, don't they?'

'I have no idea *what* you are talking about!' said François, leaning forward, his right hand slipping across the edge of the desk to a drawer. Suddenly he yanked it open, but Drew lunged over, slamming it shut with such force on the driver's wrist that he began to scream, the roar cut short by Latham's fist smashing into François's mouth. The Frenchman fell back, chair and body crashing to the floor. Drew was instantly over him, grabbing him by his throat and pulling him up, slamming him against the wall, the weapon in the drawer now in Drew's hand.

'We're going to talk, Wheelman, and your conversation had better be enlightening, or your life is over.'

'I have a family, monsieur, a wife and children! How can you *do* this?'

'Have you any idea how many families – fathers, mothers,

children, and grandchildren – were torn apart in the fucking camps, forced to walk naked into cement compounds only to emerge as corpses, you son of a *bitch*!'

'I was not even *alive* then!'

'You never heard of those things? Thousands were *French*, rounded up and sent to their deaths! That never *bothered* you?'

'You don't understand, monsieur. They have ways to make you cooperate.'

'Such as? And if you lie, I won't bother to use your gun, I'll simply snap the carotid arteries on both sides of your neck and it's *finis* time. You see, like the radar specialist in Beauvais when he looks at his screen, I can tell by the eyes. I hope I don't make a mistake . . . Jacques Bergeron is a neo, *isn't* he?'

'Yes . . . How could you possibly *know*?'

'When you're tired and you're lost, you go back over everything. It had to be someone who had access to all the information, someone who knew where the players were every moment. At first we thought it was Moreau; he was on a list that made us afraid to work with him; hell, *I* couldn't tell him a damn thing. Then he was cleared by the only man who *could* clear him, my boss. So who was it? Who knew where I was, whether it was a restaurant in Villejuif with my brother, or one hotel or another when I kept moving? Who knew that Karin and I were in a side-walk café one night with Claude, where we were all nearly killed except the owner got us out of there? Who faked the Metro incident with Dr Kroeger, the gunshots, the man who claimed he saw "Harry Latham" on the train that sped away? There *was* no Harry Latham, because *I* was Harry and I wasn't there! The answer to every one of those queries was a man called Jacques.'

'I don't know of these things, I swear by the sight of a bleeding Christ on a cross, I do not *know*!'

'But you know he's a neo, don't you? A deep – perhaps the deepest Nazi – in France. Am I *right*?'

'Yes.' François exhaled his breath until there was none left. 'I had no choice but to keep silent and do his bidding.'

'*Why?*'

'I killed a man and Jacques saw me do it.'

'How?'

'I strangled him. Try to understand, monsieur, I work long hours, sometimes I am away for days at a time, my family is neglected – what can I say?'

'A hell of a lot more,' said Drew.

'My wife found a lover. I could tell, as every husband can, when darkness envelops the bed. I used the resources of the Deuxième to find out who he was.'

'Not exactly official business, right?'

'Certainly not. But what I did not know was that Jacques was monitoring my every inquiry, my every telephone call ... I set up a meeting with this individual, a rotten hairdresser with a record of debts and failed salons, and we met in an alley in the Montparnasse. He made obscene references to my wife's behaviour, laughing as he did so. I went mad and attacked him, killed him viciously. As I walked out of the alley, Bergeron greeted me.'

'So he had you.'

'The rest of my life in prison was the alternative. He had taken photographs with an infrared night camera.'

'Yet you and your wife are back together, isn't that so?'

'We are French, monsieur. I am not a saint either. We have made peace with each other and our marriage is solid. We have our children.'

'But you worked with Bergeron, a *Nazi*. How can you *justify* that?'

The rest of my life in prison – how would *you* justify it? My wife, my children, my family. And, monsieur, I never killed for him, *never*! He had others to do that, I refused.'

Latham released the man from the wall and gestured for him to sit down. 'Okay, Wheelman, you and I are going to make a deal or we're not. Unless I'm really wrong, and I don't think I am, you and Jacques are the only neos here, and you are a reluctant one. Any more would be too dangerous. One master, one slave, a perfect combination. You can prove your reluctance by doing what I say; if you don't, you're dead meat and I'll blow you away myself. Got it?'

'What is it you want me to do? And should I accept, what guarantee do I have that those photographs will not send me to prison?'

'None actually, but the odds are on your side. I have an idea that Bergeron will be far more interested in saving his ass from a firing squad than in condemning you to one.'

'We have no such executions here in France, monsieur.'

'You're really an innocent, aren't you? These things aren't formal, François, they just happen.'

'What is it, then?' asked the driver, swallowing.

'Jacques is in another wing on this floor, if I remember correctly.'

'You do. This section is for subordinate personnel.'

'But you have access, don't you? I mean, you have the run of the place, am I right?'

'If you mean can I take you to his office, yes, I can.'

'Without announcing either of us?'

'Of course, I am permanently assigned to him. There is a rear hallway in this section that is entered by a pass code; it leads to the high executive offices. I have it, naturally.'

'Naturally. Let's go.'

'What am I to do, then?'

'Come back here, stay here, and hope for the best.'

'And you, Monsieur Lat'am?'

'I'm going to hope for the best too.'

Captain Christian Dietz put the handheld radio out of sight on a bookshelf and positioned himself at the left side of the hotel suite's central door. His acute hearing picked up the sound of muffled footsteps outside in the corridor, followed by silence. His weapon at the ready, he wondered if the would-be intruders had procured a master key somewhere, or whether they would chance an assault on the door.

The latter, apparently. The silence was shattered by a thunderous crash as the door was broken off its latch and smashed back into the commando. The two men rushed into the room, guns in their hands, their heads turning right and left, left and right, unsure of what to do next. Dietz solved their dilemma by shouting, 'Drop your weapons or you're *dead*!'

The first man turned violently and a silenced spit exploded from the barrel of his gun. The commando lurched forward on the floor and shot back, hitting the intruder in the stomach, causing him to double over and collapse. The second would-be killer, stunned, lowered his gun as three marines burst through the open door.

Suddenly Karin de Vries ran out of the bedroom in her nightgown.

'Get *back* there!' roared Dietz.

As Karin lunged towards the bedroom door, the second intruder raised his weapon and fired. Blood spurted out from the edge of her left shoulder as the marines levelled their weapons.

'*Hold* it!' roared Dietz. 'He's no good to us dead!'

'Neither are *we*, buddy!' cried a marine sergeant, his Colt .45 aimed at the neo's head. '*Drop* it, you worm, or it's all over!'

The neo let the gun fall to the floor as Dietz got to his feet and reached across the room to the prone, bleeding Karin de Vries, kicking the Nazi's weapon away as he passed over it. 'Don't move,' he ordered, tearing the night-gown strap off the shoulder and cradling Karin. 'It's not bad,' he concluded, studying the wound. 'The bullet creased the flesh, but that's all. Stay put and I'll get some towels.'

'I'll find them,' said the nearest marine. 'Where?'

'Through that door to the bathroom. Pick up three clean small ones and tie them together.'

'A tourniquet?'

'Not exactly, but close. We want to keep the skin flat. Then get some ice from the bar.'

'On my way.'

'Don't tell me you're a doctor too,' said Karin, holding up the corner of her nightgown and smiling weakly.

'This isn't brain surgery, Mrs de Vries, just a flesh wound. You were lucky; a second or two sooner and you'd have had a problem. Does it hurt?'

'More numb than painful, Captain.'

'We'll get you to the embassy doctor.'

'Where is *Drew*? That comes first. And Gerry, where is *he*?'

'Please don't put me through this, Mrs D.V. Mr Latham gave us orders and he's running the show. He and Anthony went to the Deuxième Bureau – I lost the toss with Gerry.'

'The Deuxième? *Why?*'

'Cons-Op told us he thought he'd figured out who the rat in the attic was.'

'The rat in the attic?'

'The Nazi mole who was wired into all of us.'

'At the *Deuxième*?'

'That's what he said.'

'He mentioned something in Beauvais, but when I questioned him in the van, he shrugged it off, telling me it was only a guess. But *you* knew?'

'I don't think he wanted you to be involved.'

'Here are the towels, sir!' said the marine, running from a bedroom door, then turning quickly to help his colleagues with the two neos, one dead or unconscious, the other hostile, necessitating several blows to his chest. 'We'll be in touch, Captain – you are the captain, aren't you, sir?'

'Rank doesn't count for much here, Corporal. See you later.'

'We've got to get the hell out of here, you understand that. Sorry about the ice—'

'Then *get* out!' ordered Dietz as the marine unit fled down the hall to the fire stairs with the two prisoners. The telephone rang. 'I'm lowering you to the floor,' said the commando as he secured towels around Karin's shoulder and gently placed her on the carpet. 'I've got to answer the phone.'

'If it's Drew, tell him I'm furious!'

It was not Latham; it was the hotel's front desk. 'You must *leave!*' shouted the concierge in French. 'We will cooperate with the Deuxième only so far! The switchboard is crowded with calls about loud crashes or gunshots!'

'*La passion du coeur!*' replied Dietz firmly. 'Seal off the room and we'll cover you. Give me five minutes and call the police, but I *need* five minutes.'

'We'll do our best.'

'Come on,' said the captain, hanging up the telephone and returning to Karin. 'I'll carry you out of here—'

'I can walk, actually,' interrupted De Vries.

'Glad to hear it. We'll go down the stairs, it's only one flight.'

'What about our clothes, our luggage? Surely you don't want them here for the police to find.'

'*Shit!* ... Excuse me, ma'am, but you've got a hell of a point.' The captain raced back to the phone, immediately dialling the concierge. 'If you want us out of here, send the quickest bellman up to pack the suitcases and bring them to the departure area. Also, tell him if he doesn't steal too much, he's got five hundred francs!'

'*Naturellement.*'

'*D'accord.*'

'Let's go!' said the commando, slamming down the phone and running back to Karin, suddenly stopping and grabbing a man's raincoat off a chair. 'Here, put this on, I'll help you. Get up slowly, your arm around my shoulder ... That's good, can you walk?'

'Yes, of course. It's just the arm that hurts.'

'It will until we get you to the doctor. He'll take care of that. Steady, now.'

'But what about Drew and Gerry? What's *happening?*'

'I don't know, Mrs D.V., but I'll tell you this much. That Cons-Op friend of yours, whom I didn't think too much of, frankly, is first rate. He looks beyond the fogs, you know what I mean?'

'Not really, Captain,' said Karin, being held by the commando as they walked down the hallway towards the stairs. 'What are the fogs?'

'The smoke that covers the truth. He shoots through it because he has that gut instinct that tells him it's there.'

'He's very thorough, isn't he?'

'It's more than thorough, Mrs D.V., it's a talent. I'd go undercover for him anytime. He's my kind of control.'

'Mine too, Captain, although I'd prefer another title.'

Drew approached the unmarked door of the Deuxième Bureau's newly appointed director. Without knocking he opened it swiftly, stepped inside, and closed it firmly. Jacques Bergeron was standing by a window, looking outside; he spun around, astonished at the sight of Latham.

'*Drew!*' he cried in a stunned voice. 'No one told me you were here!'

'I didn't want you to know.'

'But why?'

'Because you might have found some reason not to see me, like when I called you a couple of hours ago to tell you where we were. I was put through to François.'

'For God's *sake*, man, I've got a thousand problems to attend to! Also, I've made François my temporary chief aide; he'll be moving into the executive offices tomorrow.'

'That'll be cosy.'

'I beg your pardon . . . *Écoutez*, I apologize if I offended you, but I really think you should try to understand. I've been forced to put my calls on hold, except for the President and a few members of the Chamber, for I simply cannot respond to everyone. There are so many questions I cannot answer until I put our investigative teams to work. I must have time to think!'

'That's very good, Jacques, but I have an idea you've been thinking a lot, for a long, long time. For years, in fact. Incidentally, François confirmed it for me. You probably set up that hairdresser-Romeo with his wife – just one more expendable human being.'

The soft, vulnerable face of the Deuxième chief suddenly became mottled granite, the pleasant eyes two glass orbs of loathing. 'What have you done?' he asked quietly, so quietly he could barely be heard.

'I won't bore you with the circuitous routes that led me to you, other than to say it was kind of brilliant. The Sancho Panza to Moreau's Don Quixote, the adoring lackey who worshipped his master, who wormed his way into his master's trust and affection, helping him with his daily schedule – every day and every evening. No one but you could have known where I was at given times, where my brother was, where Karin and Moreau's poor secretary were, and you rolled fifty-fifty with the dice. You killed Harry and Moreau's secretary, but you blew it with Karin and me.'

'You're a dead man, Drew,' said the director of the Deuxième almost pleasantly. 'You're in my territory and you're dead.'

'I wouldn't jump to conclusions if I were you. Lieutenant Anthony – you know the lieutenant – is outside with your receptionist. By now I'm sure he's used her telephone to reach Ambassador Courtland, who has requested an emergency conference with the President of France and his Cabinet. Sort of a power breakfast, I imagine you'd call it.'

'On what *basis*?'

'Because after I saw François, I didn't come out and tell Anthony not to. We agreed on eight minutes; it was a safe number. You know, you really blew it when you sent those goons to the hotel, "gumballs", the marine unit called them. No one else in Paris knew where we were except you, and, by extension, François.'

'A marine unit . . . ?'

'I don't believe in a hero's death, Jacques. When you think about it, it's stupid if you don't have to go through with it.'

'You have only your word, and against mine it is *nothing*! The President himself appointed me!'

'You're a Sonnenkind, you bastard.'

'Outrageous! What evidence could you possibly have for such a preposterous *lie*?'

'It's circumstantial, granted, but put together with other things, it's pretty convincing. You see, when I began to zero in on you, I gave you the benefit of the doubt. Last night, in that military van from Beauvais, I got in touch with a whiz kid named Joel in our supercomputer complex and asked him to run an eye-dent on you. Fifty-one years ago you were legally adopted by a childless couple, a Monsieur and Madame Bergeron in Lauterbourg, near the German border. You were a terrific student, scholarships yours for the asking, right through the University of Paris and its graduate school. You could have gone into a dozen professions that would have made you a very rich man, but you didn't. You chose civil service, the intelligence branch. Not exactly a winner in the financial sweepstakes.'

'It was my interest, my *profound* interest!'

'You bet it was. With time and the years you were in the right place at the *right* time. You couldn't do anything about it because you'd left before we figured out the gliders, but how did you take it when Water Lightning fizzled? *Ein Volk, ein Reich, ein* pissant.'

'You are *insane*! Everything you say is a *lie*!'

'No, it isn't. It was in your own words, your humble confession in Beauvais. One way or another you knew you had to get out; sooner or later the rope would be circling around your neck. You really didn't expect to be named director of the Deuxième; it was the only honest thing you said because you knew there were better men in other intelligence agencies. So you declared to all of us, "I am not a leader, I am a follower who obeys orders." . . . You were repeating, ad nauseam, the terrible words we've heard too

714

often, the Nazi credo. That's what made me pull in our supercomputer expert, just on a chance.'

'I repeat,' said Jacques Bergeron icily, 'I was a war orphan, my parents were French, killed in a bombing raid, and my academic records are there for all to see. You are nothing more than a paranoid American troublemaker, and I'll see you expelled from France.'

'Can't happen, Jacques. You killed my brother, or, should I say, you had him killed. I won't let you go. I'm going to jam your severed head on the highest pike of the Pont Neuf, just the way the fans of the guillotine liked it. For all your scholastic achievements, you overlooked something. Lauterbourg was never bombed, either by the Allies or the Germans. You were smuggled across the Rhine to start a new life – as a Sonnenkind.'

Bergeron stood immobile, studying Latham, a thin, cold smile creasing his soft face. 'You're really quite talented, Drew,' he said quietly. 'But, of course, you will not get out of here alive, so your talent has been wasted, *n'est-ce pas*? A paranoid American, a man with a record of violence, comes in to assassinate the director of the Deuxième – who is the Sonnenkind? After all, my predecessor, Moreau, never trusted you. He told me you lied to him consistently; it's in his notes which I alone dutifully transcribed into his computer.'

'*You* transcribed?'

'They're there, that's all that matters. I am the only one who has the access key to his classified material. Whatever is there is his alone.'

'Why did you kill him! *Why* did you have Claude killed?'

'Because, like you, he had begun to peel away the layers and was centring in on the truth. It started with the killing of Monique, his secretary, and that ludicrous night at the café when a zealous idiot shot the driver of the American vehicle. It was a gargantuan error, unforgivable, for Moreau came to realize that I was the only other one who knew where you were . . . Monique could have – and *would* have – given false information.'

'Funny,' said Latham, 'that's when it began for me too. That and the fact that when my brother flew in from London, he was supposedly under the Deuxième's surveillance.'

'Easily rearranged, as it was,' said Bergeron, his pencil-thin smile broader.

'Question,' interrupted Drew angrily. 'When Moreau – and *you* – learned that I was impersonating Harry, why didn't you alert Berlin or Bonn?'

'Now you're foolish,' replied Bergeron. 'The circle was extraordinarily tight, especially here at the Deuxième. Only Claude and I knew, and there was no way to tell how restricted it was elsewhere. A leak traced to the Deuxième would compromise me.'

'That's pretty weak, Jacques,' said Drew, staring at the Sonnenkind.

'Again your talent shines through, monsieur. Better that others make mistakes, and one crashes through the mists of errors with the reality, proclaiming himself the true Valkyrie . . . Quite simply, I was waiting for the proper time. Your American politicians know all about that.'

'Very good, Jacky-baby. And suppose I told you that everything said in here has been recorded, the frequency tuned to Lieutenant Anthony's machine in the lobby. High tech is wonderful, isn't it?'

CHAPTER FORTY-TWO

Jacques Bergeron, Sonnenkind, screamed hysterically while lurching to his desk and picking up a heavy paperweight; he threw it into his window, shattering the glass. Then, with strength that belied his medium-size compact physique, he raised his chair and hurled it at Latham, who pulled François's gun out of his belt.

'Don't *do* it!' shouted Drew. 'I don't want to *kill* you! We need your records! For *Christ's* sake, *listen* to me!'

It was too late. Jacques Bergeron whipped out a small weapon from his chest holster and fired indiscriminately, everywhere, anywhere. Latham dived to the floor as Bergeron ran to the door, yanked it open, and raced outside.

'*Stop* him!' roared Drew, lunging towards the hallway. 'No, *wait! Don't* stop him! He's got a *gun!* Get out of his way!'

The corridor was in chaos. Two more gunshots exploded as the crowds streamed out of cubicles. A man and a woman fell wounded or killed. Latham got to his feet and ran after the Nazi, crisscrossing the intersecting hallways, shouting, '*Gerry*, he'll have to get out through there! Shoot him in the legs, keep him *alive!*'

That order was also too late. Bergeron crashed through the reception room's door as an ear-shattering bell echoed off the walls and Lieutenant Anthony emerged from the second elevator. The Nazi fired; it was the last shell in his magazine as the following clicks announced, but the bullet pierced the commando's right arm. Anthony grabbed his elbow, released it, and awkwardly, in pain, fumbled for his weapon while the woman behind the desk hysterically dropped to the floor.

'You're not going *anywhere*,' yelled the lieutenant, trying to reach his gun with his right hand, his arm in agony, 'because neither are those elevators! I alarmed both of them.'

'You are quite wrong!' screamed the neo, racing into the nearest elevator; in barely seconds the panels began to close and the deafening bell was abruptly silent. 'It is *you* who are not going anywhere, monsieur!' were the Nazi's last words.

Drew burst through the anteroom's door. 'Where *is* he?' asked Latham furiously.

'In that elevator,' replied the commando, wincing. 'I thought I shorted both of them out, but I guess I didn't.'

'Christ, you've been hit!'

'I can handle it, check the lady.'

'Are you all *right*?' said Drew, rushing to the receptionist, who was slowly getting to her feet.

'I'll be better when I deliver my resignation, monsieur,' she answered, trembling and breathless as Latham helped her up.

'Can we stop the elevator?'

'*Non. Les directeurs* – forgive me, the directors and their deputies have emergency codes that put the lifts into express cycles. No stops until they reach their floors.'

'Can we prevent him from leaving the building?'

'On what authority, sir? He is the director of the Deuxième Bureau.'

'*Il est un Nazi d'Allemagne!*' cried the lieutenant.

The receptionist stared at Anthony. 'I will try, Major.' The woman reached for the telephone on her desk and pressed three numbers. 'There is an emergency, have you seen the director?' she asked in French. '*Merci.*' She depressed the lever, dialled again, and spoke, repeating the same question. '*Merci.*' The receptionist hung up and looked at Drew and the commando. 'I first called the parking area where Monsieur Bergeron keeps his sports car. He did not go through the gate. I then reached our first-floor counter. The guard said the new director just left in a great hurry. I'm sorry.'

'Thank you for trying,' said Gerald Anthony, holding his bleeding right arm.

'If I may,' asked Latham, 'why *did* you try? We're Americans, not French.'

'Director Moreau held you in extremely high regard, monsieur. He said as much to me when you came to see him.'

'That was enough?'

'No . . . Jacques Bergeron was all smiles and courtesy when in the company of Monsieur Moreau, but by himself he was an arrogant pig. I prefer to believe your explanation, and, after all, he shot your very charming Major.'

They were back in Ambassador Courtland's private quarters at the embassy, Drew, Karin with her wounded shoulder strapped, and Stanley Witkowski, who had flown in from London. The two commandos, the lieutenant's arm attended to and in a sling, were at the hotel, alternately resting and placing generous orders for room service.

'He's disappeared,' said Daniel Courtland, sitting in a chair near the colonel and opposite Drew and Karin on the couch. 'Every police and intelligence agency in France is looking for Jacques Bergeron and nothing's turned up. Every public and private airport and customs checkpoint in Europe has his photograph with a dozen computerized composites of what he may be disguised as – *nothing*. He's no doubt safely back in Germany among his own, wherever they are.'

'We have to find out where that is, Mr Ambassador,' said Latham. 'This Water Lightning failed, but what's next, and will *it* fail? Their long-range plans may be on hold, but the Nazi movement isn't stopped. Somewhere there are records and we have to *find* them. Those bastards are all over our world, and they're not calling off their act. Just yesterday a synagogue in Los Angeles and a black church in Mississippi were burned to the ground. Several senators and congressmen who rose to denounce those incidents were accused of covering up their own sympathies. It's all a goddamn mess!'

'I know, Drew, we all know. Here in Paris, in the predominantly Jewish arrondissements, shopkeepers' windows were smashed, the word *Kristallnacht* spray-painted on the walls. It's becoming a very ugly world. Very ugly.'

'When I left London this morning,' said Witkowski quietly, 'the papers were filled with the slaughter of several West Indian children, their faces hacked off with bayonets – their *faces*. The German "*Neger*" was written in coloured crayons around the corpses.'

'In God's name, when will it *stop!*' exclaimed Karin.

'When we find out who they are and where they are,' replied Drew.

The telephone rang on the ambassador's antique table that he used as a desk. 'Shall I answer it, sir?' asked the colonel.

'No, thanks, I'll get it,' said Courtland, getting out of the chair and crossing to the table. 'Yes? ... It's for you, Latham, someone called François.'

'He's the last person I ever expected to hear from again,' said Drew, rising and walking quickly to the table. He took the phone from the ambassador. 'François ... ?'

'Monsieur Lat'am, we must meet somewhere privately.'

'There's nothing more private than this telephone, believe me. You just spoke to the American ambassador, and his phone is as sterile as any can be.'

'I believe you, for you have kept your word. I am interrogated, but only for everything I know, not for what I was.'

'You were in a lousy, untenable position, and as long as you cooperate to the fullest, you can go home to your family.'

'My gratitude is beyond words, monsieur, as is my wife's. We have discussed everything – I withheld nothing from her

720

– and together we decided I must make this call, for what it may be worth to you.'

'What is it?'

'I must take you back to the night old Jodelle killed himself in the theatre where the actor Jean-Pierre Villier was performing. Do you recall?'

'I'll never forget it,' said Drew firmly. 'What about that night?'

'It was early morning, actually, when *Sous-directeur* Bergeron ordered me to come immediately to his office at the Deuxième. I did so, but he was not there. However, I knew he was in the building, for the guards at the gate made sarcastic comments about his rudeness to them, and how he interrupted my sleep, no doubt to assist him to the toilet. I was afraid to leave. I waited until he showed up; he did so carrying a very old file from the cellar archives, so old it had not been entered into the computers. The folder itself was yellow with age.'

'Isn't that unusual?' asked Latham.

'There are thousands upon thousands of files in the archives, monsieur. Much work has been done in transposing them, but it will take years before the job is complete.'

'Why is that?'

'Experts, among them historians, are called in to validate their inclusion, and as with governments everywhere, funds are limited.'

'Go on. What happened?'

'Jacques instructed me to take the file and deliver it personally to a château in the Loire Valley, using a Deuxième vehicle with papers he signed himself that overrode any police interference in the event I was stopped for speeding, which he ordered me to do. I casually asked him why it was so necessary at this hour, could it not wait until morning? He became furious and shouted at me, yelling that we – he and I – owed everything to this place, this man. That it was our sanctuary, our refuge.'

'What place? What man?'

'*Le Nid de l'Aigle* is the château. General André Monluc, the man.'

'The something "eagle" . . . ?'

'The Eagle's Nest, monsieur. Monluc, I'm told, was a great general of France, honoured by De Gaulle himself.'

'So you think Bergeron may have escaped there?' said Drew.

'*Sanctuary* and *refuge* are the words that come back to me. Also, Jacques is an intelligence expert; he knows the multiple barriers he must surmount to leave the country. He will need help from resourceful associates, and the *combinaison* of a great general and a château in the Loire would appear to fit his situation. I hope this will be of some assistance to you.'

'It will, and I hope we won't have to see or speak to each other again. Thank you, François.' Latham hung up the phone and turned to the others. 'We've got the name of the general Jodelle was hunting, the traitor who he said fooled De Gaulle. Also where he lives, if he's alive.'

'That was a pretty strange one-sided conversation, *chłopak*. Why don't you fill us in?'

'Back off, Stanley, I made a deal. That man's been living in his own personal hell far longer than he deserved, and he never killed anyone for the Nazis. He was a water boy and a messenger with a gun to his family's collective head. Bottom line: I made a deal.'

'I've made more than I can count,' said the ambassador. 'Tell us what we have to know, Drew.'

'The general's name is Monluc, André Monluc—'

'*André*,' interrupted Karin. 'That's where the code name came from.'

'Right. The château's called the Eagle's Nest, in the Loire Valley. François thinks Bergeron may have fled there because he once called it a sanctuary in a moment of anger and perhaps fear.'

'*When?*' Witkowski broke in. 'When did he call it that?'

'Very astute, Stanley,' replied Drew. 'When Bergeron

ordered an old, buried file on Monluc to be delivered there – the night Jodelle killed himself in the theatre.'

'Thus removing any possible connection between Jodelle and the general,' said the ambassador. 'Does anyone know anything about this Monluc?'

'Not by name,' answered Latham, 'because the classified files that contained it were also removed from Washington. But the preliminary documentation on Jodelle detailed his accusation, an accusation that lacked any evidence, to say nothing of proof. It's why DC intelligence considered him a madman. He claimed that a French general, a leader of the Résistance, was in reality a traitor who worked for the Nazis. It was Monluc, of course, the man who ordered Jodelle's wife and children executed, and had Jodelle sent to a death camp.'

'The younger child who survived being Jean-Pierre Villier,' added Karin.

'Exactly. According to Villier's father – the only father he ever knew – Jodelle's suspicions obviously reached the unknown general, who protected his cover while becoming rich with Nazi gifts of gold and expropriated valuables.'

'I think I should have that mythical meeting with the French President,' said Courtland. 'Write a complete report on everything, Drew. Dictate it to a secretary or two, whatever you need, just do it quickly, say in an hour or so, and have it on my desk downstairs.'

Latham and Witkowski exchanged glances. The colonel nodded at Drew. 'That won't work, sir,' said Latham.

'What?'

'To begin with, there isn't time, and then we don't know who the President will confer with, but we do know there are neos in the Quai d'Orsay, possibly in the President's inner circle. We don't even know whom we can call for help, or who *he* might call.'

'Are you suggesting that we take action *ourselves*, American Embassy personnel in a foreign country? If so, you've lost your senses, Drew.'

'Mr Ambassador, if there's anything to learn in that château, any records, papers, telephone numbers, names, we can't take the chance of their being destroyed. Forget Bergeron for the moment, if that place is a sanctuary or a refuge, there's got to be more than beer and sausages and Horst Wessel songs. We're not talking just about France here, we're talking about all of Europe and the United States.'

'I understand that, but we *can't* take unilateral *American* action in a host country!'

'If Claude Moreau were alive, the situation would be different,' interrupted Witkowski. 'He could and would accept the mantle of a French covert operation in the interests of France. Our FBI accepts that kind of thing all the time!'

'Moreau's *not* alive, Colonel.'

'I realize that, sir, but there may be a way.' Witkowski turned to Latham. 'This François you just spoke to, he owes you, doesn't he?'

'Get off it, Stosh, I won't involve him.'

'I don't know why not. You just made a pretty good case for serious diplomatic interference, serious enough to have an ambassador replaced.'

'What's your point?' said Drew, staring at the colonel.

'The Deuxième works with the Service d'Etranger – that's the French foreign service, Mr Ambassador – and their lines of authority frequently cross, not unlike our CIA and FBI and DIA. That's understandable, isn't it?'

'Go ahead, Colonel.'

'Both the blessing and the curse of all intelligence bureaucracies is the confusion that results from these conflicts—'

'What the hell is your *point*, Stanley?'

'Simple, *chłopak*. Have this François call someone he knows pretty well at the Etranger and repeat, say, half the story he told you.'

'Which half?'

'That he suddenly remembered that Bergeron, who everybody's looking for, sent him with some old file to that château in the Loire. That's all he has to say.'

'Why wouldn't he give the information to his own people at the Deuxième?'

'Because no one's in charge. Moreau was killed yesterday, Bergeron disappeared a few hours ago, and he doesn't know whom to trust.'

'Then what?'

'I'll take care of the rest,' replied Witkowski softly.

'I beg your pardon?' said Courtland.

'Well, sir, there are always things a man in your position can legitimately deny because he didn't know about them.'

'Tell me about it,' interrupted the ambassador. 'It seems I spend considerable time learning about those things I'm not supposed to know about. What can you tell me now that will still support my deniability?'

'Very innocuous, sir. I have friends, let's say professional colleagues, at the higher levels of the Etranger. There could have been times when American criminals, say members of organized crime or drug barons, were in France, and we've kept better track of them than they have ... I've been generous with our information.'

'That's about as oblique as you can get, Colonel.'

'Thank you, Mr Ambassador.'

'To repeat,' said an agitated Latham, 'what's your *point*?'

'As long as the information comes from a French intelligence source, I can move in. The Frenchies will jump at it, and we'll have whatever support personnel we might need in an emergency. Above all, we'll have the secrecy that's vital because we have to move quickly.'

'How can you be sure of these things, Colonel?'

'Because, sir, we in the clandestine services love to propagate the myth of our invincibility. We especially like it if we come up with astonishing results when nobody knew we were there. It's idiosyncratic, Mr Ambassador, and in this case, that works in our favour. You see, we're on top of the information, we orchestrate, and the French take all the credit. It's heaven-sent.'

'I'm not sure I understood a word you've said.'

'You're not supposed to, sir,' said the veteran G-2 officer.

'What about me?' asked De Vries. 'I'll be with you, of course.'

'Yes, you will, my dear.' Witkowski smiled gently, glancing at Drew. 'We'll study the area charts – the Etranger has every square foot of France mapped – and find some high ground within sight of the château. You'll be on the radio.'

'That's nonsense. I deserve to be *with* you.'

'Don't be unfair, Karin,' said Latham. 'You've been hurt and no amount of painkillers can bring you up to a hundred per cent. In plain words, on the scene you'd be more of a concern than an asset. Certainly to me.'

'Do you know,' said De Vries quietly, her eyes level with Drew's, 'I can understand that and accept it.'

'Thanks. Besides, our lieutenant will be of very little use and will stay way back in the boondocks. He's worse off than you; the only way he can fire a gun is if it's cemented to his hand.'

'He can be on the radio with Karin, a backup relay,' added the colonel. 'Coordinators, so we don't have to be in constant communication, just open earplugs.'

'That sounds terribly patronizing, Stanley.'

'Maybe it is, Karin, but you never know.'

The career senior deputy of the Service d'Etranger was an ambitious forty-one-year-old analyst whose good fortune was to know François the Wheelman. He had been a suitor of François's wife, Yvonne, before her marriage, and although he had travelled faster and further up the government ladder than François, they remained friends and François knew why. The opportunistic analyst never stopped probing about the secretive Deuxième.

'I know just the man to call,' François had said in answer

726

to Latham's request. 'It's the least I can do for you, and, I imagine, for him, after all those expensive lunches and dinners where he learned nothing. He's paid very well, you know; he graduated from university and is quite intelligent. I think he'll be most enthusiastic.'

They all knew that analysts were not field men, nor did they pretend to be. Even so, given a specific operation and hypothetical circumstances, they could usually provide precedents and strategies that were frequently very valuable. *Directeur Adjoint* Cloche, for that was his name and it fitted, met with the N-2 unit at the Plaza-Athénée.

'*Ah*, Stanley!' he exclaimed, walking into the suite with a briefcase. 'When you telephoned soon after François's rather hysterical call, I was so relieved. It is all so tragic, so *catastrophique*, but with your sense of control, well, I *was* relieved.'

'Thanks, Clément, it's good to see you. Let me introduce you.' Introductions were made, and they all sat around the circular dining room table. 'Were you able to bring what I asked you for?' continued the colonel.

'Everything, but I must tell you, I did so on the basis of *fichiers confidentiels*.'

'What's that?' asked Drew, his tone of voice bordering on the discourteous.

'The copies were made for Monsieur Cloche in terms of confidential extrusion,' explained Karin.

'What's *that*?'

'I believe your American agents call it "solo",' clarified the senior deputy of the Etranger. 'I gave no reason for removing them – in concert with what my friend Stanley told me. *Mon Dieu*, neo-*Nazis* in the most secret areas of the government! The Deuxième *itself*. Incredible! ... I took considerable risk, but if we can find this traitor, Bergeron, my superiors can only applaud me.'

'And if we don't?' asked Lieutenant Anthony, his sling across the table like a webbed claw.

'Well, I acted on behalf of a distraught subordinate of the leaderless Deuxième and our dearest allies, the Americans.'

'Have you ever been in deep-cover incursion, sir?' asked Captain Dietz.

'*Non, Capitaine*, I am an analyst. I direct, I do not engage in such activities.'

'Then you're not going with us?'

'*Jamais.*'

'*C'est bon*, sir.'

'*All* right,' Witkowski interrupted, flashing a disagreeable glance at Dietz, 'let's get down to business. Have you got the maps, Clément?'

'More than simple maps. Elevations that you asked for, faxed from the zoning and assessment bureaus of the Loire.' Cloche opened his briefcase, lifted out several folded pages, and spread them across the table. 'This is *Le Nid de l'Aigle*, the château known as Eagle's Nest. It comprises three hundred and seventy acres, certainly not the largest but hardly the smallest of the inherited estates. It was originally granted by royal decree to a minor duke in the sixteenth century, to the family—'

'We don't need the history, sir,' interrupted Latham. 'What is it *now*? Forgive me, but we're in a hell of a hurry.'

'Very well, although the history is relevant in terms of its fortifications, natural and otherwise.'

'What fortifications?' said Karin, standing up, her eyes on the map.

'Here, here, here, and here,' said Cloche, also standing, as everyone else suddenly did, and pointing to sections on the unfolded map. 'They're deep-trenched, soft-bedded canals surrounding three-fifths of the château and fed by the river. They are filled with reeds and wild grass, as if crossing the waters were simple, but those ancient nobles who constantly were at war with each other knew the instruments of defence when under attack. Any army of bowmen and cannoneers who rushed into those seemingly shallow streams sank into the mud and drowned, taking their artillery with them.'

'That's pretty damned strategic,' said Witkowski.

'Kind of awesome for so many centuries ago,' agreed Captain Dietz.

'How many times have I told you to look at the past?' said Lieutenant Anthony, nudging the captain with his right arm and then wincing in pain. 'They worked with what they had, and history repeats itself.'

'I believe that's an oversimplification, Gerry,' objected Karin, her eyes still on the map. 'Those canal streams would have dried up years and years ago by attrition and sediment because they were *not* natural. They were dug out and constantly re-dredged. But you were right. Lieutenant, whoever owns this château studied its history and channelled them again, dredging out the old sources to the Loire River . . . Am I right, Monsieur Cloche?'

'It is what I determined, madame, but no one gave me a chance to explain.'

'You have it now,' said Latham, 'and I apologize. We'll take anything you can give us.'

'Very well, *merci*. There are basically two avenues of entry, the front gates, of course, and the northeast side. Unfortunately, at ground level, a twelve-foot-high stone wall surrounds the entire château with only one break in addition to the gates. It is at the rear, a strolling path leading to a large open patio that overlooks parts of the valley. It is the wall that will give you the most difficulty. Incidentally, it was built forty-nine years ago, shortly after the liberation of France.'

'It's probably tripped at the top with angled barbed wire, possibly electrified,' mused Captain Dietz.

'Undoubtedly, *Capitaine*. The assumption must be that the entire compound, grounds and all, are heavily guarded.'

'Even the old canals?' interrupted the lieutenant.

'Less so perhaps, but if we learned about them, others could also.'

'What about the strolling path?' asked Drew. 'How can it be reached?'

'According to the elevations,' replied Cloche, pointing to a green-and-grey-striped area of the map, 'there is a promontory, the edge of a steep hill, to be exact, that looks down on the path roughly three hundred metres below. Crawling down it is one way, but even if there are no alarm wires, which there probably are, there is still the wall.'

'How high is that promontory?' pressed Latham.

'I just told you, three hundred metres above the path.'

'What I mean is, could someone see *over* the wall from that vantage point?'

The Etranger deputy leaned forward and studied the geometrics on the map. 'I would say yes, but that judgement is based on the accuracy of what I am reading. If one draws a line from the height of the hill to the elevation of the wall, a downward *straight* line, it would appear to be so.'

'I can read you like a book, boss man,' said Lieutenant Gerald Anthony. 'That's my perch.'

'Right on, Thin Man,' agreed Drew. 'Observation Post Number One, or whatever you military types call it.'

'I think it should be *mine*,' said Karin with conviction. 'If there's trouble, I can fire a weapon, Gerry can barely hold one.'

'Come on, Mrs D.V., you got shot too!'

'My right shoulder, and I'm left-handed.'

'We'll discuss that among ourselves,' admonished Witkowski, turning to Latham. 'It's my turn to ask what *your* point is.'

'I'm surprised I have to explain it, Colonel Great Spy. We're back in the water again, only this time, instead of a big river, we're in the narrow channel of an old canal, reeds and tall wild grass are our cover. We hit the bank below the strolling path, and our experienced scout on the high ground lets us know when we can scale the wall because no guards are patrolling beyond it.'

'Scale it with *what*?'

'Grappling hooks,' answered Captain Dietz. 'What else? The solid, thick lucite types with hard rubber tips. They're quiet, stronger than steel, and the ropes can be short, only six to eight feet.'

'Suppose the hooks hit barbed wire?' said Witkowski, glowering. 'That wall's a bitch.'

'It's not the cliffs at Omaha Beach, Stanley, it's only twelve feet high. Stretching our arms over our heads, our hands are within four feet of the top. Given ten or twelve seconds, Dietz and I can be over and on the ground, taking time to negotiate any wire.'

'You and *Dietz*?'

'We'll discuss that later, Colonel.' Latham hurriedly turned to Cloche. 'What's beyond the wall?' he asked quickly.

'Look for yourself,' said the Etranger deputy, again gesturing at the map and leaning forward, his index finger poking at specific areas. 'As you can see, in every direction the wall is roughly eighty metres from the château's foundation, allowing for a pool, several patios, and a tennis court, all surrounded by lawns and gardens. Very civilized as well as secure, with what must be a lovely scenic view of the rising hills beyond the wall.'

'What's in the area behind the strolling path gate?'

'According to these schematics, there is the pool with a row of cabanas on both sides, beyond which are three entrances to the main structure, here, here, and here.'

'Right, centre, and left,' said Lieutenant Anthony. 'Where do the doors lead to?'

'The right leads to what appears to be an enormous kitchen, the far left to the closed-in north veranda, and the central door opens into a very large common room.'

'Like a big living room?'

'A very large one, Lieutenant,' agreed Cloche.

'Are these schematics, as you call them, up-to-date?' asked Drew.

'Within two years. You must remember, monsieur, that under a Socialist regime, the rich and especially the very rich

731

are under constant scrutiny by the Bureau of Taxation, which bases its levies on zoning and assessment.'

'Bless 'em,' said Latham.

'The cabanas?' mused Dietz.

'They'd be the first to be searched, with weapons on rapid fire,' said Anthony.

'Then once over the wall, the captain and I will head for the right and left doors, keeping in whatever shadows we can find after throwing the hooks back over the wall.'

'What about *me*?' said Witkowski.

'I just told you. Colonel, we'll discuss that later. What's our backup, Monsieur Cloche?'

'As we agreed, ten experienced *agents du combat* will be concealed just a hundred metres down the road, prepared to assault the château at your radio command.'

'Make sure they're completely out of sight. We know these people; even the slightest hint of intruders and they'll torch every document in the place. It's vital that we bring out whatever's there.'

'I share your concerns, monsieur, but a two-man operation strikes me as – how would you Americans say it? – the opposite of "overkill".'

'Underkill,' said Dietz. 'He's right, Cons-Op.'

'Who mentioned anything about a *two*-man operation?' an agitated Witkowski interrupted.

'Oh, for Christ's sake, Stanley!' Latham glared at the G-2 veteran. 'I checked. You're over sixty and I'm not going to be responsible for you catching a bullet in your skull because you didn't duck in time.'

'I can take you on *any*time, *chłopak*!'

'Spare me the machismo. We'll signal you to come over when it makes sense.'

'May I return to my objection,' broke in the deputy director of the Etranger. 'I have managed like assaults in the Middle East – Oman, Abu Dhabi, Bahrain, and elsewhere – when we employed the Foreign Legion. At minimum, you should have two additional personnel, if, for nothing else, to cover your rear flanks.'

'He's got a damn good point, sir,' said Lieutenant Anthony.

'Anything less would be ludicrous, if not suicidal,' added Karin.

Drew looked up from the map at Cloche. 'Maybe I wasn't thinking too clearly,' he said. 'Okay, two others. Who have you got?'

'Any one of the ten would be more than adequate, but there are three recruited from the Legion who have worked for the United Nations Security Forces.'

'Pick two of them and have them here in a couple of hours . . . Now, let's get to our equipment, and help me out here, Stosh.'

'Outside of the grappling hooks and the rope, those new MAC-10s with auto-repeat silencers, thirty rounds a clip, four clips a man,' began Witkowski. 'Also a black PVC raft, small blue penlights, UHF military radios, camouflaged fatigues, night binoculars, weighted hunting knives, garrottes, four small Beretta automatics, and in case of real trouble, three grenades apiece.'

'Can you handle that, Monsieur Cloche?'

'If it is repeated slowly, it is done. Now, as to when—'

'Tonight,' Latham broke in, 'when it's darkest.'

CHAPTER FORTY-THREE

The ancient château was a Gothic remnant, an eerie silhouette against the clear night sky, the moonlight of the Loire Valley glancing off its turrets and spires. It was, in essence, more a small castle than a château, the egotistical manifestation of a lesser noble who aspired to greater lineage. It was made of ragged stone interspersed with precision brickwork, the centuries layered upon one another, constantly remodelled as the generations progressed. There was something hypnotic about the juxtaposition of large, high television dishes with stone walls built in the fifteen-hundreds, something even awesome, as if civilization were on an inevitable march from the earth to the sky, from crossbows and cannons to space stations and nuclear warheads. Which was better and where would it end?

It was shortly before two o'clock in the morning, the breezes soft, the sounds of nocturnal animals muted, as the N-2 unit plus two *agents du combat*, formerly of the French Foreign Legion, moved into their positions. Following a terrain map under the dim blue wash of his penlight, Lieutenant Gerald Anthony led Karin de Vries through the underbrush of the steep hill towards the promontory. Along the way Karin whispered, 'Gerry, stop!'

'What is it?'

'Look, down here.' She reached into the branches of a shrub and pulled out a soiled old cap, more rag than headpiece. She turned it over, her blue penlight shining inside the torn lining. She gasped at what she saw.

'What's the *matter*?' whispered the lieutenant.

'Look!' Karin handed the cap to Anthony.

'*Jesus!*' gasped the commando. In shakily written print, inked deeply as in an act of intense possessiveness, was the name 'Jodelle'. 'The old guy had to have been up here,' whispered the lieutenant.

'It certainly fills in a few empty spaces. Here, give it back and I'll put it in my pocket . . . Let's *go!*'

Far below, in the shallow, swamplike marshes and hidden by the reeds of tall grass, the five men huddled together in the cramped black rubber life raft. Latham and Captain Dietz were at the bow, behind each his Etranger *agent du combat*, named simply One and Two, as such personnel preferred anonymity. At the stern of the small craft was an angry Colonel Stanley Witkowski, and if looks could explode an environment, the occupants would have been blown out of the marsh water.

Drew parted the bulrushes, his eyes on the promontory of the steep hill. The signal came. Two flashes of dim blue light. 'Let's *go!*' he whispered. 'They're in place.'

Using the two miniature black paddles, the Etranger agents propelled the PVC raft through the reeds and into the relatively open, shallow stream of the ancient canal. Slowly, stroke by stroke, they made their way to the opposite embankment roughly sixty yards away, past a circular brick tunnel that allowed the diverted water from the Loire River to flow into the marsh.

'You were right, Cons-Op,' said the commando captain, his voice low. 'Look over there, two strings of wire on the poles going across the opening. Five'll get you ten both are tripped with magnetic fields. River refuse can get through, but not the density of a human body.'

'It had to be, Dietz,' whispered Latham. 'Otherwise there was an open route along the bank to this crazy half-medieval-castle, half-estate.'

'Like I said to Mrs D.V., you've got the real smarts.'

'The hell I do. I had a brother who taught me to study a

problem, then study it over and over, and finally to look at it again and figure out what I missed.'

'That's the "Harry" we've heard about, isn't it?'

'That's the Harry, Captain.'

'He's why you're here, right?'

'Half right, Dietz. The other half is what he found.'

The PVC raft pulled into the embankment. Silently, the unit lifted the coiled ropes and grappling hooks out of the bottom and waded into the muddy bank of the marsh canal below the strolling path roughly twenty feet above them. Drew pulled the UHF radio out of the side pocket of his camouflage fatigues and pressed the transmission button.

'Yes?' came Karin's whispered voice over the tiny speaker.

'What's your visibility?' asked Latham

'Seventy, seventy-five per cent. With our binoculars we can scan most of the pool area and the south section, but only a partial on the north side.'

'Not bad.'

'Very good, I'd say.'

'Any signs of movement? Any lights?'

'Affirmative to both,' the lieutenant's whisper broke in. 'Like clockwork, two guards lockstep around the rear area then circle back to the midsections of the north and south sides. They're carrying small semis, probably Uzis or German adaptations, and have radios attached to their belts—'

'What are they wearing?' interrupted Drew.

'What else? Paramilitary black trousers and shirts and those crazy red armbands with the lightning bolts through the swastikas. Regular delinquents playing *Soldaten*, butch haircuts and all. You can't miss 'em, boss man.'

'Lights?'

'Four windows, two on the first floor, one each on the second and third.'

'Activity?'

'Other than the two guards, only the kitchen area, that's the south side, first floor.'

'Yes, I remember the maps. Any ideas about our penetration?'

'Definitely. Both patrols head into the midsection shadows out of sight for not less than thirteen seconds nor more than nineteen. You get by the wall, I give you two shots of the transmitter, and you go over – *fast*! There are three open cabanas, so I take back what I said before; split up and head into them. Wait for the guards to return, take them out however you can, and hoist the bodies over the wall or drag 'em into the cabanas, whatever's the quickest and easiest. When that's done, you've got limited free access and can signal the colonel.'

'That's damn good, Lieutenant. Where are the delinquents now?'

'Separating and heading back to the sides. Get up to the wall!'

'Be careful, Drew!' said De Vries.

'We'll all be careful, Karin . . . Come *on*.' Like disciplined ants climbing a mound of dirt, the five men scrambled up the embankment to the high brick wall and the even higher iron gate of the strollers' path. Latham crawled forward and examined it; the 'gate' was made of thick, heavy steel, rising above the wall, no slits or spaces for keys. It could be opened only from inside. Drew lurched back to the others, shaking his head in the moonlight. Each nodded, accepting the foregone conclusion that the wall had to be scaled.

Suddenly they heard the sound of boots on stone, and then two voices floated above them.

'*Zigarette?*'

'*Nein, ist schlecht!*'

'*Unsinn.*'

The tattoo of boots continued; the French *agents du combat* stood up, stepped back, and lifted the grappling hooks and the short coils of rope from the ground. They braced themselves and waited; silently, without breathing, they all waited. Then it came, the two short, muted bursts from Latham's radio. The Frenchmen hurled the solid plastic hooks over the wall, tugged at them, then held the ropes taut as Drew and Captain Dietz lunged up like primates, their weapons strapped across their shoulders, climbing hand over hand with pounding knees against the brick until their bodies disappeared over the top. The instant they did so, the Etranger agents leapt up, clamouring after the Americans; four seconds later the grappling hooks came flying back, embedding themselves in the moist dirt of the embankment and narrowly missing a furious Witkowski.

On the other side of the wall, Latham gestured for the American commando and his French backup to head for the farthest open cabana as he and his agent raced into the first. The cabanas were simple wood-framed structures, tentlike, and covered with brightly coloured striped canvas, the entrances no more than weighted flaps that could be pushed back and remain open for ventilation. The pool itself was dark, the sound of the filtering machinery barely a hum in the distance. Inside the first cabana, Drew turned to Etranger One. 'You know what comes next, don't you?' he asked.

'*Oui*, monsieur, I do,' said the Frenchman, unsheathing his long-bladed knife from its scabbard as Latham did the same. '*S'il vous plaît, non*,' added the agent, holding Drew's wrist. '*Vous êtes courageux*, but my colleague and I are more experienced in these matters, monsieur. Le capitaine and we discussed this. You are too valuable to take the risk.'

'I wouldn't ask you to do anything I wouldn't do!'

'You've displayed that, but you know what to look for, we do not.'

'You *discussed* this . . . ?'

'*Shh!*' whispered the agent. 'Here they come.'

The following minutes were like a marionette show performed at three speeds: slow motion, stop, and fast forward. The two Etranger agents crawled slowly out of their respective cabanas, moving around them, and staying close to the ground until each was behind his target, like two stalking animals. Suddenly the north guard spotted the south side *agent du combat* and made a mistake. He squinted to make sure his startled, unsuspecting eyes were not playing tricks on him. He swung the semiautomatic off his shoulder and was about to shoot, when Number Two was on him, his clawlike left hand around the patrol's throat, the knife surgically penetrating his back. The astonished south guard spun around as Number One raced forward, his knife held head high, cutting off all sound as the blade slashed through the Nazi's throat.

All movement stopped, those seconds so necessary to assess the moment. Silence. Results positive. The Frenchmen then began to drag the dead guards to the edge of the wall nearest each, prepared to shove the bodies over it, when Latham ran out of the first cabana. '*No!*' he whispered so loudly it could have been a roar. 'Bring them both back *here!*'

Inside, the three men stood around Drew, bewildered and not a little angry. 'What the hell are you *doing*, Cons-Op?' said the American commando Dietz. 'We don't want anybody to find these jokers, for Christ's sake!'

'I think you missed something, Captain. Their *sizes*.'

'One's pretty big, the other isn't. So?'

'You and me, Captain. They won't be perfect fits, but I'll bet we could squeeze into those idiot uniforms – *over* our fatigues. Even the shirts – it's dark out there.'

'I'll be goddamned,' said Dietz slowly. 'You may have a point. In this light they'd be better camouflage than what we're wearing.'

'*Dépêche-toi* – hurry!' said Etranger Number One as he and his colleague knelt down and began stripping the bloodstained Nazi uniforms off the corpses.

'There's a problem,' interrupted the captain, all eyes riveted upon him. 'I speak German, they speak German, but you don't, Cons-Op.'

'I don't intend to play bridge or have a drink with anybody.'

'But say we're stopped, these aren't the only clowns on guard here, take my word for it, dark or not.'

'A moment, please,' said Number Two. 'Monsieur Lat'am, can you say the word "*Halsweh*"?'

'Sure, halls-fay.'

'Try again, Cons-Op,' said Dietz, nodding approvingly at the Frenchmen. 'That's terrific, guys . . . *Halsweh*, go on.'

'Halls-vay,' mumbled Latham.

'Good enough,' said the commando. 'If anyone stops us, I'll talk. If they specifically address you, you cough, strain your voice, hold your throat, and scratch out the word "*Halsweh*", got it?'

'What the hell have I *got*?'

'It is German for sore throat, monsieur. The pollen season, you know. Many people come down with sore throats and wet eyes.'

'Thanks, Two, if I need a doctor, I'll call you.'

'Enough. Put on the clothes.'

Four minutes later, Latham and Dietz were reasonable facsimiles of the neo-Nazi patrols, bulges, bloodstains, and all. Neither would fool anyone in a harsh glare of light, but in shadows and quasi-darkness both could get away with the ruse. Discarding the German semiautomatic weapons, they replaced them with their own silenced equipment, switching to single-shot action in case a situation called for a lone kill, not rapid fire.

'One of you get Witkowski,' ordered Drew. 'Caw once like a bird and watch out or a grappling hook will crash down on your neck. He's not a happy camper.'

'I'll go,' said Dietz, starting out of the cabana.

'No, you won't,' said Latham, stopping the commando. 'He sees that uniform, he might blow your head off. You go, Number One. You and he talked a lot during our session this afternoon; he'll know you.'

'*Oui*, monsieur.'

Ninety-six seconds later, the imposing figure of Colonel Stanley Witkowski entered the cabana. 'I see you've been occupied,' he said, glancing down at the two stripped corpses. 'What are those silly costumes for?'

'We're going hunting, Stosh, and you're going to stay with our French buddies here. They'll be on our rear flank, and our lives will depend on the three of you.'

'What are you going to do?'

'Start looking, what else?'

'I thought you might screw it up without specific references,' said Witkowski, yanking a large folded piece of paper out of his jacket and, rather obscenely, unfolding it and placing it over the back of one of the corpses. He switched on his blue pencil light; it was a reduced diagram of the Eagle's Nest château. 'I had our Deputy Cloche make this for me in Paris. At least, you won't be hunting blind.'

'You son of a bitch, Stanley!' Drew looked gratefully at Witkowski, 'you had to one-up me again. All those put-together pages came down to this. How did you figure?'

'You're good, *chłopak*, but you're behind the times. You need a little help from the old mastodons, that's all.'

'Thanks, Stosh. Where do we start, give me a clue?'

'The optimum would be to take a hostage and learn whatever you can. You need more than two-year-old plans on a piece of paper.'

Latham reached under the black Nazi shirt and pulled out his radio. 'Karin?' he whispered, pressing the transmission button.

'Where *are* you?' answered De Vries.

'We're inside.'

'We *know* that,' the lieutenant broke in, 'we watched that little exercise our new recruits pulled off. You still around the pool?'

'Yes.'

'What do you need?' asked Karin.

'We want to take a prisoner and ask some questions. Any warm bodies in sight?'

'Not in the open,' said Anthony, 'but that kitchen's got

741

two or three inside; they keep passing by the rear window. It looks pretty busy, kind of strange for this hour.'

'Berchtesgaden,' said Witkowski, his voice low and hollow.

'What?' said Dietz as he and the others looked at the colonel.

'It's a replication of Hitler's Berchtesgaden, where the *Oberführer* studs and their multiple mistresses romped night and day, not knowing that Hitler had their rooms wired, listening for traitors.'

'How do you know that?' asked Drew.

'Testimony from the Nuremberg trials. That kitchen won't close down; the party boys need a break now and then and they're always hungry.'

'Out,' said Latham into the radio and replacing it under his shirt. 'Okay, fellas, how do we pull someone out of there?'

'It has to be me,' replied Dietz, turning on his penlight and studying the plans of the château. 'Whoever they are in there, they're either German or French. You don't speak German and your French is barely understandable, and the others are dressed wrong ... There's a door here on the side. I'll stick my head in and ask for a cup of coffee, for someone to please bring it out to me. In German – the two patrols were German.'

'Suppose they see you're not the same guard?'

'I'll say the other guy got sick and I'm relieving him. It's why I need the coffee, I'm still half asleep.' Dietz hurriedly left the cabana and walked rapidly down the south area towards the kitchen door, Latham and Witkowski crouched in front of the tentlike flap, watching him. The commando abruptly stopped, froze, as two bright floodlights on the side of the château suddenly came on. Dietz was fully exposed, the black shirt and trousers revealed for the misfits they were. A couple strode into the wash of bright light from the cavernous shadows beyond, a young miniskirted woman and a tall middle-aged man. The man reacted to the sight of the captain with alarm, then fury. He reached under his jacket; the commando had no choice. He fired a single silenced round into the man's head as he rushed to the woman whose scream was aborted by Dietz's chop to her throat. As she collapsed, the commando raised his weapon; two more spits exploded the floodlights. He then lifted the woman, throwing her over his shoulder, and started back to the cabana.

'Get the *casualty*!' whispered the colonel sharply, pulling the flap back, addressing the Frenchman.

'I'll go,' said Drew, racing forward. He reached the shadows; the body of the dead man was vaguely outlined by the moonlight, which was in large measure blocked by the rising sides of the castle. He ran to the corpse as the door to the kitchen crashed open. Latham spun away, out of the line of sight, his weapon gripped firmly, his back against the wall. A face beneath a chef's hat peered outside and squinted at the darkness; the head shrugged and the cook went back into the kitchen. Perspiring, Drew strapped his gun over his shoulder and ran to the fallen man; he leaned down, grabbed his feet, and started to drag the body back to the cabana.

'*Que faites-vous?*' said a female voice from the darkness.

'Halls-vay,' answered Latham haltingly, out of breath, adding hoarsely, '*trop de whisky.*'

'*Ah, un allemand! Votre français est médiocre.*' A woman dressed in a long white diaphanous gown emerged in the dim moonlight. She laughed, staggering slightly, and continued in French. 'Too much whisky, you say? Who hasn't? I've a mind to throw myself into the pool.'

'*Gut,*' said Drew, understanding half of what she said.

'Shall I help you?'

'*Nein, danke.*'

'Oh, it is Heinemann you have there. He's a bull of a German, a perfect boor.' Suddenly the woman gasped as Latham dragged the man named Heinemann into the open area, where the moonlight was brighter; she saw the blood-drenched head. Drew dropped the dead man's feet and yanked the small Beretta out of his pocket.

'You raise your voice, I'll have to kill you,' he said in English. 'Can you understand me?'

'I understand perfectly,' answered the woman, her English fluent, her weaving all but absent with her terror.

The two Etranger agents rushed up to them. Without speaking, Number Two pulled the corpse to the side of the wall, removing items from its pockets, while Number One walked behind the woman and shoved her towards the cabana, his hand gripping her neck. Latham followed, startled to realize that the bodies of the dead neo guards were no longer inside. 'What happened . . . ?'

'Our previous visitors had urgent appointments,' replied Witkowski. 'They flew away.'

'Damn good work, Cons-Op,' said Captain Dietz, sitting next to his captive, both in striped canvas chairs, the small enclosure dimly lit by upturned blue penlights. 'Real cosy in here, isn't it?' he added as Etranger Two came back in.

The two women stared at each other. '*Adrienne?*' said Latham's prisoner.

'*Allô*, Elyse,' Dietz's prize responded despondently. 'We are *finis*, *n-est-ce pas?*'

'You're Nazi whores!' accused Number One.

'Don't be foolish!' objected Elyse. 'We work where the money is best, politics have nothing to do with us.'

'Do you know who these people *are?*' said Number Two. 'The beasts of the world! My grandfather died fighting them!'

'History,' dismissed the cool, gowned Elyse. 'Decades before either of us was born.'

'You haven't heard the *stories?*' Number One spat out. 'They're history also, and they also happen to be the truth. They're Fascists, they slaughter whole races of people. They would kill me and my entire family if they could, simply because we are *Jews!*'

'And we are merely temporary companions, here for a week or so every few months. We never discuss such issues. Besides, I frequently travel to many cities in Europe, and most of the Germans I've come to know are charming, courteous gentlemen.'

'I'm sure they are,' interrupted Witkowski, 'but these aren't . . . We're wasting time. We were looking for a man who worked here and instead we ended up with two females who are visiting the place. Not very encouraging.'

'I don't know about that, Colonel.' Drew gripped his captive's arm. 'Elyse here said that she, and I assume her friend, visit here for a week or so every few months, isn't that right, lady?'

'That is the arrangement, yes, monsieur,' agreed the woman, shaking off Latham's hand.

'Then what?' pressed Drew.

'After proper medical attention, we go elsewhere. I know nothing – *we* know nothing. Our job is to provide companionship, which, I trust, you will not be so tasteless as to inquire about.'

'Don't trust anything, lady. They killed my brother, so I haven't got much trust left.' Latham again gripped the woman's arm, now far more firmly, vicelike. The plans of the château were on a hastily retrieved drinks table from the poolside area. Drew swung her towards it, grabbed a penlight, and angled it down at the diagrams. 'You and your friend are going to tell us exactly who and what's in every room, and let me explain why you'd better not lie or be evasive . . . Less than a minute away, down the road, is a French intelligence assault team ready to blow up the front gates, run in here, and take into custody everyone on the premises. I'd advise you to help us, and you might live long enough to make a deal for yourself since you've been travelling the circuit. *Entendu?*'

'Your French improves, monsieur,' said the gowned courtesan, her cold, frightened eyes locked with Latham's. 'It's all a question of survival, isn't it? . . . Come, Adrienne, study these plans with me.' The innocent-looking mini-skirted girl beside Dietz got out of the chair and joined her associate. 'Incidentally, monsieur,' said Elyse, 'I will read these quite easily. *Mes études* at the Sorbonne were in architecture.'

'Holy *shit*,' exclaimed Captain Dietz quietly.

Minutes passed as the former Sorbonne student examined the diagrams. Finally, she spoke. 'As you can see, the first floor is obvious – the north veranda, the large common area in the centre which also serves as a dining room, and the kitchen, large enough for a popular restaurant on the Rive Droite. The second and third floors are suites for visiting dignitaries, which Adrienne and I can describe down to a mattress.'

'Who's in them now?' asked Witkowski.

'Herr Heinemann was with you, Adrienne, right, *mon chou?*'

'*Oui*,' said the girl. 'Such a bad man!'

'Two other suites on that floor are occupied by Colette and Jeanne, their companions are businessmen from Munich and Baden-Baden; and on the third floor there is myself and a terribly nervous man, so upset he drank himself into a stupor and could not perform. I was grateful, naturally, and decided to go for a walk – where I met you, monsieur. The other rooms are not occupied.'

'The man with you, what does he look like?' asked Latham. Elyse described him, and Drew said quietly, 'That's our man. It's Bergeron.'

'He's terrified of something.'

'He should be. He's a liability and he knows it . . . You've described three floors; there's a fourth. What's up there?'

'It's completely off limits to everyone but a select few who wear black suits with the red swastika armbands. They're all tall, like you, and their bearing is quite military. The help, even the guards, are frightened to death of them.'

'The fourth floor?'

'It would appear to be a tomb, monsieur, the living grave of a great pharaoh, but instead of being buried in the bowels of the pyramid, it is at the highest point, nearest to the sun and the heavens.'

'Clarification, please?'

'I said it was off limits, *verboten*, but I should also add that it is *sealed* off. This very-much-inhabited tomb comprises the entire top floor and every door is made of steel. No one goes in there but the men in dark suits. They insert their hands into spaces in the walls and press their palms down for a particular door to open.'

'Electronic print-scan releases,' said Witkowski. 'There's no way to bypass those photoelectric cells.'

'If you've never been up there, how do you know all this?' asked Drew.

'Because the front and back staircases to the top floor, as well as the hallways, are constantly patrolled. Even the guards need relaxation, monsieur, and some are very attractive.'

'Ah, *oui*,' piped the young miniskirt brightly. 'The blond Erich asks me to please see him whenever I am free, and I do.'

'It's an unfair world,' mumbed Dietz.

'Who's the pharaoh on the top floor?' pressed Latham.

'That is no secret,' answered Elyse. 'An old man, a *very* old man they all worship. No one is permitted to speak to him other than his dark-suited aides, but every morning he's brought down in an elevator, his face shrouded in a heavy veil, and wheeled to what they call the "meditation path", beyond the pool. They open the gate and he dismisses everyone, orders them away. He then gets out of his chair, stands erect, denying his years, and literally marches out to a place none of us has ever seen. It is said he calls it his "eagle's nest", where he can contemplate and make wise decisions while having his morning coffee and brandy.'

'Monluc,' said Drew. 'My God, he's still alive!'

'Whoever he is, he is the treasure they *keep* alive.'

'*Is* he a treasure?' asked Witkowski. 'Or in reality a figurehead to be manipulated for their own purposes?'

'I can't presume to give you an answer,' said the educated, high-priced call girl, 'but I doubt he's manipulated by anyone. Just as the help are frightened of his aides, those same aides appear to be terrified of him. He constantly berates them, and when he threatens them with dismissal, they virtually cower before him.'

'Could they be playing their roles?' Latham studied the courtesan's face in the dull blue light.

'If they are, we'd know it, for we must constantly play our own parts. Impostors can rarely fool other impostors.'

'You're impostors?'

'In many more ways than you can imagine, monsieur.'

'Still, there has to be talk. That kind of behaviour doesn't go unnoticed.'

'Gossip, yes. The most persistent rumour is that the old man controls enormous wealth, extraordinary funds that only he can disperse. It's further said that he wears electronic devices under his robes that monitor him constantly, sending signals to medical equipment on the fourth floor, which in turn are relayed to unknown locations in Europe.'

'At his age, I can understand it. He's got to be over ninety.'

'They say he's over a hundred.'

'And still with all his faculties?'

'If he plays chess, monsieur, I would not wager heavily against him.'

'The relay machines, *chłopak*,' interrupted the colonel. 'If they're programmed to retransmit, they can be torn apart and those unknown locations traced.'

'If nothing else, they'd lead us to the money sources, the transfer points. That's why he's monitored wherever he goes. If he drops deep dead, the vaults slam shut until other orders come.'

'And if we can trace the locations, we'll know where those orders come from,' added Witkowski. 'We've got to get up there!'

Drew turned to the cool but still frightened Elyse. 'If you're lying, you'll spend the rest of your life in a cell.'

'Why would I lie at a time like this, monsieur? You've made it clear that I will be pleading for my freedom in any event.'

'I don't know. You're bright, maybe you figure we'll be killed trying to get up there, your fall-back position being well-paid whores who don't know a damn thing. That could play.'

'Then she will be dead, *mon supérieur*,' said Etranger Two. 'I will strap her to the gate in the wall with *plastique* between her legs, exploded by my electronic *contrôle*.'

'Christ, I didn't know you had that sort of thing!'

'I added a couple of things, *chłopak*.'

'I offer you a better solution,' said the courtesan, reaching out and holding the young girl's shoulder. 'I offer you both of us.'

'*Et moi?*' squeaked the miniskirt. 'What are you *saying*, Elyse?'

'Be quiet, *ma petite* . . . You wish to get into the Eagle's Nest, *n'est-ce pas*? I suggest it would be easier with us than without us.'

'How so?' asked Latham.

'We are familiar – accept that as you care to – with many of the help and most of the guards. We can get you through the kitchen and into *le grand foyer*, where the main staircase is. The backstairs, as you can see by the plans, are through lesser parlours on the right. We can do this much and something more, something most vital. You will need one of the old man's aides to get into the top floor – if you even reach it. There are five, all armed, and their quarters are also on the fourth floor, but one or another is always on duty. He stays in the library, in the front of the château, where he can be reached instantly by the *patron*, or anyone on the staff. I'll point out the door to you.'

'What about us?' said Etranger One. 'How do you explain *us*?'

'I've been considering that. The security here is immense and varied. Technicians and others arrive and depart to check the equipment. I will say you are exterior patrols who have been sent to cover the grounds outside the wall. Your clothing will support the lie.'

'*Sehr gut*,' said Dietz.

'You speak German?'

'*Einigermassen.*'

'Then you tell whoever may ask, it will be more authoritative.'

'I'm not dressed like them.'

'You obviously are under those clothes you removed from the guards.'

'Jean-Pierre Villier . . . !' said Drew, as if the name had suddenly struck him out of thin air. '"Clothes are the chameleon", or something like that.'

'What are you talking about, *chłopak*?'

'We're going about this the wrong way . . . Strip, Captain, down to your shorts!'

Four minutes later, Latham and Dietz, minus their fatigues, were in the far-better-fitting paramilitary uniforms of the neo-Nazi guards. The black cloth covered the bloodstains and the single rip in the commando's back, while the webbed belts accommodated both their knives, garrottes, and small automatic Berettas.

'Tuck in your shirts, especially the rear,' ordered the colonel. 'Looks more tailored that way.'

'Heil Hitler,' said Dietz, glancing approvingly at what he could see of himself in the dim blue light of the cabana.

'You mean Heil Jäger,' Drew corrected him, equally pleased with his appearance.

'The only thing you say is "*Halsweh*", Cons-Op.'

'Remember, Frenchmen, I'm your commanding officer,' said Witkowski. 'If any questions are asked, I answer them.'

'*Très bien, mon Colonel*,' agreed Etranger Two.

'Ready, guys?' said Dietz, picking up the two semi-automatics and handing one to Latham.

'As ready as we'll ever be.' Drew turned to the women, who rose together from the canvas chairs, the young

Adrienne frightened, trembling, the older Elyse pale and resigned. 'I don't make judgements, only practical observations as I see them,' continued Latham. 'You're afraid, and so am I, because what these two younger fellows do, I usually don't – I've been forced to. Believe me, somebody has to, that's all I can tell you. Remember, if we get out of this, we'll be on your side with the authorities . . . Let's *go*.'

CHAPTER FORTY-FOUR

The first of the kitchen help to see the uniformed Latham and Dietz come through the door were two men at a long butcher-block table, one chopping vegetables, the other straining liquid through a sieve. Startled, they looked at each other, then back at Drew and the captain, who instantly separated in military fashion, permitting the camouflaged Witkowski to walk and stop between them. Grim-faced, they bent their elbows quickly in the informal Nazi salute, as if the colonel were a man of considerable stature, an impression the G-2 veteran reenforced. '*Sprechen Sie Deutsch? Falls nicht, parlez-vous français?*' he barked.

'*Deutsch, mein Herr!*' said the astonished vegetable chef, continuing in German. 'This is a place for food, sir, and only we can be trusted . . . If I may, sir, who – who are you, sir?'

'This is *Oberst* Wachner of the Fourth Reich!' announced Dietz in clipped German, his eyes looking straight ahead. 'He and his security colleagues were ordered by Berlin to inspect the outer grounds without notification. *Kommen Sie her!*'

On command, the Etranger agents, gripping the arms of the two courtesans of the Eagle's Nest, marched through the open door.

'Can you identify these women?' fairly snarled Witkowski. 'We found them walking freely around the pool and the tennis court. It is *very* lax here!'

'We are permitted to do so, you fool!' cried the white-gowned Elyse. 'I don't care who you are, tell your apes to take their hands off us, or start paying money!'

'*Well?*' shouted '*Oberst* Wachner,' staring at the kitchen help.

'Oh, yes, sir,' said one chef, 'they are guests here.'

'And our contract does not include servicing strangers, only other guests to whom we have been properly introduced!' Elyse glared at Witkowski. The colonel nodded; the *agent du combat* removed his hand, as did One from the miniskirted Adrienne. 'I believe you owe us an apology,' said the older, far more intelligent call girl.

'*Madame.*' The colonel elaborately clicked his heels and bowed his head barely an inch or two, immediately turning back to the cooks. 'As you may gather, our assignment here is to analyse the security measures without interference from those who would cover up the flaws if they knew we were here. If you like, call Berlin to verify our presence.'

'*Ach, nein, mein Herr!* This happened before, several years ago, and we certainly understand. We are merely kitchen chefs, and would *never* interfere.'

'*Sehr gut!* Are you the only ones on duty?'

'At the moment, yes, sir. Our associate, Stoltz, left for his room an hour ago. He must be up at six o'clock to prepare the breakfast buffet – what we have not prepared for him.'

'Very well, we shall continue our inspection beyond here. Should anyone inquire about us, you don't know what they're talking about. *Remember* that, or *Berlin* will remember you.'

'*Wir haben verstanden*,' said the vegetable man fearfully, nodding repeatedly. 'But, if I may, *mein Herr*, for I wish to cooperate fully with Berlin, the guards inside are trained to fire on unannounced intruders. I would not care to have your lives on my conscience – or on my record. *Verstanden?*'

'Don't be concerned,' replied Stanley Witkowski, whipping his American identification out of his pocket and proclaiming with the panache of a long-ago Polish royal, 'If nothing else, this will put away their weapons.' He swiftly repocketed his USA embassy credentials. 'Also, we'll take the ladies with us. The big bitch has a sharp, loud mouth. We'll be fine!'

Latham and Dietz leading the procession, the French-American invaders walked through the double doors into the great hall of the château. A circular staircase, dimly lit by wall sconces, rose from the centre of the huge, polished wood foyer. There was an archway straight ahead leading to other darkened, high-ceilinged rooms, and on the right, to the left of the large double doors of the entrance, a smaller door, light shining through the space between the lintel and the bottom panel.

'That is the library, monsieur,' whispered Elyse to Drew. 'Whatever aide is on duty will be in there, but you must be quick and cautious. There are alarms everywhere. I know, for I have frequently thought of using several of them myself.'

'*Halt!*' cried the voice of a silhouetted figure emerging on the first landing.

'We are a special force from Berlin!' exclaimed Dietz, sotto voce in German as he raced up the staircase.

'*Was ist los?*' The guard raised his weapon as the commando fired two silenced rounds in rapid succession, and without breaking his stride reached the fallen patrol, dragging him to the steps and rolling him down the staircase.

The library door opened, revealing a tall man in a dark suit, a long cigarette holder in his left hand. 'What is the racket?' he asked in German. Latham yanked the garrotte from his belt, instantly arcing it over the head of Monluc's aide, twisting it and pivoting the man's body so that he was behind the Nazi. He loosened the leather strap and spoke.

'You do exactly what I tell you to do or I roll the straps and you're dead!'

'*Amerikaner!*' choked the neo, dropping his holder. '*You* are the one who is *dead*!'

'*Oberst* Klaus Wachner,' said Witkowski, approaching the aide and staring at his contorted face. 'The stories of your obscene security appear to be true,' he continued in harsh German. 'Berlin – even *Bonn* – knows about them! We penetrated your measures, and if we could, our enemies can do so also!'

'You're insane, *a traitor*. The man choking me is an American!'

'A prized soldier of the Fourth Reich, *mein Herr*. A Sonnenkind!'

'*Ach! Nein!*'

'*Doch*. You will follow his orders or I will let him have his way with you. He loathes incompetence.' Witkowski nodded for Latham to further unloosen the straps of the garrotte.

'*Danke*,' coughed Monluc's aide, grabbing his throat.

'*Two*,' said Drew, nodding at the second Etranger agent. 'Take over this clown! Go up the backstairs; they're through those other rooms—'

'I know where they are, monsieur,' the Frenchman broke in. 'I simply do not know *who* is there.'

'I'll go with him,' said Dietz. 'I speak the language and my semi's in front of us both.'

'Put it on rapid-fire,' ordered Latham.

'It's on it, Cons-Op.'

'According to the plans,' continued Drew, 'there's a walled corridor around the entire floor. Once you're up there, bring him around to the centre.'

'*Unless* we're all in trouble,' countered the commando.

'What do you mean, Captain?'

'You don't know what's up those staircases any more than I do. Say you catch total fire, one of us has to blow the place apart. I shove this bastard's hand into a door slot, open it, and throw in grenades.'

'You can't *do* that, and that's an *order*!'

'It's standard, Cons-Op. We don't risk our lives to come up with zero!'

'We've got to get whatever's up there, goddammit, we can't blow it apart! Before I do that, I'll radio the assault unit down the road.'

'There won't be time, for Christ's sake! The neos will do it *themselves!*'

'*Stop*, both of you!' cried Elyse. 'I offered you the two of us and that offer remains. Adrienne will precede your captain and the Nazi on the backstairs, and I shall climb in front of you, monsieur. The patrols will hesitate to shoot either of us, for there are constant assignations between men and women here.'

'*Berchtesgaden,*' said Witkowski quietly. 'An alpine whorehouse run by a *Führer* who claimed to be purer than a newborn lamb . . . She's right, *chłopak*. The sight of the girls gives us the split-second advantage, front and back. *Take* it.'

'Okay! . . . Let's go, and I hope to hell I'm giving the right order.'

'You don't have a choice, young man,' said the colonel softly. 'You're the leader, and like all leaders, you listen to your staff, evaluate, and make your own decision. It's not easy.'

'Cut the military bullshit, Stanley, I'd rather play hockey.'

Elyse, in her diaphanous white gown, started regally up the circular staircase; Drew, the colonel, and Etranger One followed ten steps behind her in the shadows.

'*Liebling!*' whispered a guard in the hallway beyond the landing, his voice exuberant. 'You got rid of that drunk from Paris, no?'

'*Ja, Liebste*, I came only for you. I am so bored.'

'All is quiet, come with me – *ach*, who are *they*? *Behind* you!'

Etranger One fired a single silenced shot. The guard collapsed on the railing, fell over it, and plummeted down to the marble floor below.

The backstairs were dark; the only light, far above, created shadows within darker shadows. The terrified Adrienne climbed step by quiet step up the steep staircase, her body trembling, her wide eyes filled with fear. They reached the second floor.

'*Was ist?*' came the strident voice from above as the sudden glare of a powerful flashlight filled the entire staircase. '*Liebchen? . . . Nein!*'

Etranger Two fired; the Nazi guard fell over, his head caught in the banister. 'Go *on!*' ordered Captain Dietz. 'Two more floors to go.'

They crawled ahead, the child-whore named Adrienne crying copiously, blowing her nose on the cloth of her blouse.

'It is not that far, *ma chérie*,' whispered Etranger Two gently to the young girl. 'You are very brave and we will tell everyone that.'

'Please tell my *father!*' whimpered the young girl. 'He *hates* me so!'

'I shall do so myself. For you are a true hero of France.'

'*Am* I?'

'Keep going, child.'

Latham, Etranger One, and the colonel stopped abruptly on the staircase at the sight of Elyse's hand waving behind her; it was a warning. They stepped back on the descending steps against the dark shadowed wall and waited. A blond guard walked rapidly out on the third-floor landing; he was agitated, angry. 'Fräulein, have you seen Adrienne?' he asked in German. 'She's not in the room with that pig, Heinemann. He's not there either, and the door is open.'

'They probably went for a walk, Erich.'

'That Heinemann is an ugly fellow, Elyse!'

'Surely you're not jealous, my dear. You know what we are, what we do. Only our bodies are involved, not our hearts, our feelings.'

'My God, she's too *young!*'

'Even I've told her that.'

'You know Heinemann is a pervert, don't you? He demands terrible things.'

'Don't think about them.'

'I *hate* this place!'

'Why do you stay?'

'I have no choice. My father enrolled me when I was in middle school and I was very impressed. The uniforms, the camaraderie, the fact that we were outcasts together. They said I was special and selected me to carry the banners at the meetings. They took photographs of me.'

'You can still leave, my friend.'

'No, I cannot. They paid for my years at university and I know too much. They would hunt me down and kill me.'

'*Erich!*' shouted a male voice from a hallway beyond the landing. '*Kommen Sie her!*'

'*Ach*, that one, he's always yelling. Do this, do that! He doesn't like me because I went to university and I really don't think he can read.'

'When I see Adrienne, I'll tell her you are – concerned. Remember, young man, it is only the body, not the heart.'

'You are a good friend, Fräulein.'

'I hope to be a better one someday.' The guard named Erich ran off the landing as Elyse came down several steps and whispered to the three intruders against the wall. 'Don't kill that one. He could be of use to you.'

'What's she talking about?' said Drew.

The colonel explained as Elyse continued up the staircase. 'She said not to waste him, and she's right.'

'Why?'

'He wants out of here and he knows a lot. Go *on!*'

The fourth-floor landing was not, to use Witkowski's words, very encouraging. A large twenty-foot archway was the open space between the wall that wrapped around the entire top floor. Presumably, it was the same for the back staircase. Two guards stood in the frame, another visible behind them, seated on a bench. Again Latham, E-One, and the colonel stayed out of sight as Elyse stepped up into view of the guards.

'*Halt!*' roared the neo patrol on the right, whipping his pistol out of its holster and aiming at the call girl's head.

'What are you *doing* up here? It is forbidden for anyone to come up these stairs!'

'Then you had better check with Herr What's-his-name in the library. He called me away from the new man from Paris and ordered me to be here as soon as I could disengage myself. What more can I *say*?'

'*Was ist los?*' yelled the guard in the rear bench, rising and rushing forward between the two men. 'Who *are* you?' he shouted.

'We are first names only, you know that,' replied the courtesan angrily. 'I am Elyse, and I will not tolerate your discourtesy! I was instructed by that ghoul of a man in the library to come here, and, like you, I follow orders!' Suddenly Elyse sprang away from the line of fire and shouted, '*Now!*'

The repeated spits of muted explosions filled the upper regions of the château as the three guards fell. The assault team, led by Drew, raced up the stairs, checking each body for signs of deadly life. Satisfied, they waited, their backs against the inner wall. 'Get out of here!' ordered Latham, addressing the white-gowned Elyse, who had crawled up the steps to the archway. 'You've got your freedom, lady, if I have to blow up the Quai d'Orsay to get it.'

'*Merci*, monsieur. Your French improves with every hour.'

'Go back to the kitchen,' said Witkowski. 'Tell them funny stories about us, and keep everyone calm.'

'It is not a problem, *mon colonel*. I will sit on a table and raise my skirt. They will be calm on the outside, preoccupied on the inside . . . *Au revoir*.'

'As your *capitaine* said, it is definitely an unfair world,' mumbled Etranger One as Elyse disappeared.

'Where *are* they?' said Drew. 'They should *be* here by now!'

On the narrow backstairs, Etranger Two, hammerlocking General Monluc's aide, the garrotte in place, propelled him up the staircase after Dietz and the child prostitute. They came to a stop.

'*Bist Du es*, Adrienne?' said the quiet voice on the third floor. 'What are you *doing* here?'

'I wanted to see you, Manfried,' whined the girl. 'Everyone is so mean to me and I knew you were here.'

'How could you know that, *Liebste*? The posts are secret.'

'The aides talk when they have too many schnapps.'

'They will be disciplined for it, my lovely little girl. Come up here, there is a soft rug and we will make use of it. Did I tell you that your breasts grow more beautiful each time you come here?'

'*Kill* him!' screamed Adrienne, flattening herself against the wall of the staircase.

Two muted gunshots and the guard named Manfried fell. The garrotte tightened, they proceeded to the last and final floor. At first sight the approach appeared to be insurmountable. Around the corner of the staircase there was a ten-foot archway, a single guard stationed in the centre, another behind him, dozing on a bench.

'Do you *know* him?' whispered Dietz in French into Adrienne's ear.

'*Non*, monsieur. He is new. I have seen him, that is all.'

'Do you know if he's German or French?'

'Most definitely German, sir. Almost all of the guards are German, but many speak French, the more educated ones.'

'I'm going to do something that may shock you, but I want you to stay calm and quiet, do you understand me?'

'What will you *do*?'

'There'll be a big, bright fire, but it won't last long, it was the colonel's idea.'

'*Le colonel?*'

'The big fellow who speaks German.'

'Oh, *oui*! What is it?'

'It's called a flare,' said Dietz, pulling out a short cardboard-covered tube from his right pocket and lighting the fuse with a cupped match. He peered around the corner banister, paused, his eyes on the fuse, then heaved it up the narrow steps past the guard's body. Stunned, the neo-Nazi whipped around at the sound of the flare passing him and hitting the floor; before he could adjust, the blinding explosion of a thousand white-hot sparks penetrated his eyes and his flesh. He screamed as the dozing guard behind lurched to his feet in consternation, his figure outlined beyond the moving sheets of flame. In panic, he fired repeatedly with his semiautomatic, the bullets filling the narrow staircase. The girl, Adrienne, yelled in pain; she had been hit in the leg. Dietz pulled her back as Monluc's aide, held firmly by Etranger Two, released all breath sharply, his head falling forward; he had been shot in the skull. The commando angled his weapon around the banister, his gun on rapid-fire, spraying the opening. The second guard spun around in circles, finally collapsing on the flare itself. Swirling black smoke was everywhere as Dietz grabbed the young girl by the legs, carrying her up the steps cradle-fashion.

'Bring that son of a bitch up here!' he ordered Etranger Two in French.

'*Il est mort, mon capitaine.*'

'I don't give a damn about his future, I just want his hand, and not too cold either!'

In the fourth-floor corridor, the backstairs detail raced to their left, Dietz throwing Adrienne over his shoulder, the French commando dragging the Nazi at his side. Six seconds later they came to the central archway that broke the wall. Latham, Witkowski, and Etranger One were waiting. Dietz gently lowered the girl to the floor; mercifully, she was unconscious.

'It's nasty,' said the colonel, examining the wound, 'but the blood's not gushing.' He yanked out his garrotte, and swiftly wrapped it around the girl's leg and tightened the straps. 'That'll hold for a while.'

Etranger One and Two had pinned the dead Nazi aide against the inner wall to the left of what had to be the electronic print-scan release, a dimly lit space large enough for a hand to be inserted, the palm pressed downward. If the imprint matched a computerized previous entry, the huge steel door would presumably open. However, if a mismatched imprint were made, an alarm would go off in the thick-walled, vaultlike quarters beyond.

'Ready, monsieur?' asked E-Two, gripping the neo-Nazi's lifeless right wrist.

'Wait a minute!' said Latham. 'Suppose he's left-handed?'

'So?'

'The photoelectric cells would reject it and the alarm would go off. That's the way these things work.'

'We can't wake him up to ask him, monsieur.'

'That cigarette holder – it was in his left hand . . . Let's look in his pockets.' The search of the dead man proceeded. 'Coins and money clip – left trouser pocket,' continued Drew, 'pack of cigarettes, left jacket pocket; two ballpoint pens, *right* inside jacket pocket, and the suit's custom-made, not off the rack.'

'I don't understand—'

'Left-handed people prefer to reach for pencils and pens on their right side, just as someone like me, who's right-handed, reaches over to the left. It's easier, that's all.'

'Your decision, monsieur?'

'I've got to go with my gut on this,' said Latham, breathing deeply. 'Move him over to the other side and I'll stick his left hand in there.'

The Frenchmen slid the corpse along the wall to the right side of the space. Drew grabbed the left wrist, and, as though he were dismantling a complicated bomb, he inserted the hand and slowly, cautiously, pressed the palm down on the inside surface. No one breathed until the large steel door silently opened. The dead Nazi fell to the floor and the four men walked inside. The chamber they entered was more a horrifying nightmare than someone's living quarters.

The massive room was octagonal in shape with a glass

dome that let the moonlight stream through. The courtesan, Elyse, had called it a pharaoh's tomb, an inhabited grave, and in several ways she was correct. It was eerily silent, no sound permitted from the outside, and instead of a pharaoh's possessions to see him across the river of death, there was a wall of medical equipment to prevent him from entering those waters. There were eight doors, one for each immense panel of the octagon. Elyse had told them that General Monluc's aides had their rooms within the tomb; five doors had to belong to the dark suits, leaving three unknown, one presumably a bathroom, two . . . question marks.

All this registered upon second and third glances, but what first assaulted the eyes of a stranger were the grotesquely enlarged photographs on the walls everywhere, all bathed in bloodred light that shone up from the baseboards. They were a record of Nazi atrocities; it was like a dark corridor in a Holocaust museum – the horrors visited upon the Jews and 'undesirables' by the madmen of Hitler's messianic hordes, with photographs of dead naked bodies piled in heaps. Next to them were pictures of blond men and women – presumably traitors – hanging by their necks from ropes, the faces contorted in agony, reminders that all dissent, no matter how minor, was prohibited. Only the sickest of minds could wake up in the night and be instantly gratified by the obscene panoply.

The most mesmerizing sight, however, was the night-shirted figure on the bed. It was bathed in dull white light, in contrast to the magenta-red wash illuminating the walls. A very, *very* old man reclined on soft pillows that dwarfed his body, his wizened face sunk in the billowing silk as if he were in a casket. And that *face*. The closer one looked, the more hypnotic it became.

The sunken cheeks, the deep-set eyeballs! Both skeletal with age. The short moustache beneath the nostrils, now snow white but clipped precisely; the pale face, easily remembered as having been flushed with oratorical rage – it was all there! Even the famous twitch in the right eye that had developed after the assassination attempt at Wolf-sschanze. All *there*! It was the aged face of *Adolf Hitler*!

'Jesus Christ!' whispered Witkowski. 'Is it *possible*?'

'It's not *im*possible, Stanley. It would answer a lot of questions that have been asked for over fifty years. Especially two: Who really were the charred bodies in that bunker pit, and how did the rumour start that the *Führer* had made it to an airport disguised as an old woman? I mean how, *why*? . . . No time now, Stosh, we've got to secure this pharaoh's tomb before it becomes one.'

'Call in the French unit.'

'Not until we make sure nothing here can self-destruct. Because if there *is* anything here, it's in these rooms . . . We'll pull our pharaoh's four other aides out.'

'How do you propose to do that, *chłopak*?'

'One customer at a time, Colonel. The doors have knobs and you can bet your ass they're not locked on the inside. Not in the Fourth Reich, where privacy is hardly a priority in the upper ranks, specifically as Monluc – or whoever he is – is surrounded by them.'

'Good point,' admitted Witkowski, 'you're growing up, lad, getting pretty damn smart.'

'I'll treasure that comment.' Latham silently signalled for Dietz and the French agents to join him and the colonel by the steel door. He whispered his instructions and the three men went to work as a team. One by one the doors were opened and closed, the beams of dull blue penlights crisscrossing one another while the doors were being closed. When the last of the eight had been visited, Captain Dietz reported to Drew.

'None of those mothers will move for a couple of hours.'

'You're sure of that? Are they tied securely, no glass or knives or razors around?'

'They're tied all right, Cons-Op, but we really didn't have to.'

'What do you mean?'

The commando removed a hypodermic needle and a vial

of liquid from his pocket. 'About a quarter of an inch apiece, right, Colonel?'

'*What?*'

'Well, you can't think of everything, *chłopak*. It was just a backup . . . Into the left-arm arteries, correct, Captain?'

'Yes, sir. Number Two squeezed 'em so I couldn't miss.'

'You're very big with surprises, Stanley. Anything else you haven't told me?'

'I'd have to think about it.'

'Please, forget it,' whispered Latham, turning to the commando. 'What was in the other three rooms?'

'The one nearest the bed is the biggest bathroom you've ever seen, chrome bars everywhere so the old guy can get around. The other two are actually one room. The wall's been taken down, and it's loaded with computer stuff.'

'*Bingo*,' said Drew. 'Now all we need is an expert with that equipment.'

'I thought we had one. Her name's Karin, in case you've forgotten.'

'My God, you're right! Now, listen to me, Dietz. You, our Colonel Great Spy here, and E-One and E-Two, stay on both sides of old Monluc's bed—'

'You say he's Monluc,' interrupted Dietz, 'but I say he's somebody else, and I don't even want to *think* about it!'

'Then don't. Just flank him and if he wakes up, don't let him touch *anything*. Not a button, a switch, a wire he might pull out, anything! We've got to invade those computers and learn whatever's there.'

'Why not use the colonel's magic needle, Cons-Op?'

'What . . . ?'

'Instead of a quarter of an inch, maybe an inch.'

'I don't know, Captain,' said Witkowski, 'I'm not a doctor. At his age, that stuff might not be exactly restorative.'

'So we go back to a quarter, what's the difference?'

'Not a bad idea,' whispered Drew. '*If* you can do it.'

'Hey, that Number Two's a whiz with the veins. I think he must have been a medic.'

'All Foreign Legionnaires have medic training,' explained the colonel. 'What are *you* going to do, Mr Cons-Op?'

'What you want me to do. I'm closing that steel door and calling in the assault unit. Then I'll reach Karin and our lieutenant and tell them to follow.' Latham pulled out his radio, switched military frequencies, and ordered the French Etranger unit to blow out the front gates and use its loudspeaker equipment before attacking the château. He switched back to the promontory. 'Listen up, you two. The French are coming in. When the place is secure, I'll call you back; and, Karin, come up to the top floor as fast as you can, but *only* when *everything's* under control! Not before! Understood?'

'Yes,' replied the lieutenant. 'Then you guys made it?'

'We made it, Gerry, but it's far from over. These people are Fascist maniacs; they'll hide in corners just to take one of us out. Don't let Karin get ahead of you—'

'I'm quite capable of making those decisions—'

'Oh, shut up! Out!' Drew raced over to Monluc's bed as Etranger Two and Dietz prepared to fully sedate the withered old man.

'*Now!*' said the commando. E-Two gripped the thin left arm, pressing the flesh of the inside elbow. 'Where's the *vein?*' cried Dietz in French.

'He's old. The first blue you see, hit the centre!'

'*Mein Gott!*' screamed the bedridden ancient, his eyes suddenly bulging, his mouth twisted, the twitch in his right eye going spastic. What followed caused Witkowski to blanch, his whole body trembling. The diatribe in shrieking German was electrifying, the voice strident beyond any normal use of vocal cords. 'If they will bomb *Berlin*, we shall destroy *London!* They send a hundred planes, we will send thousands upon *thousands* until the city is no more than blood and rubble! We shall teach the English a lesson in *death!* We shall—' The old man collapsed back into the silk pillows.

'Check his pulse!' said Latham. 'He's got to stay alive.'

'It is rapid, but it is there, monsieur,' said Etranger Two.

'Do you know what that son of a bitch just recited?' asked Stanley Witkowski, his face pale. 'He gave Hitler's response to the first bombing of Berlin. Word for *word!* . . . I can't *believe* this.'

Below, outside on the road in front of the château, armoured trucks of the assault unit fired their rockets, blowing apart the gates. A voice from a loudspeaker filled the night, heard thousands of yards away. 'All inside throw down your arms or be killed! Come outside and show yourselves without your weapons! The government of France has so ordered and our men will sweep this château, firing on any personnel who remain inside. You have two minutes to comply with our demands!'

Slowly, in fear, dozens of men and women walked out, their hands raised in surrender. They lined up in the circular drive, guards, cooks, waiters, and whores. The voice from the loudspeaker continued. 'If any are left inside, we tell you now – you are dead!'

Suddenly a blond man broke a window on the third floor and shouted. 'I will come down, sirs, but I must find someone. Shoot me if you will, but I must *find* her! You have my word, my weapons!' A further crash of glass preceded the hurling out of a pistol and a semiautomatic; they crashed on the drive and the figure disappeared.

'*Entrez!*' cried the voice on the loudspeaker as eight men in combat gear raced into the various entrances like spiders crawling swiftly towards insects caught in their webs. There was sporadic gunfire, not a great deal, as a few fanatic diehards died in pursuit of the obscene. At the last, an Etranger officer emerged from the front doors, a drunken Jacques Bergeron stumbling before him.

'We have our traitor from the Deuxième!' he announced in French. 'And he is as drunk as a politician.'

'*Enough.* Let the two others inside.'

Karin and Lieutenant Anthony ran through the shattered

dual gates heading for the central entrance. 'He said to go up the staircase!' yelled De Vries, in front of the lieutenant.

'For Christ's sake, will you please *wait* for me? I'm supposed to protect you!'

'If you're slow, Gerry, that's not my fault.'

'If you get shot, Cons-Op will blow my privates off!'

'I've got a gun, Lieutenant, don't you worry about a thing!'

'Thanks a bunch, *amazon*. My God, this arm hurts!'

Suddenly they both stopped, arrested by what they saw on the third-floor landing. A blond-haired guard held a young woman in his arms, carrying her down the staircase, tears in his eyes. 'She's hurt quite badly,' he said in German, 'but she is alive.'

'You were the man in the window, *ja?*' asked Anthony, also in German.

'Yes, sir. She and I were friends, and she should never have been in this terrible place.'

'Take her downstairs and tell the others to get her to a doctor,' said the lieutenant. 'Hurry up!'

'*Danke.*'

'Sure, but if you're a liar, I'll kill you myself.'

'I am not a liar, sir. I have been many bad things, but I do not lie.'

'I believe him,' said Karin, 'let him go.' They reached the top floor, but there was no way to open the steel door, no bell, no signal, nothing at all. 'Drew was emphatic, he wanted me here, but how do I get *in*?'

'Trust a young old lieutenant,' replied Anthony, having spotted the palm-release space in the wall. 'We're going to set off an alarm . . . These things were old hat a couple of *years* ago.'

'What are you talking about?'

'Watch me.' Gerald Anthony inserted his hand in the opening and pressed his palm down. In seconds the steel door was opened by a startled Latham, the alarm inside ear-shattering.

'What the hell have you *done*?' shouted Drew.

'Shut the door, boss man, and it will go off.'

Latham did so and the bell went off. 'How did you know that?' he asked.

'Hell, it's not even high tech. Simple circuit-breakers that don't roll over.'

'How did you know *that*?'

'I didn't actually, but rollovers in these systems are relatively new. This is a pretty old place, so I took a chance. What the hey, we've got the place secured anyway.'

'Don't argue with him, Drew,' said Karin, briefly embracing Latham. 'I know, I *know*, it's no time for emotions. Why do you want me here so quickly?'

'There's a room – two rooms actually – all filled with computers. We have to break into them.'

An hour passed and a perspiring Karin de Vries walked out of the door. 'You caught it in time, my dear,' she said, standing in front of Latham. 'On the premise that this isolated château in the Loire Valley could never have been unearthed, all the records are kept here. 'There are nearly two thousand printouts, who is and who isn't a member of the Nazi movement. All over the world.'

'Then we've *got* them!'

'Many of them, yes, my darling, but not all, never all. These are merely the leaders who shout and scream, rousing crowds to hate, to despise anyone but their own. And many do it in subtle ways, pretending generosity on the surface but hating underneath.'

'That's philosophical, lady, I'm talking about indictments, goddamned *Nazis*!

'Those you now have, Drew. Go after them, but understand what follows them.'

In a top-secret government laboratory in the hills of the Shenandoah Valley, a besmocked doctor of forensic pathology looked across the table at his much younger colleague, both studying their computer screens. 'Are you coming up with what I am?' asked the first pathologist quietly.

'I don't want to believe it,' said the second. 'A *switch*, the switch of all *history*!'

'The reports from Berlin can't lie, young man, they're right before our eyes. DNA wasn't known in the forties, it is now. They match ... Start the fires, Doctor, the world doesn't have to put up with this. We'd only fuel a legend, and that obscene old man died last night.'

'Exactly my thoughts. You fuel a legend, you only transfer the fuel, giving rise to other legends.'

'Worse, you glorify them, immortalize them.'

'Right on, Doctor. Hitler shot himself in that bunker over fifty years ago. We're all screwed up enough without believing the impossible, which the fanatics would latch on to in a second, glorifying it. The worst son of a bitch in the world swallowed cyanide and put a bullet in his head when the Russians were outside of Berlin. Everyone believes it, why contradict accepted history?'

The contrary evidence was destroyed by two Bunsen burners in the Shenandoah Valley.

EPILOGUE

The directors of the intelligence agencies of France, England, Germany, and the United States, under the instructions of their civilian leaders, moved swiftly, silently, and finally efficiently throughout their countries, for they had the truth, not speculation. Over two thousand computer printouts identifying the bona fide adherents to *Die Brüderschaft der Wacht*. According to the combined agreements among the four nations, the government press releases would essentially say the same thing, as exemplified by the Paris edition of the *Herald Tribune*. *Backbone of Neo-Nazi Movement Broken.*

All the articles went on to report that numerous men and women in and out of governments had been taken secretly into custody, their names, known only to a few, withheld until indictments were returned. The frenzied media went briefly apoplectic, but the government authorities would not budge in the area of naming names, which only the few could provide but did not, and eventually the frustrated media went on to other, more fruitful 'exposés'. Within two months the attention spans of their readers, listeners, and watchers waned, and the Nazi witch-hunts withered as rapidly as had the paranoid search for Communists when the loathsome McCarthy fell from power. The entrepreneurs understood that you did not get advertisers or ratings when you bored the public. So it was back to partisan political-bashing, and maybe that *was* Elvis Presley in a cornfield!

'I'm a goddamned *millionaire!*' explained Drew Latham,

771

walking hand in hand with Karin up the dirt road in Granby, Colorado. 'I still can't get over it!'

'Harry loved you very much,' said De Vries, looking above, awestruck at the majestic Rocky Mountains. 'You never doubted that, did you?'

'I never verbalized it either. Except for a few hundred thousand for Mother and Dad, which they'll never use, he left it all to *me*.'

'What surprises you so?'

'Where the hell did he *get* it?'

'The lawyers explained that, my dear. Harry was a single man with few expenses, studied the various markets both here and in Europe, and made some rather brilliant investments. That's not unlike him.'

'*Harry*,' mused Drew quietly, drawing out the name. 'Kroeger implanted that goddamned awful thing in his brain. The autopsy said that it was a new science and could be duplicated. Then it blew his head apart – after he died. Suppose he *hadn't*?'

'The doctors and the scientists say it could not be perfected for decades, if ever.'

'They've been wrong before.'

'Yes, they have . . . I forgot to tell you, we received a telegram from Jean-Pierre Villier. He's reopening *Coriolanus* and wants us both there in Paris on the first night.'

'How can you put it gracefully that a lot of French caterwauling doesn't exactly thrill me?'

'I'll phrase it another way.'

'Christ, there are still so many *questions*!'

'You don't have to burden yourself with them, my darling. *Ever*. We're free. Let others do the cleanup, your work is finished.'

'I can't help it . . . Harry said a nurse in the Brotherhood valley alerted the Antinayous that he was coming out. Who was she, and what happened to her?'

'It's in the Mettmach report, the one you only glanced at—'

'It was too painful,' Latham broke in. 'I will one day, but all that medical stuff about my brother – well, I just didn't want to read it.'

'The nurse was an assistant to Greta Frisch, Kroeger's wife. She had been forced to sleep with Von Schnabe, the commandant, on orders from the new Lebensborn. She got pregnant, and took her own life in the Vaclabruck forest.'

'The *Lebensborn*, such a lovely pastoral sound, yet so brutal, so warped ... Still, we found Mettmach in the Vaclabruck. My God, almost a full-blown military base in a backwoods wilderness!'

'It's become a five-thousand-acre penal colony where the prisoners, male and female, are issued only neo-Nazi uniforms, red armbands included. The armbands, however, are sewn in the front of their clothing, not on their arms, the way they made the Jews wear the Star of David during the Third Reich.'

'It's wild, really wild.'

'It was Ambassador Kreitz's idea. He said it will remind them why they are there as prisoners, not privileged members of society.'

'Yes, I know, and I'm still not sure I buy it. Couldn't it work the other way, uniformed prisoners of war bonding together? Swearing undying loyalty to their cause?'

'Not with their workloads, schedules, and constant lectures about the Nazi past which are accompanied by films and slides of the most brutal atrocities. They're instructed to write papers on what they observed. We hear that many come out of those lectures weeping and falling on their knees in prayer. Remember, Drew, the heavy work aside, no one acts harshly towards the inmates. Everything is completely firm but courteous.'

'The head doctors are going to have a prolonged psychiatric field day. It could be the beginning of a whole new prison system.'

'Then something decent could come out of an indecent madness.'

'Maybe, but don't count on it. There are always others waiting in the wings. Their names may be different, the cultures different, but the common denominator is always the same. "Do it *our* way, under *our* authority, no deviations permitted."'

'So we must, all of us everywhere, be on the alert for such people, such causes, hoping our leaders will perceive them and have the courage to move swiftly, but not irrationally.'

'Don't you get tired of always summing things up so well?'

'My husband – when he was my husband in the early days – usually said, "Will you please stop being so boringly academic." I guess he was right. The only life I ever had was academic, it was all that was offered me.'

'I'd never say anything like that to you . . . By the way, you did more of the follow-up than I did—'

'Naturally,' interrupted Karin, 'you had to fly back to your mother and father. They need their surviving child in their grief.'

'Yes.' Latham looked at her in the bright afternoon Colorado sunlight. 'Yes . . .' He took his eyes off her and continued. 'Did Knox Talbot find out who broke into the AA computers?'

'Of course, they were on the Eagle's Nest printouts. A man and a woman who'd worked their way up for sixteen years in the Agency. Boy Scouts, Girl Scouts, church acolytes, one from a farm – Four H, whatever that is – and the other the offspring of a suburban couple who taught Sunday school.'

'Sonnenkinder,' said Drew.

'Precisely. Right down to choir practice and your Rotary Clubs.'

'What about the files on Monluc that were stolen from the OSI?'

'One of the directors who posed as a Jewish historian. Who could suspect him?'

'Sonnenkind.'

'Naturally.'

'What about that financial shark in Paris who was buying up real estate in the Loire Valley with German money?'

'His house of cards collapsed. Bonn stepped in with some very creative foreign accounting procedures that saved a lot of German money. He was a swindler preying upon old misguided loyalties.'

Karin glanced up at Latham. 'Why are you looking at me like that? So questioningly?'

'A moment ago you mentioned my mother and father, and that made me suddenly think. You've never told me about your parents, *your* mother and father, who gave you all that academic training. I don't even know what your name is, your maiden name. Why is that?'

'Does it matter?'

'*Hell*, no! But I'm curious, isn't that normal? I guess, in my imagination, I always thought that when and if I was ever going to ask a woman to marry me, I'd have to go to her father and say something like, "Yes, sir, I can support her and I love her" – in that order. Can I do that, Karin?'

'No, I'm afraid you can't, so I might as well tell you the truth . . . My grandmother was a Danish woman, abducted by the Nazis and forced into the Lebensborn. When her daughter, my mother, was born, she stole her away, and with a tenacity that is beyond understanding, she made her way back into Denmark with that child, and hid herself in a small village on the outskirts of Hanstholm on the North Sea. She found a man, an anti-Nazi, who married her and accepted the child, my mother.'

'So what you're saying—'

'Yes, Drew Latham, but for the driven stubbornness of a woman's ferocity, I might have become a Sonnenkind, not unlike Janine Clunes. Unfortunately, the Nazis kept meticulous records, and my grandmother and her husband had to keep running, never having a permanent home of their own, or access to normal educational facilities. Finally, after the war, they moved to Belgium, where the barely literate child grew up, got married, and had me in 1962. Because my mother had been denied any formal education, my schooling became an obsession with her.'

'Where are they now?'

'My father deserted us when I was nine years old and, looking back, I can understand why. My mother had my grandmother's intensity of purpose. As *her* mother had risked everything, including a public hanging, to steal her own child away from the Lebensborn, my mother was consumed by me. She had no time for her husband, her whole focus was on *her* daughter. I had to read constantly, feverishly, attain the highest grades of anyone in the academies, study, study, study, until I myself caught the fever. I became as obsessed with my scholarship as she was.'

'No wonder you and Harry got along. Is your mother alive?'

'She's in a nursing home in Antwerp. You could say she burned herself out, and now barely recognizes me.'

'Your father?'

'Who knows? I never tried to find him. Later I thought often of trying, for, as I say, I understood why he left. At the first chance, you see, I myself left before I was completely smothered, and how accurately does the English language create that word. Then Freddie came along and I was "out like a shot," as you Americans say.'

'Well, that's over with!' said Drew, smiling and squeezing her hand. 'Now I feel I know you well enough to carry on the Latham dynasty.'

'How generous of you, I'll try to be worthy.'

'Worthy? For you it's a step or two down, but I want you to know that the first thing I'm ordering for the library is a set of encyclopaedias.'

'What library?'

'In the house.'

'What house?'

'*Our* house. Right around the bend on this old road, which, naturally, I'll have surfaced now that I can afford to.'

'What *are* you talking about?'

'This is kind of a back entrance to the property.'

'What property?'

'*Our* property. You said you liked mountains.'

'I do. Look up there, they're so grand, so breathtaking!'

'Then, come on, mountain lover, we're almost there.'

'*Where?*'

'Well, you see,' said Drew as they walked left around the dirt curve, 'I have a friend in Fort Collins who told me about this place. "Nails" is *really* rich – we called him Nails in college 'cause he could nail down anything, from a date to a deal – and he said it was the only acreage left, if I could come up with the price. Then, also very much like Nails, he added that he could help me if it was a problem.'

'What does he do?'

'I don't think anyone really knows. He has a bunch of computers and deals in stocks and bonds and commodities, those kinds of things. But the proudest moment came when I said to him, "It's no problem, Nails. If I like it, I'll buy it."'

'What did *he* say?'

'"On a government salary, buddy?" And I said, "No, old buddy, I've put a lot of my per diems into the European markets," and *he* said, "Let's have lunch, or dinner, or stay at my place for as long as you like."'

'You're shameless, Drew Latham!' They rounded the bend in the road, and what lay before them caused Karin to flush with astonishment. It was a huge, pristine blue-green lake, several white sails skimming the water, and in the distance a number of exquisitely designed houses with protruding docks below their manicured lawns. Above, glistening in the sunlight, were the receding mountains, like heavenly fortresses protecting a beautiful earthly enclave. And to their right was a large expanse of lakefront fields, uninhabited, filled with high grass and wildflowers.

'There you are, lady, that's our house. Can't you see it? A couple of miles over there is the southwest entrance to the Rocky Mountain National Park.'

'Oh, my darling, I can't *believe* it!'

'Believe, it's there. It's ours. And in a year the *house* will be there – after you approve the plans, of course. Nails got me the finest architect in Colorado.'

'But, Drew,' laughed Karin, racing down the hill of grass towards the water's edge and the stream that bordered the property. 'It will take so long, what are we going to *do*?'

'I was thinking of pitching a pretty big tent, like squatters, but it wouldn't work!' yelled Latham, catching up with her.

'Why not? I'd *love* it!'

'No, you wouldn't,' said Drew, breathless, holding her by the shoulders. 'Guess who's flying out to oversee the initial construction because the *chłopak* isn't capable?'

The *colonel*?'

'Right on, lady.'

'He, too, loves you very much.'

'I think you've got an edge in that department. He was granted his full pension, but he hasn't anywhere else to go. His children are grown, with kids of their own, and after a few days with them, he's at a loss. He's got to keep moving, Karin. Let him stay with us for a while until he has to move again, okay?'

'I could never say no.'

'Thank you. Nails rented us a house about ten miles down Route 34, and I've agreed to fly to Washington for five days a month, no more than that. Only consultation, no field duty.'

'Are you sure of that? Can you live with that?'

'Yes, because I've done my best and I have nothing else to prove – to Harry or anybody.'

'What will *we* do? You're a young man, Drew, and I'm younger than you. What are we going to *do*?'

'I don't know. First, we build our house, which will take a couple of years, actually, and then – well, then we'll have to think about things.'

'Are you really going to resign from Consular Operations?'

'That's up to Sorenson. Outside of five days a month, I'm on leave until March of next year.'

'Then you haven't made up your mind. It's not Sorenson's decision; it's yours.'

'Wesley understands. He's been where I've been and he quit.'

'Where is that?' asked Karin softly, holding Latham, her face against his chest.

'I'm not sure,' replied Drew, his arms around her. 'Thanks to Beth's genes, I'm a pretty big guy and relatively capable of taking care of myself, but I also learned something over the past three months, and you're part of it, a major part . . . I don't like being afraid for both of us around the clock. To tell you the truth, I really don't like guns, although they've saved our lives more than once. I'm sick of the dictum Kill or be killed. I don't care to play anymore, and I sure as hell don't want you to.'

'It was war, my darling, you said that yourself and you were right. But for us it's over, we're going to live like normal human beings. Also, I can't wait to see Stanley!'

As if on a perfect cue, an agitated figure appeared on the dirt road above. 'Son of a *bitch*!' roared Colonel Stanley Witkowski, perspiring and out of breath. 'The damned taxi refused to come *up* here! . . . Nice terrain, not bad. Already I've got some ideas – lots of glass and wood. Also, *chłopak*, Wes Sorenson phoned me. We're a pretty good team, the three of us, and there's a situation he thought we might find interesting under your new arrangement with Cons-Op.'

'Nothing changes,' said Latham, still holding Karin. ' . . . Forget it, Colonel!'

'He was thinking of you, young fella, we both were,' continued Witkowski, walking down the hill of grass, wiping his forehead. 'You're too young to retire, you've got to work, and what the hell else do you know? I'd say the hockey rink's pretty much out of the question; you've been away too long.'

'I said forget it.'

'I'm flying back with you next week and Wesley will lay it

779

all out. It sounds like a piece of cake, damn fine per diems and contingency funds, and we can all take turns coming back to check on the construction here.'

'The answer is no, Stanley!'

'We'll talk . . . My dear Karin, you look wonderful.'

'Thank you,' said De Vries, embracing the colonel. 'You look a bit tired.'

'It's a hell of a walk.'

'No, no, *no!*'

'We'll just talk, *chłopak* . . . Now, let's survey the grounds.'

Have you read them all?

The **Covert-One** *thrillers listed in the order in which they first appeared:*

The Hades Factor

Introducing Lt. Col. Jon Smith, a research scientist with the US army. An unknown virus takes the life of his fiancée. But this was no accident. Millions of lives are threatened. Smith must find the virus' evil-genius creator.

The Cassandra Compact

Lt. Col. Jon Smith is now an agent with the highly secretive Covert-One agency. His colleague is gunned down in Venice. Smith's investigations lead to a deadly bacteria. And a terrifying global conspiracy.

The Paris Option

A science lab in Paris is destroyed. A 'super computer' is assumed lost. But then US fighter jets disappear from radar screens. Utilities cease functioning. Lt. Col. Jon Smith must uncover the evil plot.

The Altman Code

The docks of Shanghai: a photographer records cargo being secretly loaded. He is killed. Lt. Col. Jon Smith races against time to uncover the truth about the ship and its deadly cargo.

The Lazarus Vendetta

Anti-technology protestors turn violent at a research institute in Santa Fe. Their leader is Lazarus. Lt. Col. Jon Smith must uncover his identity. And prevent him from making his most deadly move yet.

The Moscow Vector

One of the world's wealthiest men has created an incurable bioweapon. Lt. Col. Jon Smith must stop the murderous conspiracy. And thwart the Kremlin's bid to restore Russia to her former power.

The Arctic Event

The wreckage of an old Soviet bomber lies on a mountain glacier. Its cargo is weaponised anthrax. Lt. Col. Jon Smith discovers that it also contains a devastating secret that could trigger a Third World War.